11/22/63

is

" . . . not typical Stephen King. It is extraordinary Stephen King."
—*USA Today*

" . . . filled with immediacy, pathos, and suspense."
—*The New York Times*

" . . . thought-provoking, with its unexpectedly poignant ending."
—*BookPage*

More praise for Stephen King's
#1 *New York Times* bestseller

"Richly layered with the pleasures we've come to expect [from King]: characters of good heart and wounded lives, whose adventures into the fantastic are made plausible because they are anchored in reality, in the conversations and sense of place that take us effortlessly into the story. . . . [Here] are the memorable characters who populate so much of King's work—people who touch us viscerally and for whom we root. . . . And there is that powerful sense of place: in the stores, songs, clothes and cars, in the details that make this fantasy seem plausible."
—*The Washington Post*

"Ingenious. . . . [An] intoxicating, early-King bouquet of ambition and swagger."
—*Booklist*

"The work of a master craftsman."
—*Time*

"*11/22/63* is quite possibly King's most ambitious and accomplished book to date."
—NPR

"A delightful blend of history and fantasy."
—Associated Press

"Tight and energetic from start to finish. . . . Hard as this thing is to hoist, it's even harder to put down."

—*The New York Times*

"Seven words: the best yet from the best ever. America's greatest living novelist delivers his masterpiece."

—Lee Child

"The sort of book for which the phrase 'page-turner' was coined."

—*Miami Herald*

"Wildly entertaining."

—*People* (3 ½ stars)

"One of his most powerful novels ever . . . and our stock of literature in the great American Gothic tradition is brilliantly replenished because of it."

—*The Washington Post*

"Moves so fast and grips the reader so tightly that it's practically incapacitating."

—*New York Newsday*

STEPHEN KING

11/22/63

A NOVEL

GALLERY BOOKS

New York   London   Toronto   Sydney   New Delhi

G

GALLERY BOOKS
A Division of Simon & Schuster, Inc.
1230 Avenue of the Americas
New York, NY 10020

This Gallery paperback edition August 2012

For information about special discounts for bulk purchases,
please contact Simon & Schuster Special Sales at 1-866-506-1949
or business@simonandschuster.com.

The Simon & Schuster Speakers Bureau can bring authors to your live event.
For more information or to book an event, contact the Simon & Schuster Speakers Bureau
at 1-866-248-3049 or visit our website at www.simonspeakers.com.

DESIGNED BY ERICH HOBBING

Manufactured in the United States of America

29   30   28

ISBN 978-1-4516-2729-9
ISBN 978-1-4516-2730-5 (ebook)

For Zelda

Hey, honey, welcome to the party.

It is virtually not assimilable to our reason that a small lonely man felled a giant in the midst of his limousines, his legions, his throng, and his security. If such a non-entity destroyed the leader of the most powerful nation on earth, then a world of disproportion engulfs us, and we live in a universe that is absurd.

—Norman Mailer

If there is love, smallpox scars are as pretty as dimples.

—Japanese proverb

Dancing is life.

CONTENTS

11/22/63

I have never been what you'd call a crying man.

My ex-wife said that my "nonexistent emotional gradient" was the main reason she was leaving me (as if the guy she met in her AA meetings was beside the point). Christy said she supposed she could forgive me not crying at her father's funeral; I had only known him for six years and couldn't understand what a wonderful, giving man he had been (a Mustang convertible as a high school graduation present, for instance). But then, when I didn't cry at my own parents' funerals—they died just two years apart, Dad of stomach cancer and Mom of a thunderclap heart attack while walking on a Florida beach—she began to understand the nonexistent gradient thing. I was "unable to feel my feelings," in AA-speak.

"I have *never* seen you shed tears," she said, speaking in the flat tones people use when they are expressing the absolute final deal-breaker in a relationship. "Even when you told me I had to go to rehab or you were leaving." This conversation happened about six weeks before she packed her things, drove them across town, and moved in with Mel Thompson. "Boy meets girl on the AA campus"—that's another saying they have in those meetings.

I didn't cry when I saw her off. I didn't cry when I went back inside the little house with the great big mortgage, either. The house where no baby had come, or now ever would. I just lay down on the bed that now belonged to me alone, and put my arm over my eyes, and mourned.

Tearlessly.

But I'm not emotionally blocked. Christy was wrong about that. One day when I was nine, my mother met me at the door when I came home from school. She told me my collie, Rags, had been struck and killed by a truck that hadn't even bothered to stop. I didn't cry when we buried him, although my dad told me nobody would think less of me if I did, but I cried when she told me. Partly because it was my first experience of death; mostly because it had been my responsibility to make sure he was safely penned up in our backyard.

And I cried when Mom's doctor called me and told me what had happened that day on the beach. "I'm sorry, but there was no chance," he said. "Sometimes it's very sudden, and doctors tend to see that as a blessing."

Christy wasn't there—she had to stay late at school that day and meet with a mother who had questions about her son's last report card—but I cried, all right. I went into our little laundry room and took a dirty sheet out of the basket and cried into that. Not for long, but the tears came. I could have told her about them later, but I didn't see the point, partly because she would have thought I was pity-fishing (that's not an AA term, but maybe it should be), and partly because I don't think the ability to bust out bawling pretty much on cue should be a requirement for successful marriage.

I never saw my dad cry at all, now that I think about it; at his most emotional, he might fetch a heavy sigh or grunt out a few reluctant chuckles—no breast-beating or belly-laughs for William Epping. He was the strong silent type, and for the most part, my mother was the same. So maybe the not-crying-easily thing is genetic. But blocked? Unable to feel my feelings? No, I have never been those things.

Other than when I got the news about Mom, I can only remember one other time when I cried as an adult, and that was when I read the story of the janitor's father. I was sitting alone in the teachers' room at Lisbon High School, working my way through a stack of themes that my Adult English class had written. Down the hall I could hear the thud of basketballs, the blare of the time-out horn, and the shouts of the crowd as the sports-beasts fought: Lisbon Greyhounds versus Jay Tigers.

Who can know when life hangs in the balance, or why?

The subject I'd assigned was "The Day That Changed My Life." Most of the responses were heartfelt but awful: sentimental tales of a kindly aunt who'd taken in a pregnant teenager, an Army buddy who had demonstrated the true meaning of bravery, a chance meeting with a celebrity (*Jeopardy!* host Alex Trebek, I think it was, but maybe it was Karl Malden). The teachers among you who have picked up an extra three or four thousand a year by taking on a class of adults studying for their General Equivalency Diploma will know what a dispiriting job reading such themes can be. The grading process hardly figures into it, or at least it didn't for me; I passed everybody, because I never had an adult student who did less than try his or her ass off. If you turned in a paper with writing on it, you were guaranteed a hook from Jake Epping of the LHS English Department, and if the writing was organized into actual paragraphs, you got at least a B-minus.

What made the job hard was that the red pen became my primary teaching tool instead of my mouth, and I practically wore it out. What made the job dispiriting was that you knew that very little of that red-pen teaching was apt to stick; if you reach the age of twenty-five or thirty without knowing how to spell (*totally,* not *todilly*), or capitalize in the proper places (*White House,* not *white-house*), or write a sentence containing both a noun *and* a verb, you're probably never going to know. Yet we soldier on, gamely circling the misused word in sentences like *My husband was to quick to judge me* or crossing out *swum* and replacing it with *swam* in the sentence *I swum out to the float often after that.*

It was such hopeless, trudging work I was doing that night, while not far away another high school basketball game wound down toward another final buzzer, world without end, amen. It was not long after Christy got out of rehab, and I suppose if I was thinking anything, it was to hope that I'd come home and find her sober (which I did; she's held onto her sobriety better than she held onto her husband). I remember I had a little headache and was rubbing my temples the way you do when you're trying to keep a little nagger from turning into a big thumper. I remember thinking, *Three more of these, just three, and I can get out of here. I can go home, fix myself a big cup of instant cocoa, and dive into the new John Irving novel without these sincere but poorly made things hanging over my head.*

There were no violins or warning bells when I pulled the janitor's theme off the top of the stack and set it before me, no sense that my little life was about to change. But we never know, do we? Life turns on a dime.

He had written in cheap ballpoint ink that had blotted the five pages in many places. His handwriting was a looping but legible scrawl, and he must have been bearing down hard, because the words were actually engraved into the cheap notebook pages; if I'd closed my eyes and run my fingertips over the backs of those torn-out sheets, it would have been like reading Braille. There was a little squiggle, like a flourish, at the end of every lower-case *y*. I remember that with particular clarity.

I remember how his theme started, too. I remember it word for word.

It wasnt a day but a night. The night that change my life was the night my father murdirt my mother and two brothers and hurt me bad. He hurt my sister too, so bad she went into a comah. In three years she died without waking up. Her name was Ellen and I loved her very much. She love to pick flouers and put them in vayses.

Halfway down the first page, my eyes began to sting and I put my trusty red pen down. It was when I got to the part about him crawling under the bed with the blood running in his eyes (*it also run down my throat and tasted horible*) that I began to cry—Christy would have been so proud. I read all the way to the end without making a single mark, wiping my eyes so the tears wouldn't fall on the pages that had obviously cost him so much effort. Had I thought he was slower than the rest, maybe only half a step above what used to be called "educable retarded"? Well, by God, there was a reason for that, wasn't there? And a reason for the limp, too. It was a miracle that he was alive at all. But he was. A nice man who always had a smile and never raised his voice to the kids. A nice man who had been through hell and was working—humbly and hopefully, as most of them do—to get a high school diploma. Although he would be a janitor for the rest of his life, just a guy in green or brown khakis, either pushing a broom or scraping gum up off the floor with the putty knife he always kept in his back pocket. Maybe once he could have been something different, but one night his life turned on a dime and now he was just a guy in Carhartts that the kids called Hoptoad Harry because of the way he walked.

So I cried. Those were real tears, the kind that come from deep inside. Down the hall, I could hear the Lisbon band strike up their victory song—so the home team had won, and good for them. Later, perhaps, Harry and a couple of his colleagues would roll up the bleachers and sweep away the crap that had been dropped beneath them.

I stroked a big red A on top of his paper. Looked at it for a moment or two, then added a big red +. Because it was good, and because his pain had evoked an emotional reaction in me, his reader. And isn't that what A+ writing is supposed to do? Evoke a response?

As for me, I only wish the former Christy Epping had been correct. I wish I had been emotionally blocked, after all. Because everything that followed—every terrible thing—flowed from those tears.

PART 1

WATERSHED
MOMENT

CHAPTER 1

1

Harry Dunning graduated with flying colors. I went to the little GED ceremony in the LHS gym, at his invitation. He really had no one else, and I was happy to do it.

After the benediction (spoken by Father Bandy, who rarely missed an LHS function), I made my way through the milling friends and relatives to where Harry was standing alone in his billowy black gown, holding his diploma in one hand and his rented mortarboard in the other. I took his hat so I could shake his hand. He grinned, exposing a set of teeth with many gaps and several leaners. But a sunny and engaging grin, for all that.

"Thanks for coming, Mr. Epping. Thanks so much."

"It was my pleasure. And you can call me Jake. It's a little perk I accord to students who are old enough to be my father."

He looked puzzled for a minute, then laughed. "I guess I am, ain't I? Sheesh!" I laughed, too. Lots of people were laughing all around us. And there were tears, of course. What's hard for me comes easily to a great many people.

"And that A-plus! Sheesh! I never got an A-plus in my whole life! Never expected one, either!"

"You deserved it, Harry. So what's the first thing you're going to do as a high school graduate?"

His smile dimmed for a second—this was a prospect he hadn't considered. "I guess I'll go back home. I got a little house I rent on Goddard Street, you know." He raised the diploma, holding it carefully by the fingertips, as if the ink might smear. "I'll frame this and hang it on the wall. Then I guess I'll pour myself a glass of wine and sit on the couch and just admire it until bedtime."

"Sounds like a plan," I said, "but would you like to have a burger and some fries with me first? We could go down to Al's."

I expected a wince at that, but of course I was judging Harry by my colleagues. Not to mention most of the kids we taught; they avoided Al's like the plague and tended to patronize either the Dairy Queen across from the school or the Hi-Hat out on 196, near where the old Lisbon Drive-In used to be.

"That'd be great, Mr. Epping. Thanks!"

"Jake, remember?"

"Jake, you bet."

So I took Harry to Al's, where I was the only faculty regular, and although he actually had a waitress that summer, Al served us himself. As usual, a cigarette (illegal in public eating establishments, but that never stopped Al) smoldered in one corner of his mouth and the eye on that side squinted against the smoke. When he saw the folded-up graduation robe and realized what the occasion was, he insisted on picking up the check (what check there was; the meals at Al's were always remarkably cheap, which had given rise to rumors about the fate of certain stray animals in the vicinity). He also took a picture of us, which he later hung on what he called the Town Wall of Celebrity. Other "celebrities" represented included the late Albert Dunton, founder of Dunton Jewelry; Earl Higgins, a former LHS principal; John Crafts, founder of John Crafts Auto Sales; and, of course, Father Bandy of St. Cyril's. (The Father was paired with Pope John XXIII—the latter not local, but revered by Al Templeton, who called himself "a good Catlick.") The picture Al took that day showed Harry Dunning with a big smile on his face. I was standing next to him, and we were both holding his diploma. His tie was pulled slightly askew. I remember that because it made me think of those little squiggles he put on the ends of his lower-case *y*'s. I remember it all. I remember it very well.

2

Two years later, on the last day of the school year, I was sitting in that very same teachers' room and reading my way through a batch of final essays my American Poetry honors seminar had written. The kids themselves had already left, turned loose for another summer, and soon I would do the same. But for the time being I was happy enough where I was, enjoying the unaccustomed quiet. I thought I might even clean out the snack cupboard before I left. *Someone* ought to do it, I thought.

Earlier that day, Harry Dunning had limped up to me after homeroom period (which had been particularly screechy, as all homerooms and study halls tend to be on the last day of school) and offered me his hand.

"I just want to thank you for everything," he said.

I grinned. "You already did that, as I remember."

"Yeah, but this is my last day. I'm retiring. So I wanted to make sure and thank you again."

As I shook his hand, a kid cruising by—no more than a sophomore, judging by the fresh crop of pimples and the serio-comic straggle on his chin that aspired to goateehood—muttered, "Hoptoad Harry, hoppin down the av-a-*new.*"

I grabbed for him, my intention to make him apologize, but Harry stopped me. His smile was easy and unoffended. "Nah, don't bother. I'm used to it. They're just kids."

"That's right," I said. "And it's our job to teach them."

"I know, and you're good at it. But it's not my job to be anybody's whatchacallit—teachable moment. Especially not today. I hope you'll take care of yourself, Mr. Epping." He might be old enough to be my father, but *Jake* was apparently always going to be beyond him.

"You too, Harry."

"I'll never forget that A-plus. I framed that, too. Got it right up beside my diploma."

"Good for you."

And it was. It was all good. His essay had been primitive art, but every bit as powerful and true as any painting by Grandma Moses. It was certainly better than the stuff I was currently reading. The spelling in the honors essays was mostly correct, and the diction was clear (although my cautious college-bound don't-take-a-chancers had an irritating tendency to fall back on the passive voice), but the writing was pallid. Boring. My honors kids were juniors—Mac Steadman, the department head, awarded the seniors to himself—but they wrote like little old men and little old ladies, all pursey-mouthed and *ooo, don't slip on that icy patch, Mildred.* In spite of his grammatical lapses and painstaking cursive, Harry Dunning had written like a hero. On one occasion, at least.

As I was musing on the difference between offensive and defensive writing, the intercom on the wall cleared its throat. "Is Mr. Epping in the west wing teachers' room? You by any chance still there, Jake?"

I got up, thumbed the button, and said: "Still here, Gloria. For my sins. Can I help you?"

"You have a phone call. Guy named Al Templeton? I can transfer it, if you want. Or I can tell him you left for the day."

Al Templeton, owner and operator of Al's Diner, where all LHS faculty save for yours truly refused to go. Even my esteemed department head—who tried to talk like a Cambridge don and was approaching retirement age himself—had been known to refer to the specialty of the house as Al's Famous Catburger instead of Al's Famous Fatburger.

Well of course it's not really cat, people would say, *or probably not cat, but it can't be beef, not at a dollar-nineteen.*

"Jake? Did you fall asleep on me?"

"Nope, wide awake." Also curious as to why Al would call me at school. Why he'd call me at all, for that matter. Ours had always been strictly a cook-and-client relationship. I appreciated his chow, and he appreciated my patronage. "Go on and put him through."

"Why are you still here, anyway?"

"I'm flagellating myself."

"Ooo!" Gloria said, and I could imagine her fluttering her long lashes. "I love it when you talk dirty. Hold on and wait for the ringy-dingy."

She clicked off. The extension rang and I picked it up.

"Jake? You on there, buddy?"

At first I thought Gloria must have gotten the name wrong. That voice couldn't belong to Al. Not even the world's worst cold could have produced such a croak.

"Who is this?"

"Al Templeton, didn't she tellya? Christ, that hold music really sucks. Whatever happened to Connie Francis?" He began to ratchet coughs loud enough to make me hold the phone away from my ear a little.

"You sound like you got the flu."

He laughed. He also kept coughing. The combination was fairly gruesome. "I got something, all right."

"It must have hit you fast." I had been in just yesterday, to grab an early supper. A Fatburger, fries, and a strawberry milkshake. I believe it's important for a guy living on his own to hit all the major food groups.

"You could say that. Or you could say it took awhile. Either one would be right."

I didn't know how to respond to that. I'd had a lot of conversations with Al in the six or seven years I'd been going to the diner, and he could be odd—insisted on referring to the New England Patriots as the Boston Patriots, for instance, and talked about Ted Williams as if he'd known him like a brudda—but I'd never had a conversation as weird as this.

"Jake, I need to see you. It's important."

"Can I ask—"

"I expect you to ask plenty, and I'll answer, but not over the phone."

I didn't know how many answers he'd be able to give before his voice gave out, but I promised I'd come down in an hour or so.

13

"Thanks. Make it even sooner, if you can. Time is, as they say, of the essence." And he hung up, just like that, without even a goodbye.

I worked my way through two more of the honors essays, and there were only four more in the stack, but it was no good. I'd lost my groove. So I swept the stack into my briefcase and left. It crossed my mind to go upstairs to the office and wish Gloria a good summer, but I didn't bother. She'd be in all next week, closing the books on another school year, and I was going to come in on Monday and clean out the snack cupboard—that was a promise I'd made to myself. Otherwise the teachers who used the west wing teachers' room during summer session would find it crawling with bugs.

If I'd known what the future held for me, I certainly would have gone up to see her. I might even have given her the kiss that had been flirting in the air between us for the last couple of months. But of course I didn't know. Life turns on a dime.

3

Al's Diner was housed in a silver trailer across the tracks from Main Street, in the shadow of the old Worumbo mill. Places like that can look tacky, but Al had disguised the concrete blocks upon which his establishment stood with pretty beds of flowers. There was even a neat square of lawn, which he barbered himself with an old push-type lawn mower. The lawn mower was as well tended as the flowers and the lawn; not a speck of rust on the whirring, brightly painted blades. It might have been purchased at the local Western Auto store the week before . . . if there had still been a Western Auto in The Falls, that was. There was once, but it fell victim to the big-box stores back around the turn of the century.

I went up the paved walk, up the steps, then paused, frowning. The sign reading WELCOME TO AL'S DINER, HOME OF THE FATBURGER! was gone. In its place was a square of cardboard reading CLOSED & WILL NOT REOPEN DUE TO ILLNESS. THANK YOU FOR YOUR BUSINESS OVER THE YEARS & GOD BLESS.

I had not yet entered the fog of unreality that would soon swallow me, but the first tendrils were seeping around me, and I felt them. It wasn't a summer cold that had caused the hoarseness I'd heard in Al's voice, nor the croaking cough. Not the flu, either. Judging by the sign, it was something more serious. But what kind of serious illness came on in a mere twenty-four hours? Less than that, really. It was two-thirty. I had left Al's last night at five forty-five, and he'd been fine. Almost manic, in fact. I remembered asking him if he'd been drinking too much of his own coffee, and he said no, he was just thinking about taking a vacation. Do people who are getting sick—sick enough to close the businesses they've run single-handed for over twenty years—talk about taking vacations? Some, maybe, but probably not many.

The door opened while I was still reaching for the handle, and Al stood there looking at me, not smiling. I looked back, feeling that fog of unreality thicken around me. The day was warm but the fog was cold. At that point I still could have turned and walked out of it, back into the June sunshine, and part of me wanted to do that. Mostly, though, I was frozen by wonder and dismay. Also horror, I might as well admit it. Because serious illness *does* horrify us, doesn't it, and Al was seriously ill. I could see that in a single glance. And *mortally* was probably more like it.

It wasn't just that his normally ruddy cheeks had gone slack and sallow. It wasn't the rheum that coated his blue eyes, which now looked washed-out and nearsightedly peering. It wasn't even his hair, formerly almost all black, and now almost all white— after all, he might have been using one of those vanity products and decided on the spur of the moment to shampoo it out and go natural.

The impossible part was that in the twenty-two hours since I'd last seen him, Al Templeton appeared to have lost at least thirty pounds. Maybe even forty, which would have been a quarter of his previous body weight. Nobody loses thirty or forty pounds in less than a day, *nobody*. But I was looking at it. And this, I think, is where that fog of unreality swallowed me whole.

Al smiled, and I saw he had lost teeth as well as weight. His gums looked pale and unhealthy. "How do you like the new me, Jake?" And he began to cough, thick chaining sounds that came from deep inside him.

I opened my mouth. No words came out. The idea of flight again came to some craven, disgusted part of my mind, but even if that part had been in control, I couldn't have done it. I was rooted to the spot.

Al got the coughing under control and pulled a handkerchief from his back pocket. He wiped first his mouth and then the palm of his hand with it. Before he put it back, I saw it was streaked with red.

"Come in," he said. "I've got a lot to talk about, and I think you're the only one who might listen. Will you listen?"

"Al," I said. My voice was so low and strengthless I could hardly hear it myself. "What's happened to you?"

"Will you listen?"

"Of course."

"You'll have questions, and I'll answer as many as I can, but try to keep them to a minimum. I don't have much voice left. Hell, I don't have much *strength* left. Come on in here."

I came in. The diner was dark and cool and empty. The counter was polished and crumbless; the chrome on the stools gleamed; the coffee urn was polished to a high gloss; the sign reading IF YOU DON'T LIKE OUR TOWN, LOOK FOR A TIMETABLE was in its accustomed place by the Sweda register. The only thing missing was the customers.

Well, and the cook-proprietor, of course. Al Templeton had been replaced by an elderly, ailing ghost. When he turned the door's thumb-latch, locking us in, the sound was very loud.

4

"Lung cancer," he said matter-of-factly, after leading us to a booth at the far end of the diner. He tapped the pocket of his shirt, and I saw it was empty. The ever-present pack of Camel straights was gone. "No big surprise. I started when I was eleven, and smoked right up to the day I got the diagnosis. Over fifty damn years. Three packs a day until the price went way up in '07. Then I made a sacrifice and cut back to two a day." He laughed wheezily.

I thought of telling him that his math had to be wrong, because I knew his actual age. When I'd come in one day in the late winter and asked him why he was working the grill with a kid's birthday hat on, he'd said *Because today I'm fifty-seven, buddy. Which makes me an official Heinz.* But he'd asked me not to ask questions unless I absolutely had to, and I assumed the request included not butting in to make corrections.

"If I were you—and I wish I was, although I'd never wish being me on you, not in my current situation—I'd be thinking, 'Something's screwy here, nobody gets advanced lung cancer overnight.' Is that about right?"

I nodded. That was exactly right.

"The answer is simple enough. It wasn't overnight. I started coughing my brains out about seven months ago, back in May."

This was news to me; if he'd been doing any coughing, it hadn't been while I was around. Also, he was doing that bad-math thing again. "Al, hello? It's June. Seven months ago it was December."

He waved a hand at me—the fingers thin, his Marine Corps ring hanging on a digit that used to clasp it cozily—as if to say *Pass that by for now, just pass it.*

"At first I thought I just had a bad cold. But there was no fever, and instead of going away, the cough got worse. Then I started losing weight. Well, I ain't stupid, buddy, and I always knew the big C might be in the cards for me . . . although my father and mother smoked like goddam chimneys and lived into their eighties. I guess we always find excuses to keep on with our bad habits, don't we?"

He started coughing again, and pulled out the handkerchief. When the hacking subsided, he said: "I can't get off on a sidetrack, but I've been doing it my whole life and it's hard to stop. Harder than stopping with the cigarettes, actually. Next time I start wandering off-course, just kind of saw a finger across your throat, would you?"

"Okay," I said, agreeably enough. It had occurred to me by then that I was dreaming all of this. If so, it was an extremely vivid dream, right down to the shadows thrown by the revolving ceiling fan, marching across the place mats reading OUR MOST VALUABLE ASSET IS *YOU*!

"Long story short, I went to a doctor and got an X-ray, and there they were, big as billy-be-damned. Two tumors. Advanced necrosis. Inoperable."

An X-ray, I thought—*did they still use those to diagnose cancer?*

"I hung in for awhile, but in the end I had to come back."

"From where? Lewiston? Central Maine General?"

"From my vacation." His eyes looked fixedly at me from the dark hollows into which they were disappearing. "Except it was no vacation."

"Al, none of this makes any sense to me. Yesterday you were here and you were *fine.*"

"Take a good close look at my face. Start with my hair and work your way down. Try to ignore what the cancer's doing to me—it plays hell with a person's looks, no doubt about that—and then tell me I'm the same man you saw yesterday."

"Well, you obviously washed the dye out—"

"Never used any. I won't bother directing your attention to the teeth I lost while I was . . . away. I know you saw those. You think an X-ray machine did that? Or strontium-90 in the milk? I don't even *drink* milk, except for a splash in my last cup of coffee of the day."

"Strontium *what?*"

"Never mind. Get in touch with your, you know, feminine side. Look at me the way women look at other women when they're judging age."

I tried to do what he said, and while what I observed would never have stood up in court, it convinced me. There were web-works of lines spraying out from the corners of his eyes, and the lids had the tiny, delicately ruffled wrinkles you see on people who no longer have to flash their Senior Discount Cards when they step up to the multiplex box office. Skin-grooves that hadn't been there yesterday evening now made sine-waves across Al's brow. Two more lines—much deeper ones—bracketed his mouth. His chin was sharper, and the skin on his neck had grown loose. The sharp chin and wattled throat could have been caused by Al's cat-astrophic weight loss, but those lines . . . and if he wasn't lying about his hair . . .

He was smiling a little. It was a grim smile, but not without actual humor. Which somehow made it worse. "Remember my birthday last March? 'Don't worry, Al,' you said, 'if that stupid party hat catches on fire while you're hanging over the grill, I'll grab the fire extinguisher and put you out.' Remember that?"

I did. "You said you were an official Heinz."

"So I did. And now I'm sixty-two. I know the cancer makes me look even older, but these . . . and these . . ." He touched his fore-head, then the corner of one eye. "These are authentic age-tattoos. Badges of honor, in a way."

"Al . . . can I have a glass of water?"

"Of course. Shock, isn't it?" He looked at me sympathetically. "You're thinking, 'Either I'm crazy, he's crazy, or we both are.' I know. I've been there."

He levered himself out of the booth with an effort, his right hand going up beneath his left armpit, as if he were trying to hold himself together, somehow. Then he led me around the counter. As he did so, I put my finger on another element of this unreal encounter: except for the occasions when I shared a pew with him at St. Cyril's (these were rare; although I was raised in the faith, I'm not much of a Catlick) or happened to meet him on the street, I'd never seen Al out of his cook's apron.

He took a sparkling glass down and drew me a glass of water from a sparkling chrome-plated tap. I thanked him and turned to go back to the booth, but he tapped me on the shoulder. I wish he hadn't done that. It was like being tapped by Coleridge's Ancient Mariner, who stoppeth one of three.

"I want you to see something before we sit down again. It'll be quicker that way. Only *seeing* isn't the right word. I guess *experiencing* is a lot closer. Drink up, buddy."

I drank half the water. It was cool and good, but I never took my eye off him. That craven part of me was expecting to be jumped, like the first unwitting victim in one of those maniac-on-the-loose movies that always seem to have numbers in their titles. But Al only stood there with one hand propped on the counter. The hand was wrinkled, the knuckles big. It didn't look like the hand of a man in his fifties, even one with cancer, and—

"Did the radiation do that?" I asked suddenly.

"Do what?"

"You have a *tan*. Not to mention those dark spots on the backs of your hands. You get those either from radiation or too much sun."

"Well, since I haven't had any radiation treatments, that leaves the sun. I've gotten quite a lot of it over the last four years."

So far as I knew, Al had spent most of the last four years flipping burgers and making milkshakes under fluorescent lights, but I didn't say so. I just drank the rest of my water. When I set the glass down on the Formica counter, I noticed my hand was shaking slightly.

"Okay, what is it you want me to see? Or to experience?"

"Come this way."

He led me down the long, narrow galley area, past the double grill, the Fry-O-Lators, the sink, the FrostKing fridge, and the humming waist-high freezer. He stopped in front of the silent dishwasher and pointed to the door at the far end of the kitchen. It was low; Al would have to duck his head going through it, and he was only five-seven or so. I'm six-four—some of the kids called me Helicopter Epping.

"That's it," he said. "Through that door."

"Isn't that your pantry?" Strictly a rhetorical question; I'd seen him bring out enough cans, sacks of potatoes, and bags of dry goods over the years to know damn well what it was.

Al seemed not to have heard. "Did you know I originally opened this joint in Auburn?"

"No."

He nodded, and just that was enough to kick off another bout of coughing. He stifled it with the increasingly gruesome handkerchief. When the latest fit finally tapered off, he tossed the handkerchief into a handy trash can, then grabbed a swatch of napkins from a dispenser on the counter.

"It's an Aluminaire, made in the thirties and as art deco as they come. Wanted one ever since my dad took me to the Chat 'N Chew in Bloomington, back when I was a kid. Bought it fully outfitted and opened up on Pine Street. I was at that location for almost a year, and I saw that if I stayed, I'd be bankrupt in another year. There were too many other quick-bite joints in the neighborhood, some good, some not so good, all of em with their regulars. I was like a kid fresh out of law school who hangs out his shingle in a town that already has a dozen well-established shysters. Also, in those days Al's Famous Fatburger sold for two-fifty. Even back in 1990 two and a half was the best I could do."

"Then how in hell do you sell it for less than half that now? Unless it really *is* cat."

He snorted, a sound that produced a phlegmy echo of itself deep in his chest. "Buddy, what I sell is a hundred percent pure American beef, the best in the world. Do I know what people say? Sure. I shrug it off. What else can you do? Stop people from talking? You might as well try to stop the wind from blowing."

I ran a finger across my throat. Al smiled.

"Yeah, gettin off on one of those sidetracks, I know, but at least this one's part of the story.

"I could have kept beating my head against the wall on Pine Street, but Yvonne Templeton didn't raise any fools. 'Better to run away and fight again some other day,' she used to tell us kids. I took the last of my capital, wheedled the bank into loaning me another five grand—don't ask me how—and moved here to The Falls. Business still hasn't been great, not with the economy the way it is and not with all that stupid talk about Al's Catburgers or Dogburgers or Skunkburgers or whatever tickles people's fancy, but it turns out I'm no longer tied to the economy the way other people are. And it's all because of what's behind that pantry door. It wasn't there when I was set up in Auburn, I'd swear to that on a stack of Bibles ten feet high. It only showed up here."

"What are you talking about?"

He looked at me steadily from his watery, newly old eyes. "Talking's done for now. You need to find out for yourself. Go on, open it."

I looked at him doubtfully.

"Think of it as a dying man's last request," he said. "Go on, buddy. If you really are my buddy, that is. Open the door."

5

I'd be lying if I said my heart didn't kick into a higher gear when I turned the knob and pulled. I had no idea what I might be faced with (although I seem to remember having a brief image of dead cats, skinned and ready for the electric meat grinder), but when Al reached past my shoulder and turned on the light, what I saw was—

Well, a pantry.

It was small, and as neat as the rest of the diner. There were shelves stacked with big restaurant-sized cans on both walls. At the far end of the room, where the roof curved down, were some cleaning supplies, although the broom and mop had to lie flat because that part of the cubby was no more than three feet high. The floor was the same dark gray linoleum as the floor of the diner, but rather than the faint odor of cooked meat, in here there was the scent of coffee, vegetables, and spices. There was another smell, too, faint and not so pleasant.

"Okay," I said. "It's the pantry. Neat and fully stocked. You get an A in supply management, if there is such a thing."

"What do you smell?"

"Spices, mostly. Coffee. Maybe air freshener, too, I'm not sure."

"Uh-huh, I use Glade. Because of the other smell. Are you saying you don't smell anything else?"

"Yeah, there's something. Kind of sulphury. Makes me think of burnt matches." It also made me think of the poison gas I and my family had put out after my mom's Saturday night bean suppers, but I didn't like to say so. Did cancer treatments make you fart?

"It is sulphur. Other stuff, too, none of it Chanel No. 5. It's the smell of the mill, buddy."

More craziness, but all I said (in a tone of absurd cocktail-party politeness) was, "Really?"

He smiled again, exposing those gaps where teeth had been the day before. "What you're too polite to say is that Worumbo has been closed since Hector was a pup. That in fact it mostly burned to the ground back in the late eighties, and what's standing out there now"—he jerked a thumb back over his shoulder—"is nothing but a mill outlet store. Your basic Vacationland tourist stop, like the Kennebec Fruit Company during Moxie Days. You're also thinking it's about time you grabbed your cell phone and called for the men in the white coats. That about the size of it, buddy?"

"I'm not calling anybody, because you're not crazy." I was far from sure of that. "But this is just a pantry, and it's true that Worumbo Mills and Weaving hasn't turned out a bolt of cloth in the last quarter century."

"You aren't going to call anybody, you're right about that, because I want you to give me your cell phone, your wallet, and all the money you have in your pockets, coins included. It ain't a robbery; you'll get it all back. Will you do that?"

"How long is this going to take, Al? Because I've got some honors themes to correct before I can close up my grade book for the school year."

"It'll take as long as you want," he said, "because it'll only take two minutes. It *always* takes two minutes. Take an hour and really look around, if you want, but I wouldn't, not the first time, because it's a shock to the system. You'll see. Will you trust me on this?" Something he saw on my face tightened his lips over that reduced set of teeth. "Please. *Please,* Jake. Dying man's request."

I was sure he was crazy, but I was equally sure that he was telling the truth about his condition. His eyes seemed to have retreated deeper into their sockets in the short time we'd been talking. Also, he was exhausted. Just the two dozen steps from the booth at one end of the diner to the pantry at the other had left him swaying on his feet. And the bloody handkerchief, I reminded myself. Don't forget the bloody handkerchief.

Also . . . sometimes it's just easier to go along, don't you think? "Let go and let God," they like to say in the meetings my ex-wife goes to, but I decided this was going to be a case of let go and let Al. Up to a point, at any rate. And hey, I told myself, you have to go through more rigamarole than this just to get on an airplane these days. He isn't even asking me to put my shoes on a conveyor.

I unclipped my phone from my belt and put it on top of a canned tuna carton. I added my wallet, a little fold of paper money, a dollar fifty or so in change, and my key ring.

"Keep the keys, they don't matter."

Well, they did to me, but I kept my mouth shut.

Al reached into his pocket and brought out a sheaf of bills considerably thicker than the one I'd deposited on top of the carton. He held the wad out to me. "Mad money. In case you want to buy a souvenir, or something. Go on and take it."

"Why wouldn't I use my own money for that?" I sounded quite reasonable, I thought. Just as if this crazy conversation made sense.

"Never mind that now," he said. "The experience will answer most of your questions better than I could even if I was feeling tip-top, and right now I'm on the absolute other side of the world from tip-top. Take the money."

I took the money and thumbed through it. There were ones on top and they looked okay. Then I came to a five, and that looked both okay and not okay. It said **SILVER CERTIFI-CATE** above Abe Lincoln's picture, and to his left there was a big blue 5. I held it up to the light.

"It ain't counterfeit, if that's what you're thinking." Al sounded wearily amused.

Maybe not—it felt as real as it looked—but there was no bleed-through image.

"If it's real, it's old," I said.

"Just put the money in your pocket, Jake."

I did.

"Are you carrying a pocket calculator? Any other electronics?"

"Nope."

"I guess you're good to go, then. Turn around so you're looking at the back of the pantry." Before I could do it, he slapped his forehead and said, "Oh God, where are my brains? I forgot the Yellow Card Man."

"The who? The what?"

"The Yellow Card Man. That's just what I call him, I don't know his real name. Here, take this." He rummaged in his pocket, then handed me a fifty-cent piece. I hadn't seen one in years. Maybe not since I was a kid.

I hefted it. "I don't think you want to give me this. It's probably valuable."

"Of course it's valuable, it's worth half a buck."

He got coughing, and this time it shook him like a hard wind, but he waved me off when I started toward him. He leaned on the stack of cartons with my stuff on top, spat into the wad of napkins, looked, winced, and then closed his fist around them. His haggard face was now running with sweat.

"Hot flash, or somethin like it. Damn cancer's screwing with my thermostat along with the rest of my shit. About the Yellow Card Man. He's a wino, and he's harmless, but he's not like anyone else. It's like he *knows* something. I think it's only a coincidence—because he happens to be plumped down not far from where you're gonna come out—but I wanted to give you a heads-up about him."

"Well you're not doing a very good job," I said. "I have no fucking idea what you're talking about."

"He's gonna say, 'I got a yellow card from the greenfront, so gimme a buck because today's double-money day.' You got that?"

"Got it." The shit kept getting deeper.

"And he *does* have a yellow card, tucked in the brim of his hat. Probably nothing but a taxi company card or maybe a Red & White coupon he found in the gutter, but his brains are shot on cheap wine and he seems to thinks it's like Willy Wonka's Golden Ticket. So *you* say, 'I can't spare a buck but here's half a rock,' and you give it to him. Then he may say . . ." Al raised one of his now skeletal fingers. "He *may* say something like, 'Why are you here' or 'Where did you come from.' He may even say something like, 'You're not the same guy.' I don't think so, but it's possible. There's so much about this I don't know. Whatever he says, just leave him there by the drying shed—which is where he's sitting—and go out the gate. When you go he'll probably say, 'I *know* you could spare a buck, you cheap bastard,' but pay no attention. Don't look back. Cross the tracks and you'll be at the intersection of Main and Lisbon." He gave me an ironic smile. "After that, buddy, the world is yours."

"Drying shed?" I thought I vaguely remembered *something* near the place where the diner now stood, and I supposed it might have been the old Worumbo drying shed, but whatever it had been, it was gone now. If there had been a window at the back of the Aluminaire's cozy little pantry, it would have been looking out on nothing but a brick courtyard and an outerwear shop called Your Maine Snuggery. I had treated myself to a North Face parka there shortly after Christmas, and got it at a real bargain price.

"Never mind the drying shed, just remember what I told you. Now turn around again—that's right—and take two or three steps forward. Little ones. Baby steps. Pretend you're trying to find the top of a staircase with all the lights out—careful like that."

I did as he asked, feeling like the world's biggest dope. One step . . . lowering my head to keep from scraping it on the aluminum ceiling . . . two steps . . . now actually crouching a little. A few more steps and I'd have to get on my knees. That I had no intention of doing, dying man's request or not.

"Al, this is stupid. Unless you want me to bring you a carton of fruit cocktail or some of these little jelly packets, there's nothing I can do in h—"

That was when my foot went down, the way your foot does when you're starting down a flight of steps. Except my foot was still firmly on the dark gray linoleum floor. I could see it.

"There you go," Al said. The gravel had gone out of his voice, at least temporarily; the words were soft with satisfaction. "You found it, buddy."

But what had I found? What exactly was I experiencing? The power of suggestion seemed the most likely answer, since no matter what I felt, I could see my foot on the floor. Except . . .

You know how, on a bright day, you can close your eyes and see an afterimage of whatever you were just looking at? It was like that. When I looked at my foot, I saw it on the floor. But when I *blinked*—either a millisecond before or a millisecond after my eyes closed, I couldn't tell which—I caught a glimpse of my foot on a step. And it wasn't in the dim light of a sixty-watt bulb, either. It was in bright sunshine.

I froze.

"Go on," Al said. "Nothing's going to happen to you, buddy. Just go on." He coughed harshly, then said in a kind of desperate growl: "*I need you to do this.*"

So I did.

God help me, I did.

CHAPTER 2

1

I took another step forward and went down another step. My eyes still told me I was standing on the floor in the pantry of Al's Diner, but I was standing straight and the top of my head no longer scraped the roof of the pantry. Which was of course impossible. My stomach lurched unhappily in response to my sensory confusion, and I could feel the egg salad sandwich and the piece of apple pie I'd eaten for lunch preparing to push the ejector button.

From behind me—yet a little distant, as if he were standing fifteen yards away instead of only five feet—Al said, "Close your eyes, buddy, it's easier that way."

When I did it, the sensory confusion disappeared at once. It was like uncrossing your eyes. Or putting on the special glasses in a 3-D movie, that might be closer. I moved my right foot and went down another step. It *was* steps; with my vision shut off, my body had no doubt about that.

"Two more, then open em," Al said. He sounded farther away than ever. At the other end of the diner instead of standing in the pantry door.

I went down with my left foot. Went down with my right foot again, and all at once there was a pop inside my head, exactly like the kind you hear when you're in an airplane and the pressure changes suddenly. The dark field inside my eyelids turned red, and there was warmth on my skin. It was sunlight. No question about

29

it. And that faint sulphurous smell had grown thicker, moving up the olfactory scale from barely there to actively unpleasant. There was no question about that, either.

I opened my eyes.

I was no longer in the pantry. I was no longer in Al's Diner, either. Although there was no door from the pantry to the outside world, I *was* outside. I was in the courtyard. But it was no longer brick, and there were no outlet stores surrounding it. I was standing on crumbling, dirty cement. Several huge metal receptacles stood against the blank white wall where Your Maine Snuggery should have been. They were piled high with something and covered with sail-size sheets of rough brown burlap cloth.

I turned around to look at the big silver trailer which housed Al's Diner, but the diner was gone.

2

Where it should have been was the vast Dickensian bulk of Worumbo Mills and Weaving, and it was in full operation. I could hear the thunder of the dyers and dryers, the *shat-HOOSH, shat-HOOSH* of the huge weaving flats that had once filled the second floor (I had seen pictures of these machines, tended by women who wore kerchiefs and coveralls, in the tiny Lisbon Historical Society building on upper Main Street). Whitish-gray smoke poured from three tall stacks that had come down during a big windstorm in the eighties.

I was standing beside a large, green-painted cube of a building— the drying shed, I assumed. It filled half the courtyard and rose to a height of about twenty feet. I had come down a flight of stairs, but now there were no stairs. No way back. I felt a surge of panic.

"Jake?" It was Al's voice, but very faint. It seemed to arrive in my ears by a mere trick of acoustics, like a voice winding for miles down a long, narrow canyon. "You can come back the same way you got there. Feel for the steps."

I lifted my left foot, put it down, and felt a step. My panic eased.

"Go on." Faint. A voice seemingly powered by its own echoes. "Look around a little, then come back."

I didn't go anywhere at first, just stood still, wiping my mouth with the palm of my hand. My eyes felt like they were bugging out of their sockets. My scalp and a narrow strip of skin all the way down the middle of my back was crawling. I was scared— almost terrified—but balancing that off and keeping panic at bay (for the moment) was a powerful curiosity. I could see my shadow on the concrete, as clear as something cut from black cloth. I could see flakes of rust on the chain that closed the drying shed off from the rest of the courtyard. I could smell the powerful effluent pouring from the triple stacks, strong enough to make my eyes sting. An EPA inspector would have taken one sniff of that shit and shut the whole operation down in a New England minute. Except . . . I didn't think there were any EPA inspectors in the vicinity. I wasn't even sure the EPA had been invented yet. I knew where I was; Lisbon Falls, Maine, deep in the heart of Androscoggin County.

The real question was *when* I was.

3

A sign I couldn't read hung from the chain—the message was facing the wrong way. I started toward it, then turned around. I closed my eyes and shuffled forward, reminding myself to take baby steps. When my left foot clunked against the bottom step that went back up to the pantry of Al's Diner (or so I devoutly hoped), I felt in my back pocket and brought out a folded sheet of paper: my exalted department head's "Have a nice summer and don't forget the July in-service day" memo. I briefly wondered how he'd feel about Jake Epping teaching a six-week block called The Literature of Time Travel next year. Then I tore a strip from the top, crumpled it, and dropped it on the first step of the invisible stairway. It landed on the ground, of course, but either way it

marked the spot. It was a warm, still afternoon and I didn't think
it would blow away, but I found a little chunk of concrete and
used it as a paperweight, just to be sure. It landed on the step, but
it also landed on the scrap of memo. Because there *was* no step. A
snatch of some old pop song drifted through my head: *First there is
a mountain, then there is no mountain, then there is.*

Look around a little, Al had said, and I decided that was what
I'd do. I figured if I hadn't lost my mind already, I was probably
going to be okay for awhile longer. Unless I saw a parade of pink
elephants or a UFO hovering over John Crafts Auto, that was. I
tried to tell myself this wasn't happening, *couldn't* be happening,
but it wouldn't wash. Philosophers and psychologists may argue
over what's real and what isn't, but most of us living ordinary lives
know and accept the texture of the world around us. This was happening. All else aside, it was too goddam stinky to be a hallucination.

I walked to the chain, which hung at thigh level, and ducked
beneath it. Stenciled in black paint on the other side was **NO
ADMITTANCE BEYOND THIS POINT UNTIL SEWER
PIPE IS REPAIRED**. I looked back again, saw no indication that
repairs were in the immediate offing, walked around the corner
of the drying shed, and almost stumbled over the man sunning
himself there. Not that he could expect to get much of a tan.
He was wearing an old black overcoat that puddled around him
like an amorphous shadow. There were dried crackles of snot on
both sleeves. The body inside the coat was scrawny to the point of
emaciation. His iron-gray hair hung in snaggles around his beard-
scruffy cheeks. He was a wino if ever a wino there was.

Cocked back on his head was a filthy fedora that looked straight
out of a 1950s film noir, the kind where all the women have big
bazonkas and all the men talk fast around the cigarettes stuck in
the corners of their mouths. And yep, poking up from the fedora's
hatband, like an old-fashioned reporter's press pass, was a yellow
card. Once it had probably been a bright yellow, but much handling by grimy fingers had turned it bleary.

When my shadow fell across his lap, the Yellow Card Man turned and surveyed me with bleary eyes.

"Who the fuck're you?" he asked, only it came out *Hoo-a fuck-a you?*

Al hadn't given me detailed instructions on how to answer questions, so I said what seemed safest. "None of your fucking business."

"Well fuck you, too."

"Fine," I said. "We are in accord."

"Huh?"

"Have a nice day." I started toward the gate, which stood open on a steel track. Beyond it, to the left, was a parking lot that had never been there before. It was full of cars, most of them battered and all of them old enough to belong in a car museum. There were Buicks with portholes and Fords with torpedo noses. *Those belong to actual millworkers,* I thought. *Actual millworkers who are inside now, working for hourly wages.*

"I got a yellow card from the greenfront," the wino said. He sounded both truculent and troubled. "So gimme a buck because today's double-money day."

I held the fifty-cent piece out to him. Feeling like an actor who only has one line in the play, I said: "I can't spare a buck, but here's half a rock."

Then you give it to him, Al had said, but I didn't need to. The Yellow Card Man snatched it from me and held it close to his face. For a moment I thought he was actually going to bite into it, but he just closed his long-fingered hand around it in a fist, making it disappear. He peered at me again, his face almost comic with distrust.

"Who are you? What are you doing here?"

"I'll be damned if I know," I said, and turned back to the gate. I expected him to hurl more questions after me, but there was only silence. I went out through the gate.

4

The newest car in the lot was a Plymouth Fury from—I think—the mid- or late fifties. The plate on it looked like an impossibly antique version of the one on the back of my Subaru; that plate came, at my ex-wife's request, with a pink breast cancer ribbon. The one I was looking at now *did* say VACATIONLAND, but it was orange instead of white. As in most states, Maine plates now come with letters—the one on my Subaru is 23383 IY—but the one on the back of the almost-new white-over-red Fury was 90-811. No letters.

I touched the trunk. It was hard and warm from the sun. It was real.

Cross the tracks and you'll be at the intersection of Main and Lisbon. After that, buddy, the world is yours.

There were no railroad tracks passing in front of the old mill—not in my time, there weren't—but they were here, all right. Not just leftover artifacts, either. They were polished, gleaming. And somewhere in the distance I could hear the *wuff-chuff* of an actual train. When was the last time trains had passed through Lisbon Falls? Probably not since the mill closed and U.S. Gypsum (known to the locals as U.S. Gyp 'Em) was running round the clock.

Except it is running round the clock, I thought. *I'd bet money on it. And so is the mill. Because this is no longer the second decade of the twenty-first century.*

I had started walking again without even realizing it—walking like a man in a dream. Now I stood on the corner of Main Street and Route 196, also known as the Old Lewiston Road. Only now there was nothing old about it. And diagonally across the intersection, on the opposite corner—

It was the Kennebec Fruit Company, which was certainly a grandiose name for a store that had been tottering on the edge of oblivion—or so it seemed to me—for the ten years I'd been teaching at LHS. Its unlikely raison d'être and only means of survival was Moxie, that weirdest of soft drinks. The proprietor of the Fruit Company, an elderly sweet-natured man named Frank Anicetti, had once told me the world's population divided naturally (and probably by genetic inheritance) into two groups: the tiny but blessed elect who prized Moxie above all other potables . . . and everybody else. Frank called everybody else "the unfortunately handicapped majority."

The Kennebec Fruit Company of my time was a faded yellow-and-green box with a dirty show window barren of goods . . . unless the cat that sometimes sleeps there is for sale. The roof is sway-backed from many snowy winters. There's little on offer inside except for Moxie souvenirs: bright orange tee-shirts reading I'VE GOT MOXIE!, bright orange hats, vintage calendars, tin signs that *looked* vintage but were probably made last year in China. For most of the year the place is devoid of customers, most of the shelves denuded of goods . . . although you can still get a few sugary snack foods or a bag of potato chips (if you like the salt-and-vinegar kind, that is). The soft-drink cooler is stocked with nothing but Moxie. The beer cooler is empty.

Each July, Lisbon Falls hosts the Maine Moxie Festival. There are bands, fireworks, and a parade featuring—I swear this is true—Moxie floats and local beauty queens dressed in Moxie-colored tank bathing suits, which means an orange so bright it can cause retinal burns. The parade marshal is always dressed as the Moxie Doc, which means a white coat, a stethoscope, and one of those funky mirrors on a headband. Two years ago the marshal was LHS principal Stella Langley, and she'll never live it down.

During the festival, the Kennebec Fruit Company comes alive and does excellent business, mostly provided by bemused tourists on their way to the western Maine resort areas. The rest of the year it is little more than a husk haunted by the faint odor of Moxie, a smell that has always reminded me—probably because I belong to the unfortunately handicapped majority—of Musterole, the fabulously stinky stuff my mother insisted on rubbing into my throat and chest when I had a cold.

What I was looking at now from the far side of the Old Lewiston Road was a thriving business in the prime of life. The sign hung over the door (FRESH UP WITH 7-UP on top, WELCOME TO THE KENNEBEC FRUIT CO. below) was bright enough to throw arrows of sun at my eyes. The paint was fresh, the roof unbowed by the weather. People were going in and coming out. And in the show window, instead of a cat . . .

Oranges, by God. The Kennebec Fruit Company once sold actual fruit. Who knew?

I started across the street, then pulled back as an inter-city bus snored toward me. The route sign above the divided windshield read LEWISTON EXPRESS. When the bus braked to a stop at the railroad crossing, I saw that most of the passengers were smoking. The atmosphere in there must have been roughly akin to the atmosphere of Saturn.

Once the bus had gone on its way (leaving behind a smell of half-cooked diesel to mix with the rotten-egg stench belching from the Worumbo's stacks), I crossed the street, wondering briefly what would happen if I were hit by a car. Would I blink out of existence? Wake up lying on the floor of Al's pantry? Probably neither. Probably I would just die here, in a past for which a lot of people probably felt nostalgic. Possibly because they had forgotten how bad the past smelled, or because they had never considered that aspect of the Nifty Fifties in the first place.

A kid was standing outside the Fruit Company with one black-booted foot cocked back against the wood siding. The collar of his shirt was turned up at the nape of his neck, and his hair was combed in a style I recognized (from old movies, mostly) as Early Elvis. Unlike the boys I was used to seeing in my classes, he sported no goatee, not even a flavor patch below the chin. I realized that in the world I was now visiting (I *hoped* I was only visiting), he'd be kicked out of LHS for showing up with even a single strand of facial hair. Instantly.

I nodded to him. James Dean nodded back and said, "Hi-ho, Daddy-O."

I went inside. A bell jingled above the door. Instead of dust and gently decaying wood, I smelled oranges, apples, coffee, and fragrant tobacco. To my right was a rack of comic books with their covers torn off—*Archie, Batman, Captain Marvel, Plastic Man, Tales from the Crypt.* The hand-printed sign above this trove, which would have sent any eBay aficionado into paroxysms, read COMIX 5¢ EA THREE FOR 10¢ NINE FOR A QUARTER *PLEASE DON'T HANDLE UNLESS YOU INTEND TO BUY.*

On the left was a rack of newspapers. No *New York Times,* but there were copies of the *Portland Press Herald* and one leftover *Boston Globe.* The *Globe*'s headline trumpeted, **DULLES HINTS CONCESSIONS IF RED CHINA RENOUNCES USE OF FORCE IN FORMOSA**. The dates on both were Tuesday, September 9, 1958.

5

I took the *Globe,* which sold for eight cents, and walked toward a marble-topped soda fountain that did not exist in my time. Standing behind it was Frank Anicetti. It was him all right, right down to the distinguished wings of gray above his ears. Only this version—call him Frank 1.0—was thin instead of plump, and wearing rimless bifocals. He was also taller. Feeling like a stranger in my own body, I slid onto one of the stools.

He nodded at the paper. "That going to do you, or can I get you something from the fountain?"

"Anything cold that's not Moxie," I heard myself say.

Frank 1.0 smiled at that. "Don't carry it, son. How about a root beer instead?"

"Sounds good." And it did. My throat was dry and my head was hot. I felt like I was running a fever.

"Five or ten?"

"I beg your pardon?"

"Five- or ten-cent beer?" He said it the Maine way: *beeyah.*

"Oh. Ten, I guess."

"Well, I guess you guess right." He opened an ice cream freezer and removed a frosty mug roughly the size of a lemonade pitcher. He filled it from a tap and I could smell the root beer, rich and strong. He scraped the foam off the top with the handle of a wooden spoon, then filled it all the way to the top and set it down on the counter. "There you go. That and the paper's eighteen cents. Plus a penny for the governor."

I handed over one of Al's vintage dollars, and Frank 1.0 made change.

I sipped through the foam on top, and was amazed. It was . . . *full.* Tasty all the way through. I don't know how to express it any better than that. This fifty-years-gone world smelled worse than I ever would have expected, but it tasted a whole hell of a lot better.

"This is wonderful," I said.

"Ayuh? Glad you like it. Not from around here, are you?"

"No."

"Out-of-stater?"

"Wisconsin," I said. Not entirely a lie; my family lived in Milwaukee until I was eleven, when my father got a job teaching English at the University of Southern Maine. I'd been knocking around the state ever since.

"Well, you picked the right time to come," Anicetti said. "Most of the summer people are gone, and as soon as that happens, prices go down. What you're drinkin, for example. After Labor Day, a ten-cent root beer only costs a dime."

The bell over the door jangled; the floorboards creaked. It was a companionable creak. The last time I'd ventured into the Kennebec Fruit, hoping for a roll of Tums (I was disappointed), they had groaned.

A boy who might have been seventeen slipped behind the counter. His dark hair was cropped close, not quite a crewcut. His resemblance to the man who had served me was unmistakable, and I realized that this was *my* Frank Anicetti. The guy who had lopped the head of foam off my root beer was his father. Frank 2.0 didn't give me so much as a glance; to him I was just another customer.

"Titus has got the truck up on the lift," he told his dad. "Says it'll be ready by five."

"Well, that's good," Anicetti Senior said, and lit a cigarette. For the first time I noticed the marble top of the soda fountain was lined with small ceramic ashtrays. Written on the sides was WINSTON TASTES GOOD LIKE A CIGARETTE SHOULD! He looked back at me and said, "You want a scoop of vanilla in your beer? On the house. We like to treat tourists right, especially when they turn up late."

"Thanks, but this is fine," I said, and it was. Any more sweetness and I thought my head would explode. And it was *strong*—like drinking carbonated espresso.

The kid gave me a grin that was as sweet as the stuff in the frosted mug—there was none of the amused disdain I'd felt emanating from the Elvis wannabe outside. "We read a story in school," he said, "where the locals eat the tourists if they show up after the season's over."

"Frankie, that's a hell of a thing to tell a visitor," Mr. Anicetti said. But he was smiling when he said it.

"It's okay," I said. "I've taught that story myself. Shirley Jackson, right? 'The Summer People.' "

"That's the one," Frank agreed. "I didn't really get it, but I liked it."

I took another pull on my root beer, and when I set it down (it made a satisfyingly thick chunk on the marble counter), I wasn't exactly surprised to see it was almost gone. *I could get addicted to these,* I thought. *It beats the living shit out of Moxie.*

The elder Anicetti exhaled a plume of smoke toward the ceiling, where an overhead paddle fan pulled it into lazy blue rafters. "Do you teach out in Wisconsin, Mr.—?"

"Epping," I said. I was too caught by surprise to even think of giving a fake name. "I do, actually. But this is my sabbatical year."

"That means he's taking a year off," Frank said.

"I know what it means," Anicetti said. He was trying to sound irritated and doing a bad job of it. I decided I liked these two as much as I liked the root beer. I even liked the aspiring teenage hood outside, if only because he didn't know he was already a cliché. There was a sense of safety here, a sense of—I don't know—preordination. It was surely false, this world was as dangerous as any other, but I possessed one piece of knowledge I would before this afternoon have believed was reserved only for God: I knew that the smiling boy who had enjoyed the Shirley Jackson story (even though he didn't "get it") was going to live through that day and over fifty years of days to come. He wasn't going to be killed in a car crash, have a heart attack, or contract lung cancer from breathing his father's secondhand smoke. Frank Anicetti was good to go.

I glanced at the clock on the wall (START YOUR DAY WITH A SMILE, the face said, DRINK CHEER-UP COFFEE). It read 12:22. That was nothing to me, but I pretended to be startled. I drank off the rest of my beeyah and stood up. "Got to get moving if I'm going to meet my friends in Castle Rock on time."

"Well, take it easy on Route 117," Anicetti said. "That road's a bugger." It came out *buggah.* I hadn't heard such a thick Maine accent in years. Then I realized that was literally true, and I almost laughed out loud.

"I will," I said. "Thanks. And son? About that Shirley Jackson story."

"Yes, sir?" *Sir,* yet. And nothing sarcastic about it. I was deciding that 1958 had been a pretty good year. Aside from the stench of the mill and the cigarette smoke, that was.

"There's nothing to get."

"No? That's not what Mr. Marchant says."

"With all due respect to Mr. Marchant, you tell him Jake Epping says that sometimes a cigar is just a smoke and a story's just a story."

He laughed. "I will! Period three tomorrow morning!"

"Good." I nodded to the father, wishing I could tell him that, thanks to Moxie (which he didn't carry . . . yet), his business was going to be standing on the corner of Main Street and the Old Lewiston Road long after he was gone. "Thanks for the root beer."

"Come back anytime, son. I'm thinking about lowering the price on the large."

"To a dime?"

He grinned. Like his son's, it was easy and open. "Now you're cooking with gas."

The bell jingled. Three ladies came in. No slacks; they wore dresses with hemlines that dropped halfway down their shins. And hats! Two with little fluffs of white veil. They began rummaging through the open crates of fruit, looking for perfection. I started away from the soda fountain, then had a thought and turned back.

"Can you tell me what a greenfront is?"

The father and the son exchanged an amused glance that made me think of an old joke. Tourist from Chicago driving a fancy sportscar pulls up to a farmhouse way out in the country. Old farmer's sitting on the porch, smoking a corncob pipe. Tourist leans out of his Jaguar and asks, "Say, oldtimer, can you tell me how to get to East Machias?" Old farmer puffs thoughtfully on his pipe a time or two, then says, "Don'tcha move a goddam inch."

"You really are an out-of-stater, aren't you?" Frank asked. His accent wasn't as thick as his father's. *Probably watches more TV,* I thought. *There's nothing like TV when it comes to eroding a regional accent.*

"I am," I said.

"That's funny, because I could swear I hear a little Yankee twang."

"It's a Yooper thing," I said. "You know, the Upper Peninsula?" Except—dang!—the UP was Michigan.

But neither of them seemed to realize it. In fact young Frank turned away and started doing dishes. By hand, I noticed.

"The greenfront's the liquor store," Anicetti said. "Right across the street, if you're wanting to pick up a pint of something."

"I think the root beer's good enough for me," I said. "I was just wondering. Have a nice day."

"You too, my friend. Come back and see us."

I passed the fruit-examining trio, murmuring "Ladies" as I went by. And wishing I had a hat to tip. A fedora, maybe.

Like the ones you see in the old movies.

6

The aspiring hoodlum had left his post, and I thought about walking up Main Street to see what else had changed, but only for a second. No sense pressing my luck. Suppose someone asked about my clothes? I thought my sport coat and slacks looked more or less all right, but did I know that for sure? And then there was my hair, which touched my collar. In my own time that would be considered perfectly okay for a high school teacher—conservative, even—but it might garner glances in a decade where shaving the back of the neck was considered a normal part of the barbering service and sideburns were reserved for rockabilly dudes like the one who had called me Daddy-O. Of course I could say I was a tourist, that all men wore their hair a little long in Wisconsin, it was quite the coming thing, but hair and clothes—that feeling of standing out, like some space alien in an imperfectly assumed human disguise—was only part of it.

Mostly I was just plain freaked. Not mentally tottering, I think a human mind that's moderately well-adjusted can absorb a lot of strangeness before it actually totters, but freaked, yes. I kept thinking about the ladies in their long dresses and hats, ladies who would be embarrassed to show so much as the edge of a bra strap in public. And the taste of that root beer. How *full* it had been.

Directly across the street was a modest storefront with MAINE STATE LIQUOR STORE printed in raised letters over the small show window. And yes, the façade was a light green. Inside I could just make out my pal from the drying shed. His long black coat hung from his coathanger shoulders; he had taken off his hat and his hair stood out around his head like that of a cartoon nebbish who has just inserted Finger A in Electric Socket B. He was gesticulating at the clerk with both hands, and I could see his precious yellow card in one. I felt certain that Al Templeton's half a rock was in the other. The clerk, who was wearing a short white tunic that looked quite a bit like the one the Moxie Doc wore in the annual parade, looked singularly unimpressed.

I walked to the corner, waited on traffic, and crossed back to the Worumbo side of the Old Lewiston Road. A couple of men were pushing a dolly loaded with bales of cloth across the courtyard, smoking and laughing. I wondered if they had any idea what the combination of cigarette smoke and mill pollution was doing to their innards, and supposed not. Probably that was a blessing, although it was more a question for a philosophy teacher than for a guy who earned his daily bread exposing sixteen-year-olds to the wonders of Shakespeare, Steinbeck, and Shirley Jackson.

When they had entered the mill, rolling their dolly between the rusty metal jaws of doors three stories high, I crossed back to the chain with the **NO ADMITTANCE BEYOND THIS POINT** sign hanging from it. I told myself not to walk too fast, and not to peer all around me—not to do *anything* that would attract attention—but it was hard. Now that I was almost back to where I came in, the urge to hurry was almost irresistible. My mouth was dry, and the big root beer I'd drunk roiled in my stomach. What if I couldn't get back? What if the marker I'd dropped was gone? What if it was still there, but the stairs weren't?

Easy, I told myself. *Easy.*

I couldn't resist one quick survey before ducking under the chain, but the courtyard was entirely mine. Somewhere distant, like a sound heard in a dream, I could again hear that low diesel *wuff-chuff*. It called to mind another line from another song: *This train has got the disappearing railroad blues.*

I walked down the green flank of the drying shed, heart beating hard and high up in my chest. The torn scrap of paper with the chunk of concrete on top of it was still there; so far so good. I kicked at it gently, thinking *Please God let this work, please God let me get back.*

The toe of my shoe kicked the chunk of concrete—I saw it go skittering away—but it also thumped to a dead stop against the step. Those things were mutually exclusive, but they both happened. I took one more look around, even though no one in the courtyard could see me in this narrow lane unless they happened to be passing directly in front of it at one end or the other. No one was.

I went up one step. My foot could feel it, even though my eyes told me I was still standing on the cracked paving of the courtyard. The root beer took another warning lurch in my stomach. I closed my eyes and that was a little better. I took the second step, then the third. They were shallow, those steps. When I took the fourth one, the summer heat disappeared from the back of my neck and the dark behind my eyelids became deeper. I tried to take the fifth step, only there was no fifth step. I bumped my head on the low pantry ceiling instead. A hand grasped my forearm and I almost screamed.

"Relax," Al said. "Relax, Jake. You're back."

7

He offered me a cup of coffee, but I shook my head. My stomach was still sudsing. He poured himself one, and we went back to the booth where we had begun this madman's journey. My wallet, cell phone, and money were piled in the middle of the table. Al sat down with a gasp of pain and relief. He looked a little less drawn and a little more relaxed.

"So," he said. "You went and you came back. What do you think?"

"Al, I don't know what to think. I'm rocked right down to my foundations. You found this by accident?"

"Totally. Less than a month after I got myself set up here. I must have still had Pine Street dust on the heels of my shoes. The first time, I actually *fell* down those stairs, like Alice into the rabbit-hole. I thought I'd gone insane."

I could imagine. I'd had at least some preparation, poor though it had been. And really, was there any adequate way to prepare a person for a trip back in time?

"How long was I gone?"

"Two minutes. I told you, it's always two minutes. No matter how long you stay." He coughed, spat into a fresh wad of napkins, and folded them away in his pocket. "And when you go down the steps, it's always 11:58 A.M. on the morning of September ninth, 1958. Every trip is the first trip. Where did you go?"

"The Kennebec Fruit. I had a root beer. It was fantastic."

"Yeah, things taste better there. Less preservatives, or something."

"You know Frank Anicetti? I met him as a kid of seventeen."

Somehow, in spite of everything, I expected Al to laugh, but he took it as a matter of course. "Sure. I've met Frank many times. But he only meets me once—back then, I mean. For Frank, every time is the first time. He comes in, right? From the Chevron. 'Titus has got the truck up on the lift,' he tells his dad. 'Says it'll be ready by five.' I've heard that fifty times, at least. Not that I always go into the Fruit when I go back, but when I do, I hear it. Then the ladies come in to pick over the fruit. Mrs. Symonds and her friends. It's like going to the same movie over and over and over again."

"Every time is the first time." I said it slowly, putting a space around each word. Trying to get them to make sense in my mind.

"Right."

"And every person you meet is meeting *you* for the first time, no matter how many times you've met before."

"Right."

"I could go back and have the same conversation with Frank and his dad and they wouldn't know."

"Right again. Or you could change something—order a banana split instead of a root beer, say—and the rest of the conversation would go a different way. The only one who seems to suspect something's off is the Yellow Card Man, and he's too booze-fucked

45

to know what he's feeling. If I'm right, that is, and he feels anything. If he does, it's because he just happens to be sitting near the rabbit-hole. Or whatever it is. Maybe it puts out some kind of energy field. He—"

But he got coughing again and couldn't go on. Watching him doubled over, holding his side and trying not to show me how bad it hurt—how it was tearing him up inside—was painful itself. *He can't go on this way,* I thought. *He's no more than a week from the hospital, and probably just days.* And wasn't that why he'd called me? Because he had to pass on this amazing secret to somebody before the cancer shut his lips forever?

"I thought I could give you the entire lowdown this afternoon, but I can't," Al said when he had control of himself again. "I need to go home, take some of my dope, and put my feet up. I've never taken anything stronger than aspirin in my whole life, and that Oxy crap puts me out like a light. I'll sleep for six hours or so and then feel better for awhile. A little stronger. Can you come by my place around nine-thirty?"

"I could if I knew where you live," I said.

"Little cottage on Vining Street. Number nineteen. Look for the lawn gnome beside the porch. You can't miss it. He's waving a flag."

"What have we got to talk about, Al? I mean . . . you *showed* me. I believe you now." So I did . . . but for how long? Already my brief visit to 1958 had taken on the fading texture of a dream. A few hours (or a few days) and I'd probably be able to convince myself that I *had* dreamed it.

"We've got a lot to talk about, buddy. Will you come?" He didn't repeat *dying man's request,* but I read it in his eyes.

"All right. Do you want a ride to your place?"

His eyes flashed at that. "I've got my truck, and it's only five blocks. I can drive myself that far."

"Sure you can," I said, hoping I sounded more convinced than I felt. I got up and started putting my stuff back into my pockets. I encountered the wad of cash he'd given me and took it out. Now

I understood the changes in the five-spot. There were probably changes in the other bills, as well.

I held it out and he shook his head. "Nah, keep it, I got plenty."

But I put it down on the table. "If every time's the first time, how can you keep the money you bring back? How come it isn't erased the next time you go?"

"No clue, buddy. I told you, there's all kinds of stuff I don't know. There are rules, and I've figured out a few, but not many." His face lit in a wan but genuinely amused smile. "You brought back your root beer, didn't you? Still sloshing around in your belly, isn't it?"

As a matter of fact it was.

"Well there you go. I'll see you tonight, Jake. I'll be rested and we'll talk this out."

"One more question?"

He flicked a hand at me, a go-ahead gesture. I noticed that his nails, which he always kept scrupulously clean, were yellow and cracked. Another bad sign. Not as telling as the thirty-pound weight loss, but still bad. My dad used to say you can tell a lot about a person's health just by the state of his or her fingernails.

"The Famous Fatburger."

"What about it?" But there was a smile playing at the corners of his mouth.

"You can sell cheap because you buy cheap, isn't that right?"

"Ground chuck from the Red & White," he said. "Fifty-four cents a pound. I go in every week. Or I did until my latest adventure, which took me a long way from The Falls. I trade with Mr. Warren, the butcher. If I ask him for ten pounds of ground chuck, he says, 'Coming right up.' If I ask for twelve or fourteen, he says, 'Going to have to give me a minute to grind you up some fresh. Having a family get-together?'"

"Always the same."

"Yes."

"Because it's always the first time."

"Correct. It's like the story of the loaves and fishes in the Bible, when you think of it. I buy the same ground chuck week after week. I've fed it to hundreds or thousands of people, in spite of those stupid catburger rumors, and it always renews itself."

"You buy the same meat, over and over." Trying to get it through my skull.

"The same meat, at the same time, from the same butcher. Who always says the same things, unless I say something different. I'll admit, buddy, that it's sometimes crossed my mind to walk up to him and say, 'How's it going there, Mr. Warren, you old bald bastard? Been fucking any warm chicken-holes lately?' He'd never remember. But I never have. Because he's a nice man. Most people I've met back then are nice folks." At this he looked a little wistful.

"I don't understand how you can buy meat there . . . serve it here . . . then buy it again."

"Join the club, buddy. I just appreciate like hell that you're still here—I could have lost you. For that matter, you didn't have to answer the phone when I called the school."

Part of me wished I hadn't, but I didn't say that. Probably I didn't have to. He was sick, not blind.

"Come to the house tonight. I'll tell you what I've got in mind, and then you can do whatever you think is best. But you'll have to decide pretty fast, because time is short. Kind of ironic, wouldn't you say, considering where the invisible steps in my pantry come out?"

More slowly than ever, I said: "Every . . . time . . . is . . . the . . . first time."

He smiled again. "I think you've got that part. I'll see you tonight, okay? Nineteen Vining Street. Look for the gnome with the flag."

8

I left Al's Diner at three-thirty. The six hours between then and nine-thirty weren't as weird as visiting Lisbon Falls fifty-three years ago, but almost. Time seemed simultaneously to drag and speed by. I drove back to the house I was buying in Sabattus (Christy and I sold the one we'd owned in The Falls and split the take when our marital corporation dissolved). I thought I'd take a nap, but of course I couldn't sleep. After twenty minutes of lying on my back, straight as a poker, and staring up at the ceiling, I went into the bathroom to take a leak. As I watched the urine splash into the bowl, I thought: *That's processed root beer from 1958.* But at the same time I was thinking that was bullshit, Al had hypnotized me somehow.

That doubling thing, see?

I tried to finish reading the last of the honors essays, and wasn't a bit surprised to find I couldn't do it. Wield Mr. Epping's fearsome red pen? Pass critical judgments? That was a laugh. I couldn't even make the words connect. So I turned on the tube (throwback slang from the Nifty Fifties; televisions no longer *have* tubes) and channel-surfed for awhile. On TMC I came across an old movie called *Drag-strip Girl.* I found myself watching the old cars and angst-ridden teens so intently it was giving me a headache, and I turned it off. I made myself a stir-fry, then couldn't eat it even though I was hungry. I sat there, looking at it on the plate, thinking about Al Templeton serving the same dozen or so pounds of hamburger over and over, year after year. It really *was* like the miracle of the loaves and fishes, and so what if catburger and dogburger rumors circulated due to his low prices? Given what he was paying for meat, he had to be making an absurd profit on every Fatburger he did sell.

When I realized I was pacing around my kitchen—unable to sleep, unable to read, unable to watch TV, a perfectly good stir-fry turned down the sink-pig—I got in my car and drove back to town. It was quarter to seven by then, and there were plenty of parking spaces on Main Street. I pulled in across from the Kennebec Fruit and sat behind the wheel, staring at a paint-peeling relic that had once been a thriving smalltown business. Closed for the day, it looked ready for the wrecking ball. The only sign of human habitation were a few Moxie signs in the dusty show window

(DRINK MOXIE FOR *HEALTH!,* read the biggest), and they were so old-fashioned they could have been left behind for years.

The Fruit's shadow stretched across the street to touch my car. To my right, where the liquor store had been, there was now a tidy brick building that housed a branch of Key Bank. Who needed a greenfront when you could bop into any grocery store in the state and bop back out with a pint of Jack or a quart of coffee brandy? Not in a flimsy paper bag, either; in these modern times we use plastic, son. Lasts a thousand years. And speaking of grocery stores, I had never heard of one called the Red & White. If you wanted to shop for food in The Falls, you went to the IGA a block down on 196. It was right across from the old railroad station. Which was now a combination tee-shirt shop and tattoo parlor.

All the same, the past felt very close just then—maybe it was just the golden cast of the declining summer light, which has always struck me as slightly supernatural. It was as if 1958 were still right here, only hidden beneath a flimsy film of intervening years. And, if I hadn't imagined what had happened to me this afternoon, that was true.

He wants me to do something. Something he would have done himself, but the cancer stopped him. He said he went back and stayed for four years (at least I thought that was what he'd said), *but four years wasn't long enough.*

Was I willing to go back down those stairs and stay for four-plus years? Basically take up residence? Come back two minutes later . . . only in my forties, with strands of gray starting to show up in my hair? I couldn't imagine doing that, but I couldn't imagine what Al had found so important back there in the first place. The one thing I did know was that four or six or eight years of my life was too much to ask, even for a dying man.

I still had over two hours before I was scheduled to show up at Al's. I decided I'd go back home, make myself another meal, and this time force myself to eat it. After that, I'd take another shot at finishing my honors essays. I might be one of the very few people who had ever traveled back in time—for that matter, Al and

I might be the only ones who had ever done it in the history of the world—but my poetry students were still going to want their final grades.

I hadn't had the radio on when I drove to town, but I turned it on now. Like my TV, it gets its programming from computer-driven space voyagers that go whirling around the earth at a height of twenty-two thousand miles, an idea that surely would have been greeted with wide-eyed wonder (but probably not outright disbelief) by the teenager Frank Anicetti had been back in the day. I tuned to the Sixties on Six and caught Danny & the Juniors working out on "Rock and Roll Is Here to Stay"—three or four urgent, harmonic voices singing over a jackhammer piano. They were followed by Little Richard screaming "Lucille" at the top of his lungs, and then Ernie K-Doe more or less moaning "Mother-in-Law": *She thinks her advice is a contribution, but if she would leave that would be the solution.* It all sounded as fresh and sweet as the oranges Mrs. Symonds and her friends had been picking over that early afternoon.

It sounded *new.*

Did I want to spend years in the past? No. But I *did* want to go back. If only to hear how Little Richard sounded when he was still top of the pops. Or get on a Trans World Airlines plane without having to take off my shoes, submit to a full-body scan, and go through a metal detector.

And I wanted another root beer.

CHAPTER 3

1

The gnome did indeed have a flag, but not an American one. Not even the Maine flag with the moose on it. The one the gnome was holding had a vertical blue stripe and two fat horizontal stripes, the top one white and the bottom one red. It also had a single star. I gave the gnome a pat on his pointy hat as I went past and mounted the front steps of Al's little house on Vining Street, thinking about an amusing song by Ray Wylie Hubbard: "Screw You, We're from Texas."

The door opened before I could ring the bell. Al was wearing a bathrobe over pajamas, and his newly white hair was in corkscrew tangles—a serious case of bedhead if I'd ever seen one. But the sleep (and the painkillers, of course) had done him some good. He still looked sick, but the lines around his mouth weren't so deep and his gait, as he led me down the short stub of a hall and into his living room, seemed surer. He was no longer pressing his right hand into his left armpit, as if trying to hold himself together.

"Look a little more like my old self, do I?" he asked in his gravelly voice as he sat down in the easy chair in front of the TV. Only he didn't really sit, just kind of positioned himself and dropped.

"You do. What have the doctors told you?"

"The one I saw in Portland says there's no hope, not even with chemo and radiation. Exactly what the doc I saw in Dallas said.

In 1962, that was. Nice to think some things don't change, don't you think?"

I opened my mouth, then closed it again. Sometimes there's nothing to say. Sometimes you're just stumped.

"No sense beating around the bush about it," he said. "I know death's embarrassing to folks, especially when the one dying has nothing but his own bad habits to blame, but I can't waste time being delicate. I'll be in the hospital soon enough, if for no other reason than I won't be able to get back and forth to the bathroom on my own. I'll be damned if I'll sit around coughing my brains out and hip deep in my own shit."

"What happens to the diner?"

"The diner's finished, buddy. Even if I was healthy as a horse, it would be gone by the end of this month. You know I always just rented that space, don't you?"

I didn't, but it made sense. Although Worumbo was still called Worumbo, it was now your basic trendy shopping center, so that meant Al had been paying rent to some corporation.

"My lease is up for renewal, and Mill Associates wants that space to put in something called—you're going to love this—an L.L. Bean Express. Besides, they say my little Aluminaire's an eyesore."

"That's ridiculous!" I said, and with such genuine indignation that Al chuckled. The chuckles tried to morph into a coughing fit and he stifled them. Here in the privacy of his own home, he wasn't using tissues, handkerchiefs, or napkins to deal with that cough; there was a box of maxi pads on the table beside his chair. My eyes kept straying to them. I'd urge them away, perhaps to look at the photo on the wall of Al with his arm around a good-looking woman, then find them straying back. Here is one of the great truths of the human condition: when you need Stayfree Maxi Pads to absorb the expectorants produced by your insulted body, you are in serious fucking trouble.

"Thanks for saying that, buddy. We could have a drink on it. My alcohol days are over, but there's iced tea in the fridge. Maybe you'd do the honors."

2

He used sturdy generic glassware at the restaurant, but the pitcher holding the iced tea looked like Waterford to me. A whole lemon bobbed placidly on top, the skin cut to let the flavor seep out. I choked a couple of glasses with ice, poured, and went back into the living room. Al took a long, deep swallow of his and closed his eyes gratefully.

"Boy, is that good. Right this minute everything in Al World is good. That dope's wonderful stuff. Addictive as hell, of course, but wonderful. It even suppresses the coughing a little. The pain'll start creeping in again by midnight, but that should give us enough time to talk this through." He sipped again and gave me a look of rueful amusement. "Human things are terrific right to the end, it seems like. I never would have guessed."

"Al, what happens to that . . . that hole into the past, if they pull your trailer and build an outlet store where it was?"

"I don't know that any more than I know how I can buy the same meat over and over again. What I *think* is it'll disappear. I think it's as much a freak of nature as Old Faithful, or that weird balancing rock they've got in western Australia, or a river that runs backward at certain phases of the moon. Things like that are delicate, buddy. A little shift in the earth's crust, a change in the temperature, a few sticks of dynamite, and they're gone."

"So you don't think there'll be . . . I don't know . . . some kind of cataclysm?" What I was picturing in my mind was a breach in the cabin of an airliner cruising at thirty-six thousand feet, and everything being sucked out, including the passengers. I saw that in a movie once.

"I don't think so, but who can tell? All I know is that there's nothing I can do about it, either way. Unless you want me to deed the place over to you, that is. I could do that. Then you could go to the National Historical Preservation Society and tell them, 'Hey, guys, you can't let them put up an outlet store in the courtyard of the old Worumbo mill. There's a time tunnel there. I know it's hard to believe, but let me show you.'"

For a moment I actually considered this, because Al was probably right: the fissure leading into the past was almost certainly delicate. For all I knew (or *he* did), it could pop like a soap bubble if the Aluminaire was even joggled hard. Then I thought of the federal government discovering they could send special ops into the past to change whatever they wanted. I didn't know if that were possible, but if so, the folks who gave us fun stuff like bio-weapons and computer-guided smart bombs were the last folks I'd want carrying their various agendas into living, unarmored history.

The minute this idea occurred to me—no, the very *second*—I knew what Al had in mind. Only the specifics were missing. I set my iced tea aside and stood up.

"No. Absolutely not. Uh-uh."

He took this calmly. I could say it was because he was stoned on OxyContin, but I knew better. He could see I didn't mean to just walk out no matter what I said. My curiosity (not to mention my fascination) was probably sticking out like porcupine quills. Because part of me *did* want to know the specifics.

"I see I can skip the introductory material and get right down to business," Al said. "That's good. Sit down, Jake, and I'll let you in on my only reason for not just taking my whole supply of little pink pills at once." And when I stayed on my feet: "You know you want to hear this, and what harm? Even if I could make you do something here in 2011—which I can't—I couldn't make you do anything back there. Once you get back there, Al Templeton's a four-year-old kid in Bloomington, Indiana, racing around his backyard in a Lone Ranger mask and still a bit iffy in the old toilet-training department. So sit down. Like they say in the infomercials, you're under no obligation."

Right. On the other hand, my mother would have said *the devil's voice is sweet.*

But I sat down.

3

"Do you know the phrase *watershed moment,* buddy?"

I nodded. You didn't have to be an English teacher to know that one; you didn't even have to be literate. It was one of those annoying linguistic shortcuts that show up on cable TV news shows, day in and day out. Others include *connect the dots* and *at this point in time.* The most annoying of all (I have inveighed against it to my clearly bored students time and time and time again) is the totally meaningless *some people say,* or *many people believe.*

"Do you know where it comes from? The origin?"

"Nope."

"Cartography. A watershed is an area of land, usually mountains or forests, that drains into a river. History is also a river. Wouldn't you say so?"

"Yes. I suppose I would." I drank some of my tea.

"Sometimes the events that change history are widespread—like heavy, prolonged rains over an entire watershed that can send a river out of its banks. But rivers can flood even on sunny days. All it takes is a heavy, prolonged downpour in *one small area* of the watershed. There are flash floods in history, too. Want some examples? How about 9/11? Or what about Bush beating Gore in 2000?"

"You can't compare a national election to a flash flood, Al."

"Maybe not most of them, but the 2000 presidential election was in a class by itself. Suppose you could go back to Florida in the fall of Double-O and spend two hundred thousand dollars or so on Al Gore's behalf?"

"Couple of problems with that," I said. "First, I don't have two hundred thousand dollars. Second, I'm a schoolteacher. I can tell you all about Thomas Wolfe's mother fixation, but when it comes to politics I'm a babe in the woods."

He gave an impatient flap of his hand, which almost sent his Marine Corps ring flying off his reduced finger. "Money's not a problem. You'll just have to trust me on that for now. And advance knowledge usually trumps the shit out of experience. The difference in Florida was supposedly less than six hundred votes. Do you think you could buy six hundred votes on Election Day with two hundred grand, if buying was what it came down to?"

"Maybe," I said. "Probably. I guess I'd isolate some communities where there's a lot of apathy and the voting turnout's traditionally light—it wouldn't take all that much research—then go in with the old cashola."

Al grinned, revealing his missing teeth and unhealthy gums. "Why not? It worked in Chicago for years."

The idea of buying the presidency for less than the cost of two Mercedes-Benz sedans silenced me.

"But when it comes to the river of history, the watershed moments most susceptible to change are assassinations—the ones that succeeded and the ones that failed. Archduke Franz Ferdinand of Austria gets shot by a mentally unstable pipsqueak named Gavrilo Princip and there's your kickoff to World War I. On the other hand, after Claus von Stauffenberg failed to kill Hitler in 1944—close, but no cigar—the war continued and millions more died."

I had seen that movie, too.

Al said, "There's nothing we can do about Archduke Ferdinand or Adolf Hitler. They're out of our reach."

I thought of accusing him of making pronounal assumptions and kept my mouth shut. I felt a little like a man reading a very grim book. A Thomas Hardy novel, say. You know how it's going to end, but instead of spoiling things, that somehow increases your fascination. It's like watching a kid run his electric train faster and faster and waiting for it to derail on one of the curves.

"As for 9/11, if you wanted to fix that one, you'd have to wait around for forty-three years. You'd be pushing eighty, if you made it at all."

Now the lone-star flag the gnome had been holding made sense. It was a souvenir of Al's last jaunt into the past. "You couldn't even make it to '63, could you?"

To this he didn't reply, just watched me. His eyes, which had looked rheumy and vague when he let me into the diner that afternoon, now looked bright. Almost young.

"Because that's what you're talking about, right? Dallas in 1963?"

"That's right," he said. "I had to opt out. But *you're* not sick, buddy. You're healthy and in the prime of life. You can go back, and you can stop it."

He leaned forward, his eyes not just bright; they were blazing.

"You can change history, Jake. Do you understand that? *John Kennedy can live.*"

4

I know the basics of suspense fiction—I ought to, I've read enough thrillers in my lifetime—and the prime rule is to keep the reader guessing. But if you've gotten any feel for my character at all, based on that day's extraordinary events, you'll know that I wanted to be convinced. Christy Epping had become Christy Thompson (boy meets girl on the AA campus, remember?), and I was a man on his own. We didn't even have any kids to fight over. I had a job I was good at, but if I told you it was challenging, it would be a lie. Hitchhiking around Canada with a buddy after my senior year of college was the closest thing to an adventure I'd ever had, and given the cheerful, helpful nature of most Canadians, it wasn't much of an adventure. Now, all of a sudden, I'd been offered a chance to become a major player not just in American history but in the history of the *world*. So yes, yes, yes, I wanted to be convinced.

But I was also afraid.

"What if it went wrong?" I drank down the rest of my iced tea in four long swallows, the ice cubes clicking against my teeth. "What if I managed, God knows how, to stop it from happening and made things worse instead of better? What if I came back and discovered America had become a fascist regime? Or that the pollution had gotten so bad everybody was walking around in gas masks?"

"Then you'd go back again," he said. "Back to two minutes of twelve on September ninth of 1958. Cancel the whole thing out. Every trip is the first trip, remember?"

"Sounds good, but what if the changes were so radical your little diner wasn't even there anymore?"

He grinned. "Then you'd have to live your life in the past. But would that be so bad? As an English teacher, you'd still have a marketable skill, and you wouldn't even need it. I was there for four years, Jake, and I made a small fortune. Do you know how?"

I could have taken an educated guess, but I shook my head.

"Betting. I was careful—I didn't want to raise any suspicions, and I sure didn't want some bookie's leg-breakers coming after me—but when you've studied up on who won every big sporting event between the summer of 1958 and the fall of 1963, you can afford to be careful. I won't say you can live like a king, because that's living dangerously. But there's no reason you can't live well. And I think the diner'll still be there. It has been for me, and I changed plenty of things. Anybody does. Just walking around the block to buy a loaf of bread and a quart of milk changes the future. Ever hear of the butterfly effect? It's a fancy-shmancy scientific theory that basically boils down to the idea that—"

He started coughing again, the first protracted fit since he'd let me in. He grabbed one of the maxis from the box, plastered it across his mouth like a gag, and then doubled over. Gruesome retching sounds came up from his chest. It sounded as if half his works had come loose and were slamming around in there like bumper cars at an amusement park. Finally it abated. He glanced at the pad, winced, folded it up, and threw it away.

"Sorry, buddy. This oral menstruation's a bitch."

"Jesus, Al!"

He shrugged. "If you can't joke about it, what's the point of anything? Now where was I?"

"Butterfly effect."

"Right. It means small events can have large, whatchama-dingit, ramifications. The idea is that if some guy kills a butterfly in China, maybe forty years later—or four hundred—there's an earthquake in Peru. That sound as crazy to you as it does to me?"

It did, but I remembered a hoary old time-travel paradox and pulled it out. "Yeah, but what if you went back and killed your own grandfather?"

He stared at me, baffled. "Why the fuck would you do that?"

That was a good question, so I just told him to go on.

"You changed the past this afternoon in all sorts of little ways, just by walking into the Kennebec Fruit . . . but the stairs leading up into the pantry and back into 2011 were still there, weren't they? And The Falls is the same as when you left it."

"So it seems, yes. But you're talking about something a little more major. To wit, saving JFK's life."

"Oh, I'm talking about a lot more than that, because this ain't some butterfly in China, buddy. I'm also talking about saving RFK's life, because if John lives in Dallas, Robert probably doesn't run for president in 1968. The country wouldn't have been ready to replace one Kennedy with another."

"You don't know that for sure."

"No, but listen. Do you think that if you save John Kennedy's life, his brother Robert is still at the Ambassador Hotel at twelve-fifteen in the morning on June fifth, 1968? And even if he is, is Sirhan Sirhan still working in the kitchen?"

Maybe, but the chances had to be awfully small. If you introduced a million variables into an equation, of course the answer was going to change.

"Or what about Martin Luther King? Is he still in Memphis in April of '68? Even if he is, is he still standing on the balcony of the Lorraine Motel at exactly the right time for James Earl Ray to shoot him? What do you think?"

"If that butterfly theory is right, probably not."

"That's what I think, too. And if MLK lives, the race riots that followed his death don't happen. Maybe Fred Hampton doesn't get shot in Chicago."

"Who?"

He ignored me. "For that matter, maybe there's no Symbionese Liberation Army. No SLA, no Patty Hearst kidnapping. No Patty Hearst kidnapping, a small but maybe significant reduction in black fear among middle-class whites."

"You're losing me. Remember, I was an English major."

"I'm losing you because you know more about the Civil War in the nineteenth century than you do about the one that ripped this country apart after the Kennedy assassination in Dallas. If I asked you who starred in *The Graduate,* I'm sure you could tell me. But if I asked you to tell me who Lee Oswald tried to assassinate only a few months before gunning Kennedy down, you'd go 'Huh?' Because somehow all that stuff has gotten lost."

"Oswald tried to kill someone *before* Kennedy?" This was news to me, but most of my knowledge of the Kennedy assassination came from an Oliver Stone movie. In any case, Al didn't answer. Al was on a roll.

"Or what about Vietnam? Johnson was the one who started all the insane escalation. Kennedy was a cold warrior, no doubt about it, but Johnson took it to the next level. He had the same my-balls-are-bigger-than-yours complex that Dubya showed off when he stood in front of the cameras and said 'Bring it on.' Kennedy might have changed his mind. Johnson and Nixon were incapable of that. Thanks to them, we lost almost sixty thousand American soldiers in Nam. The Vietnamese, North and South, lost *millions.* Is the butcher's bill that high if Kennedy doesn't die in Dallas?"

"I don't know. And neither do you, Al."

"That's true, but I've become quite the student of recent American history, and I think the chances of improving things by saving him are very good. And really, there's no downside. If things turn to shit, you just take it all back. Easy as erasing a dirty word off a chalkboard."

"Or I can't get back, in which case I never know."

"Bullshit. You're young. As long as you don't get run over by a taxicab or have a heart attack, you'd live long enough to know how things turn out."

I sat silent, looking down at my lap and thinking. Al let me. At last I raised my head again.

"You must have read a lot about the assassination and about Oswald."

"Everything I could get my hands on, buddy."

"How sure are you that he did it? Because there are about a thousand conspiracy theories. Even I know that. What if I went back and stopped him and some other guy popped Kennedy from the Grassy Hill, or whatever it was?"

"Grassy Knoll. And I'm close to positive it was all Oswald. The conspiracy theories were all pretty crazy to begin with, and most of them have been disproved over the years. The idea that the shooter wasn't Oswald at all, but someone who looked like him, for instance. The body was exhumed in 1981 and DNA tested. It was him, all right. The poisonous little fuck." He paused, then added: "I met him, you know."

I stared at him. "Bullshit!"

"Oh yes. He spoke to me. This was in Fort Worth. He and Marina—his wife, she was Russian—were visiting Oswald's brother in Fort Worth. If Lee ever loved anybody, it was his brother Bobby. I was standing outside the picket fence around Bobby Oswald's yard, leaning against a phone pole, smoking a cigarette and pretending to read the paper. My heart was hammering what felt like two hundred beats a minute. Lee and Marina came out together. She was carrying their daughter, June. Just a mite of a thing, less than a year old. The kid was asleep. Ozzie was wearing khaki pants and a button-down Ivy League shirt that was all frayed around the collar. The slacks had a sharp crease, but they were dirty. He'd given up his Marine cut, but his hair would still have been way too short to grab. Marina—holy Christ, what a knockout! Dark hair, bright blue eyes, flawless skin. She looks like a goddam movie star. If you do this, you'll see for yourself. She said something to him in Russian as they came down the walk. He said something back. He was smiling when he said it, but then he pushed her. She almost fell over. The kid woke up and started to cry. All this time, Oswald kept smiling."

"You saw this. You actually did. You saw *him*." In spite of my own trip back in time, I was at least half-convinced that this had to be either a delusion or an outright lie.

"I did. She came out through the gate and walked past me with her head down, holding the baby against her breasts. Like I wasn't there. But he walked right up to me, close enough for me to smell the Old Spice he was wearing to try and cover up the smell of his sweat. There were blackheads all over his nose. You could tell looking at his clothes—and his shoes, which were scuffed and busted down at the backs—that he didn't have a pot to piss in or a window to throw it out of, but when you looked in his face, you knew that didn't matter. Not to him, it didn't. He thought he was a big deal."

Al considered briefly, then shook his head.

"No, I take that back. He *knew* he was a big deal. It was just a matter of waiting for the rest of the world to catch up on that. So there he is, in my face—choking distance, and don't think the idea didn't cross my mind—"

"Why didn't you? Or just cut to the chase and shoot him?"

"In front of his wife and baby? Could you do that, Jake?"

I didn't have to consider it for long. "Guess not."

"Me either. I had other reasons, too. One of them was an aversion to state prison . . . or the electric chair. We were out on the street, remember."

"Ah."

"Ah is right. He still had that little smile on his face when he walked up to me. Arrogant and prissy, both at the same time. He's wearing that smile in just about every photograph anybody ever took of him. He's wearing it in the Dallas police station after they arrested him for killing the president and a motor patrolman who happened to cross his path when he was trying to get away. He says to me, 'What are you looking at, sir?' I say 'Nothing, buddy.' And he says, 'Then mind your beeswax.'

"Marina was waiting for him maybe twenty feet down the sidewalk, trying to soothe the baby back to sleep. It was hotter than hell that day, but she was wearing a kerchief over her hair, the way lots of European women do back then. He went to her and grabbed her elbow—like a cop instead of her husband—and says, *'Pokhoda! Pokhoda!'* Walk, walk. She said something to him, maybe asking if he'd carry the baby for awhile. That's my guess, anyway. But he just pushed her away and said, *'Pokhoda, cyka!'* Walk, bitch. She did. They went off down toward the bus stop. And that was it."

"You speak Russian?"

"No, but I have a good ear and a computer. Back here I do, anyway."

"You saw him other times?"

"Only from a distance. By then I was getting real sick." He grinned. "There's no Texas barbecue as good as Fort Worth barbecue, and I couldn't eat it. It's a cruel world, sometimes. I went to a doctor, got a diagnosis I could have made myself by then, and came back to the twenty-first century. Basically, there was nothing more to see, anyway. Just a skinny little wife-abuser waiting to be famous."

He leaned forward.

"You know what the man who changed American history was like? He was the kind of kid who throws stones at other kids and then runs away. By the time he joined the Marines—to be like his brother Bobby, he idolized Bobby—he'd lived in almost two dozen different places, from New Orleans to New York City. He had big ideas and couldn't understand why people wouldn't listen to them. He was mad about that, furious, but he never lost that pissy, prissy little smile of his. Do you know what William Manchester called him?"

"No." I didn't even know who William Manchester was.

"A wretched waif. Manchester was talking about all the conspiracy theories that bloomed in the aftermath of the assassination . . . and after Oswald himself was shot and killed. I mean, you know that, right?"

"Of course," I said, a little annoyed. "A guy named Jack Ruby did it." But given the holes in my knowledge I'd already demonstrated, I suppose he had a right to wonder.

"Manchester said that if you put the murdered president on one side of a scale and Oswald—the wretched waif—on the other, it didn't balance. No way did it balance. If you wanted to give Kennedy's death some meaning, you'd have to add something heavier. Which explains the proliferation of conspiracy theories. Like the Mafia did it—Carlos Marcello ordered the hit. Or the KGB did it. Or Castro, to get back at the CIA for trying to load him up with poison cigars. There are people to this day who believe Lyndon Johnson did it so he could be president. But in the end . . ." Al shook his head. "It was almost certainly Oswald. You've heard of Occam's Razor, haven't you?"

It was nice to know something for sure. "It's a basic truism sometimes known as the law of parsimony. 'All other things being equal, the simplest explanation is usually the right one.' So why didn't you kill him when he *wasn't* on the street with his wife and kid? You were a Marine, too. When you knew how sick you were, why didn't you just kill the little motherfucker yourself?"

"Because being ninety-five percent sure isn't a hundred. Because, shithead or not, he was a family man. Because after he was arrested, Oswald said he was a patsy and I wanted to be sure he was lying. I don't think anybody can ever be a hundred percent sure of anything in this wicked world, but I wanted to get up to ninety-eight. I had no intention of waiting until November twenty-second and then stopping him at the Texas School Book Depository, though— that would have been cutting it way too fine, for one big reason I'll have to tell you about."

His eyes no longer looked so bright, and the lines on his face were deepening again. I was scared by how shallow his reserves of strength had become.

"I've written all this stuff down. I want you to read it. Actually, I want you to cram like a bastard. Look on top of the TV, buddy. Would you do that?" He gave me a tired smile and added, "I got my sittin-britches on."

It was a thick blue notebook. The price stamped on the paper cover was twenty-five cents. The brand was foreign to me. "What's Kresge's?"

"The department store chain now known as Kmart. Never mind what's on the cover, just pay attention to what's inside. It's an Oswald timeline, plus all the evidence piled up against him . . . which you don't really have to read if you take me up on this, because you're going to stop the little weasel in April of 1963, over half a year before Kennedy comes to Dallas."

"Why April?"

"Because that's when somebody tried to kill General Edwin Walker . . . only he wasn't a general anymore by then. He got cashiered in 1961, by JFK himself. General Eddie was handing out segregationist literature to his troops and ordering them to read the stuff."

"It was Oswald who tried to shoot him?"

"That's what you need to make sure of. Same rifle, no doubt about that, ballistics proved it. I was waiting to see him take the shot. I could afford not to interfere, because that time Oswald missed. The bullet deflected off the wood strip in the middle of Walker's kitchen window. Not much, but just enough. The bullet literally parted his hair and flying wood splinters from the munting cut his arm a little. That was his only wound. I won't say the man deserved to die—very few men are evil enough to deserve being shot from ambush—but I would have traded Walker for Kennedy any day of the week."

I paid little attention to that last. I was thumbing through Al's Oswald Book, page after page of closely written notes. They were completely legible at the beginning, less so toward the end. The last few pages were the scrawls of a very sick man. I snapped the cover closed and said, "If you could confirm that Oswald was the shooter in the General Walker attempt, that would have settled your doubts?"

"Yes. I needed to make sure he's capable of doing it. Ozzie's a bad man, Jake—what people back in '58 call a louse—but beating on your wife and keeping her a virtual prisoner because she doesn't speak the language don't justify murder. And something else. Even if I hadn't come down with the big C, I knew I might not get another chance to make it right if I killed Oswald and someone else shot the president anyway. By the time a man's in his sixties, he's pretty much off the warranty, if you see what I mean."

"Would it have to be killing? Couldn't you just . . . I don't know . . . frame him for something?"

"Maybe, but by then I was sick. I don't know if I could have done it even if I was well. On the whole it seemed simpler to just end him, once I was sure. Like swatting a wasp before it can sting you."

I was quiet, thinking. The clock on the wall said ten-thirty. Al had opened the conversation by saying he'd be good to go until midnight, but I only had to look at him to know that had been wildly optimistic.

I took his glass and mine out to the kitchen, rinsed them, and put them in the dish drainer. It felt like there was a tornado funnel behind my forehead. Instead of cows and fenceposts and scraps of paper, what it was sucking up and spinning around were names: Lee Oswald, Bobby Oswald, Marina Oswald, Edwin Walker, Fred Hampton, Patty Hearst. There were bright acronyms in that whirl, too, circling like chrome hood ornaments ripped off luxury cars: JFK, RFK, MLK, SLA. The cyclone even had a sound, two Russian words spoken over and over again in a flat Southern drawl: *pokhoda, cyka.*

Walk, bitch.

5

"How long have I got to decide?" I asked.

"Not long. The diner goes at the end of the month. I talked to a lawyer about buying some more time—tying them up in a suit, or something—but he wasn't hopeful. Ever seen a sign in a furniture store saying LOST OUR LEASE, EVERYTHING MUST GO?"

"Sure."

"Nine cases out of ten that's just sales-pitch bullshit, but this is the tenth case. And I'm not talking about some discount dollar store bumping to get in, I'm talking about Bean's, and when it comes to Maine retail, L.L. Bean is the biggest ape in the jungle. Come July first, the diner's gone like Enron. But that isn't the big thing. By July first, *I* might be gone. I could catch a cold and be dead of pneumonia in three days. I could have a heart attack or a stroke. Or I could kill myself with these damn OxyContin pills by accident. The visiting nurse who comes in asks me every day if I'm being careful not to exceed the dosage, and I *am* careful, but I can see she's still worried she'll walk in some morning and find me dead, probably because I got stoned and lost count. Plus the pills inhibit respiration, and my lungs are shot. On top of all that, I've lost a lot of weight."

"Really? I hadn't noticed."

"Nobody loves a smartass, buddy—when you get to be my age, you'll know. In any case, I want you to take this as well as the notebook." He held out a key. "It's to the diner. If you should call me tomorrow and hear from the nurse that I passed away in the night, you'll have to move fast. Always assuming you decide to move at all, that is."

"Al, you're not planning—"

"Just trying to be careful. Because this matters, Jake. As far as I'm concerned, it matters more than anything else. If you ever wanted to change the world, this is your chance. Save Kennedy, save his brother. Save Martin Luther King. Stop the race riots. Stop Vietnam, maybe." He leaned forward. "Get rid of one wretched waif, buddy, and you could save millions of lives."

"It's a hell of a sales pitch," I said, "but I don't need the key. When the sun comes up tomorrow, you'll still be on the big blue bus."

"Ninety-five percent probability. But that's not good enough. Take the goddam key."

I took the goddam key and put it in my pocket. "I'll let you get some rest."

"One more thing before you go. I need to tell you about Carolyn Poulin and Andy Cullum. Sit down again, Jake. This'll take a few minutes."

I stayed on my feet. "Uh-uh. You're used up. You need to sleep."

"I'll sleep when I'm dead. Sit down."

6

After discovering what he called the rabbit-hole, Al said, he was at first content to use it to buy supplies, make a few bets with a bookie he found in Lewiston, and build up his stash of fifties cash. He also took the occasional midweek holiday on Sebago Lake, which was teeming with fish that were tasty and perfectly safe to eat. People worried about fallout from A-bomb tests, he said, but fears of getting mercury poisoning from tainted fish were still in the future. He called these jaunts (usually Tuesdays and Wednesdays, but he would sometimes stay all the way to Friday) his mini-vacations. The weather was always good (because it was always the same weather) and the fishing was always terrific (he probably caught at least some of the same fish over and over).

"I know exactly how you feel about all this, Jake, because I was pretty much in shock those first few years. You want to know what's a mind-blower? Going down those stairs at the height of a January nor'easter and coming out in that bright September sunshine. Shirtsleeve weather, am I right?"

I nodded and told him to go on. The little bit of color that had been in his cheeks when I came in was all gone, and he was coughing steadily again.

"But if you give a man some time, he can get used to anything, and when the shock finally started to wear off, I started to think

I'd found that old rabbit-hole for a reason. That's when I started to think about Kennedy. But your question reared its ugly head: can you change the past? I wasn't concerned about the consequences—at least not to start with—but only about whether or not it could be done at all. On one of my Sebago trips, I took out my knife and carved AL T. FROM 2007 on a tree near the cabin where I stayed. When I got back here, I jumped in my car and drove on over to Sebago Lake. The cabins where I stayed are gone; there's a tourist hotel there now. But the tree is still there. So was what I carved into it. Old and smooth, but still there: AL T. FROM 2007. So I knew it could be done. *Then* I started thinking about the butterfly effect.

"There's a newspaper in The Falls back then, the *Lisbon Weekly Enterprise,* and the library scanned all their microfilm into the computer in '05. Speeds things up a lot. I was looking for an accident in the fall or early winter of 1958. A certain kind of accident. I would have gone all the way into early 1959 if necessary, but I found what I was looking for on November fifteenth of '58. A twelve-year-old girl named Carolyn Poulin was hunting with her father across the river, in the part of Durham that's called Bowie Hill. Around two o'clock that afternoon—it was a Saturday—a hunter from Durham named Andrew Cullum shot at a deer in that same section of the woods. He missed the deer, hit the girl. Even though she was a quarter of a mile away, he hit the girl. I think about that, you know. When Oswald shot at General Walker, the range was less than a hundred yards. But the bullet clipped the wood sash in the middle of a window and he missed. The bullet that paralyzed the Poulin girl traveled over four hundred yards—*much* farther than the shot that killed Kennedy—and missed every tree trunk and branch along the way. If it had even clipped a twig, it almost surely would have missed her. So sure, I think about it."

That was the first time the phrase *life turns on a dime* crossed my mind. It wasn't the last. Al grabbed another maxi pad, coughed, spat, tossed it in the wastebasket. Then he drew in the closest thing to a deep breath he could manage, and labored on. I didn't try to stop him. I was fascinated all over again.

"I plugged her name into the *Enterprise*'s search database and found a few more stories about her. She graduated from Lisbon High School in 1965—a year behind the rest of her class, but she made it—and went to the University of Maine. Business major. Became an accountant. She lives in Gray, less than ten miles from Sebago Lake, where I used to go on my minivacations, and she still works as a freelance. Want to guess who one of her biggest clients is?"

I shook my head.

"John Crafts, right here in The Falls. Squiggy Wheaton, one of the salesmen, is a regular customer at the diner, and when he told me one day that they were doing their annual inventory and 'the numbers lady' was there going over the books, I made it my business to roll on up and get an eyes-on. She's sixty-five now, and . . . you know how some women that age can be really beautiful?"

"Yes," I said. I was thinking of Christy's mother, who didn't fully come into her looks until she was in her fifties.

"Carolyn Poulin is that way. Her face is a classic, the kind a painter from two or three hundred years ago would love, and she's got snow white hair that she wears long, down her back."

"Sounds like you're in love, Al."

He had enough strength left to shoot me the bird.

"She's in great physical shape, too—well, you'd almost expect that, wouldn't you, an unmarried woman hauling herself in and out of a wheelchair every day and getting in and out of the specially equipped van she drives. Not to mention in and out of bed, in and out of the shower, all the rest. And she does—Squiggy says she's completely self-sufficient. I was impressed."

"So you decided to save her. As a test case."

"I went back down the rabbit-hole, only this time I stayed in the Sebago cabin over two months. Told the owner I'd come into some money when my uncle died. You ought to remember that, buddy—the rich uncle thing is tried and true. Everybody believes it because everybody wants one. So comes the day: November fifteenth, 1958. I don't mess with the Poulins. Given my idea about stopping Oswald, I'm much more interested in Cullum, the shooter. I'd researched him, too, and found out he lived about a mile from Bowie Hill, near the old Durham grange hall. I thought I'd get there before he left for the woods. Didn't quite work out that way.

"I left my cabin on Sebago really early, which was a good thing for me, because I wasn't a mile down the road before the Hertz car I was driving came up with a flat shoe. I took out the spare, put it on, and although it looked absolutely fine, I hadn't gone another mile before that one went flat, too.

"I hitched a ride to the Esso station in Naples, where the guy in the service bay told me he had too damn much work to come out and put a new tire on a Hertz Chevrolet. I think he was pissed about missing the Saturday hunting. A twenty-dollar tip changed his mind, but I never got into Durham until past noon. I took the old Runaround Pond Road because that's the quickest way to go, and guess what? The bridge over Chuckle Brook had fallen into the goddam water. Big red and white sawhorses; smudgepots; big orange sign reading ROAD CLOSED. By then I had a pretty good idea of what was going on, and I had a sinking feeling that I wasn't going to be able to do what I'd set out that morning to do. Keep in mind that I left at eight A.M., just to be on the safe side, and it took me over four hours to get eighteen miles. But I didn't give up. I went around by Methodist Church Road instead, hammering that rent-a-dent for all it was worth, pulling up this long rooster-tail of dust behind me—all the roads out that way are dirt back then.

"Okay, so I'm seeing cars and trucks parked off to the sides or at the start of woods roads every here and there, and I'm also seeing hunters walking with their guns broken open over their arms. Every single one of them lifted his hand to me—folks are friendlier in '58, there's no doubt about that. I waved back, too, but what I was really waiting for was another flat. Or a blowout. That would probably have sent me right off the road and into the ditch, because I was doing sixty at least. I remember one of the hunters patting the air with his hands, the way you do when you're telling someone to slow down, but I paid no attention.

"I flew up Bowie Hill, and just past the old Friends' Meeting House, I spied a pickemup parked by the graveyard. POULIN CONSTRUCTION AND CARPENTRY painted on the door. Truck empty. Poulin and his girl in the woods, maybe sitting in a clearing somewhere, eating their lunch and talking the way fathers and daughters do. Or at least how I imagine they do, never having had one myself—"

Another long fit of coughing, which ended with a terrible wet gagging sound.

"Ah *shit,* don't that *hurt,*" he groaned.

"Al, you need to stop."

He shook his head and wiped a slick of blood off his lower lip with the heel of his palm. "What I need is to get this out, so shut up and let me do it.

"I gave the truck a good long stare, still rolling at sixty or so all the while, and when I looked back at the road, I saw there was a tree down across it. I stopped just in time to keep from crashing into it. It wasn't a big tree, and before the cancer went to work on me, I was pretty strong. Also, I was mad as hell. I got out and started wrestling with it. While I was doing that—also cussing my head off—a car came along from the other direction. Man gets out, wearing an orange hunting vest. I don't know for sure if it's *my* man or not—the *Enterprise* never printed his picture—but he looks like the right age.

"He says, 'Let me help you with that, oldtimer.'

" 'Thank you very much,' I says, and holds out my hand. 'Bill Laidlaw.'

"He shakes it and says, 'Andy Cullum.' So it was him. Given all the trouble I'd had getting to Durham, I could hardly believe it. I felt like I'd won the lottery. We grabbed the tree, and between us we got it shifted. When it was, I sat down on the road and grabbed my chest. He asked me if I was okay. 'Well, I don't know,' I says. 'I never had a heart attack, but this sure feels like one.' Which is why Mr. Andy Cullum never got any hunting done on that November afternoon, Jake, and why he never shot any little girl, either. He

74

was busy taking poor old Bill Laidlaw up to Central Maine General in Lewiston."

"You did it? You actually did it?"

"Bet your ass. I told em at the hospital that I'd had a big old hero for lunch—what's called an Italian sandwich back then—and the diagnosis was 'acute indigestion.' I paid twenty-five dollars in cash and they sprung me. Cullum waited around and took me back to my Hertz car, how's that for neighborly? I returned home to 2011 that very night . . . only of course I came back only two minutes after I left. Shit like that'll give you jet-lag without ever getting on a plane.

"My first stop was the town library, where I looked up the story of the 1965 high school graduation again. Before, there'd been a photo of Carolyn Poulin to go with it. The principal back then—Earl Higgins, he's long since gone to his reward—was bending over to hand her her diploma as she sat in her wheelchair, all dressed up in her cap and gown. The caption underneath said, *Carolyn Poulin reaches a major goal on her long road to recovery.*"

"Was it still there?"

"The story about the graduation was, you bet. Graduation day always makes the front page in smalltown newspapers, you know that, buddy. But after I came back from '58, the picture was of a boy with a half-assed Beatle haircut standing at the podium and the caption said, *Valedictorian Trevor "Buddy" Briggs speaks to graduation assemblage.* They listed every graduate—there were only a hundred or so—and Carolyn Poulin wasn't among em. So I checked the graduation story from '64, which was the year she would have graduated if she hadn't been busy getting better from being shot in the spine. And bingo. No picture and no special mention, but she was listed right between David Platt and Stephanie Routhier."

"Just another kid marching to 'Pomp and Circumstance,' right?"

"Right. Then I plugged her name into the *Enterprise*'s search function, and got some hits after 1964. Not many, three or four. About what you'd expect for an ordinary woman living an ordinary life. She went to the University of Maine, majored in business administration, then went to grad school in New Hampshire. I found one more story, from 1979, not long before the *Enterprise* folded. FORMER LISBON RESIDENT STUDENT WINS NATIONAL DAYLILY COMPETITION, it said. There was a picture of her, standing on her own two good legs, with the winning lily. She lives . . . lived . . . I don't know which way is right, maybe both . . . in a town outside of Albany, New York."

"Married? Kids?"

"Don't think so. In the picture, she's holding up the winning daylily and there are no rings on her left hand. I know what you're thinking, not much that changed except for being able to walk. But who can really tell? She was living in a different place and influenced the lives of who knows how many different people. Ones she never would have known if Cullum had shot her and she'd stayed in The Falls. See what I mean?"

What I saw was it was really impossible to tell, one way or another, but I agreed with him, because I wanted to finish with this before he collapsed. And I intended to see him safely into his bed before I left.

"What I'm telling you, Jake, is that you *can* change the past, but it's not as easy as you might think. That morning I felt like a man trying to fight his way out of a nylon stocking. It would give a little, then snap back just as tight as before. Finally, though, I managed to rip it open."

"Why would it be hard? Because the past doesn't *want* to be changed?"

"*Something* doesn't want it to be changed, I'm pretty sure of that. But it can be. If you take the resistance into account, it can be." Al was looking at me, eyes bright in his haggard face. "All in all, the story of Carolyn Poulin ends with 'And she lived happily ever after,' wouldn't you say?"

"Yes."

"Look inside the back cover of the notebook I gave you, buddy, and you might change your mind. Little something I printed out today."

I did as he asked and found a cardboard pocket. For storing things like office memos and business cards, I assumed. A single sheet of paper was folded into it. I took it out, opened it up, and looked for a long time. It was a computer printout of page 1 of the *Weekly Lisbon Enterprise.* The date below the masthead was June 18, 1965. The headline read: **LHS CLASS OF '65 GOES FORTH IN TEARS, LAUGHTER**. In the photograph, a bald man (his mortarboard tucked under his arm so it wouldn't tumble off his head) was bending over a smiling girl in a wheelchair. He was holding one side of her diploma; she was holding the other. *Carolyn Poulin reaches a major goal on her long road to recovery,* the caption read.

I looked up at Al, confused. "If you changed the future and saved her, how can you have this?"

"Every trip's a reset, buddy. Remember?"

"Oh my God. When you went back to stop Oswald, everything you did to save Poulin got erased."

"Yes . . . and no."

"What do you mean, yes *and* no?"

"The trip back to save Kennedy was going to be the last trip, but I was in no hurry to get down to Texas. Why would I be? In September of 1958, Ozzie Rabbit—that's what his fellow Marines called him—isn't even in America. He's steaming gaily around the South Pacific with his unit, keeping Japan and Formosa safe for democracy. So I went back to the Shadyside Cabins in Sebago and hung out there until November fifteenth. Again. But when it rolled around, I left even earlier in the morning, which was a good fucking call on my part, because I didn't just have a couple of flat tires that time. My goddam rental Chevy threw a rod. Ended up paying the service station guy in Naples sixty bucks to use his car for the day, and left him my Marine Corps ring as extra security. Had some other adventures, which I won't bother recapping—"

"Was the bridge still out in Durham?"

"Don't know, buddy, I didn't even try going that way. A person who doesn't learn from the past is an idiot, in my estimation. One thing *I* learned was which way Andrew Cullum would be coming, and I wasted no time getting there. The tree was down across the road, just like before, and when he came along, I was wrestling with it, just like before. Pretty soon I'm having chest pains, just like before. We played out the whole comedy, Carolyn Poulin had her Saturday in the woods with her dad, and a couple of weeks later I said yahoo and got on a train for Texas."

"Then how can I still have this picture of her graduating in a wheelchair?"

"Because every trip down the rabbit-hole's a reset." Then Al just looked at me, to see if I got it. After a minute, I did.

"I—?"

"That's right, buddy. You bought yourself a dime root beer this afternoon. You also put Carolyn Poulin back in a wheelchair."

CHAPTER 4

1

Al let me help him into his bedroom, and even muttered "Thanks, buddy" when I knelt to unlace his shoes and pull them off. He only balked when I offered to help him into the bathroom.

"Making the world a better place is important, but so is being able to get to the john under your own power."

"Just as long as you're sure you *can* make it."

"I'm sure I can tonight, and I'll worry about tomorrow tomorrow. Go home, Jake. Start reading the notebook—there's a lot there. Sleep on it. Come see me in the morning and tell me what you decided. I'll still be here."

"Ninety-five percent probability?"

"At least ninety-seven. On the whole, I'm feeling pretty chipper. I wasn't sure I'd even get this far with you. Just telling it—and having you believe it—is a load off my mind."

I wasn't sure I *did* believe it, even after my adventure that afternoon, but I didn't say so. I told him goodnight, reminded him not to lose count of his pills ("Yeah, yeah"), and left. I stood outside looking at the gnome with his Lone Star flag for a minute before going down the walk to my car.

Don't mess with Texas, I thought . . . but maybe I was going to. And given Al's difficulties with changing the past—the blown tires, the blown engine, the collapsed bridge—I had an idea that if I went ahead, Texas was going to mess with me.

79

2

After all that, I didn't think I'd be able to get to sleep before two or three in the morning, and there was a fair likelihood that I wouldn't be able to get to sleep at all. But sometimes the body asserts its own imperatives. By the time I got home and fixed myself a weak drink (being able to have liquor in the house again was one of several small pluses in my return to the single state), I was heavy-eyed; by the time I had finished the scotch and read the first nine or ten pages of Al's Oswald Book, I could barely keep them open.

I rinsed my glass in the sink, went into the bedroom (leaving a trail of clothes behind me as I walked, a thing Christy would have given me hell about), and fell onto the double bed where I now slept single. I thought about reaching over to turn off the bedside lamp, but my arm felt heavy, heavy. Correcting honors essays in the strangely quiet teachers' room now seemed like something that had happened a very long time ago. Nor was that strange; everyone knows that, for such an unforgiving thing, time is uniquely malleable.

I crippled that girl. Put her back in a wheelchair.

When you went down those steps from the pantry this afternoon, you didn't even know who Carolyn Poulin was, so don't be an ass. Besides, maybe somewhere she's still walking. Maybe going through that hole creates alternate realities, or time-streams, or some damn thing.

Carolyn Poulin, sitting in her wheelchair and getting her diploma. Back in the year when "Hang On Sloopy" by the McCoys was top of the pops.

Carolyn Poulin, walking through her garden of daylilies in 1979, when "Y.M.C.A." by the Village People was top of the pops; occasionally dropping to one knee to pull some weeds, then springing up again and walking on.

Carolyn Poulin in the woods with her dad, soon to be crippled.

Carolyn Poulin in the woods with her dad, soon to walk into an ordinary smalltown adolescence. Where had she been on that time-stream, I wondered, when the radio and TV bulletins announced that the thirty-fifth President of the United States had been shot in Dallas?

John Kennedy can live. You can save him, Jake.

And would that really make things better? There were no guarantees.

I felt like a man trying to fight his way out of a nylon stocking.

I closed my eyes and saw pages flying off a calendar—the kind of corny transition they used in old movies. I saw them flying out my bedroom window like birds.

One more thought came before I dropped off: the dopey sophomore with the even dopier straggle of goatee on his chin, grinning and muttering, *Hoptoad Harry, hoppin down the av-a-*new. And Harry stopping me when I went to call the kid on it. *Nah, don't bother,* he'd said. *I'm used to it.*

Then I was gone, down for the count.

3

I woke up to early light and twittering birdsong, pawing at my face, sure I had cried just before waking. I'd had a dream, and although I couldn't remember what it was, it must have been a very sad one, because I have never been what you'd call a crying man.

Dry cheeks. No tears.

I turned my head on the pillow to look at the clock on the nightstand and saw it lacked just two minutes of 6:00 A.M. Given the quality of the light, it was going to be a beautiful June morning, and school was out. The first day of summer vacation is usually as happy for teachers as it is for students, but I felt sad. Sad. And not just because I had a tough decision to make.

Halfway to the shower, three words popped into my mind: *Kowabunga, Buffalo Bob!*

I stopped, naked and looking at my own wide-eyed reflection

in the mirror over the dresser. Now I remembered the dream, and it was no wonder I'd awoken feeling sad. I'd dreamed I was in the teachers' room, reading Adult English themes while down the hall in the gymnasium, another high school basketball game wound down toward another final buzzer. My wife was just out of rehab. I was hoping that she'd be home when I got there and I wouldn't have to spend an hour on the phone before locating her and fishing her out of some local waterhole.

In the dream, I had shifted Harry Dunning's essay to the top of the pile and begun to read: *It wasnt a day but a night. The night that change my life was the night my father murdirt my mother and two brothers. . . .*

That had gotten my full attention, and in a hurry. Well, it would get anybody's, wouldn't it? But my eyes had only begun to sting when I got to the part about what he'd been wearing. The outfit made perfect sense, too. When kids went out on that special fall night, carrying empty bags they hoped to bring back filled with sweet swag, their costumes always reflected the current craze. Five years ago, it seemed that every second boy who showed up at my door was wearing Harry Potter eyeglasses and a lightning-bolt-scar decal on his forehead. On my own maiden voyage as a candy-beggar, many moons ago, I'd gone clanking down the sidewalk (with my mother trailing ten feet behind me, at my urgent request) dressed as a snowtrooper from *The Empire Strikes Back*. So was it surprising that Harry Dunning had been wearing buckskin?

"Kowabunga, Buffalo Bob," I told my reflection, and suddenly ran for my study. I don't keep all student work, no teacher does—you'd drown in it!—but I made a habit of photocopying the best essays. They make great teaching tools. I never would have used Harry's in class, it was far too personal for that, but I thought I remembered making a copy of it just the same, because it had provoked such a strong emotional reaction in me. I pulled open the bottom drawer and began thumbing through the rat's nest of folders and loose papers. After fifteen sweaty minutes, I found it. I sat down in my desk chair and began to read.

4

It wasnt a day but a night. The night that change my life was the night my father murdirt my mother and two brothers and hurt me bad. He hurt my sister too, so bad she went into a comah. In three years she died without waking up. Her name was Ellen and I loved her very much. She love to pick flowers and put them in vayses. What happen was like a horra movie. I never go see horra movies because on Halloween night in 1958 I lived thru one.

My brother Troy was to old for trick and treat (15). He was watching TV with my mother and said he would help us eat our candy when we came back and Ellen, she said no you won't, dress up and get your own, and everybody laughed because we all loved Ellen, she was only 7 but she was a real Lucile Ball, she could make anybody laugh, even my father (if he was sober that is, when he was drunk he was always mad). She was going as Princess Summerfall Winterspring (I look it up and that's how you spell it) and I was going as Buffalo Bob, both from THE HOWDY DOODY SHOW we like to watch. "Say kids what time is it?" and "Let's hear from the Penut Galery" and "Kowabunga, Buffalo Bob!!!" Me and Ellen love that show. She love the Princess and I love Buffalo Bob and we both love Howdy! We wanted my brother Tugga (his name was Arthur but everyone called him Tugga, I dont remember why) to go as "Mayor Fineus T. Bluster" but he wouldnt, he said Howdy Doody was a baby show, he was going as "Frankinstine" even though Ellen she said that mask was to scary. Also, Tugga, he gave me some s--t about taking my Daisy air rifle because he said Buffalo Bob didnt have any guns on the TV show, and my mother she said, "You take it if you want to Harry its not a real gun or even shoot preten bullets so Buffalo Bob wouldnt mind." That was the last thing she ever said to me and I'm glad it was a nice thing because she could be strick.

So we was getting ready to go and I said wait a sec I have to go to the bathroom because I was so excited. They all laugh at me, even

Mom and Troy on the couch but going to pee then save my life because that was when my dad come in with that hammer. My dad he was mean when he drank and beat up my mom "time and again." One time when Troy try to stop him by argueing him out of it, he broke Troys arm. That time he almost went to jail (my dad I mean). Anyway my mom and dad were "separated" at this time I'm writing about, and she was thinking about divorcing him, but that wasn't so easy back in 1958 like it is now.

Anyway, he came in the door and I was in the bathroom peeing and I heard my mother say "Get out of here with that thing, youre not suppose to be here." The next thing was she start to scream. Then after that they was all screaming.

There was more—three terrible pages—but it wasn't me who had to read them.

5

It was still a few minutes shy of six-thirty, but I found Al in the phone book and punched in his number without hesitation. I didn't wake him up, either. He answered on the first ring, his voice more like a dog's bark than human speech.

"Hey, buddy, ain't you the early bird?"

"I've got something to show you. A student theme. You even know who wrote it. You ought to; you've got his picture on your Celebrity Wall."

He coughed, then said: "I've got a lot of pictures on the Celebrity Wall, buddy. I think there might even be one of Frank Anicetti, back around the time of the first Moxie Festival. Help me out a little here."

"I'd rather show you. Can I come over?"

"If you can take me in my bathrobe, you can come over. But I got to ask you straight up, now that you've had a night to sleep on it. Have you decided?"

"I think I have to make another trip back first."

I hung up before he could ask any more questions.

6

He looked worse than ever in the early light flooding in through his living room window. His white terrycloth robe hung around him like a deflated parachute. Passing up the chemo had allowed him to keep his hair, but it was thinning and baby-fine. His eyes appeared to have retreated even farther into their sockets. He read Harry Dunning's theme twice, started to put it down, then read it again. At last he looked up at me and said, "Jesus H. Christ on a chariot-driven crutch."

"The first time I read it, I cried."

"I don't blame you. The part about the Daisy air rifle is what really gets me. Back in the fifties, there was an ad for Daisy air rifles on the back of just about every goddam comic book that hit the stands. Every kid on my block—every boy, anyway—wanted just two things: a Daisy air rifle and a Davy Crockett coonskin cap. He's right, there were no bullets, even pretend ones, but we used to tip a little Johnson's Baby Oil down the barrel. Then when you pumped air into it and pulled the trigger, you got a puff of blue smoke." He looked down at the photocopied pages again. "Son of a bitch killed his wife and three of his kids with a *hammer*? Jee-*zus*."

He just start laying on with it, Harry had written. *I run back into the living room and there was blood all over the walls and white stuff on the couch. That was my mother's brains. Ellen, she was laying on the floor with the rocker-chair on top of her legs and blood coming out of her ears and hair. The TV was still on, it was this show my mom liked about Elerie Queen, who solve crimes.*

The crime that night had been nothing like the bloodlessly elegant problems Ellery Queen unraveled; it had been a slaughter. The ten-year-old boy who stopped to pee before going out trick-or-treating came back from the bathroom in time to see his drunken, roaring father split the head of Arthur "Tugga" Dunning as Tugga tried to crawl into the kitchen. Then he turned and saw Harry, who raised the Daisy air rifle and said, "Leave me alone, Daddy, or I'll shoot you."

Dunning rushed at the boy, swinging the bloody hammer. Harry fired the air rifle at him (I could hear the *ka-chow* sound it must have made, even if I had never fired one myself), then dropped it and ran for the bedroom he shared with the now-deceased Tugga. His father had neglected to shut the front door when he came in, and somewhere—"it sounded 1000 miles away," the janitor had written—neighbors were shouting and trick-or-treating kids were screaming.

Dunning would almost certainly have killed the remaining son as well, if he hadn't tripped on the overturned "rocker-chair." He went sprawling, got up, and ran down to his younger sons' room. Harry was trying to crawl under the bed. His father hauled him out and fetched him a lick on the side of the head that surely would have killed the boy if the father's hand hadn't slipped on the bloody handle; instead of splitting Harry's skull, the hammerhead had only caved in part of it above the right ear.

I didnt pass out but almost. I kept crawling for under the bed and I hardly felt him hit my leg at all but he did and broke it in 4 diferent places.

A man from down the block who had been out canvassing the neighborhood for candy with his daughter came running in at that point. In spite of the slaughter in the living room, the neighbor had the presence of mind to grab the ash shovel out of the tool bucket beside the kitchen woodstove. He slugged Dunning in the back of the head with it while the man was trying to turn the bed over and get at his bleeding, semiconscious son.

Afterwards I went uncontchus like Ellen only I was lucky I woke up. The doctors said they might have to ampantate my leg but in the end they didnt.

No, he had kept the leg and eventually become a janitor at Lisbon High School, known to generations of students as Hoptoad

Harry. Would the kids have been kinder if they'd known the origin of the limp? Probably not. Although emotionally delicate and eminently bruisable, teenagers are short on empathy. That comes later in life, if it comes at all.

"October of 1958," Al said in his harsh dog-bark voice. "Am I supposed to believe that's a coincidence?"

I remembered what I'd said to the teenage version of Frank Anicetti about the Shirley Jackson story and smiled. "Sometimes a cigar is just a smoke and a coincidence is just a coincidence. All I know is that we're talking about another watershed moment."

"And I didn't find this story in the *Enterprise* because?"

"It didn't happen around here. It happened in Derry, upstate. When Harry was well enough to get out of the hospital, he went to live with his uncle and aunt in Haven, about twenty-five miles south of Derry. They adopted him and put him to work on the family farm when it became clear he couldn't keep up in school."

"Sounds like *Oliver Twist,* or something."

"No, they were good to him. Remember there were no remedial classes in those days, and the phrase 'mentally challenged' hadn't been invented yet—"

"I know," Al said dryly. "Back then, mentally challenged means you're either a feeb, a dummy, or just plain addlepated."

"But he wasn't then and he isn't now," I said. "Not really. I think mostly it was the shock, you know? The trauma. It took him years to recover from that night, and by the time he did, school was behind him."

"At least until he went back for his GED, and by then he was middle-aged going on old." Al shook his head. "What a waste."

"Bullshit," I said. "A good life is never wasted. Could it have been better? Yes. Can I make that happen? Based on yesterday, maybe I can. But that's really not the point."

"Then what is? Because to me this looks like Carolyn Poulin all over again, and that case is already proved. Yes, you can change the past. And no, the world doesn't just pop like a balloon when you do it. Would you pour me a fresh cup of coffee, Jake? And get yourself one while you're at it. It's hot, and you look like you could use one."

While I was pouring the coffee, I spied some sweet rolls. When I offered him one, he shook his head. "Solid food hurts going down. But if you're determined to make me swallow calories, there's a six-pack of Ensure in the fridge. In my opinion it tastes like chilled snot, but I can choke it down."

When I brought it in one of the wine goblets I'd spied in his cupboard, he laughed hard. "Think that'll make it taste any better?"

"Maybe. If you pretend it's pinot noir."

He drank half of it, and I could see him struggling with his gorge to keep it down. That was a battle he won, but he pushed the goblet away and picked up the coffee mug again. Didn't drink from it, just wrapped his hands around it, as if trying to take some of its warmth into himself. Watching this, I recalculated the amount of time he might have left.

"So," he said. "Why is this different?"

If he hadn't been so sick, he would have seen it for himself. He was a bright guy. "Because Carolyn Poulin was never a very good test case. You didn't save her life, Al, only her legs. She went on to have a good but completely normal existence on both tracks—the one where Cullum shot her and the one where you stepped in. She never married on either track. There were no kids on either track. It's like . . ." I fumbled. "No offense, Al, but what you did was like a doctor saving an infected appendix. Great for the appendix, but it's never going to do anything vital even if it's healthy. Do you see what I'm saying?"

"Yes." But I thought he looked a little peeved. "Carolyn Poulin looked like the best I could do, buddy. At my age, time is limited even when you're healthy. I had my eyes on a bigger prize."

"I'm not criticizing. But the Dunning family makes a better test case, because it's not just a young girl paralyzed, terrible as something like that must have been for her and her family. We're talking about four people murdered and a fifth maimed for life. Also, we know him. After he got his GED, I brought him down to the diner for a burger, and when you saw his cap and gown, you paid. Remember that?"

"Yeah. That's when I took the picture for my Wall."

"If I can do this—if I can stop his old man from swinging that hammer—do you think that picture will still be there?"

"I don't know," Al said. "Maybe not. I might not even remember it was there in the first place."

That was a little too theoretical for me, and I passed it without comment. "And think about the three other kids—Troy, Ellen, and Tugga. Surely some of *them* will get married if they live to grow up. And maybe Ellen becomes a famous comedian. Doesn't he say in there that she was as funny as Lucille Ball?" I leaned forward. "The only thing I want is a better example of what happens when you change a watershed moment. I need that before I go monkeying with something as big as the Kennedy assassination. What do you say, Al?"

"I say that I see your point." Al struggled to his feet. It was painful to watch him, but when I started to get up, he waved me back. "Nah, stay there. I've got something for you. It's in the other room. I'll get it."

7

It was a tin box. He handed it to me and told me to carry it into the kitchen. He said it would be easier to lay stuff out on the table. When we were seated, he unlocked it with a key he wore around his neck. The first thing he took out was a bulky manila envelope. He opened it and shook out a large and untidy pile of paper money. I plucked one leaf from all that lettuce and looked at it wonderingly. It was a twenty, but instead of Andrew Jackson on the face, I saw Grover Cleveland, who would probably not be on anyone's top ten list of great American presidents. On the back was a locomotive and a steamship that looked destined for a collision beneath the words **FEDERAL RESERVE NOTE**.

"This looks like Monopoly money."

"It's not. And there's not as much there as it probably looks like, because there are no bills bigger than a twenty. These days, when a fill-up can run you thirty, thirty-five dollars, a fifty raises no eyebrows even at a convenience store. Back then it's different, and raised eyebrows you don't need."

"This is your gambling dough?"

"Some. It's mostly my savings. I worked as a cook between '58 and '62, same as here, and a man on his own can save a lot, especially if he don't run with expensive women. Which I didn't. Or cheap ones, for that matter. I stayed on friendly terms with everybody and got close to nobody. I advise you to do the same. In Derry, and in Dallas, if you go there." He stirred the money with one thin finger. "There's a little over nine grand, best I can remember. It buys what sixty would today."

I stared at the cash. "Money comes back. It stays, no matter how many times you use the rabbit-hole." We'd been over this point, but I was still trying to get it through my head.

"Yeah, although it's still back there, too—complete reset, remember?"

"Isn't that a paradox?"

He looked at me, haggard, patience wearing thin. "I don't know. Asking questions that don't have answers is a waste of time, and I don't have much."

"Sorry, sorry. What else have you got in there?"

"Not much. But the beauty of it is that you don't need much. It was a very different time, Jake. You can read about it in the history books, but you can't really understand it until you've lived there for awhile." He passed me a Social Security card. The number was 005-52-0223. The name was George T. Amberson. Al took a pen out of the box and handed it to me. "Sign it."

I took the pen, which was a promotional giveaway. Written on the barrel was TRUST YOUR CAR TO THE MAN WHO WEARS THE STAR **TEXACO**. Feeling a little like Daniel Webster making his pact with the devil, I signed the card. When I tried to give it back to him, he shook his head.

The next item was George T. Amberson's Maine driver's license, which stated I was six feet five, blue eyes, brown hair, weight one-ninety. I had been born on April 22, 1923, and lived at 19 Blue-bird Lane in Sabattus, which happened to be my 2011 address.

"Six-five about right?" Al asked. "I had to guess."

"Close enough." I signed the driver's license, which was your basic piece of cardboard. Color: Bureaucratic Beige. "No photo?"

"State of Maine's years away on that, buddy. The other forty-eight, too."

"Forty-*eight*?"

"Hawaii won't be a state until next year."

"Oh." I felt a little out of breath, as if someone had just punched me in the gut. "So . . . you get stopped for speeding, and the cop just assumes you are who this card claims you are?"

"Why not? If you say something about a terrorist attack in 1958, people are gonna think you're talking about teenagers tipping cows. Sign these, too."

He handed me a Hertz Courtesy Card, a Cities Service gas card, a Diners Club card, and an American Express card. The Amex was celluloid, the Diners Club cardboard. George Amberson's name was on them. Typed, not printed.

"You can get a genuine plastic Amex card next year, if you want."

I smiled. "No checkbook?"

"I coulda got you one, but what good would it do you? Any paperwork I filled out on George Amberson's behalf would be lost in the next reset. Also any cash I put into the account."

"Oh." I felt like a dummy. "Right."

"Don't get down on yourself, all this is still new to you. You'll want to start an account, though. I'd suggest no more than a thousand. Keep most of the dough in cash, and where you can grab it."

"In case I have to come back in a hurry."

"Right. And the credit cards are just identity-backers. The actual accounts I opened to get them are going to be wiped out when you go back through. They might come in handy, though— you can never tell."

"Does George get his mail at Nineteen Bluebird Lane?"

"In 1958, Bluebird Lane's just an address on a Sabattus plat map, buddy. The development where you live hasn't been built yet. If anybody asks you about that, just say it's a business thing. They'll buy it. Business is like a god in '58—everybody worships it but nobody understands it. Here."

He tossed me a gorgeous man's wallet. I gaped at it. "Is this *ostrich?*"

"I wanted you to look prosperous," Al said. "Find some pictures to put in it along with your identification. I got you some other odds and ends, too. More ballpoint pens, one a fad item with a combination letter-opener and ruler on the end. A Scripto mechanical pencil. A pocket protector. In '58 they're considered necessary, not nerdy. A Bulova watch on a Speidel chrome expansion band—all the cool cats will dig that one, daddy. You can sort the rest out for yourself." He coughed long and hard, wincing. When he stopped, sweat was standing out on his face in large drops.

"Al, when did you put all this together?"

"When I realized I wasn't going to make it into 1963, I left Texas and came home. I already had you in mind. Divorced, no children, smart, best of all, young. Oh, here, almost forgot. This is the seed everything else grew from. Got the name off a gravestone in the St. Cyril's boneyard and just wrote an application letter to the Maine Secretary of State."

He handed me my birth certificate. I ran my fingers over the embossed franking. It had a silky official feel.

When I looked up, I saw he'd put another sheet of paper on the table. It was headed SPORTS 1958–1963. "Don't lose it. Not only because it's your meal ticket, but because you'd have a lot of questions to answer if it fell into the wrong hands. Especially when the picks start to prove out."

I started to put everything back into the box, and he shook his head. "I've got a Lord Buxton briefcase for you in my closet, all nicely battered around the edges."

"I don't need it—I've got my backpack. It's in the trunk of my car."

He looked amused. "Where you're going, nobody wears backpacks except Boy Scouts, and they only wear them when they're going on hikes and Camporees. You've got a lot to learn, buddy, but if you step careful and don't take chances, you'll get there."

I realized I was really going to do this, and it was going to happen right away, with almost no preparation. I felt like a visitor to the London docks of the seventeenth century who suddenly becomes aware he's about to be shanghaied.

"But what do I do?" This came out in a near bleat.

He raised his eyebrows—bushy and now as white as the thinning hair on his head. "You save the Dunning family. Isn't that what we've been talking about?"

"I don't mean that. What do I do when people ask me how I make my *living*? What do I say?"

"Your rich uncle died, remember? Tell them you're piecing your windfall inheritance out a little at a time, making it last long enough for you to write a book. Isn't there a frustrated writer inside every English teacher? Or am I wrong about that?"

Actually, he wasn't.

He sat looking at me—haggard, far too thin, but not without sympathy. Perhaps even pity. At last he said, very softly, "It's big, isn't it?"

"It is," I said. "And Al . . . man . . . I'm just a *little* guy."

"You could say the same of Oswald. A pipsqueak who shot from ambush. And according to Harry Dunning's theme, his father's just a mean drunk with a hammer."

"He's not even that anymore. He died of acute stomach poisoning in Shawshank State Prison. Harry said it was probably bad squeeze. That's—"

"I know what squeeze is. I saw plenty when I was stationed in the Philippines. Even drank some, to my sorrow. But he's not dead where you're going. Oswald, either."

"Al . . . I know you're sick, and I know you're in pain. But can you come down to the diner with me? I . . ." For the first and last time, I used his habitual form of address. "Buddy, I don't want to start this alone. I'm scared."

"Wouldn't miss it." He hooked a hand under his armpit and stood up with a grimace that rolled his lips back to the gumlines. "You get the briefcase. I'll get dressed."

8

It was quarter to eight when Al unlocked the door of the silver trailer that the Famous Fatburger called home. The glimmering chrome fixtures behind the counter looked ghostly. The stools seemed to whisper *no one will sit on us again.* The big old-fashioned sugar shakers seemed to whisper back *no one will pour from us again—the party's over.*

"Make way for L.L. Bean," I said.

"That's right," Al said. "The fucking march of progress."

He was out of breath, panting, but didn't pause to rest. He led me behind the counter and to the pantry door. I followed, switching the briefcase with my new life inside it from one hand to the other. It was the old-fashioned kind, with buckles. If I'd carried it into my homeroom at LHS, most of the kids would have laughed. A few others—those with an emerging sense of style—might have applauded its retro funk.

Al opened the door on the smells of vegetables, spices, coffee. He once more reached past my shoulder to turn on the light. I gazed at the gray linoleum floor the way a man might stare at a pool that could well be filled with hungry sharks, and when Al tapped me on the shoulder, I jumped.

"Sorry," he said, "but you ought to take this." He was holding out a fifty-cent piece. Half a rock. "The Yellow Card Man, remember him?"

"Sure I do." Actually I'd forgotten all about him. My heart was beating hard enough to make my eyeballs feel like they were pulsing in their sockets. My tongue tasted like an old piece of carpet, and when he handed me the coin, I almost dropped it.

He gave me a final critical look. "The jeans are okay for now, but you ought to stop at Mason's Menswear on upper Main Street and get some slacks before you head north. Pendletons or khaki twill is fine for everyday. Ban-Lon for dress."

"Ban-Lon?"

"Just ask, they'll know. You'll also need to get some dress shirts. Eventually a suit. Also some ties and a tie clip. Buy yourself a hat, too. *Not* a baseball cap, a nice summer straw."

There were tears leaking from the corners of his eyes. This frightened me more thoroughly than anything he'd said.

"Al? What's wrong?"

"I'm just scared, same as you are. No need for an emotional parting scene, though. If you're coming back, you'll be here in two minutes no matter how long you stay in '58. Just time enough for me to start the coffeemaker. If it works out, we'll have a nice cup together, and you can tell me all about it."

If. What a big word.

"You could say a prayer, too. There'd be time for that, wouldn't there?"

"Sure. I'll be praying that it goes nice and smooth. Don't get so dazed by where you are that you forget you're dealing with a dangerous man. More dangerous than Oswald, maybe."

"I'll be careful."

"Okay. Keep your mouth shut as much as you can until you pick up the lingo and the feel of the place. Go slow. Don't make waves."

I tried to smile, but I'm not sure I made it. The briefcase felt very heavy, as if it were filled with rocks instead of money and bogus ID. I thought I might faint. And yet, God help me, part of me still wanted to go. Couldn't *wait* to go. I wanted to see the USA in my Chevrolet; America was asking me to call.

Al held out his thin and trembling hand. "Good luck, Jake. God bless."

"George, you mean."

"George, right. Now get going. As they say back then, it's time for you to split the scene."

I turned and walked slowly into the pantry, moving like a man trying to locate the top of a staircase with the lights out.

On my third step, I found it.

PART 2

THE JANITOR'S FATHER

CHAPTER 5

1

I walked along the side of the drying shed, just like before. I ducked under the chain with the **NO ADMITTANCE BEYOND THIS POINT** sign hanging from it, just like before. I walked around the corner of the big green-painted cube of a building just like before, and then something smacked into me. I'm not particularly heavy for my height, but I've got some meat on my bones—"You won't blow away in a high wind," my father used to say—and still the Yellow Card Man almost knocked me over. It was like being attacked by a black overcoat full of flapping birds. He was yelling something, but I was too startled (not scared, exactly, it was all too quick for that) to have any idea what it was.

I pushed him away and he stumbled back against the drying shed with his coat swirling around his legs. There was a bonk sound when the back of his head struck the metal, and his filthy fedora tumbled to the ground. He followed it down, not in a tumble but in a kind of accordion collapse. I was sorry for what I'd done even before my heart had a chance to settle into a more normal rhythm, and sorrier still when he picked up his hat and began brushing at it with one dirty hand. The hat was never going to be clean again, and, in all probability, neither was he.

"Are you okay?" I asked, but when I bent down to touch his shoulder, he went scuttering away from me along the side of the shed, pushing with his hands and sliding on his butt. I'd say he looked like a crippled spider, but he didn't. He looked like what he was: a wino with a brain that was damp going on wet. A man who might be as close to death as Al Templeton was, because in this fifty-plus-years-ago America there were probably no charity-supported shelters or rehabs for guys like him. The VA might take him if he'd ever worn the uniform, but who would take him to the VA? Nobody, probably, although someone—a mill foreman would be the most likely—might call the cops on him. They'd put him in the drunk tank for twenty-four or forty-eight hours. If he didn't die of DT-induced convulsions while he was in there, they'd turn him loose to start the next cycle. I found myself wishing my ex-wife was here—she could find an AA meeting and take him to it. Only Christy wouldn't be born for another twenty-one years.

I put the briefcase between my feet and held my hands out to show him they were empty, but he cringed even further down the side of the drying shed. Spittle gleamed on his stubbly chin. I looked around to be sure we weren't attracting attention, saw that we had this part of the millyard to ourselves, and tried again. "I only pushed you because you startled me."

"Who the fuck *are* you?" he asked, his voice cracking through about five different registers. If I hadn't heard the question on my last visit, I wouldn't have had any idea what he was asking . . . and although the slur was the same, wasn't the inflection a little different this time? I wasn't sure, but I thought so. *He's harmless, but he's not like anyone else,* Al had said. *It's like he* knows *something.* Al thought it was because he happened to be sunning himself near the rabbit-hole at 11:58 in the morning on September 9, 1958, and was susceptible to its influence. The way you can produce static on a TV screen if you run a mixer close to it. Maybe that was it. Or, hell, maybe it was just the booze.

"Nobody important," I said in my most soothing voice. "Nobody you need to concern yourself with. My name's George. What's yours?"

"Motherfucker!" he snarled, and scrambled yet further from me.

If that was his name, it was certainly an unusual one. "You're not supposed to be here!"

"Don't worry, I'm leaving," I said. I picked up the briefcase to demonstrate my sincerity, and he hunched his thin shoulders all the way up to his ears, as if he expected me to hurl it at him. He was like a dog that's been beaten so often it expects no other treatment. "No harm and no foul, okay?"

"Get out, bastard-ball! Go back to where you came from *and leave me alone!*"

"It's a deal." I was still recovering from the startle he'd given me, and the residual adrenaline mixed badly with the pity I felt— not to mention the exasperation. The same exasperation I'd felt with Christy when I came home to discover she was drunk-going-on-shitfaced again in spite of all her promises to straighten up, fly right, and quit the booze once and for all. The combination of emotions added to the heat of this late summer midday was making me feel a little sick to my stomach. Probably not the best way to start a rescue mission.

I thought of the Kennebec Fruit and how good that root beer had been; I could see the gasp of vapor from the ice cream freezer as Frank Anicetti Senior pulled out the big mug. Also, it had been blessedly cool in there. I started in that direction with no further ado, my new (but carefully aged around the edges) briefcase banging against the side of my knee.

"Hey! Hey, you, whatsyaface!"

I turned. The wino was struggling to his feet, using the side of the drying shed as a support. He had snagged his hat and was holding it crushed against his midsection. Now he began to fumble at it. "I got a yellow card from the greenfront, so gimme a buck, motherfucker. Today's double-money day."

We were back on message. That was comforting. Nonetheless, I took pains not to approach him too closely. I didn't want to scare him again or provoke another attack. I stopped six feet away and held out my hand. The coin Al had given me gleamed on my palm. "I can't spare a buck, but here's half a rock."

He hesitated, now holding his hat in his left hand. "You better not want a suck-job."

"Tempting, but I think I can resist."

"Huh?" He looked from the fifty-cent piece to my face, then back down at the money again. He raised his right hand to wipe the slick of drool off his chin, and I saw another difference from before. Nothing earth-shattering, but enough to make me wonder about the solidity of Al's claim that each time was a complete reset.

"I don't care if you take it or leave it, but make up your mind," I said. "I've got things to do."

He snatched the coin, then cowered back against the drying shed again. His eyes were large and wet. The slick of drool had reappeared on his chin. There's really nothing in the world that can match the glamour of a late-stage alcoholic; I can't think why Jim Beam, Seagram's, and Mike's Hard Lemonade don't use them in their magazine ads. Drink Beam and see a better class of bugs.

"Who are you? What are you doing here?"

"A job, I hope. Listen, have you tried AA for that little problem you've got with the boo—"

"Fuck off, Jimla!"

I had no idea what a jimla might be, the *fuck off* part came through loud and clear. I headed for the gate, expecting him to hurl more questions after me. He hadn't before, but this encounter had been markedly different.

Because he wasn't the Yellow Card Man, not this time. When he raised his hand to wipe his chin, the card clutched in it had no longer been yellow.

This time it was a dirty but still bright orange.

2

I threaded my way through the mill parking lot, once again tapping the trunk of the white-over-red Plymouth Fury for good luck. I was certainly going to need all of that I could get. I crossed the train tracks, once again hearing the *wuff-chuff* of a train, only this time it sounded a little more distant, because this time my encounter with the Yellow Card Man—who was now the Orange Card Man—had taken a bit longer. The air stank of mill effluent as it had before, and the same inter-city bus snored past. Because I was a little late this time, I couldn't read the route sign, but I remembered what it said: LEWISTON EXPRESS. I wondered idly how many times Al had seen that same bus, with the same passengers looking out the windows.

I hurried across the street, waving away the blue cloud of bus exhaust as best I could. The rockabilly rebel was at his post outside the door, and I wondered briefly what he'd say if I stole his line. But in a way that would be as mean as terrorizing the drying shed wino on purpose; if you stole the secret language belonging to kids like this, they didn't have much left. This one couldn't even go back and pound on the Xbox. So I just nodded.

He nodded back. "Hi-ho, Daddy-O."

I went inside. The bell jingled. I went past the discount comic books and straight to the soda fountain where Frank Anicetti Senior was standing. "What can I do for you today, my friend?"

For a moment I was stumped, because that wasn't what he'd said before. Then I realized it wouldn't be. Last time I'd grabbed a newspaper out of the rack. This time I hadn't. Maybe each trip back to 1958 reset the odometer back to all zeros (with the exception of the Yellow Card Man), but the first time you varied something, everything was up for grabs. The idea was both scary and liberating.

"I could use a root beer," I said.

"And I can use the custom, so we've got a meeting of the minds. Five- or ten-cent beer?"

"Ten, I guess."

"Well, I think you guess right."

The frost-coated mug came out of the freezer. He used the handle of the wooden spoon to scrape off the foam. He filled it to the top and set it in front of me. All just like before.

"That's a dime, plus one for the governor."

I handed over one of Al's vintage dollars, and while Frank 1.0 made change, I looked over my shoulder and saw the former Yellow Card Man standing outside the liquor store—the *greenfront*—and swaying from side to side. He made me think of a Hindu fakir I'd seen in some old movie, tooting a horn to coax a cobra out of a wicker basket. And, coming up the sidewalk, right on schedule, was Anicetti the Younger.

I turned back, sipped my root beer, and sighed. "This hits the spot."

"Yep, nothing like a cold beer on a hot day. Not from around here, are you?"

"No, Wisconsin." I held out my hand. "George Amberson."

He shook it as the bell over the door jangled. "Frank Anicetti. And there comes my boy. Frank Junior. Say hello to Mr. Amberson from Wisconsin, Frankie."

"Hello, sir." He gave me a smile and a nod, then turned to his dad. "Titus has got the truck up on the lift. Says it'll be ready by five."

"Well, that's good." I waited for Anicetti 1.0 to light a cigarette and wasn't disappointed. He inhaled, then turned back to me. "Are you traveling on business or for pleasure?"

For a moment I didn't respond, but not because I was stumped for an answer. What was throwing me was the way this scene kept diverging from and then returning to the original script. In any case, Anicetti didn't seem to notice.

"Either way, you picked the right time to come. Most of the summer people are gone, and when that happens we all relax. You want a scoop of vanilla ice cream in your beer? Usually it's five cents extra, but on Tuesdays I reduce the price to a nickel."

"You wore that one out ten years ago, Pop," Frank Junior said amiably.

"Thanks, but this is fine," I said. "I'm on business, actually. A real estate closing up in . . . Sabattus? I think that's it. Do you know that town?"

104

"Only my whole life," Frank said. He jetted smoke from his nostrils, then gave me a shrewd look. "Long way to come for a real estate closing."

I returned a smile that was supposed to communicate *if you knew what I know.* It must have gotten across, because he tipped me a wink. The bell over the door jingled and the fruit-shopping ladies came in. The DRINK CHEER-UP COFFEE wall clock read 12:28. Apparently the part of the script where Frank Junior and I discussed the Shirley Jackson story had been cut from this draft. I finished my root beer in three long swallows, and as I did, a cramp tightened my bowels. In novels characters rarely have to go potty, but in real life, mental stress often provokes a physical reaction.

"Say, you don't happen to have a men's room, do you?"

"Sorry, no," Frank Senior said. "Keep meaning to put one in, but in the summer we're too busy and in the winter there never seems to be enough cash for the renovations."

"You can go around the corner to Titus," Frank Junior said. He was scooping ice cream into a metal cylinder, getting ready to make himself a milkshake. He hadn't done that before, and I thought with some unease about the so-called butterfly effect. I thought I was watching that butterfly unfurl its wings right before my eyes. We were changing the world. Only in small ways—infinitesimal ways—but yes, we were changing it.

"Mister?"

"I'm sorry," I said. "Had a senior moment."

He looked puzzled, then laughed. "Never heard that one before, but it's pretty good." Because it was, he might repeat it the next time he lost his own train of thought. And a phrase that otherwise wouldn't enter the bright flow of American slanguage until the seventies or eighties would make an early debut. You couldn't say a *premature* debut, exactly, because on this time-stream it would be right on schedule.

"Titus Chevron is around the corner on your right," Anicetti Senior said. "If it's . . . uh . . . urgent, you're welcome to use our bathroom upstairs."

105

"No, I'm fine," I said, and although I'd already looked at the wall clock, I took an ostentatious glance at my Bulova on the cool Speidel band. It was a good thing they couldn't see the face, because I'd forgotten to reset it and it was still on 2011 time. "But I've got to be going. Errands to run. Unless I'm very lucky, they'll tie me up for more than a day. Can you recommend a good motel around here?"

"Do you mean a motor court?" Anicetti Senior asked. He butted his cigarette in one of the WINSTON TASTES GOOD ashtrays that lined the counter.

"Yes." This time my smile felt foolish rather than in-the-know . . . and my bowels cramped again. If I didn't take care of that problem soon, it was going to develop into an authentic 911 situation. "Motels are what we call them in Wisconsin."

"Well I'd say the Tamarack Motor Court, about five miles up 196 on your way to Lewiston," Anicetti Senior said. "It's near the drive-in movie."

"Thanks for the tip," I said, getting up.

"You bet. And if you want to get trimmed up before any of your meetings, try Baumer's Barber Shop. He does a real fine job."

"Thanks. Another good tip."

"Tips are free, root beers are sold American. Enjoy your time in Maine, Mr. Amberson. And Frankie? You drink that milkshake and get on back to school."

"You bet, Pop." This time it was Junior who tipped a wink in my direction.

"Frank?" one of the ladies called in a yoo-hoo voice. "Are these oranges fresh?"

"As fresh as your smile, Leola," he replied, and the ladies tee-hee'd. I'm not trying to be cute here; they actually tee-hee'd.

I passed them, murmuring "Ladies" as I went by. The bell jingled and I went out into the world that had existed before my birth. But this time instead of crossing the street to the courtyard where the rabbit-hole was, I walked deeper into that world. Across the street, the wino in the long black coat was gesticulating at the tunic-wearing clerk. The card he was waving might be orange instead of yellow, but otherwise he was back on script.

I took that as a good sign.

3

Titus Chevron was beyond the Red & White Supermarket, where Al had bought the same supplies for his diner over and over again. According to the sign in the window, lobster was going for sixty-nine cents a pound. Across from the market, standing on a patch of ground that was vacant in 2011, was a big maroon barn with the doors standing open and all sorts of used furniture on display—cribs, cane rockers, and overstuffed easy chairs of the "Dad's relaxin'" type seemed in particularly abundant supply. The sign over the door read **THE JOLLY WHITE ELEPHANT**. An additional sign, this one an A-frame propped to catch the eye of folks on the road to Lewiston, made the audacious claim that **IF WE DON'T HAVE IT, YOU DON'T NEED IT**. A fellow I took to be the proprietor was sitting in one of the rocking chairs, smoking a pipe and looking across at me. He wore a strap-style tee-shirt and baggy brown slacks. He also wore a goatee, which I thought equally audacious for this particular island in the time-stream. His hair, although combed back and held in place with some sort of grease, curled down to the nape of his neck and made me think of some old rock-and-roll video I'd seen: Jerry Lee Lewis jumping on his piano as he sang "Great Balls of Fire." The proprietor of the Jolly White Elephant probably had a reputation as the town beatnik.

I tipped a finger to him. He gave me the faintest of nods and went on puffing his pipe.

At the Chevron (where regular was selling for 19.9 cents a gallon and "super" was a penny more), a man in blue coveralls and a strenuous crewcut was working on a truck—the Anicettis', I presumed—that was up on the lift.

"Mr. Titus?"

He glanced over his shoulder. "Ayuh?"

"Mr. Anicetti said I could use your restroom?"

"Key's inside the front door." *Doe-ah.*

"Thank you."

The key was attached to a wooden paddle with MEN printed on it. The other key had GIRLS printed on the paddle. My ex-wife would have shit a brick at that, I thought, and not without glee.

The restroom was clean but smoky-smelling. There was an urn-style ashtray beside the commode. From the number of butts studding it, I would guess a good many visitors to this tidy little room enjoyed puffing as they pooped.

When I came out, I saw two dozen or so used cars in a small lot next to the station. A line of colored pennants fluttered above them in a light breeze. Cars that would have sold for thousands —as classics, no less—in 2011 were priced at seventy-five and a hundred dollars. A Caddy that looked in nearly mint condition was going for eight hundred. The sign over the little sales booth (inside, a gum-chewing, ponytailed cutie was absorbed in *Photoplay*) read: ALL THESE CARS RUN GOOD AND COME WITH THE BILL TITUS GUARENTEE **WE SERVICE WHAT WE SELL!**

I hung the key up, thanked Titus (who grunted without turning from the truck on the lift), and started back toward Main Street, thinking it would be a good idea to get my hair cut before visiting the bank. That made me remember the goatee-wearing beatnik, and on impulse I crossed the street to the used furniture emporium.

"Morning," I said.

"Well, it's actually afternoon, but whatever makes you happy." He puffed his pipe, and that light late-summer breeze brought me a whiff of Cherry Blend. Also a memory of my grandfather, who used to smoke it when I was a kid. He sometimes blew it in my ear to quell the earache, a treatment that was probably not AMA-approved.

"Do you sell suitcases?"

"Oh, I got a few in my kick. No more'n two hundred, I'd say. Walk all the way to the back and look on your right."

"If I buy one, could I leave it here for a couple of hours, while I do some shopping?"

"I'm open until five," he said, and turned his face up into the sun. "After that you're on your own."

4

I traded two of Al's vintage dollars for a leather valise, left it behind the beatnik's counter, then walked up to Main Street with my briefcase banging my leg. I glanced into the greenfront and saw the clerk sitting beside the cash register and reading a newspaper. There was no sign of my pal in the black overcoat.

It would have been hard to get lost in the shopping district; it was only a block long. Three of four storefronts up from the Kennebec Fruit, I came to Baumer's Barber Shop. A red-and-white barber pole twirled in the window. Next to it was a political poster featuring Edmund Muskie. I remembered him as a tired, slope-shouldered old man, but this version of him looked almost too young to vote, let alone get elected to anything. The poster read, SEND ED MUSKIE TO THE U.S. SENATE, VOTE DEMOCRAT! Someone had put a bright white band around the bottom. Hand-printed on it was THEY SAID IT COULDN'T BE DONE IN MAINE BUT *WE DID IT!* NEXT UP: HUMPHREY IN 1960!

Inside, two old parties were sitting against the wall while an equally old third party got his tonsure trimmed. Both of the waiting men were puffing like choo-choos. So was the barber (Baumer, I assumed), with one eye squinted against the rising smoke as he clipped. All four studied me in a way I was familiar with: the not-quite-mistrustful look of appraisal that Christy once called the Yankee Glare. It was nice to know that some things hadn't changed.

"I'm from out of town, but I'm a friend," I told them. "Voted the straight Democratic ticket my whole life." I raised my hand in a so-help-me-God gesture.

Baumer grunted with amusement. Ash tumbled from his cigarette. He brushed it absently off his smock and onto the floor, where there were several crushed butts among the cut hair. "Harold there's a Republican. You want to watch out he don't bitecha."

"He ain't got the choppers for it nummore," one of the others said, and they all cackled.

"Where you from, mister?" Harold the Republican asked.

"Wisconsin." I picked up a copy of *Man's Adventure* to forestall further conversation. On the cover, a subhuman Asian gent with a whip in one gloved hand was approaching a blonde lovely tied to a post. The story that went with it was called JAP SEX-SLAVES OF THE PACIFIC. The barbershop's smell was a sweet and completely wonderful mixture of talcum powder, pomade, and cigarette smoke. By the time Baumer motioned me to the chair, I was deep into the sex-slaves story. It wasn't as exciting as the cover.

"Been doin some traveling, Mr. Wisconsin?" he asked as he settled a white rayon cloth over my front and wrapped a paper collar around my neck.

"Quite a lot," I said truthfully.

"Well, you're in God's country now. How short do you want it?"

"Short enough so I don't look like"—a *hippie,* I almost finished, but Baumer wouldn't know what that was—"like a beatnik."

"Let it get a little out of control, I guess." He began to clip. "Leave it much longer and you'd look like that faggot who runs the Jolly White Elephant."

"I wouldn't want that," I said.

"Nosir, he's a sight, that one." *That-un.*

When Baumer finished, he powdered the back of my neck, asked me if I wanted Vitalis, Brylcreem, or Wildroot Cream Oil, and charged me forty cents.

I call that a deal.

5

My thousand-dollar deposit at the Hometown Trust raised no eye-brows. The freshly barbered look probably helped, but I think it was mostly being in a cash-and-carry society where credit cards were still in their infancy . . . and probably regarded with some suspicion by thrifty Yankees. A severely pretty teller with her hair done up in tight rolls and a cameo at her throat counted my money, entered the amount in a ledger, then called over the assistant manager, who counted it again, checked the ledger, and then wrote out a receipt that showed both the deposit and the total in my new checking account.

"If you don't mind me saying so, that's a mighty big amount to be carrying in checking, Mr. Amberson. Would you like to open a savings account? We're currently offering three percent interest, compounded quarterly." He widened his eyes to show me what a wonderful deal this was. He looked like that old-time Cuban bandleader, Xavier Cugat.

"Thanks, but I've got a fair amount of business to transact." I lowered my voice. "Real estate closing. Or so I hope."

"Good luck," he said, lowering his own to the same confidential pitch. "Lorraine will fix you up with checks. Fifty enough to go on with?"

"Fifty would be fine."

"Later on, we can have some printed with your name and your address." He raised his eyebrows, turning it into a question.

"I expect to be in Derry. I'll be in touch."

"Fine. I'm at Drexel eight four-seven-seven-seven."

I had no idea what he was talking about until he slid a business card through the window. Gregory Dusen, Assistant Manager, was engraved on it, and **DRexel 8-4777**.

Lorraine got my checks and a faux alligator checkbook to put them in. I thanked her and dropped them into my briefcase. At the door I paused for a look back. A couple of the tellers were working adding machines, but otherwise the transactions were all of the pen-and-elbow-grease variety. It occurred to me that, with a few exceptions, Charles Dickens would have felt at home here. It also occurred to me that living in the past was a little like living underwater and breathing through a tube.

6

I got the clothes Al had recommended at Mason's Menswear, and the clerk told me yes, they would be more than happy to take a check, providing it was drawn on a local bank. Thanks to Lorraine, I could oblige in that regard.

Back at the Jolly White Elephant, the beatnik watched silently as I transferred the contents of three shopping bags to my new valise. When I snapped it shut, he finally offered an opinion. "Funny way to shop, man."

"I guess so," I said. "But it's a funny old world, isn't it?"

He cracked a smile at that. "In my opinion, that's a big you-bet. Slip me some skin, Jackson." He extended his hand, palm up.

For a moment it was like trying to figure out what the word *Drexel* attached to some numbers was all about. Then I remembered *Dragstrip Girl,* and understood the beatnik was offering the fifties version of a fist-bump. I dragged my palm across his, feeling the warmth and the sweat, thinking again: *This is real. This is happening.*

"Skin, man," I said.

7

I crossed back to Titus Chevron, swinging the newly loaded valise from one hand and the briefcase from the other. It was only mid-morning in the 2011 world I'd come from, but I felt tired out. There was a telephone booth between the service station and the adjacent car lot. I went in, shut the door, and read the hand-printed sign over the old-fashioned pay phone: REMEMBER PHONE CALLS NOW A DIME COURTESY OF "MA" BELL.

I thumbed through the Yellow Pages in the local phone book and found Lisbon Taxi. Their ad featured a cartoon cab with eyes for headlights and a big smile on its grille. It promised FAST, COURTEOUS SERVICE. That sounded good to me. I grubbed for my change, but the first thing I came up with was something I should have left behind: my Nokia cell phone. It was antique by the standards of the year I'd come from—I'd been meaning to trade up to an iPhone—but it had no business here. If someone saw it, I'd be asked a hundred questions I couldn't answer. I stowed it in the briefcase. It would be okay there for the time being, I guessed, but I'd have to get rid of it eventually. Keeping it would be like walking around with an unexploded bomb.

I found a dime, dropped it in the slot, and it went right through to the coin return. I fished it out, and one look was enough to pin-point the problem. Like my Nokia, the dime had come from the future; it was a copper sandwich, really no more than a penny with pretensions. I pulled out all my coins, poked through them, and found a 1953 dime I'd probably got in change from the root beer I'd bought at the Kennebec Fruit. I started to put it in, then had a thought that made me feel cold. What if my 2002 dime had got-ten stuck in the phone's throat instead of falling through to the coin return? And what if the AT&T man who serviced the pay phones in Lisbon Falls had found it?

He would have thought it was a joke, that's all. Just some elaborate prank.

I somehow doubted this—the dime was too perfect. He would have shown it around; there might even eventually have been an item about it in the newspaper. I had gotten lucky this time, but next time I might not. I needed to be careful. I thought of my cell phone again, with deepening unease. Then I put the 1953 dime in the coin slot and was rewarded with a dial tone. I placed the call slowly and carefully, trying to remember if I'd ever used a phone with a rotary dial before. I thought not. Each time I released it, the phone made a weird clucking sound as the dial spun back.

"Lisbon Taxi," a woman said, "where the mileage is always smileage. How may we help you today?"

8

While I waited for my ride, I window-shopped my way through Titus's car lot. I was particularly taken by a red '54 Ford convertible—a Sunliner, according to the script below the chrome headlight on the driver's side. It had whitewall tires and a genuine canvas roof that the cool cats in *Dragstrip Girl* would have called a ragtop.

"That ain't a bad one, mister," Bill Titus said from behind me. "Goes like a house afire, that I can testify to personally."

I turned. He was wiping his hands on a red rag that looked almost as greasy as his hands.

"Some rust on the rocker panels," I said.

"Yeah, well, this climate." He gave a whattaya-gonna-do shrug. "Main thing is, the motor's in nifty shape and those tires are almost new."

"V-8?"

"Y-block," he said, and I nodded as if I understood this perfectly. "Bought it from Arlene Hadley over Durham after her husband died. If there was one thing Bill Hadley knew, it was how to take care of a car . . . but you won't know them because you're not from around here, are you?"

"No. Wisconsin. George Amberson." I held out my hand.

He shook his head, smiling a little. "Good to meet you, Mr. Amberson, but I don't want to getcha all over grease. Consider it shook. You a buyer or a looker?"

"I don't know yet," I said, but this was disingenuous. I thought the Sunliner was the coolest car I'd ever seen in my life. I opened my mouth to ask what kind of mileage it got, then realized it was a question almost without meaning in a world where you could fill your tank for two dollars. Instead I asked him if it was a standard.

"Oh, ayuh. And when you catch second, you want to watch out for the cops. She goes like a bastid in second. Want to take er out for a spin?"

"I can't," I said. "I just called a cab."

"That's no way to travel," Titus said. "If you bought this, you could go back to Wisconsin·in style and never mind the train."

"How much are you asking? This one doesn't have a price on the windshield."

"Nope, just took it in trade day before yest'y. Haven't got around to it." *Gut.* He took out his cigarettes. "I'm carryin it at three-fifty, but tell you what, I'd dicker." *Dicka.*

I clamped my teeth together to keep my jaw from dropping and told him I'd think it over. If my thinking went the right way, I said, I'd come back tomorrow.

"Better come early, Mr. Amberson, this one ain't gonna be on the lot for long."

I was again comforted. I had coins that wouldn't work in pay phones, banking was still done mostly by hand, and the phones made an odd chuckling sound in your ear when you dialed, but some things didn't change.

9

The taxi driver was a fat man who wore a battered hat with a badge on it reading LICENSED LIVERY. He smoked Luckies one after the other and played WJAB on the radio. We listened to "Sugartime" by the McGuire Sisters, "Bird Dog" by the Everly Brothers, and "Purple People Eater," by some creature called a Sheb Wooley. That one I could have done without. After every other song, a trio of out-of-tune young women sang: *"Four-teen for-ty, WJA-beee . . . the Big Jab!"* I learned that Romanow's was having their annual end-of-summer blowout sale, and F. W. Woolworth's had just gotten a fresh order of Hula Hoops, a steal at $1.39.

"Goddam things don't do nothin but teach kids how to bump their hips," the cabbie said, and let the wing window suck ash from the end of his cigarette. It was his only stab at conversation between Titus Chevron and the Tamarack Motor Court.

I unrolled my window to get away from the cigarette smog a little and watched a different world roll by. The urban sprawl between Lisbon Falls and the Lewiston city line didn't exist. Other than a few gas stations, the Hi-Hat Drive-In, and the outdoor movie theater (the marquee advertised a double feature consisting of *Vertigo* and *The Long, Hot Summer*—both in CinemaScope and Technicolor), we were in pure Maine countryside. I saw more cows than people.

The motor court was set back from the highway and shaded not by tamaracks but by huge and stately elms. It wasn't like seeing a herd of dinosaurs, but almost. I gawked at them while Mr. Licensed Livery lit up another smoke. "Need a hand witcher bags, sir?"

"No, I'm fine." The fare on his meter wasn't as stately as the elms, but still rated a double take. I gave the guy two dollars and asked fifty cents back. He seemed satisfied with that; the tip was enough to buy a pack of Luckies.

10

I checked in (no problem there; cash on the counter and no ID required) and took a long nap in a room where the air-conditioning was a fan on the windowsill. I awoke refreshed (good) and then found it impossible to get to sleep that night (not good). There was next to no traffic on the highway after sundown, and the quiet was so deep it was disquieting. The television was a Zenith table model that must have weighed a hundred pounds. Sitting on top was a pair of rabbit ears. Propped against them was a sign reading

ADJUST ANTENNA BY HAND *DO NOT USE "TINFOIL!"* THANKS FROM MANAGEMENT.

There were three stations. The NBC affiliate was too snowy to watch no matter how much I fiddled with the rabbit ears, and on CBS the picture rolled; adjusting the vertical hold had no effect. ABC, which came in clear as a bell, was showing *The Life and Legend of Wyatt Earp,* starring Hugh O'Brian. He shot a few outlaws and then an ad for Viceroy cigarettes came on. Steve McQueen explained that Viceroys had a thinking man's filter and a smoking man's taste. While he was lighting up, I got off the bed and turned the TV off.

Then there was just the sound of the crickets.

I stripped to my shorts, lay down, and tried to sleep. My mind turned to my mother and father. Dad was currently six years old and living in Eau Claire. My mom, only five, was living in an Iowa farmhouse that would burn to the ground three or four years from now. Her family would then move to Wisconsin, and closer to the intersection of lives that would eventually produce . . . me.

I'm crazy, I thought. *Crazy and having a terribly involved hallucination in a mental hospital somewhere. Perhaps some doctor will write me up for a psychiatric journal. Instead of The Man Who Mistook His Wife for a Hat, I'll be The Man Who Thought He Was in 1958.*

But I ran my hand over the nubby fabric of the bedspread, which I had yet to turn back, and knew that it was all true. I thought of Lee Harvey Oswald, but Oswald still belonged to the future and he wasn't what was troubling me in this museum piece of a motel room.

I sat on the edge of the bed, opened the briefcase, and took out my cell phone, a time-traveling gadget that was absolutely worthless here. Nevertheless, I could not resist flipping it open and pushing the power button. NO SERVICE popped up in the window, of course—what had I expected? Five bars? A plaintive voice saying *Come home, Jake, before you cause damage you can't undo?* Stupid, superstitious idea. If I did damage, I *could* undo it, because every trip was a reset. You could say that time-travel came with a built-in safety switch.

117

That was comforting, but having a phone like this in a world where color TV was the biggest technological breakthrough in consumer electronics wasn't comforting at all. I wouldn't be hung as a witch if I was found with it, but I might be arrested by the local cops and held in a jail cell until some of J. Edgar Hoover's boys could arrive from Washington to question me.

I put it on the bed, then pulled all of my change out of my right front pocket. I separated the coins into two piles. Those from 1958 and earlier went back into my pocket. Those from the future went into one of the envelopes I found in the desk drawer (along with a Gideon Bible and a Hi-Hat takeout menu). I got dressed, took my key, and left the room.

The crickets were much louder outside. A broken piece of moon hung in the sky. Away from its glow, the stars had never seemed so bright or close. A truck droned past on 196, and then the road was still. This was the countryside, and the countryside was sleeping. In the distance, a freight train whistled a hole in the night.

There were only two cars in the courtyard, and the units they belonged to were dark. So was the office. Feeling like a criminal, I walked into the field behind the motor court. High grass whickered against the legs of my jeans, which I would swap tomorrow for my new Ban-Lon slacks.

There was a smoothwire fence marking the edge of the Tamarack's property. Beyond it was a small pond, what rural people call a tank. Nearby, half a dozen cows were sleeping in the warm night. One of them looked up at me as I worked my way under the fence and walked to the tank. After that it lost interest and lowered its head again. It didn't raise it when my Nokia cell phone splashed into the pond. I sealed the envelope with my coins inside it and sent it after the phone. Then I went back the way I came, pausing at the rear of the motel to make sure the courtyard was still empty. It was.

I let myself into my room, undressed, and was asleep almost instantly.

CHAPTER 6

1

The same chain-smoking cabbie picked me up the next morning, and when he dropped me off at Titus Chevron, the convertible was there. I had expected this, but it was still a relief. I was wearing a nondescript gray sport coat I'd bought off the rack at Mason's Menswear. My new ostrich wallet was safe in its inner pocket, and lined with five hundred dollars of Al's cash. Titus came over to me while I was admiring the Ford, wiping his hands on what looked like the same rag he'd been using on them yesterday.

"I slept on it, and I want it," I said.

"That's good," he said, then assumed an air of regret. "But I slept on it, too, Mr. Amberson, and I guess I told you a lie when I said there might be some room for dickerin. Do you know what my wife said this morning while we were eatin our pancakes n bacon? She said 'Bill, you'd be a damn fool to let that Sunliner go for less'n three-fifty.' In fact, she said I was a damn fool for pricin it that low to start with."

I nodded as if I'd expected nothing else. "Okay," I said.

He looked surprised.

"Here's what I can do, Mr. Titus. I can write you a check for three hundred and fifty—good check, Hometown Trust, you can call them and see—or I can give you three hundred in cash right out of my wallet. Less paperwork if we do it like that. What do you say?"

He grinned, revealing teeth of startling whiteness. "I say they know how to drive a bargain out there in Wisconsin. If you make it three-twenty, I'll put on a sticker and a fourteen-day plate and off you go."

"Three-ten."

"Aw, don't make me squirm," Titus said, but he wasn't squirming; he was enjoying himself. "Add a fin onto that and we'll call it a deal."

I held out my hand. "Three hundred and fifteen works for me."

"Yowza." This time he shook with me, never minding the grease. Then he pointed to the sales booth. Today the ponytailed cutie was reading *Confidential*. "You'll want to pay the young lady, who happens to be my daughter. She'll write up the sale. When you're done, come around and I'll put on that sticker. Throw in a tank of gas, too."

Forty minutes later, behind the wheel of a 1954 Ford ragtop that now belonged to me, I was headed north toward Derry. I learned on a standard, so that was no problem, but this was the first car I'd ever driven with the gearshift on the column. It was weird at first, but once I got used to it (I would also have to get used to operating the headlight dimmer switch with my left foot), I liked it. And Bill Titus had been right about second gear; in second, the Sunliner went like a bastid. In Augusta, I stopped long enough to haul the top down. In Waterville, I grabbed a fine meatloaf dinner that cost ninety-five cents, apple pie à la mode included. It made the Fatburger look overpriced. I hummed along with the Skyliners, the Coasters, the Del Vikings, the Elegants. The sun was warm, the breeze ruffled my new short haircut, and the turnpike (nicknamed "The Mile-A-Minute Highway," according to the billboards) was pretty much all mine. I seemed to have left my doubts of the night before sunk in the cow-tank along with my cell phone and futuristic change. I felt good.

Until I saw Derry.

2

There was something wrong with that town, and I think I knew it from the first.

I took Route 7 when The Mile-A-Minute Highway petered down to an asphalt-patched two-lane, and twenty miles or so north of Newport, I came over a rise and saw Derry hulking on the west bank of the Kenduskeag under a cloud of pollution from God knew how many paper and textile mills, all operating full bore. There was an artery of green running through the center of town. From a distance it looked like a scar. The town around that jagged greenbelt seemed to consist solely of sooty grays and blacks under a sky that had been stained urine yellow by the stuff billowing from all those smokestacks.

I drove past several produce stands where the people minding the counters (or just standing side o' the road and gaping as I drove past) looked more like inbred hillbillies from *Deliverance* than Maine farmers. As I passed the last of them, BOWERS ROAD-SIDE PRODUCE, a large mongrel raced out from behind several heaped baskets of tomatoes and chased me, drooling and snapping at the Sunliner's rear tires. It looked like a misbegotten bulldog. Before I lost sight of it, I saw a scrawny woman in overalls approach it and begin beating it with a piece of board.

This was the town where Harry Dunning had grown up, and I hated it from the first. No concrete reason; I just did. The downtown shopping area, situated at the bottom of three steep hills, felt pitlike and claustrophobic. My cherry-red Ford seemed like the brightest thing on the street, a distracting (and unwelcome, judging by most of the glances it was attracting) splash of color amid the black Plymouths, brown Chevrolets, and grimy delivery trucks. Running through the center of town was a canal filled almost to the top of its moss-splotched concrete retaining walls with black water.

I found a parking space on Canal Street. A nickel in the meter bought me an hour's worth of shopping time. I'd forgotten to buy a hat in Lisbon Falls, and two or three storefronts up I saw an outfit called Derry Dress & Everyday, Central Maine's Most Debonair Haberdashery. I doubted there was much competition in that regard.

I had parked in front of the drugstore, and paused to examine the sign in the window. Somehow it sums up my feelings about Derry—the sour mistrust, the sense of barely withheld violence—better than anything else, although I was there for almost two months and (with the possible exception of a few people I happened to meet) disliked everything about it. The sign read:

SHOPLIFTING IS NOT A "KICK" OR A "GROOVE" OR A "GASSER"!
SHOPLIFTING IS A *CRIME*, AND WE WILL PROSECUTE!
NORBERT KEENE
OWNER & MANAGER

And the thin, bespectacled man in the white smock who was looking out at me just about had to be Mr. Keene. His expression did not say *Come on in, stranger, poke around and buy something, maybe have an ice cream soda.* Those hard eyes and that turned-down mouth said *Go away, there's nothing here for the likes of you.* Part of me thought I was making that up; most of me knew I wasn't. As an experiment, I raised my hand in a hello gesture.

The man in the white smock did not raise his in return.

I realized that the canal I'd seen must run directly beneath this peculiar sunken downtown, and I was standing on top of it. I could feel hidden water in my feet, thrumming the sidewalk. It was a vaguely unpleasant feeling, as if this little piece of the world had gone soft.

A male mannequin wearing a tuxedo stood in the window of Derry Dress & Everyday. There was a monocle in one eye and a school pennant in one plaster hand. The pennant read DERRY TIGERS WILL SLAUGHTER BANGOR RAMS! Even though I was a fan of school spirit, this struck me as a little over the top. Beat the Bangor Rams, sure—but slaughter them?

Just a figure of speech, I told myself, and went in.

A clerk with a tape measure around his neck approached me. His duds were much nicer than mine, but the dim overhead bulbs made his complexion look yellow. I felt an absurd urge to ask, *Can you sell me a nice summer straw hat, or should I just go fuck myself?* Then he smiled, asked how he could help me, and everything seemed almost normal. He had the required item, and I took possession of it for a mere three dollars and seventy cents.

"A shame you'll have such a short time to wear it before the weather turns cold," he said.

I put the hat on and adjusted it in the mirror beside the counter. "Maybe we'll get a good stretch of Indian summer."

Gently and rather apologetically, he tilted the hat the other way. It was a matter of two inches or less, but I stopped looking like a clodhopper on a visit to the big city and started to look like . . . well . . . central Maine's most debonair time-traveler. I thanked him.

"Not at all, Mr.—?"

"Amberson," I said, and held out my hand. His grip was short, limp, and powdery with some sort of talcum. I restrained an urge to rub my hand on my sport coat after he released it.

"In Derry on business?"

"Yes. Are you from here yourself?"

"Lifelong resident," he said, and sighed as if this were a burden. Based on my own first impressions, I guessed it might be. "What's your game, Mr. Amberson, if you don't mind me asking?"

"Real estate. But while I'm here, I thought I'd look up an old Army buddy. His name is Dunning. I don't recall his first name, we just used to call him Skip." The Skip part was a fabrication, but it was true that I didn't know the first name of Harry Dunning's father. Harry had named his brothers and sister in his theme, but the man with the hammer had always been "my father" or "my dad."

"I'm afraid I couldn't help you there, sir." Now he sounded distant. Business was done, and although the store was empty of other customers, he wanted me gone.

"Well, maybe you can with something else. What's the best hotel in town?"

"That would be the Derry Town House. Just turn back to Kenduskeag Avenue, take your right, and go up Up-Mile Hill to Main Street. Look for the carriage lamps out front."

"Up-Mile Hill?"

"That's what we call it, yes sir. If there's nothing else, I have several alterations to make out back."

When I left, the light had begun to drain from the sky. One thing I remember vividly about the time I spent in Derry during September and October of 1958 was how evening always seemed to come early.

One storefront down from Derry Dress & Everyday was Machen's Sporting Goods, where THE FALL GUN SALE was under way. Inside, I saw two men sighting hunting rifles while an elderly clerk with a string tie (and a stringy neck to go with it) looked on approvingly. The other side of Canal appeared to be lined with workingmen's bars, the kind where you could get a beer and a shot for fifty cents and all the music on the Rock-Ola would be C & W. There was the Happy Nook, the Wishing Well (which the habitués called the Bucket of Blood, I later learned), Two Brothers, the Golden Spoke, and the Sleepy Silver Dollar.

Standing outside the latter, a quartet of bluecollar gents was taking the afternoon air and staring at my convertible. They were equipped with mugs of beer and cigarettes. Their faces were shaded beneath flat caps of tweed and cotton. Their feet were clad in the big no-color workboots my 2011 students called shitkickers. Three of the four were wearing suspenders. They watched me with no expression on their faces. I thought for a moment of the mongrel that had chased my car, snapping and drooling, then crossed the street.

"Gents," I said. "What's on tap in there?"

For a moment none of them answered. Just when I thought

none of them would, the one sans suspenders said, "Bud and Mick, what else? You from away?"

"Wisconsin," I said.

"Bully for you," one of them muttered.

"Late in the year for tourists," another said.

"I'm in town on business, but I thought I might look up an old service buddy while I'm here." No response to this, unless one of the men dropping his cigarette butt onto the sidewalk and then putting it out with a snot-loogie the size of a small mussel could be termed an answer. Nevertheless, I pushed on. "Skip Dunning's his name. Do any of you fellows know a Dunning?"

"Should hope to smile n kiss a pig," No Suspenders said.

"I beg pardon?"

He rolled his eyes and turned down the corners of his mouth, the out-of-patience expression a man gives to a stupid person with no hope of ever being smart. "Derry's full of Dunnings. Check the damn phone book." He started inside. His posse followed. No Suspenders opened the door for them, then turned back to me. "What's that Ford got in it?" *Gut* for *got*. "V-8?"

"Y-block." Hoping I sounded as if I knew what it meant.

"Pretty good goer?"

"Not bad."

"Then maybe you should climb in and go 'er right on up the hill. They got some nice joints there. These bars are for millies." No Suspenders assessed me in a cold way I came to expect in Derry, but never got used to. "You'd get stared at. P'raps more, when the 'leven-to-seven lets out from Striar's and Boutillier's."

"Thanks. That's very kind of you."

The cold assessment continued. "You don't know much, do you?" he remarked, then went inside.

I walked back to my convertible. On that gray street, with the smell of industrial smokes in the air and the afternoon bleeding away to evening, downtown Derry looked only marginally more charming than a dead hooker in a church pew. I got in, engaged the clutch, started the engine, and felt a strong urge to just drive away. Drive back to Lisbon Falls, climb up through the rabbit-hole, and tell Al Templeton to find another boy. Only he couldn't, could he? He was out of strength and almost out of time. I was, as the New England saying goes, the trapper's last shot.

I drove up to Main Street, saw the carriage lamps (they came on for the night just as I spotted them), and pulled into the turn-around in front of the Derry Town House. Five minutes later, I was checked in. My time in Derry had begun.

3

By the time I got my new possessions unpacked (some of the remaining cash went into my wallet, the rest into the lining of my new valise) I was good and hungry, but before going down to dinner, I checked the telephone book. What I saw caused my heart to sink. Mr. No Suspenders might not have been very welcoming, but he was right about Dunnings selling cheap in Derry and the four or five surrounding hamlets that were also included in the directory. There was almost a full page of them. It wasn't that surprising, because in small towns certain names seem to sprout like dandelions on a lawn in June. In my last five years teaching English at LHS, I must have had two dozen Starbirds and Lemkes, some of them siblings, most of them first, second, or third cousins. They intermarried and made more.

Before leaving for the past I should have taken time to call Harry Dunning and ask him his father's first name—it would have been so simple. I surely would have, if I hadn't been so utterly and completely gobsmacked by what Al had shown me, and what he was asking me to do. *But,* I thought, *how hard can it be?* It shouldn't take Sherlock Holmes to find a family with kids named Troy, Arthur (alias Tugga), Ellen, and Harry.

With this thought to cheer me, I went down to the hotel res-taurant and ordered a shore dinner, which came with clams and a lobster roughly the size of an outboard motor. I skipped dessert in favor of a beer in the bar. In the detective novels I read, bartenders were often excellent sources of information. Of course, if the one working the Town House stick was like the other people I'd met so far in this grim little burg, I wouldn't get far.

He wasn't. The man who left off his glass-polishing duties to serve me was young and stocky, with a cheery full moon of a face below his flattop haircut. "What can I get you, friend?"

The f-word sounded good to me, and I returned his smile with enthusiasm. "Miller Lite?"

He looked puzzled. "Never heard of that one, but I've got High Life."

Of course he hadn't heard of Miller Lite; it hadn't been invented yet. "That would be fine. Guess I forgot I was on the East Coast there for a second."

"Where you from?" He used a church key to whisk the top off a bottle, and set a frosted glass in front of me.

"Wisconsin, but I'll be here for awhile." Although we were alone, I lowered my voice. It seemed to inspire confidence. "Real estate stuff. Got to look around a little."

He nodded respectfully and poured for me before I could. "Good luck to you. God knows there's plenty for sale in these parts, and most of it going cheap. I'm getting out, myself. End of the month. Heading for a place with a little less edge to it."

"It *doesn't* seem all that welcoming," I said, "but I thought that was just a Yankee thing. We're friendlier in Wisconsin, and just to prove it, I'll buy you a beer."

"Never drink alcohol on the job, but I might have a Coke."

"Go for it."

"Thanks very much. It's nice to have a gent on a slow night." I watched as he made the Coke by pumping syrup into a glass, adding soda water, and then stirring. He took a sip and smacked his lips. "I like em sweet."

Judging by the belly he was getting, I wasn't surprised.

"That stuff about Yankees being stand-offy is bullshit, anyway," he said. "I grew up in Fork Kent, and it's the friendliest little town you'd ever want to visit. Why, when tourists get off the Boston and Maine up there, we just about kiss em hello. Went to bartending school there, then headed south to seek my fortune. This looked like a good place to start, and the pay's not bad, but—" He looked around, saw no one, but still lowered his own voice. "You want the truth, Jackson? This town stinks."

"I know what you mean. All those mills."

"It's a lot more than that. Look around. What do you see?"

I did as he asked. There was a fellow who looked like a salesman in the corner, drinking a whiskey sour, but that was it.

"Not much," I said.

"That's the way it is all through the week. The pay's good because there's no tips. The beerjoints downtown do a booming business, and we get some folks in on Friday and Saturday nights, but otherwise, that's just about it. The carriage trade does its drinking at home, I guess." He lowered his voice further. Soon he'd be whispering. "We had a bad summer here, my friend. Local folks keep it as quiet as they can—even the newspaper doesn't play it up—but there was some nasty work. Murders. Half a dozen at least. Kids. Found one down in the Barrens just recently. Patrick Hockstetter, his name was. All decayed."

"The Barrens?"

"It's this swampy patch that runs right through the center of town. You probably saw it when you flew in."

I'd been in a car, but I still knew what he was talking about.

The bartender's eyes widened. "That's not the real estate you're interested in, is it?"

"Can't say," I told him. "If word got around, I'd be looking for a new job."

"Understood, understood." He drank half his Coke, then stifled a belch with the back of his hand. "But I hope it is. They ought to pave that goddam thing over. It's nothing but stinkwater and mosquitoes. You'd be doing this town a favor. Sweeten it up a little bit."

"Other kids found down there?" I asked. A serial child-murderer would explain a lot about the gloom I'd been feeling ever since I crossed the town line.

"Not that I know of, but people say that's where some of the disappeared ones went, because that's where all the big sewage pumping stations are. I've heard people say there are so many sewer pipes under Derry—most of em laid in the Great Depression—that nobody knows where all of em are. And you know how kids are."

"Adventurous."

He nodded emphatically. "Right with Eversharp. There's people who say it was some vag who's since moved on. Other folks say he was a local who dressed up like a clown to keep from being recognized. The first of the victims—this was last year, before I came—they found him at the intersection of Witcham and Jackson with his arm ripped clean off. Denbrough was his name, George Denbrough. Poor little tyke." He gave me a meaningful look. "And he was found right next to one of those sewer drains. The ones that dump into the Barrens."

"Christ."

"Yeah."

"I hear you using the past tense about all this stuff."

I got ready to explain what I meant, but apparently this guy had been listening in English class as well as bartending school. "It seems to've stopped, knock on wood." He rapped his knuckles on the bar. "Maybe whoever was doing it packed up and moved on. Or maybe the sonofabitch killed himself, sometimes they do that. That'd be good. But it wasn't any homicidal maniac in a clown suit who killed the little Corcoran boy. The clown who did *that* murder was the kid's own father, if you can believe it."

That was close enough to why I was here to feel like fate rather than coincidence. I took a careful sip of my beer. "Is that so?"

"You bet it is. Dorsey Corcoran, that was the kid's name. Only four years old, and you know what his goddam father did? Beat him to death with a recoilless hammer."

A hammer. He did it with a hammer. I maintained my look of polite interest—at least I hope I did—but I felt gooseflesh go marching up my arms. "That's awful."

"Yeah, and not the wor—" He broke off and looked over my shoulder. "Get you another, sir?"

It was the businessman. "Not me," he said, and handed over a dollar bill. "I'm going to bed, and tomorrow I'm blowing this pop-shop. I hope they remember how to order hardware in Waterville and Augusta, because they sure don't here. Keep the change, son, buy yourself a DeSoto." He plodded out with his head down.

"See? That's a perfect example of what we get at this oasis." The bartender looked sadly after his departing customer. "One drink, off to bed, and tomorrow it's seeya later, alligator, after awhile, crocodile. If it keeps up, this burg's gonna be a ghost town." He stood up straight and tried to square his shoulders—an impossible task, because they were as round as the rest of him. "But who gives a rip? Come October first, I'm gone. Down the road. Happy trails to you, until we meet again."

"The father of this boy, Dorsey . . . he didn't kill any of the others?"

"Naw, he was alibi'd up. I guess he was the kid's stepfather, now that I think about it. Dicky Macklin. Johnny Keeson at the desk—he probably checked you in—told me he used to come in here and drink sometimes, until he got banned for trying to pick up a stewardess and getting nasty when she told him to go peddle his papers. After that I guess he did his drinking at the Spoke or the Bucket. They'll have anybody in those places."

He leaned over close enough for me to smell the Aqua Velva on his cheeks.

"You want to know the worst?"

I didn't, but thought I ought to. So I nodded.

"There was also an *older* brother in that fucked-up family. Eddie. He disappeared last June. Just poof. Gone, no forwarding, if you dig what I'm saying. Some people think he ran off to get away from Macklin, but anybody with any sense knows he would have turned up in Portland or Castle Rock or Portsmouth if that was the case—no way a ten-year-old can stay out of sight for long. Take it from me, Eddie Corcoran got the hammer just like his little brother. Macklin just won't own up to it." He grinned, a sudden and sunny grin that made his moon face almost handsome. "Have I talked you out of buying real estate in Derry yet, mister?"

"That's not up to me," I said. I was flying on autopilot by then. Hadn't I heard or read about a series of child-murders in this part of Maine? Or maybe watched it on TV, with only a quarter of my brain turned on while the rest of it was waiting for the sound of my problematic wife walking—or staggering—up to the house after another "girls' night out"? I thought so, but the only thing I remembered for sure about Derry was that there was going to be a flood in the mid-eighties that would destroy half the town.

"It's not?"

"No, I'm just the middleman."

"Well, good luck to you. This town isn't as bad as it was— last July, folks were strung as tight as Doris Day's chastity belt— but it's still a long way from right. I'm a friendly guy, and I like friendly people. I'm splitting."

"Good luck to you, too," I said, and dropped two dollars on the bar.

"Gee, sir, that's way too much!"

"I always pay a surcharge for good conversation." Actually, the surcharge was for a friendly face. The conversation had been disquieting.

"Well, thanks!" He beamed, then stuck out his hand. "I never introduced myself. Fred Toomey."

"Nice to meet you, Fred. I'm George Amberson." He had a good grip. No talcum powder.

"Want a piece of advice?"

"Sure."

"While you're in town, be careful about talking to kids. After last summer, a strange man talking to kids is apt to get a visit from the police if people see him doing it. Or he could take a beating. That sure wouldn't be out of the question."

"Even without the clown suit, huh?"

131

"Well, that's the thing about dressing up in an outfit, isn't it?" His smile was gone. Now he looked pale and grim. Like everyone else in Derry, in other words. "When you put on a clown suit and a rubber nose, nobody has any idea what you look like inside."

4

I thought about that while the old-fashioned elevator creaked its way up to the third floor. It was true. And if the rest of what Fred Toomey had said was also true, would anybody be surprised if another father went to work on his family with a hammer? I thought not. I thought people would say it was just another case of Derry being Derry. And they might be right.

As I let myself into my room, I had an authentically horrible idea: suppose I changed things just enough in the next seven weeks so that Harry's father killed Harry, too, instead of just leaving him with a limp and a partially fogged-over brain?

That won't happen, I told myself. *I won't let it happen. Like Hillary Clinton said in 2008, I'm in it to win it.*

Except, of course, she had lost.

5

I ate breakfast the following morning in the hotel's Riverview Restaurant, which was deserted except for me and the hardware salesman from last night. He was buried in the local newspaper. When he left it on the table, I snagged it. I wasn't interested in the front page, which was devoted to more saber-rattling in the Philippines (although I did wonder briefly if Lee Oswald was in the vicinity). What I wanted was the local section. In 2011, I'd been a reader of the Lewiston *Sun Journal,* and the last page of the B section was always headed "School Doin's." In it, proud parents could see their kids' names in print if they had won an award, gone on a class trip, or been part of a community cleanup project. If the Derry *Daily News* had such a feature, it wasn't impossible that I'd find one of the Dunning kids listed.

The last page of the *News,* however, contained only obituaries.

I tried the sports pages, and read about the weekend's big upcoming football game: Derry Tigers versus Bangor Rams. Troy Dunning was fifteen, according to the janitor's essay. A fifteen-year-old could easily be a part of the team, although probably not a starter.

I didn't find his name, and although I read every word of a smaller story about the town's Peewee Football team (the Tiger Cubs), I didn't find Arthur "Tugga" Dunning, either.

I paid for my breakfast and went back up to my room with the borrowed newspaper under my arm, thinking that I made a lousy detective. After counting the Dunnings in the phone book (ninety-six), something else occurred to me: I had been hobbled, perhaps even crippled, by a pervasive internet society I had come to depend on and take for granted. How hard would it have been to locate the right Dunning family in 2011? Just plugging *Tugga Dunning* and *Derry* into my favorite search engine probably would have done the trick; hit enter and let Google, that twenty-first-century Big Brother, take care of the rest.

In the Derry of 1958, the most up-to-date computers were the size of small housing developments, and the local paper was no help. What did that leave? I remembered a sociology prof I'd had in college—a sarcastic old bastard—who used to say, *When all else fails, give up and go to the library.*

I went there.

6

Late that afternoon, hopes dashed (at least for the time being), I walked slowly up Up-Mile Hill, pausing briefly at the intersection of Jackson and Witcham to look at the sewer drain where a little boy named George Denbrough had lost his arm and his life (at least according to Fred Toomey). By the time I got to the top of the hill, my heart was pounding and I was puffing. It wasn't being out of shape; it was the stench of the mills.

I was dispirited and a bit scared. It was true that I still had plenty of time to locate the right Dunning family, and I was confident I would—if calling all the Dunnings in the phone book was what it took, that was what I'd do, even at the risk of alerting Harry's time bomb of a father—but I was starting to sense what Al had sensed: something working against me.

I walked along Kansas Street, so deep in thought that at first I didn't realize there were no more houses on my right. The ground now dropped away steeply into that tangled green riot of swampy ground that Toomey had called the Barrens. Only a rickety white fence separated the sidewalk from the drop. I planted my hands on it, staring into the undisciplined growth below. I could see gleams of murky standing water, patches of reeds so tall they looked prehistoric, and snarls of billowing brambles. The trees would be stunted down there, fighting for sunlight. There would be poison ivy, litters of garbage, and quite likely the occasional hobo camp. There would also be paths only some of the local kids would know. The adventurous ones.

I stood and looked without seeing, aware but hardly registering the faint lilt of music—something with horns in it. I was thinking about how little I had accomplished this morning. *You* can *change the past,* Al had told me, *but it's not as easy as you might think.*

What *was* that music? Something cheery, with a little jump to it. It made me think of Christy, back in the early days, when I was besotted with her. When we were besotted with each other. *Bah-dah-dah . . . bah-dah-da-dee-dum . . .* Glenn Miller, maybe?

I had gone to the library hoping to get a look at the census records. The last national one would have taken place eight years ago, in 1950, and would have shown three of the four Dunning kids: Troy, Arthur, and Harold. Only Ellen, who would be seven at the time of the murders, hadn't been around to be counted in

1950. There would be an address. It was true the family might have moved in the intervening eight years, but if so, one of the neighbors would be able to tell me where they'd gone. It was a small city.

Only the census records weren't there. The librarian, a pleasant woman named Mrs. Starrett, told me that in her opinion those records certainly *belonged* in the library, but the town council had for some reason decided they belonged in City Hall. They'd been moved there in 1954, she said.

"That doesn't sound good," I told her, smiling. "You know what they say—you can't fight City Hall."

Mrs. Starrett didn't return the smile. She was helpful, even charming, but she had the same watchful reserve as everyone else I'd met in this queer place—Fred Toomey being the exception that proved the rule. "Don't be silly, Mr. Amberson. There's nothing private about the United States Census. You march right over there and tell the city clerk that Regina Starrett sent you. Her name is Marcia Guay. She'll help you out. Although they probably stored them in the basement, which is *not* where they ought to be. It's damp, and I shouldn't be surprised if there are mice. If you have any trouble—any trouble at all—you come back and see me."

So I went to City Hall, where a poster in the foyer said PARENTS, REMIND YOUR CHILDREN NOT TO TALK TO STRANGERS AND TO ALWAYS PLAY WITH FRIENDS. Several people were lined up at the various windows. (Most of them smoking. Of course.) Marcia Guay greeted me with an embarrassed smile. Mrs. Starrett had called ahead on my behalf, and had been suitably horrified when Miss Guay told her what she now told me: the 1950 census records were gone, along with almost all of the other documents that had been stored in the City Hall basement.

"We had terrible rains last year," she said. "They went on for a whole week. The canal overflowed, and everything down in the Low Town—that's what the oldtimers call the city center, Mr. Amberson—everything in the Low Town flooded. Our basement looked like the Grand Canal in Venice for almost a month. Mrs. Starrett was right, those records never should have been moved, and no one seems to know why they were or who authorized it. I'm awfully sorry."

It was impossible not to feel what Al had felt while trying to save Carolyn Poulin: that I was inside a kind of prison with flexible walls. Was I supposed to hang around the local schools, hoping to spot a boy who looked like the sixty-years-plus janitor who had just retired? Look for a seven-year-old girl who kept her classmates in stitches? Wait to hear some kid yell, *Hey Tugga, wait up?*

Right. A newcomer hanging around the schools in a town where the first thing you saw at City Hall was a poster warning parents about stranger-danger. If there was such a thing as flying directly *into* the radar, that would be it.

One thing was for sure—I had to get out of the Derry Town House. At 1958 prices I could well afford to stay there for weeks, but that might cause talk. I decided to look through the classified ads and find myself a room I could rent by the month. I turned back toward the Low Town, then stopped.

Bah-dah-dah . . . bah-dah-da-dee-dum . . .

That *was* Glenn Miller. It was "In the Mood," a tune I had reason to know well. Curious, I walked toward the sound of the music.

7

There was a little picnic area at the end of the rickety fence between the Kansas Street sidewalk and the drop into the Barrens. It contained a stone barbecue and two picnic tables with a rusty trash barrel standing between them. A portable phonograph was parked on one of the picnic tables. A big black 78-rpm record spun on the turntable.

On the grass, a gangly boy in tape-mended glasses and an absolutely gorgeous redheaded girl were dancing. At LHS we called the incoming freshmen "tweenagers," and that's what these kids were, if that. But they were dancing with grown-up grace. Not jitterbugging, either; they were swing-dancing. I was charmed, but I was also . . . what? Scared? A little bit, maybe. I was scared for almost all the time I spent in Derry. But it was something else, too, something bigger. A kind of awe, as if I had gripped the rim of some vast understanding. Or peered (through a glass darkly, you understand) into the actual clockwork of the universe.

Because, you see, I had met Christy at a swing-dancing class in Lewiston, and this was one of the tunes we had learned to. Later—in our best year, six months before the marriage and six months after—we had danced in competitions, once taking fourth prize (also known as "first also-ran," according to Christy) in the New England Swing-Dancing Competition. Our tune was a slightly slowed-down dance-mix version of KC and the Sunshine Band's "Boogie Shoes."

This isn't a coincidence, I thought, watching them. The boy was wearing blue jeans and a crew-neck shirt; she had on a white blouse with the tails hanging down over faded red clamdiggers. That amazing hair was pulled back in the same impudently cute ponytail Christy had always worn when we danced competitively. Along with her bobby sox and vintage poodle skirt, of course.

This cannot be a coincidence.

They were doing a Lindy variation I knew as the Hellzapoppin. It's supposed to be a fast dance—lightning-fast, if you have the physical stamina and grace to bring it off—but they were dancing it slow because they were still learning their steps. I could see inside every move. I knew them all, although I hadn't actually danced any of them in five years or more. Come together, both hands clasped. He stoops a little and kicks with his left foot while she does the same, both of them twisting at the waist so that they appear to be going in opposite directions. Move apart, hands still clasped, then she twirls, first to the left and then to the right—

But they goofed up the return spin and she went sprawling on the grass. "Jesus, Richie, you never get that right! *Gah,* you're

137

hopeless!" She was laughing, though. She flopped on her back and stared up at the sky.

"I'se sorry, Miss Scawlett!" the boy cried in a screechy pickaninny voice that would have gone over like a lead balloon in the politically correct twenty-first century. "I'se just a clodhoppin country boy, but I intends to learn dis-yere dance if it kills me!"

"I'm the one it's likely to kill," she said. "Start the record again before I lose my—" Then they both saw me.

It was a strange moment. There was a veil in Derry—I came to know that veil so well I could almost see it. The locals were on one side; people from away (like Fred Toomey, like me) were on the other. Sometimes the locals came out from behind it, as Mrs. Starrett the librarian had when expressing her irritation about the misplaced census records, but if you asked too many questions— and certainly if you startled them—they retreated behind it again.

Yet I had startled these kids, and they didn't retreat behind the veil. Instead of closing up, their faces remained wide open, full of curiosity and interest.

"Sorry, sorry," I said. "Didn't mean to surprise you. I heard the music and then I saw you lindy-hopping."

"*Trying* to lindy-hop, is what you mean," the boy said. He helped the girl to her feet. He made a bow. "Richie Tozier, at your service. My friends all say 'Richie-Richie, he live in a ditchie,' but what do they know?"

"Nice to meet you," I said. "George Amberson." And then—it just popped out—"*My* friends all say 'Georgie-Georgie, he wash his clothes in a Norgie,' but they don't know anything, either."

The girl collapsed on one of the picnic table benches, giggling. The boy raised his hands in the air and bugled: "Strange grown-up gets off a good one! Wacka-wacka-wacka! *Dee*-lightful! Ed McMahon, what have we got for this wonderful fella? Well, Johnny, today's prizes on *Who Do You Trust* are a complete set of *Encyclopaedia Britannica* and an Electrolux vacuum cleaner to suck em up wi—"

"Beep-beep, Richie," the girl said. She was wiping the corners of her eyes.

This caused an unfortunate reversion to the screeching pickaninny voice. "I'se sorry, Miss Scawlett, don't be whuppin on me! I'se still got scabs from de las' time!"

"Who are you, Miss?" I asked.

"Bevvie-Bevvie, I live on the levee," she said, and started giggling again. "Sorry—Richie's a fool, but I have no excuse. Beverly Marsh. You're not from around here, are you?"

A thing everybody seemed to know immediately. "Nope, and you two don't seem like you are, either. You're the first two Derryites I've met who don't seem . . . grumpy."

"Yowza, it's a grumpy-ass town," Richie said, and took the tone arm off the record. It had been bumping on the final groove over and over.

"I understand folks're particularly worried about the children," I said. "Notice I'm keeping my distance. You guys on grass, me on sidewalk."

"They weren't all that worried when the murders were going on," Richie grumbled. "You know about the murders?"

I nodded. "I'm staying at the Town House. Someone who works there told me."

"Yeah, now that they're over, people are all concerned about the kids." He sat down next to Bevvie who lived on the levee. "But when they were going on, you didn't hear jack spit."

"Richie," she said. "Beep-beep."

This time the boy tried on a really atrocious Humphrey Bogart imitation. "Well it's true, schweetheart. And you know it's true."

"All that's over," Bevvie told me. She was as earnest as a Chamber of Commerce booster. "They just don't know it yet."

"*They* meaning the townspeople or just grown-ups in general?"

She shrugged as if to say *what's the difference.*

"But you do know."

"As a matter of fact, we do," Richie said. He looked at me challengingly, but behind his mended glasses, that glint of maniacal humor was still in his eyes. I had an idea it never completely left them.

I stepped onto the grass. Neither child fled, screaming. In fact, Beverly shoved over on the bench (elbowing Richie so he would do the same) and made room for me. They were either very brave or very stupid, and they didn't look stupid.

Then the girl said something that flabbergasted me. "Do I know you? Do *we* know you?"

Before I could answer, Richie spoke up. "No, it's not that. It's . . . I dunno. Do you want something, Mr. Amberson? Is that it?"

"Actually, I do. Some information. But how did you know that? And how do you know I'm not dangerous?"

They looked at each other, and something passed between them. It was impossible to know just what, yet I felt sure of two things: they had sensed an otherness about me that went way beyond just being a stranger in town . . . but, unlike the Yellow Card Man, they weren't afraid of it. Quite the opposite; they were fascinated by it. I thought those two attractive, fearless kids could have told some stories if they wanted to. I've always remained curious about what those stories might have been.

"You're just not," Richie said, and when he looked to the girl, she nodded agreement.

"And you're sure that the . . . the bad times . . . are over?"

"Mostly," Beverly said. "Things'll get better. In Derry I think the bad times are over, Mr. Amberson—it's a hard place in a lot of ways."

"Suppose I told you—just hypothetically—that there was one more bad thing on the horizon? Something like what happened to a little boy named Dorsey Corcoran."

They winced as if I had pinched a place where the nerves lay close to the surface. Beverly turned to Richie and whispered in his ear. I'm not positive about what she said, it was quick and low, but it might have been *That wasn't the clown.* Then she looked back at me.

"What bad thing? Like when Dorsey's father—"

"Never mind. You don't have to know." It was time to jump. These were the ones. I didn't know how I knew it, but I did. "Do you know some kids named Dunning?" I ticked them off on my fingers. "Troy, Arthur, Harry, and Ellen. Only Arthur's also called—"

"Tugga," Beverly said matter-of-factly. "Sure we know him, he goes to our school. We're practicing the Lindy for the school talent show, it's just before Thanksgiving—"

"Miss Scawlett, she b'leeve in gittin an *early* start on de practicin," Richie said.

Beverly Marsh took no notice. "Tugga's signed up for the show, too. He's going to lip-synch to 'Splish Splash.'" She rolled her eyes. She was good at that.

"Where does he live? Do you know?"

They knew, all right, but neither of them said. And if I didn't give them a little more, they wouldn't. I could see that in their faces.

"Suppose I told you there's a good chance Tugga's never going to be in the talent show unless somebody watches out for him? His brothers and his sister, too? Would you believe a thing like that?"

The kids looked at each other again, conversing with their eyes. It went on a long time—ten seconds, maybe. It was the sort of long gaze that lovers indulge in, but these tweenagers couldn't be lovers. Friends, though, for sure. Close friends who'd been through something together.

"Tugga and his family live on Cossut Street," Richie said finally. That's what it sounded like, anyway.

"Cossut?"

"That's how people around here say it," Beverly told me. "K-O-S-S-U-T-H. Cossut."

"Got it." Now the only question was how much these kids were going to blab about our weird conversation on the edge of the Barrens.

Beverly was looking at me with earnest, troubled eyes. "But Mr. Amberson, I've met Tugga's dad. He works at the Center Street Market. He's a *nice* man. Always smiling. He—"

"The nice man doesn't live at home anymore," Richie interrupted. "His wife kicked im out."

She turned to him, eyes wide. "Tug told you that?"

"Nope. Ben Hanscom. Tug told *him.*"

"He's still a nice man," Beverly said in a small voice. "Always joking around and stuff but never touchy-grabby."

"Clowns joke around a lot, too," I said. They both jumped, as if I had pinched that vulnerable bundle of nerves again. "That doesn't make them nice."

"We know," Beverly whispered. She was looking at her hands. Then she raised her eyes to me. "Do you know about the Turtle?" She said *turtle* in a way that made it sound like a proper noun.

I thought of saying *I know about the Teenage Mutant Ninja Turtles,* and didn't. It was decades too early for Leonardo, Donatello, Raphael, and Michelangelo. So I just shook my head.

She looked doubtfully at Richie. He looked at me, then back at her. "But he's good. I'm pretty sure he's good." She touched my wrist. Her fingers were cold. "Mr. Dunning's a *nice* man. And just because he doesn't live at home anymore doesn't mean he isn't."

That hit home. My wife had left me, but not because I wasn't nice. "I know that." I stood up. "I'm going to be around Derry for a little while, and it would be good not to attract too much attention. Can you two keep quiet about this? I know it's a lot to ask, but—"

They looked at each other and burst into laughter.

When she could speak, Beverly said: "We can keep a secret."

I nodded. "I'm sure you can. Kept a few this summer, I bet."

They didn't reply to this.

I cocked a thumb at the Barrens. "Ever play down there?"

"Once," Richie said. "Not anymore." He stood up and brushed off the seat of his blue jeans. "It's been nice talking to you, Mr. Amberson. Don't take any wooden Indians." He hesitated. "And be careful in Derry. It's better now, but I don't think it's ever gonna be, you know, completely right."

"Thanks. Thank you both. Maybe someday the Dunning family will have something to thank you for, too, but if things go the way I hope they will—"

"—they'll never know a thing," Beverly finished for me.

"Exactly." Then, remembering something Fred Toomey had said: "Right with Eversharp. You two take care of yourselves."

"We will," Beverly said, then began to giggle again. "Keep washing those clothes in your Norgie, Georgie."

I skimmed a salute off the brim of my new summer straw and started to walk away. Then I had an idea and turned back to them. "Does that phonograph play at thirty-three and a third?"

"Like for LPs?" Richie asked. "Naw. Our hi-fi at home does, but Bevvie's is just a baby one that runs on batteries."

"Watch what you call my record player, Tozier," Beverly said. "I saved up for it." Then, to me: "It just plays seventy-eights and forty-fives. Only I lost the plastic thingie for the hole in the forty-fives, so now it only plays seventy-eights."

"Forty-five rpm should do," I said. "Start the record again, but play it at that speed." Slowing down the tempo while getting the hang of swing-dance steps was something Christy and I had learned in our classes.

"Crazy, daddy," Richie said. He switched the speed-control lever beside the turntable and started the record again. This time it sounded like everyone in Glenn Miller's band had swallowed Quaaludes.

"Okay." I held out my hands to Beverly. "You watch, Richie."

She took my hands with complete trust, looking up at me with wide blue amused eyes. I wondered where she was and who she was in 2011. If she was even alive. Supposing she was, would she remember that a strange man who asked strange questions had once danced with her to a draggy version of "In the Mood" on a sunny September afternoon?

I said, "You guys were doing it slow before, and this will slow you down even more, but you can still keep the beat. Plenty of time for each step."

Time. Plenty of time. Start the record again but slow it down.

I pulled her toward me by our clasped hands. Let her go back. We both bent like people under water, and kicked to the left while the Glenn Miller Orchestra played *bahhhh . . . dahhh . . . dahhhh*

143

. . . bahhhh . . . dahhhh . . . daaaa . . . deee . . . dummmmmm. At that same slow speed, like a windup toy that's almost unwound, she twirled to the left under my upraised hands.

"Stop!" I said, and she froze with her back to me and our hands still linked. "Now squeeze my right hand to remind me what comes next."

She squeezed, then rotated smoothly back and all the way around to the right.

"Cool!" she said. "Now I'm supposed to go under, then you bring me back. And I flip over. That's why we're doing it on the grass, so if I mess it up I don't break my neck."

"I'll leave that part up to you," I said. "I'm too ancient to be flipping anything but hamburgers."

Richie once more raised his hands to the sides of his face. "Wacka-wacka-wacka! Strange grown-up gets off *another*—"

"Beep-beep, Richie," I said. That made him laugh. "Now you try it. And work out hand signals for any other moves that go beyond the jitterbug two-step they do in the local soda shop. That way even if you don't win the talent show contest, you'll look good."

Richie took Beverly's hands and tried it. In and out, side to side, around to the left, around to the right. Perfect. She slipped feet-first between Richie's spread legs, supple as a fish, and then he brought her back. She finished with a showy flip that brought her to her feet again. Richie took her hands and they repeated the whole thing. It was even better the second time.

"We lose the beat on the under-and-out," Richie complained.

"You won't when the record's playing at normal speed. Trust me."

"I like it," Beverly said. "It's like having the whole thing under glass." She did a little spin on the toes of her sneakers. "I feel like Loretta Young at the start of her show, when she comes in wearing a swirly dress."

"They call me Arthur Murray, I'm from Miz-OOO-ri," Richie said. He also looked pleased.

"I'm going to speed the record up," I said. "Remember your signals. And keep time. It's all about time."

Glenn Miller played that old sweet song, and the kids danced. On the grass, their shadows danced beside them. Out . . . in . . . dip . . . kick . . . spin left . . . spin right . . . go under . . . pop out . . . and *flip*. They weren't perfect this time, and they'd screw up the steps many times before they nailed them (if they ever did), but they weren't bad.

Oh, to hell with that. They were beautiful. For the first time since I'd topped that rise on Route 7 and saw Derry hulking on the west bank of the Kenduskeag, I was happy. That was a good feeling to go on, so I walked away from them, giving myself the old advice as I went: don't look back, never look back. How often do people tell themselves that after an experience that is exceptionally good (or exceptionally bad)? Often, I suppose. And the advice usually goes unheeded. Humans were built to look back; that's why we have that swivel joint in our necks.

I went half a block, then turned around, thinking they would be staring at me. But they weren't. They were still dancing. And that was good.

8

There was a Cities Service station a couple of blocks down on Kansas Street, and I went into the office to ask directions to Kossuth Street, pronounced Cossut. I could hear the whir of an air compressor and the tinny jangle of pop music from the garage bay, but the office was empty. That was fine with me, because I saw something useful next to the cash register: a wire stand filled with maps. The top pocket held a single city map that looked dirty and forgotten. On the front was a photo of an exceptionally ugly Paul Bunyan statue cast in plastic. Paul had his axe over his shoulder and was grinning up into the summer sun. *Only Derry*, I thought, *would take a plastic statue of a mythical logger as its icon.*

There was a newspaper dispenser just beyond the gas pumps. I took a copy of the *Daily News* as a prop, and flipped a nickel on top of the pile of papers to join the other coins scattered there. I don't know if they're more honest in 1958, but they're a hell of a lot more trusting.

According to the map, Kossuth Street was on the Kansas Street side of town, and turned out to be just a pleasant fifteen-minute stroll from the gas station. I walked under elm trees that had yet to be touched by the blight that would take almost all of them by the seventies, trees that were still as green as they had been in July. Kids tore past me on bikes or played jacks in driveways. Little clusters of adults gathered at corner bus stops, marked by white stripes on telephone poles. Derry went about its business and I went about mine—just a fellow in a nondescript sport coat with his summer straw pushed back a little on his head, a fellow with a folded newspaper in one hand. He might be looking for a yard or garage sale; he might be checking for plummy real estate. Certainly he looked like he belonged here.

So I hoped.

Kossuth was a hedge-lined street of old-fashioned New England saltbox houses. Sprinklers twirled on lawns. Two boys ran past me, tossing a football back and forth. A woman with her hair bound up in a kerchief (and the inevitable cigarette dangling from her lower lip) was washing the family car and occasionally spraying the family dog, who backed away, barking. Kossuth Street looked like an exterior scene from some old fuzzy sitcom.

Two little girls were twirling a skip-rope while a third danced nimbly in and out, stutter-stepping effortlessly as she chanted: "Charlie Chaplin went to *France*! Just to watch the ladies *dance*! Salute to the *Cap'un*! Salute to the *Queen*! My old man drives a sub-ma-rine!" The skip-rope slap-slap-slapped on the pavement. I felt eyes on me. The woman in the kerchief had paused in her labors, the hose in one hand, a big soapy sponge in the other. She was watching me approach the skipping girls. I gave them a wide berth, and saw her go back to work.

You took a hell of a chance talking to those kids on Kansas Street, I thought. Only I didn't believe it. Walking a little too close to the skip-rope girls . . . *that* would have been taking a hell of a chance. But Richie and Bev had been the right ones. I had known it almost as soon as I laid eyes on them, and they had known it, too. We had seen eye to eye.

Do we know you? the girl had asked. Bevvie-Bevvie, who lived on the levee.

Kossuth dead-ended at a big building called the West Side Recreation Hall. It was deserted, with a FOR SALE BY CITY sign on the crabgrassy lawn. Surely an object of interest for any self-respecting real estate hunter. Two houses down from it on the right, a little girl with carrot-colored hair and a faceful of freckles was riding a bicycle with training wheels up and down an asphalt driveway. She sang variations of the same phrase over and over as she rode: "Bing-bang, I saw the whole gang, ding-dang, I saw the whole gang, ring-rang, I saw the whole gang. . . ."

I walked toward the Rec, as though there was nothing in the world I wanted to see more, but from the corner of my eye I continued to track Li'l Carrot-Top. She was swaying from side to side on the bicycle seat, trying to find out how much she could get away with before toppling over. Based on her scabby shins, this probably wasn't the first time she'd played the game. There was no name on the mailbox of her house, just the number 379.

I walked to the FOR SALE sign and jotted information down on my newspaper. Then I turned around and headed back the way I'd come. As I passed 379 Kossuth (on the far side of the street, and pretending to be absorbed in my paper), a woman came out on the stoop. A boy was with her. He was munching something wrapped in a napkin, and in his free hand he was holding the Daisy air rifle with which, not so long from now, he would try to scare off his rampaging father.

"Ellen!" the woman called. "Get off that thing before you fall off! Come in and get a cookie."

Ellen Dunning dismounted, dropped her bike on its side in the driveway, and ran into the house, bugling: "Sing-*sang*, I saw the whole gang!" at the top of her considerable lungs. Her hair, a shade of red far more unfortunate than Beverly Marsh's, bounced like bedsprings in revolt.

The boy, who'd grow up to write a painfully composed essay that would bring me to tears, followed her. The boy who was going to be the only surviving member of his family.

Unless I changed it. And now that I had seen them, real people living their real lives, there seemed to be no other choice.

CHAPTER 7

1

How should I tell you about my seven weeks in Derry? How to explain the way I came to hate and fear it?

It wasn't because it kept secrets (although it did), and it wasn't because terrible crimes, some of them still unsolved, had happened there (although they had). *All that's over,* the girl named Beverly had said, the boy named Richie had agreed, and I came to believe that, too . . . although I also came to believe the shadow never completely left that city with its odd sunken downtown.

It was a sense of impending failure that made me hate it. And that feeling of being in a prison with elastic walls. If I wanted to leave, it would let me go (willingly!), but if I stayed, it would squeeze me tighter. It would squeeze me until I couldn't breathe. And—here's the bad part—leaving wasn't an option, because now I had seen Harry before the limp and before the trusting but slightly dazed smile. I had seen him before he became Hoptoad Harry, hoppin down the av-a-*new.*

I had seen his sister, too. Now she was more than just a name in a painstakingly written essay, a faceless little girl who loved to pick flowers and put them in vases. Sometimes I lay awake thinking of how she planned to go trick-or-treating as Princess Summerfall Winterspring. Unless I did something, that was never going to happen. There was a coffin waiting for her after a long and fruitless struggle for life. There was a coffin waiting for her mother, whose first name I still didn't know. And for Troy. And for Arthur, known as Tugga.

If I let that happen, I didn't see how I could live with myself. So I stayed, but it wasn't easy. And every time I thought of putting myself through this again, in Dallas, my mind threatened to freeze up. At least, I told myself, Dallas wouldn't be like Derry. Because no place on earth could be like Derry.

How should I tell you, then?

In my life as a teacher, I used to hammer away at the idea of simplicity. In both fiction and nonfiction, there's only one question and one answer. *What happened?* the reader asks. *This is what happened,* the writer responds. *This . . . and this . . . and this, too.* Keep it simple. It's the only sure way home.

So I'll try, although you must always keep in mind that in Derry, reality is a thin skim of ice over a deep lake of dark water. But still:

What happened?

This happened. And this. And this, too.

2

On Friday, my second full day in Derry, I went down to the Center Street Market. I waited until five in the afternoon, because I thought that was when the place would be busiest—Friday's payday, after all, and for a lot of people (by which I mean wives; one of the rules of life in 1958 is Men Don't Buy Groceries) that meant shopping day. Lots of shoppers would make it easier for me to blend in. To help in that regard, I went to W. T. Grant's and supplemented my wardrobe with some chinos and blue workshirts. Remembering No Suspenders and his buddies outside the Sleepy Silver Dollar, I also bought a pair of Wolverine workboots. On my way to the market, I kicked them repeatedly against the curbing until the toes were scuffed.

The place was every bit as busy as I'd hoped, with a line at all three cash registers and the aisles full of women pushing shopping carts. The few men I saw only had baskets, so that was what I took. I put a bag of apples in mine (dirt cheap), and a bag of oranges (almost as expensive as 2011 oranges). Beneath my feet, the oiled wooden floor creaked.

What exactly did Mr. Dunning *do* in the Center Street Market? Bevvie-on-the-levee hadn't said. He wasn't the manager; a glance into the glassed-in booth just beyond the produce section showed a white-haired gentleman who could have claimed Ellen Dunning as a granddaughter, perhaps, but not as a daughter. And the sign on his desk said MR. CURRIE.

As I walked along the back of the store, past the dairy case (I was amused by a sign reading HAVE YOU TRIED "YOGHURT?" IF NOT YOU WILL LOVE IT WHEN YOU DO), I began to hear laughter. Female laughter of the immediately identifiable oh-you-rascal variety. I turned into the far aisle and saw a covey of women, dressed in much the same style as the ladies in the Kennebec Fruit, clustered around the meat counter. THE BUTCHERY, read the handmade wooden sign hanging down on decorative chrome chains. HOME-STYLE CUTS. And, at the bottom: FRANK DUNNING, HEAD BUTCHER.

Sometimes life coughs up coincidences no writer of fiction would dare copy.

It was Frank Dunning who was making the ladies laugh. The resemblance to the janitor who had taken my GED English course was close enough to be eerie. He was Harry to the life, except this version's hair was almost completely black instead of almost all gray, and the sweet, slightly puzzled smile had been replaced by a raffish, razzle-dazzle grin. It was no wonder the ladies were all aflutter. Even Bevvie-on-the-levee thought he was the cat's meow, and why not? She might only be twelve or thirteen, but she was female, and Frank Dunning was a charmer. He knew it, too. There had to be reasons for the flowers of Derry womanhood to spend their husbands' paychecks at the downtown market instead of at the slightly cheaper A&P, and one of them was right here. Mr. Dunning was handsome, Mr. Dunning wore spandy-clean clean whites (slightly bloodstained at the cuffs, but he was a butcher, after all), Mr. Dunning wore a stylish white hat that looked like a cross between a chef's toque and an artist's beret. It hung down to just above one eyebrow. A fashion statement, by God.

All in all, Mr. Frank Dunning, with his rosy, clean-shaven cheeks and his immaculately barbered black hair, was God's gift to the Little Woman. As I strolled toward him, he tied off a package of meat with a length of string drawn from a roll on a spindle beside his scale and wrote the price on it with a flourish of his black marker. He handed it to a lady of about fifty summers who was wearing a housedress with big pink roses blooming on it, seamed nylons, and a schoolgirl blush.

"There you are, Mrs. Levesque, one pound of German bologna, sliced thin." He leaned confidentially over the counter, close enough so that Mrs. Levesque (and the other ladies) would be able to whiff on the entrancing aroma of his cologne. Was it Aqua Velva, Fred Toomey's brand? I thought not. I thought a fascinator like Frank Dunning would go for something a little more expensive. "Do you know the problem with German bologna?"

"No," she said, dragging it out a little so it became *Noo-oo.* The other ladies twittered in anticipation.

Dunning's eyes flicked briefly to me and saw nothing to interest him. When he looked back at Mrs. Levesque, they once more picked up their patented twinkle.

"An hour after you eat some, you're hungry for power."

I'm not sure all the ladies got it, but they all shrieked with appreciation. Dunning sent Mrs. Levesque happily on her way, and as I passed out of hearing, he was turning his attention to a Mrs. Bowie. Who would, I was sure, be equally happy to receive it.

He's a nice man. Always joking around and stuff.

But the nice man had cold eyes. When interacting with his fascinated lady-harem, they had been blue. But when he turned his attention to me—however briefly—I could have sworn that they turned gray, the color of water beneath a sky from which snow will soon fall.

3

The market closed at 6:00 P.M., and when I left with my few items, it was only twenty past five. There was a U-Needa-Lunch on Witcham Street, just around the corner. I ordered a hamburger, a fountain Coke, and a piece of chocolate pie. The pie was excellent—real chocolate, real cream. It filled my mouth the way Frank Anicetti's root beer had. I dawdled as long as I could, then strolled down to the canal, where there were some benches. There was also a sightline—narrow but adequate—to the Center Street Market. I was full but ate one of my oranges anyway, casting bits of peel over the cement embankment and watching the water carry them away.

Promptly at six, the lights in the market's big front windows went out. By quarter past, the last of the ladies had exited, toting their carry-alls either up Up-Mile Hill or clustering at one of those phone poles with the painted white stripe. A bus marked ROUNDABOUT ONE FARE came along and scooped them up. At quarter to seven, the market employees began leaving. The last two to exit were Mr. Currie, the manager, and Dunning. They shook hands and parted, Currie going up the alley between the market and the shoe store next to it, probably to get his car, and Dunning to the bus stop.

By then there were only two other people there and I didn't want to join them. Thanks to the one-way traffic pattern in the Low Town, I didn't have to. I walked to another white-painted pole, this one handy to The Strand (where the current double feature was *Machine-Gun Kelly* and *Reform School Girl*; the marquee promised BLAZING ACTION), and waited with some working joes who were talking about possible World Series matchups. I could have told them plenty about that, but kept my mouth shut.

A city bus came along and stopped across from the Center Street Market. Dunning got on. It came the rest of the way down the hill and pulled up at the movie-theater stop. I let the working joes go ahead of me, so I could watch how much money they put in the pole-mounted coin receptacle next to the driver's seat. I felt like an alien in a science fiction movie, one who's trying to masquerade as an earthling. It was stupid—I wanted to ride the city bus, not blow up the White House with a death-ray—but that didn't change the feeling.

One of the guys who got on ahead of me flashed a canary-colored bus pass that made me think fleetingly of the Yellow Card Man. The others put fifteen cents into the coin receptacle, which clicked and dinged. I did the same, although it took me a bit longer because my dime was stuck to my sweaty palm. I thought I could feel every eye on me, but when I looked up, everyone was either reading the newspaper or staring vacantly out the windows. The interior of the bus was a fug of blue-gray smoke.

Frank Dunning was halfway down on the right, now wearing tailored gray slacks, a white shirt, and a dark blue tie. Natty. He was busy lighting a cigarette and didn't look at me as I passed him and took a seat near the back. The bus groaned its way around the circuit of Low Town one-way streets, then mounted Up-Mile Hill on Witcham. Once we were in the west side residential area, riders began to get off. They were all men; presumably the women were back at home putting away their groceries or getting supper on the table. As the bus emptied and Frank Dunning went on sitting where he was, smoking his cigarette, I wondered if we were going to end up being the last two riders.

I needn't have worried. When the bus angled toward the stop at the corner of Witcham Street and Charity Avenue (Derry also had Faith and Hope Avenues, I later learned), Dunning dropped his cigarette on the floor, crushed it with his shoe, and rose from his seat. He walked easily up the aisle, not using the grab-handles but swaying with the movements of the slowing bus. Some men don't lose the physical graces of their adolescence until relatively late in life. Dunning appeared to be one of them. He would have made an excellent swing-dancer.

He clapped the bus driver on the shoulder and started telling him a joke. It was short, and most of it was lost in the chuff of the airbrakes, but I caught the phrase *three jigs stuck in an elevator* and decided it wasn't one he'd have told to his Housedress Harem. The driver exploded with laughter, then yanked the long chrome lever that opened the front doors. "See you Monday, Frank," he said.

"If the creek don't rise," Dunning responded, then ran down the two steps and jumped across the grass verge to the sidewalk. I could see muscles ripple under his shirt. What chance would a woman and four children have against him? *Not much* was my first thought on the subject, but that was wrong. The correct answer was *none.*

As the bus drew away, I saw Dunning mount the steps of the first building down from the corner on Charity Avenue. There were eight or nine men and women sitting in rockers on the wide front porch. Several of them greeted the butcher, who started shaking hands like a visiting politician. The house was a three-story New England Victorian, with a sign hanging from the porch eave. I just had time to read it:

EDNA PRICE ROOMS
BY THE WEEK OR THE MONTH
EFFICIENCY KITCHENS AVAILABLE
NO PETS!

Below this, hanging from the big sign on hooks, was a smaller orange sign reading NO VACANCY.

Two stops further down the line, I exited the bus. I thanked the driver, who uttered a surly grunt in return. This, I was discovering, was what passed for courteous discourse in Derry, Maine. Unless, of course, you happened to know a few jokes about jigs stuck in an elevator or maybe the Polish navy.

I walked slowly back toward town, jogging two blocks out of my way to keep clear of Edna Price's establishment, where those in residence gathered on the porch after supper just like folks in one of those Ray Bradbury stories about bucolic Greentown, Illinois. And did not Frank Dunning resemble one of those good folks?

He did, he did. But there had been hidden horrors in Bradbury's Greentown, too.

The nice man doesn't live at home anymore, Richie-from-the-ditchie had said, and he'd had the straight dope on that one. The nice man lived in a rooming house where everybody seemed to think he was the cat's ass.

By my estimation, Price's Rooms was no more than five blocks west of 379 Kossuth Street, and maybe closer. Did Frank Dunning sit in his rented room after the other tenants had gone to bed, facing east like one of the faithful turning toward Qiblah? If so, did he do it with his hey-great-to-see-you smile on his face? I thought no. And were his eyes blue, or did they turn that cold and thoughtful gray? How did he explain leaving his hearth and home to the folks taking the evening air on Edna Price's porch? Did he have a story, one where his wife was either a little bit cracked or an outright villain? I thought yes. And did people believe it? The answer to that one was easy. It doesn't matter if you're talking 1958, 1985, or 2011. In America, where surface has always passed for substance, people always believe guys like Frank Dunning.

4

On the following Tuesday, I rented an apartment advertised in the Derry *News* as "semi-furnished, in a good neighborhood," and on Wednesday the seventeenth of September, Mr. George Amberson moved in. Goodbye, Derry Town House, hello Harris Avenue. I had been living in 1958 for over a week, and was beginning to feel comfortable there, if not exactly a native.

The semi-furnishings consisted of a bed (which came with a slightly stained mattress but no linen), a sofa, a kitchen table with one leg that needed to be shimmed so it didn't teeter, and a single chair with a yellow plastic seat that made a weird *smook* sound as it reluctantly released its grip on the seat of one's pants. There was a stove and a clattery fridge. In the kitchen pantry, I discovered the apartment's air-conditioning unit: a GE fan with a frayed plug that looked absolutely lethal.

I felt that the apartment, which was directly beneath the flight path of planes landing at Derry Airport, was a bit overpriced at sixty-five dollars a month, but agreed to it because Mrs. Joplin, the landlady, was willing to overlook Mr. Amberson's lack of references. It helped that he could offer three months' rent in cash. She nevertheless insisted on copying the information from my driver's license. If she found it strange that a real estate freelancer from Wisconsin was carrying a Maine license, she didn't say so.

I was glad Al had given me lots of cash. Cash is so soothing to strangers.

It goes a lot farther in '58, too. For only three hundred dollars, I was able to turn my semi-furnished apartment into one that was fully furnished. Ninety of the three hundred went for a second-hand RCA table-model television. That night I watched *The Steve Allen Show* in beautiful black-and-white, then turned it off and sat at the kitchen table, listening to a plane settle earthward in a roar of propellers. From my back pocket I took a Blue Horse notebook I'd bought in the Low Town drugstore (the one where shoplifting was not a kick, groove, or gasser). I turned to the first page and clicked out the tip of my equally new Parker ballpoint. I sat that way for maybe fifteen minutes—long enough for another plane to clatter earthward, seemingly so close that I almost expected to feel a thump as the wheels scraped the roof.

The page remained blank. So did my mind. Every time I tried to throw it into gear, the only coherent thought I could manage was *the past doesn't want to be changed.*

Not helpful.

At last I got up, took the fan from its shelf in the pantry, and set it on the counter. I wasn't sure it would work, but it did, and the hum of the motor was strangely soothing. Also, it masked the fridge's annoying rumble.

When I sat down again, my mind was clearer, and this time a few words came.

OPTIONS

1. *Tell police*
2. *Anonymous call to butcher (Say "I'm watching you, mf, if you do something I'll tell")*
3. *Frame butcher for something*
4. *Incapacitate butcher somehow*

I stopped there. The fridge clicked off. There were no descending planes and no traffic on Harris Avenue. For the time being it was just me and my fan and my incomplete list. At last I wrote the final item:

5. *Kill butcher*

Then I crumpled it, opened the box of kitchen matches that sat beside the stove to light the burners and the oven, and scratched one. The fan promptly whiffed it out and I thought again how hard it was to change some things. I turned the fan off, lit another match, and touched it to the ball of notepaper. When it was blazing, I dropped it into the sink, waited for it to go out, then washed the ashes down the drain.

After that, Mr. George Amberson went to bed.

But he did not sleep for a long time.

5

When the last plane of the night skimmed over the rooftop at twelve-thirty, I was still awake and thinking of my list. Telling the police was out. It might work with Oswald, who would declare his undying love for Fidel Castro in both Dallas and New Orleans, but Dunning was a different matter. He was a well-liked and well-respected member of the community. Who was I? The new guy in a town that didn't like outsiders. That afternoon, after coming out of the drugstore, I had once again seen No Suspenders and his crew outside the Sleepy Silver Dollar. I was wearing my working-man clothes, but they had given me that same flat-eyed *who the fuck're you* look.

Even if I'd been living in Derry for eight years instead of eight days, just what would I say to the police, anyway? That I'd had a vision of Frank Dunning killing his family on Halloween night? That would certainly go over well.

I liked the idea of placing an anonymous call to the butcher himself a little better, but it was a scary option. Once I called Frank Dunning—either at work or at Edna Price's, where he would no doubt be summoned to the communal phone in the parlor—I would have changed events. Such a call might stop him from kill-ing his family, but I thought it just as likely it would have the opposite effect, tipping him over the precarious edge of sanity he must be walking behind the affable George Clooney smile. Instead of preventing the murders, I might only succeed in making them happen sooner. As it was, I knew where and when. If I warned him, all bets were off.

Frame him for something? It might work in a spy novel, but I wasn't a CIA agent; I was a goddam English teacher.

Incapacitate butcher was next on the list. Okay, but how? Smack him with the Sunliner, maybe as he walked from Charity Avenue to Kossuth Street with a hammer in his hand and murder on his mind? Unless I had amazing luck, I'd be caught and jailed. There was this, too. Incapacitated people usually get better. He might try again once he did. As I lay there in the dark, I found that sce-nario all too plausible. Because the past didn't like to be changed. It was obdurate.

The only sure way was to follow him, wait until he was alone, and then kill him. Keep it simple, stupid.

But there were problems with this, too. The biggest was that I didn't know if I could go through with it. I thought I could in hot blood—to protect myself or another—but in cold blood? Even if I knew that my potential victim was going to kill his own wife and children if he weren't stopped?

And . . . what if I did it and then got caught before I could escape to the future where I was Jake Epping instead of George Amberson? I'd be tried, found guilty, sent to Shawshank State Prison. And that was where I'd be on the day John F. Kennedy was killed in Dallas.

Even that wasn't the absolute bottom of the matter. I got up, paced through the kitchen to my phone booth of a bathroom, went to the toilet, then sat on the seat with my forehead propped on the heels of my palms. I had assumed Harry's essay was the truth. Al had, too. It probably was, because Harry was two or three degrees on the dim side of normal, and people like that are less liable to try passing off fantasies like the murder of an entire family as reality. Still . . .

Ninety-five percent probability isn't a hundred, Al had said, and that was Oswald himself he'd been talking about. Just about the only person the killer *could* have been, once you set aside all the conspiracy babble, and yet Al still had those last lingering doubts.

It would have been easy to check out Harry's story in the computer-friendly world of 2011, but I never had. And even if it was completely true, there might be crucial details he'd gotten wrong or not mentioned at all. Things that could trip me up. What if, instead of riding to the rescue like Sir Galahad, I only managed to get killed along with them? That would change the future in all sorts of interesting ways, but I wouldn't be around to discover what they were.

A new idea popped into my head, one that was crazily attractive. I could station myself across from 379 Kossuth on Halloween night . . . *and just watch.* To make sure it really happened, yes, but also to note all the details the only living witness—a traumatized child—might have missed. Then I could drive back to Lisbon Falls, go up through the rabbit-hole, and immediately return to September 9 at 11:58 in the morning. I'd buy the Sunliner again and go to Derry again, this time loaded with information. It was true I'd already spent a fair amount of Al's currency, but there was enough left to get by on.

The idea ran well out of the gate but stumbled before it even got to the first turn. The whole purpose of this trip had been to find out what effect saving the janitor's family would have on the future, and if I let Frank Dunning go through with the murders, I wouldn't know. And I was already faced with having to do this again, because there would be one of those resets when—*if*—I went back through the rabbit-hole to stop Oswald. Once was bad. Twice would be worse. Three times was unthinkable.

And one other thing. Harry Dunning's family had already died once. Was I going to condemn them to die a second time? Even if each time was a reset and they didn't know? And who was to say that on some deep level they didn't?

The pain. The blood. Li'l Carrot-Top lying on the floor under the rocker. Harry trying to scare the lunatic off with a Daisy air gun: "Leave me alone, Daddy, or I'll shoot you."

I shuffled back through the kitchen, pausing to look at the chair with the yellow plastic seat. "I hate you, chair," I told it, then went to bed again.

That time I fell asleep almost immediately. When I woke up the next morning, a nine-o'clock sun was shining in my as-yet-curtainless bedroom window, birds were twittering self-importantly, and I thought I knew what I had to do. Keep it simple, stupid.

6

At noon I put on my tie, set my straw hat at the correct rakish angle, and took myself down to Machen's Sporting Goods, where THE FALL GUN SALE was still going on. I told the clerk I was interested in buying a handgun, because I was in the real estate business and occasionally I had to carry quite large amounts of cash. He showed me several, including a Colt .38 Police Special revolver. The price was $9.99. That seemed absurdly low until I remembered that, according to Al's notes, the Italian mail-order rifle Oswald had used to change history had cost less than twenty.

"This is a fine piece of protection," the clerk said, rolling out the barrel and giving it a spin: *clickclickclickclick.* "Dead accurate up to fifteen yards, guaranteed, and anyone stupid enough to try mugging you out of your cash is going to be a lot closer than that."

"Sold."

I braced for an examination of my scant paperwork, but had once again forgotten to take into account the relaxed and unterrified atmosphere of the America where I was now living. The way the deal worked was this: I paid my money and walked out with the gun. There was no paperwork and no waiting period. I didn't even have to give my current address.

Oswald had wrapped his gun in a blanket and hidden it in the garage of the house where his wife was staying with a woman named Ruth Paine. But when I walked out of Machen's with mine in my briefcase, I thought I knew how he must have felt: like a man with a powerful secret. A man who owned his own private tornado.

A guy who should have been at work in one of the mills was standing in the doorway of the Sleepy Silver Dollar, smoking a cigarette and reading the paper. Appearing to read the paper, at least. I couldn't swear he was watching me, but then again I couldn't swear he wasn't.

It was No Suspenders.

7

That evening, I once more took up a position close to The Strand, where the marquee read OPENS TOMORROW! **THUNDER ROAD** (MITCHUM) & **THE VIKINGS** (DOUGLAS)! More BLAZING ACTION in the offing for Derry filmgoers.

Dunning once more crossed to the bus stop and climbed aboard.

This time I didn't follow. There was no need; I knew where he was going. I walked back to my new apartment, looking around every now and then for No Suspenders. There was no sign of him, and I told myself that seeing him across from the sporting goods store had just been a coincidence. Not a big one, either. The Sleepy was his joint of choice, after all. Because the Derry mills ran six days a week, the workers had rotating off-days. Thursday could have been one of this guy's. Next week he might be hanging at the Sleepy on Friday. Or Tuesday.

The following evening I was once more at The Strand, pretending to study the poster for *Thunder Road (Robert Mitchum Roars Down the Hottest Highway on Earth!)*, mostly because I had nowhere else to go; Halloween was still six weeks away, and I seemed to have entered the time-killing phase of our program. But this time instead of crossing to the bus stop, Frank Dunning walked down to the three-way intersection of Center, Kansas, and Witcham and stood there as if undecided. He was once more looking reet in dark slacks, white shirt, blue tie, and a sport coat in a light gray windowpane check. His hat was cocked back on his head. For a moment I thought he was going to head for the movies and check out the hottest highway on earth, in which case I would stroll casually away toward Canal Street. But he turned left, onto Witcham. I could hear him whistling. He was a good whistler.

There was no need to follow him; he wasn't going to commit any hammer murders on the nineteenth of September. But I was curious, and I had nothing better to do. He went into a bar and grill called The Lamplighter, not as upper-crust as the one at the Town House, but nowhere near as grotty as the ones on Canal. In every small city there are one or two borderland joints where blue-collar and whitecollar workers meet as equals, and this looked like that kind of place. Usually the menu features some local delicacy that makes outsiders scratch their head in puzzlement. The Lamplighter's specialty seemed to be something called Fried Lobster Pickin's.

I passed the wide front windows, lounging rather than walking, and saw Dunning greet his way across the room. He shook hands; he patted cheeks; he took one man's hat and scaled it to a guy standing at the Bowl Mor machine, who caught it deftly and to general hilarity. A nice man. Always joking around. Laugh-and-the-whole-world-laughs-with-you type of thing.

I saw him sit down at a table close to the Bowl Mor and almost walked on. But I was thirsty. A beer would go down fine just about now, and The Lamplighter's bar was all the way across a crowded room from the large table where Dunning was sitting with the all-male group he had joined. He wouldn't see me, but I could keep an eye on him in the mirror. Not that I was apt to see anything too startling.

Besides, if I was going to be here for another six weeks, it was time to start *belonging* here. So I turned around and entered the sounds of cheerful voices, slightly inebriated laughter, and Dean Martin singing "That's Amore." Waitresses circulated with steins of beer and heaped platters of what had to be Fried Lobster Pickin's. And there were rising rafters of blue smoke, of course.

In 1958, there's always smoke.

8

"See you glancin at that table back there," a voice said at my elbow. I had been at The Lamplighter long enough to have ordered my second beer and a "junior platter" of Lobster Pickin's. I figured if I didn't at least try them, I'd always wonder.

I looked around and saw a small man with slicked-back hair, a round face, and lively black eyes. He looked like a cheerful chipmunk. He grinned at me and stuck out a child-sized hand. On his forearm, a bare-breasted mermaid flapped her flippy tail and winked one eye. "Charles Frati. But you can call me Chaz. Everyone does."

I shook. "George Amberson, but you can call me George. Everyone does that, too."

He laughed. So did I. It's considered bad form to laugh at your own jokes (especially when they're teensy ones), but some people are so engaging they never have to laugh alone. Chaz Frati was one of those. The waitress brought him a beer, and he raised it. "Here's to you, George."

"I'll drink to that," I said, and clicked the rim of my glass against his.

"Anybody you know?" he asked, looking at the big rear table in the backbar mirror.

"Nope." I wiped foam from my upper lip. "They just seem to be having more fun than anybody else in the place, that's all."

Chaz smiled. "That's Tony Tracker's table. Might as well have his name engraved on it. Tony and his brother Phil own a freight-hauling company. They also own more acres in this town—and the towns around it—than Carter has liver pills. Phil don't show up here much, he's mostly on the road, but Tony don't miss many Friday or Saturday nights. Has lots of friends, too. They always have a good time, but nobody makes a party go like Frankie Dunning. He's the guy tellin jokes. Everybody likes old Tones, but they *love* Frankie."

"You sound like you know them all."

"For years. Know most of the people in Derry, but I don't know you."

"That's because I just got here. I'm in real estate."

"Business real estate, I take it."

"You take it right." The waitress deposited my Lobster Pickin's and hustled away. The heap on the platter looked like roadkill, but it smelled terrific and tasted better. Probably a billion grams of cholesterol in every bite, but in 1958, nobody worries about that, which is restful. "Help me with this," I said.

"Nope, they're all yours. You out of Boston? New York?"

I shrugged and he laughed.

"Playin it cagey, huh? Don't blame you, cuz. Loose lips sink ships. But I have a pretty good idea what you're up to."

I paused with a forkful of Lobster Pickin's halfway to my mouth.

It was warm in The Lamplighter, but I felt suddenly chilly. "Is that so?"

He leaned close. I could smell Vitalis on his slicked-back hair and Sen-Sen on his breath. "If I said 'possible mall site,' would that be a bingo?"

I felt a gust of relief. The idea that I was in Derry looking for a place to put a shopping mall had never crossed my mind, but it was a good one. I dropped Chaz Frati a wink. "Can't say."

"No, no, course you couldn't. Business is as business does, I always say. We'll drop the subject. But if you'd ever consider letting one of the local yokels in on a good thing, I'd love to listen. And just to show you that my heart is in the right place, I'll give you a little tip. If you haven't checked out the old Kitchener Ironworks yet, you ought to. Perfect spot. And malls? Do you know what malls are, my son?"

"The wave of the future," I said.

He pointed a finger at me like a gun and winked. I laughed again, just couldn't help it. Part of it was the simple relief of finding out that not every grown-up in Derry had forgotten how to be friendly to a stranger. "Hole in one."

"And who owns the land the old Kitchener Ironworks sits on, Chaz? The Tracker brothers, I suppose?"

"I said they own most of the land around here, not all of it." He looked down at the mermaid. "Milly, should I tell George who owns that prime business-zoned real estate only two miles from the center of this metropolis?"

Milly wagged her scaly tail and jiggled her teacup breasts. Chaz Frati didn't clench his hand into a fist to make this happen; the muscles in his forearm seemed to move on their own. It was a good trick. I wondered if he also pulled rabbits out of hats.

"All right, dear." He looked up at me again. "Actually, that would be yours truly. I buy the best and let the Tracker brothers have the rest. Business is as business does. May I give you my card, George?"

"Absolutely."

He did. The card simply said CHARLES "CHAZ" FRATI BUY SELL TRADE. I tucked it into my shirt pocket.

"If you know all those people and they know you, why aren't you over there instead of sitting at the bar with the new kid on the block?" I asked.

He looked surprised, then amused all over again. "Was you born in a trunk and then threw off a train, cuz?"

"Just new in town. Haven't learned the ropes. Don't hold it against me."

"Never would. They do business with me because I own half this town's motor courts, both downtown movie theaters and the drive-in, one of the banks, and all of the pawnshops in eastern and central Maine. But they don't eat with me or drink with me or invite me into their homes or their country club because I'm a member of the Tribe."

"You lost me."

"I'm a Jew, cuz."

He saw my expression and grinned. "You didn't know. Even when I wouldn't eat any of your lobster, you didn't know. I'm touched."

"I'm just trying to figure out why it should make a difference," I said.

He laughed as though this were the best joke he'd heard all year. "Then you was born under a cabbage leaf instead of in a trunk."

In the mirror, Frank Dunning was talking. Tony Tracker and his friends were listening with big grins on their faces. When they exploded into bull roars of laughter, I wondered if it had been the one about the three jigs stuck in the elevator or maybe something even more amusing and satiric—three Yids on a golf course, maybe.

Chaz saw me looking. "Frank knows how to make a party go, all right. You know where he works? No, you're new in town, I forgot. Center Street Market. He's the head butcher. Also half-owner, although he don't advertise it. You know what? He's half the reason that place stands up and makes a profit. Draws the ladies like bees to honey."

"Does he, now?"

"Yep, and the men like him, too. That's not always the case. Fellas don't always like a ladies' man."

That made me think of my ex-wife's fierce Johnny Depp fixation.

"But it's not like the old days when he'd drink with em until closin, then play poker with em down at the freight depot until the crack of dawn. These days he'll have one beer—maybe two—and then he's out the door. You watch."

It was a behavior pattern I knew about firsthand from Christy's sporadic efforts to control her booze intake rather than stop altogether. It would work for awhile, but sooner or later she always went off the deep end.

"Drinking problem?" I asked.

"Don't know about that, but he's sure got a temper problem." He looked down at the tattoo on his forearm. "Milly, you ever notice how many funny fellas have got a mean streak?"

Milly flipped her tail. Chaz looked at me solemnly. "See? The women always know." He snuck a Lobster Pickin' and shot his eyes comically from side to side. He was a very amusing fellow, and it never crossed my mind that he was anything other than what he claimed to be. But, as Chaz himself had implied, I was a bit on the naïve side. Certainly for Derry. "Don't tell Rabbi Snoresalot."

"Your secret's safe with me."

By the way the men at the Tracker table were leaning toward Frank, he had launched into another joke. He was the kind of man who talked a lot with his hands. They were big hands. It was easy to imagine one of them holding the haft of a Craftsman hammer.

"He ripped and roared something terrible back in high school," Chaz said. "You're looking at a guy who knows, because I went to the old County Consolidated with him. But I mostly kept out of his way. Suspensions left and right. Always for fighting. He was supposed to go to the University of Maine, but he got a girl pregnant and ended up getting married instead. After a year or two of it, she collected the baby and scrammed. Probably a smart idea, the way he was then. Frankie was the kind of guy, fighting the Germans or the Japs probably would have been good for im—get all that mad out, you know. But he came up 4-F. I never heard why. Flat feet? Heart murmur? The high blood? No way of telling. But you probably don't want to hear all this old gossip."

"I do," I said. "It's interesting." It sure was. I'd come into The Lamplighter to wet my whistle and had stumbled into a gold mine instead. "Have another Lobster Pickin'."

"Twist my arm," he said, and popped one into his mouth. He jerked a thumb at the mirror as he chewed. "And why shouldn't I? Just look at those guys back there—half of em Catholics and still chowing up on burgers n BLTs n sausage subs. On Friday! Who can make sense of religion, cuz?"

"You got me," I said. "I'm a lapsed Methodist. Guess Mr. Dunning never got that college education, huh?"

"Nope, by the time his first wife done her midnight flit, he was gettin a graduate degree in cuttin meat, and he was good at it. Got into some more trouble—and yeah, drinkin was somewhat involved from what I heard, people gossip terrible, y'know, and a man who owns pawnshops hears it all—so Mr. Vollander, him who owned the market back in those days, he sat down and had a Dutch uncle talk with ole Frankie." Chaz shook his head and picked another Pickin'. "If Benny Vollander had ever known Frankie Dunning was gonna own half the place by the time that Korea shit was over, he probably would have had a brain hemorrhage. Good thing we can't see the future, isn't it?"

"That would complicate things, all right."

Chaz was warming to his story, and when I told the waitress to bring another couple of beers, he didn't tell her no.

"Benny Vollander said Frankie was the best 'prentice butcher he'd ever had, but if he got in any more trouble with the cops—fightin if anyone farted sideways, in other words—he'd have to let him go. A word to the wise is sufficient, they say, and Frankie straightened up. Divorced that first wife of his on grounds of desertion after she was gone a year or two, then remarried not long after. The war was goin full steam by then and he could have had his pick of the ladies—he has that charm, you know, and most of the competition was overseas, anyway—but he settled on Doris McKinney. Lovely girl she was."

"And still is, I'm sure."

"Absolutely, cuz. Pretty as a picture. They've got three or four kids. Nice family." Chaz leaned close again. "But Frankie still loses his temper now and then, and he must have lost it at her last spring, because she turned up at church with bruises on her face and a week later he was out the door. He's living in a rooming house as close as he could get to the old homestead. Hopin she'll take him back, I imagine. And sooner or later, she will. He's got that charming way of—whoops, lookie there, what'd I tell you? He's a gone cat."

Dunning was getting up. The other men were bellowing for him to sit back down, but he was shaking his head and pointing to his watch. He tipped the last swallow of his beer down his throat, then bent and kissed one man's bald head. This brought a room-shaking roar of approval and Dunning surfed on it toward the door.

He slapped Chaz on the back as he went by and said, "Keep that nose clean, Chazzy—it's too long to get dirty."

Then he was gone. Chaz looked at me. He was giving me the cheerful chipmunk grin, but his eyes weren't smiling. "Ain't he a card?"

"Sure," I said.

9

I'm one of those people who doesn't really know what he thinks until he writes it down, so I spent most of that weekend making notes about what I'd seen in Derry, what I'd done, and what I planned to do. They expanded into an explanation of how I'd gotten to Derry in the first place, and by Sunday I realized that I'd started a job that was too big for a pocket notebook and ballpoint pen. On Monday I went out and bought a portable typewriter. My intention had been to go to the local business supply store, but then I saw Chaz Frati's card on the kitchen table, and went there instead. It was on East Side Drive, a pawnshop almost as big as a department store. The three gold balls were over the door, as was traditional, but there was something else, as well: a plaster mermaid flapping her flippy tail and winking one eye. This one, being out in public, was wearing a bra top. Frati himself was not in evidence, but I got a terrific Smith-Corona for twelve dollars. I told the clerk to tell Mr. Frati that George the real estate guy had been in.

"Happy to do it, sir. Would you like to leave your card?"

Shit. I'd have to have some of those printed . . . which meant a visit to Derry Business Supply after all. "Left them in my other suit coat," I said, "but I think he'll remember me. We had a drink at The Lamplighter."

That afternoon I began expanding my notes.

10

I got used to the planes coming in for a landing directly over my head. I arranged for newspaper and milk delivery: thick glass bottles brought right to your doorstep. Like the root beer Frank Anicetti had served me on my first jaunt into 1958, the milk tasted incredibly full and rich. The cream was even better. I didn't know if artificial creamers had been invented yet, and had no intention of finding out. Not with this stuff around.

The days slipped by. I read Al Templeton's notes on Oswald until I could have quoted long passages by heart. I visited the library and read about the murders and the disappearances that had plagued Derry in 1957 and 1958. I looked for stories about Frank Dunning and his famous bad temper, but found none; if he had ever been arrested, the story hadn't made it into the newspaper's Police Beat column, which was good-sized on most days and usually expanded to a full page on Mondays, when it contained a full summary of the weekend's didoes (most of which happened after the bars closed). The only story I found about the janitor's father concerned a 1955 charity drive. The Center Street Market had contributed ten percent of their profits that fall to the Red Cross, to help out after hurricanes Connie and Diane slammed into the East Coast, killing two hundred and causing extensive flood damage in New England. There was a picture of Harry's father handing an oversized check to the regional head of the Red Cross. Dunning was flashing that movie-star smile.

I made no more shopping trips to the Center Street Market, but on two weekends—the last in September and the first in October—I followed Derry's favorite butcher after he finished his half-day Saturday stint behind the meat counter. I rented nondescript Hertz Chevrolets from the airport for this chore. The Sunliner, I felt, was a little too conspicuous for shadowing.

On the first Saturday afternoon, he went to a Brewer flea market in a Pontiac he kept in a downtown pay-by-the-month garage and rarely used during the workweek. On the following Sunday, he drove to his house on Kossuth Street, collected his kids, and took them to a Disney double feature at the Aladdin. Even at a distance, Troy, the eldest, looked bored out of his mind both going into the theater and coming out.

Dunning didn't enter the house for either the pickup or the drop-off. He honked for the kids when he arrived and let them off at the curb when they came back, watching until all four were inside. He didn't drive off immediately even then, only sat behind the wheel of the idling Bonneville, smoking a cigarette. Maybe hoping the lovely Doris might want to come out and talk. When he was sure she wouldn't, he used a neighbor's driveway to turn around in and sped off, squealing his tires hard enough to send up little splurts of blue smoke.

I slumped in the seat of my rental, but I needn't have bothered. He never looked in my direction as he passed, and when he was a good distance down Witcham Street, I followed along after. He returned his car to the garage where he kept it, went to The Lamplighter for a single beer at the nearly deserted bar, then trudged back to Edna Price's rooms on Charity Avenue with his head down.

The following Saturday, October fourth, he collected his kids and took them to the football game at the University of Maine in Orono, some thirty miles away. I parked on Stillwater Avenue and waited for the game to be over. On the way back they stopped at the Ninety-Fiver for dinner. I parked at the far end of the parking lot and waited for them to come out, reflecting that the life of a private eye must be a boring one, no matter what the movies would have us believe.

When Dunning delivered his children back home, dusk was creeping over Kossuth Street. Troy had clearly enjoyed football more than the adventures of Cinderella; he exited his father's Pontiac grinning and waving a Black Bears pennant. Tugga and Harry also had pennants and also seemed energized. Ellen, not so much. She was fast asleep. Dunning carried her to the door of the house in his arms. This time Mrs. Dunning made a brief appearance—just long enough to take the little girl into her own arms.

Dunning said something to Doris. Her reply didn't seem to please him. The distance was too great to read his expression, but he was wagging a finger at her as he spoke. She listened, shook her head, turned, and went inside. He stood there a moment or two, then took off his hat and slapped it against his leg.

All interesting—and instructive of the relationship—but no help otherwise. Not what I was looking for.

I got that the following day. I had decided to make only two reconnaissance passes that Sunday, feeling that, even in a dark brown rental unit that almost faded into the landscape, more would be risking notice. I saw nothing on the first one and figured he was probably in for the day, and why not? The weather had turned gray and drizzly. He was probably watching sports on TV with the rest of the boarders, all of them smoking up a storm in the parlor.

But I was wrong. Just as I turned onto Witcham for my second pass, I saw him walking toward downtown, today dressed in blue jeans, a windbreaker, and a wide-brimmed waterproof hat. I drove past him and parked on Main Street about a block up from the garage he used. Twenty minutes later I was following him out of town to the west. Traffic was light, and I kept well back.

His destination turned out to be Longview Cemetery, two miles past the Derry Drive-In. He stopped at a flower stand across from it, and as I drove by, I saw him buying two baskets of fall flowers from an old lady who held a big black umbrella over both of them during the transaction. I watched in my rearview mirror as he put the flowers on the passenger seat of his car, got back in, and drove up the cemetery's access road.

I turned around and drove back to Longview. This was taking a risk, but I had to chance it, because this looked good. The parking lot was empty except for two pickups loaded with groundkeeping equipment under tarps and a dinged-up old payloader that looked like war surplus. No sign of Dunning's Pontiac. I drove across the lot toward the gravel lane leading into the cemetery itself, which was huge, sprawling over as many as a dozen hilly acres.

In the cemetery proper, smaller lanes split off from the main one. Groundfog was rising up from the dips and valleys, and the drizzle was thickening into rain. Not a good day for visiting the dear departed, all in all, and Dunning had the place to himself. His Pontiac, parked halfway up a hill on one of the feeder lanes, was easy to spot. He was placing the flower baskets before two side-by-side graves. His parents', I assumed, but I didn't really care. I turned my car around and left him to it.

By the time I got back to my Harris Avenue apartment, that fall's first hard rain was pounding the city. Downtown, the canal would be roaring, and the peculiar thrumming that came up through the concrete in the Low Town would be more noticeable than ever. Indian summer seemed to be over. I didn't care about that, either. I opened my notebook, flipped almost to the end before I found a blank page, and wrote *October 5th, 3:45 PM, Dunning to Longview Cem, puts flowers on parents' (?) graves. Rain.*

I had what I wanted.

CHAPTER 8

1

In the weeks before Halloween, Mr. George Amberson inspected almost every commercial-zoned piece of property in Derry and the surrounding towns.

I knew better than to believe that I'd ever be accepted as a townie on short notice, but I wanted to get the locals accustomed to the sight of my sporty red Sunliner convertible, just part of the scenery. *There goes that real estate fella, been here almost a month now. If he knows what he's doin, there might be some money in it for someone.*

When people asked me what I was looking for, I'd give a wink and a smile. When people asked me how long I'd be staying, I told them it was hard to say. I learned the geography of the town, and I began to learn the verbal geography of 1958. I learned, for instance, that *the war* meant World War II; *the conflict* meant Korea. Both were over, and good riddance. People worried about Russia and the so-called "missile gap," but not too much. People worried about juvenile delinquency, but not too much. There was a recession, but people had seen worse. When you bargained with someone, it was absolutely okay to say that you jewed em down (or got gypped). Penny candy included dots, wax lips, and niggerbabies. In the South, Jim Crow ruled. In Moscow, Nikita Khrushchev bellowed threats. In Washington, President Eisenhower droned good cheer.

I made a point of checking out the defunct Kitchener Ironworks not long after speaking with Chaz Frati. It was in a large overgrown stretch of empty to the north of town, and yes, it would be the perfect spot for a shopping mall once the extension of the Mile-A-Minute Highway reached it. But on the day I visited—leaving my car and walking when the road turned to axle-smashing rubble— it could have been the ruin of an ancient civilization: look on my works, ye mighty, and despair. Heaps of brick and rusty chunks of old machinery poked out of the high grass. In the middle was a long-collapsed ceramic smokestack, its sides blackened by soot, its huge bore full of darkness. If I'd lowered my head and hunched over, I could have walked into it, and I am not a short man.

I saw a lot of Derry in those weeks before Halloween, and I *felt* a lot of Derry. Longtime residents were pleasant to me, but—with one exception—never chummy. Chaz Frati was that exception, and in retrospect I guess his unprompted revelations should have struck me as odd, but I had a great many things on my mind, and Frati didn't seem all that important. I thought, *sometimes you just meet a friendly guy, that's all,* and let it go at that. Certainly I had no idea that a man named Bill Turcotte had put Frati up to it.

Bill Turcotte, aka No Suspenders.

2

Bevvie-from-the-levee had said she thought the bad times in Derry were over, but the more of it I saw (and the more I felt— that especially), the more I came to believe that Derry wasn't like other places. Derry wasn't right. At first I tried to tell myself that it was me, not the town. I was a man out of joint, a temporal bedouin, and any place would have felt a little strange to me, a little skewed—like the cities that seem so much like bad dreams in those strange Paul Bowles novels. This was persuasive at first, but as the days passed and I continued to explore my new environment, it became less so. I even began to question Beverly Marsh's assertion that the bad times were over, and imagined (on nights when I couldn't sleep, and there were quite a few of those) that she questioned it herself. Hadn't I glimpsed a seed of doubt in her eyes? The look of someone who doesn't quite believe but wants to? Maybe even needs to?

Something wrong, something bad.

Certain empty houses that seemed to stare like the faces of people suffering from terrible mental illness. An empty barn on the outskirts of town, the hayloft door swinging slowly open and closed on rusty hinges, first disclosing darkness, then hiding it, then disclosing it again. A splintered fence on Kossuth Street, just a block away from the house where Mrs. Dunning and her children lived. To me that fence looked as if something—or some*one*—had been hurled through it and into the Barrens below. An empty playground with the roundy-round slowly spinning even though there were no kids to push it and no appreciable wind to turn it. It screamed on its hidden bearings as it moved. One day I saw a roughly carved Jesus go floating down the canal and into the tunnel that ran beneath Canal Street. It was three feet long. The teeth peeped from lips parted in a snarling grin. A crown of thorns, jauntily askew, circled the forehead; bloody tears had been painted below the thing's weird white eyes. It looked like a juju fetish. On the so-called Kissing Bridge in Bassey Park, amid the declarations of school spirit and undying love, someone had carved the words I WILL KILL MY MOTHER SOON, and below it someone had added: NOT SOON ENOUGH SHES FULL OF DISEEZE. One afternoon while walking on the east side of the Barrens, I heard a terrible squealing and looked up to see the silhouette of a thin man standing on the GS & WM railroad trestle not far away. A stick rose and fell in his hand. He was beating something. The squealing stopped and I thought, *It was a dog and he's finished with it. He took it out there on a rope leash and beat it until it was dead.* There was no way I could have known such a thing, of course . . . and yet I did. I was sure then, and I am now.

Something wrong.

Something bad.

Do any of those things bear on the story I'm telling? The story of the janitor's father, and of Lee Harvey Oswald (he of the smirky little I-know-a-secret smile and gray eyes that would never quite meet yours)? I don't know for sure, but I can tell you one more thing: there was something inside that fallen chimney at the Kitchener Ironworks. I don't know what and I don't *want* to know, but at the mouth of the thing I saw a heap of gnawed bones and a tiny chewed collar with a bell on it. A collar that had surely belonged to some child's beloved kitten. And from inside the pipe—deep in that oversized bore—something moved and shuffled.

Come in and see, that something seemed to whisper in my head. *Never mind all the rest of it, Jake—come in and see. Come in and visit. Time doesn't matter in here; in here, time just floats away. You know you want to, you know you're curious. Maybe it's even another rabbit-hole. Another* portal.

Maybe it was, but I don't think so. I think it was *Derry* in there—everything that was wrong with it, everything that was askew, hiding in that pipe. Hibernating. Letting people believe the bad times were over, waiting for them to relax and forget there had ever been bad times at all.

I left in a hurry, and to that part of Derry I never went back.

3

One day in the second week of October—by then the oaks and elms on Kossuth Street were a riot of gold and red—I once more visited the defunct West Side Rec. No self-respecting real estate bounty hunter would fail to fully investigate the possibilities of such a prime site, and I asked several people on the street what it was like inside (the door was padlocked, of course) and when it had closed.

One of the people I spoke to was Doris Dunning. *Pretty as a picture,* Chaz Frati had said. A generally meaningless cliché, but true in this case. The years had put fine lines around her eyes and deeper ones at the corners of her mouth, but she had exquisite skin and a terrific full-breasted figure (in 1958, the heyday of Jayne Mansfield, full breasts are considered attractive rather than embarrassing). We spoke on the stoop. To invite me in with the house empty and the kids at school would have been improper and no doubt the subject of neighborly gossip, especially with her husband "living out." She had a dustrag in one hand and a cigarette in the other. There was a bottle of furniture polish poking out of her apron pocket. Like most folks in Derry, she was polite but distant.

Yes, she said, when it was still up and running, West Side Rec had been a fine facility for the kiddos. It was so nice to have a place like that close by where they could go after school and race around to their hearts' content. She could see the playground and the basketball court from her kitchen window, and it was very sad to see them empty. She said she thought the Rec had been closed in a round of budget cuts, but the way her eyes shifted and her mouth tucked in suggested something else to me: that it had been closed during the round of child-murders and disappearances. Budget concerns might have been secondary.

I thanked her and handed her one of my recently printed business cards. She took it, gave me a distracted smile, and closed the door. It was a gentle close, not a slam, but I heard a rattle from behind it and knew she was putting on the chain.

I thought the Rec might do for my purposes when Halloween came, although I didn't completely love it. I anticipated no problems getting inside, and one of the front windows would give me a fine view of the street. Dunning might come in his car rather than on foot, but I knew what it looked like. It would be after dark, according to Harry's essay, but there were streetlights.

Of course, that visibility thing cut both ways. Unless he was totally fixated on what he'd come to do, Dunning would almost certainly see me running at him. I had the pistol, but it was only dead accurate up to fifteen yards. I'd need to be even closer before I dared risk a shot, because on Halloween night, Kossuth Street was sure to be alive with pint-sized ghosts and goblins. Yet I couldn't wait until he actually got in the house before breaking cover, because according to the essay, Doris Dunning's estranged husband had gone to work right away. By the time Harry came out of the bathroom, all of them were down and all but Ellen were dead. If I waited, I was apt to see what Harry had seen: his mother's brains soaking into the couch.

I hadn't traveled across more than half a century to save just one of them. And so what if he saw me coming? I was the man with the gun, he was the man with the hammer—probably filched from the tool drawer at his boardinghouse. If he ran at me, that would be good. I'd be like a rodeo clown, distracting the bull. I'd caper and yell until he got in range, then put two in his chest.

Assuming I was able to pull the trigger, that was.

And assuming the gun worked. I'd test-fired it in a gravel pit on the outskirts of town, and it seemed fine . . . but the past is obdurate.

It doesn't want to change.

4

Upon further consideration, I thought there might be an even better location for my Halloween-night stakeout. I'd need a little luck, but maybe not too much. *God knows there's plenty for sale in these parts,* bartender Fred Toomey had said on my first night in Derry. My explorations had borne that out. In the wake of the murders (and the big flood of '57, don't forget that), it seemed that half the town was for sale. In a less standoffish burg, a supposed real-estate buyer like myself probably would have been given a key to the city and a wild weekend with Miss Derry by now.

One street I hadn't checked out was Wyemore Lane, a block south of Kossuth Street. That meant the Wyemore backyards would abut on Kossuth backyards. It couldn't hurt to check.

Though 206 Wyemore, the house directly behind the Dunnings', was occupied, the one next to it on the left—202—looked like an answered prayer. The gray paint was fresh and the shingles were new, but the shutters were closed up tight. On the freshly raked lawn was a yellow-and-green sign I'd seen all over town: FOR SALE BY DERRY HOME REAL ESTATE SPECIALISTS. This one invited me to call Specialist Keith Haney and discuss financing. I had no intention of doing that, but I parked my Sunliner in the newly asphalted driveway (someone was going all-out to sell this one) and walked into the backyard, head up, shoulders back, big as Billy-be-damned. I had discovered many things while exploring my new environment, and one of them was that if you acted like you belonged in a certain place, people thought you did.

The backyard was nicely mowed, the leaves raked away to showcase the velvety green. A push lawnmower had been stored under the garage overhang with a swatch of green tarpaulin tucked neatly over the rotary blades. Beside the cellar bulkhead was a doghouse with a sign on it that showed Keith Haney at his don't-miss-a-trick best: YOUR POOCH BELONGS HERE. Inside was a pile of unused leaf-bags with a garden trowel and a pair of hedge clippers to hold them down. In 2011, the tools would have been locked away; in 1958, someone had taken care to see they were out of the rain and called it good. I was sure the house was locked, but that was okay. I had no interest in breaking and entering.

At the far end of 202 Wyemore's backyard was a hedge about six feet tall. Not quite as tall as I was, in other words, and although it was luxuriant, a man could force his way through easily enough if he didn't mind a few scratches. Best of all, when I walked down to the far right corner, which was behind the garage, I was able to look on a diagonal into the backyard of the Dunning house. I saw two bicycles. One was a boy's Schwinn, leaning on its kickstand. The other, lying on its side like a dead pony, was Ellen Dunning's. There was no mistaking the training wheels.

There was also a litter of toys. One of them was Harry Dunning's Daisy air rifle.

5

If you've ever acted in an amateur stage company—or directed student theatricals, which I had several times while at LHS—you'll know what the days leading up to Halloween were like for me. At first, rehearsals have a lazy feel. There's improvisation, joking, horseplay, and a good deal of flirting as sexual polarities are established. If someone flubs a line or misses a cue in those early rehearsals, it's an occasion for laughter. If an actor shows up fifteen minutes late, he or she might get a mild reprimand, but probably nothing more.

Then opening night begins to seem like an actual possibility instead of a foolish dream. Improv falls away. So does the horseplay, and although the jokes remain, the laughter that greets them has a nervous energy that was missing before. Flubbed lines and missed cues begin to seem exasperating rather than amusing. An actor arriving late for rehearsal once the sets are up and opening night is only days away is apt to get a serious reaming from the director.

The big night comes. The actors put on their costumes and makeup. Some are outright terrified; all feel not quite prepared. Soon they will have to face a roomful of people who have come to see them strut their stuff. What seemed distant in the days of bare-stage blocking has come after all. And before the curtain goes up, some Hamlet, Willy Loman, or Blanche DuBois will have to rush into the nearest bathroom and be sick. It never fails.

Trust me on the sickness part. I know.

6

In the small hours of Halloween morning, I found myself not in Derry but on the ocean. A *stormy* ocean. I was clinging to the rail of a large vessel—a yacht, I think—that was on the verge of foundering. Rain driven by a howling gale was sheeting into my face. Huge waves, black at their bases and a curdled, foamy green on top, rushed toward me. The yacht rose, twisted, then plummeted down again with a wild corkscrewing motion.

I woke from this dream with my heart pounding and my hands still curled from trying to hold onto the rail my brain had dreamed up. Only it wasn't just my brain, because the bed was still going up and down. My stomach seemed to have come unmoored from the muscles that were supposed to hold it in place.

At such moments, the body is almost always wiser than the brain. I threw back the covers and sprinted for the bathroom, kicking over the hateful yellow chair as I sped through the kitchen. My toes would be sore later, but right then I barely felt it. I tried to lock my throat shut, but only partially succeeded. I could hear a weird sound seeping through it and into my mouth. *Ulk-ulk-urp-ulk* was what it sounded like. My stomach was the yacht, first rising and then taking those horrible corkscrew drops. I fell on my knees in front of the toilet and threw up my dinner. Next came lunch and yesterday's breakfast: oh God, ham and eggs. At the thought of all that shining grease, I retched again. There was a pause, and then what felt like everything I'd eaten for the last week left the building.

Just as I began to hope it was over, my bowels gave a terrible liquid wrench. I stumbled to my feet, batted down the toilet ring, and managed to sit before everything fell out in a watery splat.

But no. Not everything, not yet. My stomach took another giddy heave just as my bowels went to work again. There was only one thing to do, and I did it: leaned forward and vomited into the sink.

It went on like that until noon of Halloween day. By then both of my ejection-ports were producing nothing but watery gruel. Each time I threw up, each time my bowels cramped, I thought the same thing: *The past does not want to be changed. The past is obdurate.*

But when Frank Dunning arrived tonight, I meant to be there.

Even if I was still heaving and shitting graywater, I meant to be there. Even if it killed me, I meant to be there.

7

Mr. Norbert Keene, proprietor of the Center Street Drug, was behind the counter when I came in on that Friday afternoon. The wooden paddle-fan over his head lifted what remained of his hair in a wavery dance: cobwebs in a summer breeze. Just looking at that made my abused stomach give another warning lurch. He was skinny inside his white cotton smock—almost emaciated—and when he saw me coming, his pale lips creased in a smile.

"You look a little under the weather, my friend."

"Kaopectate," I said in a hoarse voice that didn't sound like my own. "Do you have it?" Wondering if it had even been invented yet.

"Are we suffering a little touch of the bug?" The overhead light caught in the lenses of his small rimless spectacles and skated around when he moved his head. *Like butter across a skillet,* I thought, and at that my stomach gave another lunge. "It's been going around town. You're in for a nasty twenty-four hours, I'm afraid. Probably a germ, but you may have used a public convenience and forgotten to wash your hands. So many people are lazy about th—"

"Do you have Kaopectate or not?"

"Of course. Second aisle."

"Continence pants—what about those?"

The thin-lipped grin spread out. Continence pants are funny, of course they are. Unless, of course, you're the one who needs them. "Fifth aisle. Although if you stay close to home, you won't need them. Based on your pallor, sir . . . and the way you're sweating . . . it might be wiser to do that."

"Thanks," I said, and imagined socking him square in the mouth and knocking his dentures down his throat. *Suck on a little Polident, pal.*

I shopped slowly, not wanting to joggle my liquefied guts any more than necessary. Got the Kaopectate (Large Economy Size? check), then the continence pants (Adult Large? check). The pants were in Ostomy Supplies, between the enema bags and brooding yellow coils of plastic hose whose function I didn't want to know about. There were also adult diapers, but at those I balked. If necessary, I would stuff the continence pants with dish towels. This struck me as funny, and despite my misery I had to struggle not to laugh. Laughing in my current delicate state might bring on disaster.

As if sensing my distress, the skeletal druggist rang up my items in slow motion. I paid him, holding out a five-dollar bill with a hand that was shaking appreciably.

"Anything else?"

"Just one thing. I'm miserable, you can see I'm miserable, so why the hell are you grinning at me?"

Mr. Keene took a step backward, the smile falling from his lips. "I assure you, I wasn't *grinning.* I certainly hope you feel better."

My bowels cramped. I staggered a little, grabbing the paper bag with my stuff inside it and holding onto the counter with my free hand. "Do you have a bathroom?"

The smile reappeared. "Not for customers, I'm afraid. Why not try one of the . . . the establishments across the street?"

"You're quite the bastard, aren't you? The perfect goddam Derry citizen."

He stiffened, then turned away and stalked into the nether regions where his pills, powders, and syrups were kept.

I walked slowly past the soda fountain and out the door. I felt like a man made of glass. The day was cool, no more than forty-five degrees, but the sun felt hot on my skin. And sticky. My bowels cramped again. I stood stock-still for a moment with my head down, one foot on the sidewalk and one in the gutter. The cramp passed. I crossed the street without looking for traffic, and someone honked at me. I restrained myself from flipping the bird at the honker, but only because I had enough trouble. I couldn't risk getting into a fight; I was in one already.

The cramp struck again, a double knife to the lower gut. I broke into a run. The Sleepy Silver Dollar was closest, so that was the door I jerked open, hustling my unhappy body into semidarkness and the yeasty smell of beer. On the jukebox, Conway Twitty was moaning that it was only make-believe. I wished he were right.

The place was empty except for one patron sitting at an empty table, looking at me with startled eyes, and the bartender leaning at the end of the stick, doing the crossword puzzle in the daily paper. He looked up at me.

"Bathroom," I said. "Quick."

He pointed to the back, and I sprinted toward the doors marked BUOYS and GULLS. I straight-armed BUOYS like a fullback looking for open field to run in. The place stank of shit, cigarette smoke, and eye-watering chlorine. The single toilet stall had no door, which was probably good. I tore my pants open like Superman late for a bank robbery, turned, and dropped.

Just in time.

When the latest throe had passed, I took the giant bottle of Kaopectate out of the paper bag and chugged three long swallows. My stomach heaved. I fought it back into place. When I was sure the first dose was going to stay down, I slugged another one, belched, and slowly screwed the cap back into place. On the wall to my left, someone had drawn a penis and testicles. The testicles were split open, and blood was gushing from them. Below this charming image, the artist had written: HENRY CASTONGUAY NEXT TIME YOU FUCK MY WIFE THIS IS WHAT YOU GET.

I closed my eyes, and when I did, I saw the startled patron who had watched my charge to the bathroom. But was he a patron? There had been nothing on his table; he had just been sitting there. With my eyes closed, I could see that face clearly. It was one I knew.

When I went back into the bar, Ferlin Husky had replaced Conway Twitty, and No Suspenders was gone. I went to the bartender and said, "There was a guy sitting over there when I came in. Who was it?"

He looked up from his puzzle. "I didn't see no one."

I took out my wallet, removed a five, and put it on the bar beside a Narragansett coaster. "The name."

He held a brief silent dialogue with himself, glanced at the tip jar beside the one holding pickled eggs, saw nothing inside but one lonely dime, and made the five disappear. "That was Bill Turcotte."

The name meant nothing to me. The empty table might mean nothing, either, but on the other hand . . .

I put Honest Abe's twin brother on the bar. "Did he come in here to watch me?" If the answer to that was yes, it meant he had been following me. Maybe not just today, either. But why?

The bartender pushed the five back. "All I know is what he usually comes in for is beer and a lot of it."

"Then why did he leave without having one?"

"Maybe he looked in his wallet and didn't see nothing but his liberry card. Do I look like fuckin Bridey Murphy? Now that you've stunk up my bathroom, why don't you either order something or leave?"

"It was stinking just fine before I got there, my friend."

Not much of an exit line, but the best I could do under the circumstances. I went out and stood on the sidewalk, looking for Turcotte. There was no sign of him, but Norbert Keene was standing in the window of his drugstore, hands clasped behind his back, watching me. His smile was gone.

8

At five-twenty that afternoon, I parked my Sunliner in the lot adjacent to the Witcham Street Baptist Church. It had plenty of company; according to the signboard, there was a 5:00 P.M. AA meeting at this particular church. In the Ford's trunk were all the possessions I'd collected during my seven weeks as a resident of what I had come to think of as the Peculiar Little City. The only indispensable items were in the Lord Buxton briefcase Al had given me: his notes, my notes, and the remaining cash. Thank God I'd kept most of it in portable form.

Beside me on the seat was a paper bag containing my bottle of Kaopectate—now three-quarters empty—and the continence pants. Thankfully, I didn't think I was going to need those. My stomach and bowels seemed to have settled, and the shakes had left my hands. There were half a dozen Payday candybars in the glove compartment lying on top of my Police Special. I added these items to the bag. Later, when I was in position between the garage and the hedge at 202 Wyemore Lane, I'd load the gun and stuff it into my belt. Like a cheap gunsel in the kind of B pictures that played The Strand.

There was one other item in the glove compartment: an issue of *TV Guide* with Fred Astaire and Barrie Chase on the cover. For probably the dozenth time since I'd bought the magazine at the newsstand on upper Main Street, I turned to the Friday listings.

8 PM, Channel 2: **The New Adventures of Ellery Queen,** George Nader, Les Tremayne. "So Rich, So Lovely, So Dead." A conniving stockbroker (Whit Bissell) stalks a wealthy heiress (Eva Gabor) as Ellery and his father investigate.

I put it into the bag with the other stuff—mostly for good luck—then got out, locked my car, and set out for Wyemore Lane. I passed a few mommies and daddies trick-or-treating with children too young to be out on their own. Carved pumpkins grinned cheerfully from many stoops, and a couple of stuffed straw-hat-wearing dummies stared at me blankly.

I walked down Wyemore Lane in the middle of the sidewalk as if I had every right to be there. When a father approached, holding the hand of a little girl wearing dangly gypsy earrings, mom's bright red lipstick, and big black plastic ears clapped over a curly-haired wig, I tipped my hat to Dad and bent down to the child, who was carrying a paper bag of her own.

"Who are *you*, honey?"

"Annette Foonijello," she said. "She's the *prettiest* Mouseketeer."

"And you're just as pretty," I told her. "Now what do you say?"

She looked puzzled, so her father leaned over and whispered in her ear. She brightened into a smile. "Trigger-treat!"

"Right," I said. "But no tricks tonight." Except for the one I hoped to play on the man with the hammer.

I took a Payday from my bag (I had to paw past the gun to get it), and held it out. She opened her bag and I dropped it in. I was just a guy on the street, a perfect stranger in a town that had been beset by terrible crimes not long ago, but I saw the same childlike trust on the faces of both father and daughter. The days of candy doctored with LSD were far in the future—as were those of DO NOT USE IF SEAL IS BROKEN.

The father whispered again.

"Thank you, mister," Annette Foonijello said.

"Very welcome." I winked to Dad. "You two have a great night."

"She'll probably have a bellyache tomorrow," Dad said, but he smiled. "Come on, Punkin."

"I'm *Annette*!" she said.

"Sorry, sorry. Come on, Annette." He gave me a grin, tipped his own hat, and they were off again, in search of plunder.

I continued on to 202, not too fast. I would have whistled if my lips hadn't been so dry. At the driveway I risked one quick look around. I saw a few trick-or-treaters on the other side of the street, but no one who was paying the slightest attention to me. Excellent. I walked briskly up the driveway. Once I was behind the house, I breathed a sigh of relief so deep it seemed to come all the way from my heels. I took up my position in the far right corner of the backyard, safely hidden between the garage and the hedge. Or so I thought.

I peered into the Dunnings' backyard. The bikes were gone. Most of the toys were still there—a child's bow and some arrows with suction-cup tips, a baseball bat with its handle wrapped in friction tape, a green Hula Hoop—but the Daisy air rifle was missing. Harry had taken it inside. He meant to bring it when he went out trick-or-treating as Buffalo Bob.

Had Tugga given him shit about that yet? Had his mother already said *you take it if you want to, it's not a real gun?* If not, they would. Their lines had already been written. My stomach cramped, this time not from the twenty-four-hour bug that was going around, but because total realization—the kind you feel in your gut—had finally arrived in all its bald-ass glory. This was actually going to happen. In fact, it was happening already. The show had started.

I glanced at my watch. It seemed to me that I'd left the car in the church parking lot an hour ago, but it was only quarter to six. In the Dunning house, the family would be sitting down to supper . . . although if I knew kids, the younger ones would be too excited to eat much, and Ellen would already be wearing her Princess Summerfall Winterspring outfit. She'd probably jumped into it as soon as she got home from school, and would be driving her mother crazy with requests to help her put on her warpaint.

I sat down with my back propped against the rear wall of the garage, rummaged in my bag, and brought out a Payday. I held it up and considered poor old J. Alfred Prufrock. I wasn't so different, although it was a candybar I wasn't sure I dared to eat. On the other hand, I had a lot to do in the next three hours or so, and my stomach was a rumbling hollow.

Fuck it, I thought, and unwrapped the candybar. It was wonderful—sweet, salty, and chewy. I gobbled most of it in two bites. I was getting ready to pop the rest of it into my mouth (and wondering why in God's name I hadn't packed a sandwich and a bottle of Coke), when I saw movement from the corner of my left eye. I started to turn, reaching into the bag for the gun at the same time, but I was too late. Something cold and sharp pricked the hollow of my left temple.

"Take your hand out of that bag."

I knew the voice at once. *Should hope to smile n kiss a pig,* its owner had said when I asked if he or any of his friends knew a fellow named Dunning. He had said Derry was full of Dunnings, and I verified that for myself not long after, but he'd had a good idea which one I was after right from the get-go, hadn't he? And this was the proof.

The point of the blade dug a little deeper, and I felt a trickle of blood run down the side of my face. It was warm against my chilly skin. Almost hot.

"Take it out *now,* chum. I think I know what's in there, and if your hand don't come out empty, your Halloween treat's gonna be eighteen inches of Jap steel. This thing's plenty sharp. It'll pop right out the other side of your head."

I took my hand out of the bag—empty—and turned to look at No Suspenders. His hair tumbled over his ears and forehead in greasy locks. His dark eyes swam in his pale, stubbly face. I felt a dismay so great it was almost despair. Almost . . . but not quite. *Even if it kills me,* I thought again. *Even if.*

"There's nothing in the bag but candybars," I said mildly. "If you want one, Mr. Turcotte, all you have to do is ask. I'll give you one."

He snatched the bag before I could reach in. He used the hand that wasn't holding the weapon, which turned out to be a bayonet. I don't know if it was Japanese or not, but from the way it gleamed in the fading dusklight, I was willing to stipulate that it was plenty sharp.

He rummaged and brought out my Police Special. "Nothing but candybars, huh? This don't look like candy to me, *Mister* Amberson."

"I need that."

"Yeah, and people in hell need icewater, but they don't get it."

"Keep your voice down," I said.

He put my gun in his belt—exactly where I had imagined I'd put it, once I'd shoved through the hedge and into the Dunning backyard—then poked the bayonet toward my eyes. It took willpower to keep from flinching back. "Don't you tell me what to—" He staggered on his feet. He rubbed first his stomach, then his chest, then the stubble-rough column of his neck, as if something were caught in there. I heard a click in his throat as he swallowed.

"Mr. Turcotte? Are you all right?"

"How do you know my name?" And then, without waiting for an answer: "It was Pete, wasn't it? The bartender in the Sleepy. He told you."

"Yes. Now I've got a question for you. How long have you been following me? And why?"

He grinned humorlessly, revealing a pair of missing teeth. "That's two questions."

"Just answer them."

"You act like"—he winced again, swallowed again, and leaned against the back wall of the garage—"like you're the one in charge."

I gauged Turcotte's pallor and distress. Mr. Keene might be a bastard with a streak of sadism, but I thought that as a diagnostician he wasn't too bad. After all, who's more apt to know what's going around than the local druggist? I was pretty sure I wasn't going to need the rest of the Kaopectate, but Bill Turcotte might. Not to mention the continence pants, once that bug really went to work.

This could be very good or very bad, I thought. But that was bullshit. There was nothing good about it.

Never mind. Keep him talking. And once the puking starts—assuming it does before he cuts my throat or shoots me with my own gun—jump him.

"Just tell me," I said. "I think I have a right to know, since I haven't done anything to you."

"It's *him* you mean to do something to, that's what I think. All that real estate stuff you've been spouting around town—so much crap. You came here looking for *him.*" He nodded in the direction of the house on the other side of the hedge. "I knew it the minute his name jumped out of your mouth."

"How could you? This town is full of Dunnings, you said so yourself."

"Yeah, but only one I care about." He raised the hand holding the bayonet and wiped sweat off his brow with his sleeve. I think

I could have taken him right then, but I was afraid the sound of a scuffle might attract attention. And if the gun went off, I'd probably be the one to take the bullet.

Also, I was curious.

"He must have done you a hell of a good turn somewhere along the way to turn you into his guardian angel," I said.

He voiced a humorless yap of a laugh. "That's a hot one, bub, but in a way it's true. I guess I am sort of his guardian angel. At least for now."

"What do you mean?"

"I mean he's mine, Amberson. That son of a bitch killed my little sister, and if anyone puts a bullet in him . . . or a blade"—he brandished the bayonet in front of his pale, grim face—"it's going to be me."

9

I stared at him with my mouth open. Somewhere in the distance there was a rattle of pops as some Halloween miscreant set off a string of firecrackers. Kids were shouting their way up and down Witcham Street. But here it was just the two of us. Christy and her fellow alcoholics called themselves the Friends of Bill; we were the Enemies of Frank. A perfect team, you would say . . . except Bill "No Suspenders" Turcotte didn't look like much of a team player.

"You . . ." I stopped and shook my head. "Tell me."

"If you're half as bright as you think you are, you should be able to put it together for yourself. Or didn't Chazzy tell you enough?"

At first that didn't compute. Then it did. The little man with the mermaid on his forearm and the cheerful chipmunk face. Only that face hadn't looked so cheerful when Frank Dunning had clapped him on the back and told him to keep his nose clean, because it was too long to get dirty. Before that, while Frank was still telling jokes at the Tracker brothers' bullshit table at the back of The Lamplighter, Chaz Frati had filled me in about Dunning's bad temper . . . which, thanks to the janitor's essay, was no news to me. *He got a girl pregnant. After a year or two, she collected the baby and scrammed.*

"Is somethin comin through on the radio waves, Commander Cody? Looks like it might be."

"Frank Dunning's first wife was your sister."

"Well there. The man says the secret woid and wins a hunnert dollars."

"Mr. Frati said she took the baby and ran out on him. Because she got enough of him turning ugly when he drank."

"Yeah, that's what he told you, and that's what most people in town believe—what Chazzy believes, for all I know—but I know better. Clara n me was always close. Growin up it was me for her and her for me. You probably don't know about a thing like that, you strike me as a mighty cold fish, but that's how it was."

I thought about that one good year I'd had with Christy—six months before the marriage and six months after. "Not that cold. I know what you're talking about."

He was rubbing at himself again, although I don't think he was aware of it: belly to chest, chest to throat, back down to the chest again. His face was paler than ever. I wondered what he'd had for lunch, but didn't think I'd have to wonder for long; soon I'd be able to see for myself.

"Yeah? Then maybe you'd think it's a little funny that she never wrote me after her n Mikey got settled somewhere. Not so much as a postcard. Me, I think it's a lot more than funny. Because she woulda. *She* knew how I felt about her. And she knew how much I loved that kiddo. She was twenty and Mikey was sixteen months old when that joke-tellin cuntwipe reported em missin. That was the summer of '38. She'd be forty now, and my nephew'd be twenty-one. Old enough to fuckin vote. And you want to tell me she'd never write a single *line* to the brother who kep Nosey Royce from stickin his wrinkled old meat inside her back when we was kids? Or to ask for a little money to help her get set up in Boston or New Haven or wherever? Mister, I would have——"

He winced, made a little *urk-ulp* sound I was very familiar with, and staggered back against the garage wall.

"You need to sit down," I said. "You're sick."

"I never get sick. I ain't even had a cold since I was in sixth grade."

If so, that bug would blitzkrieg him like the Germans rolling into Warsaw.

"It's stomach flu, Turcotte. I was up all night with it. Mr. Keene at the drugstore says it's going around."

"That narrow-ass ole lady don't know nothin. I'm fine." He gave his greasy clumps of hair a toss to show me how fine he was. His face was paler than ever. The hand holding the Japanese bayonet was shaking the way mine had until noon today. "Do you want to hear this or not?"

"Sure." I snuck a glance at my watch. It was ten past six. The time that had been dragging so slowly was now speeding up. Where was Frank Dunning right now? Still at the market? I thought not. I thought he had left early today, maybe saying he was going to take his kids trick-or-treating. Only that wasn't the plan. He was in a bar somewhere, and not The Lamplighter. That was where he went for a single beer, two at the most. Which he could handle, although—if my wife was a fair example, and I thought she was—he would always leave dry-mouthed, with his brain raging for more.

No, when he felt the need to really take a bath in the stuff, he'd want to do it in one of Derry's down-and-dirty bars: the Spoke, the Sleepy, the Bucket. Maybe even one of the absolute dives that hung over the polluted Kenduskeag—Wally's or the scabrous Paramount Lounge, where ancient whores with waxwork faces still populated most of the stools at the bar. And did he tell jokes that got the whole place laughing? Did people even approach him as he went about the job of pouring grain alcohol onto the coals of rage at the back of his brain? Not unless they wanted impromptu dental work.

"When my sister n nephew disappeared, them n Dunning was

livin in a little rented house out by the Cashman town line. He was drinkin heavy, and when he drinks heavy, he exercises his fuckin fists. I seen the bruises on her, and once Mikey was black n blue all the way up his little right arm from the wrist to the elbow. I says, 'Sis, is he beatin on you n the baby? Because if he is, I'll beat on *him.*' She says no, but she wouldn't look at me when she said it. She says, 'You stay away from him, Billy. He's strong. You are too, I know it, but you're skinny. A hard wind would blow you away. He'd hurt you.' It wasn't six months after that when she disappeared. Took off, that's what *he* said. But there's a lot of woods out that side of town. Hell, once you get into Cashman, there's nothing *but* woods. Woods n swamp. You know what really happened, don't you?"

I did. Others might not believe it because Dunning was now a well-respected citizen who seemed to have controlled his drinking a long time ago. Also because he had charm to spare. But I had inside information, didn't I?

"I think he snapped. I think he came home drunk and she said the wrong thing, maybe something completely innocuous—"

"Inocku-*what?*"

I peered through the hedge into the backyard. Beyond it, a woman passed the kitchen window and was gone. In *casa* Dunning, dinner was served. Would they be having dessert? Jell-O with Dream Whip? Ritz cracker pie? I thought not. Who needs dessert on Halloween night? "What I'm saying is that he killed them. Isn't that what you think?"

"Yeah . . ." He looked both taken aback and suspicious. I think obsessives always look that way when they hear the things that have kept them up long nights not just articulated but corroborated. *It has to be a trick,* they think. Only this was no trick. And it certainly wasn't a treat.

I said, "Dunning was what, twenty-two? Whole life ahead of him. He must have been thinking, 'Well, I did an awful thing here, but I can clean it up. We're out in the woods, nearest neighbors a mile away. . . .' *Were* they a mile away, Turcotte?"

"At least." He said it grudgingly. One hand was massaging the base of his throat. The bayonet had sagged. Grabbing it with my right hand would have been simple, and grabbing the revolver out of his belt with the other wouldn't have been out of the question, but I didn't want to. I thought the bug would take care of Mr. Bill Turcotte. I really thought it would be that simple. You see how easy it is to forget the obduracy of the past?

"So he took the bodies out in the woods and buried them and said they'd run off. There couldn't have been much of an investigation."

Turcotte turned his head and spat. "He come from a good old Derry fambly. Mine come down from the Saint John Valley in a rusty ole pickup truck when I was ten n Clara was eight. Just on parle trash. What do *you* think?"

I thought it was another case of Derry being Derry—that's what *I* thought. And while I understood Turcotte's love and sympathized with his loss, he was talking about an old crime. It was the one that was scheduled to happen in less than two hours that concerned me.

"You set me up with Frati, didn't you?" This was now obvious, but still disappointing. I'd thought the guy was just being friendly, passing on a little local gossip over beer and Lobster Pickin's. Wrong. "Pal of yours?"

Turcotte smiled, but it looked more like a grimace. "Me friends with a rich kike pawnbroker? That's a laugh. You want to hear a little story?"

I took another peek at my watch and saw I still had some time to spare. While Turcotte was talking, that old stomach virus would be hard at work. The first time he bent over to puke, I intended to pounce.

"Why not?"

"Me, Dunning, and Chaz Frati are all the same age—forty-two. You believe that?"

"Sure." But Turcotte, who had lived hard (and was now getting sick, little as he wanted to admit it), looked ten years older than either of them.

"When we was all seniors at the old Consolidated, I was assistant manager of the football team. Tiger Bill, they called me—ain't that cute? I tried out for the team when I was a freshman and then again when I was a sophomore, but I got cut both times. Too skinny for the line, too slow for the backfield. Story of my fuckin life, mister. But I loved the game, and I couldn't afford the dime to buy a ticket—my fambly didn't have *nothin*—so I took on bein assistant manager. Nice name, but do you know what it means?"

Sure I did. In my Jake Epping life, I wasn't Mr. Real Estate but Mr. High School, and some things don't change. "You were the waterboy."

"Yeah, I brought em water. And held the puke-bucket if someone got sick after runnin laps on a hot day or took a helmet in the nuts. Also the guy who stayed late to pick up all their crud on the field and fished their shit-stained jocks off the shower room floor."

He grimaced. I imagined his stomach turning into a yacht on a stormy sea. Up she goes, mateys . . . then the corkscrew plunge.

"So one day in September or October of '34, I'm out there after practice all on my lonesome, pickin up dropped pads and elastic bandages and all the other stuff they used to leave behind, puttin it all in my wheelie-basket, and what do I see but Chaz Frati tearassin across the football field, droppin his books behind him. A bunch of boys was chasin him and—*Christ,* what was that?"

He stared around, eyes bulging in his pale face. Once again I maybe could have grabbed the pistol, and the bayonet for sure, but I didn't. His hand was rubbing his chest again. Not his stomach, but his chest. That probably should have told me something, but I had too much on my mind. His story was not the least of it. That's the curse of the reading class. We can be seduced by a good story even at the least opportune moments.

"Relax, Turcotte. It's just kids shooting off firecrackers. Halloween, remember?"

"I don't feel so good. Maybe you're right about that bug."

If he thought he might be getting sick enough to be incapacitated, he might do something rash. "Never mind the bug just now. Tell me about Frati."

He grinned. It was an unsettling expression on that pale, sweaty, stubbly face. "Ole Chazzy ran like hell, but they caught up with him. There was a ravine about twenty yards past the goalposts at the south end of the field, and they pushed him down into it. Would you be s'prized to know that Frankie Dunning was one of em?"

I shook my head.

"They got him down in there, and they pantsed him. Then they started pushin him around and takin smacks at him. I yelled for em to quit it, and one of em looks up at me and yells, 'Come on down and make us, fuckface. We'll give you double what we're givin him.' So I ran for the locker room and told some of the football players that a bunch of yeggs were bullyin up on a kid and maybe they wanted to put a stop to it. Well, they didn't give a shit about who was gettin bullied and who wasn't, but those guys were always up for a fight. They run on out, some of em not wearin nothin but their underwear. And you want to know somethin really funny, Amberson?"

"Sure." I took another quick glance at my watch. Almost quarter of seven now. In the Dunning house, Doris would be doing the dishes and maybe listening to Huntley-Brinkley on the television.

"You late for somethin?" Turcotte asked. "Got a fuckin train to catch?"

"You were going to tell me something funny."

"Oh. Yeah. They was singin the school song! How do you like that?"

In my mind's eye I could see eight or ten beefy half-dressed boys churning across the field, eager to do a little post-practice hitting, and singing *Hail Derry Tigers, we hold your banner high.* It *was* sort of funny.

Turcotte saw my grin and answered with one of his own. It was strained but genuine. "The footballies baffed a couple of those guys around pretty good. Not Frankie Dunning, though; that yellabelly saw they was gonna be outnumbered and run into the woods. Chazzy was layin on the ground, holdin his arm. It was broke. Could have been a lot worse, though. They woulda put him in the hospital. One of the footballies looks at him layin there and kinda toes at him—the way you might toe a cow patty you almost stepped in—and he says, 'We ran all the way out here to save a jewboy's bacon?' And a bunch of em laughed, because it was kind of a joke, you see. Jewboy? Bacon?" He peered at me through clumps of his Brylcreem-shiny hair.

"I get it," I said.

"'Aw, who gives a fuck,' another of em says. 'I got to kick some ass and that's good enough for me.' They went on back, and I helped ole Chaz up the ravine. I even walked home with im, because I thought he might faint or somethin. I was scared Frankie and his friends might come back—he was, too—but I stuck with him. Fuck if I know just why. You should have seen the house he lived in—a fuckin palace. That hockshop business must really pay. When we got there, he thanked me. Meant it, too. He was just about bawlin. I says, 'Don't mention it, I just didn't like seeing six-on-one.' Which was true. But you know what they say about Jews: they never forget a debt or a favor."

"Which you called in to find out what I was doing."

"I had a pretty good idea what you were doin, chum. I just wanted to make sure. Chaz told me to leave it alone—he said he thought you were a nice guy—but when it comes to Frankie Dunning, I don't leave it alone. Nobody messes with Frankie Dunning but me. He's *mine*."

He winced and went back to rubbing his chest. And this time the penny dropped.

"Turcotte—*is* it your stomach?"

"Naw, chest. Feels all tight."

That didn't sound good, and the thought that went through my mind was *now he's in the nylon stocking, too.*

"Sit down before you fall down." I started toward him. He pulled the gun. The skin between my nipples—where the bullet would go—began to itch madly. *I could have disarmed him,* I thought. *I really could have. But no, I had to hear the story. I had to know.*

"*You* sit down, brother. Unlax, as they say in the funnypages."

"If you're having a heart attack—"

"I ain't havin no fuckin heart attack. Now sit *down*."

I sat and looked up at him as he leaned against the garage. His lips had gone a bluish shade I did not associate with good health.

"What do you want with him?" Turcotte asked. "That's what I want to know. That's what I *got* to know, before I can decide what to do with you."

I thought carefully about how to answer this. As if my life depended on it. Maybe it did. I didn't think Turcotte had outright murder in him, no matter what *he* thought, or Frank Dunning would have been planted next to his parents a long time ago. But Turcotte had my gun, and he was a sick man. He might pull the trigger by accident. Whatever force there was that wanted things to stay the same might even help him do it.

If I told him just the right way—leaving out the crazy stuff, in other words—he might believe it. Because of what he believed already. What he knew in his heart.

"He's going to do it again."

He started to ask what I meant, then didn't have to. His eyes widened. "You mean . . . her?" He looked toward the hedge. Until then, I hadn't even been sure he knew what was beyond it.

"Not just her."

"One of the kids, too?"

"Not one, *all*. He's out drinking right now, Turcotte. Working himself into another of his blind rages. You know all about those, don't you? Only this time there won't be any covering up afterward. He doesn't care, either. This has been building ever since his last binge, when Doris finally got tired of being knocked around. She showed him the door, did you know that?"

"Everybody knows. He's livin in a roomin house over on Charity."

"He's been trying to get back into her good graces, but the

charming act doesn't work on her anymore. She wants a divorce, and since he finally understands he can't talk her out of it, he's going to give her one with a hammer. Then he's going to divorce his kids the same way."

He frowned at me. Bayonet in one hand, gun in the other. *A hard wind would blow you away,* his sister had told him all those years ago, but I didn't think it would take much more than a breeze tonight. "How could you know that?"

"I don't have time to explain, but I know, all right. I'm here to stop it. So give me back my gun and let me do it. For your sister. For your nephew. And because I think down deep, you're a pretty nice guy." This was bullshit, but if you're going to lay it on, my father used to say, you might as well lay it on thick. "Why else would you have stopped Dunning and his friends from beating Chaz Frati half to death?"

He was thinking. I could almost hear the wheels turning and the cogs clicking. Then a light went on in his eyes. Perhaps it was only the last remains of the sunset, but to me it looked like the candles that would now be flickering inside of jack-o'-lanterns all over town. He began to smile. What he said next could only have come from a man who was mentally ill . . . or who had lived too long in Derry . . . or both.

"Gonna go after em, is he? Okay, let im."

"What?"

He pointed the .38 at me. "Sit back down, Amberson. Take a load off."

I reluctantly settled back. It was now past 7:00 P.M. and he was turning into a shadow-man. "Mr. Turcotte—Bill—I know you don't feel good, so maybe you don't fully understand the situation. There's a woman and four little kids in there. The little girl is only seven, for God's sake."

"My nephew was a lot younger'n that." Turcotte spoke weightily, a man articulating a great truth that explains everything. And justifies it, as well. "I'm too sick to take im on, and you ain't got the guts. I can see that just lookin at you."

I thought he was wrong about that. He might have been right about Jake Epping of Lisbon Falls, but that fellow had changed. "Why not let me try? What harm to you?"

"Because even if you killed his ass, it wouldn't be enough. I just figured that out. It come to me like—" He snapped his fingers. "Like out of thin air."

"You're not making sense."

"That's because you ain't had twenty years of seeing men like Tony and Phil Tracker treat him like King Shit. Twenty years of seeing women bat their eyes at him like he was Frank Sinatra. He's been drivin a Pontiac while I worked my ass off in about six different mills for minimum wage, suckin fabric fibers down my throat until I can't hardly get up in the morning." Hand at his chest. Rubbing and rubbing. His face a pale smear in the back-yard gloom of 202 Wyemore. "Killin's too good for that cuntwipe. What he needs is forty years or so in the Shank, where if he drops the soap in the shower, he won't fuckin dare to bend over and pick it up. Where the only booze he gets'll be prune squeeze." His voice dropped. "And you know what else?"

"What?" I felt cold all over.

"When he sobers up, he'll miss em. He'll be sorry he did it. He'll wish he could take it back." Now almost whispering—a hoarse and phlegmy sound. It's how the irretrievably mad must talk to themselves late at night in places like Juniper Hill, when their meds wear off. "Maybe he wun't regret the wife s'much, but the kiddies, sure." He laughed, then grimaced as if it hurt him. "You're probably fulla shit, but you know what? I hope you're not. We'll wait and see."

"Turcotte, those kids are innocent."

"So was Clara. So was little Mikey." His shadow-shoulders went up and down in a shrug. "Fuck em."

"You don't mean th—"

"Shut up. We'll wait."

10

There were glow-in-the-dark hands on the watch Al had given me, and I watched with horror and resignation as the long hand moved down toward the bottom of the dial, then started up once more. Twenty-five minutes until the start of *The New Adventures of Ellery Queen*. Then twenty. Then fifteen. I tried to talk to him and he told me to shut up. He kept rubbing his chest, only stopping long enough to take his cigarettes from his breast pocket.

"Oh, that's a good idea," I said. "That'll help your heart a lot."

"Put a sock in it."

He stuck the bayonet in the gravel behind the garage and lit his cigarette with a battered Zippo. In the momentary flicker of flame, I saw sweat running down his cheeks, even though the night was chilly. His eyes seemed to have receded into their sockets, making his face look like a skull. He sucked in smoke, coughed it out. His thin body shook, but the gun remained steady. Pointed at my chest. Overhead, the stars were out. It was now ten of eight. How far along had *Ellery Queen* been when Dunning arrived? Harry's theme hadn't said, but I was guessing not long. There was no school tomorrow, but Doris Dunning still wouldn't want seven-year-old Ellen out much later than ten, even if she was with Tugga and Harry.

Five minutes of eight.

And suddenly an idea occurred to me. It had the clarity of undisputed truth, and I spoke while it was still bright.

"You chickenshit."

"*What?*" He straightened as if he'd been goosed.

"You heard me." I mimicked him. " 'Nobody messes with Frankie Dunning but me. He's *mine*.' You've been telling yourself that for twenty years, haven't you? And you haven't messed with him yet."

"I told you to shut up."

"Hell, twenty-two! You didn't mess with him when he went

after Chaz Frati, either, did you? You ran away like a little girl and got the football players."

"There was six of em!"

"Sure, but Dunning's been on his own plenty of times since, and you haven't even put a banana peel down on the sidewalk and hoped he'd slip on it. You're a chickenshit coward, Turcotte. Hiding over here like a rabbit in a hole."

"Shut up!"

"Telling yourself some bullshit about how seeing him in prison would be the best revenge, so you don't have to face the fact—"

"Shut up!"

"—that you're a nutless wonder who's let his sister's murderer walk around free for over twenty years—"

"I'm warning you!" He cocked the revolver's hammer.

I thumped the middle of my chest. "Go on. Do it. Everybody'll hear the shot, the police will come, Dunning'll see the ruckus and turn right around, and *you'll* be the one in Shawshank. I bet they got a mill there, too. You can work in it for a nickel an hour instead of a buck-twenty. Only you'll *like* that, because you won't have to try and explain to yourself why you just stood by all those years. If your sister was alive, she'd *spit* on y—"

He thrust the gun forward, meaning to press the muzzle against my chest, and stumbled on his own damn bayonet. I batted the pistol aside with the back of my hand and it went off. The bullet must have gone into the ground less than an inch from my leg, because a little spray of stones struck my pants. I grabbed the gun and pointed it at him, ready to shoot if he made the slightest move to grab the fallen bayonet.

What he did was slump against the garage wall. Now both hands were plastered over the left side of his chest, and he was making a low gagging sound.

Somewhere not too far away—on Kossuth, not Wyemore—a man bellowed: "Fun's fun, you kids, but one more cherry bomb and I'm calling the cops! A word to the wise!"

I let out my breath. Turcotte was letting his out as well, but in hitching gasps. The gagging sounds continued as he slid down the side of the garage and sprawled on the gravel. I took the bayonet, considered putting it in my belt, and decided I'd only gash my leg with it when I pushed through the hedge: the past hard at work, trying to stop me. I hucked it into the dark yard instead, and heard a low clunk as it hit something. Maybe the side of the YOUR POOCH BELONGS HERE doghouse.

"Ambulance," Turcotte croaked. His eyes gleamed with what might have been tears. "Please, Amberson. Hurts bad."

Ambulance. Good idea. And here's something hilarious. I'd been in Derry—in *1958*—for almost two months, but I still plunged my hand into my right front pants pocket, where I always kept my cell phone when I wasn't wearing a sport coat. My fingers found nothing there but some change and the keys to the Sunliner.

"Sorry, Turcotte. You were born in the wrong era for instant rescue."

"What?"

According to the Bulova, *The New Adventures of Ellery Queen* was now being telecast to a waiting America. "Tough it out," I said, and shoved through the hedge, the hand not holding the gun raised to protect my eyes from the stiff, raking branches.

11

I tripped over the sandbox in the middle of the Dunning backyard, fell full length, and found myself face-to-face with a blank-eyed doll wearing a tiara and nothing else. The revolver flew out of my hand. I went searching for it on my hands and knees, thinking I would never find it; this was the obdurate past's final trick. A small one, compared to raging stomach flu and Bill Turcotte, but a good one. Then, just as I spotted it lying at the edge of a trapezoidal length of light thrown by the kitchen window, I heard a car coming down Kossuth Street. It was moving far faster than any reasonable driver would have dared to travel on a street that was no doubt full of children wearing masks and carrying trick-or-treat bags. I knew who it was even before it screeched to a stop.

Inside 379, Doris Dunning was sitting on the couch with Troy while Ellen pranced around in her Indian princess costume, wild to get going. Troy had just told her that he would help eat the candy when she, Tugga, and Harry came back. Ellen was replying, "No, you won't, dress up and get your own." Everybody would laugh at that, even Harry, who was in the bathroom taking a last-minute whiz. Because Ellen was a real Lucille Ball who could make anybody laugh.

I snatched at the gun. It slipped through my sweat-slick fingers and landed in the grass again. My shin was howling where I'd barked it on the side of the sandbox. On the other side of the house, a car door slammed and rapid footsteps rattled on concrete. I remember thinking, *Bar the door, Mom, that's not just your bad-tempered husband; that's Derry itself coming up the walk.*

I grabbed the gun, staggered upright, stumbled over my own stupid feet, almost went down again, found my balance, and ran for the back door. The cellar bulkhead was in my path. I detoured around it, convinced that if I put my weight on it, it would give way. The air itself seemed to have turned syrupy, as if it were also trying to slow me down.

Even if it kills me, I thought. *Even if it kills me and Oswald goes through with it and millions die. Even then. Because this is* now. *This is* them.

The back door would be locked. I was so sure of this that I almost tumbled off the stoop when the knob turned and it swung outward. I stepped into a kitchen that still smelled of the pot roast Mrs. Dunning had cooked in her Hotpoint. The sink was stacked with dishes. There was a gravy boat on the counter; beside it, a platter of cold noodles. From the TV came a trembling violin soundtrack—what Christy used to call "murder music." Very fitting. Lying on the counter was the rubber Frankenstein mask

STEPHEN KING

Tugga meant to wear when he went out trick-or-treating. Next to it was a paper swag-bag with **TUGGA'S CANDY DO NOT TOUCH** printed on the side in black crayon.

In his theme, Harry had quoted his mother as saying, "Get out of here with that thing, you're not suppose to be here." What I heard her actually say as I ran across the linoleum toward the arch between the kitchen and the living room was, "Frank? What are you doing here?" Her voice began to rise. "What's that? Why have you . . . *get out of here!*"

Then she screamed.

12

As I came through the arch, a child said: "Who are you? Why is my mom yelling? Is my daddy here?"

I turned my head and saw ten-year-old Harry Dunning standing in the door of a small water closet in the far corner of the kitchen. He was dressed in buckskin and carrying his air rifle in one hand. With the other he was pulling at his fly. Then Doris Dunning screamed again. The other two boys were yelling. There was a thud—a heavy, sickening sound—and the scream was cut off.

"No, Daddy, don't, you're HURRRTING her!" Ellen shrieked.

I ran through the arch and stopped there with my mouth open. Based on Harry's theme, I had always assumed that I'd have to stop a man swinging the sort of hammer guys kept in their toolboxes. That wasn't what he had. What he had was a sledgehammer with a twenty-pound head, and he was handling it as if it were a toy. His sleeves were rolled up, and I could see the bulge of muscles that had been built up by twenty years of cutting meat and toting carcasses. Doris was on the living room rug. He had already broken her arm—the bone was sticking out through a rip in the sleeve of her dress—and dislocated her shoulder as well, from the look. Her face was pale and dazed. She was crawling across the rug in front of the TV with her hair hanging in her face. Dunning was slinging

210

back the hammer. This time he'd connect with her head, crushing her skull and sending her brains flying onto the couch cushions.

Ellen was a little dervish, trying to push him back out the door. *"Stop, Daddy, stop!"*

He grabbed her by her hair and heaved her. She went reeling, feathers flying out of her headdress. She struck the rocking chair and knocked it over.

"Dunning!" I shouted. *"Stop it!"*

He looked at me with red, streaming eyes. He was drunk. He was crying. Snot hung from his nostrils and spit slicked his chin. His face was a cramp of rage, woe, and bewilderment.

"Who the fuck're you?" he asked, then charged at me without waiting for an answer.

I pulled the trigger of the revolver, thinking, *This time it won't fire, it's a Derry gun and it won't fire.*

But it did. The bullet took him in the shoulder. A red rose bloomed on his white shirt. He twisted sideways with the impact, then came on again. He raised the sledge. The bloom on his shirt spread, but he didn't seem to feel it.

I pulled the trigger again, but someone jostled me just as I did, and the bullet went high and wild. It was Harry. *"Stop it, Daddy!"* His voice was shrill. *"Stop or I'll shoot you!"*

Arthur "Tugga" Dunning was crawling toward me, toward the kitchen. Just as Harry fired his air rifle—*ka-chow!*—Dunning brought the sledge down on Tugga's head. The boy's face was obliterated in a sheet of blood. Bone fragments and clumps of hair leaped high in the air; droplets of blood spattered the overhead light fixture. Ellen and Mrs. Dunning were shrieking, shrieking.

I caught my balance and fired a third time. This one tore off Dunning's right cheek all the way up to the ear, but it still didn't stop him. *He's not human* is what I thought then, and what I still think now. All I saw in his gushing eyes and gnashing mouth—he seemed to be chewing the air rather than breathing it—was a kind of blabbering emptiness.

"Who the fuck're you?" he repeated, then: "You're trespassing."

He slung the sledge back and brought it around in a whistling horizontal arc. I bent at the knees, ducking as I did it, and
although the twenty-pound head seemed to miss me entirely—I
felt no pain, not then—a wave of heat flashed across the top of my
head. The gun flew out of my hand, struck the wall, and bounced
into the corner. Something warm was running down the side of my
face. Did I understand he'd clipped me just enough to tear a six-
inch-long gash in my scalp? That he'd missed either knocking me
unconscious or outright killing me by maybe as little as an eighth
of an inch? I can't say. All of this happened in less than a minute;
maybe it was only thirty seconds. Life turns on a dime, and when
it does, it turns fast.

"Get out!" I shouted at Troy. *"Take your sister and get out! Yell for
help! Yell your head o—"*

Dunning swung the sledge. I jumped back, and the head buried itself in the wall, smashing laths and sending a puff of plaster
into the air to join the gunsmoke. The TV was still playing. Still
violins, still murder music.

As Dunning struggled to pull his sledge out of the wall, something flew past me. It was the Daisy air rifle. Harry had thrown it.
The barrel struck Frank Dunning in his torn-open cheek and he
screamed with pain.

"You little bastard! I'll kill you for that!"

Troy was carrying Ellen to the door. *So that's all right,* I thought,
I changed things at least that much—

But before he could get her out, someone first filled the door
and then came stumbling in, knocking Troy Dunning and the
little girl to the floor. I barely had time to see this, because Frank
had pulled the sledge free and was coming for me. I backed up,
shoving Harry into the kitchen with one hand.

"Out the back door, son. Fast. I'll hold him off until you—"

Frank Dunning shrieked and stiffened. All at once something
was poking out through his chest. It was like a magic trick. The
thing was so coated with blood it took a second for me to realize
what it was: the point of a bayonet.

"That's for my sister, you fuck," Bill Turcotte rasped. "That's for Clara."

13

Dunning went down, feet in the living room, head in the arch-way between the living room and the kitchen. But not all the way down. The tip of the blade dug into the floor and held him up. One of his feet kicked a single time, then he was still. He looked like he'd died trying to do a push-up.

Everyone was screaming. The air stank of gunsmoke, plaster, and blood. Doris was lurching crookedly toward her dead son with her hair hanging in her face. I didn't want her to see that—Tugga's head had been split open all the way down to the jaw—but there was no way I could stop her.

"I'll do better next time, Mrs. Dunning," I croaked. "That's a promise."

There was blood all over my face; I had to wipe it out of my left eye in order to see on that side. Since I was still conscious, I thought I wasn't hurt too badly, and I knew that scalp wounds bleed like a bitch. But I was a mess, and if there was ever going to be a next time, I had to get out of here this time, unseen and in a hurry.

But I had to talk to Turcotte before I left. Or at least try. He had collapsed against the wall by Dunning's splayed feet. He was holding his chest and gasping. His face was corpse-white except for his lips, now as purple as those of a kid who has been gobbling huckleberries. I reached for his hand. He grasped it with panicky tightness, but there was a tiny glint of humor in his eyes.

"Who's the chickenshit now, Amberson?"

"Not you," I said. "You're a hero."

"Yeah," he wheezed. "Just toss the fuckin medal in my coffin."

Doris was cradling her dead son. Behind her, Troy was walk-ing in circles with Ellen's head pressed tight against his chest. He didn't look toward us, didn't seem to realize we were there. The little girl was wailing.

"You'll be okay," I said. As if I knew. "Now listen, because this is important: forget my name."

"What name? You never gave it."

"Right. And . . . you know my car?"

"Ford." He was losing his voice, but his eyes were still fixed on mine. "Nice one. Convert. Y-block engine. Fifty-four or—five."

"You never saw it. That's the most important thing of all, Turcotte. I need it to get downstate tonight and I'll have to take the turnpike most of the way because I don't know any of the other roads. If I can get down to central Maine, I'll be free and clear. Do you understand what I'm telling you?"

"Never saw your car," he said, then winced. "Ah, fuck, don't that *hurt.*"

I put my fingers on his stubble-prickly throat and felt his pulse. It was rapid and wildly uneven. In the distance I could hear wailing sirens. "You did the right thing."

His eyes rolled. "Almost didn't. I don't know what I was thinkin of. I must have been crazy. Listen, buddy. If they do run you down, don't tell em what I . . . you know, what I—"

"I never would. You took care of him, Turcotte. He was a mad dog and you put him down. Your sister would be proud."

He smiled and closed his eyes.

14

I went into the bathroom, grabbed a towel, soaked it in the basin, and scrubbed my bloody face. I tossed the towel in the tub, grabbed two more, and stepped out into the kitchen.

The boy who had brought me here was standing on the faded linoleum by the stove and watching me. Although it had probably been six years since he'd sucked his thumb, he was sucking it now.

His eyes were wide and solemn, swimming with tears. Freckles of blood spattered his cheeks and brow. Here was a boy who had just experienced something that would no doubt traumatize him, but he was also a boy who would never grow up to become Hoptoad Harry. Or to write a theme that would make me cry.

"Who are you, mister?" he asked.

"Nobody." I walked past him to the door. He deserved more than that, though. The sirens were closer now, but I turned back. "Your good angel," I said. Then I slipped out the back door and into Halloween night of 1958.

15

I walked up Wyemore to Witcham, saw flashing blue lights heading for Kossuth Street, and kept on walking. Two blocks further into the residential district, I turned right on Gerard Avenue. People were standing out on the sidewalks, turned toward the sound of the sirens.

"Mister, do you know what happened?" a man asked me. He was holding the hand of a sneaker-wearing Snow White.

"I heard kids setting off cherry bombs," I said. "Maybe they started a fire." I kept walking and made sure to keep the left side of my face away from him, because there was a streetlight nearby and my scalp was still oozing blood.

Four blocks down, I turned back toward Witcham. This far south of Kossuth, Witcham Street was dark and quiet. All the available police cars were probably now at the scene. Good. I had almost reached the corner of Grove and Witcham when my knees turned to rubber. I looked around, saw no trick-or-treaters, and sat down on the curb. I couldn't afford to stop, but I had to. I'd thrown up everything in my stomach, I hadn't had anything to eat all day except for one lousy candybar (and couldn't remember if I'd even managed to get all of that down before Turcotte jumped me), and I'd just been through a violent interlude in which I had been wounded—how badly I still didn't know. It was either stop now and let my body regroup or pass out on the sidewalk.

I put my head between my knees and drew a series of deep slow breaths, as I'd learned in the Red Cross course I'd taken to get a lifeguard certification back in college. At first I kept seeing Tugga Dunning's head as it exploded under the smashing downward force of the hammer, and that made the faintness worse. Then I thought of Harry, who had been splashed with his brother's blood but was otherwise unhurt. And Ellen, who wasn't deep in a coma from which she would never emerge. And Troy. And Doris. Her badly broken arm might hurt her for the rest of her life, but at least she was going to *have* a life.

"I did it, Al," I whispered.

But what had I done in 2011? What had I done *to* 2011? Those were questions that still had to be answered. If something terrible had happened because of the butterfly effect, I could always go back and erase it . . . unless, in changing the course of the Dunning family's lives, I had somehow changed the course of Al Templeton's as well. Suppose the diner was no longer where I'd left it? Suppose it turned out he'd never moved it from Auburn? Or never opened a diner at all? It didn't seem likely . . . but here I was, sitting on a 1958 curb with blood oozing out of my 1958 haircut, and how likely was *that*?

I rose to my feet, staggered, then got moving. To my right, down Witcham Street, I could see the flash and strobe of blue lights. A crowd had gathered on the corner of Kossuth, but their backs were to me. The church where I'd left my car was just across the street. The Sunliner was alone in the parking lot now, but it looked okay; no Halloween pranksters had let the air out of my tires. Then I saw a yellow square under one of the windshield wipers. My thoughts flashed to the Yellow Card Man, and my gut tightened. I snatched it, then exhaled a sigh of relief when I read what was written there: JOIN YOUR FRIENDS AND NEIGHBORS FOR WORSHIP THIS SUNDAY AT 9 AM NEWCOMERS ALWAYS

WELCOME! REMEMBER, "LIFE IS THE QUESTION, JESUS IS THE ANSWER."

"I thought hard drugs were the answer, and I could sure use some right now," I muttered, and unlocked the driver's door. I thought of the paper bag I'd left behind the garage of the house on Wyemore Lane. The cops investigating the area were apt to discover it. Inside they'd find a few candybars, a mostly empty bottle of Kaopectate . . . and a stack of what amounted to adult diapers.

I wondered what they'd make of that.

But not too much.

16

By the time I reached the turnpike, my head was aching fiercely, but even if this hadn't been before the era of twenty-four-hour convenience stores, I'm not sure I would have dared to stop; my shirt was stiff with drying blood on the lefthand side. At least I'd remembered to fill the gas tank.

Once I tried exploring the gash on my head with the tips of my fingers and was rewarded with a blaze of pain that persuaded me not to make a second attempt.

I did stop at the rest area outside of Augusta. By then it was past ten o'clock and the place was deserted. I turned on the dome light and checked my pupils in the rearview mirror. They looked the same size, which was a relief. There was a snacks vending machine outside the men's privy, where ten cents bought me a cream-stuffed chocolate whoopie pie. I gobbled it as I drove, and my headache abated somewhat.

It was after midnight when I got to Lisbon Falls. Main Street was dark, but both the Worumbo and U.S. Gypsum mills were running full tilt, huffing and chuffing, throwing their stinks into the air and spilling their acid wastes into the river. The clusters of shining lights made them look like spaceships. I parked the Sunliner outside the Kennebec Fruit, where it would stay until someone peeked inside and saw the spots of blood on the seat, driver's door, and steering wheel. Then the police would be called. I supposed they'd dust the Ford for fingerprints. It was possible they'd match prints found on a certain .38 Police Special at a murder scene in Derry. The name George Amberson might emerge in Derry and then down here in the Falls. But if the rabbit-hole was still where I'd left it, George was going to leave no trail to follow, and the fingerprints belonged to a man who wasn't going to be born for another eighteen years.

I opened the trunk, took out the briefcase, and decided to leave everything else. For all I knew, it might end up being sold at the Jolly White Elephant, the secondhand store not far from Titus Chevron. I crossed the street toward the mill's dragon-breath, a *shat-HOOSH, shat-HOOSH* that would continue around the clock until Reagan-era free trade rendered pricey American textiles obsolete.

The drying shed was lit by a white fluorescent glow from the dirty dyehouse windows. I spotted the chain blocking off the drying shed from the rest of the courtyard. It was too dark to read the sign hanging from it, and it had been almost two months since I'd seen it, but I remembered what it said: **NO ADMITTANCE BEYOND THIS POINT UNTIL SEWER PIPE IS REPAIRED**. There was no sign of the Yellow Card Man—or the Orange Card Man, if that's what he was now.

Headlights flooded the courtyard, illuminating me like an ant on a plate. My shadow jumped out long and scrawny in front of me. I froze as a big transport truck trundled toward me. I expected the driver to stop, lean out, and ask me what the hell I was doing here. He slowed but didn't stop. Raised a hand to me. I raised mine in return, and he drove on toward the loading docks with dozens of empty barrels clunking around in back. I headed for the chain, took one quick look around, and ducked under it.

I walked down the flank of the drying shed, heart beating hard in my chest. The gash on my head pounded in harmony. This time there was no chunk of concrete to mark the spot. *Slow,* I told myself. *Slow.* The step is right . . . *here.*

Only it wasn't. There was nothing but the pavement under my testing, tapping shoe.

I went a little farther, and there was still nothing. It was cold enough to see a thin vapor when I exhaled, but a light, greasy sweat had broken out on my arms and neck. I went a little farther, but was now almost sure I had gone too far. Either the rabbit-hole was gone or it had never been there in the first place, which meant that my whole life as Jake Epping—everything from my prize-winning FFA garden in grammar school to my abandoned novel in college to my marriage to a basically sweet woman who'd almost drowned my love for her in alcohol—had been a crazy hallucination. I'd been George Amberson all along.

I went a little farther, then stopped, breathing hard. Somewhere—maybe in the dyehouse, maybe in one of the weaving rooms—someone shouted *"Fuck me sideways!"* I jumped, then jumped again at the bull roar of laughter that followed the exclamation.

Not here.

Gone.

Or never was.

And did I feel disappointment? Terror? Outright panic? None of those, actually. What I felt was a sneaking sense of relief. What I thought was, *I could live here. And quite easily. Happily, even.*

Was that true? Yes. *Yes.*

It stank near the mills and on public conveyances where everybody smoked their heads off, but in most places the air smelled incredibly sweet. Incredibly *new.* Food tasted good; milk was delivered directly to your door. After a period of withdrawal from my computer, I'd gained enough perspective to realize just how addicted to that fucking thing I'd become, spending hours reading stupid email attachments and visiting websites for the same reason mountaineers wanted to climb Everest: because they were there. My cell phone never rang because I *had* no cell phone, and what a relief that had been. Outside of the big cities, most folks were still on party lines, and did the majority lock their doors at night? Balls they did. They worried about nuclear war, but I was safe in the knowledge that the people of 1958 would grow old and die without ever hearing of an A-bomb being exploded in anything but a test. No one worried about global warming or suicide bombers flying hijacked jets into skyscrapers.

And if my 2011 life *wasn't* a hallucination (in my heart I knew this), I could still stop Oswald. I just wouldn't know the ultimate result. I thought I could live with that.

Okay. The first thing to do was to return to the Sunliner and get out of Lisbon Falls. I'd drive to Lewiston, find the bus station, and buy a ticket to New York. I'd take a train to Dallas from there . . . or hell, why not fly? I still had plenty of cash, and no airline clerk was going to demand a picture ID. All I had to do was fork over the price of a ticket and Trans World Airlines would welcome me aboard.

The relief of this decision was so great that my legs again went rubbery. The weakness wasn't as bad as it had been in Derry, when I'd had to sit down, but I leaned against the drying shed for support. My elbow struck it, making a soft *bong* sound. And a voice spoke to me out of thin air. Hoarse. Almost a growl. A voice from the future, as it were.

"Jake? Is that you?" This was followed by a fusillade of dry, barking coughs.

I almost kept silent. I *could* have kept silent. Then I thought of how much of his life Al had invested in this project, and how I was now the only thing he had left to hope for.

I turned toward the sound of those coughs and spoke in a low voice. "Al? Talk to me. Count off." I could have added, *Or just keep coughing.*

He began to count. I went toward the sound of the numbers, feeling with my foot. After ten steps—far beyond the place where I had given up—the toe of my shoe simultaneously took a step forward and struck something that stopped it cold. I took one more look around. Took one more breath of the chemical-stenchy air. Then I closed my eyes and started climbing steps I couldn't see.

On the fourth one, the chilly night air was replaced with stuffy warmth and the smells of coffee and spices. At least that was the case with my top half. Below the waist, I could still feel the night.

I stood there for maybe three seconds, half in the present and half in the past. Then I opened my eyes, saw Al's haggard, anxious, too-thin face, and stepped back into 2011.

PART 3

LIVING IN THE PAST

CHAPTER 9

1

I would have said I was beyond surprise by then, but what I saw just to Al's left dropped my jaw: a cigarette smoldering in an ashtray. I reached past him and stubbed it out. "Do you want to cough up whatever working lung tissue you've got left?"

He didn't respond to that. I'm not sure he even heard it. He was staring at me, wide-eyed. "Jesus God, Jake—who scalped you?"

"No one. Let's get out of here before I strangle on your second-hand smoke." But that was empty scolding. During the weeks I'd spent in Derry, I'd gotten used to the smell of burning cigarettes. Soon I'd be picking up the habit myself, if I didn't watch out.

"You *are* scalped," he said. "You just don't know it. There's a piece of your hair hanging down behind your ear, and . . . how much did you bleed, anyway? A quart? And who did it to you?"

"A, less than a quart. B, Frank Dunning. If that takes care of your questions, now *I've* got one. You said you were going to pray. Why were you smoking instead?"

"Because I was nervous. And because it doesn't matter now. The horse is out of the barn."

I could hardly argue on that score.

2

Al made his way slowly behind the counter, where he opened a cabinet and took out a plastic box with a red cross on it. I sat on one of the stools and looked at the clock. It had been quarter to eight when Al unlocked the door and led us into the diner. Probably five of when I went down the rabbit-hole and emerged in Wonderland circa 1958. Al claimed every trip took exactly two minutes, and the clock on the wall seemed to bear that out. I'd spent fifty-two days in 1958, but here it was 7:59 in the morning.

Al was assembling gauze, tape, disinfectant. "Bend down here so I can see it," he said. "Put your chin right on the counter."

"You can skip the hydrogen peroxide. It happened four hours ago, and it's clotted. See?"

"Better safe than sorry," he said, then set the top of my head on fire. *"Ahhh!"*

"Hurts, don't it? Because it's still open. You want some 1958 sawbones treating you for an infected scalp before you head down to Big D? Believe me, buddy, you don't. Hold still. I have to snip some hair or the tape won't hold. Thank God you kept it short."

Clip-clip-clip. Then he added to the pain—insult to injury, as they say—by pressing gauze to the laceration and taping it down.

"You can take the gauze off in a day or two, but you'll want to keep your hat over it until then. Gonna look a little mangy up top there for awhile, but if the hair doesn't grow back, you can always comb it over. Want some aspirin?"

"Yes. And a cup of coffee. Can you rustle that?" Although coffee would only help for a little while. What I needed was sleep.

"I can." He flicked the switch on the Bunn-o-Matic, then began rummaging in the first aid kit again. "You look like you've lost some weight."

You should talk, I thought. "I've been sick. Caught a twenty-four-hour—" That was where I stopped.

"Jake, what's wrong?"

I was looking at Al's framed photographs. When I'd gone down the rabbit-hole, there had been a picture of Harry Dunning and me up there. We were smiling and holding up Harry's GED diploma for the camera.

It was gone.

3

"Jake? Buddy? What is it?"

I took the aspirin he'd put on the counter, stuck them in my mouth, dry-swallowed. Then I got up and walked slowly over to the Wall of Celebrity. I felt like a man made of glass. Where the picture of Harry and me had hung for the last two years, there was now one of Al shaking hands with Mike Michaud, the U.S. Representative from Maine's Second District. Michaud must have been running for re-election, because Al was wearing two buttons on his cook's apron. One said MICHAUD FOR CONGRESS. The other said LISBON LUVS MIKE. The honorable Representative was wearing a bright orange Moxie tee-shirt and holding up a dripping Fatburger for the camera.

I lifted the photo from its hook. "How long has this been here?"

He looked at it, frowning. "I've never seen that picture in my life. God knows I supported Michaud in his last two runs—hell, I support any Democrat who ain't been caught screwing his campaign aides—and I met him at a rally in double-oh-eight, but that was in Castle Rock. He's never been in the diner."

"Apparently he has been. That's your counter, isn't it?"

He took the picture in hands now so scrawny they were little more than talons, and held it close to his face. "Yuh," he said. "It sure is."

"So there is a butterfly effect. This photo's proof."

He looked at it fixedly, smiling a little. In wonder, I think. Or maybe awe. Then he handed it back to me and went behind the counter to pour the coffee.

"Al? You still remember Harry, don't you? Harry Dunning?"

"Of course I do. Isn't he why you went to Derry and almost got your head knocked off?"

"For him and the rest of his family, yes."

"And did you save them?"

"All but one. His father got Tugga before we could stop him."

"Who's we?"

"I'll tell you everything, but first I'm going home to bed."

"Buddy, we don't have a whole lot of time."

"I *know* that," I said, thinking *All I have to do is look at you, Al.* "But I'm dead for sleep. For me, it's one-thirty in the morning, and I've had . . ."—my mouth opened in a huge yawn—". . . had quite a night."

"All right." He brought coffee—a full cup for me, black, half a cup for him, liberally dosed with cream. "Tell me what you can while you drink this."

"First, explain to me how you can remember Harry if he was never a janitor at LHS and never bought a Fatburger from you in his whole life. Second, explain to me why you *don't* remember Mike Michaud visiting the diner when that picture says he did."

"You don't know for a fact that Harry Dunning's not still in town," Al said. "In fact, you don't know for sure he's not still janitoring at Lisbon High."

"It'd be a hell of a coincidence if he was. I changed the past big-time, Al—with some help from a guy named Bill Turcotte. Harry wouldn't have gone to live with his aunt and uncle in Haven, because his mother didn't die. Neither did his brother Troy or his sister, Ellen. And Dunning never got near Harry himself with that hammer of his. If Harry still lives in The Falls after all those changes, I'd be the most surprised guy on earth."

"There's a way to check," Al said. "I've got a laptop computer in my office. Come on back." He led the way, coughing and holding onto things. I carried my cup of coffee with me; he left his behind.

Office was far too grand a name for the closet-sized cubbyhole off the kitchen. It was hardly big enough for both of us. The walls were papered with memos, permits, and health directives from both the state of Maine and the feds. If the people who passed on rumors and gossip about the Famous Catburger had seen all that paperwork—which included a Class A Certification of Cleanliness following the last inspection by the State of Maine Restaurant Commission—they might have been forced to rethink their position.

Al's MacBook sat on the sort of desk I remember using in the third grade. He collapsed into a chair of about the same size with a grunt of pain and relief. "High school's got a website, doesn't it?"

"Sure."

While we waited for the laptop to boot, I wondered how many emails had piled up during my fifty-two-day absence. Then I remembered I'd actually been gone only two minutes. Silly me. "I think I'm losing it, Al," I said.

"I know the feeling. Just hang on, buddy, you'll—wait, here we go. Let's see. Courses . . . summer schedule . . . faculty . . . administration . . . custodial staff."

"Hit it," I said.

He massaged the touch pad, muttered, nodded, clicked on something, then stared into the computer screen like a swami consulting his crystal ball.

"Well? Don't keep me hanging."

He turned the laptop so I could look. LHS CUSTODIAL STAFF, it said. THE BEST IN MAINE! There was a photograph of two men and a woman standing at center court in the gymnasium. They were all smiling. They were all wearing Lisbon Greyhounds sweatshirts. None of them was Harry Dunning.

4

"You remember him in his life as a janitor and as your student because you're the one who went down the rabbit-hole," Al said. We were back in the diner again, sitting in one of the booths. "I remember him either because I've used the rabbit-hole myself or just because I'm near it." He considered. "That's probably it. A kind of radiation. The Yellow Card Man's also near it, only on the other side, and he feels it, too. You've seen him, so you know."

"He's the Orange Card Man now."

"What are you talking about?"

I yawned again. "If I tried to tell you now, I'd make a total mess of everything. I want to drive you home, then go home myself. I'm going to get something to eat, because I'm hungry as a bear—"

"I'll scramble you up some eggs," he said. He started to rise, then sat back down with a thump and began to cough. Each inhale was a hacking wheeze that shook his whole body. Something rattled in his throat like a playing card in the spokes of a bicycle wheel.

I put my hand on his arm. "What you'll do is go back home, take some dope, and rest. Sleep if you can. I know *I* can. Eight hours. I'll set the alarm."

He stopped coughing, but I could still hear that playing card rattling in his throat. "Sleep. The good kind. I remember that. I envy you, buddy."

"I'll be back at your place by seven tonight. No, let's say eight. That'll give me a chance to check a few things on the internet."

"And if everything looks jake?" He smiled faintly at this pun . . . which I, of course, had heard at least a thousand times.

"Then I'll go back again tomorrow and get ready to do the deed."

"No," he said. "You're going to *undo* the deed." He squeezed my hand. His fingers were thin, but there was still strength in his grip. "That's what this is all about. Finding Oswald, undoing his fuckery, and wiping that self-satisfied smirk off his face."

5

When I started my car, the first thing I did was reach for the stubby Ford gearshift on the column and punch for the springy Ford clutch with my left foot. When my fingers closed around nothing but air and my shoe thumped on nothing but floormat, I laughed. I couldn't help it.

"What?" Al asked from his place in the shotgun seat.

I missed my nifty Ford Sunliner, that was what, but it was okay; soon I'd buy it again. Although since next time I'd be shorter of funds, at least to start with (my deposit at the Hometown Trust would be gone, lost in the next reset), I might dicker a little more with Bill Titus.

I thought I could do that.

I was different now.

"Jake? Something funny?"

"It's nothing."

I looked for changes on Main Street, but all the usual buildings were present and accounted for, including the Kennebec Fruit, which looked—as usual—about two unpaid bills away from financial collapse. The statue of Chief Worumbo still stood in the town park, and the banner in the window of Cabell's Furniture still assured the world that WE WILL NOT BE UNDERSOLD.

"Al, you remember the chain you have to duck under to get back to the rabbit-hole, don't you?"

"Sure."

"And the sign hanging from it?"

"The one about the sewer pipe." He was sitting like a soldier who thinks the road ahead may be mined, and every time we went over a bump, he winced.

"When you came back from Dallas—when you realized you were too sick to make it—was that sign still there?"

"Yeah," he said after a moment's reflection. "It was. That's kind of funny, isn't it? Who takes four years to fix a busted sewer pipe?"

"Nobody. Not in a millyard where trucks are coming and going all day and all night. So why doesn't it attract attention?"

He shook his head. "No idea."

"It might be there to keep people from wandering into the rabbit-hole by accident. But, if so, who put it there?"

"I don't know. I don't even know if what you're saying is right."

I turned onto his street, hoping I could see him safely inside and then manage the seven or eight miles out to Sabattus without falling asleep behind the wheel. But one other thing was on my mind, and I needed to say it. If only so he wouldn't get his hopes up too high.

"The past is obdurate, Al. It doesn't want to be changed."

"I know. I told *you*."

"You did. But what I think now is that the resistance to change is proportional to how much the future might be altered by any given act."

He looked at me. The patches beneath his eyes were darker than ever, and the eyes themselves shone with pain. "Could you give it to me in English?"

"Changing the Dunning family's future was harder than changing Carolyn Poulin's future, partly because there were more people involved, but mostly because the Poulin girl would have lived, either way. Doris Dunning and her kids all would have died . . . and one of them died anyway, although I intend to remedy that."

A ghost of a smile touched his lips. "Good for you. Just make sure that next time you duck a little more. Save yourself from having to deal with an embarrassing scar where the hair may not grow back."

I had ideas about that, but didn't bother saying so. I nosed my car up his driveway. "What I'm saying is that I may not be able to stop Oswald. At least not the first time." I laughed. "But what the hell, I flunked my driver's test the first time, too."

"So did I, but they didn't make me wait five years to take it again."

He had a point there.

"What are you, Jake, thirty? Thirty-two?"

"Thirty-five." And two months closer to thirty-six than I had been earlier this morning, but what was a couple of months between friends?

"If you screwed the pooch and had to start over, you'd be *forty-five* when the merry-go-round came back to the brass ring the second time. A lot can happen in ten years, especially if the past's against you."

"I know," I said. "Look what happened to you."

"I got lung cancer from smoking, that's all." He coughed as if to prove this, but I saw doubt as well as pain in his eyes.

"Probably that's all it was. I *hope* that's all it was. But it's one more thing we don't kn—"

His front door banged open. A large young woman wearing a lime-green smock and white Nancy Nurse shoes came half-running down the driveway. She saw Al slumped in the passenger seat of my Toyota and yanked open the door. "Mr. Templeton, where have you been? I came in to give you your meds, and when I found the house empty, I thought—"

He managed a smile. "I know what you thought, but I'm okay. Not beautiful, but okay."

She looked at me. "And you. What are you doing driving him around? Can't you see how fragile he is?"

Of course I could. But since I could hardly tell her what we'd been doing, I kept my mouth shut and prepared to take my scolding like a man.

"We had an important matter to discuss," Al said. "Okay? Got it?"

"Just the same—"

He opened the car door. "Help me inside, Doris. Jake's got to get home."

Doris.

As in Dunning.

He didn't notice the coincidence—and surely that was what it was, it's a common enough name—but it clanged in my head just the same.

233

6

I made it home, and this time it was the Sunliner's emergency brake I found myself reaching for. As I turned off the engine I thought about what a cramped, niggardly, basically unpleasant plastic-and-fiberglass shitbox my Toyota was compared to the car I'd gotten used to in Derry. I let myself in, started to feed my cat, and saw the food in his dish was still fresh and moist. Why wouldn't it be? In 2011, it had been in the bowl for only an hour and a half.

"Eat that, Elmore," I said. "There are cats starving in China who'd love a bowl of Friskies Choice Cuts."

Elmore gave me the look that one deserved and oiled out through the cat door. I nuked a couple of Stouffer's frozen dinners (thinking like Frankenstein's monster learning to talk: *microwave good, modern cars bad*). I ate everything, disposed of the trash, and went into the bedroom. I took off my plain white 1958 shirt (thanking God Al's Doris had been too mad to notice the blood-spatters on it), sat on the side of the bed to unlace my sensible 1958 shoes, and then let myself fall backward. I'm pretty sure I fell asleep while I was still in midair.

7

I forgot all about setting the alarm and might have slept long past 5:00 P.M., but Elmore jumped on my chest at quarter past four and began to sniff at my face. That meant he'd cleaned his dish and was requesting a refill. I provided more food for the feline, splashed my face with cold water, then ate a bowl of Special K, thinking it would be days before I could get the proper order of my meals reestablished.

With my belly full, I went into the study and booted up my computer. The town library was my first cyber-stop. Al was right—they had the entire run of the *Lisbon Weekly Enterprise* in their database. I had to become a Friend of the Library before I could access the goodies, which cost ten dollars, but given the circumstances, that seemed a small price to pay.

The issue of the *Enterprise* I was looking for was dated November 7. On page 2, sandwiched between an item about a fatal car wreck and one concerning a case of suspected arson, was a story headlined LOCAL POLICE SEEK MYSTERY MAN. The mystery man was me . . . or rather my Eisenhower-era alter ego. The Sunliner convertible had been found, the bloodstains duly noted. Bill Titus identified the Ford as one he had sold to a Mr. George Amberson. The tone of the article touched my heart: simple concern for a missing (and possibly injured) man's whereabouts. Gregory Dusen, my Hometown Trust banker, described me as "a well-spoken and polite fellow." Eddie Baumer, proprietor of Baumer's Barber Shop, said essentially the same thing. Not a single whiff of suspicion accrued to the Amberson name. Things might have been different if I'd been linked to a certain sensational case in Derry, but I hadn't been.

Nor was I in the following week's issue, where I had been reduced to a mere squib in the Police Beat: SEARCH FOR MISSING WISCONSIN MAN CONTINUES. In the issue following that, the *Weekly Enterprise* had gone gaga for the upcoming holiday season, and George Amberson disappeared from the paper entirely. *But I had been there.* Al carved his name on a tree. I'd found mine in the pages of an old newspaper. I'd expected it, but looking at the actual proof was still awe-inspiring.

I next went to the Derry *Daily News* website. It cost me considerably more to access their archives—$34.50—but within a matter of minutes I was looking at the front page of the issue for the first of November, 1958.

You would expect a sensational local crime to headline the front page of a local newspaper, but in Derry—the Peculiar Little City—they kept as quiet as possible about their atrocities. The big story that day had to do with Russia, Great Britain, and the United States

235

meeting in Geneva to discuss a possible nuclear test-ban treaty. Below this was a story about a fourteen-year-old chess prodigy named Bobby Fischer. At the very bottom of the front page, on the lefthand side (where, media experts tell us, people are apt to look last, if at all), was a story headlined MURDEROUS RAMPAGE ENDS IN 2 DEATHS. According to the story, Frank Dunning, "a prominent member of the business community and active in many charity drives," had arrived at the home of his estranged wife "in a state of inebriation" shortly after 8:00 P.M. on Friday night. After an argument with his wife (which I certainly did not hear . . . and I was there), Dunning struck her with a hammer, breaking her arm, and then killed his twelve-year-old son, Arthur Dunning, when Arthur tried to defend his mother.

The story was continued on page 12. When I turned there, I was greeted by a snapshot of my old frenemy Bill Turcotte. According to the story, "Mr. Turcotte was passing by when he heard shouts and screams from the Dunning residence." He rushed up the walk, saw what was going on through the open door, and told Mr. Frank Dunning "to stop laying about with that hammer." Dunning refused; Mr. Turcotte spotted a sheathed hunting knife on Dunning's belt and pulled it free; Dunning rounded on Mr. Turcotte, who grappled with him; during the ensuing struggle, Dunning was stabbed to death. Only moments later, the heroic Mr. Turcotte suffered a heart attack.

I sat looking at the old snapshot—Turcotte standing with one foot placed proudly on the bumper of a late forties sedan, cigarette in the corner of his mouth—and drumming my fingers on my thighs. Dunning had been stabbed from the back, not from the front, and with a bayonet, not a hunting knife. Dunning hadn't even *had* a hunting knife. The sledgehammer—which was not identified as such—had been his only weapon. Could the police have missed such glaring details? I didn't see how, unless they were as blind as Ray Charles. Yet for Derry as I had come to know it, all this made perfect sense.

I think I was smiling. The story was so crazy it was admirable.

All the loose ends were tied up. You had your crazy drunk husband, your cowering, terrified family, and your heroic passerby (no indication what he'd been passing by on his way *to*). What else did you need? And there was no mention of a certain Mysterious Stranger at the scene. It was all so *Derry*.

I rummaged in the fridge, found some leftover chocolate pudding, and hoovered it up while standing at the counter and looking out into my backyard. I picked up Elmore and petted him until he wriggled to be put down. I returned to my computer, tapped a key to magic away the screensaver, and looked at the picture of Bill Turcotte some more. The heroic intervener who had saved the family and suffered a heart attack for his pains.

At last I went to the telephone and dialed directory assistance.

8

There was no listing for Doris, Troy, or Harold Dunning in Derry. As a last resort I tried Ellen, not expecting anything; even if she were still in town, she'd probably taken the name of her husband. But sometimes longshots are lucky shots (Lee Harvey Oswald being a particularly malignant case in point). I was so surprised when the phone-robot coughed up a number that I wasn't even holding my pencil. Rather than redial directory assistance, I pushed 1 to call the number I'd requested. Given time to think about it, I'm not sure I would have done that. Sometimes we don't want to know, do we? Sometimes we're afraid to know. We go just so far, then turn back. But I held bravely onto the receiver and listened as a phone in Derry rang once, twice, three times. The answering machine would probably kick on after the next one, and I decided I didn't want to leave a message. I had no idea what to say.

But halfway through the fourth ring, a woman said: "Hello?"

"Is this Ellen Dunning?"

"Well, I guess that depends on who's calling." She sounded cautiously amused. The voice was smoky and a little insinuating. If I didn't know better, I would have imagined a woman in her thirties rather than one who was now either sixty or pushing it hard. *It was the voice,* I thought, *of someone who used it professionally. A singer? An actress? Maybe a comedian (or comedienne) after all?* None of them seemed likely in Derry.

"My name is George Amberson. I knew your brother Harry a long time ago. I was back in Maine, and I thought maybe I'd try to get in touch."

"Harry?" She sounded startled. "Oh my God! Was it in the Army?"

Had it been? I thought fast and decided that couldn't be my story. Too many potential pitfalls.

"No, no, back in Derry. When we were kids." Inspiration struck. "We used to play at the Rec. Same teams. Palled around a lot."

"Well, I'm sorry to tell you this, Mr. Amberson, but Harry's dead."

For a moment I was dumbstruck. Only that doesn't work on the phone, does it? I managed to say, "Oh God, I'm so sorry."

"It was a long time ago. In Vietnam. During the Tet Offensive."

I sat down, feeling sick to my stomach. I'd saved him from a limp and some mental fogginess only to cut his lifespan by forty years or so? Terrific. The surgery was a success, but the patient died.

Meanwhile, the show had to go on.

"What about Troy? And you, how are you? You were just a little kid back then, riding a bike with training wheels. And singing. You were always singing." I essayed a feeble laugh. "Gosh, you used to drive us crazy."

"The only singing I do these days is on Karaoke Night at Bennigan's Pub, but I never did get tired of running my mouth. I'm a jock on WKIT up in Bangor. You know, a disc jockey?"

"Uh-huh. And Troy?"

"Living *la vida loca* in Palm Springs. He's the rich fella in the family. Made a bundle in the computer biz. Got in on the ground floor back in the seventies. Goes to lunch with Steve Jobs and stuff." She laughed. It was a terrific laugh. I bet people all over eastern Maine tuned in just to hear it. But when she spoke again, her tone was lower and all the humor had gone out of it. Sun to shade, just like that. "Who are you really, Mr. Amberson?"

"What do you mean?"

"I do call-in shows on the weekends. A yard-sale show on Saturdays—'I've got a rototiller, Ellen, almost brand-new, but I can't make the payments and I'll take the best offer over fifty bucks.' Like that. On Sundays, it's politics. Folks call in to flay Rush Limbaugh or talk about how Glenn Beck should run for president. I know voices. If you'd been friends with Harry back in the Rec days, you'd be in your sixties, but you're not. You sound like you're no more than thirty-five."

Jesus, right on the money. "People tell me I sound a lot younger than my age. I bet they tell you the same."

"Nice try," she said flatly, and all at once she *did* sound older. "I've had years of training to put that sunshine in my voice. Have you?"

I couldn't think of a response, so I kept silent.

"Also, no one calls to check up on someone they chummed around with when they were in grammar school. Not fifty years later, they don't."

Might as well hang up, I thought. *I got what I called for, and more than I bargained for. I'll just hang up.* But the phone felt glued to my ear. I'm not sure I could have dropped it if I'd seen fire racing up my living room curtains.

When she spoke again, there was a catch in her voice. "Are you him?"

"I don't know what you—"

"There was somebody else there that night. Harry saw him and so did I. Are you him?"

"What night?" Only it came out *whu-nigh,* because my lips had gone numb. It felt as if someone had put a mask over my face. One lined with snow.

"Harry said it was his good angel. I think you're him. So where were you?"

Now she was the one who sounded unclear, because she'd begun crying.

"Ma'am . . . Ellen . . . you're not making any sen—"

"I took him to the airport after he got his orders and his leave was over. He was going to Nam, and I told him to watch his ass. He said, 'Don't worry, Sis, I've got a guardian angel to watch out for me, remember?' So where were you on the sixth of February in 1968, Mr. Angel? Where were you when my brother died at Khe Sanh? *Where were you then, you son of a bitch?*"

She said something else, but I don't know what it was. By then she was crying too hard. I hung up the phone. I went into the bathroom. I got into the bathtub, pulled the curtain, and put my head between my knees so I was looking at the rubber mat with the yellow daisies on it. Then I screamed. Once. Twice. Three times. And here is the worst: I didn't just wish Al had never spoken to me about his goddamned rabbit-hole. It went farther than that. I wished him dead.

9

I got a bad feeling when I pulled into his driveway and saw the house was entirely dark. It got worse when I tried the door and found it unlocked.

"Al?"

Nothing.

I found a light switch and flipped it. The main living area had the sterile neatness of rooms that are cleaned regularly but no longer much used. The walls were covered with framed photographs. Almost all were of people I didn't know—Al's relatives, I assumed—but I recognized the couple in the one hanging over the couch: John and Jacqueline Kennedy. They were at the seashore, probably Hyannis Port, and had their arms around each other. There was a smell of Glade in the air, not quite masking the sickroom smell coming from deeper in the house. Somewhere, very low, The Temptations were singing "My Girl." Sunshine on a cloudy day, and all of that.

"Al? You here?"

Where else? Studio Nine in Portland, dancing disco and trying to pick up college girls? I knew better. I had made a wish, and sometimes wishes are granted.

I fumbled for the kitchen switches, found them, and flooded the room with enough fluorescent light to take out an appendix by. On the table was a plastic medicine-caddy, the kind that holds a week's worth of pills. Most of those caddies are small enough to fit into a pocket or purse, but this one was almost as big as an encyclopedia. Next to it was a message scribbled on a piece of Ziggy notepaper: *If you forget your 8-o'clockies, I'LL KILL YOU!!!! Doris.*

"My Girl" finished and "Just My Imagination" started. I followed the music into the sickroom stench. Al was in bed. He looked relatively peaceful. At the end, a single tear had trickled from the outer corner of each closed eye. The tracks were still wet enough to gleam. The multidisc CD player was on the night table to his left. There was a note on the table, too, with a pill bottle on top to hold it down. It wouldn't have served as much of a paperweight in even a light draft, because it was empty. I looked at the label: OxyContin, twenty milligrams. I picked up the note.

Sorry, buddy, couldn't wait. Too much pain. You have the key to the diner and you know what to do. Don't kid yourself that you can try again, either, because too much can happen. Do it right the first time. Maybe you're mad at me for getting you into this. I would be, in your shoes. But don't back down. Please don't do that. Tin box is under the bed. There's another $500 or so inside that I saved back.

It's on you, buddy. About 2 hours after Doris finds me in the morning, the landlord will probably padlock the diner, so it has to be tonight. Save him, okay? Save Kennedy and everything changes.

Please.

Al

You bastard, I thought. *You knew I might have second thoughts, and this is how you took care of them, right?*

Sure I'd had second thoughts. But thoughts are not choices. If he'd had the idea I might back out, he was wrong. Stop Oswald? Sure. But Oswald was strictly secondary at that point, part of a misty future. A funny way to put it when you were thinking about 1963, but completely accurate. It was the Dunning family that was on my mind.

Arthur, also known as Tugga: I could still save him. Harry, too.

Kennedy might have changed his mind, Al had said. He'd been speaking of Vietnam.

Even if Kennedy didn't change his mind and pull out, would Harry be in the exact same place at the exact same time on February 6, 1968? I didn't think so.

"Okay," I said. "Okay." I bent over Al and kissed his cheek. I could taste the faint saltiness of that last tear. "Sleep well, buddy."

10

Back at my place, I inventoried the contents of my Lord Buxton briefcase and fancy-Dan ostrich wallet. I had Al's exhaustive notes on Oswald's movements after he mustered out of the Marines on September 11, 1959. My ID was still all present and accounted for. My cash situation was better than I'd expected; with the extra money Al had saved back, added to what I already had, my net worth was still over five thousand dollars.

There was hamburger in the meat drawer of my refrigerator. I cooked up some of it and put it in Elmore's dish. I stroked him as he ate. "If I don't come back, go next door to the Ritters'," I said. "They'll take care of you."

Elmore took no notice of this, of course, but I knew he'd do it if I wasn't there to feed him. Cats are survivors. I picked up the briefcase, went to the door, and fought off a brief but strong urge to run into my bedroom and hide under the covers. Would my cat and my house even be here when I came back, if I succeeded in what I was setting out to do? And if they were, would they still belong to me? No way of telling. Want to know something funny? Even people capable of living in the past don't really know what the future holds.

"Hey, Ozzie," I said softly. "I'm coming for you, you fuck."

I closed the door and went out.

11

The diner was weird without Al, because it felt as if Al was still there—his ghost, I mean. The faces on his Town Wall of Celebrity seemed to stare down at me, asking what I was doing here, telling me I didn't belong here, exhorting me to leave well enough alone before I snapped the universe's mainspring. There was something particularly unsettling about the picture of Al and Mike Michaud, hanging where the photo of Harry and me belonged.

I went into the pantry and began to take small, shuffling steps forward. *Pretend you're trying to find the top of a staircase with the lights out,* Al had said. *Close your eyes, buddy, it's easier that way.*

I did. Two steps down, I heard that pressure-equalizing pop deep in my ears. Warmth hit my skin; sunlight shone through my closed eyelids; I heard the *shat-HOOSH, shat-HOOSH* of the weaving flats. It was September 9, 1958, two minutes before noon. Tugga Dunning was alive again, and Mrs. Dunning's arm had not yet been broken. Not far from here, at Titus Chevron, a nifty red Ford Sunliner convertible was waiting for me.

But first, there was the former Yellow Card Man to deal with. This time he was going to get the dollar he requested, because I had neglected to put a fifty-cent piece in my pocket. I ducked under the chain and paused long enough to put a dollar bill in my right front pants pocket.

That was where it stayed, because when I came around the corner of the drying shed, I found the Yellow Card Man sprawled on the concrete with his eyes open and a pool of blood spreading around his head. His throat was slashed from ear to ear. In one hand was the jagged shard of green wine bottle he had used to do the job. In the other he held his card, the one that supposedly had something to do with it being double-money day at the green-front. The card that had once been yellow, then orange, was now dead black.

CHAPTER 10

1

I crossed the employee parking lot for the third time, not quite running. I once more rapped on the trunk of the white-over-red Plymouth Fury as I went by. For good luck, I guess. In the weeks, months, and years to come, I was going to need all the good luck I could get.

This time I didn't visit the Kennebec Fruit, and I had no intention of shopping for clothes or a car. Tomorrow or the next day would do for that, but today might be a bad day to be a stranger in The Falls. Very shortly someone was going to find a dead body in the millyard, and a stranger might be questioned. George Amberson's ID wouldn't stand up to that, especially when his driver's license was for a house on Bluebird Lane that hadn't been built yet.

I made it to the millworkers' bus stop outside the parking lot just as the bus with LEWISTON EXPRESS in its destination window came snoring along. I got on and handed over the dollar bill I'd meant to give to the Yellow Card Man. The driver clicked a handful of silver out of the chrome change-maker he wore on his belt. I dropped fifteen cents into the fare box and made my way down the swaying aisle to a seat near the back, behind two pimply sailors—probably from the Brunswick Naval Air Station—who were talking about the girls they hoped to see at a strip joint called the Holly. Their conversation was punctuated by an exchange of hefty shoulder-punches and a great deal of snorkeling laughter.

I watched Route 196 unroll almost without seeing it. I kept thinking about the dead man. And the card, which was now dead black. I'd wanted to put distance between myself and that troubling corpse as quickly as possible, but I had paused long enough to touch the card. It wasn't cardboard, as I had first assumed. Not plastic, either. Celluloid, maybe . . . except it hadn't exactly felt like that, either. What it felt like was dead skin—the kind you might pare off a callus. There had been no writing on it, at least none that I could see.

Al had assumed the Yellow Card Man was just a wet-brain who'd been driven crazy by an unlucky combination of booze and proximity to the rabbit-hole. I hadn't questioned that until the card turned orange. Now I more than questioned it; I flat-out didn't believe it. What *was* he, anyway?

Dead, that's what he is. And that's all he is. So let it go. You've got a lot to do.

When we passed the Lisbon Drive-In, I yanked the stop-cord. The driver pulled over at the next white-painted telephone pole.

"Have a nice day," I told him as he pulled the lever that flopped the doors open.

"Ain't nothin nice about this run except a cold beer at quittin time," he said, and lit a cigarette.

A few seconds later I was standing on the gravel shoulder of the highway with my briefcase dangling from my left hand, watching the bus lumber off toward Lewiston, trailing a cloud of exhaust. On the back was an ad-card showing a housewife who held a gleaming pot in one hand and an S.O.S. Magic Scouring Pad in the other. Her huge blue eyes and toothy red-lipsticked grin suggested a woman who might be only minutes away from a catastrophic mental breakdown.

The sky was cloudless. Crickets sang in the high grass. Somewhere a cow lowed. With the diesel stink of the bus whisked away by a light breeze, the air smelled sweet and fresh and new. I started trudging the quarter mile or so to the Tamarack Motor Court. Just a short walk, but before I got to my destination, two people pulled over and asked me if I wanted a ride. I thanked them and said I was fine. And I was. By the time I reached the Tamarack I was whistling.

September of '58, United States of America.

Yellow Card Man or no Yellow Card Man, it was good to be back.

2

I spent the rest of that day in my room, going over Al's Oswald notes for the umpteenth time, this time paying special attention to the two pages at the end marked *CONCLUSIONS ON HOW TO PROCEDE.* Trying to watch the TV, which essentially got just one channel, was an exercise in absurdity, so when dusk came I ambled down to the drive-in and paid a special walk-in price of thirty cents. There were folding chairs set up in front of the snack-bar. I bought a bag of popcorn plus a tasty cinnamon-flavored soft drink called Pepsol, and watched *The Long, Hot Summer* with several other walk-ins, mostly elderly people who knew each other and chatted companionably. The air had turned chilly by the time *Vertigo* started, and I had no jacket. I walked back to the motor court and slept soundly.

The next morning I took the bus back to Lisbon Falls (no cabs; I considered myself on a budget, at least for the time being), and made the Jolly White Elephant my first stop. It was early, and still cool, so the beatnik was inside, sitting on a ratty couch and reading *Argosy.*

"Hi, neighbor," he said.

"Hi yourself. I guess you sell suitcases?"

"Oh, I got a few in stock. No more'n two-three hundred. Walk all the way to the back—"

"And look on the right," I said.

"That's right. Have you been here before?"

"We've *all* been here before," I said. "This thing is bigger than pro football."

He laughed. "Groovy, Jackson. Go pick yourself a winner."

I picked the same leather valise. Then I went across the street and bought the Sunliner again. This time I bargained harder and got it for three hundred. When the dickering was done, Bill Titus sent me over to his daughter.

"You don't sound like you're from around here," she said.

"Wisconsin originally, but I've been in Maine for quite awhile. Business."

"Guess you weren't around The Falls yesterday, huh?" When I said I hadn't been, she popped her gum and said: "You missed some excitement. They found an old boozer dead outside the drying shed over at the mill." She lowered her voice. "Suicide. Cut his own throat with a piece of glass. Can you imagine?"

"That's awful," I said, tucking the Sunliner's bill of sale into my wallet. I bounced the car keys on my palm. "Local guy?"

"Nope, and no ID. He probably came down from The County in a boxcar, that's what my dad says. For the apple picking over in Castle Rock, maybe. Mr. Cady—he's the clerk at the greenfront— told my dad the guy came in yesterday morning and tried to buy a pint, but he was drunk and smelly, so Mr. Cady kicked him out. Then he must have went over to the millyard to drink up whatever he had left, and when it was gone, he broke the bottle and cut his throat with one of the pieces." She repeated: "Can you *imagine?*"

I skipped the haircut, and I skipped the bank, too, but I once more bought clothes at Mason's Menswear.

"You must like that shade of blue," the clerk commented, and held up the shirt on top of my pile. "Same color as the one you're wearing."

In fact it *was* the shirt I was wearing, but I didn't say so. It would only have confused us both.

3

I drove up the Mile-A-Minute Highway that Thursday afternoon. This time I didn't need to buy a hat when I got to Derry, because I'd remembered to add a nice summer straw to the purchases I made at Mason's. I registered at the Derry Town House, had a meal in the dining room, then went into the bar and ordered a beer from Fred Toomey. On this go-round I made no effort to engage him in conversation.

The following day I rented my old apartment on Harris Avenue, and far from keeping me awake, the sound of the descending planes actually lulled me to sleep. The day after that, I went down to Machen's Sporting Goods and told the clerk I was interested in buying a handgun because I was in the real estate business and blah blah blah. The clerk brought out my .38 Police Special and once more told me it was a fine piece of protection. I bought it and put it in my briefcase. I thought about walking out Kansas Street to the little picnic area so I could watch Richie-from-the-ditchie and Bevvie-from-the-levee practice their Jump Street moves, then realized I'd missed them. I wished I'd thought to check the late November issues of the *Daily News* during my brief return to 2011; I could have found out if they'd won their talent show.

I made it a habit to drop into The Lamplighter for an early-evening beer, before the place started to fill up. Sometimes I ordered Lobster Pickin's. I never saw Frank Dunning there, nor wanted to. I had another reason for making The Lamplighter a regular stop. If all went well, I'd soon be heading for Texas, and I wanted to build up my personal treasury before I went. I made friends with Jeff the bartender, and one evening toward the end of September, he brought up a subject I'd been planning to raise myself.

"Who do you like in the Series, George?"

"Yankees, of course," I said.

"You say that? A guy from *Wisconsin*?"

"Home-state pride has nothing to do with it. The Yankees are a team of destiny this year."

"Never happen. Their pitchers are old. Their defense is leaky. Mantle's got bad wheels. The Bronx Bomber dynasty is over. Milwaukee might even sweep."

I laughed. "You make a few good points, Jeff, I can see you're a student of the game, but 'fess up—you hate the Yanks just like everybody else in New England, and it's destroyed your perspective."

"You want to put your money where your mouth is?"

"Sure. A fin. I make it a point not to take any more than a five-spot from the wage-slaves. Are we on?"

"We are." And we shook on it.

"Okay," I said, "now that we've got that accomplished, and since we're on the subjects of baseball and betting—the two great American pastimes—I wonder if you could tell me where I could find some serious action in this town. If I may wax poetic, I want to lay a major wager. Bring me another beer and draw one for yourself."

I said *major wager* Maine-style—*majah wajah*—and he laughed as he drew a couple of Narragansetts (which I had learned to call Nasty Gansett; when in Rome, one should, as much as possible, speak as the Romans do).

We clinked glasses, and Jeff asked me what I meant by serious action. I pretended to consider, then told him.

"Five hundred smacks? On the *Yankees*? When the Braves've got Spahn and Burdette? Not to mention Hank Aaron and Steady Eddie Mathews? You're nuts."

"Maybe yes, maybe no. We'll see starting October first, won't we? *Is* there anyone in Derry who'll fade a bet of that size?"

Did I know what he was going to say next? No. I'm not that prescient. Was I surprised? No again. Because the past isn't just obdurate; it's in harmony with both itself and the future. I experienced that harmony time and again.

"Chaz Frati. You've probably seen him in here. He owns a bunch of hockshops. I wouldn't exactly call him a bookie, but he keeps plenty busy at World Series time and during high school football and basketball season."

"And you think he'll take my action."

"Sure. Give you odds and everything. Just . . ." He looked around, saw we still had the bar to ourselves, but dropped his voice to a whisper anyway. "Just don't stiff him, George. He knows people. *Strong* people."

"I hear you," I said. "Thanks for the tip. In fact, I'm going to do you a favor and not hold you to that five when the Yankees win the Series."

4

The following day I entered Chaz Frati's Mermaid Pawn & Loan, where I was confronted by a large, stone-faced lady of perhaps three hundred pounds. She wore a purple dress, Indian beads, and moccasins on her swollen feet. I told her I was interested in discussing a rather large sports-oriented business proposal with Mr. Frati.

"Is that a bet in regular talk?" she asked.

"Are you a cop?" I asked.

"Yes," she said, bringing a Tiparillo out of one dress pocket and lighting it with a Zippo. "I'm J. Edgar Hoover, my son."

"Well, Mr. Hoover, you got me. I'm talking about a bet."

"World Series or Tigers football?"

"I'm not from town, and wouldn't know a Derry Tiger from a Bangor Baboon. It's baseball."

The woman stuck her head through a curtained-off doorway at the back of the room, presenting me with what was surely one of central Maine's largest backsides, and hollered, "Hey Chazzy, come out here. You got a live one."

Frati came out and kissed the large lady on the cheek. "Thank you, my love." His sleeves were rolled up, and I could see the mermaid. "May I help you?"

"I hope so. George Amberson's the name." I offered my hand. "I'm from Wisconsin, and although my heart's with the hometown boys, when it comes to the Series my wallet's with the Yankees."

He turned to the shelf behind him, but the large lady already had what he wanted—a scuffed green ledger with PERSONAL LOANS on the front. He opened it and paged to a blank sheet, periodically wetting the tip of his finger. "How much of your wallet are we talking about, cuz?"

"What kind of odds could I get on five hundred to win?"

The fat woman laughed and blew out smoke.

"On the Bombers? Even-up, cuz. Strictly even-up."

"What kind of odds could I get on five hundred, Yankees in seven?"

He considered, then turned to the large lady. She shook her head, still looking amused. "Won't go," she said. "If you don't believe me, send a telegram and check the line in New York."

I sighed and drummed my fingers on a glass case filled with watches and rings. "Okay, how about this—five hundred and the Yankees come back from three games to one."

He laughed. "Some sensayuma, cuz. Just let me consult with the boss."

He and the large lady (Frati looked like a Tolkien dwarf next to her) consulted in whispers, then he came back to the counter. "If you mean what I think you mean, I'll take your action at four-to-one. But if the Yankees don't go down three-to-one and then bounce all the way back, you lose the bundle. I just like to get the terms of the wager straight."

"Straight as can be," I said. "And—no offense to either you or your friend—"

"We're married," the large lady said, "so don't call us friends." And she laughed some more.

"No offense to either you or your wife, but four-to-one doesn't make it. *Eight*-to-one, though . . . then it's a nice piece of action for both sides."

"I'll give you five-to-one, but that's where it stops," Frati said. "For me this is just a sideline. You want Vegas, go to Vegas."

"Seven," I said. "Come on, Mr. Frati, work with me on this."

He and the large lady conferred. Then he came back and offered six-to-one, which I accepted. It was still low odds for such a crazy bet, but I didn't want to hurt Frati too badly. It was true that he'd set me up for Bill Turcotte, but he'd had his reasons.

Besides, that was in another life.

5

Back then, baseball was played as it was meant to be played—in bright afternoon sunshine, and on days in the early fall when it still felt like summer. People gathered in front of Benton's Appliance Store down in the Low Town to watch the games on three twenty-one-inch Zeniths perched on pedestals in the show window. Above them was a sign reading WHY WATCH ON THE STREET WHEN YOU CAN WATCH AT HOME? *EASY CREDIT TERMS!*

Ah, yes. Easy credit terms. That was more like the America I had grown up in.

On October first, Milwaukee beat the Yankees four to three, behind Warren Spahn. On October second, Milwaukee buried the Bombers, thirteen to five. On the fourth of October, when the Series returned to the Bronx, Don Larsen blanked Milwaukee four-zip, with relief help from Ryne Duren, who had no idea where the ball was going once it left his hand, and consequently scared the living shit out of the batters who had to face him. The perfect closer, in other words.

I listened to the first part of that game on the radio in my apartment, and watched the last couple of innings with the crowd gathered in front of Benton's. When it was over, I went into the drugstore and purchased Kaopectate (probably the same giant economy size bottle as on my last trip). Mr. Keene once more asked me if I was suffering a touch of the bug. When I told him that I felt fine, the old bastard looked disappointed. I *did* feel fine, and I didn't expect that the past would throw me exactly the same Ryne Duren fastballs, but I felt it best to be prepared.

On my way out of the drugstore, my eye was attracted by a display with a sign over it that read TAKE HOME A LITTLE BIT O' MAINE! There were postcards, inflatable toy lobsters, sweet-smelling bags of soft pine duff, replicas of the town's Paul Bunyan statue, and small decorative pillows with the Derry Standpipe on them—the Standpipe being a circular tower that held the town's drinking water. I bought one of these.

"For my nephew in Oklahoma City," I told Mr. Keene.

The Yankees had won the third game of the Series by the time I pulled into the Texaco station on the Harris Avenue Extension. There was a sign in front of the pumps saying MECHANIC ON DUTY 7 DAYS A WEEK—TRUST YOUR CAR TO THE MAN WHO WEARS THE STAR!

While the pump-jockey filled the tank and washed the Sunliner's windshield, I wandered into the garage bay, found a mechanic by the name of Randy Baker on duty, and did a little dickering with him. Baker was puzzled, but agreeable to my proposal. Twenty dollars changed hands. He gave me the numbers of both the station and his home. I left with a full tank, a clean windshield, and a satisfied mind. Well . . . *relatively* satisfied. It was impossible to plan for every contingency.

Because of my preparations for the following day, I dropped by The Lamplighter for my evening beer later than usual, but there was no risk of encountering Frank Dunning. It was his day to take his kids to the football game in Orono, and on the way back they were going to stop at the Ninety-Fiver for fried clams and milk-shakes.

Chaz Frati was at the bar, sipping rye and water. "You better hope the Braves win tomorrow, or you're out five hundred," he said.

They *were* going to win, but I had bigger things on my mind. I'd stay in Derry long enough to collect my three grand from Mr. Frati, but I intended to finish my real business the following day. If things went as I hoped, I'd be done in Derry before Milwaukee scored what would prove to be the only run they needed in the sixth inning.

"Well," I said, ordering a beer and some Lobster Pickin's, "we'll just have to see, won't we?"

"That's right, cuz. It's the joy of the wager. Mind if I ask you a question?"

"Nope. Just as long as you won't be offended if I don't answer."

"That's what I like about you, cuz—that sensayuma. Must be a Wisconsin thing. What I'm curious about is why you're in our fair city."

"Real estate. I thought I told you that."

He leaned close. I could smell Vitalis on his slicked-back hair and Sen-Sen on his breath. "And if I said 'possible mall site,' would that be a bingo?"

So we talked for awhile, but you already know that part.

6

I've said I stayed away from The Lamplighter when I thought Frank Dunning might be there because I already knew everything about him that I needed to know. It's the truth, but not *all* of the truth. I need to make that clear. If I don't, you'll never understand why I behaved as I did in Texas.

Imagine coming into a room and seeing a complex, multistory house of cards on the table. Your mission is to knock it over. If that was all, it would be easy, wouldn't it? A hard stamp of the foot or a big puff of air—the kind you muster when it's time to blow out all the birthday candles—would be enough to do the job. But that's *not* all. The thing is, you have to knock that house of cards down at a specific moment in time. Until then, it must stand.

I knew where Dunning was going to be on the afternoon of Sunday, October 5, 1958, and I didn't want to risk changing his course by so much as a single jot or tittle. Even crossing eyes with him in The Lamplighter might have done that. You could snort and call me excessively cautious; you could say such a minor matter would be very unlikely to knock events off-course. But the past is as fragile as a butterfly's wing. Or a house of cards.

I had come back to Derry to knock Frank Dunning's house of cards down, but until then I had to protect it.

7

I bade Chaz Frati goodnight and went back to my apartment. My bottle of Kaopectate was in the bathroom medicine cabinet, and my new souvenir pillow with the Standpipe embroidered on it in gold thread was on the kitchen table. I took a knife from the silverware drawer and carefully cut the pillow along a diagonal. I put my revolver inside, shoving it deep into the stuffing.

I wasn't sure I'd sleep, but I did, and soundly. *Do your best and let God do the rest* is just one of many sayings Christy dragged back from her AA meetings. I don't know if there's a God or not—for Jake Epping, the jury's still out on that one—but when I went to bed that night, I was pretty sure I'd done my best. All I could do now was get some sleep and hope my best was enough.

8

There was no stomach flu. This time I awoke at first light with the most paralyzing headache of my life. A migraine, I supposed. I didn't know for sure, because I'd never had one. Looking into even dim light produced a sick, rolling thud from the nape of my neck to the base of my sinuses. My eyes gushed senseless tears.

I got up (even that hurt), put on a pair of cheap sunglasses I'd picked up on my trip north to Derry, and took five aspirin. They helped just enough for me to be able to get dressed and into my overcoat. Which I would need; the morning was chilly and gray, threatening rain. In a way, that was a plus. I'm not sure I could have survived in sunlight.

I needed a shave, but skipped it; I thought standing under a bright light—one doubled in the bathroom mirror—might cause my brains simply to disintegrate. I couldn't imagine how I was going to get through this day, so I didn't try. *One step at a time,* I told myself as I walked slowly down the stairs. I was clutching the railing with one hand and my souvenir pillow with the other. I must have looked like an overgrown child with a teddy bear. *One step at a ti—*

The banister snapped.

For a moment I tilted forward, head thudding, hands waving wildly in the air. I dropped the pillow (the gun inside clunked) and clawed at the wall above my head. In the last second before my tilt would have become a bone-breaking tumble, my fingers clutched one of the old-fashioned wall sconces screwed into the plaster. It pulled free, but the electrical wire held just long enough for me to regain my balance.

I sat down on the steps with my throbbing head on my knees. The pain pulsed in sync with the jackhammer beat of my heart. My watering eyes felt too big for their sockets. I could tell you I wanted to creep back to my apartment and give it all up, but that wouldn't be the truth. The truth was I wanted to die right there on the stairs and have done with it. Are there people who have such headaches not just occasionally but *frequently*? If so, God help them.

There was only one thing that could get me back on my feet, and I forced my aching brains not just to think of it but see it: Tugga Dunning's face suddenly obliterated as he crawled toward me. His hair and brains leaping into the air.

"Okay," I said. "Okay, yeah, okay."

I picked up the souvenir pillow and tottered the rest of the way down the stairs. I emerged into an overcast day that seemed as bright as a Sahara afternoon. I felt for my keys. They weren't there. What I found where they should have been was a good-sized hole in my right front pants pocket. It hadn't been there the night before, I was almost sure of that. I turned around in small, jerky steps. The keys were lying on the stoop in a litter of spilled change. I bent down, wincing as a lead weight slid forward inside my head. I picked up the keys and made my way to the Sunliner. And when I tried the ignition, my previously reliable Ford refused to start. There was a click from the solenoid. That was all.

I had prepared for this eventuality; what I hadn't prepared for was having to drag my poisoned head up the stairs again. Never in my life had I wished so fervently for my Nokia. With it, I could have called from behind the wheel, then just sat quietly with my eyes closed until Randy Baker came.

Somehow, I got back up the stairs, past the broken banister and the light fixture that dangled against the torn plaster like a dead head on a broken neck. There was no answer at the service station—it was early and it was Sunday—so I tried Baker's home number.

He's probably dead, I thought. *Had a heart attack in the middle of the night. Killed by the obdurate past, with Jake Epping as the unindicted co-conspirator.*

My mechanic wasn't dead. He answered on the second ring, voice sleepy, and when I told him my car wouldn't start, he asked the logical question: "How'd you know yesterday?"

"I'm a good guesser," I said. "Get here as soon as you can, okay? There'll be another twenty in it for you, if you can get it going."

9

When Baker replaced the battery cable that had mysteriously come loose in the night (maybe at the same moment that hole was appearing in the pocket of my slacks) and the Sunliner still wouldn't start, he checked the plugs and found two that were badly corroded. He had extras in his large green toolkit, and when they were in place, my chariot roared to life.

"It's probably not my business, but the only place you should be going is back to bed. Or to a doctor. You're as pale as a ghost."

"It's just a migraine. I'll be okay. Let's look in the trunk. I want to check the spare."

We checked the spare. Flat.

I followed him to the Texaco through what had become a light, steady drizzle. The cars we passed had their headlights on, and even with the sunglasses, each pair seemed to bore holes through my brain. Baker unlocked the service bay and tried to blow up my spare. No go. It hissed air from half a dozen cracks almost as fine as pores in human skin.

"Huh," he said. "Never seen that before. Tire must be defective."

"Put another one on the rim," I said.

I went around to the back of the station while he did it. I couldn't stand the sound of the compressor. I leaned against the cinderblock and turned my face up, letting cold mist fall on my hot skin. *One step at a time,* I told myself. *One step at a time.*

When I tried to pay Randy Baker for the tire, he shook his head. "You already give me half a week's pay. I'd be a dog to take more. I'm just worried you'll run off the road, or something. Is it really that important?"

"Sick relative."

"You're sick yourself, man."

I couldn't deny it.

10

I drove out of town on Route 7, slowing to look both ways at every intersection whether I had the right of way or not. This turned out to be an excellent idea, because a fully loaded gravel truck blew through a red at the intersection of 7 and the Old Derry Road. If I hadn't come to an almost complete stop in spite of a green light, my Ford would have been demolished. With me turned to hamburger inside it. I laid on my horn in spite of the pain in my head, but the driver paid no attention. He looked like a zombie behind the wheel.

I'll never be able to do this, I thought. But if I couldn't stop Frank Dunning, how could I even hope to stop Oswald? Why go to Texas at all?

That wasn't what kept me moving, though. It was the thought of Tugga that did that. Not to mention the other three kids. I had saved them once. If I didn't save them again, how could I escape the sure knowledge that I had participated in murdering them, just by triggering another reset?

I approached the Derry Drive-In, and turned into the gravel drive leading to the shuttered box office. The drive was lined with decorative fir trees. I parked behind them, turned off the engine, and tried to get out of the car. I couldn't. The door wouldn't open. I slammed my shoulder against it a couple of times, and when it still wouldn't open, I saw the lock was pushed down even though this was long before the era of self-locking cars, and I hadn't pushed it down myself. I pulled on it. It wouldn't come up. I wiggled it. It wouldn't come up. I unrolled my window, leaned out, and managed to use my key on the door lock below the chrome thumb-button on the outside handle. This time the lock popped up. I got out, then reached in for the souvenir pillow.

Resistance to change is proportional to how much the future might be altered by any given act, I had told Al in my best school-lecture voice, and it was true. But I'd had no idea of the personal cost. Now I did.

I walked slowly up Route 7, my collar raised against the rain and my hat pulled low over my ears. When cars came—they were infrequent—I faded back into the trees that lined my side of the road. I think that once or twice I put my hands on the sides of my head to make sure it wasn't swelling. It *felt* like it was.

At last, the trees pulled back. They were replaced by a rock wall. Beyond the wall were manicured rolling hills dotted with headstones and monuments. I had come to Longview Cemetery. I breasted a hill, and there was the flower stand on the other side of the road. It was shuttered and dark. Weekends would ordinarily be busy visiting-the-dead-relatives days, but in weather like this, business would be slow, and I supposed the old lady who ran the place was sleeping in a little bit. She would open later, though. I had seen that for myself.

I climbed the wall, expecting it to give way beneath me, but it didn't. And once I was actually in Longview, a wonderful thing happened: the headache began to abate. I sat on a gravestone beneath an overhanging elm tree, closed my eyes, and checked the pain level. What had been a screaming 10—maybe even turned up to 11, like a Spinal Tap amplifier—had gone back to 8.

"I think I broke through, Al," I said. "I think I might be on the other side."

Still, I moved carefully, alert for more tricks—falling trees, graverobbing thugs, maybe even a flaming meteor. There was nothing. By the time I reached the side-by-side graves marked ALTHEA PIERCE DUNNING and JAMES ALLEN DUN-NING, the pain in my head was down to a 5.

I looked around and saw a mausoleum with a familiar name engraved on the pink granite: TRACKER. I went to it and tried the iron gate. In 2011 it would have been locked, but this was 1958 and it swung open easily . . . although with a horror-movie squall of rusty hinges.

I went inside, kicking my way through a drift of old brittle leaves. There was a stone meditation bench running up the center of the vault; on either side were stone storage lockers for Track-ers going all the way back to 1831. According to the copper plate on the front of that earliest one, the bones of Monsieur Jean Paul Traiche lay within.

I closed my eyes.

Lay down on the meditation bench and dozed.

Slept.

When I woke up it was close to noon. I went to the front door of the Tracker vault to wait for Dunning . . . just as Oswald, five years from now, would no doubt wait for the Kennedy motorcade in his shooter's blind on the sixth floor of the Texas School Book Depository.

My headache was gone.

11

Dunning's Pontiac appeared around the same time Red Schoendienst was scoring that day's winning run for the Milwaukee Braves. Dunning parked on the closest feeder lane, got out, turned up his collar, then bent back in to get the flower baskets. He walked down the hill to his parents' graves carrying one in each hand.

Now that the time had come, I was pretty much okay. I had gotten on the other side of whatever had been trying to hold me back. The souvenir pillow was under my coat. My hand was inside. The wet grass muffled my footsteps. There was no sun to cast my shadow. He didn't know I was behind him until I spoke his name. Then he turned around.

"When I'm visiting my folks, I don't like company," he said. "Who the hell are you, anyway? And what's that?" He was looking at the pillow, which I had taken out. I was wearing it like a glove.

I chose to answer the first question only. "My name's Jake Epping. I came out here to ask you a question."

"So ask and then leave me alone." Rain was dripping off the brim of his hat. Mine, too.

"What's the most important thing in life, Dunning?"

"What?"

"To a man, I mean."

"What are you, wacky? What's with the pillow, anyway?"

"Humor me. Answer the question."

He shrugged. "His family, I suppose."

"I think so, too," I said, and pulled the trigger twice. The first report was a muffled thump, like hitting a rug with a carpet beater. The second was a little louder. I thought the pillow might catch on fire—I saw that in *Godfather 2*—but it only smoldered a little. Dunning fell over, crushing the basket of flowers he'd placed on his father's grave. I knelt beside him, my knee squelching up water from the wet earth, placed the torn end of the pillow against his temple, and fired again. Just to make sure.

12

I dragged him into the Tracker mausoleum and dropped the scorched pillow on his face. When I left, a couple of cars were driving slowly through the cemetery, and a few people were standing under umbrellas at gravesites, but nobody was paying any attention to me. I walked without haste toward the rock wall, pausing every now and then to look at a grave or monument. Once I was screened by trees, I jogged back to my Ford. When I heard cars coming, I slipped into the woods. On one of those retreats, I buried the gun under a foot of earth and leaves. The Sunliner was waiting undisturbed where I'd left it, and it started on the first crank. I drove back to my apartment and listened to the end of the baseball game. I cried a little, I think. Those were tears of relief, not remorse. No matter what happened to me, the Dunning family was safe.

I slept like a baby that night.

13

There was plenty about the World Series in Monday's Derry *Daily News,* including a nice pic of Schoendienst sliding home with the winning run after a Tony Kubek error. According to Red Barber's column, the Bronx Bombers were finished. "Stick a fork in em," he opined. "The Yanks are dead, long live the Yanks."

Nothing about Frank Dunning to start Derry's workweek, but he was front-page material in Tuesday's paper, along with a photo that showed him grinning with the-ladies-love-me good cheer. His devilish George Clooney twinkle was all present and accounted for.

BUSINESSMAN FOUND MURDERED IN LOCAL CEMETERY
Dunning Was Prominent in Many Charity Drives

According to the Derry Chief of Police, the department was following up all sorts of good leads and an arrest was expected soon. Reached by phone, Doris Dunning declared herself to be "shocked and devastated." There was no mention of the fact that she and the decedent had been living apart. Various friends and co-workers at the Center Street Market expressed similar shock. Everyone seemed in agreement that Frank Dunning had been an absolutely terrific guy, and no one could guess why someone would want to shoot him.

Tony Tracker was especially outraged (possibly because the corpse had been found in the family body-bank). "For this guy, they ought to bring back the death penalty," he said.

On Wednesday, the eighth of October, the Yankees squeezed out a four-to-three win over the Braves at County Stadium; on Thursday they broke a two-two tie in the eighth, scoring four runs and closing the Series out. On Friday, I went back to the Mermaid Pawn & Loan, expecting to be met there by Mrs. Grump and Mr. Gloom. The large lady more than lived up to my expectations— she curled her lip when she saw me and shouted, "Chazzy! Mr. Moneybags is here!" Then she shoved through the curtained-off doorway and out of my life.

Frati came out wearing the same chipmunk grin I'd first encountered in The Lamplighter, on my previous trip into Derry's colorful past. In one hand he was holding a well-stuffed envelope with G. AMBERSON printed on the front.

"There you are, cuz," he said, "big as life and twice as handsome. And here's your loot. Feel free to count it."

"I trust you," I said, and put the envelope in my pocket. "You're mighty cheery for a fellow who just forked over three large."

"I won't deny that you cut into this year's Fall Classic take," he said. "*Seriously* cut into it, although I still made a few bucks. I always do. But I'm mostly in the game because it's a whattayacall-lit, public service. People are gonna bet, people are always gonna bet, and I give em a prompt payoff when a payoff's due. Also, I like taking bets. It's a kind of hobby with me. And do you know when I like it best?"

"No."

"When someone like you comes along, a real stampeder who bucks the odds and comes through. That restores my faith in the random nature of the universe."

I wondered how random he'd think it was if he could see Al Templeton's cheat sheet.

"Your wife's view doesn't appear to be so, um, catholic."

He laughed, and his small black eyes sparkled. Win, lose, or draw, the little man with the mermaid on his arm flat-out enjoyed life. I admired that. "Oh, Marjorie. When some sad sack comes in here with his wife's engagement ring and a sob story, she turns into a pile of goo. But on the sports-book stuff, she's a different lady. That she takes personal."

"You love her a lot, don't you, Mr. Frati?"

"Like the moon and the stars, cuz. Like the moon and the stars."

Marjorie had been reading that day's paper, and it was still on the glass-topped counter containing the rings and things. The headline read HUNT FOR MYSTERY KILLER GOES ON AS FRANK DUNNING IS LAID TO REST.

"What do you reckon *that* was about?" I asked.

"Dunno, but I'll tell you something." He leaned forward, and the smile was gone. "He wasn't the saint the local rag is makin him out to be. I could tell you stories, cuz."

"Go ahead. I've got all day."

The smile reappeared. "Nah. In Derry, we keep ourselves to our-selves."

"So I've noticed," I said.

14

I wanted to go back to Kossuth Street. I knew the cops might be watching the Dunning house to see if anyone showed an unusual interest in the family, but the desire was very strong, just the same. It wasn't Harry I wanted to see; it was his little sister. There were things I wanted to tell her.

That she should go out trick-or-treating on Halloween no matter how sad she felt about her daddy.

That she'd be the prettiest, most magical Indian princess anyone had ever seen, and would come home with a mountain of candy.

That she had at least fifty-three long and busy years ahead of her, and probably many more.

Most of all that someday her brother Harry was going to want to put on a uniform and go for a soldier and she must do her very, very, very best to talk him out of it.

Only kids forget. Every teacher knows this.

And they think they're going to live forever.

15

It was time to leave Derry, but I had one final little chore to take care of before I went. I waited until Monday. That afternoon, the thirteenth of October, I threw my valise into the Sunliner's trunk, then sat behind the wheel long enough to scribble a brief note. I tucked it into an envelope, sealed it, and printed the recipient's name on the front.

I drove down to the Low Town, parked, and walked into the Sleepy Silver Dollar. It was empty except for Pete the bartender, as I had expected. He was washing glasses and watching *Love of Life* on the boob tube. He turned to me reluctantly, keeping one eye on John and Marsha, or whatever their names were.

"What can I get you?"

"Nothing, but you can do me a favor. For which I will compensate you to the tune of five American dollars."

He looked unimpressed. "Really. What's the favor?"

I put the envelope on the bar. "Pass this over when the proper party comes in."

He looked at the name on the front of the envelope. "What do you want with Billy Turcotte? And why don't you give it to him yourself?"

"It's a simple enough assignment, Pete. Do you want the five, or not?"

"Sure. Long as it won't do no harm. Billy's a good enough soul."

"It won't do him any harm. It might even do him some good."

I put a fin on top of the envelope. Pete made it disappear and went back to his soap opera. I left. Turcotte probably got the envelope. Whether or not he did anything after he read what was inside is another question, one of many to which I will never have answers. This is what I wrote:

Dear Bill—

There is something wrong with your heart. You must go to the doctor soon, or it will be too late. You might think this is a joke, but it is not. You might think I couldn't know such a thing, but I do. I know it as surely as you know Frank Dunning murdered your sister Clara and your nephew Mikey. PLEASE BELIEVE ME AND GO TO THE DOCTOR!

A Friend

16

I got into my Sunliner, and as I backed out of the slant parking slot, I saw Mr. Keene's narrow and mistrustful face peering out at me from the drugstore. I unrolled my window, stuck out my arm, and shot him the bird. Then I drove up Up-Mile Hill and out of Derry for the last time.

CHAPTER 11

As I drove south on the Mile-A-Minute Highway, I tried to convince myself that I needn't bother with Carolyn Poulin. I told myself she was Al Templeton's experiment, not mine, and his experiment, like his life, was now over. I reminded myself that the Poulin girl's case was very different from that of Doris, Troy, Tugga, and Ellen. Yes, Carolyn was going to be paralyzed from the waist down, and yes, that was a terrible thing. But being paralyzed by a bullet is not the same as being beaten to death with a sledgehammer. In a wheelchair or out of it, Carolyn Poulin was going to live a full and fruitful life. I told myself it would be crazy to risk my real mission by yet again daring the obdurate past to reach out, grab me, and chew me up.

None of it would wash.

I had meant to spend my first night on the road in Boston, but the image of Dunning on his father's grave, with the crushed basket of flowers beneath him, kept recurring. He had deserved to die—hell, *needed* to—but on October 5 he had as yet done nothing to his family. Not to his second one, anyway. I could tell myself (and did!) that he'd done plenty to his first one, that on October 13 of 1958 he was already a murderer twice over, one of his victims little more than an infant, but I had only Bill Turcotte's word for that.

I guess in the end, I wanted to balance something that felt bad, no matter how necessary, with something that felt good. So instead of driving to Boston, I got off the turnpike at Auburn and drove

269

west into Maine's lakes region. I checked into the cabins where Al had stayed, just before nightfall. I got the largest of the four water-side accommodations at a ridiculous off-season rate.

Those five weeks may have been the best of my life. I saw no one but the couple who ran the local store, where I bought a few simple groceries twice a week, and Mr. Winchell, who owned the cabins. He stopped in on Sundays to make sure I was okay and having a good time. Every time he asked, I told him I was, and it was no lie. He gave me a key to the equipment shed, and I took a canoe out every morning and evening when the water was calm. I remember watching the full moon rise silently over the trees on one of those evenings, and how it beat a silver avenue across the water while the reflection of my canoe hung below me like a drowned twin. A loon cried somewhere, and was answered by a pal or a mate. Soon others joined the conversation. I shipped my paddle and just sat there three hundred yards out from shore, watching the moon and listening to the loons converse. I remember thinking if there was a heaven somewhere and it wasn't like this, then I didn't want to go.

The fall colors began to bloom—first timid yellow, then orange, then blazing, strumpet red as autumn burned away another Maine summer. There were cardboard boxes filled with coverless paper-backs at the market, and I must have read three dozen or more: mysteries by Ed McBain, John D. MacDonald, Chester Himes, and Richard S. Prather; steamy melodramas like *Peyton Place* and *A Stone for Danny Fisher*; westerns by the score; and one science-fiction novel called *The Lincoln Hunters,* which concerned time-travelers trying to record a "forgotten" speech by Abraham Lincoln.

When I wasn't reading or canoeing, I was walking in the woods. Long autumn afternoons, most hazy and warm. Dusty gilded light slanting down through the trees. At night, a quiet so vast it seemed almost to reverberate. Few cars passed on Route 114, and after ten o'clock or so there were none at all. After ten, the part of the world where I had come to rest belonged only to the loons and the wind in the fir trees. Little by little, the image of Frank Dunning lying on his father's grave began to fade, and I found myself less likely to recall at odd moments how I had dropped the souvenir pillow, still smoldering, over his staring eyes in the Tracker mausoleum.

By the end of October, as the last of the leaves were swirling down from the trees and the nighttime temperatures began to dip into the thirties, I started driving into Durham, getting the lay of the land around Bowie Hill, where a shooting was going to occur in another two weeks. The Friends' Meeting House Al had mentioned made a convenient landmark. Not far past it, a dead tree was leaning toward the road, probably the one Al had been struggling with when Andrew Cullum came along, already wearing his orange hunting vest. I also made it a point to locate the accidental shooter's home, and to trace his probable course from there to Bowie Hill.

My plan was no plan at all, really; I'd just follow the trail Al had already blazed. I'd drive to Durham early in the day, park near the fallen tree, struggle with it, then pretend to have a heart attack when Cullum came along and pitched in. But after locating Cullum's house, I happened to stop for a cold drink at Brownie's Store half a mile away, and saw a poster in the window that gave me an idea. It was crazy, but sort of interesting.

The poster was headed ANDROSCOGGIN COUNTY CRIBBAGE TOURNAMENT RESULTS. There followed a list of about fifty names. The tourney winner, from West Minot, had scored ten thousand "pegs," whatever they were. The runner-up had scored ninety-five hundred. In third place, with 8,722 pegs—the name had been circled in red, which was what drew my attention in the first place—was Andy Cullum.

Coincidences happen, but I've come to believe they are actually quite rare. Something is at work, okay? Somewhere in the universe (or behind it), a great machine is ticking and turning its fabulous gears.

The next day, I drove back to Cullum's house just shy of five in the afternoon. I parked behind his Ford woody station wagon and went to the door.

A pleasant-faced woman wearing a ruffled apron and holding a baby in the crook of her arm opened to my knock, and I knew just looking at her that I was doing the right thing. Because Carolyn Poulin wasn't going to be the only victim on the fifteenth of November, just the one who'd end up in a wheelchair.

"Yes?"

"My name's George Amberson, ma'am." I tipped my hat to her. "I wonder if I could speak to your husband."

Sure I could. He'd already come up behind her and put an arm around her shoulders. A young guy, not yet thirty, now wearing an expression of pleasant inquiry. His baby reached for his face, and when Cullum kissed the kid's fingers, she laughed. Cullum extended his hand to me, and I shook it.

"What can I do for you, Mr. Amberson?"

I held up the cribbage board. "I noticed at Brownie's that you're quite the player. So I have a proposal for you."

Mrs. Cullum looked alarmed. "My husband and I are Methodists, Mr. Amberson. The tournaments are just for fun. He won a trophy, and I'm happy to polish it for him so it looks good on the mantel, but if you want to play cards for money, you've come to the wrong household." She smiled. I could see it cost her an effort, but it was still a good one. I liked her. I liked both of them.

"She's right." Cullum sounded regretful but firm. "I used to play penny-a-peg back when I was working in the woods, but that was before I met Marnie."

"I'd be crazy to play you for money," I said, "because I don't play at all. But I want to learn."

"In that case, come on in," he said. "I'll be happy to teach you. Won't take but fifteen minutes, and it's an hour yet before we eat our dinner. Shoot a pickle, if you can add to fifteen and count to thirty-one, you can play cribbage."

"I'm sure there's more to it than a little counting and adding, or you wouldn't have placed third in the Androscoggin Tournament," I said. "And I actually want a little more than to just learn

272

the rules. I want to buy a day of your time. November the fifteenth, to be exact. From ten in the morning until four in the afternoon, let's say."

Now his wife began to look scared. She was holding the baby close to her chest.

"For those six hours of your time, I'll pay you two hundred dollars."

Cullum frowned. "What's your game, mister?"

"I'm hoping to make it cribbage." That, however, wasn't going to be enough. I saw it on their faces. "Look, I'm not going to try and kid you that there isn't more to it, but if I tried to explain, you'd think I was crazy."

"I think that already," Marnie Cullum said. "Send him on his way, Andy."

I turned to her. "It's nothing bad, it's nothing illegal, it's not a scam, and it's not dangerous. I take my oath on it." But I was starting to think it wasn't going to work, oath or no oath. It had been a bad idea. Cullum would be doubly suspicious when he met me near the Friends' Meeting House on the afternoon of the fifteenth.

But I kept pushing. It was a thing I'd learned to do in Derry.

"It's just *cribbage*," I said. "You teach me the game, we play for a few hours, I give you two hundred bucks, and we all part friends. What do you say?"

"Where are you from, Mr. Amberson?"

"Upstate in Derry, most recently. I'm in commercial real estate. Right now I'm vacationing on Sebago Lake before heading back down south. Do you want some names? References, so to speak?" I smiled. "People who'll tell you I'm not nuts?"

"He goes out in the woods on Saturdays during hunting season," Mrs. Cullum said. "It's the only chance he gets, because he works all week and when he gets home it's so close to dark it doesn't even pay to load a gun."

She still looked mistrustful, but now I saw something else on her face that gave me hope. When you're young and have a kid, when your husband works manual labor—which his chapped, callused hands said he did—two hundred bucks can mean a lot of groceries. Or, in 1958, two and a half house payments.

"I could miss an afternoon in the woods," Cullum said. "Town's pretty well hunted out, anyway. The only place left where you can get a damn deer is Bowie Hill."

"Watch your language around the baby, Mr. Cullum," she said. Her tone was sharp, but she smiled when he kissed her cheek.

"Mr. Amberson, I need to talk to m'wife," Cullum said. "Do you mind standing on the stoop for a minute or two?"

"I'll do better than that," I said. "I'll go down to Brownie's and get myself a dope." That was what most Derryites called sodas. "Can I bring either of you back a cold drink?"

They declined with thanks, and then Marnie Cullum closed the door in my face. I drove to Brownie's, where I bought an Orange Crush for myself and a licorice whip I thought the baby might like, if she was old enough to have such things. The Cullums were going to turn me down, I thought. With thanks, but firmly. I was a strange man with a strange proposal. I had hoped that changing the past might be easier this time, because Al had already changed it twice. Apparently that wasn't going to be the case.

But I got a surprise. Cullum said yes, and his wife allowed me to give the licorice to the little girl, who received it with a gleeful chortle, sucked on it, then ran it through her hair like a comb. They even invited me to stay for the evening meal, which I declined. I offered Andy Cullum a fifty-dollar retainer, which *he* declined . . . until his wife insisted that he take it.

I went back to Sebago feeling exultant, but as I drove back to Durham on the morning of November fifteenth (the fields white with a frost so thick that the orange-clad hunters, who were already out in force, left tracks), my mood had changed. *He will have called the State Police or the local constable,* I thought. *And while they're questioning me in the nearest police station, trying to find out what kind of loony I am, Cullum will be off hunting in the Bowie Hill woods.*

But there was no police car in the driveway, just Andy Cullum's

Ford woody. I took my new cribbage board and went to the door. He opened it and said, "Ready for your lesson, Mr. Amberson?"

I smiled. "Yes, sir, I am."

He took me out to the back porch; I don't think the missus wanted me in the house with her and the baby. The rules were simple. Pegs were points, and a game was two laps around the board. I learned about the right jack, double runs, being stuck in the mudhole, and what Andy called "mystic nineteen"—the so-called impossible hand. Then we played. I kept track of the score to begin with, but quit once Cullum pulled four hundred points ahead. Every now and then some hunter would bang off a distant round, and Cullum would look toward the woods beyond his small backyard.

"Next Saturday," I said on one of these occasions. "You'll be out there next Saturday, for sure."

"It'll probably rain," he said, then laughed. "I should complain, huh? I'm having fun and making money. And you're getting better, George."

Marnie gave us lunch at noon—big tuna sandwiches and bowls of homemade tomato soup. We ate in the kitchen, and when we were done, she suggested we bring our game inside. She had decided I wasn't dangerous, after all. That made me happy. They were nice people, the Cullums. A nice couple with a nice baby. I thought of them sometimes when I heard Lee and Marina Oswald screaming at each other in their low-end apartments . . . or saw them, on at least one occasion, carry their animus out onto the street. The past harmonizes; it also tries to balance, and mostly succeeds. The Cullums were at one end of the seesaw; the Oswalds were at the other.

And Jake Epping, also known as George Amberson? He was the tipping point.

Toward the end of our marathon session, I won my first game. Three games later, at just a few minutes past four, I actually skunked him, and laughed with delight. Baby Jenna laughed right along with me, then leaned forward from her highchair and gave my hair a companionable tug.

"That's it!" I cried, laughing. The three Cullums were laughing right along with me. "That's the one I stop on!" I took out my wallet and laid three fifties down on the red-and-white checked oilcloth covering the kitchen table. "And worth every cent!"

Andy pushed it back to my side. "Put it in your billfold where it belongs, George. I had too much fun to take your money."

I nodded as if I agreed, then pushed the bills to Marnie, who snatched them up. "Thank you, Mr. Amberson." She looked reproachfully at her husband, then back at me. "We can really use this."

"Good." I got up and stretched, hearing my spine crackle. Somewhere—five miles from here, maybe seven—Carolyn Poulin and her father were getting back into a pickemup with POULIN CONSTRUCTION AND CARPENTRY painted on the door. Maybe they'd gotten a deer, maybe not. Either way, I was sure they'd had a nice afternoon in the woods, talking about whatever fathers and daughters talk about, and good for them.

"Stay for supper, George," Marnie said. "I've got beans and hot-dogs."

So I stayed, and afterward we watched the news on the Cullums' little table-model TV. There had been a hunting accident in New Hampshire, but none in Maine. I allowed myself to be talked into a second dish of Marnie's apple cobbler, although I was full to bursting, then stood and thanked them very much for their hospitality.

Andy Cullum put out his hand. "Next time we play for free, all right?"

"You bet." There was going to be no next time, and I think he knew that.

His wife did, too, it turned out. She caught up to me just before I got into my car. She had swaddled a blanket around the baby and put a little hat on her head, but Marnie had no coat on herself. I could see her breath, and she was shivering.

"Mrs. Cullum, you should go in before you catch your death of c—"

"What did you save him from?"

"I beg pardon?"

"I know that's why you came. I prayed on it while you and Andy were out there on the porch. God sent me an answer, but not the *whole* answer. What did you save him from?"

I put my hands on her shivering shoulders and looked into her eyes. "Marnie . . . if God had wanted you to know that part, He would have told you."

Abruptly she put her arms around me and hugged me. Surprised, I hugged her back. Baby Jenna, caught in between, goggled up at us.

"Whatever it was, thank you," Marnie whispered in my ear. Her warm breath gave me goosebumps.

"Go inside, hon. Before you freeze."

The front door opened. Andy was standing there, holding a can of beer. "Marnie? Marn?"

She stepped back. Her eyes were wide and dark. "God brought us a guardian angel," she said. "I won't speak of this, but I'll hold it. And ponder it in my heart." Then she hurried up the walk to where her husband was waiting.

Angel. It was the second time I'd heard that, and I pondered the word in my own heart, both that night while I lay in my cabin, waiting for sleep, and the next day as I drifted my canoe across still Sunday waters under a cold blue tilting-to-winter sky.

Guardian angel.

On Monday the seventeenth of November, I saw the first whirling flurries of snow, and took them as a sign. I packed up, drove down to Sebago Village, and found Mr. Winchell drinking coffee and eating doughnuts at the Lakeside Restaurant (in 1958, folks eat a lot of doughnuts). I gave him my keys and told him I'd had a wonderful, restorative time. His face lit up.

"That's good, Mr. Amberson. That's just how it's s'posed to be. You're paid until the end of the month. Give me an address where I can send you a refund for your last two weeks, and I'll put a check in the mail."

"I won't be entirely sure where I'm going until the brass in the home office makes up its corporate mind," I said, "but I'll be sure to write you." Time-travelers lie a lot.

He held out his hand. "Been a pleasure having you."

I shook it. "The pleasure was all mine."

I got in my car and drove south. That night I registered at Boston's Parker House, and checked out the infamous Combat Zone. After the weeks of peace on Sebago, the neon jangled my eyes and the surging crowds of night prowlers—mostly young, mostly male, many wearing uniforms—made me feel both agoraphobic and homesick for those peaceful nights in western Maine, when the few stores closed at six and traffic dried up at ten.

I spent the following night at the Hotel Harrington, in D.C. Three days later I was on the west coast of Florida.

CHAPTER 12

1

I took US 1 south. I ate in a lot of roadside restaurants featuring Mom's Home Cooking, places where the Blue Plate Special, including fruit cup to start and pie à la mode for dessert, cost eighty cents. I never saw a single fast-food franchise, unless you count Howard Johnson's, with its 28 Flavors and Simple Simon logo. I saw a troop of Boy Scouts tending a bonfire of fall leaves with their Scoutmaster; I saw women wearing overcoats and galoshes taking in laundry on a gray afternoon when rain threatened; I saw long passenger trains with names like *The Southern Flyer* and *Star of Tampa* charging toward those American climes where winter is not allowed. I saw old men smoking pipes on benches in town squares. I saw a million churches, and a cemetery where a congregation at least a hundred strong stood in a circle around an open grave singing "The Old Rugged Cross." I saw men building barns. I saw people helping people. Two of them in a pickup truck stopped to help me when the Sunliner's radiator popped its top and I was broken down by the side of the road. That was in Virginia, around four o'clock in the afternoon, and one of them asked me if I needed a place to sleep. I guess I can imagine that happening in 2011, but it's a stretch.

And one more thing. In North Carolina, I stopped to gas up at a Humble Oil station, then walked around the corner to use the toilet. There were two doors and three signs. **MEN** was neatly stenciled over one door, **LADIES** over the other. The third sign was an arrow on a stick. It pointed toward the brush-covered slope behind the station. It said *COLORED*. Curious, I walked down the path, being careful to sidle at a couple of points where the oily, green-shading-to-maroon leaves of poison ivy were unmistakable. I hoped the dads and moms who might have led their children down to whatever facility waited below were able to identify those troublesome bushes for what they were, because in the late fifties most children wear short pants.

There *was* no facility. What I found at the end of the path was a narrow stream with a board laid across it on a couple of crumbling concrete posts. A man who had to urinate could just stand on the bank, unzip, and let fly. A woman could hold onto a bush (assuming it wasn't poison ivy or poison oak) and squat. The board was what you sat on if you had to take a shit. Maybe in the pouring rain.

If I ever gave you the idea that 1958's all Andy-n-Opie, remember the path, okay? The one lined with poison ivy. And the board over the stream.

2

I settled sixty miles south of Tampa, in the town of Sunset Point. For eighty dollars a month, I rented a conch shack on the most beautiful (and mostly deserted) beach I had ever seen. There were four similar shacks on my stretch of sand, all as humble as my own. Of the nouveau-ugly McMansions that would later sprout like concrete toadstools in this part of the state, I saw none. There was a supermarket ten miles south, in Nokomis, and a sleepy shopping district in Venice. Route 41, the Tamiami Trail, was little more than a country road. You had to go slow on it, particularly toward dusk, because that's when the gators and the armadillos liked to cross. Between Sarasota and Venice, there were fruit stands, roadside markets, a couple of bars, and a dancehall called Blackie's.

Beyond Venice, brother, you were mostly on your own, at least until you got to Fort Myers.

I left George Amberson's real estate persona behind. By the spring of 1959, recessionary times had come to America. On Florida's Gulf Coast, everybody was selling and nobody was buying, so George Amberson became exactly what Al had envisioned: an authorial wannabe whose moderately rich uncle had left him enough to live on, at least for awhile.

I *did* write, and not on one project but two. In the mornings, when I was freshest, I began work on the manuscript you're now reading (if there ever *is* a you). In the evenings I worked on a novel that I tentatively called *The Murder Place.* The place in question was Derry, of course, although I called it Dawson in my book. I began it solely as set decoration, so I'd have something to show if I made friends and one of them asked to see what I was working on (I kept my "morning manuscript" in a steel lockbox under my bed). Eventually *The Murder Place* became more than camouflage. I began to think it was good, and to dream that someday it might even see print.

An hour on the memoir in the morning and an hour on the novel at night still left a lot of time to be filled. I tried fishing, and there were plenty of fish to be caught, but I didn't like it and gave it up. Walking was fine at dawn and sunset, but not in the heat of the day. I became a regular patron of Sarasota's one bookstore, and I spent long (and mostly happy) hours at the little libraries in Nokomis and Osprey.

I read and reread Al's Oswald stuff, too. Finally I recognized this for the obsessive behavior it was, and put the notebook in the lockbox with my "morning manuscript." I have called those notes exhaustive, and so they seemed to me then, but as time—the conveyor belt on which we all must ride—brought me closer and closer to the point where my life might converge with that of the young assassin-to-be, they began to seem less so. There were holes.

Sometimes I cursed Al for forcing me into this mission willy-nilly, but in more clearheaded moments, I realized that extra time wouldn't have made any difference. It might have made things worse, and Al probably knew it. Even if he hadn't committed suicide, I would only have had a week or two, and how many books have been written about the chain of events leading up to that day in Dallas? A hundred? Three hundred? Probably closer to a thousand. Some agreeing with Al's belief that Oswald acted alone, some claiming he'd been part of an elaborate conspiracy, some stating with utter certainty that he hadn't pulled the trigger at all and was exactly what he called himself after his arrest, a patsy. By committing suicide, Al had taken away the scholar's greatest weakness: calling hesitation research.

3

I made occasional trips to Tampa, where discreet questioning led me to a bookmaker named Eduardo Gutierrez. Once he was sure I wasn't a cop, he was delighted to take my action. I first bet the Minneapolis Lakers to beat the Celtics in the '59 championship series, thereby establishing my bona fides as a sucker; the Lakers didn't win a single game. I also bet four hundred on the Canadiens to beat the Maple Leafs in the Stanley Cup Series, and won . . . but that was even money. Chump change, cuz, my pal Chaz Frati would have said.

My single large strike came in the spring of 1960, when I bet on Venetian Way to beat Bally Ache, the heavy favorite in the Kentucky Derby. Gutierrez said he'd give me four-to-one on a gee, five-to-one on a double gee. I went for the double after making the appropriate noises of hesitation, and came away ten thousand richer. He paid off with Frati-esque good cheer, but there was a steely glint in his eyes that I didn't care for.

Gutierrez was a Cubano who probably didn't weigh one-forty soaking wet, but he was also an expat from the New Orleans Mob, run in those days by a bad boy named Carlos Marcello. I got this bit of gossip in the billiard parlor next to the barbershop where

Gutierrez ran his book (and an apparently never-ending backroom poker game under a photograph of a barely clad Diana Dors). The man with whom I'd been playing nineball leaned forward, looked around to make sure we had the corner table to ourselves, then murmured, "You know what they say about the Mob, George— once in, never out."

I would have liked to have spoken to Gutierrez about his years in New Orleans, but I didn't think it would be wise to be too curious, especially after my big Derby payday. If I *had* dared—and if I could have thought of a plausible way to raise the subject— I would have asked Gutierrez if he'd ever been acquainted with another reputed member of the Marcello organization, an ex-pug named Charles "Dutz" Murret. I somehow think the answer would have been yes, because the past harmonizes with itself. Dutz Murret's wife was Marguerite Oswald's sister. Which made him Lee Harvey Oswald's uncle.

4

One day in the spring of 1959 (there *is* spring in Florida; the natives told me it sometimes lasts as long as a week), I opened my mailbox and discovered a call-card from the Nokomis Public Library. I had reserved a copy of *The Disenchanted,* the new Budd Schulberg novel, and it had just come in. I jumped in my Sunliner—no better car for what was then becoming known as the Sun Coast—and drove up to get it.

On my way out, I noticed a new poster on the cluttered bulletin board in the foyer. It would have been hard to miss; it was bright blue and featured a shivering cartoon man who was looking at an oversized thermometer where the mercury was registering ten below zero. GOT A DEGREE PROBLEM? the poster demanded. YOU MAY BE ELIGIBLE FOR A MAIL-ORDER CERTIFI-CATE FROM UNITED COLLEGE OF OKLAHOMA! WRITE FOR DETAILS!

United College of Oklahoma sounded fishier than a mackerel stew, but it gave me an idea. Mostly because I was bored. Oswald was still in the Marines, and wouldn't be discharged until September, when he would head for Russia. His first move would be an effort to renounce his American citizenship. He wouldn't succeed, but after a showy—and probably bogus—suicide attempt in a Moscow hotel, the Russians were going to let him stay in their country. "On approval," so to speak. He'd be there for thirty months or so, working at a radio factory in Minsk. And at a party he would meet a girl named Marina Prusakova. *Red dress, white slippers,* Al had written in his notes. *Pretty. Dressed for dancing.*

Fine for him, but what was I going to do in the meantime? United College offered one possibility. I wrote for details, and received a prompt response. The catalogue touted an absolute plethora of degrees. I was fascinated to discover that, for three hundred dollars (cash or money order), I could receive a bachelor's in English. All I had to do was pass a test consisting of fifty multiple choice questions.

I got the money order, mentally kissed my three hundred goodbye, and sent in an application. Two weeks later, I received a thin manila envelope from United College. Inside were two smearily mimeographed sheets. The questions were wonderful. Here are two of my favorites:

22. What was "Moby's" last name?
   A. Tom
   B. Dick
   C. Harry
   D. John
37. Who wrote "The House of 7 Tables"?
   A. Charles Dickens
   B. Henry James
   C. Ann Bradstreet
   D. Nathaniel Hawthorne
   E. None of these

When I finished enjoying this wonderful test, I filled out the answers (with the occasional cry of "You've *got* to be shitting me!") and sent it back to Enid, Oklahoma. I got a postcard by return mail congratulating me on passing my exam. After I had paid an additional fifty-dollar "administration fee," I was informed, I would be sent my degree. So I was told, and lo, so it came to pass. The degree was a good deal better looking than the test had been, and came with an impressive gold seal. When I presented it to a representative of the Sarasota County Schoolboard, that worthy accepted it without question and put me on the substitute list.

Which is how I ended up teaching again for one or two days each week during the 1959–1960 academic year. It was good to be back. I enjoyed the students—boys with flattop crewcuts, girls with ponytails and shin-length poodle skirts—although I was painfully aware that the faces I saw in the various classrooms I visited were all of the plain vanilla variety. Those days of substituting reacquainted me with a basic fact of my personality: I liked writing, and had discovered I was good at it, but what I loved was teaching. It filled me up in some way I can't explain. Or want to. Explanations are such cheap poetry.

My best day as a sub came at West Sarasota High, after I'd told an American Lit class the basic story of *The Catcher in the Rye* (a book which was not, of course, allowed in the school library and would have been confiscated if brought into those sacred halls by a student) and then encouraged them to talk about Holden Caulfield's chief complaint: that school, grown-ups, and American life in general were all phony. The kids started slow, but by the time the bell rang, everyone was trying to talk at once, and half a dozen risked tardiness at their next classes to offer some final opinion on what was wrong with the society they saw around them and the lives their parents had planned for them. Their eyes were bright, their faces flushed with excitement. I had no doubt there was going to be a run on a certain dark red paperback at the area bookstores. The last one to leave was a muscular kid wearing a football sweater. To me he looked like Moose Mason in the Archie comic books.

"Ah wish you was here all the time, Mr. Amberson," he said in his soft Southern accent. "Ah dig you the most."

He didn't just dig me; he dug me the *most.* Nothing can compare to hearing something like that from a seventeen-year-old kid who looks like he might be fully awake for the first time in his academic career.

Later that month, the principal called me into his office, offered some pleasantries and a Co'-Cola, then asked: "Son, are you a subversive?" I assured him I was not. I told him I'd voted for Ike. He seemed satisfied, but suggested I might stick more to the "generally accepted reading list" in the future. Hairstyles change, and skirt lengths, and slang, but high school administrations? Never.

5

In a college class once (this was at the University of Maine, a real college from which I had obtained a real BS degree), I heard a psychology prof opine that humans actually *do* possess a sixth sense. He called it *hunch-think,* and said it was most well developed in mystics and outlaws. I was no mystic, but I was both an exile from my own time and a murderer (I might consider the shooting of Frank Dunning justified, but the police certainly wouldn't see it that way). If those things didn't make me an outlaw, nothing could.

"My advice to you in situations where danger appears to threaten," the prof said that day in 1995, "is heed the hunch."

I decided to do just that in July of 1960. I was becoming increasingly uneasy about Eduardo Gutierrez. He was a little guy, but there were those reputed Mob connections to consider . . . and the glint in his eyes when he'd paid off on my Derby bet, which I now considered foolishly large. Why had I made it, when I was still far from broke? It wasn't greed; it was more the way a good hitter feels, I suppose, when he is presented with a hanging curveball. In some cases, you just can't help swinging for the fences. I swang, as Leo "The Lip" Durocher used to put it in his colorful radio broadcasts, but now I regretted it.

I purposely lost the last two wagers I put down with Gutierrez, trying my best to make myself look foolish, just a garden-variety plunger who happened to get lucky once and would presently lose it all back, but my hunch-think told me it wasn't playing very well. My hunch-think didn't like it when Gutierrez started greeting me with, "Oh, see! Here comes my Yanqui from Yankeeland." Not *the* Yanqui; *my* Yanqui.

Suppose he had detailed one of his poker-playing friends to follow me back to Sunset Point from Tampa? Was it possible he might send some of his other poker-playing friends—or a couple of muscle boys hungry to get out from under whatever loan-shark vig Gutierrez was currently charging—to do a little salvage operation and get back whatever remained of that ten thousand? My front mind thought that was the sort of lame plot device that turned up on PI shows like *77 Sunset Strip,* but hunch said something different. Hunch said that the little man with the thinning hair was perfectly capable of green-lighting a home invasion, and telling the black-baggers to beat the shit out of me if I tried to object. I didn't want to get beaten up and I didn't want to be robbed. Most of all, I didn't want to risk my pages falling into the hands of a Mob-connected bookie. I didn't like the idea of running away with my tail between my legs, but hell, I had to make my way to Texas sooner or later in any case, so why not sooner? Besides, discretion is the better part of valor. I learned that at my mother's knee.

So after a mostly sleepless July night when the sonar pings of hunch had been particularly strong, I packed my worldly goods (the lockbox containing my memoir and my cash I hid beneath the Sunliner's spare tire), left a note and a final rent check for my landlord, and headed north on US 19. I spent my first night on the road in a decaying DeFuniak Springs motor court. The screens had holes in them, and until I turned out my room's one light (an unshaded bulb dangling on a length of electrical cord), I was beset by mosquitoes the size of fighter planes.

Yet I slept like a baby. There were no nightmares, and the pings of my interior radar had fallen silent. That was good enough for me.

I spent the first of August in Gulfport, although the first place I stopped at, on the town's outskirts, refused to take me. The clerk of the Red Top Inn explained to me that it was for Negroes only, and directed me to The Southern Hospitality, which he called "Guff-pote's finest." Maybe so, but on the whole, I think I would have preferred the Red Top. The slide guitar coming from the bar-and-barbecue next door had sounded terrific.

6

New Orleans wasn't precisely on my way to Big D, but with the hunch-sonar quiet, I found myself in a touristy frame of mind . . . although it wasn't the French Quarter, the Bienville Street steamboat landing, or the Vieux Carré I wanted to visit.

I bought a map from a street-vendor and found my way to the one destination that did interest me. I parked and after a five-minute walk found myself standing in front of 4905 Magazine Street, where Lee and Marina Oswald would be living with their daughter, June, in the last spring and summer of John Kennedy's life. It was a shambling not-quite-wreck of a building with a waist-high iron fence surrounding an overgrown yard. The paint on the lower story, once white, was now a peeling shade of urine yellow. The upper story was unpainted gray barnboard. A piece of cardboard blocking a broken window up there read 4-RENT CALL MU3-4192. Rusty screens enclosed the porch where, in September of 1963, Lee Oswald would sit in his underwear after dark, whispering *"Pow! Pow! Pow!"* under his breath and dry-firing what was going to become the most famous rifle in American history at passing pedestrians.

I was thinking of this when someone tapped me on the shoulder, and I almost screamed. I guess I *did* jump, because the young black man who had accosted me took a respectful step backward, raising his open hands.

"Sorry, sah. Sorry, sho din mean to make you stahtle."

"It's all right," I said. "Totally my fault."

This declaration seemed to make him uneasy, but he had business on his mind and pressed ahead with it . . . although he had to come close again, because his business entailed a tone of voice lower than the conversational. He wanted to know if I might be interested in buying a few joysticks. I thought I knew what he was talking about, but wasn't entirely sure until he added, "Ha-quality swampweed, sah."

I told him I'd pass, but if he could direct me to a good hotel in the Paris of the South, it would be worth half a rock to me. When he spoke again, his speech was a good deal crisper. "Opinions differ, but I'd say the Hotel Monteleone." He gave me good directions.

"Thanks," I said, and handed over the coin. It disappeared into one of his many pockets.

"Say, what you lookin at that place for, anyway?" He nodded toward the ramshackle apartment house. "You thinkin bout buyin it?"

A little twinkle of the old George Amberson surfaced. "You must live around here. Do you think it would be a good deal?"

"Some on this street might be, but not that one. To me it looks haunted."

"Not yet," I said, and headed for my car, leaving him to look after me, perplexed.

7

I took the lockbox out of the trunk and put it on the Sunliner's passenger seat, meaning to hand-carry it up to my room at the Monteleone, and I did just that. But while the doorman was getting the rest of my bags, I spotted something on the floor of the backseat that made me flush with a sense of guilt that was far out of proportion to what the object was. But childhood teachings are the strongest teachings, and another thing I was taught at my mother's knee was to always return library books on time.

"Mr. Doorman, would you hand me that book, please?" I asked.

"Yes, sah! Happy to!"

It was *The Chapman Report,* which I'd borrowed from the Nokomis Public Library a week or so before deciding it was time to put on my traveling shoes. The sticker in the corner of the transparent protective cover—*7 DAYS ONLY, BE KIND TO THE NEXT BORROWER*—reproached me.

When I got to my room, I checked my watch and saw it was only 6:00 P.M. In the summer, the library didn't open until noon but stayed open until eight. Long distance is one of the few things more expensive in 1960 than in 2011, but that childish sense of guilt was still on me. I called the hotel operator and gave her the Nokomis Library's telephone number, reading it off the card-pocket pasted to the back flyleaf of the book. The little message below it, *Please Call if You Will Be More Than 3 Days Late in Your Return,* made me feel more like a dog than ever.

My operator talked to another operator. Behind them, faint voices babbled. I realized that in the time I came from, most of those distant speakers would be dead. Then the phone began to ring on the other end.

"Hello, Nokomis Public Library." It was Hattie Wilkerson's voice, but that sweet old lady sounded like she was stuck in a very large steel barrel.

"Hello, Mrs. Wilkerson—"

"Hello? *Hello?* Do you hear me? *Drat* long distance!"

"Hattie?" I was shouting now. "It's George Amberson calling!"

"George *Amberson?* Oh, my soul! Where are you calling from, George?"

I almost told her the truth, but the hunch-radar gave out a single very loud ping and I bellowed, "Baton Rouge!"

"In Louisiana?"

"Yes! I have one of your books! I just realized! I'm going to send it ba—"

"You don't need to shout, George, the connection is *much* better now. The operator must not have stuck our little plug in the whole way. I am *so* glad to hear from you. It's God's providence that you weren't there. We were worried even though the fire chief said the house was empty."

"What are you talking about, Hattie? My place on the beach?"

But really, what else?

"Yes! Someone threw a flaming bottle of gasoline through the window. The whole thing went up in a matter of minutes. Chief Durand thinks it was kids who were out drinking and carousing. There are so many bad apples now. It's because they're afraid of the Bomb, that's what my husband says."

So.

"George? Are you still there?"

"Yes," I said.

"Which book do you have?"

"What?"

"Which *book* do you have? Don't make me check the card catalogue."

"Oh. *The Chapman Report.*"

"Well, send it back as soon as you can, won't you? We have quite a few people waiting for that one. Irving Wallace is extremely popular."

"Yes," I said. "I'll be sure to do that."

"And I'm very sorry about your house. Did you lose your things?"

"I have everything important with me."

"Thank God for that. Will you be coming back s—"

There was a click loud enough to sting my ear, then the burr of an open line. I replaced the receiver in the cradle. Would I be coming back soon? I saw no need to call back and answer that question. But I would watch out for the past, because it senses change-agents, and it has teeth.

I sent *The Chapman Report* back to the Nokomis Library first thing in the morning.

Then I left for Dallas.

8

Three days later I was sitting on a bench in Dealey Plaza and looking at the square brick cube of the Texas School Book Depository. It was late afternoon, and blazingly hot. I had pulled down my tie (if you don't wear one in 1960, even on hot days, you're apt to attract unwanted attention) and unbuttoned the top button of my plain white shirt, but it didn't help much. Neither did the scant shade of the elm behind my bench.

When I checked into the Adolphus Hotel on Commerce Street, I was offered a choice: air-conditioning or no air-conditioning. I paid the extra five bucks for a room where the window-unit lowered the temperature all the way to seventy-eight, and if I had a brain in my head, I'd go back to it now, before I keeled over with heatstroke. When night came, maybe it would cool off. Just a little.

But that brick cube held my gaze, and the windows—especially the one on the right corner of the sixth floor—seemed to be examining me. There was a palpable sense of wrongness about the building. You—if there ever *is* a you—might scoff at that, calling it nothing but the effect of my unique foreknowledge, but that didn't account for what was really holding me on that bench in spite of the beating heat. What did that was the sense that I had seen the building before.

It reminded me of the Kitchener Ironworks, in Derry.

The Book Depository wasn't a ruin, but it conveyed the same sense of sentient menace. I remembered coming on that submerged, soot-blackened smokestack, lying in the weeds like a giant prehistoric snake dozing in the sun. I remembered looking into its dark bore, so large I could have walked into it. And I remembered feeling that something was in there. Something alive. Something that *wanted* me to walk into it. So I could visit. Maybe for a long, long time.

Come on in, the sixth-floor window whispered. *Take a look around. The place is empty now, the skeleton crew that works here in the summer has gone home, but if you walk around to the loading dock by the railroad tracks, you'll find an open door, I'm quite sure of it. After all, what is there in here to protect? Nothing but schoolbooks, and even the students they're meant for don't really want them. As you well know, Jake. So come in. Come on up to the sixth floor. In your time there's a museum here, people come from all over the world and some of them still weep for the man who was killed and all he might have done, but this is 1960, Kennedy's still a senator, and Jake Epping doesn't exist. Only George Amberson exists, a man with a short haircut and a sweaty shirt and a pulled-down tie. A man of his time, so to speak. So come on up. Are you afraid of ghosts? How can you be, when the crime hasn't happened yet?*

But there *were* ghosts up there. Maybe not on Magazine Street in New Orleans, but there? Oh yes. Only I'd never have to face them, because I was going to enter the Book Depository no more than I had ventured into that fallen smokestack in Derry. Oswald would get his job stacking textbooks just a month or so before the assassination, and waiting that long would be cutting things far too close. No, I intended to follow the plan Al had roughed out in the closing section of his notes, the one titled *CONCLUSIONS ON HOW TO PROCEDE.*

Sure as he was about his lone gunman theory, Al had held onto a small but statistically significant possibility that he was wrong. In his notes, he called it "the window of uncertainty."

As in sixth-floor window.

He had meant to close that window for good on April 10, 1963, over half a year before Kennedy's trip to Dallas, and I thought his idea made sense. Possibly later that April, more likely on the night of the tenth—why wait?—I would kill the husband of Marina and the father of June just as I had Frank Dunning. And with no more compunction. If you saw a spider scuttering across the floor toward your baby's crib, you might hesitate. You might even consider trapping it in a bottle and putting it out in the yard so it could go on living its little life. But if you were sure that spider was poisonous? A black widow? In that case, you wouldn't hesitate. Not if you were sane.

You'd put your foot on it and crush it.

9

I had a plan of my own for the years between August of 1960 and April of 1963. I'd keep my eye on Oswald when he came back from Russia, but I wouldn't interfere. Because of the butterfly effect, I couldn't afford to. If there's a stupider metaphor than *a chain of events* in the English language, I don't know what it is. Chains (other than the ones we all learned to make out of strips of colored paper in kindergarten, I suppose) are strong. We use them to pull engine blocks out of trucks and to bind the arms and legs of dangerous prisoners. That was no longer reality as I understood it. Events are flimsy, I tell you, they are houses of cards, and by approaching Oswald—let alone trying to warn him off a crime which he had not yet even conceived—I would be giving away my only advantage. The butterfly would spread its wings, and Oswald's course would change.

Little changes at first, maybe, but as the Bruce Springsteen song tells us, from small things, baby, big things one day come. They might be good changes, ones that would save the man who was now the junior senator from Massachusetts. But I didn't believe that. Because the past is obdurate. In 1962, according to one of Al's scribbled marginal notes, Kennedy was going to be in Houston, at Rice University, making a speech about going to the moon. *Open auditorium, no bullet-pr'f podium,* Al had written. Houston was less than three hundred miles from Dallas. What if Oswald decided to shoot the president there?

Or suppose Oswald was exactly what he claimed to be, a patsy? What if I scared him out of Dallas and back to New Orleans and Kennedy *still* died, the victim of some crazy Mafia or CIA plot? Would I have courage enough to go back through the rabbit-hole and start all over? Save the Dunning family again? Save Carolyn Poulin again? I had already given nearly two years to this mission. Would I be willing to invest five more, with the outcome as uncertain as ever?

Better not to have to find out.

Better to make sure.

On my way to Texas from New Orleans, I had decided the best way to monitor Oswald without getting in his way would be to live in Dallas while he was in the sister city of Fort Worth, then relocate to Fort Worth when Oswald moved his family to Dallas. The idea had the virtue of simplicity, but it wouldn't work. I realized that in the weeks after looking at the Texas School Book Depository for the first time and feeling very strongly that it was—like Nietzsche's abyss—looking back at me.

I spent August and September of that presidential election year driving the Sunliner around Dallas, apartment-hunting (even after all this time sorely missing my GPS unit and frequently stopping to ask for directions). Nothing seemed right. At first I thought that was about the apartments themselves. Then, as I began to get a better sense of the city, I realized it was about me.

The simple truth was that I didn't like Dallas, and eight weeks of hard study was enough to make me believe there was a lot not to like. The *Times Herald* (which many Dallas-ites routinely called the *Slimes Herald*) was a tiresome juggernaut of nickel boosterism. The *Morning News* might wax lyrical, talking about how Dallas and Houston were "in a race to the heavens," but the skyscrapers of which the editorial spoke were an island of architectural blah surrounded by rings of what I came to think of as The Great American Flatcult. The newspapers ignored the slum neighborhoods where the divisions along racial lines were just beginning to melt a little. Further out were endless middle-class housing developments, mostly owned by veterans of World War II and Korea. The vets had wives who spent their days Pledging the furniture and Maytagging the clothes. Most had 2.5 children. The teenagers mowed lawns, delivered the *Slimes Herald* on bicycles, Turtle Waxed the family car, and listened (furtively) to Chuck Berry on transistor radios. Maybe telling their anxious parents he was white.

Beyond the suburban houses with their whirling lawn-sprinklers were those vast flat tracts of empty. Here and there rolling irrigators still serviced cotton crops, but mostly King Cotton was dead, replaced by endless acres of corn and soybeans. The real Dallas County crops were electronics, textiles, bullshit, and black money petro-dollars. There weren't many derricks in the area, but when the wind blew from the west, where the Permian Basin is, the twin cities stank of oil and natural gas.

The downtown business district was full of sharpies hustling around in what I came to think of as the Full Dallas: checked sport coats, narrow neckwear held down with bloated tie clips (these clips, the sixties version of bling, usually came with diamonds or plausible substitutes sparkling in their centers), white Sansabelt pants, and gaudy boots with complex stitching. They worked in banks and investment companies. They sold soybean futures and oil leases and real estate to the west of the city, land where nothing would grow except jimson and tumbleweed. They clapped each other on the shoulders with beringed hands and called each other *son*. On their belts, where businessmen in 2011 carry their cell phones, many carried handguns in hand-tooled holsters.

There were billboards advocating the impeachment of Supreme Court Chief Justice Earl Warren; billboards showing a snarling Nikita Khrushchev (NYET, COMRADE KHRUSHCHEV, the billboard copy read, WE WILL BURY *YOU!*); there was one on

West Commerce Street that read THE AMERICAN COMMU-
NIST PARTY FAVORS INTEGRATION. **THINK ABOUT IT!**
That one had been paid for by something called The Tea Party
Society. Twice, on businesses whose names suggested they were
Jewish-owned, I saw soaped swastikas.

I didn't like Dallas. No sir, no ma'am, no way. I hadn't liked it
from the moment I checked into the Adolphus and saw the restaurant maître d' gripping a cringing young waiter by the arm and
shouting into his face. Nevertheless, my business was here, and
here I would stay. That was what I thought then.

10

On the twenty-second of September, I finally found a place that
looked livable. It was on Blackwell Street in North Dallas, a
detached garage that had been converted into a pretty nice duplex
apartment. Greatest advantage: air-conditioning. Greatest dis-
advantage: the owner-landlord, Ray Mack Johnson, was a racist
who shared with me that if I took the place, it would be wise
to stay away from nearby Greenville Avenue, where there were a
lot of mixed-race jukejoints and coons with the kind of knives he
called "switchers."

"I got ary thing in the world against niggers," he told me.
"Nosir. It was God who cursed them to their position, not me.
You know that, don't you?"

"I guess I missed that part of the Bible."

He squinted suspiciously. "What are you, Methodist?"

"Yes," I said. It seemed a lot safer than saying I was, denomina-
tionally speaking, nothing.

"You need to get in the Baptist way of churching, son. Ours
welcomes newcomers. You take this place, and maybe some Sunday you can come with me n my wife."

"Maybe so," I agreed, reminding myself to be in a coma that
Sunday. Possibly dead.

Mr. Johnson, meanwhile, had returned to his original scripture.

"You see, Noah got drunk this one time on the Ark, and he was a-layin on his bed, naked as a jaybird. Two of his sons wouldn't look at him, they just turned the other way and put a blanket over him. I don't know, it might've been a sheet. But Ham—he was the coon of the family—looked on his father in his nakedness, and God cursed him and all his race to be hewers of wood and drawers of water. So there it is. That's what's behind it. Genesis, chapter nine. You go on and look it up, Mr. Amberson."

"Uh-huh," I said, telling myself that I had to go *someplace,* I couldn't afford to stay at the Adolphus indefinitely. Telling myself I could live with a little racism, that I wouldn't melt. Telling myself it was the temper of the times, and it was probably the same just about everywhere. Only I didn't quite believe it. "I'll think it over and let you know in a day or two, Mr. Johnson."

"You don't want to wait too long, son. This place will go fast. You have a blessed day, now."

11

The blessed day was another scorcher, and apartment-hunting was thirsty work. After leaving Ray Mack Johnson's learned company, I felt in need of a beer. I decided to get one on Greenville Avenue. If Mr. Johnson discouraged the neighborhood, I thought I ought to check it out.

He was correct on two counts: the street was integrated (more or less), and it was rough. It was also lively. I parked and strolled, savoring the carny atmosphere. I passed almost two dozen bars, a few second-run movie houses (COME IN IT'S "KOOL" INSIDE, read the banners flapping from the marquees in a hot, oil-smelling Texas wind), and a striptease joint where a streetside barker yelled "Girls, girls, girls, best burley-q in the whole damn world! Best burley-q you've ever *seen*! These ladies *shave,* if you know what I mean!" I also passed three or four check-cashing-and-quickie-loan storefronts. Standing bold as brass in front of one—Faith Financial, Where Trust Is Our Watchword—was a chalkboard with THE DAILY LINE printed at the top and FOR AMUSEMENT ONLY at the bottom. Men in straw hats and suspenders (a look only dedicated punters can pull off) were standing around it, discussing the posted odds. Some had racing forms; some had the *Morning News* sports section.

For amusement only, I thought. *Yeah, right.* For a moment I thought of my beachfront shack burning in the night, the flames pulled high into the starry black by the wind off the Gulf. Amusement had its drawbacks, especially when it came to betting.

Music and the smell of beer wafted out of open doorways. I heard Jerry Lee Lewis singing "Whole Lotta Shakin' Goin' On" from one juke and Ferlin Husky emoting "Wings of a Dove" from the one next door. I was propositioned by four hookers and a sidewalk vendor who was selling hubcaps, rhinestone-glittery straight razors, and Lone Star State flags embossed with the words DON'T MESS WITH TEXAS. Try translating that one into Latin.

That troubling sense of déjà vu was very strong, that feeling that things were wrong here just as they had been wrong before. Which was crazy—I'd never been on Greenville Avenue in my life—but it was also undeniable, a thing of the heart rather than the head. All at once I decided I didn't want a beer. And I didn't want to rent Mr. Johnson's converted garage, either, no matter how good the air-conditioning was.

I had just passed a watering hole called the Desert Rose, where the Rock-Ola was blasting Muddy Waters. As I turned to start back to where my car was parked, a man came flying out the door. He stumbled and went sprawling on the sidewalk. There was a burst of laughter from the bar's dark interior. A woman yelled, "And don't come back, you dickless wonder!" This produced more (and heartier) laughter.

The ejected patron was bleeding from the nose—which was bent severely to one side—and also from a scrape that ran down the left side of his face from temple to jawline. His eyes were huge and shocked. His untucked shirt flapped almost to his knees as he grabbed a lamppost and pulled himself to his feet. Once on them, he glared around at everything, seeing nothing.

I took a step or two toward him, but before I could get there, one of the women who'd asked me if I'd like a date came swaying up on stiletto heels. Only she wasn't a woman, not really. She couldn't have been more than sixteen, with large dark eyes and smooth coffee-colored skin. She was smiling, but not in a mean way, and when the man with the bloody face staggered, she took his arm. "Easy, sweetheart," she said. "You need to settle down before you—"

He raked up the hanging tails of his shirt. The pearl-handled grip of a pistol—much smaller than the one I'd bought at Machen's Sporting Goods, really not much more than a toy—lay against the pale fat hanging over the beltless waistband of his gabardine slacks. His fly was half-unzipped and I could see boxer shorts with red racing cars on them. I remember that. He pulled the gun, pressed the muzzle against the streetwalker's midriff, and pulled the trigger. There was a stupid little pop, the sound of a ladyfinger firecracker going off in a tin can, no more than that. The woman screamed and sat down on the sidewalk with her hands laced over her belly.

"You *shot* me!" She sounded more outraged than hurt, but blood had begun to spill through her fingers. "You *shot* me, you pissant bugger, why did you *shoot* me?"

He took no notice, only yanked open the door of the Desert Rose. I was still standing where I'd been when he shot the pretty young hooker, partly because I was frozen by shock, but mostly because all of this happened in a matter of seconds. Longer than it would take Oswald to kill the President of the United States, maybe, but not much.

"Is this what you want, Linda?" he shouted. "If this is what you want, I'll give you what you want!"

He put the muzzle of the gun into his ear and pulled the trigger.

12

I folded my handkerchief and pressed it gently over the hole in the young girl's red dress. I don't know how badly she was hurt, but she was lively enough to produce a steady stream of colorful phrases she had probably not learned from her mother (on the other hand, who knows). And when one man in the gathering crowd moved a little too close to suit her, she snarled: "Quit lookin up my dress, you nosy bastard. For that you pay."

"This pore ole sumbitch here is dead as can be," someone remarked. He was kneeling beside the man who had been thrown out of the Desert Rose. A woman began to shriek.

Approaching sirens: they were shrieking, too. I noticed one of the other ladies who had approached me during my stroll down Greenville Avenue, a redhead in capri pants. I beckoned to her. She touched her chest in a *who, me?* gesture, and I nodded. Yes, you. "Hold this handkerchief on the wound," I told her. "Try to stop the bleeding. I've got to go."

She gave me a wise little smile. "Don't want to hang around for the cops?"

"Not really. I don't know any of these people. I was just passing by."

The redhead knelt by the bleeding, cursing girl on the sidewalk, and pressed down on the sodden handkerchief. "Honey," she said, "aren't we all."

13

I couldn't sleep that night. I'd start to drift, then see Ray Mack Johnson's sweat-oily, complacent face as he blamed two thousand years of slavery, murder, and exploitation on some teenage kid eyeballing his father's gearshift. I'd jerk awake, settle back, drift . . . and see the little man with the unzipped fly sticking the muzzle of his hideout gun in his ear. *Is this what you want, Linda?* One final burst of petulance before the big sleep. And I'd start awake again. Next time it was men in a black sedan throwing a gasoline bomb through the front window of my place on Sunset Point: Eduardo Gutierrez attempting to get rid of his Yanqui from Yankeeland. Why? Because he didn't like to lose big, that was all. For him, that was enough.

Finally I gave up and sat down by the window, where the hotel air-conditioner was rattling gamely away. In Maine the night would be crisp enough to start bringing color to the trees, but here in Dallas it was still seventy-five at two-thirty in the morning. And humid.

"Dallas, Derry," I said as I looked down into the silent ditch of Commerce Street. The brick cube of the Book Depository wasn't visible, but it was close by. Walking distance.

"Derry, Dallas."

Each name comprised of two syllables that broke on the double letter like a stick of kindling over a bent knee. I couldn't stay here. Another thirty months in Big D would send me crazy. How long would it be before I started seeing graffiti like I WILL KILL MY MOTHER SOON? Or glimpsed a juju Jesus floating down the Trinity River? Fort Worth might be better, but Fort Worth was still too close.

Why do I have to stay in either?

This thought came to me shortly after 3:00 A.M., and with the force of a revelation. I had a fine car—a car I'd sort of fallen in love with, to tell you the truth—and there was no shortage of good fast roads in central Texas, many of them recently built. By the turn of the twenty-first century, they would probably be choked with traffic, but in 1960 they were almost eerily deserted. There were speed limits, but they weren't enforced. In Texas, even the state cops were believers in the gospel of put the pedal to the metal and let er bellow.

I could move out from beneath the suffocating shadow I felt over this city. I could find a place that was smaller and less daunting, a place that didn't feel so filled with hate and violence. In broad daylight I could tell myself I was imagining those things, but not in the ditch of the morning. There were undoubtedly good people in Dallas, thousands upon thousands of them, the great majority, but that underchord was there, and sometimes it broke out. As it had outside the Desert Rose.

Bevvie-from-the-levee had said that *In Derry I think the bad times are over.* I wasn't convinced about Derry, and I felt the same way about Dallas, even with its worst day still over three years away.

"I'll commute," I said. "George wants a nice quiet place to work on his book, but since the book is about a city—a *haunted* city—he really has to commute, doesn't he? To get material."

It was no wonder it took me almost two months to think of this; life's simplest answers are often the easiest to overlook. I went back to bed and fell asleep almost at once.

14

The next day I drove south out of Dallas on Highway 77. An hour and a half took me into Denholm County. I turned west onto State Road 109 mostly because I liked the billboard marking the intersection. It showcased a heroic young football player wearing a gold helmet, black jersey, and gold leggings. DENHOLM LIONS, the billboard proclaimed. 3-TIME DISTRICT CHAMPS! STATE CHAMPIONSHIP BOUND IN 1960! "WE'VE GOT JIM POWER!"

Whatever that is, I thought. But of course every high school has its secret signs and signals; it's what makes kids feel like they're on the inside.

Five miles up Highway 109, I came to the town of Jodie. POP. 1280, the sign said. WELCOME, STRANGER! Halfway up the wide, tree-lined Main Street I saw a little restaurant with a sign in the window reading BEST SHAKES, FRIES, AND BURGERS IN ALL OF TEXAS! It was called Al's Diner.

Of course it was.

I parked in one of the slant spaces out front, went in, and ordered the Pronghorn Special, which turned out to be a double cheeseburger with barbecue sauce. It came with Mesquite Fries and a Rodeo Thickshake—your choice of vanilla, chocolate, or strawberry. A Pronghorn wasn't quite as good as a Fatburger, but it wasn't bad, and the fries were just the way I like them: crispy, salty, and a little overdone.

Al turned out to be Al Stevens, a skinny middle-aged guy who looked nothing like Al Templeton. He had a rockabilly hairdo, a gray-streaked bandido mustache, a thick Texas drawl, and a paper hat worn jauntily cocked over one eye. When I asked him if there was much to rent in the town of Jodie, he laughed and said, "Take your pick. But when it comes to jobs, this ain't exactly a center of commerce. Ranchland, mostly, and you'll pardon me sayin, but you don't look like the cowboy type."

"I'm not," I said. "Actually, I'm more the book-writing type."

"Get out! Anything I might have read?"

"Not yet," I said. "I'm still trying. I've got about half of a novel written, and a couple of publishers have shown some interest. I'm looking for a quiet place to finish."

"Well, Jodie's quiet, all right." Al rolled his eyes. "When it comes to quiet, I reckon we could take out a patent. Only gets noisy on Friday nights."

"Football?"

"Yessir, whole town goes. Halftime comes, they all roar like lions, then give out with the Jim Yell. You can hear em two miles away. It's pretty comical."

"Who's Jim?"

"LaDue, the quarterback. We've had us some good teams, but ain't never been a QB like LaDue on a Denholm team. And he's only a junior. People been talkin 'bout the state championship. That seems a tad optimistic to me, with those big Dallas schools just up the road, but a little hope never hurt anybody, that's what I reckon."

"Football aside, how's the school?"

"It's real fine. Lot of people were doubtful about this consolidation thing at first—I was one of em—but it's turned out to be a good thing. They got over seven hunnerd this year. Some of em bus in an hour or more, but they don't seem to mind. Probably saves em chores at home. Is your book about high school kids? *Blackboard Jungle* kind of thing? Because there ain't no gangs or anything out here. Out here kids still mind their manners."

"Nothing like that. I've got savings, but I wouldn't mind stretching what I've got with some substitute work. I can't teach full-time and still write."

"Course not," he said respectfully.

"My degree's from Oklahoma, but . . ." I shrugged to show Oklahoma wasn't in Texas's league, but a man could hope.

"Well, you ought to talk to Deke Simmons. He's the principal. Comes in for dinner most evenins. His wife died a couple of years back."

"Sorry to hear that," I said.

"We all were. He's a nice man. Most people are in these parts, Mr.—?"

"Amberson. George Amberson."

"Well, George, we're pretty sleepy, except on Friday nights, but you could do worse. Might could even learn to roar like a lion at halftime."

"Maybe I could," I said.

"You come on back around six. That's usually the time Deke comes in." He put his arms on the counter and leaned over them. "Want a tip?"

"Sure."

"He'll probably have his lady-friend with him. Miss Corcoran, the librarian up to the school. He's kinda been sparkin her since last Christmas or so. I've heard that Mimi Corcoran's the one who *really* runs Denholm Consolidated, because she runs *him*. If you impress her, I reckon you're in like Flynn."

"I'll keep that in mind," I said.

15

Weeks of apartment-hunting in Dallas had netted me exactly one possible, which turned out to be owned by a man I didn't want to rent from. It took me three hours in Jodie to find a place that looked fine. Not an apartment, but a tidy little five-room shotgun house. It was for sale, the real estate agent told me, but the couple who owned it would be willing to rent to the right party. There was an elm-shaded backyard, a garage for the Sunliner . . . and central air-conditioning. The rent was reasonable, given the amenities.

Freddy Quinlan was the agent's name. He was curious about me—I think the Maine license plate on my car struck him as exotic—but not unduly so. Best of all, I felt I was out from under the shadow that had lain over me in Dallas, Derry, and Sunset Point, where my last long-term rental now lay in ashes.

"Well?" Quinlan asked. "What do you think?"

"I want it, but I can't give you a yes or no this afternoon. I have to see a fellow first. I don't suppose you'll be open tomorrow, will you?"

"Yessir, I will. Saturdays I'm open until noon. Then I go home and watch the Game of the Week on TV. Looks like it could be a heck of a Series this year."

"Yes," I said. "It certainly does."

Quinlan extended his hand. "It was nice meeting you, Mr. Amberson. I bet you'd like Jodie. We're good people around here. Hope it works out for you."

I shook with him. "So do I."

Like the man said, a little hope never hurt anybody.

16

That evening I returned to Al's Diner and introduced myself to the principal of Denholm Consolidated and his librarian lady-friend. They invited me to join them.

Deke Simmons was tall, bald, and sixtyish. Mimi Corcoran was bespectacled and tanned. The blue eyes behind her bifocals were sharp, looking me up and down for clues. She walked with the aid of a cane, handling it with the careless (almost contemptuous) dexterity of long use. Both of them, I was amused to see, were carrying Denholm pennants and wearing gold buttons that read WE'VE GOT JIM POWER! It was Friday night in Texas.

Simmons asked me how I was liking Jodie (a lot), how long I'd been in Dallas (since August), and if I enjoyed high school football (yes indeed). The closest he got to anything substantive was asking me if I felt confident in my ability to make kids "mind." Because, he said, a lot of substitutes had a problem with that.

"These young teachers send em to us in the office like we didn't have anything better to do," he said, and then chomped his Pronghorn Burger.

"Sauce, Deke," Mimi said, and he obediently wiped the corner of his mouth with a paper napkin from the dispenser.

She, meanwhile, was continuing her inventory of me: sport coat, tie, haircut. The shoes she'd taken a good look at as I crossed to their booth. "Do you have references, Mr. Amberson?"

"Yes, ma'am, I did quite a bit of substitute teaching in Sarasota County."

"And in Maine?"

"Not so much there, although I taught for three years in Wisconsin on a regular basis before quitting to work full-time on my book. Or as much full-time as my finances would allow." I *did* have a reference from St. Vincent's High School, in Madison. It was a good reference; I had written it myself. Of course, if anyone checked back, I'd be hung. Deke Simmons wouldn't do it, but sharp-eyed Mimi with the leathery cowboy skin might.

"And what is your novel about?"

This might also hang me, but I decided to be honest. As honest as possible, anyway, given my peculiar circumstances. "A series of murders, and their effect on the community where they happen."

"Oh my goodness," Deke said.

She tapped his wrist. "Hush. Go on, Mr. Amberson."

"My original setting was a fictional Maine city—I called it Dawson—but then I decided it might be more realistic if I set it in an *actual* city. A bigger one. I thought Tampa, at first, but it was wrong, somehow—"

She waved Tampa away. "Too pastel. Too many tourists. You were looking for something a little more insular, I suspect."

A very sharp lady. She knew more about my book than I did.

"That's right. So I decided to try Dallas. I think it's the right place, but . . ."

"But you wouldn't want to live there?"

"Exactly."

"I see." She picked at her piece of deep-fried fish. Deke was looking at her with a mildly poleaxed expression. Whatever it was he wanted as he went cantering down the backstretch of life, she appeared to have it. Not so strange; everybody loves somebody sometime, as Dean Martin would so wisely point out. But not for another few years. "And when you're not writing, what do you like to read, Mr. Amberson?"

"Oh, just about everything."

"Have you read *The Catcher in the Rye?*"

Uh-oh, I thought.

"Yes, ma'am."

She looked impatient at this. "Oh, call me Mimi. Even the kids call me Mimi, although I insist they put a Miz with it for propriety's sake. What do you think of Mr. Salinger's cri de coeur?"

Lie, or tell the truth? But it wasn't a serious question. This woman would read a lie the way I could read . . . well . . . an IMPEACH EARL WARREN billboard.

"I think it says a lot about how lousy the fifties were, and a lot about how good the sixties can be. If the Holden Caulfields of America don't lose their outrage, that is. And their courage."

"Um. Hum." Picking plenty at her fish, but not eating any that I could see. No wonder she looked like you could staple a string to the back of her dress and fly her like a kite. "Do you believe it should be in the school library?"

I sighed, thinking how much I would have enjoyed living and teaching part-time in the town of Jodie, Texas. "Actually, ma'am—Mimi—I do. Although I believe it should be checked out only to certain students, and at the librarian's discretion."

"The librarian's? Not the parents'?"

"No, ma'am. That's a slippery slope."

Mimi Corcoran burst into a wide smile and turned to her beau. "Deke, this fellow doesn't belong on the substitute list. He should be full-time."

"Mimi—"

"I know, no vacancy in the English Department. But if he sticks around, maybe he can step in after that idiot Phil Bateman retires."

"Meems, that is very indiscreet."

"Yes," she said, and actually dropped me a wink. "Also very true. Send Deke your references from Florida, Mr. Amberson. They should do nicely. Better yet, bring them in yourself, next week. The school year has started. No sense in losing time."

"Call me George," I said.

"Yes, indeed," she said. She pushed her plate away. "Deke, this is *terrible*. Why do we eat here?"

"Because I like the burgers and you like Al's strawberry short-cake."

"Oh, yes," she said. "The strawberry shortcake. Bring it on. Mr. Amberson, can you stay for the football game?"

"Not tonight," I said. "I've got to get back to Dallas. Maybe next week's game. If you think you can use me."

"If Mimi likes you, I like you," Deke Simmons said. "I can't guarantee you a day every week, but some weeks there'll be two or even three. It will all average out."

"I'm sure it will."

"The substitute salary isn't much, I'm afraid—"

"I know that, sir. I'm just looking for a way to supplement my income."

"That *Catcher* book will never be in our library," Deke said with a regretful side-glance at his purse-lipped paramour. "Schoolboard won't have it. Mimi knows that." Another big bite of his Prongburger.

"Times change," Mimi Corcoran said, pointing first to the napkin dispenser and then to the side of his mouth. "Deke. Sauce."

17

The following week I made a mistake. I should have known better; making another major wager should have been the last thing on my mind after all that had happened to me. You'll say I should have been more on my guard.

I *did* understand the risk, but I was worried about money. I had come to Texas with something less than sixteen thousand dollars. Some was the remainder of Al's stake-money, but most of it was the result of two very large bets, one placed in Derry and one in Tampa. But staying at the Adolphus for seven weeks or so had eaten up over a thousand; getting settled in a new town would easily cost another four or five hundred. Food, rent, and utilities aside, I was going to need a lot more clothes—and better ones—if I was going to look respectable in a classroom. I'd be based in Jodie for two and a half years before I could conclude my business with Lee Harvey Oswald. Fourteen thousand dollars or so wasn't going to cut it. The substitute teaching salary? Fifteen dollars and fifty cents a day. Yeehaw.

Okay, maybe I *could* have scraped through on fourteen grand, plus thirty and sometimes even fifty bucks a week as a sub. But I'd have to stay healthy and not have any accidents, and I couldn't bank on that. Because the past is sly as well as obdurate. It fights back. And yes, maybe there was an element of greed involved, too. If so, it was based less on the love of money than on the intoxicating knowledge that I could beat the usually unbeatable house whenever I wanted to.

I think now: *If Al had researched the stock market as thoroughly as who won all those baseball games, football games, and horse races . . .*

But he didn't.

I think now: *If Freddy Quinlan hadn't mentioned that the World Series was shaping up to be a doozy . . .*

But he did.

And I went back to Greenville Avenue.

I told myself that all those straw-hatted punters I'd seen standing out in front of Faith Financial (Where Trust Is Our Watchword) would be betting the Series, and some of them would be laying down serious cash. I told myself that I'd be one among many, and a middling bet from Mr. George Amberson—who'd claim to be living in a nice converted-garage duplex on Blackwell Street right here in Dallas, should anyone inquire—would attract no attention. Hell, I told myself, the guys running Faith Financial probably don't know Señor Eduardo Gutierrez of Tampa from Adam. Or from Noah's son, Ham, for that matter.

Oh, I told myself lots of things, and they all boiled down to the same two things: that it was perfectly safe, and that it was perfectly reasonable to want more money even though I currently had enough to live on. Dumb. But stupidity is one of two things we see most clearly in retrospect. The other is missed chances.

18

On September twenty-eighth, a week before the Series was scheduled to start, I walked into Faith Financial and—after some dancing—put down six hundred dollars on the Pittsburgh Pirates to beat the Yankees in seven. I accepted two-to-one odds, which was outrageous considering how heavily favored the Yankees were. On the day after Bill Mazeroski hit his unlikely ninth-inning home run to seal the deal for the Buckos, I drove back to Dallas and Greenville Avenue. I think that if Faith Financial had been deserted, I would have turned around and driven right *back* to Jodie . . . or maybe that's just what I tell myself now. I don't know for sure.

What I *do* know is there was a queue of bettors waiting to collect, and I joined it. That group was a Martin Luther King dream come true: fifty percent black, fifty percent white, a hundred percent happy. Most guys came out with nothing but a few fives or maybe a double sawbuck or two, but I saw several who were counting C-notes. An armed robber who had chosen that day to hit Faith Financial would have done well, indeed.

The money-man was a stocky fellow wearing a green eyeshade. He asked me the standard first question ("Are you a cop? If you are, you have to show me your ID"), and when I answered in the negative, he asked for my name and a look at my driver's license. It was a brand-new one, which I had received by registered mail the week before; finally a piece of Texas identification to add to my collection. And I was careful to hold my thumb over the Jodie address.

He paid me my twelve hundred. I stuffed it in my pocket and walked quickly to my car. When I was back on Highway 77, with Dallas falling behind and Jodie growing closer with every turn of the wheels, I finally relaxed.

Stupid me.

19

We're going to take another leap forward in time (narratives also contain rabbit-holes, when you stop to think of it), but I need to recount one more thing from 1960, first.

Fort Worth. November sixteenth, 1960. Kennedy the president-elect for a little over a week. The corner of Ballinger and West Seventh. The day was cold and overcast. Cars puffed white exhaust. The weatherman on KLIF ("All the hits, all the time") was forecasting rain that might thicken to sleet by midnight, so be careful on the highways, all you rockers and rollers.

I was bundled into a rawhide ranch coat; a felt cap with flaps was jammed down over my ears. I was sitting on a bench in front of the Texas Cattle Raisers' Association, looking down West Seventh. I had been there for almost an hour, and I didn't think the young man would visit with his mother much longer than that; according to Al Templeton's notes, all three of her boys had gotten away from her as soon as they possibly could. What I was hoping was that she might come out of her apartment building with him. She was recently back in the area after several months in Waco, where she had been working as a ladies' home companion.

My patience was rewarded. The door of the Rotary Apartments opened and a skinny man who bore an eerie resemblance to Lee Harvey Oswald came out. He held the door for a woman in a tartan car coat and blocky white nurse's shoes. She was only shoulder-high to him, but solidly built. Her graying hair was scrooped back from a prematurely lined face. She wore a red kerchief. Matching lipstick outlined a small mouth that looked dissatisfied and pugnacious—the mouth of a woman who believes the world is against her and has had plenty of evidence over the years to prove it. Lee Oswald's elder brother went quickly down the concrete path. The woman scurried after and grabbed the back of his topcoat. He turned to her on the sidewalk. They appeared to argue, but the woman did most of the talking. She shook her finger in his face. No way I could tell what she was scolding him about; I was a prudent block and a half away. Then he started toward the corner of West Seventh and Summit Avenue, as I had expected. He had come by bus, and that was where the nearest stop was.

The woman stood where she was for a moment, as if undecided. *Come on, Mama,* I thought, *you're not going to let him get away that easily, are you? He's just half a block down the street. Lee had to go all the way to Russia to get away from that wagging finger.*

She went after him, and as they neared the corner, she raised her voice and I heard her clearly. "*Stop,* Robert, don't walk so fast, I'm not done with you!"

He looked over his shoulder but kept walking. She caught up

to him at the bus stop and tugged on his sleeve until he looked at her. The finger resumed its tick-tock wagging. I caught isolated phrases: *you promised,* and *gave you everything* and—I think—*who are you to judge me.* I couldn't see Oswald's face because his back was to me, but his slumped shoulders said plenty. I doubted if this was the first time Mama had followed him down the street, jabbering away the whole time, oblivious of spectators. She spread a hand above the shelf of her bosom, that timeless Mom-gesture that says *Behold me, ye thankless child.*

Oswald dug into his back pocket, produced his wallet, and gave her a bill. She stuffed it in her purse without looking at it and started back toward the Rotary Apartments. Then she thought of something else and turned to him once more. I heard her clearly. Raised to shout across the fifteen or twenty yards now between them, that reedy voice was like fingernails drawn down a slate blackboard.

"And call me if you hear from Lee again, hear? I'm still on the party line, it's all I can afford until I get a better job, and that Sykes woman from downstairs is on it *all the time,* I spoke to her, I gave her a real piece of my mind, 'Mrs. Sykes,' I said—"

A man passed her. He stuck a theatrical finger in one ear, grinning. If Mama saw, she took no notice. She certainly took no notice of her son's grimace of embarrassment.

" 'Mrs. Sykes,' I said, 'you're not the only one who needs the phone, so I'd thank you to keep your calls *short.* And if you won't do it on your own, I may have to call a representative of the telephone company to *make* you do it.' That's what I said. So you call me, Rob. You know I need to hear from Lee."

Here came the bus. As it pulled up, he raised his voice to be heard over the chuff of the air-brakes. "He's a damn Commie, Ma, and he's not coming home. Get used to it."

"You call me!" she shrilled. Her grim little face was set. She stood with her feet planted apart, like a boxer ready to absorb a blow. Any blow. Every blow. Her eyes glared from behind black-rimmed harlequin glasses. Her kerchief was double-knotted beneath her

chin. The rain had begun to fall now, but she paid it no mind. She drew in breath and raised her voice to something just short of a scream. *"I need to hear from my good boy, you hear?"*

Robert Oswald bolted up the steps and into the bus without replying. It pulled away in a chuff of blue exhaust. And as it did, a smile lit her face. It did something of which I would have thought a smile incapable: it made her simultaneously younger and uglier.

A workman passed her. He didn't bump or even brush her, as far as I could see, but she snapped: "Watch where you're going! You don't own the sidewalk!"

Marguerite Oswald started back toward her apartment. When she turned away from me, she was still smiling.

I drove back to Jodie that afternoon, shaken and thoughtful. I wouldn't see Lee Oswald for another year and a half, and I remained determined to stop him, but I already felt more sympathy for him than I ever had for Frank Dunning.

CHAPTER 13

1

It was seven forty-five on the evening of May 18, 1961. The light of a long Texas dusk lay across my backyard. The window was open, and the curtains fluttered in a mild breeze. On the radio, Troy Shondell was singing "This Time." I was sitting in what had been the little house's second bedroom and was now my study. The desk was a cast-off from the high school. It had one short leg, which I had shimmed. The typewriter was a Webster portable. I was revising the first hundred and fifty or so pages of my novel, *The Murder Place,* mostly because Mimi Corcoran kept pestering me to read it, and Mimi, I had discovered, was the sort of person you could put off with excuses for only so long. The work was actually going well. I'd had no problem turning Derry into the fictional town of Dawson in my first draft, and turning Dawson into Dallas was even easier. I had started making the changes only so the work-in-progress would support my cover story when I finally let Mimi read it, but now the changes seemed both vital and inevitable. It seemed the book had wanted to be about Dallas all along.

The doorbell rang. I put a paperweight on the manuscript pages so they wouldn't blow around, and went to see who my visitor was. I remember all of this very clearly: the dancing curtains, the smooth river stone paperweight, "This Time" playing on the radio, the long light of Texas evening, which I had come to love. I *should* remember it. It was when I stopped living in the past and just starting living.

I opened the door and Michael Coslaw stood there. He was weeping. "I can't, Mr. Amberson," he said. "I just can't."

"Well, come in, Mike," I said. "Let's talk about it."

2

I wasn't surprised to see him. I had been in charge of Lisbon High's little Drama Department for five years before running away to the Era of Universal Smoking, and I'd seen plenty of stage fright in those years. Directing teenage actors is like juggling jars of nitroglycerine: exhilarating and dangerous. I've seen girls who were quick studies and beautifully natural in rehearsal freeze up completely onstage; I've seen nerdy little guys blossom and seem to grow a foot taller the first time they utter a line that gets a laugh from an audience. I've directed dedicated plodders and the occasional kid who showed a spark of talent. But I'd never had a kid like Mike Coslaw. I suspect there are high school and college faculty who've been working dramatics all their lives and never had a kid like him.

Mimi Corcoran really did run Denholm Consolidated High School, and it was she who coaxed me into taking over the junior-senior play when Alfie Norton, the math teacher who had been doing it for years, was diagnosed with acute myeloid leukemia and moved to Houston for treatments. I tried to refuse on the grounds that I was still doing research in Dallas, but I wasn't going there very much in the winter and early spring of 1961. Mimi knew it, because whenever Deke needed an English sub during that half of the school year, I was usually available. When it came to Dallas, I was basically marking time. Lee was still in Minsk, soon to marry Marina Prusakova, the girl in the red dress and white shoes.

"You've got plenty of time on your hands," Mimi had said. Her own hands were fisted on her nonexistent hips: she was in full take-no-prisoners mode that day. "And it *pays.*"

"Oh, yeah," I said. "I checked that out with Deke. Fifty bucks. I'll be living large in the hood."

"In the *what?*"

"Never mind, Mimi. For the time being, I'm doing all right for cash. Can't we leave it at that?"

No. We couldn't. Miz Mimi was a human bulldozer, and when she met a seemingly immovable object, she just lowered her blade and revved her engine higher. Without me, she said, there would *be* no junior-senior play for the first time in the high school's history. The parents would be disappointed. The schoolboard would be disappointed. "And," she added, drawing her brows together, "*I* will be *bereft.*"

"God forbid you should be bereft, Miz Mimi," I'd said. "Tell you what. If you let me pick the play—something not too controversial, I promise—I'll do it."

Her frown had disappeared into the brilliant Mimi Corcoran smile that always turned Deke Simmons into a simmering bowl of oatmeal (which, temperamentally speaking, was not a huge transformation). "Excellent! Who knows, you may find a brilliant thespian lurking in our halls."

"Yes," I said. "And pigs may whistle."

But—life is such a joke—I *had* found a brilliant thesp. A natural. And now he sat in my living room on the night before our show opened for the first of four performances, taking up almost the entire couch (which bowed humbly beneath his two hundred and seventy pounds), bawling his freaking head off. Mike Coslaw. Also known as Lennie Small in George Amberson's okay-for-high-school adaptation of John Steinbeck's *Of Mice and Men.*

If, that was, I could talk him into showing up tomorrow.

3

I thought about handing him some Kleenex and decided they weren't up to the job. I fetched a dish wiper from the kitchen drawer instead. He scrubbed his face with it, got himself under some kind of control, then looked at me desolately. His eyes were red and raw. He hadn't started crying as he approached my door; this looked like it had been going on all afternoon.

"Okay, Mike. Make me understand."

"Everybody on the team's makin fun of me, Mr. Amberson. Coach started callin me Clark Gable—this was at the Lion Pride Spring Picnic—and now *everybody's* doin it. Even Jimmy's doin it." Meaning Jim LaDue, the team's hot-rod quarterback and Mike's best friend.

I wasn't surprised about Coach Borman; he was a thud who preached the gospel of gung-ho and didn't like anyone poaching on his territory either in season or out. And Mike had been called far worse; while hall-monitoring, I'd heard him called Bohunk Mike, George of the Jungle, and Godzilla. He laughed the nicknames off. That amused, even absentminded reaction to slurs and japes may be the greatest gift height and size conveys on large boys, and at six-seven and two-seventy, Mike made me look like Mickey Rooney.

There was only one star on the Lions' football team, and that was Jim LaDue—didn't he have his own billboard, at the intersection of Highway 77 and Route 109? But if there was any player who made it *possible* for Jim to star, it was Mike Coslaw, who planned to sign with Texas A&M as soon as his senior high school season was over. LaDue would be rolling with the 'Bama Crimson Tide (as both he and his father would be happy to tell you), but if someone had asked me to pick the one most likely to go pro, I would have put my money on Mike. I liked Jim, but to me he looked like a knee injury or shoulder separation waiting to happen. Mike, on the other hand, seemed built for the long haul.

"What does Bobbi Jill say?" Mike and Bobbi Jill Allnut were practically joined at the hip. Gorgeous girl? Check. Blonde? Check. Cheerleader? Why even ask?

He grinned. "Bobbi Jill's behind me a thousand percent. Says to man up and stop letting those other guys get my goat."

"Sounds like a sensible young lady."

"Yeah, she's the absolute best."

"Anyway, I suspect a little name-calling isn't what's really on your mind." And when he didn't reply: "Mike? Talk to me."

"I'm gonna get up there in front of all those people and make a fool of myself. Jimmy told me so."

"Jimmy's a helluva quarterback, and I know the two of you are pals, but when it comes to acting, he doesn't know jack shit." Mike blinked. In 1961 you usually didn't hear the word *shit* from teachers, even if they had a mouthful. But of course I was only a substitute, and that freed me up some. "I think you know that. As they say in these parts, you may stagger, but you ain't stupid."

"People *think* I am," he said in a low voice. "And I'm strictly a C student. Maybe you don't know that, maybe subs don't get to see the records, but I am."

"I made it a point to see yours after the second week of rehearsals, when I saw what you could do onstage. You're a C student because, as a football player, you're *supposed* to be a C student. It's part of the ethos."

"The what?"

"Figure it out from the context and save the dumb act for your friends. Not to mention Coach Borman, who probably has to tie a string on his whistle so he can remember which end to blow."

Mike snickered at that, red eyes and all.

"Listen to me. People automatically think anyone as big as you is stupid. Tell me different if you want to; according to what I hear, you've been walking around in that body since you were twelve, so you should know."

He didn't tell me different. What he said was, "Everybody on the team tried out for Lennie. It was a joke. A goof." He added hastily. "Nothin against you, Mr. A. Everybody on the team likes you. Even Coach likes you."

A bunch of players *had* crashed the tryouts, intimidating the more scholarly aspirants into silence and all claiming they wanted to read for the part of George Milton's big dumb friend. Of course it had been a joke, but Mike's reading of Lennie had been the farthest thing in the world from funny. What it had been was a goddam revelation. I would have used an electric cattle prod to keep him in the room, if that's what it took, but of course there was no need of such extreme measures. Want to know the best thing about teaching? Seeing that moment when a kid discovers his or her gift. There's no feeling on earth like it. Mike knew his teammates would make fun of him, but he took the part anyway.

And of course Coach Borman didn't like it. The Coach Bormans of the world never do. In this case, however, there wasn't much he could do about it, especially with Mimi Corcoran on my side. He certainly couldn't claim he needed Mike for football practice in April and May. So he was reduced to calling his best lineman Clark Gable. There are guys who can't rid themselves of the idea that acting is for girls and queers who sort of *wish* they were girls. Gavin Borman was that kind of guy. At Don Haggarty's annual April Fool's keg-party, he had whined to me about "putting ideas in that big galoot's head."

I told him he was certainly welcome to his opinion; like assholes, everybody had one. Then I walked away, leaving him with a paper cup in his hand and a perplexed look on his face. The Coach Bormans of the world are also used to getting their way through a kind of jocular intimidation, and he couldn't understand why it wasn't working on the lowly sub who'd stepped into Alfie Norton's director's shoes at the last minute. I could hardly tell Borman that shooting a guy to keep him from killing his wife and kids has a way of changing a man.

Basically, Coach never had a chance. I cast some of the other football players as townspeople, but I meant to have Mike as Lennie from the moment he opened his mouth and said, "I remember about the rabbits, George!"

He *became* Lennie. He hijacked not just your eyes—because he was so damn big—but the heart in your chest. You forgot everything else, the way people forgot their everyday cares when Jim LaDue faded back to throw a pass. Mike might have been built to crash the opposing line in humble obscurity, but he had been *made*—by God, if there is such a deity; by a roll of the genetic dice if there is not—to stand on a stage and disappear into someone else.

"It was a goof for everyone but you," I said.

"Me, too. At first."

"Because at first you didn't know."

"No. I dint." Husky. Almost whispering. He lowered his head because the tears were coming again and he didn't want me to see them. The coach had called him Clark Gable, and if I called the man on it, he'd claim it was just a joke. A goof. A yuk. As if he didn't know the rest of the squad would pick up on it and pile on. As if he didn't know that shit would hurt Mike in a way being called Bohunk Mike never could. Why do people *do* that to gifted people? Is it jealousy? Fear? Both, maybe. But this kid had the advantage of knowing how good he was. And we both knew Coach Borman wasn't really the problem. The only person who could stop Mike from going onstage tomorrow night was Mike.

"You've played football in front of crowds nine times bigger than the one that'll be in that auditorium. Hell, when you boys went down to Dallas for the regionals last November, you played in front of ten or twelve thousand. And they were *not* friendly."

"Football's different. When we hit the field, we're all wearing the same uniform and helmets. Folks can only tell us apart by our numbers. Everybody's on the same side—"

"There are nine other people in this show with you, Mike, and that's not counting the townspeople I wrote in to give your football buddies something to do. They're a team, too."

"It's not the same."

"Maybe not quite. But one thing *is* the same—if you let them down, the shit falls apart and everybody loses. The actors, the crew, the Pep Club girls who did the publicity, and all the people who are planning to come in for the show, some of them from ranches fifty miles out. Not to mention me. I lose, too."

"I guess that's so," he said. He was looking at his feet, and mighty big feet they were.

"I could stand to lose Slim or Curley; I'd just send someone out with the book to read the part. I guess I could even stand to lose Curley's Wife—"

"I wish Sandy was a little better," Mike said. "She's pretty as hell, but if she ever hits her mark, it's an accident."

I allowed myself a cautious inward smile. I was starting to think this was going to be all right. "What I couldn't stand—what the *show* couldn't stand—is to lose you or Vince Knowles."

Vince was playing Lennie's road-buddy George, and actually, we *could* have stood the loss if he'd gotten the flu or broken his neck in a road accident (always a possibility, given the way he drove his daddy's farm truck). I would have gone on in Vince's place, if push came to shove, even though I was much too big for the part, and I wouldn't need just to read, either. After six weeks of rehearsals, I was as off-the-book as any of my actors. More than some. But I couldn't replace Mike. No one could replace him, with his unique combination of size and actual talent. He was the linchpin.

"What if I fuck up?" he asked, then heard what he'd said and clapped a hand to his mouth.

I sat down beside him on the couch. There wasn't much room, but I managed. Right then I wasn't thinking of John Kennedy, Al Templeton, Frank Dunning, or the world I'd come from. Right then I was thinking of nothing but this big boy . . . and my show. Because at some point it had *become* mine, just as this earlier time with its party-line telephones and cheap gas had become mine. At that moment I cared more about *Of Mice and Men* than I did about Lee Harvey Oswald.

But I cared even more about Mike.

I took his hand off his mouth. Put it on one huge thigh. Put my hands on his shoulders. Looked into his eyes. "Listen to me," I said. "Are you listening?"

"Yessir."

"You are *not* going to fuck up. Say it."

"I . . ."

"Say it."

"I'm not going to fuck up."

"What you're going to do is amaze them. I promise you that, Mike." Gripping his shoulders tighter. It was like trying to sink my fingers into stones. He could have picked me up and broken me over his knee, but he only sat there looking at me from a pair of eyes that were humble, hopeful, and still rimmed with tears. "Do you hear me? I promise."

4

The stage was a beachhead of light. Beyond it was a lake of darkness where the audience sat. George and Lennie stood on the bank of an imaginary river. The other men had been sent away, but they wouldn't be gone long; if the big, vaguely smiling hulk of a man in the overalls were to die with any dignity, George would have to see to it himself.

"George? Where them guys goin?"

Mimi Corcoran was sitting on my right. At some point she had taken my hand and was gripping it. Hard, hard, hard. We were in the first row. Next to her on her other side, Deke Simmons was staring up at the stage with his mouth slightly hung open. It was the expression of a farmer who sees dinosaur cropping grass in his north forty.

"Huntin. They're goin huntin. Siddown, Lennie."

Vince Knowles was never going to be an actor—what he was going to be, most likely, was a salesman at Jodie Chrysler-Dodge, like his father—but a great performance can lift all the actors in a production, and that had happened tonight. Vince, who in rehearsals had only once or twice achieved even low levels of believability (mostly because his ratty, intelligent little face *was* Steinbeck's George Milton), had caught something from Mike. All at once, about halfway through Act I, he finally seemed to realize what it meant to go rambling through life with a Lennie as your only friend, and he had fallen into the part. Now, watching him push an old felt hat from props back on his head, I thought that Vince looked like Henry Fonda in *The Grapes of Wrath*.

"George!"

"Yeah?"

"Ain't you gonna give me hell?"

"What do you mean?"

"You know, George." Smiling. The kind of smile that says *Yeah, I know I'm a dope, but we both know I can't help it.* Sitting down beside George on the imaginary riverbank. Taking off his own hat, tossing it aside, rumpling his short blond hair. Imitating George's voice. Mike had nailed this with eerie ease in the very first rehearsal, with no help from me. "'If I was alone, I could live so easy. I could get a job and not have no more mess.'" Resuming his own voice . . . or Lennie's, rather. "I can go away. I can go right up in the hills and find a cave, if you don't want me."

Vince Knowles lowered his head, and when he raised it and spoke his next line, his voice was thick and hitching. It was a simulacrum of sorrow he'd never approached in even his best rehearsals. "No, Lennie, I want you to stay here with me."

"Then tell me like you done before! Bout other guys, and about us!"

That was when I heard the first low sob from the audience. It was followed by another. Then a third. This I had not expected, not in my wildest dreams. A chill raced up my back, and I stole a glance at Mimi. She wasn't crying yet, but the liquid sheen in her eyes told me that she soon would be. Yes, even her—hard old baby that she was.

George hesitated, then took hold of Lennie's hand, a thing Vince never would have done in rehearsals. *That's queerboy stuff,* he would have said.

"Guys like us . . . Lennie, guys like us got no families. They got nobody that gives a hoot in hell about them." Touching the prop gun hidden under his coat with his other hand. Taking it partway out. Putting it back. Then steeling himself and taking it all the way out. Laying it along his leg.

"But not us, George! Not us! Idn't that right?"

Mike was gone. The stage was gone. Now it was only the two of them, and by the time Lennie was asking George to tell him about the little ranch, and the rabbits, and living off the fat of the land, half the audience was weeping audibly. Vince was crying so hard he could hardly deliver his final lines, telling poor stupid Lennie to look over there, the ranch they were going to live on was over there. If he looked hard enough, he could see it.

The stage lensed slowly to full dark, Cindy McComas for once running the lights perfectly. Birdie Jamieson, the school janitor, fired a blank cartridge. Some woman in the audience gave a little scream. That sort of reaction is usually followed by nervous laughter, but tonight there was only the sound of people weeping in their seats. Otherwise, silence. It went on for ten seconds. Or maybe it was only five. Whatever it was, to me it seemed forever. Then the applause broke. It was the best thunder I ever heard in my life. The house lights went up. The entire audience was on its feet. The front two rows were reserved for faculty, and I happened to glance at Coach Borman. Damned if he wasn't crying, too.

Two rows back, where all the school jocks were sitting together, Jim LaDue leaped to his feet. *"You rock, Coslaw!"* he shouted. This elicited cheers and laughter.

The cast came out to take their bows: first the football-player townspeople, then Curley and Curley's Wife, then Candy and Slim and the rest of the farmhands. The applause started to die a little and then Vince came out, flushed and happy, his own cheeks still wet. Mike Coslaw came last, shuffling as if embarrassed, then looking out in comical amazement as Mimi shouted "Bravo!"

Others echoed it, and soon the auditorium resounded with it: *Bravo, Bravo, Bravo*. Mike bowed, sweeping his hat so low it brushed the stage. When he stood again, he was smiling. But it was more than a smile; his face was transformed with the happiness that's reserved for those who are finally allowed to reach all the way up.

Then he shouted, "Mr. Amberson! Come up here, Mr. Amberson!"

The cast took up the chant of "Director! Director!"

"Don't kill the applause," Mimi growled from beside me. "Get up there, you goofball!"

So I did, and the applause swelled again. Mike grabbed me, hugged me, lifted me off my feet, then set me down and gave me a hearty smack on the cheek. Everyone laughed, including me. We all grabbed hands, lifted them to the audience, and bowed. As I listened to the applause, a thought occurred to me, one that darkened my heart. In Minsk, there were newlyweds. Lee and Marina had been man and wife for exactly nineteen days.

5

Three weeks later, just before school let out for the summer, I went to Dallas to take some photographs of the three apartments where Lee and Marina would live together. I used a small Minox, holding it in the palm of my hand and allowing the lens to peep out between two spread fingers. I felt ridiculous—more like the trench-coated caricatures in *Mad* magazine's *Spy vs Spy* feature than James Bond—but I had learned to be careful about such things.

When I returned to my house, Mimi Corcoran's sky-blue Nash Rambler was parked at the curb and Mimi was just sliding in behind the wheel. When she saw me, she got out again. A brief grimace tightened her face—pain or effort—but when she came up the drive, she was wearing her usual dry smile. As if I amused her, but in a good way. In her hands she was carrying a bulky manila envelope, which contained the hundred and fifty pages of *The Murder Place*. I'd finally given in to her pesterings . . . but that had been only the day before.

"Either you liked it one hell of a lot, or you never got past page ten," I said, taking the envelope. "Which was it?"

Her smile now looked enigmatic as well as amused. "Like most librarians, I'm a fast reader. Can we go inside and talk about it? It isn't even the middle of June, and it's already so hot."

Yes, and she was sweating, something I'd never seen before. Also, she looked as if she'd lost weight. Not a good thing for a lady who had no pounds to give away.

Sitting in my living room with big glasses of iced coffee—me in the easy chair, she on the couch—Mimi gave her opinion. "I enjoyed the stuff about the killer dressed up as a clown. Call me twisted, but I found that deliciously creepy."

"If you're twisted, I am, too."

She smiled. "I'm sure you'll find a publisher for it. On the whole, I liked it very much."

I felt a little hurt. *The Murder Place* might have begun as camouflage, but it had become more important to me as I got deeper into it. It was like a secret memoir. One of the nerves. "That 'on the whole' stuff reminds me of Alexander Pope—you know, damning with faint praise?"

"I didn't quite mean it that way." More qualification. "It's just that . . . goddammit, George, this isn't what you were meant to do. You were meant to teach. And if you publish a book like this, no school department in the United States will hire you." She paused. "Except maybe in Massachusetts."

I didn't reply. I was speechless.

"What you did with Mike Coslaw—what you did *for* Mike Coslaw—was the most amazing and wonderful thing I've ever seen."

"Mimi, it wasn't me. He's just naturally tal—"

"I *know* he's naturally talented, that was obvious from the moment he walked onstage and opened his mouth, but I'll tell you something, my friend. Something forty years in high schools and sixty years of living has taught me and taught me well. Artistic talent is far more common than the talent to *nurture* artistic talent. Any parent with a hard hand can crush it, but to nurture it is much more difficult. That's a talent you have, and in much greater supply than the one that drove this." She tapped the sheaf of pages on the coffee table in front of her.

"I don't know what to say."

"Say thank you, and compliment me on my acute judgment."

"Thanks. And your insight is only exceeded by your good looks."

That brought the smile back, dryer than ever. "Don't exceed your brief, George."

"Yes, Miz Mimi."

The smile disappeared. She leaned forward. The blue eyes behind her glasses were too big, swimming in her face. The skin under her tan was yellowish, and her formerly taut cheeks were hollow. When had this happened? Had Deke noticed? But that was ridic, as the kids said. Deke wouldn't notice that his socks were mismatched until he took them off at night. Probably not even then.

She said, "Phil Bateman is no longer just threatening to retire, he's done pulled the pin and tossed the grenade, as our delightful Coach Borman would say. Which means there's a vacancy on the English faculty. Come and teach full-time at DCHS, George. The kids like you, and after the junior-senior play, the community thinks you're the second coming of Alfred Hitchcock. Deke is just waiting to see your application—he told me so just last night. Please. Publish this under a pseudonym, if you have to, but come and teach. That's what you were meant to do."

I wanted badly to say yes, because she was right. My job wasn't writing books, and it certainly wasn't killing people, no matter how much they deserved killing. And there was Jodie. I'd come to it as a stranger who had been displaced from his home era as well as his hometown, and the first words spoken to me here—by Al

Stevens, at the diner—had been friendly words. If you've ever been homesick, or felt exiled from all the things and people that once defined you, you'll know how important welcoming words and friendly smiles can be. Jodie was the anti-Dallas, and now one of its leading citizens was asking me to be a resident instead of a visitor. But the watershed moment was approaching. Only it wasn't here yet. Maybe . . .

"George? You have the most *peculiar* look on your face."

"That's called thinking. Will you let me do it, please?"

She put her hands to her cheeks and rounded her mouth in a comic O of apology. "Well braid my hair and call me Buckwheat."

I paid no attention, because I was busy flicking through Al's notes. I no longer had to look at them to do that. When the new school year started in September, Oswald was still going to be in Russia, although he had already started what would be a lengthy paperwork battle to get back to America with his wife and daughter, June, with whom Marina would be pregnant any day now. It was a battle Oswald would eventually win, playing one superpower bureaucracy off against the other with instinctive (if rudimentary) cleverness, but they wouldn't step off the SS *Maasdam* and onto American soil until the middle of next year. And as for Texas . . .

"Meems, the school year usually ends the first week in June, doesn't it?"

"Always. The kids who need summer jobs have to nail them down."

. . . as for Texas, the Oswalds were going to arrive on the fourteenth of June, 1962.

"And any teaching contract I signed would be probationary, right? As in one year?"

"With an option to renew if all parties are satisfied, yes."

"Then you've got yourself a probationary English teacher."

She laughed, clapped her hands, got to her feet, and held her arms out. "Marvelous! Huggies for Miz Mimi!"

I hugged her, then released her quickly when I heard her gasp. "What the hell is wrong with you, ma'am?"

She went back to the couch, picked up her iced coffee, and sipped. "Let me give you two pieces of advice, George. The first is never call a Texas woman ma'am if you come from the northern climes. It sounds sarcastic. The second is never ask *any* woman what the hell is wrong with her. Try something slightly more delicate, like 'Are you feeling quite all right?'"

"Are you?"

"Why wouldn't I? I'm getting married."

At first I couldn't match this particular zig with a corresponding zag. Except the grave look in her eyes suggested she wasn't zigging at all. She was circling something. Probably not a nice something, either.

"Say 'Congratulations, Miz Mimi.'"

"Congratulations, Miz Mimi."

"Deke first popped the question almost a year ago. I put him off, saying it was too soon after his wife died, and it would cause talk. As time passes, that has become less effective as an argument. I doubt if there would have been all that much talk, anyway, given our ages. People in small towns realize that folks like Deke and me can't afford the luxury of decorum quite so much once we reach a certain, shall we say, plateau of maturity. Truth is, I liked things fine just the way they were. The old fella loves me quite a lot more than I love him, but I *like* him plenty, and—at the risk of embarrassing you—even ladies who've reached a certain plateau of maturity aren't averse to a nice boink on a Saturday night. Am I embarrassing you?"

"No," I said. "Actually, you're delighting me."

The dry smile. "Lovely. Because when I swing my feet out of bed in the morning, my first thought as they hit the floor is, 'Might there be a way I can delight George Amberson today? And if so, how shall I go about it?'"

"Don't exceed your brief, Miz Mimi."

"Spoken like a man." She sipped her iced coffee. "I had two

objectives when I came here today. I've accomplished the first. Now I'll move on to the second so you can get on with your day. Deke and I are going to be married on July twenty-first, which is a Friday. The ceremony will be a small private affair in his home— just us, the preacher, and a few family members. His parents— they're quite vigorous for dinosaurs—are coming from Alabama and my sister from San Diego. The reception will be a lawn party at my house the following day. Two P.M. until drunk o'clock. We're inviting almost everyone in town. There's going to be a piñata and lemonade for the little kiddies, barbecue and kegs of beer for the big kiddies, and even a band from San-Antone. Unlike most bands from San-Antone, I believe they are able to play 'Louie Louie' as well as 'La Paloma.' If you don't favor us with your presence—"

"You'll be bereft?"

"Indeed I will. Will you save the date?"

"Absolutely."

"Good. Deke and I will be leaving for Mexico on Sunday, by which time his hangover will have dissipated. We're a little old for a honeymoon, but there are certain resources available south of the border that are not available in the Sixgun State. Certain experimental treatments. I doubt if they work, but Deke is hopeful. And hell, it's worth a try. Life . . ." She gave a rueful sigh. "Life is too sweet to give up without a fight, don't you think?"

"Yes," I said.

"Yes. So one holds on." She looked at me closely. "Are you going to cry, George?"

"No."

"Good. Because that would embarrass me. I might even cry myself, and I don't do it well. No one would ever write a poem about my tears. I *croak*."

"How bad is it? May I ask?"

"Quite bad." She said it offhandedly. "I might have eight months. Possibly a year. Assuming the herbal treatments or peach pits or whatever down Mexico way don't effect a magical cure, that is."

"I'm very sorry to hear it."

"Thank you, George. Expressed to a nicety. Any more would be sloppy."

I smiled.

"I have another reason for inviting you to our reception, although it goes without saying that your charming company and sparkling repartee would be enough. Phil Bateman isn't the only one who's retiring."

"Mimi, don't do that. Take a leave of absence if you have to, but—"

She shook her head decisively. "Sick or well, forty years is enough. It's time for younger hands, younger eyes, and a younger mind. On my recommendation, Deke has hired a well-qualified young lady from Georgia. Her name is Sadie Clayton. She'll be at the reception, she'll know absolutely no one, and I expect you to be especially nice to her."

"Mrs. Clayton?"

"I wouldn't quite say that." Mimi looked at me guilelessly. "I believe she intends to reclaim her maiden name at some point in the near future. Following certain legal formalities."

"Mimi, are you matchmaking?"

"Not at all," she said . . . then snickered. "*Hardly* at all. Although you will be the only teacher on the English faculty who's currently unattached, and that makes you a natural to act as her mentor."

I thought that a gigantic leap into illogic, especially for such an ordered mind, but I accompanied her to the door without saying so. What I said was, "If it's as serious as you say, you should be seeking treatment *now.* And not from some quack doctor in Juaréz, either. You should be at the Cleveland Clinic." I didn't know if the Cleveland Clinic even existed yet, but just then I didn't care.

"I think not. Given the choice between dying in a hospital room somewhere, stuck full of tubes and wires, and dying in a seaside Mexican hacienda . . . that is, as you like to say, a no-brainer. And there's something else, as well." She looked at me unflinchingly. "The pain isn't too bad yet, but I'm told it will be. In Mexico, they are far less apt to strike moral poses about large doses of morphine. Or Nembutal, if it comes to that. Trust me, I know what I'm doing."

Based on what had happened to Al Templeton, I guessed that was true. I put my arms around her, this time hugging very gently. I kissed one leathery cheek.

She bore it with a smile, then slipped away. Her eyes searched my face. "I'd like to know your story, my friend."

I shrugged. "I'm an open book, Miz Mimi."

She laughed. "What a crock of shit. You say you're from Wisconsin, but you showed up in Jodie with a New England drawl in your mouth and some story about teaching in Florida. You say you're commuting to Dallas for research purposes, and your manuscript purports to be *about* Dallas, but the people in it speak like New Englanders. In fact, there are a couple of places where characters actually say *ayuh*. You might want to change those."

And I thought my rewrite had been so clever.

"Actually, Mimi, New Englanders say it *a-yuh*, not *i-yuh*."

"Noted." She continued to search my face. It was a struggle not to drop my eyes, but I managed. "Sometimes I've actually caught myself wondering if you might not be a space alien, like Michael Rennie in *The Day the Earth Stood Still*. Here to analyze the natives and report back to Alpha Centauri on whether there's still hope for us as a species or if we should be exploded by plasma rays before we can spread our germs to the rest of the galaxy."

"That's very fanciful," I said, smiling.

"Good. I'd hate to think our whole planet was being judged by Texas."

"If Jodie were used as a sample, I'm sure Earth would get a passing grade."

"You like it here, don't you?"

"Yes."

"Is George Amberson your real name?"

"No. I changed it for reasons that are important to me but wouldn't be to anyone else. I'd prefer you kept that to yourself. For obvious reasons."

She nodded. "I can do that. I'll see you around, George. The diner, the library . . . and at the party, of course. You'll be nice to Sadie Clayton, won't you?"

"Nice as pie," I said, giving it the Texas twist: *pah.* That made her laugh.

When she was gone, I sat in my living room for a long time, not reading, not watching TV. And working on either of my manuscripts was the farthest thing from my mind. I thought about the job I'd just agreed to: a year of teaching full-time English at Denholm Consolidated High School, home of the Lions. I decided I had no regrets. I could roar at halftime with the best of them.

Well, I did have one regret, but it wasn't for me. When I thought about Mimi and her current situation, I had regrets aplenty.

6

On the subject of love at first sight, I'm with the Beatles: I believe that it happens all the time. But it didn't happen that way for me and Sadie, although I held her the first time I met her, and with my right hand cupping her left breast. So I guess I'm also with Mickey and Sylvia, who said love is strange.

South-central Texas can be savagely hot in mid-July, but the Saturday of the post-wedding party was damned near perfect, with temperatures in the upper seventies and lots of fat white clouds hustling across a sky the color of faded overalls. Long shutters of sun and shadow slipped down Mimi's backyard, which was on a mild slope ending at a muddy trickle of water she called Nameless Crick.

There were streamers of yellow and silver—Denholm High's colors—strung from the trees, and there was indeed a piñata, hung temptingly low from the jutting branch of a sugar pine. No child passed near it without giving it a longing glance.

"After dinner, the kids'll get sticks and beat away on it," someone said from just behind my left shoulder. "Candy and toys for all the *niños.*"

I turned and beheld Mike Coslaw, resplendent (and a little hallucinatory) in tight black jeans and a white open-throated shirt. A sombrero on a tug-string hung down on his back, and he wore a multicolored sash around his waist. I saw a number of other football players, including Jim LaDue, dressed in the same semiridiculous manner, circulating with trays. Mike held his out with a slightly crooked smile. "Canapé, Señor Amberson?"

I took a baby shrimp on a toothpick, and dipped it in the sauce. "Nice getup. Kind of a Speedy Gonzales thing."

"Don't start. If you want to see a *real* getup, check Vince Knowles." He pointed beyond the net to where a group of teachers was playing a clumsy but enthusiastic game of volleyball. I beheld Vince dressed up in tails and a top hat. He was surrounded by fascinated children who were watching him pull scarves out of thin air. It worked well, if you were still young enough to miss the one poking out of his sleeve. His shoe-polish mustache gleamed in the sun.

"On the whole, I prefer the Cisco Kid look," Mike said.

"I'm sure you all make terrific waiters, but who in God's name persuaded you to dress up? And does Coach know?"

"He ought to, he's here."

"Oh? I haven't seen him."

"He's over by the barbecue pit, gettin hammered with the Boosters Club. As for the outfit . . . Miz Mimi can be pretty persuasive."

I thought of the contract I'd signed. "I know."

Mike lowered his voice. "We all know she's sick. Besides . . . I think of this as acting." He struck a bullfighter pose—not easy when you're carrying a tray of canapés. "*¡Arriba!*"

"Not bad, but—"

"I know, I'm not really inside the part yet. Gotta *submerge* myself, right?"

"It works for Brando. How are you guys gonna be this fall, Mike?"

"Senior year? Jim in the pocket? Me, Hank Alvarez, Chip Wiggins, and Carl Crockett on the line? We're going to State, and that gold ball's going into the trophy case."

"I like your attitude."

"Are you going to do a play this fall, Mr. Amberson?"

"That's the plan."

"Good. Great. Save me a part . . . but with football, it'll have to be a small one. Check out the band, they're not bad."

The band was a lot better than not bad. The logo on the snare drum proclaimed them The Knights. The teenage lead singer counted off, and the band launched into a hot version of "Ooh, My Head," the old Ritchie Valens song—and not really so old in the summer of '61, although Valens had been dead for almost two years.

I got my beer in a paper cup and walked closer to the bandstand. The kid's voice was familiar. So was the keyboard, which sounded like it desperately wanted to be an accordion. And suddenly it clicked. The kid was Doug Sahm, and not so many years from now he would have hits of his own: "She's About a Mover" for one, "Mendocino" for another. That would be during the British Invasion, so the band, which basically played *Tejano* rock, would take a pseudo-British name: The Sir Douglas Quintet.

"George? Come here and meet someone, would you?"

I turned. Mimi was coming down the slope of the lawn with a woman in tow. My first impression of Sadie—everyone's first impression, I have no doubt—was her height. She was wearing flats, as were most of the women here, knowing that they'd be spending the afternoon and evening traipsing around outside, but this was a woman who had probably last worn heels to her own wedding, and even for that occasion she might have picked a dress that would hide just one more pair of low- or no-heels, chosen so she wouldn't tower comically over the groom as they stood at the altar. She was six feet at least, maybe a little more. I still had her by at least three inches, but other than Coach Borman and Greg Underwood of the History Department, I was probably the only man at the party who did. And Greg was a beanpole. Sadie had, in the argot of the day, a really good built. She knew it and was self-conscious about it rather than proud. I could tell that from the way she walked.

I know I'm a little too big to be considered normal, that walk said. The set of her shoulders said more: *It's not my fault, I just growed that way. Like Topsy.* She was wearing a sleeveless dress printed over with roses. Her arms were tanned. She had dashed on a little pink lipstick, but no other makeup.

Not love at first sight, I'm pretty sure of it, but I remember that first sight with surprising clarity. If I told you I remember with similar clarity the first time I saw the former Christy Epping, I'd be lying. Of course, it was at a dance club and we were both toasted, so maybe I get a pass on that.

Sadie was good-looking in an artless what-you-see-is-what-you-get American-girl way. She was something else, as well. On the day of the party I thought that something else was plain old big-person clumsiness. Later I found out she wasn't clumsy at all. Was, in fact, the farthest thing from it.

Mimi looked good—or at least no worse than she had on the day she'd come to my house and convinced me to teach full-time—but she *was* wearing makeup, which was unusual. It didn't quite conceal the hollows under her eyes, probably caused by a combination of sleeplessness and pain, or the new lines at the corners of her mouth. But she was smiling, and why not? She had married her fella, she had thrown a party that was obviously a roaring success, and she had brought a pretty girl in a pretty summer dress to meet the school's only eligible English teacher.

"Hey, Mimi," I said, starting up the mild slope toward her, weaving my way around the card tables (borrowed from the Amvets Hall) where people would later sit to eat barbecue and watch the sunset. "Congratulations. I guess now I'll have to get used to calling you Miz Simmons."

She smiled her dry smile. "Please stick to Mimi, it's what I'm used to. I have a new faculty member I want you to meet. This is—"

Someone had neglected to push one of the folding chairs all the way back in, and the big blonde girl, already holding her hand out to me and composing her how-nice-to-meet-you smile, tripped over it and went spilling forward. The chair came with her, tipping up, and I saw the potential for a nasty accident if one of the legs speared her in the stomach.

I dropped my cup of beer in the grass, took a giant step forward, and grabbed her as she fell. My left arm went around her waist. My right hand landed higher, grabbing something warm and round and slightly yielding. Between my hand and her breast, the cotton of her dress slipped over the smooth nylon or silk of whatever she was wearing beneath. It was an intimate introduction, but we had the banging angles of the chair for a chaperone, and although I staggered a little against the momentum of her hundred and fifty or so pounds, I kept my feet and she kept hers.

I took my hand away from the part of her that is rarely grasped when strangers are introduced and said: "Hello, I'm—" *Jake.* I came within a hair of giving my twenty-first-century name, but caught it at the very last moment. "I'm George. How nice to make your acquaintance."

She was blushing to the roots of her hair. I probably was, too. But she had the good grace to laugh.

"Nice to make yours. I think you just saved me from a very nasty accident."

Probably I had. Because that was it, you see? Sadie wasn't clumsy, she was accident-prone. It was amusing until you realized what it really was: a kind of haunting. She was the girl, she told me later, who got the hem of her dress caught in a car door when she and her date arrived at the senior prom, and managed to tear her skirt right off as they headed for the gym. She was the woman around whom water fountains malfunctioned, giving her a faceful; the woman who was apt to set an entire book of matches on fire when she lit a cigarette, burning her fingers or singeing her hair; the woman whose bra strap broke during Parents' Night or who discovered huge runs in her stockings before school assemblies at which she was scheduled to speak.

She was careful to mind her head going through doors (as all sensible tall folks learn to be), but people had a tendency to open them incautiously in her face, just as she was approaching them. She had been stuck in elevators on three occasions, once for two hours, and the year before, in a Savannah department store, the recently installed escalator had gobbled one of her shoes. Of course I knew none of this then; all I knew on that July afternoon was that a good-looking woman with blonde hair and blue eyes had fallen into my arms.

"I see you and Miss Dunhill are already getting along *famously*," Mimi said. "I'll leave you to get to know one another."

So, I thought, *the change from Mrs. Clayton to Miss Dunhill had already been effected, legal formalities or not.* Meanwhile, the chair was stuck into the sod by one leg. When Sadie tried to tug it free, it wouldn't come at first. When it did, the back of the chair ran nimbly up her thigh, hiking her skirt and revealing one stocking-top all the way to the garter. Which was as pink as the roses on her dress. She gave a little cry of exasperation. Her blush darkened to an alarming shade of firebrick.

I took the chair and set it firmly aside. "Miss Dunhill . . . Sadie . . . if I ever saw a woman who could use a cold beer, that woman is you. Come with me."

"Thank you," she said. "I'm so sorry. My mother told me never to throw myself at men, but I've never learned."

As I led her toward the line of kegs, pointing out various faculty members along the way (and taking her arm to steer her around a volleyball player who looked like he was going to collide with her as he backpedaled to return a high lob), I felt sure of one thing: we could be colleagues and we could be friends, maybe good friends, but we'd never be any more than that, no matter what Mimi might hope for. In a comedy starring Rock Hudson and Doris Day, our introduction would have undoubtedly qualified as "meet cute," but in real life, in front of an audience that was still grinning, it was just awkward and embarrassing. Yes, she was pretty. Yes, it was very nice to be walking with such a tall girl and still be taller. And sure, I had enjoyed the yielding firmness of that breast, cupped inside its thin double layer of proper cotton and sexy nylon. But unless you're fifteen, an accidental grope at a lawn party does not qualify as love at first sight.

I got the newly minted (or reminted) Miss Dunhill a beer, and we stood conversing near the makeshift bar for the requisite amount of time. We laughed when the dove Vince Knowles had rented for the occasion poked its head out of his top hat and pecked his finger. I pointed out more Denholm educators (many already leaving Sobriety City on the Alcohol Express). She said she would never get to know them all and I assured her she would. I asked her to call on me if she needed help with anything. The requisite number of minutes, the expected conversational gambits. Then she thanked me again for saving her from a nasty fall, and went to see if she could help gather the kids into the piñata-bashing mob they would soon become. I watched her go, not in love but a little in lust; I'll admit I mused briefly on the stocking-top and the pink garter.

My thoughts returned to her that night as I got ready for bed. She filled a large amount of space in a very nice way, and my eye hadn't been the only one following the pleasant sway of her progress in the print dress, but really, that was it. What more could there be? I'd read a book called *A Reliable Wife* not too long before leaving on the world's strangest trip, and as I climbed into bed, a line from the novel crossed my mind: "He had lost the habit of romance."

That's me, I thought as I turned out the light. *Totally out of the habit.* And then, as the crickets sang me to sleep: *But it wasn't just the breast that was nice. It was the weight of her. The weight of her in my arms.*

As it turned out, I hadn't lost the habit of romance at all.

7

August in Jodie was an oven, with temperatures at least in the nineties every day and often breaking a hundred. The air-conditioning in my rented house on Mesa Lane was good, but not good enough to withstand that sort of sustained assault. Sometimes—if there was a cooling shower—the nights were a little better, but not by much.

I was at my desk on the morning of August 27, working away at *The Murder Place* in a pair of basketball shorts and nothing else, when the doorbell rang. I frowned. It was Sunday, I'd heard the sound of competing church bells not too long previous, and most of the people I knew attended one of the town's four or five places of worship.

I pulled on a tee-shirt, and went to the door. Coach Borman was standing there with Ellen Dockerty, the former head of the Home Ec Department and DCHS's acting principal for the coming year; to no one's surprise, Deke had tendered his resignation on the same day Mimi tendered hers. Coach was stuffed into a dark blue suit and a loud tie that looked like it was strangling his plug of a neck. Ellen was wearing a prim gray outfit relieved by a spray of lace at her throat. They looked solemn. My first thought, as persuasive as it was wild: *They know. Somehow they know who I am and where I came from. They're here to tell me.*

Coach Borman's lips were trembling, and although Ellen didn't sob, tears filled her eyes. Then I knew.

"Is it Mimi?"

Coach nodded. "Deke called me. I got Ellie—I usually take her to church—and we're letting people know. The ones she liked the best first."

"I'm sorry to hear," I said. "How's Deke?"

"He seems to be bearing up," Ellen said, then glanced at Coach with some asperity. "According to him, at least."

"Yeah, he's okay," Coach said. "Broken up, accourse."

"Sure he is," I said.

"He's going to have her cremated." Ellen's lips thinned in disapproval. "Said it was what she wanted."

I thought about it. "We should have some sort of special assembly once school's back in. Can we do that? People can speak. Maybe we could put together a slide show? People must have lots of pictures of her."

"That's a wonderful idea," Ellen said. "Could you organize it, George?"

"I'd be happy to try."

"Get Miss Dunhill to help you." And before the suspicion of more matchmaking could even begin to cross my mind, she added: "I think it will help the boys and girls who loved Meems to know her hand-picked replacement helped plan the memorial assembly. It will help Sadie, too."

Of course it would. As a newcomer, she could use a little banked goodwill to start the year with.

"Okay, I'll talk to her. Thank you both. Are you going to be okay?"

"Sure," Coach said stoutly, but his lips were still trembling. I liked him for that. They went slowly down to his car, which was parked at the curb. Coach had his hand on Ellen's elbow. I liked him for that, too.

I closed the door, sat down on the bench in the little dab of front hall, and thought about Mimi saying she would be bereft if I didn't take over the junior-senior play. And if I didn't sign on to teach full-time for at least a year. Also if I didn't come to her wedding party. Mimi, who thought *Catcher in the Rye* belonged in the school library, and who wasn't averse to a nice boink on Saturday night. She was one of those faculty members the kids remember long after graduation, and sometimes come back to visit when they are no longer kids. The kind who sometimes shows up in a troubled student's life at a critical moment and makes a critical difference.

Who can find a virtuous woman? the proverb asks. *For her price is*

above rubies. She seeketh wool and flax and worketh willingly with her
hands. She is like the merchants' ships, that bringeth food from afar.

There are more clothes than the ones you put on your body,
every teacher knows that, and food isn't just what you put in your
mouth. Miz Mimi had fed and clothed many. Including me. I sat
there on a bench I'd bought at a Fort Worth flea market with my
head lowered and my face in my hands. I thought about her, and I
was very sad, but my eyes remained dry.

I have never been what you'd call a crying man.

8

Sadie immediately agreed to help me put together a memorial
assembly. We worked on it in the final days of that hot August,
driving around town to line up speakers. I tapped Mike Coslaw
to read Proverbs 31, which describes the virtuous woman, and Al
Stevens volunteered to tell the story—which I had never heard
from Mimi herself—about how she had named the Prongburger,
his *spécialité de la maison.* We also collected over two hundred photographs. My favorite showed Mimi and Deke doing the twist at a
school dance. She looked like she was having fun; he looked like a
man with a fair-sized stick up his ass. We culled the photos in the
school library, where the nameplate on the desk now read MISS
DUNHILL instead of MIZ MIMI.

During that time Sadie and I never kissed, never held hands,
never even looked into each other's eyes for longer than a passing glance. She didn't talk about her busted marriage or her reasons for coming to Texas from Georgia. I didn't talk about my
novel or tell her about my largely made-up past. We talked about
books. We talked about Kennedy, whose foreign policy she considered jingoistic. We discussed the nascent civil rights movement.
I told her about the board across the creek at the bottom of the
path behind the Humble Oil station in North Carolina. She said
she'd seen similar toilet facilities for colored people in Georgia,

but believed their days were numbered. She thought school integration would come, but probably not until the mid-seventies. I told her I thought it would be sooner, driven by the new president and his attorney-general kid brother.

She snorted. "You have more respect for that grinning Irishman than I do. Tell me, does he ever get his hair cut?"

We didn't become lovers, but we became friends. Sometimes she tripped over things (including her own feet, which were large), and on two occasions I steadied her, but there were no catches as memorable as the first one. Sometimes she'd declare she just *had* to have a cigarette, and I'd accompany her out to the student smoking area behind the metal shop.

"I'll be sorry not to be able to come out here and sprawl on the bench in my old blue jeans," she said one day. This was less than a week before school was scheduled to start. "There's always such a *fug* in teachers' rooms."

"Someday that'll all change. Smoking will be banned on school grounds. For teachers as well as students."

She smiled. It was a good one, because her lips were rich and full. And the jeans, I must say, looked good on her. She had long, *long* legs. Not to mention just enough junk in her trunk. "A cigarette-free society . . . Negro children and white children studying side by side in perfect harmony . . . no wonder you're writing a novel, you've got one hell of an imagination. What else do you see in your crystal ball, George? Rockets to the moon?"

"Sure, but it'll probably take a little longer than integration. Who told you I was writing a novel?"

"Miz Mimi," she said, and butted her cigarette in one of the half a dozen sand-urn ashtrays. "She said it was good. And speaking of Miz Mimi, I suppose we ought to get back to work. I think we're almost there with the photographs, don't you?"

"Yes."

"And are you sure playing that *West Side Story* song over the slide show isn't going to be too corny?"

I thought "Somewhere" was cornier than Iowa and Nebraska

put together, but according to Ellen Dockerty it had been Mimi's favorite song.

I told Sadie this, and she laughed doubtfully. "I didn't know her all that well, but it sure doesn't seem like her. Maybe it's *Ellie's* favorite song."

"Now that I think about it, that seems all too likely. Listen, Sadie, do you want to go to the football game with me on Friday? Kind of show the kids that you're here before school starts on Monday?"

"I'd love to." Then she paused, looking a little uncomfortable. "As long as you don't, you know, get any ideas. I'm not ready to date just yet. Maybe not for a long time."

"Neither am I." She was probably thinking about her ex, but I was thinking about Lee Oswald. Soon he'd have his American passport back. Then it would only be a matter of wangling a Soviet exit visa for his wife. "But friends sometimes go to the game together."

"That's right, they do. And I like going places with you, George."

"Because I'm taller."

She punched my arm playfully—a big-sister kind of punch. "That's right, podna. You're the kind of man I can look up to."

9

At the game, practically *everybody* looked up to us, and with faint awe—as though we were representatives of a slightly different race of humans. I thought it was kind of nice, and for once Sadie didn't have to slouch to fit in. She wore a Lion Pride sweater and her faded jeans. With her blonde hair pulled back in a ponytail, she looked like a high school senior herself. A tall one, probably the center on the girls' basketball team.

We sat in Faculty Row and cheered as Jim LaDue riddled the Arnette Bears' defense with half a dozen short passes and then a sixty-yard bomb that brought the crowd to its feet. At halftime the score was Denholm 31, Arnette 6. As the players ran off the field and the Denholm band marched onto it with their tubas and trombones wagging, I asked Sadie if she wanted a hotdog and a Coke.

"You bet I do, but right now the line'll be all the way out to the parking lot. Wait until there's a time-out in the third quarter or something. We have to roar like lions and do the Jim Cheer."

"I think you can manage those things on your own."

She smiled at me and gripped my arm. "No, I need you to help me. I'm new here, remember?"

At her touch, I felt a warm little shiver I did not associate with friendship. And why not? Her cheeks were flushed, her eyes were sparkling; under the lights and the greeny-blue sky of a deepening Texas dusk, she was way beyond pretty. Things between us might have progressed faster than they did, except for what happened during that halftime.

The band marched around the way high school bands do, in step but not completely in tune, blaring a medley you couldn't quite figure out. When they finished, the cheerleaders trotted to the fifty-yard line, dropped their pompoms in front of their feet, and put their hands on their hips. *"Give us an L!"*

We gave them what they required, and when further importuned, we obliged with an *I,* an *O,* an *N,* and an *S.*

"What's that spell?"

"LIONS!" Everybody on the home bleachers up and clapping.

"Who's gonna win?"

"LIONS!" Given the halftime score, there wasn't much doubt about it.

"Then let us hear you roar!"

We roared in the traditional manner, turning first to the left and then to the right. Sadie gave it her all, cupping her hands around her mouth, her ponytail flying from one shoulder to the other.

What came next was the Jim Cheer. In the previous three years—yes, our Mr. LaDue had started at QB even as a freshman—

this had been pretty simple. The cheerleaders would yell some-thing like, *"Let us hear your Lion Pride! Name the man who leads our side!"* And the hometown crowd would bellow *"JIM! JIM! JIM!"* After that the cheerleaders would do a few more cartwheels and then run off the field so the other team's band could march out and tootle a tune or two. But this year, possibly in honor of Jim's valedictory season, the chant had changed.

Each time the crowd yelled *"JIM,"* the cheerleaders responded with the first syllable of his last name, drawing it out like a teas-ing musical note. It was new, but it wasn't complicated, and the crowd caught on in a hurry. Sadie was doing the chant with the best of them, until she realized I wasn't. I was just standing there with my mouth open.

"George? Are you okay?"

I couldn't answer. In fact, I barely heard her. Because most of me was back in Lisbon Falls. I had just come through the rabbit-hole. I had just walked along the side of the drying shed and ducked under the chain. I had been prepared to meet the Yellow Card Man, but not to be attacked by him. Which I was. Only he was no longer the Yellow Card Man; now he was the Orange Card Man. *You're not supposed to be here,* he had said. *Who are you? What are you doing here?* And when I'd started to ask him if he'd tried AA for his drinking problem, he'd said—

"George?" Now she sounded worried as well as concerned. "What is it? What's wrong?"

The fans had totally gotten into the call-and-response thing. The cheerleaders shouted *"JIM"* and the bleacher-creatures shouted back *"LA."*

Fuck off, Jimla! That was what the Yellow Card Man who'd become the Orange Card Man (although not yet the dead-by-his-own-hand Black Card Man) had snarled at me, and that was what I was hearing now, tossed back and forth like a medicine ball between the cheerleaders and the twenty-five hundred fans watch-ing them:

"JIMLA, JIMLA, JIMLA!"

Sadie grabbed my arm and shook me. "Talk to me, mister! Talk to me, because I'm getting scared!"

I turned to her and managed a smile. It did not come easy, believe me. "Just crashing for sugar, I guess. I'm going to grab those Cokes."

"You aren't going to faint, are you? I can walk you to the aid station if—"

"I'm fine," I said, and then, without thinking about what I was doing, I kissed the tip of her nose. Some kid shouted, *"Way to go, Mr. A!"*

Rather than looking irritated, she wriggled her nose like a rabbit, then smiled. "Get out of here, then. Before you damage my reputation. And bring me a chili dog. Lots of cheese."

"Yes, ma'am."

The past harmonizes with itself, that much I already understood. But what song was this? I didn't know, and it worried me plenty. In the concrete runway leading to the refreshment stand, the chant was magnified, making me want to put my hands over my ears to block it out.

"JIMLA, JIMLA, JIMLA."

PART 4

SADIE AND
THE GENERAL

CHAPTER 14

1

The memorial assembly was held at the end of the new school year's first day, and if one can measure success by damp hankies, the show Sadie and I put together was boffo. I'm sure it was cathartic for the kids, and I think Miz Mimi herself would have enjoyed it. *Sarcastic people tend to be marshmallows underneath the armor,* she once told me. *I'm no different.*

The teachers held it together through most of the eulogies. It was Mike who started to get to them, with his calm, heartfelt recitation from Proverbs 31. Then, during the slide show, with the accompanying schmaltz from *West Side Story,* the faculty lost it, too. I found Coach Borman particularly entertaining. With tears streaming down his red cheeks and large, quacking sobs emerging from his massive chest, Denholm's football guru reminded me of everybody's *second*-favorite cartoon duck, Baby Huey.

I whispered this observation to Sadie as we stood beside the big screen with its marching images of Miz Mimi. She was crying, too, but had to step off the stage and into the wings as laughter first fought with and then overcame her tears. Safely back in the shadows, she looked at me reproachfully . . . and then gave me the finger. I decided I deserved it. I wondered if Miz Mimi would still think Sadie and I were getting along famously.

I thought she probably would.

I picked *Twelve Angry Men* for the fall play, accidentally on purpose neglecting to inform the Samuel French Company that I intended to retitle our version *The Jury,* so I could cast some girls. I would hold tryouts in late October and start rehearsals on November 13, after the Lions' last regular-season football game. I had my eye on Vince Knowles for Juror #8—the holdout who'd been played by Henry Fonda in the movie—and Mike Coslaw for what I considered the best part in the show: bullying, abrasive Juror #3.

But I had begun to focus on a more important show, one that made the Frank Dunning affair look like a paltry vaudeville skit by comparison. Call this one *Jake and Lee in Dallas.* If things went well, it would be a tragedy in one act. I had to be ready to go onstage when the time came, and that meant starting early.

2

On the sixth of October, the Denholm Lions won their fifth football game, on their way to an undefeated season that would be dedicated to Vince Knowles, the boy who had played George in *Of Mice and Men* and who would never get a chance to act in the George Amberson version of *Twelve Angry Men*—but more of that later. It was the start of a three-day weekend, because the Monday following was Columbus Day.

I drove to Dallas on the holiday. Most businesses were open, and my first stop was one of the pawnshops on Greenville Avenue. I told the little man behind the counter that I wanted to buy the cheapest wedding ring he had in stock. I walked out with an eight-buck band of gold (at least it *looked* like gold) on the third finger of my left hand. Then I drove downtown to a place on Lower Main Street I had bird-dogged in the Dallas Yellow Pages: Silent Mike's Satellite Electronics. There I was greeted by a trim little man who wore horn-rimmed glasses and a weirdly futuristic button on his vest: TRUST NOBODY, it said.

"Are you Silent Mike?" I asked.

"Yep."

"And are you truly silent?"

He smiled. "Depends on who's listening."

"Let's assume nobody," I said, and told him what I wanted. It turned out I could have saved my eight bucks, because he had no interest at all in my supposedly cheating wife. It was the equipment I wanted to buy that interested the proprietor of Satellite Electronics. On that subject he was Loquacious Mike.

"Mister, they may have gear like that on whatever planet *you* come from, but we sure don't have it here."

That stirred a memory of Miz Mimi comparing me to the alien visitor in *The Day the Earth Stood Still*. "I don't know what you mean."

"You want a small wireless listening device? Fine. I got a bunch in that glass case right over there to your left. They're called transistor radios. I stock both Motorola and GE, but the Japanese make the best ones." He stuck out his lower lip and blew a lock of hair off his forehead. "Ain't that a kick in the behind? We beat em fifteen years ago by bombing two of their cities to radioactive dust, but do they die? No! They hide in their holes until the dust settles, then come crawling back out armed with circuit boards and soldering irons instead of Nambu machine guns. By 1985, they'll own the world. The part of it *I* live in, anyway."

"So you can't help me?"

"Whattaya, kiddin? Sure I can. Silent Mike McEachern's always happy to help fill a customer's electronic needs. But it'll cost."

"I'd be willing to pay quite a bit. It could save me even more when I get that cheating bitch into divorce court."

"Uh-huh. Wait here a minute while I get something out of the back. And turn that sign in the door over to CLOSED, wouldja? I'm going to show you something that's probably not . . . well, maybe it *is* legal, but who knows? Is Silent Mike McEachern an attorney?"

"I'm guessing not."

My guide to sixties-era electronica reappeared with a weird-looking gadget in one hand and a small cardboard box in the other.

The printing on the box was in Japanese. The gadget looked like a dildo for pixie chicks, mounted on a black plastic disc. The disc was three inches thick and about the diameter of a quarter, with a spray of wires coming out of it. He put it on the counter.

"This is an Echo. Manufactured right here in town, son. If anyone can beat the sons of Nippon at their own game, it's us. Electronics is gonna replace banking in Dallas by 1970. Mark my words." He crossed himself, pointed skyward, and added, "God bless Texas."

I picked the gadget up. "What exactly is an Echo when it's at home with its feet up on the hassock?"

"The closest thing to the kind of bug you described to me that you're gonna get. It's small because it doesn't have any vacuum tubes and doesn't run on batteries. It runs on ordinary AC house current."

"You plug it into the wall?"

"Sure, why not? Your wife and her boyfriend can look at it and say, 'How nice, someone bugged the place while we were out, let's have a nice noisy shag, then talk over all our private business.'"

He was a geek, all right. Still, patience is a virtue. And I needed what I needed.

"What do you do with it, then?"

He tapped the disc. "This goes inside the base of a lamp. Not a floor lamp, unless you're interested in recording the mice running around inside the baseboards, you dig? A table lamp, so it's up where people talk." He brushed the wires. "The red and yellow ones connect to the lamp cord, lamp cord's plugged into the wall. The bug's dead until someone turns on the lamp. When they do, bingo, you're off to the races."

"This other thing is the mike?"

"Yep, and for American-made it's a good one. Now—you see the other two wires? The blue and green ones?"

"Uh-huh."

He opened the cardboard box with the Japanese writing on it, and took out a reel-to-reel recorder. It was bigger than a pack of Sadie's Winstons, but not by much.

"Those wires hook up to this. Base unit goes in the lamp, recorder goes in a bureau drawer, maybe under your wife's scanties. Or drill a little hole in the wall and put it in the closet."

"The recorder also draws power from the lamp cord."

"Naturally."

"Could I get two of these Echoes?"

"I could get you four, if you wanted. Might take a week, though."

"Two will be fine. How much?"

"Stuff like this ain't cheap. A pair'd run you a hundred and forty. Best I can do. And it would have to be a cash deal." He spoke with a regret that suggested we had been having a nice little techno-dream for ourselves, but now the dream was almost over.

"How much more would it cost me to have you do the installation?" I saw his alarm and hastened to dispel it. "I don't mean the actual black-bag job, nothing like that. Just to put the bugs in a couple of lamps and hook up the tape recorders—could you do that?"

"Of course I could, Mr.—"

"Let's say Mr. Doe. John Doe."

His eyes sparkled as I imagine E. Howard Hunt's would when he first beheld the challenge that was the Watergate Hotel. "Good name."

"Thanks. And it would be good to have a couple of options with the wires. Something short, if I can place it close by, something longer if I need to hide it in a closet or on the other side of a wall."

"I can do that, but you don't want more than ten feet or the sound turns to mud. Also, the more wire you use, the greater the chance that someone'll find it."

Even an English teacher could understand that.

"How much for the whole deal?"

"Mmm . . . hundred and eighty?"

He looked ready to haggle, but I didn't have the time or the inclination. I put five twenties down on the counter and said, "You get the rest when I pick them up. But first we test them out and make sure they work, agreed?"

"Yeah, fine."

"One other thing. Get used lamps. Kind of grungy."

"Grungy?"

"Like they were picked up at a yard sale or a flea market for a quarter apiece." After you direct a few plays—counting the ones I'd worked on at LHS, *Of Mice and Men* had been my fifth—you learn a few things about set decoration. The last thing I wanted was someone stealing a bug-loaded lamp from a semi-furnished apartment.

For a moment he looked puzzled, then a complicitous smile dawned on his face. "*I get it. Realism.*"

"That's the plan, Stan." I started for the door, then came back, leaned my forearms on the transistor radio display case, and looked into his eyes. I can't swear that he saw the man who had killed Frank Dunning, but I can't say for sure that he didn't, either. "You're not going to talk about this, are you?"

"No! Course not!" He zipped two fingers across his lips.

"That's the way," I said. "When?"

"Give me a few days."

"I'll come back next Monday. What time do you close?"

"Five."

I calculated the distance from Jodie to Dallas and said, "An extra twenty if you stay open until seven. It's the soonest I can make it. That work for you?"

"Yeah."

"Good. Have everything ready."

"I will. Anything else?"

"Yeah. Why the hell do they call you Silent Mike?"

I was hoping he'd say *Because I can keep a secret,* but he didn't. "When I was a kid, I thought that Christmas carol was about me. It just kind of stuck."

I didn't ask, but halfway back to my car it came to me, and I started to laugh.

Silent Mike, holy Mike.

Sometimes the world we live in is a truly weird place.

3

When Lee and Marina returned to the United States, they'd live in a sad procession of low-rent apartments, including the one in New Orleans I'd already visited, but based on Al's notes, I thought there were only two I needed to focus on. One was at 214 West Neely Street, in Dallas. The other was in Fort Worth, and that was where I went after my visit to Silent Mike's.

I had a map of the city, but still had to ask directions three times. In the end it was an elderly black woman clerking at a mom-n-pop who pointed me the right way. When I finally found what I was looking for, I wasn't surprised that it had been hard to locate. The ass end of Mercedes Street was unpaved hardpan lined with crumbling houses little better than sharecroppers' shacks. It spilled into a huge, mostly empty parking lot where tumbleweeds blew across the crumbling asphalt. Beyond the lot was the back of a cinderblock warehouse. Printed on it in whitewashed letters ten feet tall was PROPERTY OF MONTGOMERY WARD and TRESPASSERS WILL BE PROSECUTED and POLICE TAKE NOTE.

The air stank of cracked petroleum from the direction of Odessa-Midland, and raw sewage much closer at hand. The sound of rock and roll spilled from open windows. I heard the Dovells, Johnny Burnette, Lee Dorsey, Chubby Checker . . . and that was in the first forty yards or so. Women were hanging clothes on rusty whirligigs. They were all wearing smocks that had probably been purchased at Zayre's or Mammoth Mart, and they all appeared to be pregnant. A filthy little boy and an equally filthy little girl stood on a cracked clay driveway and watched me go by. They were holding hands and looked too much alike not to be twins. The boy, naked except for a single sock, was holding a cap pistol. The girl was wearing a saggy diaper below a Mickey Mouse Club tee-shirt. She was clutching a plastic babydoll as filthy as she was. Two bare-chested men were throwing a football back and forth between their respective yards, both of them with cigarettes hanging from the corners of their mouths. Beyond them, a rooster and two bedraggled chickens pecked in the dust near a scrawny dog that was either sleeping or dead.

I pulled up in front of 2703, the place to which Lee would bring his wife and daughter when he could no longer stand Marguerite Oswald's pernicious brand of smotherlove. Two concrete strips led up to a bald patch of oil-stained ground where there would have been a garage in a better part of town. The wasteland of crabgrass that passed for a lawn was littered with cheap plastic toys. A little girl in ragged pink shorts was kicking a soccer ball repeatedly against the side of the house. Each time it hit the wooden siding, she said, *"Chumbah!"*

A woman with her hair in large blue rollers and a cigarette plugged in her gob shoved her head out the window and shouted, "You keep doin that, Rosette, I'm gone come out n beat you snotty!" Then she saw me. "Wha' *choo* want? If it's a bill, I cain't hep you. My husband does all that. He got work today."

"It's not a bill," I said. Rosette kicked the soccer ball at me with a snarl that became a reluctant smile when I caught it with the side of my foot and booted it gently back. "I just wanted to speak to you for a second."

"Y'all gotta wait, then. I ain't decent."

Her head disappeared. I waited. Rosette kicked the soccer ball high and wide this time (*"Chumbah!"*), but I managed to catch it on one palm before it hit the house.

"Ain't s'pozed to use your hands, dirty old sumbitch," she said. "That's a penalty."

"Rosette, what I told you about that goddam mouth?" Moms came out on the stoop, securing a filmy yellow scarf over her rollers. It made them look like cocooned insects, the kind that might be poisonous when they hatched.

"Dirty old *fucking* sumbitch!" Rosette shrieked, and then scampered up Mercedes Street in the direction of the Monkey Ward warehouse, kicking her soccer ball and laughing maniacally.

"Wha' choo want?" Moms was twenty-two going on fifty. Several of her teeth were gone, and she had the fading remains of a black eye.

"Want to ask you some questions," I said.

"What makes my bi'ness your bi'ness?"

I took out my wallet and offered her a five-dollar bill. "Ask me no questions and I'll tell you no lies."

"You ain't from around here. Soun like a Yankee."

"Do you want this money or not, Missus?"

"Depends on the questions. I ain't tellin you my goddam bra-size."

"I want to know how long you've been here, for a start."

"This place? Six weeks, I guess. Harry thought he might catch on at the Monkey Ward warehouse, but they ain't hiring. So he went on over to Manpower. You know what that is?"

"Day-labor?"

"Yeah, n he workin with a bunch of niggers." Only it wasn't *workin*, it was *woikin*. "Nine dollars a day workin with a bunch of goddam niggers side a the road. He says it's like bein at West Texas Correctional again."

"How much rent do you pay?"

"Fifty a month."

"Furnished?"

"Semi. Well, you *could* say. Got a goddam bed and a goddam gas stove gone kill us all, most likely. And I ain't takin you in, so don't ax. I don't know you from goddam Adam."

"Did it come with lamps and such?"

"You're crazy, mister."

"Did it?"

"Yeah, couple. One that works and one that duddn't. I ain't stayin here, be goddamned if I will. He tell how he don't want to move back in with my mama down Mozelle, but tough titty said the kitty. I ain't stayin here. You smell this place?"

"Yes, ma'am."

"That ain't nothin but shit, sonny jim. Not catshit, not dogshit, that's peopleshit. Work with niggers, that's one thing, but live like one? Nosir. You done?"

I wasn't, quite, although I wished I were. I was disgusted by her, and disgusted with myself for daring to judge. She was a prisoner of her time, her choices, and this shit-smelling street. But it was the rollers under the yellow headscarf that I kept looking at. Fat blue bugs waiting to hatch.

"Nobody stays here for long, I guess?"

"On 'Cedes Street?" She waved her cigarette at the hardpan leading to the deserted parking lot and the vast warehouse filled with nice things she would never own. At the elbow-to-elbow shacks with their steps of crumbling cinderblock and their broken windows blocked up with pieces of cardboard. At the roiling kids. At the old, rust-eaten Fords and Hudsons and Studebaker Larks. At the unforgiving Texas sky. Then she uttered a terrible laugh filled with amusement and despair.

"Mister, this is a bus stop on the road to nowhere. Me'n Bratty Sue's sailin back to Mozelle. If Harry won't go with us, we'll sail without him."

I took the map out of my hip pocket, tore off a strip, and scribbled my Jodie telephone number on it. Then I added another five-dollar bill. I held them out to her. She looked but didn't take.

"What I want your telephone number for? I ain't got no goddam phone. That there ain't no DFW 'shange, anyway. That's goddam long distance."

"Call me when you get ready to move out. That's all I want. You call me and say, 'Mister, this is Rosette's mama, and we're moving.' That's all it is."

I could see her calculating. It didn't take her long. Ten dollars was more than her husband would make working all day in the hot Texas sun. Because Manpower knew from nothing about time-and-a-half on holidays. And this would be ten dollars *he* knew from nothing about.

"Gimme another semny-fi cent," she said. "For the long distance."

"Here, take a buck. Live a little. And don't forget."

"I won't."

"No, you don't want to. Because if you forgot, I might just be apt to find my way to your husband and tattle. This is important business, Missus. To me it is. What's your name, anyway?"

"Ivy Templeton."

I stood there in the dirt and the weeds, smelling shit, half-cooked oil, and the big farty aroma of natural gas.

"Mister? What's wrong with you? You come over all funny."

"Nothing," I said. And maybe it *was* nothing. Templeton is far from an uncommon name. Of course a man can talk himself into anything, if he tries hard enough. I'm walking, talking proof of that.

"What's *your* name?"

"Puddentane," I said. "Ask me again and I'll tell you the same."

At this touch of grammar school raillery, she finally cracked a smile.

"You call me, Missus."

"Yeah, okay. Go on now. You was to run over that little hell-bitch of mine on your way out, you'd prolly be doin me a favor."

I drove back to Jodie and found a note thumbtacked to my door:

George—
   Would you call me? I need a favor.
                          Sadie (and that's the trouble!!)

Which meant exactly what? I went inside to call her and find out.

4

Coach Borman's mother, who lived in an Abilene nursing home, had broken her hip, and this coming Saturday was the DCHS Sadie Hawkins Dance.

"Coach talked me into chaperoning the dance with him! He said, and I quote, 'How can you resist going to a dance that's practically named after you?' Just last week, this was. And like a fool I agreed. Now he's going down to Abilene, and where does that leave me? Chaperoning two hundred sex-crazed sixteen-year-olds doing the Twist and the Philly? I don't think so! What if some of the boys bring beer?"

I thought it would be amazing if they didn't, but felt it best not to say so.

"Or what if there's a fight in the parking lot? Ellie Dockerty said a bunch of boys from Henderson crashed the dance last year and two of their kids and two of ours had to go to the hospital! George, can you help me out here? *Please?*"

"Have I just been Sadie Hawkinsed by Sadie Dunhill?" I was grinning. The idea of going to the dance with her did not exactly fill me with gloom.

"Don't joke! It's not funny!"

"Sadie, I'd be happy to go with you. Are you going to bring me a corsage?"

"I'd bring you a bottle of champagne, if that's what it took." She considered this. "Well, no. Not on my salary. A bottle of Cold Duck, though."

"Doors open at seven-thirty?" Actually I knew they did. The posters were up all over the school.

"Right."

"And it's just a record-hop. No band. That's good."

"Why?"

"Live bands can cause problems. I shapped a dance once where the drummer sold home brew beer at intermission. *That* was a pleasant experience."

"Were there fights?" She sounded horrified. Also fascinated.

"Nope, but there was a whole lot of puking. The stuff was spunky."

"This was in Florida?"

It had been at Lisbon High, in 2009, so I told her yes, in Florida. I also told her I'd be happy to co-chaperone the hop.

"Thank you so much, George."

"My pleasure, ma'am."

And it absolutely was.

5

The Pep Club was in charge of the Sadie Hawkins, and they'd done a bang-up job: lots of crepe streamers wafting down from the gymnasium rafters (silver and gold, of course), lots of ginger ale punch, lemon-snap cookies, and red velvet cupcakes provided by the Future Homemakers of America. The Art Department— small but dedicated—contributed a cartoon mural that showed the immortal Miss Hawkins herself, chasing after the eligible bachelors of Dogpatch. Mattie Shaw and Mike's girlfriend, Bobbi Jill, did most of the work, and they were justifiably proud. I wondered if they still would be seven or eight years from now, when the first wave of women's libbers started burning their bras and demonstrating for full reproductive rights. Not to mention wearing tee-shirts that said things like I AM NOT PROPERTY and A WOMAN NEEDS A MAN LIKE A FISH NEEDS A BICYCLE.

The night's DJ and master of ceremonies was Donald Bellingham, a sophomore. He arrived with a totally ginchy record collection in not one but two Samsonite suitcases. With my permission (Sadie just looked bewildered), he hooked up his Webcor phonograph and his dad's preamp to the school's PA system. The gym was big enough to provide natural reverb, and after a few preliminary feedback shrieks, he got a booming sound that was awesome. Although born in Jodie, Donald was a permanent resident of Rockville, in the state of Daddy Cool. He wore pink-rimmed specs with thick lenses, belt-in-the-back slacks, and saddle shoes so grotesquely square they were authentically crazy, man. His face was an exploding zit-factory below a Brylcreem-loaded Bobby Rydell duck's ass. He looked like he might get his first kiss from a real live girl around the age of forty-two, but he was fast and funny with the mike, and his record collection (which he called "the stack-o-wax" and "Donny B.'s round mound of sound") was, as previously noted, the ginchiest.

"Let's kick-start this party with a blast from the past, a rock n roll relic from the grooveyard of cool, a golden gasser, a platter that matters, move your feet to the real gone beat of *Danny . . . and the JOOONIERS!*"

"At the Hop" nuked the gym. The dance started as most of them do in the early sixties, just the girls jitterbugging with the girls. Feet in penny loafers flew. Petticoats swirled. After awhile, though, the floor started to fill up with boy-girl couples . . . for the fast dances, at least, more current stuff like "Hit the Road Jack" and "Quarter to Three."

Not many of the kids would have made the cut on *Dancing with the Stars,* but they were young and enthusiastic and obviously having a ball. It made me happy to see them. Later, if Donny B. didn't have the good sense to lower the lights a bit, I'd do it myself. Sadie was nervous at first, ready for trouble, but these kids had just come to have fun. There were no invading hordes from Henderson or any other school. She saw that and began to loosen up a little.

After about forty minutes of nonstop music (and four red velvet cupcakes), I leaned toward Sadie and said, "Time for Warden Amberson to do his first circuit of the building and make sure no one in the exercise yard is engaging in inappropriate behavior."

"Do you want me to come with you?"

"I want you to keep an eye on the punch bowl. If any young man approaches it with a bottle of anything, even cough syrup, I want you to threaten him with electrocution or castration, whichever you think might be more effective."

She leaned back against the wall and laughed until tears sparkled in the corners of her eyes. "Get out of here, George, you're *awful.*"

I went. I was glad I'd made her laugh, but even after three years, it was easy to forget how much more effect sexually tinged jokes have in the Land of Ago.

I caught a couple making out in one of the more shadowy nooks on the east side of the gym—he prospecting inside her sweater, she apparently trying to suck his lips off. When I tapped the young prospector on the shoulder, they leaped apart. "Save it for The Bluffs after the dance," I said. "For now, go on back to the gym. Walk slow. Cool off. Get some punch."

They went, she buttoning her sweater, he walking slightly bent over in that well-known male adolescent gait known as the Blue-Balls Scuttle.

Two dozen red fireflies winked from behind the metal shop. I waved and a couple of the kids in the smoking area waved back. I poked my head around the east corner of the woodshop and saw something I didn't like. Mike Coslaw, Jim LaDue, and Vince Knowles were huddled there, passing something back and forth. I grabbed it and heaved it over the chain-link fence before they even knew I was there.

Jim looked momentarily startled, then gave me his lazy football-hero smile. "Hello to you too, Mr. A."

"Spare me, Jim. I'm not some girl you're trying to charm out of her panties, and I'm most assuredly not your coach."

He looked shocked and a little scared, but I saw no offended sense of entitlement in his face. I think that if this had been one of the big Dallas schools, there might have been. Vince had backed away a step. Mike stood his ground, but looked downcast and embarrassed. No, it was more than embarrassment. It was outright shame.

"A bottle at a record-hop," I said. "It's not that I expect you to stick to all the rules, but why would you be so stupid when it comes to violating them? Jimmy, you get caught drinking and kicked off the football team, what happens to your 'Bama scholarship?"

"Prob'ly get red-shirted, I guess," he said. "That's all."

"Right, and sit out a year. Actually have to make grades. Same with you, Mike. And you'd get kicked out of the Drama Club. Do you want that?"

"Nosir." Hardly more than a whisper.

"Do you, Vince?"

"No, huh-uh, Mr. A. Absolutely nitzy. Are we still gonna do the jury one? Because if we are—"

"Don't you know enough to shut up when a teacher's scolding you?"

"Yessir, Mr. A."

"You boys don't get a pass from me next time, but this is your lucky night. What you get tonight is a valuable piece of advice: *Do not fuck up your futures.* Not over a pint of Five Star at a school dance you won't even remember a year from now. Do you understand that?"

"Yessir," Mike said. "I'm sorry."

"Me, too," Vince said. "Absolutely." And crossed himself, grinning. Some of them are just built that way. And maybe the world needs a cadre of smartasses to liven things up, who knows?

"Jim?"

"Yessir," he said. "Please don't tell my daddy."

"No, this is between us." I looked them over. "You boys will find plenty of places to drink next year at college. But not at our school. You hear me?"

This time they all said yessir.

"Now go back inside. Drink some punch and rinse the smell of whiskey off your breath."

They went. I gave them time, then followed at a distance, head down, hands stuffed deep in pockets, thinking hard. *Not at our school,* I had said. Ours.

Come and teach, Mimi had said. *That's what you were meant to do.*

2011 had never seemed more distant than it did then. Hell, Jake Epping had never seemed so distant. A growling tenor sax was blowing in a party-lit gym deep in the heart of Texas. A sweet

368

breeze carried it across the night. A drummer was laying down an insidious off-your-seat-and-on-your-feet shuffle.

I think that's when I decided I was never going back.

6

The growling sax and hoochie-coochie drummer were backing a group called The Diamonds. The song was "The Stroll." The kids weren't doing that dance, though. Not quite.

The Stroll was the first step Christy and I learned when we started going to Thursday-night dance classes. It's a two-by-two dance, a kind of icebreaker where each couple jives down an aisle of clapping guys and girls. What I saw when I came back into the gym was different. Here the boys and the girls came together, turned in each other's arms as if waltzing, then separated again, ending up across from where they had begun. When they were apart, their feet went back on their heels and their hips swayed forward, a move that was both charming and sexy.

As I watched from beside the snack table, Mike, Jim, and Vince joined the guys' side. Vince didn't have much—to say he danced like a white boy would be an insult to white boys everywhere—but Jim and Mike moved like the athletes they were, which is to say with unconscious grace. Pretty soon most of the girls on the other side were watching them.

"I was starting to worry about you!" Sadie shouted over the music. "Is everything all right out there?"

"Fine!" I shouted back. "What's that dance?"

"The Madison! They've been doing it on Bandstand all month! Want me to teach you?"

"Lady," I said, taking her by the arm, "I'm going to teach you."

The kids saw us coming and made room, clapping and shouting *"Way to go, Mr. A!"* and *"Show him how you work, Miz Dunhill!"* Sadie laughed and tightened the elastic holding her ponytail.

Color mounted high in her cheeks, making her more than pretty. She got back on her heels, clapping her hands and shaking her shoulders with the other girls, then came forward into my arms, her eyes turned up to mine. I was glad I was tall enough for her to do that. We turned like a wind-up bride and groom on a wedding cake, then came apart. I dipped low and spun on my toes with my hands held out like Al Jolson singing "Mammy." This brought more applause and some pre-Beatles shrieks from the girls. I wasn't showing off (okay, maybe a little); mostly I was just happy to be dancing. It had been too long.

The song ended, the growling sax fading off into that rock n roll eternity our young DJ was pleased to call the grooveyard, and we started to walk off the floor.

"God, that was fun," she said. She took my arm and squeezed it. "*You're* fun."

Before I could answer, Donald blared out through the PA. "In honor of two chaperones who can actually dance—a first in the history of our school—here's a blast from the past, gone from the charts but not from our hearts, a platter that matters, straight from my own daddy-o's record collection, which he doesn't know I brought and if any of you cool cats tell him, I'm in trouble. Dig it, all you steady rockers, this is how they did it when Mr. A. and Miz D. were in high school!"

They all turned to look at us, and . . . well . . .

You know how, when you're out at night and you see the edge of a cloud light up a bright gold, you know the moon is going to come out in a second or two? That was the feeling I had right then, standing among the gently swaying crepe streamers in the Denholm gymnasium. I knew what he was going to play, I knew we were going to dance to it, and I knew *how* we were going to dance. Then it came, that smooth brass intro:

Bah-dah-dah . . . bah-dah-da-dee-dum . . .

Glenn Miller. "In the Mood."

Sadie reached behind her and pulled the elastic, releasing the ponytail. She was still laughing and beginning to hip-sway just a little bit. Her hair slipped smoothly from one shoulder to the other.

"Can you swing?" Raising my voice to be heard over the music. Knowing she could. Knowing she *would*.

"Do you mean like the Lindy Hop?" she asked.

"That's what I mean."

"Well . . ."

"Go, Miz Dunhill," one of the girls said. "We want to see it." And two of her friends pushed Sadie toward me.

She hesitated. I did another spin and held out my hands. The kids cheered as we moved out on the floor. They gave us room. I pulled her toward me, and after the smallest of hesitations, she spun first to the left and then to the right, the A-line of the jumper she was wearing giving her just enough room to cross her feet as she went. It was the Lindy variation Richie-from-the-ditchie and Bevvie-from-the-levee had been learning that day in the fall of 1958. It was the Hellzapoppin. Of course it was. Because the past harmonizes.

I brought her to me by our clasped hands, then let her go back. We separated. Then, like people who had practiced these moves for months (possibly to a slowed-down record in a deserted picnic area), we bent and kicked, first to the left and then to the right. The kids laughed and cheered. They had formed a clapping circle around us in the middle of the polished floor.

We came together and she twirled like a hopped-up ballerina beneath our linked hands.

Now you squeeze to tell me left or right.

The light squeeze came on my right hand, as if the thought had summoned it, and she whirled back like a propeller, her hair flying out in a fan that gleamed first red, then blue in the lights. I heard several girls gasp. I caught her and went down on one heel with her bent over my arm, hoping like hell that I wouldn't pop my knee. I didn't.

I came up. She came with me. She went out, then came back into my arms. We danced under the lights.

Dancing is life.

7

The hop ended at eleven, but I didn't turn the Sunliner into Sadie's driveway until quarter past midnight on Sunday morning. One of the things nobody tells you about the glamorous job of chaperoning teenage dances is that the shaps are the ones who have to make sure everything's picked up and locked away once the music ends.

Neither of us said much on the way back. Although Donald played several other tempting big-band jump tunes and the kids pestered us to swing-dance again, we declined. Once was memorable; twice would have been indelible. Maybe not such a good thing in a small town. For me, it already was indelible. I couldn't stop thinking about the feel of her in my arms or her quick breath on my face.

I cut the engine and turned to her. *Now she'll say "Thank you for bailing me out" or "Thanks for a lovely evening," and that'll be that.*

But she didn't say either of those things. She didn't say anything. She just looked at me. Hair on her shoulders. Top two buttons of the man's Oxford-cloth shirt beneath the jumper undone. Earrings gleaming. Then we were together, first fumbling, then holding on tight. It was kissing, but it was more than kissing. It was like eating when you've been hungry or drinking when you've been thirsty. I could smell her perfume and her clean sweat under the perfume and I could taste tobacco, faint but still pungent, on her lips and tongue. Her fingers slipped through my hair (one pinky tickling for just a moment in the cup of my ear and making me shiver), then locked at the back of my neck. Her thumbs were moving, moving. Stroking bare skin at the nape that once, in another life, would have been covered by hair. I slipped my hand first beneath and then around the fullness of her breast and she murmured, "Oh, thank you, I thought I was going to fall."

"My pleasure," I said, and squeezed gently.

We necked for maybe five minutes, breathing harder as the caresses grew bolder. The windshield of my Ford steamed up.

Then she pushed me away and I saw her cheeks were wet. When in God's name had she started to cry?

"George, I'm sorry," she said. "I can't. I'm too scared." Her jumper was in her lap, revealing her garters, the hem of her slip, the lacy froth of her panties. She pulled the skirt down to her knees.

I guessed it was being married, and even if the marriage was busted, it still mattered—this was the mid-twentieth century, not the early twenty-first. Or maybe it was the neighbors. The houses looked dark and fast asleep, but you couldn't tell for sure, and in small towns, new preachers and new teachers are always interesting topics of conversation. It turned out I was wrong on both counts, but there was no way I could have known.

"Sadie, you don't have to do anything you don't want to. I'm not—"

"You don't understand. It's not that I don't want to. That's not why I'm scared. It's because I never have."

Before I could say anything else, she was out of the car and running for the house, fumbling in her purse for her key. She didn't look back.

8

I got home at twenty to one, walking from the garage to the house in my own version of the Blue-Balls Scuttle. I had no more than turned on the kitchen light when the phone began to ring. 1961 is forty years from caller ID, but only one person would be calling me at such an hour, and after such a night.

"George? It's me." She sounded composed, but her voice was thick. She had been crying. And hard, from the sound.

"Hi, Sadie. You never gave me a chance to thank you for a lovely time. During the dance, and after."

"I had a good time, too. It's been so long since I danced. I'm almost afraid to tell you who I learned to Lindy with."

"Well," I said, "I learned with my ex-wife. I'm guessing you might have learned with your estranged husband." Except it wasn't a guess; it was how these things went. I was no longer surprised by it, but if I told you I ever got used to that eerie chiming of events, I'd be lying.

"Yes." Her tone was flat. "Him. John Clayton of the Savannah Claytons. And *estranged* is just the right word, because he's a very strange man."

"How long have you been married?"

"Forever and a day. If you want to call what we had a marriage, that is." She laughed. It was Ivy Templeton's laugh, full of humor and despair. "In my case, forever and a day adds up to a little over four years. After school lets out in June, I'm going to make a discreet trip to Reno. I'll get a summer job as a waitress or something. The residency requirement is six weeks. Which means in late July or early August I'll be able to shoot this . . . this joke I got myself into . . . like a horse with a broken leg."

"I can wait," I said, but as soon as the words were out of my mouth, I wondered if they were true. Because the actors were gathering in the wings and the show would soon start. By June of '62, Lee Oswald would be back in the USA, living first with Robert and Robert's family, then with his mother. By August he'd be on Mercedes Street in Fort Worth and working at the nearby Leslie Welding Company, putting together aluminum windows and the kind of storm doors that have initials worked into them.

"I'm not sure *I* can." She spoke in a voice so low I had to strain to hear her. "I was a virgin bride at twenty-three and now I'm a virgin grass widow at twenty-eight. That's a long time for the fruit to hang on the tree, as they say back where I come from, especially when people—your own mother, for one—assume you started getting your practical experience on all that birds-and-bees stuff four years ago. I've never told anyone that, and if you repeated it, I think I'd die."

"It's between us, Sadie. And always will be. Was he impotent?"

"Not exact—" She broke off. There was silence for a moment,

and when she spoke again, her voice was full of horror. "George . . . is this a party line?"

"No. For an extra three-fifty a month, this baby is all mine."

"Thank God. But it's still nothing to be talking about on the phone. And certainly not at Al's Diner over Prongburgers. Can you come for supper? We could have a little picnic in my backyard. Say around five?"

"That would be fine. I'll bring a poundcake, or something."

"That's not what I want you to bring."

"What, then?"

"I can't say it on the phone, even if it's not a party line. Something you buy in a drugstore. But not the Jodie Drugstore."

"Sadie—"

"Don't say anything, please. I'm going to hang up and splash some cold water on my face. It feels like it's on fire."

There was a click in my ear. She was gone. I undressed and went to bed, where I lay awake a long time, thinking long thoughts. About time and love and death.

CHAPTER 15

1

At ten o'clock on that Sunday morning, I jumped into the Sunliner and drove twenty miles to Round Hill. There was a drugstore on the main drag, and it was open, but I saw a WE ROAR FOR THE DENHOLM LIONS sticker on the door and remembered Round Hill was part of Consolidated District Four. I drove on to Killeen. There, an elderly druggist who bore an eerie but probably coincidental resemblance to Mr. Keene back in Derry winked at me as he gave me a brown bag and my change. "Don't do anything against the law, son."

I returned the wink in the expected fashion and drove back to Jodie. I'd had a late night, but when I lay down and tried to nap, I didn't even get in sleep's neighborhood. So I went to the Weingarten's and bought a poundcake after all. It looked Sunday-stale, but I didn't care and didn't think Sadie would, either. Picnic supper or no picnic supper, I was pretty sure food wasn't the number one item on today's agenda. When I knocked on her door, there was a whole cloud of butterflies in my stomach.

Sadie's face was free of makeup. She wasn't even wearing lipstick. Her eyes were large, dark, and frightened. For one moment I was sure she was going to slam the door in my face and I'd hear her running away just as fast as her long legs would carry her. And that would be that.

But she didn't run. "Come on in," she said. "I made chicken

salad." Her lips began to tremble. "I hope you like . . . you like p-plenty of m-may—"

Her knees started to buckle. I dropped the box with the pound-cake inside on the floor and grabbed her. I thought she was going to faint, but she didn't. She put her arms around my neck and held tight, like a drowning woman to a floating log. I could feel her body thrumming. I stepped on the goddamned poundcake. Then she did. *Squoosh.*

"I'm scared," she said. "What if I'm no good at it?"

"What if I'm not?" This was not entirely a joke. It had been a long time. At least four years.

She didn't seem to hear me. "He never wanted me. Not the way I expected. And his way is the only way I know. The touching, then the broom."

"Calm down, Sadie. Take a deep breath."

"Did you go to the drugstore?"

"Yes, in Killeen. But we don't have to—"

"We do. *I* do. Before I lose what little courage I have left. Come on."

Her bedroom was at the end of the hall. It was spartan: a bed, a desk, a couple of prints on the walls, chintz curtains dancing in the soft breath of the window air-conditioning unit, turned down to low. Her knees started to give way again and I caught her again. It was a weird kind of swing-dancing. There were even Arthur Murray footprints on the floor. Poundcake. I kissed her and her lips fastened on mine, dry and frantic.

I pushed her away gently and braced her back against the closet door. She looked at me solemnly, her hair in her eyes. I brushed it away, then—very gently—began to lick her dry lips with the tip of my tongue. I did it slowly, being sure to get the corners.

"Better?" I asked.

She answered not with her voice but with her own tongue. Without pressing my body against hers, I began to very slowly run my hand up and down the long length of her, from where I could feel the rapid beat of her pulse on both sides of her throat, to her chest, her breasts, her stomach, the flat tilted plane of her pubic bone, around to one buttock, then down to her thigh. She was wearing jeans. The fabric whispered under my palm. She leaned back and her head bonked on the door.

"Ouch!" I said. "Are you all right?"

She closed her eyes. "I'm fine. Don't stop. Kiss me some more." Then she shook her head. "No, don't kiss me. Do my lips again. Lick me. I like that."

I did. She sighed and slipped her fingers under my belt at the small of my back. Then around to the front, where the buckle was.

2

I wanted to go fast, every part of me was yelling for speed, telling me to plunge deep, wanting that perfect *gripping* sensation that is the essence of the act, but I went slow. At least at first. Then she said, "Don't make me wait, I've had enough of that," and so I kissed the sweaty hollow of her temple and moved my hips forward. As if we were doing a horizontal version of the Madison. She gasped, retreated a little, then raised her own hips to meet me.

"Sadie? All right?"

"Ohmygodyes," she said, and I laughed. She opened her eyes and looked up at me with curiosity and hopefulness. "Is it over, or is there more?"

"A little more," I said. "I don't know how much. I haven't been with a woman in a long time."

It turned out there was quite a bit more. Only a few minutes in real time, but sometimes time is different—as no one knew better than I. At the end she began to gasp. "Oh dear, oh my dear, oh my dear dear God, oh *sugar*!"

It was the sound of greedy discovery in her voice that put me over the edge, so it wasn't quite simultaneous, but a few seconds later she lifted her head and buried her face in the hollow of my shoulder. A small fisted hand beat on my shoulder blade once, twice . . . then opened like a flower and lay still. She dropped back onto the pillows. She was staring at me with a stunned, wide-eyed expression that was a little scary.

"I came," she said.

"I noticed."

"My mother told me it didn't happen for women, only for men. She said orgasms for women were a myth." She laughed shakily. "Oh my God, what she was missing."

She got up on one elbow, then took one of my hands and put it on her breast. Beneath it, her heart was pounding and pounding. "Tell me, Mr. Amberson—how soon before we can do it again?"

3

As the reddening sun sank into the everlasting gas- and oil-smog to the west, Sadie and I sat in her tiny backyard under a nice old pecan tree, eating chicken salad sandwiches and drinking iced tea. No poundcake, of course. The poundcake was a total loss.

"Is it bad for you, having to wear those . . . you know, those drugstore things?"

"It's fine," I said. It really wasn't, and never had been. There would be improvements in a great many American products between 1961 and 2011, but take it from Jake, rubbers stay pretty much the same. They may have fancier names and even a taste-component (for those with peculiar tastes), but they remain essentially a girdle you snap on over your dick.

"I used to have a diaphragm," she said. There was no picnic table, so she had spread a blanket on the grass. Now she picked up a Tupperware container with the remains of a cucumber-and-onion salad inside it and began snapping the lid open and closed, a form of fidgeting some people would have considered Freudian. Including me.

"My mother gave it to me a week before Johnny and I were married. She even told me how to put it in, although she couldn't look me in the eye, and if you'd flicked a drop of water on one of her cheeks, I'm sure it would've sizzled. 'Don't start a baby for the first eighteen months,' she said. 'Two years, if you can make him wait. That way you can live on his salary and save yours.'"

"Not the world's worst advice." I was being cautious. We were in a minefield. She knew it as well as I did.

"Johnny's a science teacher. He's tall, although not quite as tall as you are. I was tired of going places with men who were shorter than me, and I think that's why I said yes when he first asked me out. Eventually, going out with him got to be a habit. I thought he was nice, and at the end of the night he never seemed to grow an extra pair of hands. At the time, I thought those things were love. I was very naïve, wasn't I?"

I made a seesaw gesture with my hand.

"We met at Georgia Southern and then got jobs at the same high school in Savannah. Coed, but private. I'm pretty sure his daddy pulled a wire or two to make that happen. The Claytons don't have money—not anymore, although they did once—but they're still high in Savannah society. Poor but genteel, you know?"

I didn't—questions of who was in society and who wasn't were never big issues when I was growing up—but I murmured an assent. She had been sitting on top of this for a long time, and looked almost hypnotized.

"So I had a diaphragm, yes I did. In its own little plastic lady-box with a rose on the cover. Only I never used it. Never had to. Finally threw it in the trash after one of those getting-it-outs. That's what he called it, getting it out. 'I have to get it out,' he used to say. Then the broom. You see?"

I didn't see at all.

Sadie laughed, and I was again reminded of Ivy Templeton. "Wait two years, she said! We could have waited *twenty,* and no diaphragm required!"

"What happened?" I gripped her upper arms lightly. "Did he beat you? Beat you with a broomhandle?" There was another way a broomhandle could be used—I'd read *Last Exit to Brooklyn*—but apparently he hadn't done that. She had been a virgin, all right; the proof was on the sheets.

"No," she said. "The broom wasn't for beating. George, I don't think I can talk about this anymore. Not now. I feel . . . I don't know . . . like a bottle of soda that's been shaken up. Do you know what I want?"

I thought so, but did the polite thing and asked.

"I want you to take me inside, and then take the cap off." She raised her hands over her head and stretched. She hadn't bothered putting her bra back on, and I could see her breasts lift under her blouse. Her nipples made tiny shadows, like punctuation marks, against the cloth in the late light.

She said, "I don't want to relive the past today. Today I only want to fizz."

4

An hour later I saw she was drowsing. I kissed her first on the forehead and then on the nose to wake her up. "I have to go. If only to get my car out of your driveway before your neighbors start to call their friends."

"I suppose so. It's the Sanfords next door, and Lila Sanford is this month's student librarian."

And I was pretty sure that Lila's father was on the schoolboard, but I didn't say so. Sadie was glowing, and there was no need to spoil that. For all the Sanfords knew, we were sitting on the couch with our knees together, waiting for *Dennis the Menace* to finish and Ed Sullivan's rilly big shew to come on. If my car was still in Sadie's driveway at eleven, their perceptions might change.

She watched me dress. "What happens now, George? With us?"

"I want to be with you if you want to be with me. Is that what you want?"

She sat up, the sheet puddled around her waist, and reached

for her cigarettes. "Very much. But I'm married, and that won't change until next summer in Reno. If I tried for an annulment, Johnny would fight me. Hell, his *parents* would fight me."

"If we're discreet, everything will be fine. But we have to be discreet. You know that, right?"

She laughed and lit up. "Oh yes. I know that."

"Sadie, have you had discipline problems in the library?"

"Huh? Some, sure. The usual." She shrugged; her breasts bobbed; I wished I hadn't dressed quite so fast. On the other hand, who was I kidding? James Bond might've been up for a third go-round, but Jake/George was tapped out. "I'm the new girl in school. They're testing me. It's a pain in the keister, but nothing I didn't expect. Why?"

"I think your problems are about to vanish. Students love it when teachers fall in love. Even the boys. It's like a TV show to them."

"Will they know that we've . . ."

I thought about it. "Some of the girls will. The ones with experience."

She huffed out smoke. "Great." But she didn't look entirely displeased.

"How about dinner out at The Saddle in Round Hill? Get people used to seeing us as a couple."

"All right. Tomorrow?"

"No, I have something to do in Dallas tomorrow."

"Research for your book?"

"Uh-huh." Here we were, brand-new, and I was lying already. I didn't like it, but saw no way around it. As for the future . . . I refused to think about that now. I had my own glow to protect. "Tuesday?"

"Yes. And George?"

"What?"

"We have to find a way to keep doing this."

I smiled. "Love will find a way."

"I think this part is more lust."

"It's both, maybe."

"You're a sweet man, George Amberson."

Christ, even the name was a lie.

"I'll tell you about Johnny and me. When I can. And if you want to hear."

"I want to." I thought I had to. If this was going to work, I had to understand. About her. About him. About the broom. "When you're ready."

"As our esteemed principal likes to say, 'Students, this will be challenging but worthwhile.'"

I laughed.

She butted out her cigarette. "One thing I wonder about. Would Miz Mimi approve of us?"

"I'm pretty sure she would."

"I think so, too. Drive home safe, my dear. And you better take those." She was pointing at the paper bag from the Killeen Pharmacy. It was sitting on top of her dresser. "If I had the kind of nosy company who checks the medicine cabinet after they tee-tee, I'd have some explaining to do."

"Good idea."

"But keep them handy, honey."

And she winked.

5

On the way home, I found myself thinking about those rubbers. Trojan brand . . . and ribbed for *her* pleasure, according to the box. The lady didn't have a diaphragm any longer (although I guessed she might arrange for one on her next trip to Dallas), and birth control pills wouldn't be widely available for another year or two. Even then, doctors would be wary about prescribing them, if I remembered my Modern Sociology course correctly. So for now it was Trojans. I wore them not for her pleasure but so she wouldn't have a baby. Which was amusing when you considered that I wouldn't be a baby myself for another fifteen years.

Thinking about the future is confusing in all sorts of ways.

6

The following evening I revisited Silent Mike's establishment. The sign in the door was turned to CLOSED and the place looked empty, but when I knocked, my electronics buddy let me in.

"Right on time, Mr. Doe, right on time," he said. "Let's see what you think. Me, I think I outdid myself."

I stood by the glass case filled with transistor radios and waited while he disappeared into the back room. He returned holding a lamp in each hand. The shades were grimy, as if they had been adjusted by a great many dirty fingers. The base of one was chipped so it stood crooked on the counter: the Leaning Lamp of Pisa. They were perfect, and I told him so. He grinned and put two of the boxed tape recorders next to the lamps. Also a drawstring bag containing several lengths of wire so thin it was almost invisible.

"Want a little tutorial?"

"I think I've got it," I said, and put five twenties down on the counter. I was a little touched when he tried to push one back.

"One-eighty was the price we agreed on."

"The other twenty is for you to forget I was ever here."

He considered this for a moment, then put a thumb on the stray twenty and pulled it into the group with its little green friends. "I already did that. Why don't I consider this a tip?"

As he put the stuff into a brown paper bag, I was struck by simple curiosity and asked him a question.

"Kennedy? I didn't vote for him, but as long as he doesn't go taking his orders from the Pope, I think he'll be okay. The country needs somebody younger. It's a new age, y'know?"

"If he were to come to Dallas, do you think he'd be all right?"

"Probably. Can't say for sure, though. On the whole, if I were him, I'd stay north of the Mason-Dixon line."

I grinned. "Where all is calm, all is bright?"

Silent Mike (Holy Mike) said, "Don't start."

7

There was a rack of pigeonholes for mail and school announcements in the first-floor teachers' room. On Tuesday morning, during my free period, I found a small sealed envelope in mine.

Dear George—

If you still want to take me to dinner tonight, it will have to be five-ish, because I'll have early mornings all this week and next, getting ready for the Fall Book Sale. Perhaps we could come back to my place for dessert.

I have poundcake, if you'd like a slice.

Sadie

"What are you laughing about, Amberson?" Danny Laverty asked. He was correcting themes with a hollow-eyed intensity that suggested hangover. "Tell me, I could use a giggle."

"Nah," I said. "Private joke. You wouldn't get it."

8

But *we* got it, poundcake became our name for it, and we ate plenty that fall.

We were discreet, but of course there were people who knew what was going on. There was probably some gossip, but no scandal. Smalltown folks are rarely mean folks. They knew Sadie's situation, at least in a general way, and understood we could make no public commitment, at least for awhile. She didn't come to my house; that would have caused the wrong kind of talk. I never stayed beyond ten o'clock at hers; that also would have caused the wrong kind of talk. There was no way I could have put my Sunliner in her garage and stayed the night, because her Volkswagen Beetle, small as it was, filled it almost wall-to-wall. I wouldn't have done so in any case, because someone would have known. In small towns, they always do.

I visited her after school. I dropped by for the meal she called supper. Sometimes we went to Al's Diner and ate Prongburgers or catfish fillets; sometimes we went to The Saddle; twice I took her to the Saturday-night dances at the local Grange. We saw movies at the Gem in town or at the Mesa in Round Hill or the Starlite Drive-In in Killeen (which the kids called the submarine races). At a nice restaurant like The Saddle, she might have a glass of wine before dinner and I might have a beer with, but we were careful not to be seen at any of the local taverns and certainly not at the Red Rooster, Jodie's one and only jukejoint, a place our students talked about with longing and awe. It was 1961 and segregation might finally be softening in the middle—Negroes had won the right to sit at the Woolworth's lunchcounters in Dallas, Fort Worth, and Houston—but schoolteachers didn't drink in the Red Rooster. Not if they wanted to keep their jobs. Never-never-never.

When we made love in Sadie's bedroom, she always kept a pair of slacks, a sweater, and a pair of moccasins on her side of the bed. She called it her emergency outfit. The one time the doorbell bonged while we were naked (a state she had taken to calling *in flagrante delicious*), she got into those threads in ten seconds flat. She came back, giggling and waving a copy of *The Watchtower.* "Jehovah's Witnesses. I told them I was saved and they went away."

Once, as we ate ham-steaks and okra in her kitchen afterward, she said our courtship reminded her of that movie with Audrey Hepburn and Gary Cooper—*Love in the Afternoon.* "Sometimes I wonder if it would be better at night." She said this a little wistfully. "When regular people do it."

"You'll get a chance to find out," I said. "Hang in there, baby."

She smiled and kissed the corner of my mouth. "You turn some cool phrases, George."

"Oh yes," I said, "I'm very original."

She pushed her plate aside. "I'm ready for dessert. How about you?"

9

Not long after the Jehovah's Witnesses came calling at Sadie's place—this must have been early November, because I'd finished casting my version of *Twelve Angry Men*—I was out raking my lawn when someone said, "Hello, George, how's it going?"

I turned around and saw Deke Simmons, now a widower for the second time. He had stayed in Mexico longer than anyone had thought he would, and just when folks began to believe he was going to remain there, he had come back. This was the first time I'd seen him. He was very brown, but far too thin. His clothes bagged on him, and his hair—iron-gray on the day of the wedding reception—was now almost all white and thinning on top.

I dropped my rake and hurried over to him. I meant to shake his hand, but hugged him instead. It startled him—in 1961, Real Men Don't Hug—but then he laughed.

I held him at arm's length. "You look great!"

"Nice try, George. But I feel better than I did. Meems dying . . . I knew it was going to happen, but it still knocked me for a loop. Head could never get through to heart on that one, I reckon."

"Come on in and have a cup of coffee."

"I'd like that."

We talked about his time in Mexico. We talked about school. We talked about the undefeated football team and the upcoming fall play. Then he put down his cup and said, "Ellen Dockerty asked me to pass on a word or two about you and Sadie Clayton."

Uh-oh. And I'd thought we were doing so well.

"She goes by Dunhill now. It's her maiden name."

"I know all about her situation. Knew when we hired her. She's a fine girl and you're a fine man, George. Based on what Ellie tells me, the two of you are handling a difficult situation with a fair amount of grace."

I relaxed a little.

"Ellie said she was pretty sure neither of you knew about Candlewood Bungalows just outside of Killeen. She didn't feel right about telling you, so she asked if I would."

"Candlewood Bungalows?"

"I used to take Meems there on a lot of Saturday nights." He was fiddling at his coffee cup with hands that now looked too big for his body. "It's run by a couple of retired schoolteachers from Arkansas or Alabama. One of those *A*-states, anyway. Retired *men* schoolteachers. If you know what I mean."

"I think I'm following, yes."

"They're nice fellows, very quiet about their own relationship and about the relationships of some of their guests." He looked up from his coffee cup. He was blushing a little, but also smiling. "This isn't a hot-sheet joint, if that's what you're thinking. Farthest thing from it. The rooms are nice, the prices are reasonable, and the little restaurant down the road is a-country fare. Sometimes a gal needs a place like that. And maybe a man does, too. So they don't have to be in such a hurry. And so they won't feel cheap."

"Thank you," I said.

"Very welcome. Mimi and I had many pleasant evenings at the Candlewood. Sometimes we only watched the TV in our pajamas and then went to bed, but that can be as good as anything else when you get to a certain age." He smiled ruefully. "Or almost. We'd go to sleep listening to the crickets. Or sometimes a coyote would howl, very far away, out in the sage. At the moon, you know. They really do that. They howl at the moon."

He took a handkerchief from his back pocket with an old man's slowness and mopped his cheeks with it.

I offered my hand and Deke took hold.

"She liked you, although she never could figure out what to make of you. She said you reminded her of the way they used to show ghosts in those old movies from the thirties. 'He's bright and shiny, but not all here,' she said."

"I'm no ghost," I said. "I promise you."

He smiled. "No? I finally got around to checking your references. This was after you'd been subbing for us awhile and did such a bang-up job with the play. The ones from the Sarasota School District are fine, but beyond there . . ." He shook his head, still smiling. "And your degree is from a mill in Oklahoma."

Clearing my throat did no good. I couldn't speak at all.

"And what's that to me, you ask? Not much. There was a time in this part of the world when if a man rode into town with a few books in his saddlebags, spectacles on his nose, and a tie around his neck, he could get hired on as schoolmaster and stay for twenty years. Wasn't that long ago, either. You're a damn fine teacher. The kids know it, I know it, and Meems knew it, too. And that's a *lot* to me."

"Does Ellen know I faked my other references?" Because Ellen Dockerty was acting principal, and once the schoolboard met in January, the job would be hers permanently. There were no other candidates.

"Nope, and she's not going to. Not from me, at least. I feel like she doesn't need to." He stood up. "But there's one person who *does* need to know the truth about where you've been and what you've done, and that's a certain lady librarian. If you're serious about her, that is. Are you?"

"Yes," I said, and Deke nodded as if that took care of everything.

I only wished it did.

10

Thanks to Deke Simmons, Sadie finally got to find out what it was like to make love after sundown. When I asked her how it was, she told me it had been wonderful. "But I'm looking forward to waking up next to you in the morning even more. Do you hear the wind?"

I did. It hooted around the eaves.

"Doesn't that sound make you feel cozy?"

"Yes."

"I'm going to say something now. I hope it doesn't make you uncomfortable."

"Tell me."

"I guess I've fallen in love with you. Maybe it's just the sex, I've heard that's a mistake people make, but I don't think so."

"Sadie?"

"Yes?" She was trying to smile, but she looked frightened.

"I love you, too. No maybe or mistake about it."

"Thank God," she said, and snuggled close.

11

On our second visit to the Candlewood Bungalows, she was ready to talk about Johnny Clayton. "But turn out the light, would you?"

I did as she asked. She smoked three cigarettes during the telling. Toward the end, she cried hard, probably not from remembered pain so much as simple embarrassment. For most of us, I think it's easier to admit doing wrong than being stupid. Not that she had been. There's a world of difference between stupidity and naïveté, and like most good middle-class girls who came to maturity in the nineteen-forties and -fifties, Sadie knew almost nothing about sex. She said she had never actually looked at a penis until she had looked at mine. She'd had glimpses of Johnny's, but she said if he caught her looking, he would take hold of her face and turn it away with a grip that stopped just short of painful.

"But it always *did* hurt," she said. "You know?"

John Clayton came from a conventionally religious family, nothing nutty about them. He was pleasant, attentive, reasonably attractive. He didn't have the world's greatest sense of humor (almost none might have been closer to the mark), but he seemed to adore her. Her parents adored *him*. Claire Dunhill was especially crazy about Johnny Clayton. And, of course, he was taller than Sadie, even when she was in heels. After years of beanpole jokes, that was important.

"The only troubling thing before the marriage was his compulsive neatness," Sadie said. "He had all his books alphabetized, and he got very upset if you moved them around. He was nervous if you took even one off the shelf—you could feel it, a kind of tensing. He shaved three times a day and washed his hands all the time. If someone shook with him, he'd make an excuse to rush off to the lav and wash just as soon as he could."

"Also color-coordinated clothes," I said. "On his body and in the closet, and woe to the person who moved them around. Did he alphabetize the stuff in the pantry? Or get up sometimes in the night to check that the stove burners were off and the doors were locked?"

She turned to me, her eyes wide and wondering in the dark. The bed squeaked companionably; the wind gusted; a loose windowpane rattled. "How do you know that?"

"It's a syndrome. Obsessive-compulsive disorder. OCD, for short. Howard—" I stopped. *Howard Hughes has a bad case of it,* I'd started to say, but maybe that wasn't true yet. Even if it was, people probably didn't know. "An old friend of mine had it. Howard Temple. Never mind. Did he hurt you, Sadie?"

"Not really, no beating or punching. He slapped me once, that's all. But people hurt people in other ways, don't they?"

"Yes."

"I couldn't talk to anyone about it. Certainly not my mother. Do you know what she told me on my wedding day? That if I said half a prayer before and half a prayer during, everything would be fine. *During* was as close as she could come to the word *intercourse.* I tried to talk to my friend Ruthie about it, but only once. This was after school, and she was helping me pick up the library.

'What goes on behind the bedroom door is none of my business,' she said. I stopped, because I didn't really *want* to talk about it. I was so ashamed."

Then it came in a rush. Some of what she said was blurred by tears, but I got the gist. On certain nights—maybe once a week, maybe twice—he would tell her he needed to "get it out." They would be lying side by side in bed, she in her nightgown (he insisted she wear ones that were opaque), he in a pair of boxer shorts. Boxers were the closest she ever came to seeing him naked. He would push the sheet down to his waist, and she would see his erection tenting them.

"Once he looked at that little tent himself. Only once that I remember. And do you know what he said?"

"No."

"'How disgusting we are.' Then he said, 'Get it over with so I can get some sleep.'"

She would reach beneath the sheet and masturbate him. It never took long, sometimes only seconds. On a few occasions he touched her breasts as she performed this function, but mostly his hands remained knotted high on his chest. When it was over, he would go into the bathroom, wash himself off, and come back in wearing his pajamas. He had seven pairs, all blue.

Then it was her turn to go into the bathroom and wash her hands. He insisted that she do this for at least three minutes, and under water hot enough to turn her skin red. When she came back to bed, she held her palms out to his face. If the smell of Lifebuoy wasn't strong enough to satisfy him, she would have to do it again.

"And when I came back, the broom would be there."

He would put it on top of the sheet if it was summer, on the blankets if it was winter. Running straight down the middle of the bed. His side and her side.

"If I was restless and happened to move it, he'd wake up. No matter how fast asleep he was. And he'd push me back to my side. Hard. He called it 'transgressing the broom.'"

The time he slapped her was when she asked how they would

ever have children if he never put it in her. "He was furious. That's why he slapped me. He apologized later, but what he said right then was, 'Do you think I'd put myself in your germy womanhole and bring children into this filthy world? It's all going to blow up anyway, anyone who reads the paper can see that coming, and the radiation will kill us. We'll die with sores all over our bodies, and coughing up our lungs. It could happen any day.'"

"Jesus. No wonder you left him, Sadie."

"Only after four wasted years. It took me that long to convince myself that I deserved more from life than color-coordinating my husband's sock drawer, giving him handjobs twice a week, and sleeping with a goddam broom. That was the most humiliating part, the part I was sure I could never talk about to anyone . . . because it was *funny*."

I didn't think it was funny. I thought it was somewhere in the twilight zone between neurosis and outright psychosis. I also thought I was listening to the perfect Fifties Fable. It was easy to imagine Rock Hudson and Doris Day sleeping with a broom between them. If Rock hadn't been gay, that was.

"And he hasn't come looking for you?"

"No. I applied to a dozen different schools and had the answers sent to a post office box. I felt like a woman having an affair, sneaking around. And that's how my mother and father treated me when they found out. My dad has come around a little—I think he suspects how bad it was, although of course he doesn't want to know any of the details—but my mother? Not her. She's furious with me. She had to change churches and quit the Sewing Bee. Because she couldn't hold her head up, she says."

In a way, this seemed as cruel and crazy as the broom, but I didn't say so. A different aspect of the matter interested me more than Sadie's conventional Southern parents. "*Clayton* didn't tell them you were gone? Have I got that right? Never came to see them?"

"No. My mother understood, of course." Sadie's ordinarily faint Southern accent deepened. "I just shamed that poor boy so bad that he didn't want to tell *anyone.*" She dropped the drawl. "I'm not being sarcastic, either. She understands shame, and she understands covering up. On those two things, Johnny and my mama are in perfect harmony. *She's* the one he should have married." She laughed a little hysterically. "Mama probably would have *loved* that old broom."

"Never a word from him? Not even a postcard saying, 'Hey Sadie, let's tie up the loose ends so we can get on with our lives?'"

"How could there be? He doesn't know where I am, and I'm sure he doesn't care."

"Is there anything you want from him? Because I'm sure a lawyer—"

She kissed me. "The only thing I want is here in bed with me."

I kicked the sheets down to our ankles. "Look at me, Sadie. No charge."

She looked. And then she touched.

12

I drowsed afterward. Not deep—I could still hear the wind and that one rattling windowpane—but I got far enough down to dream. Sadie and I were in an empty house. We were naked. Something was moving around upstairs—it made thudding, unpleasant noises. It might have been pacing, but it seemed as if there were too many feet. I didn't feel guilty that we were going to be discovered with our clothes off. I felt scared. Written in charcoal on the peeling plaster of one wall were the words I WILL KILL THE PRESIDENT SOON. Below it, someone had added NOT SOON ENOUGH HES FULL OF DISEEZE. This had been printed in dark lipstick. Or maybe it was blood.

Thud, clump, thud.

From overhead.

"I think it's Frank Dunning," I whispered to Sadie. I gripped her arm. It was very cold. It was like gripping the arm of a dead person. A woman who had been beaten to death with a sledgehammer, perhaps.

Sadie shook her head. She was looking up at the ceiling, her mouth trembling.

Clud, thump, clud.

Plaster-dust sifting down.

"Then it's John Clayton," I whispered.

"No," she said. "I think it's the Yellow Card Man. He brought the Jimla."

Above us, the thudding stopped abruptly.

She took hold of my arm and began to shake it. Her eyes were eating up her face. "It is! It's the Jimla! And it heard us! *The Jimla knows we're here!*"

13

"Wake up, George! Wake up!"

I opened my eyes. She was propped on one elbow beside me, her face a pale blur. "What? What time is it? Do we have to go?" But it was still dark and the wind was still high.

"No. It isn't even midnight. You were having a bad dream." She laughed, a little nervously. "Maybe about football? Because you were saying 'Jimla, Jimla.'"

"Was I?" I sat up. There was the scrape of a match and her face was momentarily illuminated as she lit a cigarette.

"Yes. You were. You said all kinds of stuff."

That was not good. "Like what?"

"Most of it I couldn't make out, but one thing was pretty clear. 'Derry is Dallas,' you said. Then you said it backwards. 'Dallas is Derry.' What was *that* about? Do you remember?"

"No." But it's hard to lie convincingly when you're fresh out of sleep, even a shallow doze, and I saw skepticism on her face. Before it could deepen into disbelief, there was a knock at the door. At quarter to midnight, a knock.

We stared at each other.

The knock came again.

It's the Jimla. This thought was very clear, very certain.

Sadie put her cigarette in the ashtray, gathered the sheet around her, and ran to the bathroom without a word. The door shut behind her.

"Who is it?" I asked.

"It's Mr. Yorrity, sir—Bud Yorrity?"

One of the gay retired teachers who ran the place.

I got out of bed and pulled on my pants. "What is it, Mr. Yorrity?"

"I have a message for you, sir. Lady said it was urgent."

I opened the door. He was a small man in a threadbare bathrobe. His hair was a sleep-frizzed cloud around his head. In one hand he held a piece of paper.

"What lady?"

"Ellen Dockerty."

I thanked him for his trouble and closed the door. I unfolded the paper and read the message.

Sadie came out of the bathroom, still clutching the sheet. Her eyes were wide and frightened. "What is it?"

"There's been an accident," I said. "Vince Knowles rolled his pickup truck outside of town. Mike Coslaw and Bobbi Jill were with him. Mike was thrown clear. He has a broken arm. Bobbi Jill has a nasty cut on her face, but Ellie says she's okay otherwise."

"Vince?"

I thought of the way everyone said Vince drove—as if there were no tomorrow. Now there wasn't. Not for him. "He's dead, Sadie."

Her mouth dropped open. "He can't be! *He's only eighteen years old!*"

"I know."

The sheet fell free of her relaxing arms and puddled around her feet. She put her hands over her face.

14

My revised version of *Twelve Angry Men* was canceled. What took its place was *Death of a Student,* a play in three acts: the viewing at the funeral parlor, the service at Grace Methodist Church, the graveside service at West Hill Cemetery. This mournful show was attended by the whole town, or near enough to make no difference.

The parents and Vince's stunned kid sister starred at the viewing, sitting in folding chairs beside the coffin. When I approached them with Sadie at my side, Mrs. Knowles rose and put her arms around me. I was almost overwhelmed by the odors of White Shoulders perfume and Yodora antiperspirant.

"You changed his life," she whispered in my ear. "He told me so. For the first time he made his grades, because he wanted to act."

"Mrs. Knowles, I'm so, so sorry," I said. Then a terrible thought crossed my mind and I hugged her tighter, as if hugging could make it go away: *Maybe it's the butterfly effect. Maybe Vince is dead because I came to Jodie.*

The coffin was flanked by photomontages of Vince's too-brief life. On an easel in front of it, all by itself, was a picture of him in his *Of Mice and Men* costume and that battered old felt hat from props. His ratty, intelligent face peered out from beneath. Vince really hadn't been much of an actor, but that photo caught him wearing an absolutely perfect wiseass smile. Sadie began to sob, and I knew why. Life turns on a dime. Sometimes toward us, but more often it spins away, flirting and flashing as it goes: *so long, honey, it was good while it lasted, wasn't it?*

And Jodie *was* good—good for me. In Derry I was an outsider, but Jodie was home. Here's home: the smell of the sage and the way the hills flush orange with Indian blanket in the summer. The faint taste of tobacco on Sadie's tongue and the squeak of the oiled wood floorboards in my homeroom. Ellie Dockerty caring enough to send us a message in the middle of the night, perhaps so we could get back to town undiscovered, probably just so we'd know.

The nearly suffocating mixture of perfume and deodorant as Mrs. Knowles hugged me. Mike putting his arm—the one not buried in a cast—around me at the cemetery, then pressing his face against my shoulder until he could get himself under control again. The ugly red slash on Bobbi Jill's face is home, too, and thinking that unless she had plastic surgery (which her family could not afford), it would leave a scar that would remind her for the rest of her life of how she had seen a boy from just down the road dead at the side of the road, his head mostly torn off his shoulders. Home is the black armband that Sadie wore, that I wore, that the whole faculty wore for a week after. And Al Stevens posting Vince's photo in the window of his diner. And Jimmy LaDue's tears as he stood up in front of the whole school and dedicated the undefeated season to Vince Knowles.

Other things, too. People saying howdy on the street, people giving me a wave from their cars, Al Stevens taking Sadie and me to the table at the back that he had started calling "our table," playing cribbage on Friday afternoons in the teachers' room with Danny Laverty for a penny a point, arguing with elderly Miss Mayer about who gave the better newscast, Chet Huntley and David Brinkley, or Walter Cronkite. My street, my shotgun house, getting used to using a typewriter again. Having a best girl and getting S&H Green Stamps with my groceries and real butter on my movie popcorn.

Home is watching the moon rise over the open, sleeping land and having someone you can call to the window, so you can look together. Home is where you dance with others, and dancing is life.

15

The Year of Our Lord 1961 was winding down. On a drizzly day about two weeks before Christmas, I came into my house after school, once more bundled into my rawhide ranch coat, and heard the phone ringing.

"This is Ivy Templeton," a woman said. "You prob'ly don't even remember me, do you?"

"I remember you very well, Miz Templeton."

"I dunno why I even bothered to call, that goddam ten bucks is long since spent. Just somethin about you stuck in my head. Rosette, too. She calls you 'the man who cotched my ball.'"

"You're moving out, Miz Templeton?"

"That's one hunderd percent goddam right. My mama's comin up from Mozelle tomorrow in the truck."

"Don't you have a car? Or did it break down?"

"Car's runnin okay for a junker, but Harry ain't goan be ridin in it. Or drivin it ever again. He was workin one of those goddam Manpower jobs last month. Fell in a ditch and a gravel truck run over him while it was backin up. Broke his spine."

I closed my eyes and saw the smashed remains of Vince's truck being hauled down Main Street behind the wrecker from Gogie's Sunoco. Blood all over the inside of the cracked windshield. "I'm sorry to hear that, Miz Templeton."

"He goan live but he ain't never goan walk again. He goan sit in a wheelchair and pee in a bag, that's what *he* goan do. But first he's goan ride down Mozelle in the back of my mama's truck. We'll steal the mattress out'n the bedroom for him to lay on. Be like takin your dog on vacation, won't it?"

She started to cry.

"I'm runnin out on two months' back rent, but that don't confront me none. You know what *does* confront me, Mr. Puddentane, Ask Me Again and I'll Tell You the Same? I got thirty-five goddam dollars and that's the end of it. Goddam asshole Harry, if he could've kep his feet I wouldn't be in this fix. I thought I was in one before, but now looka this!"

There was a long, watery snork in my ear.

"You know what? The mailman been givin me the glad eye, and I think for twenty dollars I'd roll him a fuck on the goddam livin room floor. If the goddam neighbors across the street couldn't watch us while we 'us goin at it. Can't very well take him in the bedroom, can I? That's where my brokeback husband is." She rasped out a laugh. "Tell you what, why don't you come on over in your fancy convertible? Take me to a motel sommers. Spend a little extra, get one with a settin-room. Rosette can watch TV and I'll roll *you* a fuck. You looked like you 'us doing okay."

I said nothing. I'd just had an idea that was as bright as a flash-bulb.

If the goddam neighbors across the street couldn't watch us goin at it.

There was a man *I* was supposed to be watching for. Besides Oswald himself, that was. A man whose name also happened to be George, and who was going to become Oswald's only friend.

Don't trust him, Al had written in his notes.

"You there, Mr. Puddentane? No? If not, fuck you and goodb—"

"Don't hang up, Miz Templeton. Suppose I were to pay your back rent and throw in a hundred bucks on top of that?" It was far more than I needed to pay for what I wanted, but I had it and she needed it.

"Mister, right now I'd do you with my *father* watchin for two hundred bucks."

"You don't have to do me at all, Miz Templeton. All you have to do is meet me in that parking lot at the end of the street. And bring me something."

16

It was dark by the time I got to the parking lot of the Montgomery Ward warehouse, and the rain had started to thicken a little, the way it does when it's trying to be sleet. That doesn't happen often in the hill country south of Dallas, but sometimes isn't never. I hoped I could make it back to Jodie without sliding off the road.

Ivy was sitting behind the wheel of a sad old sedan with rusty rocker panels and a cracked rear window. She got into my Ford and immediately leaned toward the heater vent, which was going full blast. She was wearing two flannel shirts instead of a coat, and shivering.

"Feels good. That Chev's colder'n a witch's tit. Heater's bust. You bring the money, Mr. Puddentane?"

I gave her an envelope. She opened it and riffled through some of the twenties that had been sitting on the top shelf of my closet ever since I'd collected on my World Series bet at Faith Financial over a year before. She lifted her substantial bottom off the seat, shoved the envelope into the back pocket of her jeans, then fumbled in the breast pocket of the shirt closer to her body. She brought out a key and slapped it into my hand.

"That do you?"

It did me very well. "It's a dupe, right?"

"Just like you told me. I had it made at the hardware store on McLaren Street. Why you want a key to that glorified shithouse? For two hundred, you could rent it for four months."

"I've got my reasons. Tell me about the neighbors across the street. The ones that could watch you and the mailman doing it on the living room floor."

She shifted uneasily and pulled her shirts a little closer across her equally substantial bosom. "I was just jokin about that."

"I know." I didn't, and I didn't care. "I just want to know if the neighbors can really see into your living room."

"Course they can, and I could see into theirs, if they didn't have curtains. Which I woulda bought for our place, could I afford em. When it comes to privacy, we all might as well be livin outside. I s'pose I coulda put up burlap, scavenged it from right over there"—she pointed to the trash bins lined up against the east side of the warehouse—"but it looks so slutty."

"The neighbors with the view live at what? Twenty-seven-oh-four?"

"Twenty-seven-oh-six. It used to be Slider Burnett n his fambly, but they moved out just after Halloween. He was a substitute rodeo clown, do you believe it? Who knew there was such a job? Now it's some fella named Hazzard and his two kids and I think his mother. Rosette won't play with the kids, says they're dirty. Which is a newsflash comin from *that* little pigpen. Ole grammy tries to talk and it comes out all mush. Side of her face won't move. Dunno what help she can be to him, draggin around like she does. If I get like that, just shoot me. Eeee, doggies!" She shook her head. "Tell you one thing, they won't be there long. No one stays on 'Cedes Street. Got a cigarette? I had to give em up. When you can't afford a quarter for fags, that's when you know for sure you're on your goddam uppers."

"I don't smoke."

She shrugged. "What the hell. I can afford my own now, can't I? I'm goddam rich. You ain't married, are you?"

"No."

"Got a girlfriend, though. I can smell perfume on this side of the car. The nice stuff."

That made me smile. "Yes, I've got a girlfriend."

"Good for you. Does she know you're sneakin around the south side of Fort Worth after dark, doin funny business?"

I said nothing, but sometimes that's answer enough.

"Nev' mind. That's between you n her. I'm warm now, so I'll go on back. If it's still rainy n cold like this tomorrow, I don't know what we're goan do about Harry in the back of my ma's truck." She looked at me, smiling. "When I was a kid I used to think I was gonna grow up to be Kim Novak. Now Rosette, she thinks she's goan replace Darlene on the Mouseketeers. Hidey-fuckin-ho."

She started to open the door and I said, "Wait."

I raked the crap out of my pockets—Life Savers, Kleenex, a book of matches Sadie had tucked in there, notes for a freshman English test I meant to give before the Christmas break—and then gave her the ranch coat. "Take this."

"I ain't takin your goddam coat!" She looked shocked.

"I've got another one at home." I didn't, but I could buy one, and that was more than she could do.

"What'm I gonna tell Harry? That I found it under a goddam cabbage leaf?"

403

I grinned. "Tell him you rolled the mailman a fuck and bought it with the proceeds. What's he going to do, chase you down the driveway and beat you up?"

She laughed, a harsh rainbird caw that was strangely charming. And took the coat.

"Regards to Rosette," I said. "Tell her I'll see her in her dreams."

She stopped smiling. "I hope not, mister. That one she had about you was a nightmare. Bout screamed the house down, she did. Woke me out of a dead sleep at two in the morning. She said the man who cotched her ball had a monster in the backseat of his car, and she was afraid it would eat her up. Scared the life out of me, she did, screamin like that."

"Did the monster have a name?" Of course it did.

"She said it was a jimla. Prob'ly meant a jinny, like in those stories about Aladdin and the Seven Veils. Anyway, I gotta go. You take care of yourself."

"You too, Ivy. Merry Christmas."

She cawed her rainbird laugh again. "Almost forgot about that. You have one, too. Don't forget to give your girl a present."

She trotted to her old car with my coat—her coat, now—thrown over her shoulders. I never saw her again.

17

The rain only froze on the bridges, and I knew from my other life—the one in New England—to be careful on those, but it was still a long drive back to Jodie. I had no more than put the water on for a cup of tea when the phone rang. This time it was Sadie.

"I've been trying to get you since suppertime to ask you about Coach Borman's Christmas Eve bash. It starts at three. I'll go if you want to take me, because then we can get away early. Say we've got dinner reservations at The Saddle, or something. I need to RSVP, though."

I saw my own invitation lying next to my typewriter, and felt a little twinge of guilt. It had been there for three days, and I hadn't even opened it.

"Do you want to go?" I asked.

"I wouldn't mind making an appearance." There was a pause. "Where have you been all this time?"

"Fort Worth." I almost added, *Christmas shopping.* But I didn't. The only thing I'd bought in Fort Worth was some information. And a housekey.

"Were you shopping?"

Again I had to fight not to lie. "I . . . Sadie, I really can't say."

There was a long, long pause. I found myself wishing I smoked. Probably I had developed a contact addiction. God knew I was smoking by proxy all day, every day. The teachers' room was a constant blue haze.

"Is it a woman, George? Another woman? Or am I being nosy?"

Well, there was Ivy, but that wasn't the kind of woman she was talking about.

"In the woman department, there's only you."

Another of those long, long pauses. In the world, Sadie could move carelessly; in her head, she never did. At last she said, "You know a lot about me, things I never thought I could tell anyone, but I know almost nothing about you. I guess I just realized that. Sadie can be stupid, George, can't she?"

"You're not stupid. And one thing you *do* know is that I love you."

"Yes . . ." She sounded doubtful. I remembered the bad dream I'd had that night at the Candlewood Bungalows, and the caution I'd seen in her face when I told her I didn't remember it. Was that same look on her face now? Or perhaps an expression a little deeper than mere caution?

"Sadie? Are we all right?"

"Yes." Sounding a little more sure now. "Sure we are. Except for Coach's party. What do you want to do about it? Remember that the whole darn School Department will be there, and most of them will be drunk on their fannies by the time Mrs. Coach puts on the buffet."

"Let's go," I said, too heartily. "Party down and kick out the jams."

"Kick out the *what*?"

"Have some fun. That's all I meant. We'll pop in for an hour, maybe an hour and a half, then pop back out. Dinner at The Saddle. That work for you?"

"Fine." We were like a couple negotiating for a second date after the first one had been inconclusive. "We'll enjoy ourselves."

I thought about Ivy Templeton smelling the ghost of Sadie's perfume and asking if my girl knew I was sneaking around south Fort Worth after dark, doing funny business. I thought about Deke Simmons saying there was one person who deserved to know the truth about where I'd been and what I'd done. But was I going to tell Sadie I'd killed Frank Dunning in cold blood so he wouldn't murder his wife and three of his four children? That I had come to Texas to prevent an assassination and change the course of history? That I knew I could do that because I came from a future where we could have been IM'ing this conversation via computer?

"Sadie, this is going to work out. I promise you that."

Again she said, "Fine." Then she said, "I'll see you tomorrow, George, in school." And hung up, very gently and politely.

I held the telephone in my hand for several seconds, staring straight ahead at nothing. A rattling began on the windows facing my backyard. The rain had turned to sleet after all.

CHAPTER 16

1

Coach Borman's Christmas Eve bash was a bust, and the ghost of Vince Knowles wasn't the only reason. On the twenty-first, Bobbi Jill Allnut got tired of looking at that red slash running all the way down the left side of her face to the jawline and took a bunch of her mother's sleeping pills. She didn't die, but she spent two nights in Parkland Memorial, the hospital where both the president and the president's assassin would expire, unless I changed things. There are probably closer hospitals in 2011—almost certainly in Killeen, maybe even in Round Hill—but not during my one year of full-time teaching at DCHS.

Dinner at The Saddle wasn't so hot, either. The place was packed and convivial with pre-Christmas cheer, but Sadie refused dessert and asked to go home early. She said she had a headache. I didn't believe her.

The New Year's Eve dance at Bountiful Grange No. 7 was a little better. There was a band from Austin called The Jokers, and they were really laying it down. Sadie and I danced beneath sagging nets filled with balloons until our feet were sore. At midnight The Jokers swung into a Ventures-style version of "Auld Lang Syne," and the band's lead man shouted "May all your dreams come *true* in nineteen hundred and sixty-*two*!"

The balloons drifted down around us. I kissed Sadie and wished her a happy New Year as we waltzed, but although she had been gay and laughing all evening, I felt no smile on her lips. "And a happy New Year to you too, George. Could I have a glass of punch? I'm very thirsty."

There was a long line at the spiked punch bowl, a shorter one at the unspiked version. I ladled the mixture of pink lemonade and ginger ale into a Dixie cup, but when I brought it back to where she had been standing, Sadie was gone.

"Think she went out for some air, champ," Carl Jacoby said. He was one of the high school's four shop teachers, and probably the best, but I wouldn't have let him within two hundred yards of a power tool that night.

I checked the smokers clustered under the fire escape. Sadie wasn't among them. I walked to the Sunliner. She was sitting in the passenger seat with her voluminous skirts billowing all the way up to the dashboard. God knows how many petticoats she was wearing. She was smoking and crying.

I got in and tried to take her in my arms. "Sadie, what is it? What is it, hon?" As if I didn't know. As if I hadn't known for some time.

"Nothing." Crying harder. "I've got my period, that's all. Take me home."

It was only three miles, but that seemed like a very long drive. We didn't talk. I turned into her driveway and cut the motor. She had stopped crying, but she still didn't say anything. Neither did I. Some silences can be comfortable. This one felt deadly.

She took her Winstons out of her handbag, looked at them, and put them back. The snick of the catch was very loud. She looked at me. Her hair was a dark cloud surrounding the white oval of her face. "Is there anything you want to tell me, George?"

What I wanted to tell her more than anything was that my name wasn't George. I had come to dislike that name. Almost to hate it.

"Two things. The first is that I love you. The second is that I'm not doing anything I'm ashamed of. Oh, and two-A: nothing *you'd* be ashamed of."

"Good. That's good. And I love you, George. But I'm going to tell *you* something, if you'll listen."

"I'll always listen." But she was scaring me.

"Everything can stay the same . . . for now. While I'm still married to John Clayton, even if it's just on paper and was never properly consummated in the first place, there are things I don't feel I have the right to ask you . . . or *of* you."

"Sadie—"

She put her fingers to my lips. "For now. But I won't ever allow another man to put a broom in the bed. Do you understand me?"

She put a quick kiss where her fingers had been, then dashed up the walk to her door, fumbling for her key.

That was how 1962 started for the man who called himself George Amberson.

2

New Year's Day dawned cold and clear, with the forecaster on the Morning Farm Report threatening freezing mist in the lowlands. I had stowed the two bugged lamps in my garage. I put one of them in my car and drove to Fort Worth. I thought if there was ever a day when the raggedy-ass carnival on Mercedes Street would be shut down, it was this one. I was right. It was as silent as . . . well, as silent as the Tracker mausoleum, when I'd dragged Frank Dunning's body into it. Overturned trikes and a few toys lay in balding front yards. Some party-boy had left a larger toy—a monstrous old Mercury—parked beside his porch. The car doors were still open. There were a few sad, leftover crepe streamers on the unpaved hardpan of the street, and a lot of beer cans—mostly Lone Star—in the gutters.

I glanced across at 2706 and saw no one looking out the large front window, but Ivy had been right: anyone standing there would have a perfect line of sight into the living room of 2703.

I parked on the concrete strips that passed for a driveway as if I had every right to be at the former home of the unlucky Templeton family. I got my lamp and a brand-new toolbox and went to the front door. I had a bad moment when the key refused to work, but it was just new. When I wetted it with some saliva and jiggled it a little, it turned and I went in.

There were four rooms if you counted the bathroom, visible through a door that hung open on one working hinge. The biggest was a combined living room and kitchen. The other two were bedrooms. In the larger one, there was no mattress on the bed. I remembered Ivy saying *Be like takin your dog on vacation, won't it?* In the smaller one, Rosette had drawn Crayola girls on walls where the plaster was decaying and the lathing showed through. They were all wearing green jumpers and big black shoes. They had out-of-proportion pigtails as long as their legs, and many were kicking soccer balls. One had a Miss America tiara perched on her hair and a big old red-lipstick smile. The house still smelled faintly of whatever fried meat Ivy had cooked for their final meal before going back to Mozelle to live with her mama, her little hellion, and her brokeback husband.

This was where Lee and Marina would begin the American phase of their marriage. They'd make love in the bigger of the two bedrooms, and he would beat her there. It was where Lee would lie awake after long days putting together storm doors and wondering why the hell he wasn't famous. Hadn't he tried? Hadn't he tried *hard*?

And in the living room, with its hilly up-and-down floor and its threadbare bile-green carpet, Lee would first meet the man I wasn't supposed to trust, the one that accounted for most if not all of the doubts Al had held onto about Oswald's role as the lone gunman. That man's name was George de Mohrenschildt, and I wanted very much to hear what he and Oswald had to say to each other.

There was an old bureau on the side of the main room that was closest to the kitchen. The drawers were a jumble of mismatched silverware and crappy cooking utensils. I pulled the bureau away from the wall and saw an electrical socket. Excellent. I put the lamp on top of the bureau and plugged it in. I knew someone might live here awhile before the Oswalds moved in, but I didn't think anyone would be apt to take the Leaning Lamp of Pisa when they decamped. If they did, I had a backup unit in my garage.

I drilled a hole through the wall to the outside with my smallest bit, pushed the bureau back into place, and tried the lamp. It worked fine. I packed up and left the house, being careful to lock the door behind me. Then I drove back to Jodie.

Sadie called and asked me if I would like to come over and have some supper. Just coldcuts, she said, but there was poundcake for dessert, if I cared for some. I went over. The dessert was as wonderful as ever, but things weren't the same. Because she was right. There was a broom in the bed. Like the jimla Rosette had seen in the back of my car, it was invisible . . . but it was there. Invisible or not, it cast a shadow.

3

Sometimes a man and a woman reach a crossroads and linger there, reluctant to take either way, knowing the wrong choice will mean the end . . . and knowing there's so much worth saving. That's the way it was with Sadie and me during that unrelenting gray winter of 1962. We still went out to dinner once or twice a week, and we still went to the Candlewood Bungalows on the occasional Saturday night. Sadie enjoyed sex, and that was one of the things that kept us together.

On three occasions we shapped hops together. Donald Bellingham was always the DJ, and sooner or later we'd be asked to reprise our first Lindy Hop. The kids always clapped and whistled when we did. Not out of politeness, either. They were authentically wowed, and some of them started to learn the moves themselves.

Were we pleased? Sure, because imitation really is the most sincere form of flattery. But we were never as good as that first time, never so intuitively smooth. Sadie's grace wavered. Once she missed her grip on a flyaway and would have gone sprawling if there hadn't been a couple of husky football players with quick reflexes standing nearby. She laughed it off, but I could see the embarrassment on her face. And the reproach. As if it had been my fault. Which in a way, it was.

There was bound to be a blow-up. It would have come sooner than it did, if not for the *Jodie Jamboree.* That was our greening, a chance to linger a little and think things over before we were forced into a decision neither of us wanted to make.

4

Ellen Dockerty came to me in February and asked me two things: first, would I please reconsider and sign a contract for the '62–'63 school year, and second, would I please direct the junior-senior play again, since last year's had been such a smash hit. I refused both requests, not without a tug of pain.

"If it's your book, you'd have all summer to work on it," she coaxed.

"It wouldn't be long enough," I said, although at that point I didn't give Shit One about *The Murder Place.*

"Sadie Dunhill says she doesn't believe you care a fig for that novel."

It was an insight she hadn't shared with me. It shook me, but I tried not to show it. "El, Sadie doesn't know everything."

"The play, then. At least do the play. As long as it doesn't involve nudity, I'll back anything you choose. Given the current composition of the schoolboard, and the fact that I myself only have a two-year contract as principal, that's a mighty big promise. You can dedicate it to Vince Knowles, if you like."

"Vince has already had a football season dedicated to his memory, Ellie. I think that's enough."

She went away, beaten.

The second request came from Mike Coslaw, who would be graduating in June and told me he intended to declare a theater major at college. "But I'd really like to do one more play here. With you, Mr. Amberson. Because you showed me the way."

Unlike Ellie Dockerty, he accepted the excuse about my bogus novel without question, which made me feel bad. Terrible, really. For a man who didn't like to lie—who had seen his marriage collapse because of all the ones he'd heard from his I-can-stop-whenever-I-want wife—I was certainly telling a passel of them, as we said in my Jodie days.

I walked Mike out to the student parking lot where his prize possession was parked (an old Buick sedan with fenderskirts), and asked him how his arm felt now that the cast was off. He said it was fine, and he was sure he'd be set for football practice this coming summer. "Although," he said, "if I got cut, it wouldn't break my heart. Then maybe I could do some community theater as well as school stuff. I want to learn everything—set design, lighting, even costumes." He laughed. "People'll start callin me queer."

"Concentrate on football, making grades, and not getting too homesick the first semester," I said. "Please. Don't screw around."

He did a zombie Frankenstein voice. "Yes . . . master . . ."

"How's Bobbi Jill?"

"Better," he said. "There she is."

Bobbi Jill was waiting by Mike's Buick. She waved at him, then saw me and immediately turned away, as if interested in the empty football field and the rangeland beyond. It was a gesture everyone in school had gotten used to. The scar from the accident had healed to a fat red string. She tried to cover it with cosmetics, which only made it more noticeable.

Mike said, "I tell her to quit with the powder already, it makes her look like an advertisement for Soames's Mortuary, but she won't listen. I also tell her I'm not going with her out of pity, or so she won't swallow any more pills. She says she believes me, and maybe she does. On sunny days."

I watched him hurry to Bobbi Jill, grab her by the waist, and swing her around. I sighed, feeling a little stupid and a lot stubborn. Part of me wanted to do the damn play. Even if it was good for nothing else, it would fill the time while I was waiting for my own show to start. But I didn't want to get hooked into the life of Jodie in more ways than I already was. Like any possible long-term future with Sadie, my relationship with the town needed to be on hold.

If everything went just right, it was possible I could wind up with the girl, the gold watch, and everything. But I couldn't count on that no matter how carefully I planned. Even if I succeeded I might have to run, and if I didn't get away, there was a good chance that my good deed on behalf of the world would be rewarded by life in prison. Or the electric chair in Huntsville.

5

It was Deke Simmons who finally trapped me into saying yes. He did it by telling me I'd be nuts to even consider it. I should have recognized that *Oh, Br'er Fox, please don't th'ow me in that briar patch* shtick, but he was very sly about it. Very subtle. A regular Br'er Rabbit, you might say.

We were in my living room drinking coffee on a Saturday afternoon while some old movie played on my snow-fuzzy TV— cowboys in Fort Hollywood standing off two thousand or so attacking Indians. Outside, more rain was falling. There must have been at least a few sunny days during the winter of '62, but I can't recall any. All I can remember are cold fingers of drizzle always finding their way to the barbered nape of my neck in spite of the turned-up collar of the sheepskin jacket I'd bought to replace the ranch coat.

"You don't want to worry about that damn play just because Ellen Dockerty's got her underwear all in a bunch about it," Deke said. "Finish your book, get a bestseller, and never look back. Live the good life in New York. Have a drink with Norman Mailer and Irwin Shaw at the White Horse Tavern."

"Uh-huh," I said. John Wayne was blowing a bugle. "I don't think Norman Mailer has to worry too much about me. Irwin Shaw, either."

"Also, you had such a success with *Of Mice and Men,*" he said. "Anything you did as a follow-up would probably be a disappointment by compar— oh, jeez, look at that! John Wayne just got an arrow through his hat! Lucky it was the twenty-gallon deluxe!"

I was more miffed by the idea that my second effort might fall short than I should have been. It made me think about how Sadie and I couldn't quite equal our first performance on the dance floor, despite our best efforts.

Deke seemed completely absorbed in the TV as he said, "Besides, Ratty Sylvester has expressed an interest in the junior-senior. He's talking about *Arsenic and Old Lace.* Says he and the wife saw it in Dallas two years ago and it was a regular ole knee-slapper."

Good God, *that* chestnut. And Fred Sylvester of the Science Department as director? I wasn't sure I'd trust Ratty to direct a grammar school fire drill. If a talented but still very damp-around-the-edges actor like Mike Coslaw ended up with Ratty at the helm, it could set his maturing process back five years. Ratty and *Arsenic and Old Lace.* Jesus wept.

"There wouldn't be time to put on anything really good, anyway," Deke went on. "So I say let Ratty take the fall. I never liked the scurrying little sumbitch, anyway."

Nobody really liked him, so far as I could tell, except maybe for Mrs. Ratty, who scurried by his side to every school and faculty function, wrapped in acres of organdy. But he wouldn't be the one to take the fall. That would be the kids.

"They could put on a variety show," I said. "There'd be time enough for that."

"Oh, Christ, George! Wallace Beery just took an arrow in the shoulder! I think he's a goner!"

"Deke?"

"No, John Wayne's dragging him to safety. This old shoot-em-up doesn't make a *lick* of sense, but I love it, don't you?"

"Did you hear what I said?"

A commercial came on. Keenan Wynn climbed down off a bull-dozer, doffed his hardhat, and told the world he'd walk a mile for a Camel. Deke turned to me. "No, I must have missed it."

Sly old fox. As if.

"I said there'd be time to put on a variety show. A revue. Songs, dances, jokes, and a bunch of sketches."

"Everything but girls doing the hootchie-koo? Or were you thinking of that, too?"

"Don't be a dope."

"So that makes it vaudeville. I always liked vaudeville. 'Good-night, Mrs. Calabash, wherever you are,' and all that."

He dragged his pipe out of the pocket of his cardigan, stuffed it with Prince Albert, and fired it up.

"You know, we actually used to do something like that down to the Grange. The show was called *Jodie Jamboree.* Not since the late forties, though. Folks got a little embarrassed by it, although no one ever came right out and said so. And vaudeville wasn't what we called it."

"What are you talking about?"

"It was a minstrel show, George. All the cowboys and farm-hands joined in. They wore blackface, sang and danced, told jokes in what they imagined was a Negro dialect. More or less based on *Amos 'n Andy.*"

I began to laugh. "Did anyone play the banjo?"

"As a matter of fact, on a couple of occasions our current prin-cipal did."

"*Ellen* played the *banjo* in a *minstrel* show?"

"Careful, you're starting to speak in iambic pentameter. That can lead to delusions of grandeur, pard."

I leaned forward. "Tell me one of the jokes."

Deke cleared his throat, and began speaking in two deep voices.

"Say dere, Brother Tambo, what did you buy dat jar of Vase-line fo'?

"Well I b'leeves it was fo'ty-nine cent!"

He looked at me expectantly, and I realized that had been the punchline.

"Did they laugh?" I almost feared the answer.

"Split their guts and hollered for more. You heard those jokes around the square for weeks after." He looked at me solemnly, but his eyes were twinkling like Christmas lights. "We're a small town. Our needs when it comes to humor are quite humble. Our idea of Rabelaisian wit is a blind feller slipping on a banana peel."

I sat thinking. The western came back on, but Deke seemed to have lost interest in it. He was watching me.

"That stuff could still work," I said.

"George, that stuff always does."

"It wouldn't need to be funny black fellers, either."

"Couldn't do it that way anymore, anyway," he said. "Maybe in Louisiana or Alabama, but not on the way to Austin, which the folks at the *Slimes Herald* call Comsymp City. And you wouldn't want to, would you?"

"No. Call me a bleeding-heart, but I find the idea repulsive. And why bother? Corny jokes . . . boys in big old suits with padded shoulders instead of cornpone overalls . . . girls in knee-high flapper dresses with lots of fringes . . . I'd love to see what Mike Coslaw could do with a comedy skit. . . ."

"Oh, he'd kill it," Deke said, as if that were a foregone conclusion. "Pretty good idea. Too bad you don't have time to try it out."

I started to say something, but then another of those lightning flashes hit me. It was just as bright as the one that had lit up my brain when Ivy Templeton had said that her neighbors across the street could see into her living room.

"George? Your mouth is open. The view is good but not appetizing."

"I could make time," I said. "If you could talk Ellie Dockerty into one condition."

He got up and snapped off the TV without a single glance, although the fighting between Duke Wayne and the Pawnee

417

Nation had now reached the critical point, with Fort Hollywood burning merry hell in the background. "Name it."

I named it, then said, "I've got to talk to Sadie. Right now."

6

She was solemn at first. Then she began to smile. The smile became a grin. And when I told her the idea that had come to me at the end of my conversation with Deke, she threw her arms around me. But that wasn't good enough for her, so she climbed until she could wrap her legs around me, as well. There was no broom between us that day.

"It's brilliant! You're a genius! Will you write the script?"

"You bet. It won't take long, either." Corny old jokes were already flying around in my head: *Coach Borman looked at the orange juice for twenty minutes because the can said CONCENTRATE. Our dog had an ingrown tail, we had to X-ray him to find out if he was happy. I rode on a plane so old that one restroom was marked Orville and the other was marked Wilbur.* "But I need plenty of help with other stuff. What it comes down to is I need a producer. I'm hoping you'll take the job."

"Sure." She slipped back to the floor with her body still pressed against mine. This produced a regrettably brief flash of bare leg as her skirt pulled up. She began to pace her living room, smoking furiously. She tripped over the easy chair (for probably the sixth or eighth time since we'd been on intimate terms) and caught her balance without even seeming to notice, although she was going to have a pretty fine bruise on her shin by nightfall.

"If you're thinking twenties-style flapper stuff, I can get Jo Peet to run up the costumes." Jo was the new head of the Home Ec Department, having succeeded to the position when Ellen Dockerty was confirmed as principal.

"That's great."

"Most of the Home Ec girls love to sew . . . and to cook. George, we'll need to serve evening meals, won't we? If the rehearsals run extra long? And they will, because we're starting awfully late."

"Yes, but just sandwiches—"

"We can do better than that. *Lots.* And music! We'll need music! It'll have to be recorded, because the band could never pull a thing like this together in time." And then, together, we said *"Donald Bellingham!"* in perfect harmony.

"What about advertising?" I asked. We were starting to sound like Mickey Rooney and Judy Garland, getting ready to put on a show in Aunt Milly's barn.

"Carl Jacoby and his Graphic Design kids. Posters not just here but all over town. Because we want the whole town to come, not just the relatives of the kids in the show. Standing room only."

"Bingo," I said, and kissed her nose. I loved her excitement. I was getting pretty excited myself.

"What do we say about the benefit aspect?" Sadie asked.

"Nothing until we're sure we can make enough money. We don't want to raise any false hopes. What do you think about taking a run to Dallas with me tomorrow and asking some questions?"

"Tomorrow's Sunday, hon. After school on Monday. Maybe even before it's out, if you can get period seven free."

"I'll get Deke to come out of retirement and cover Remedial English," I said. "He owes me."

7

Sadie and I went to Dallas on Monday, driving fast to get there before the close of business hours. The office we were looking for turned out to be on Harry Hines Boulevard, not far from Parkland Memorial. There we asked a bushel of questions, and Sadie gave a brief demonstration of what we were after. The answers were more than satisfactory, and two days later I began my second-to-last show-biz venture, as director of *Jodie Jamboree,* An All-New, All-Hilarious Vaudeville Song & Dance Show. And all to benefit

A Good Cause. We didn't say what that cause was, and nobody asked.

Two things about the Land of Ago: there's a lot less paperwork and a hell of a lot more trust.

8

Everybody in town *did* turn out, and Deke Simmons was right about one thing: those lame jokes never seemed to get old. Not fifteen hundred miles from Broadway, at least.

In the persons of Jim LaDue (who wasn't bad, and could actually sing a little) and Mike Coslaw (who was flat-out hilarious), our show was more Dean Martin and Jerry Lewis than Mr. Bones and Mr. Tambo. The skits were of the knockabout type, and with a couple of athletes to perform them, they worked better than they probably had a right to. In the audience, knees were slapped and buttons were busted. Probably a few girdles were popped, as well.

Ellen Dockerty dragged her banjo out of retirement; for a lady with blue hair, she played a mean breakdown. And there was hootchie-koo after all. Mike and Jim persuaded the rest of the football team to perform a spirited can-can wearing petticoats and bloomers down south and nothing but skin up north. Jo Peet found wigs for them, and they stopped the show. The town ladies seemed especially crazy about those bare-chested young men, wigs and all.

For the finale, the entire cast paired off and filled the gymnasium stage with frenetic swing-dancing as "In the Mood" blared from the speakers. Skirts flew; feet flashed; football players (now dressed in zoot suits and stingy-brim hats) spun limber girls. Most of the latter were cheerleaders who already knew a few things about how to cut a rug.

The music ended; the laughing, winded cast stepped forward to take their bows; and as the audience rose to its feet for the third (or maybe it was the fourth) time since the curtain went up, Donald started up "In the Mood" again. This time the boys and girls scampered to opposite sides of the stage, grabbed the dozens of cream pies waiting for them on tables in the wings, and began to pelt each other. The audience roared its approval.

This part of the show our cast had known about and looked forward to, although since no actual pies had been flung during rehearsals, I wasn't sure how it would play out. Of course it went splendidly, as cream-pie fights always do. So far as the kids knew this was the climax, but I had one more trick up my sleeve.

As they came forward to take their second bows, faces dripping cream and costumes splattered, "In the Mood" started up for the *third* time. Most of the kids looked around, puzzled, and so did not see Faculty Row rise to its feet holding the cream pies Sadie and I had stashed beneath their seats. The pies flew, and the cast was doused for the second time. Coach Borman had *two* pies, and his aim was deadly: he got both his quarterback and his star defenseman.

Mike Coslaw, face dripping cream, began to bellow: *"Mr. A! Miz D! Mr. A! Miz D!"*

The rest of the cast took it up, then the audience, clapping in rhythm. We went up onstage, hand-in-hand, and Bellingham started that goddam record yet again. The kids formed lines on either side of us, shouting *"Dance! Dance! Dance!"*

We had no choice, and although I was convinced my girlfriend would go sliding in all that cream and break her neck, we were perfect for the first time since the Sadie Hawkins. At the end of it, I squeezed both of Sadie's hands, saw her little nod—*Go on, go for it, I trust you*—and shot her between my legs. Both of her shoes flew into the first row, her skirt skidded deliriously up her thighs . . . and she came magically to her feet in one piece, with her hands first held out to the audience—which was going insane—and then to the sides of her cream-smeared skirt, in a ladylike curtsey.

The kids turned out to have a trick up their sleeves, as well, one almost certainly instigated by Mike Coslaw, although he would never own up to it. They had saved some pies back, and as we stood there, soaking up the applause, we were hit by at least a dozen, flying from all directions. And the crowd, as they say, goes wild.

Sadie pulled my ear close to her mouth, wiped whipped cream from it with her pinky, and whispered: "How can you leave all this?"

9

And it still wasn't over.

Deke and Ellen walked to center stage, finding their way almost magically around the streaks, splatters, and clots of cream. No one would have dreamed of tossing a cream pie at either of *them.*

Deke raised his hands for silence, and when Ellen Dockerty stepped forward, she spoke in a clear classroom voice that carried easily over the murmurs and residual laughter.

"Ladies and gentleman, tonight's performance of *Jodie Jamboree* will be followed by three more." This brought another wave of applause.

"These are *benefit* performances," Ellie went on when the applause died down, "and it pleases me—yes, it pleases me very much—to tell you to whom the benefit will accrue. Last fall, we lost one of our valued students, and we all mourned the passing of Vincent Knowles, which came far, far, *far* too soon."

Now there was dead silence from the audience.

"A girl you all know, one of the leading lights of our student body, was badly scarred in that accident. Mr. Amberson and Miss Dunhill have arranged for Roberta Jillian Allnut to have facial reconstructive surgery this June, in Dallas. There will be no cost to the Allnut family; I'm told by Mr. Sylvester, who has served as the *Jodie Jamboree* accountant, that Bobbi Jill's classmates—and this town—have assured that all the costs of the surgery will be paid in full."

There was a moment of quiet as they processed this, then they leaped to their feet. The applause was like summer thunder. I saw Bobbi Jill herself on the bleachers. She was weeping with her hands over her face. Her parents had their arms around her.

This was one night in a small town, one of those burgs off the main road that nobody cares about much except for the people who live there. And that's okay, because *they* care. I looked at Bobbi Jill, sobbing into her hands. I looked at Sadie. There was cream in her hair. She smiled. So did I. She mouthed *I love you, George.* I mouthed back *I love you, too.* That night I loved all of them, and myself for being with them. I never felt so alive or happy to *be* alive. How could I leave all this, indeed?

The blow-up came two weeks later.

10

It was a Saturday, grocery day. Sadie and I had gotten into the habit of doing it together at Weingarten's, on Highway 77. We'd push our carts companionably side by side while Mantovani played overhead, examining the fruit and looking for the best buys on meat. You could get almost any kind of cut you wanted, as long as it was beef or chicken. It was okay with me; even after nearly three years, I was still wowed by the rock-bottom prices.

That day I had something other than groceries on my mind: the Hazzard family living at 2706 Mercedes, a shotgun shack across the street and a little to the left of the rotting duplex that Lee Oswald would soon call home. *Jodie Jamboree* had kept me very busy, but I'd managed three trips back to Mercedes Street that spring. I parked my Ford in a lot in downtown Fort Worth and took the Winscott Road bus, which stopped less than half a mile away. On these trips I dressed in jeans, scuffed boots, and a faded denim jacket I'd picked up at a yard sale. My story, if anyone asked for it: I was looking for a cheap rent because I'd just gotten a night watchman job at Texas Sheet Metal in West Fort Worth. That made me a trustworthy individual (as long as no one checked up), and supplied a reason why the house would be quiet, with the shades drawn, during the daylight hours.

On my strolls up Mercedes Street to the Monkey Ward warehouse and back (always with a newspaper folded open to the rental section of the classifieds), I spotted Mr. Hazzard, a hulk in his mid-thirties, the two kids Rosette wouldn't play with, and an old woman with a frozen face who dragged one foot as she walked. Hazzard's mama eyed me suspiciously from the mailbox on one occasion, as I idled slowly past along the rut that served as a sidewalk, but she didn't speak.

On my third recon, I saw a rusty old trailer hooked to the back of Hazzard's pickup truck. He and the kids were loading it with boxes while the old lady stood nearby on the just-greening crabgrass, leaning on her cane and wearing a stroke-sneer that could have masked any emotion. I was betting on utter indifference. What *I* felt was happiness. The Hazzards were moving on. As soon as they did, a working stiff named George Amberson was going to rent 2706. The important thing was to make sure I was first in line.

I was trying to figure out if there was any foolproof way to do that as we went about our Saturday shopping chores. On one level I was responding to Sadie, making the right comments, kidding her when she spent too much time at the dairy case, pushing the cart loaded with groceries out to the parking lot, putting the bags in the Ford's trunk. But I was doing it all on autopilot, most of my mind worrying over the Fort Worth logistics, and that turned out to be my undoing. I wasn't paying attention to what was coming out of my mouth, and when you're living a double life, that's dangerous.

As I drove back to Sadie's place with her sitting quietly (too quietly) beside me, I was singing because the Ford's radio was on the fritz. The valves had gotten wheezy, too. The Sunliner still looked snappy, and I was attached to it for all sorts of reasons, but it was seven years downstream from the assembly line and there were over ninety thousand miles on the clock.

I carried Sadie's groceries into the kitchen in a single load, making heroic grunting noises and staggering for effect. I didn't notice that she wasn't smiling, and had no idea that our little period of greening was over. I was still thinking about Mercedes Street, and wondering what kind of a show I'd have to put on there—or rather, how much of a show. It would be delicate. I wanted to be a familiar face, because familiarity breeds disinterest as well as contempt, but I didn't want to stand out. Then there were the Oswalds. She didn't speak English and he was a cold fish by nature, all to the good, but 2706 was still awfully close. The past might be obdurate but the future was delicate, a house of cards, and I had to be very careful not to change it until I was ready. So I'd have to—

That was when Sadie spoke to me, and shortly after that, life as I had come to know it (and love it) in Jodie came crashing down.

11

"George? Can you come in the living room? I want to talk to you."

"Hadn't you better put your hamburger and pork chops in the fridge? And I think I saw ice cr—"

"Let it melt!" she shouted, and that brought me out of my head in a hurry.

I turned to her, but she was already in the living room. She picked up her cigarettes from the table beside the couch and lit one. At my gentle urgings she had been trying to cut down (at least around me), and this seemed somehow more ominous than her raised voice.

I went into the living room. "What is it, honey? What's wrong?"

"Everything. What was that song?"

Her face was pale and set. She held the cigarette in front of her mouth like a shield. I began to realize that I had slipped up, but I didn't know how or when, and that was scary. "I don't know what you m—"

"The song you were singing in the car when we were coming home. The one you were bellowing at the top of your lungs."

I tried to remember and couldn't. All I could remember was thinking I'd always have to dress like a slightly down-on-his-luck workman on Mercedes Street, so I'd fit in. Sure I'd been singing, but I often did when I was thinking about other things—doesn't everybody?

"Just some pop thing I heard on KLIF, I guess. Something that got into my head. You know how songs do that. I don't understand what's got you so upset."

"Something you heard on K-Life. With lyrics like 'I met a gin-soaked bar-room queen in Memphis, she tried to take me upstairs for a ride'?"

It wasn't just my heart that sank; everything below my neck seemed to drop five inches. "Honky Tonk Women." That's what I'd been singing. A song that wouldn't be recorded for another seven or eight years, by a group that wouldn't even have an American hit for another three. My mind had been on other things, but still—how could I have been so dumb?

" 'She blew my nose and then she blew my mind'? On the *radio*? The FCC would shut down a station that played something like that!"

I started to get angry then. Mostly at myself . . . but not *entirely* at myself. I was walking a goddam tightrope, and she was shouting at me over a Rolling Stones tune.

"Chill, Sadie. It's just a *song*. I don't know *where* I heard it."

"That's a lie, and we both know it."

"You're freaking out. I think maybe I better take my groceries and head home." I tried to keep my voice calm. The sound of it was very familiar. It was the way I'd always tried to speak to Christy when she came home with a snootful. Skirt on crooked, blouse half-untucked, hair all crazy. Not to mention the smeared lipstick. From the rim of a glass, or from some fellow barfly's lips?

Just thinking about it made me angrier. *Wrong again,* I thought. I didn't know if I meant Sadie or Christy or me, and at that moment I didn't care. We never get so mad as when we get caught, do we?

"I think maybe you better tell me where you heard that song, if you ever want to come back here. And where you heard what you said to the kid at the checkout when he said he'd double-bag your chicken so it wouldn't leak."

"I don't have any idea what—"

" 'Excellent, dude,' that's what you said. I think maybe you better tell me where you heard *that*. And *kick out the jams*. And *boogie shoes*. And *shake your bootie*. *Chill* and *freaking out*, I want to know where you heard those, too. Why you say them and no one else does. I want to know why you were so scared of that stupid Jimla chant that you talked about it in your sleep. I want to know where Derry is and why it's like Dallas. I want to know when you were married, and to who, and for how long. I want to know where you were before you were in Florida, because Ellie Dockerty says she doesn't know, that some of your references are fake. 'Appear to be fanciful' is how she put it."

I was sure Ellen hadn't found out from Deke . . . but she *had* found out. I actually wasn't too surprised, but I was infuriated that she had blabbed to Sadie. "She had no right to tell you that!"

She smashed out her cigarette, then shook her hand as bits of live coal jumped up and stung it. "Sometimes it's like you're from . . . I don't know . . . some other universe! One where they sing about screwing drunk women from M-Memphis! I tried to-to tell myself all that doesn't matter, that l-l-love conquers all, except it doesn't. It doesn't conquer lies." Her voice wavered, but she didn't cry. And her eyes stayed fixed on mine. If there had only been anger in them, it would have been a little easier. But there was pleading, too.

"Sadie, if you'd only—"

"I *won't*. Not anymore. So don't start up with the stuff about how you're not doing anything you're ashamed of and I wouldn't be, either. Those are things I need to decide for myself. It comes down to this: either the broom goes, or you'll have to."

"If you knew, you wouldn't—"

"Then tell me!"

"I *can't*." The anger popped like a pricked balloon, leaving an emotional dullness behind. I dropped my eyes from her set face, and they happened to fall on her desk. What I saw there stopped my breath.

It was a little pile of job applications for her time in Reno this coming summer. The top one was from Harrah's Hotel and Casino. On the first line she had printed her name in neat block letters. Her *full* name, including the middle one I'd never thought to ask her about.

I reached down, very slowly, and put my thumbs over her first name and the second syllable of her last name. What that left was **DORIS DUN**.

I remembered the day I had spoken to Frank Dunning's wife, pretending to be a real estate speculator with an interest in the West Side Rec. She'd been twenty years older than Sadie Doris Clayton, née Dunhill, but both women had blue eyes, exquisite skin, and fine, full-breasted figures. Both women were smokers. All of it could have been coincidental, but it wasn't. And I knew it.

"What are you doing?" The accusatory tone meant the real question was *Why do you keep dodging and evading,* but I was no longer angry. Not even close.

"Are you sure he doesn't know where you are?" I asked.

"Who? Johnny? Do you mean Johnny? Why . . ." That was when she decided it was useless. I saw it in her face. "George, you need to leave."

"But he could find out," I said. "Because your parents know, and your parents thought he was just the bees' knees, you said so yourself."

I took a step toward her. She took a step back. The way you'd step back from a person who's revealed himself to be of unsound mind. I saw the fear in her eyes, and the lack of comprehension, and still I couldn't stop. Remember that I was scared myself.

"Even if you told them not to say, he'd get it out of them. Because he's charming. Isn't he, Sadie? When he's not compulsively washing his hands, or alphabetizing his books, or talking about how disgusting it is to get an erection, he's very, very charming. He certainly charmed *you.*"

"Please go away, George." Her voice was trembling.

I took another step toward her instead. She took a compensatory step back, struck the wall . . . and *cringed*. Seeing her do that was like a slap across the face to a hysteric or a glass of cold water flung into the face of a sleepwalker. I retreated to the arch between the living room and the kitchen, my hands held up to the sides of my face, like a man surrendering. Which was what I was doing.

"I'm going. But Sadie—"

"I just don't understand how you could do it," she said. The tears had come; they were rolling slowly down her cheeks. "Or why you refuse to *un*do it. We had such a good thing."

"We still do."

She shook her head. She did it slowly but firmly.

I crossed the kitchen in what felt like a float rather than a walk, plucked the tub of vanilla ice cream from one of the bags standing on the counter, and put it in the freezer of her Coldspot. Part of me was thinking this was all just a bad dream, and I'd wake up soon. Most of me knew better.

Sadie stood in the arch, watching me. She had a fresh cigarette in one hand and the job applications in the other. Now that I saw it, the resemblance to Doris Dunning was eerie. Which raised the question of why I hadn't seen it before. Because I'd been preoccupied with other stuff? Or was it because I still hadn't fully grasped the immensity of the things I was fooling with?

I went out through the screen door and stood on the stoop, looking at her through the mesh. "Watch out for him, Sadie."

"Johnny's mixed up about a lot of things, but he's not dangerous," she said. "And my parents would never tell him where I am. They promised."

"People can break promises, and people can snap. Especially people who've been under a lot of pressure and are mentally unstable to begin with."

"You need to go, George."

"Promise me that you'll watch out for him and I will."

She shouted, *"I promise, I promise, I promise!"* The way her cigarette trembled between her fingers was bad; the combination of shock, loss, grief, and anger in her red eyes was much worse. I could feel them following me all the way back to my car.

Goddamned Rolling Stones.

CHAPTER 17

1

A few days before the end-of-year testing cycle began, Ellen Dockerty summoned me to her office. After she closed the door, she said: "I'm sorry for the trouble I've caused, George, but if I had it to do over again, I'm not sure I would behave any differently."

I said nothing. I was no longer angry, but I was still stunned. I'd gotten very little sleep since the blow-up, and I had an idea that 4:00 A.M. and I were going to be close friends in the near future.

"Clause Twenty-five of the Texas School Administrative Code," she said, as if that explained everything.

"I beg your pardon, Ellie?"

"Nina Wallingford was the one who brought it to my attention." Nina was the district nurse. She put tens of thousands of miles on her Ford Ranch Wagon each school year circling Denholm County's eight schools, three of them still of the one- or two-room variety. "Clause Twenty-five concerns the state's rules for immunization in schools. It covers teachers as well as students, and Nina pointed out she didn't have any immunization records for you. No medical records of any kind, in fact."

And there it was. The fake teacher exposed by his lack of a polio shot. Well, at least it wasn't my advanced knowledge of the Rolling Stones, or inappropriate use of disco slang.

"You being so busy with the *Jamboree* and all, I thought I'd write to the schools where you'd taught and save you the trouble. What

431

I got back from Florida was a letter stating that they don't require immunization records from substitutes. What I got from Maine and Wisconsin was 'Never heard of him.'"

She leaned forward behind her desk, looking at me. I couldn't meet her gaze for long. What I saw in her face before I redirected my gaze to the backs of my hands was an unbearable sympathy.

"Would the State Board of Education care that we had hired an imposter? Very much. They might even institute legal action to recoup your year's salary. Do I care? Absolutely not. Your work at DCHS has been exemplary. What you and Sadie did for Bobbi Jill Allnut was absolutely wonderful, the kind of thing that garners State Teacher of the Year nominations."

"Thanks," I muttered. "I guess."

"I asked myself what Mimi Corcoran would do. What Meems said to me was, 'If he had signed a contract to teach next year and the year after, you'd be forced to act. But since he's leaving in a month, it's actually in your interest—and the school's—to say nothing.' Then she added, 'But there's one person who *has* to know he's not who he says he is.'"

Ellie paused.

"I told Sadie that I was sure you'd have some reasonable explanation, but it seems you do not."

I glanced at my watch. "If you're not firing me, Miz Ellie, I ought to get back to my period five class. We're diagramming sentences. I'm thinking of trying them on a compound that goes, *I am blameless in this matter, but I cannot say why.* What do you think? Too tough?"

"Too tough for me, certainly," she said pleasantly.

"One thing," I said. "Sadie's marriage was difficult. Her husband was strange in ways I don't want to go into. His name is John Clayton. I think he might be dangerous. You need to ask Sadie if she has a picture of him, so you'll know what he looks like if he shows up and starts asking questions."

"And you think this because?"

"Because I've seen something like it before. Will that do?"

"I suppose it will have to, won't it?"

That wasn't a good enough answer. "Will you ask her?"

"Yes, George." She might mean it; she might only be humoring me. I couldn't tell.

I was at the door when she said, as if only passing the time of day: "You're breaking that young woman's heart."

"I know," I said, and left.

2

Mercedes Street. Late May.

"Welder, are you?"

I was standing on the porch of 2706 with the landlord, a fine American named Mr. Jay Baker. He was stocky, with a huge gut he called the house that Shiner built. We had just finished a quick tour of the premises, which Baker had explained to me was "Prime to the bus stop," as if that made up for the sagging ceilings, water-stained walls, cracked toilet tank, and general air of decrepitude.

"Night watchman," I said.

"Yeah? That's a good job. Plenty of time to fuck the dog on a job like that."

This seemed to require no response.

"No wife or kiddies?"

"Divorced. They're back East."

"Pay hellimony, do you?"

I shrugged.

He let it go. "So do you want the place, Amberson?"

"I guess so," I said, and sighed.

He took a long rent-book with a floppy leather cover out of his back pocket. "First month, last month, damage deposit."

"Damage deposit? You have to be kidding."

Baker went on as if he hadn't heard me. "Rent's due on the last Friday of the month. Come up short or late and you're on the street, courtesy of Fort Worth PD. Me'n them get along real good."

He took the charred cigar stub from his breast pocket, stuck the chewed end in his gob, and popped a wooden match alight with his thumbnail. It was hot on the porch. I had an idea it was going to be a long, hot summer.

I sighed again. Then—with a show of reluctance—I took out my wallet and began to remove twenty-dollar bills. "In God we trust," I said. "All others pay cash."

He laughed, puffing out clouds of acrid blue smoke as he did so. "That's good, I'll remember that. Especially on the last Friday of the month."

I couldn't believe I was going to live in this desperate shack and on this desperate street, after my nice house south of here— where I'd taken pride in keeping an actual lawn mowed. Although I hadn't even left Jodie yet, I felt a wave of homesickness.

"Give me a receipt, please," I said.

That much I got for free.

3

It was the last day of school. The classrooms and hallways were empty. The overhead fans paddled air that was already hot, although it was only the eighth of June. The Oswald family had left Russia; in another five days, according to Al Templeton's notes, the SS *Maasdam* would dock in Hoboken, where they would walk down the gangplank and onto United States soil.

The teachers' room was empty except for Danny Laverty. "Hey, champ. Understand you're going off to Dallas to finish that book of yours."

"That's the plan." Fort Worth was actually the plan, at least to begin with. I began cleaning out my pigeonhole, which was stuffed with end-of-school communiqués.

"If I was footloose and fancy-free instead of tied down to a wife, three rugrats, and a mortgage, I might try a book myself," Danny said. "I was in the war, you know."

I knew. Everyone knew, usually within ten minutes of meeting him.

"Got enough to live on?"

"I'll be okay."

I had more than enough to take me through to next April, when I expected to conclude my business with Lee Oswald. I wouldn't need to make any more expeditions to Faith Financial on Greenville Avenue. Going there even once had been incredibly stupid. If I wanted, I could try to tell myself that what had happened to my place in Florida had just been the result of a prank gone bad, but I'd also tried to tell myself that Sadie and I were doing fine, and look how *that* had turned out.

I tossed the wad of paperwork from my pigeonhole into the trash . . . and saw a small sealed envelope I had somehow missed. I knew who used envelopes like that. There was no salutation on the sheet of notepaper inside, and no signature except for the faint (perhaps even illusory) scent of her perfume. The message was brief.

Thank you for showing me how good things can be. Please don't say goodbye.

I held it for a minute, thinking, then stuck it in my back pocket and walked rapidly down to the library. I don't know what I planned to do or what I meant to tell her, but none of it mattered because the library was dark and the chairs were up on the tables. I tried the knob anyway, but the door was locked.

4

The only two cars left at the faculty end of the parking lot were Danny Laverty's Plymouth sedan and my Ford, the ragtop now

435

looking rather raggedy. I could sympathize; I felt a bit raggedy myself.

"Mr. A! Wait up, Mr. A!"

It was Mike and Bobbi Jill, hurrying across the hot parking lot toward me. Mike was carrying a small wrapped present, which he held out to me. "Bobbi n me got you something."

"Bobbi and *I*. And you shouldn't have, Mike."

"We had to, man."

I was moved to see that Bobbi Jill was crying, and pleased to see that the thick coating of Max Factor had disappeared from her face. Now that she knew the disfiguring scar's days were numbered, she had stopped trying to conceal it. She kissed me on the cheek.

"Thank you so, so, *so* much, Mr. Amberson. I'll never forget you." She looked at Mike. "*We'll* never forget you."

And they probably wouldn't. That was a good thing. It didn't make up for the locked and dark library, but yes—it was a very good thing.

"Open it," Mike said. "We hope you like it. It's for your book."

I opened the package. Inside was a wooden box about eight inches long and two inches wide. Inside the box, cradled in silk, was a Waterman fountain pen with the initials GA engraved on the clip.

"Oh, Mike," I said. "This is too much."

"It wouldn't be enough if it was solid gold," he said. "You changed my life." He looked at Bobbi. "Both our lives."

"Mike," I said, "it was my pleasure."

He hugged me, and in 1962, that is not a cheap gesture between men. I was glad to hug him back.

"You stay in touch," Bobbi Jill said. "Dallas ain't far." She paused. "*Isn't.*"

"I will," I said, but I wouldn't, and they probably wouldn't, either. They were going off into their lives, and if they were lucky, their lives would shine.

They started away, then Bobbi turned back. "It's a shame you two broke up. It makes me feel real bad."

"It makes me feel bad, too," I said, "but it's probably for the best."

I headed home to pack up my typewriter and my other belongings, which I reckoned were still few enough to fit into no more than a suitcase and a few cardboard boxes. At the one stoplight on Main Street, I opened the little box and looked at the pen. It was a beautiful thing, and I was very touched that they had given it to me. I was even more touched that they had waited to say goodbye. The light turned green. I snapped the lid of the box closed and drove on. There was a lump in my throat, but my eyes were dry.

5

Living on Mercedes Street was not an uplifting experience.

Days weren't so bad. They resounded with the shouts of children recently released from school, all dressed in too-big hand-me-downs; housewives kvetching at mailboxes or backyard clotheslines; teenagers driving rusty beaters with glasspack mufflers and radios blaring K-Life. The hours between 2:00 and 6:00 A.M. weren't so bad, either. Then a kind of stunned silence fell over the street as colicky babies finally slept in their cribs (or dresser drawers) and their daddies snored toward another day of hourly wages in the shops, factories, or outlying farms.

Between four and six in the afternoon, however, the street was a jangle of mommas screaming at kids to get the hell in and do their chores and poppas arriving home to scream at their wives, probably because they had no one else to scream at. Many of the wives gave back as good as they got. The drunkadaddies started to roll in around eight, and things really got noisy around eleven, when either the bars closed or the money ran out. Then I heard slamming doors, breaking glass, and screams of pain as some loaded drunkadaddy tuned up on the wife, the kiddies, or both. Often red lights would strobe in through my drawn curtains as the cops arrived. A couple of times there were gunshots, maybe fired at the sky, maybe not. And one early morning, when I went out to get the paper, I saw a woman with dried blood crusting the lower half of her face. She was sitting on the curb in front of a house four down from mine, drinking a can of Lone Star. I almost went down to check on her, even though I knew how unwise it would be to get involved with the life of this low-bottom working neighborhood. Then she saw me looking at her and hoisted her middle finger. I went back inside.

There was no Welcome Wagon, and no women named Muffy or Buffy trotting off to Junior League meetings. What there was on Mercedes Street was plenty of time to think. Time to miss my friends in Jodie. Time to miss the work that had kept my mind off what I had come here to do. Time to realize the teaching had done a lot more than pass the time; it had satisfied my mind the way work does when you care about it, when you feel like you might actually be making a difference.

There was even time to feel bad about my formerly spiffy convertible. Besides the nonfunctional radio and the wheezy valves, it now blatted and backfired through a rusty tailpipe and there was a crack in the windshield caused by a rock that had bounced off the back of a lumbering asphalt truck. I'd stopped washing it, and now—sad to say—it fit in perfectly with the other busted-up transpo on Mercedes Street.

Mostly there was time to think about Sadie.

You're breaking that young woman's heart, Ellie Dockerty had said, and mine wasn't doing so well, either. The idea of spilling everything to Sadie came to me one night as I lay awake listening to a drunken argument next door: *you did, I didn't, you did, I didn't, fuck you.* I rejected the idea, but it came back the following night, rejuvenated. I could see myself sitting with her at her kitchen table, drinking coffee in the strong afternoon sunlight that slanted through the window over the sink. Speaking calmly. Telling her my real name was Jacob Epping, I wouldn't actually be born for another fourteen years, I had come from the year 2011 via a fissure in time that my late friend Al Templeton called the rabbit-hole.

How would I convince her of such a thing? By telling her that a certain American defector who had changed his mind about Russia was shortly going to move in across the street from where I now lived, along with his Russian wife and their baby girl? By telling her that the Dallas Texans—not to become the Cowboys, never to become America's Team—were going to beat the Houston Oilers 20–17 this fall, in double overtime? Ridiculous. But what else did I know about the immediate future? Not much, because I'd had no time to study up. I knew a fair amount about Oswald, but that was all.

She'd think I was crazy. I could sing her lyrics from another dozen pop songs that hadn't been recorded yet, and she'd still think I was crazy. She'd accuse me of making them up myself— wasn't I a writer, after all? And suppose she *did* believe it? Did I want to drag her into the shark's mouth with me? Wasn't it bad enough that she'd be coming back to Jodie in August, and that if John Clayton was an echo of Frank Dunning, he might come looking for her?

"All right, get out then!" a woman screamed from the street, and a car accelerated away in the direction of Winscott Road. A wedge of light probed briefly through a crack in my drawn curtains and flashed across the ceiling.

"COCKSUCKER!" she yelled after it, to which a male voice, a little more distant, yelled back: "You can suck mine, lady, maybe it'll calm you down."

That was life on Mercedes Street in the summer of '62.

Leave her out of it. That was the voice of reason. *It's just too dangerous. Maybe at some point she can be a part of your life again—a life in Jodie, even—but not now.*

Only there was never going to be a life for me in Jodie. Given what Ellen now knew about my past, teaching at the high school was a fool's dream. And what else was I going to do? Pour concrete?

One morning I put on the coffeepot and went for the paper on the stoop. When I opened the front door, I saw that both of the Sunliner's rear tires were flat. Some bored out-too-late kid had slashed them with a knife. That was also life on Mercedes Street in the summer of '62.

6

On Thursday, the fourteenth of June, I dressed in jeans, a blue workshirt, and an old leather vest I'd picked up at a secondhand store on Camp Bowie Road. Then I spent the morning pacing through my house. I had no television, but I listened to the radio. According to the news, President Kennedy was planning a state trip to Mexico later in the month. The weather report called for fair skies and warm temperatures. The DJ yammered awhile, then played "Palisades Park." The screams and roller-coaster sound effects on the record clawed at my head.

At last I could stand it no longer. I was going to be early, but I didn't care. I got into the Sunliner—which now sported two retread blackwalls to go with the whitewalls on the front—and drove the forty-odd miles to Love Field in northwest Dallas. There was no short-term or long-term parking, just parking. It cost seventy-five cents a day. I clapped my old summer straw on my head and trudged approximately half a mile to the terminal building. A couple of Dallas cops stood at the curb drinking coffee, but there were no security guards inside and no metal detectors to walk through. Passengers simply showed their tickets to a guy standing by the door, then walked across the hot tarmac to planes belonging to one of five carriers: American, Delta, TWA, Frontier, and Texas Airways.

I checked the chalkboard mounted on the wall behind the Delta counter. It said that Flight 194 was on time. When I asked the clerk to make sure, she smiled and told me it had just left Atlanta. "But you're awfully early."

"I can't help it," I said. "I'll probably be early to my own funeral."

She laughed and wished me a nice day. I bought a *Time* and walked across to the restaurant, where I ordered the Cloud 9 Chef's

Salad. It was huge and I was too nervous to be hungry—it's not every day that a man gets to see the person who's going to change world history—but it gave me something to pick at while I waited for the plane carrying the Oswald family to arrive.

I was in a booth with a good view of the main terminal. It wasn't very crowded, and a young woman in a dark blue traveling suit caught my eye. Her hair was twisted into a neat bun. She had a suitcase in each hand. A Negro porter approached her. She shook her head, smiling, then banged her arm on the side of the Traveler's Aid booth as she passed it. She dropped one of her suitcases, rubbed her elbow, then picked up the case again and forged onward.

Sadie leaving to start her six-week residency in Reno.

Was I surprised? Not at all. It was that convergence thing again. I'd grown used to it. Was I almost overwhelmed by an impulse to run out of the restaurant and catch up to her before it was too late? Of course I was.

For a moment it seemed more than possible, it seemed necessary. I would tell her fate (rather than some weird time-travel harmonic) had brought us together at the airport. Stuff like that worked in the movies, didn't it? I'd ask her to wait while I bought my own ticket to Reno, and tell her that once we were there, I'd explain everything. And after the obligatory six weeks, we could buy a drink for the judge who had granted her divorce before he married us.

I actually started to get up. As I did, I happened to look at the cover of the *Time* I'd bought at the newsstand. Jacqueline Kennedy was on the cover. She was smiling, radiant, wearing a sleeveless dress with a V-neck. THE PRESIDENT'S LADY DRESSES FOR SUMMER, the caption read. As I looked at the photo, the color drained away to black and white and the expression changed from a happy smile to a vacant stare. Now she was standing next to Lyndon Johnson on *Air Force One,* and no longer wearing the pretty (and slightly sexy) summer dress. A blood-spattered wool suit had taken its place. I remembered reading—not in Al's notes, somewhere else—that not long after Mrs. Kennedy's husband had been pronounced dead, Lady Bird Johnson had moved to embrace her in the hospital corridor and had seen a glob of the dead president's brains on that suit.

A head-shot president. And all the dead who would come after, standing behind him in a ghostly file that stretched away into infinity.

I sat back down again and watched Sadie carry her suitcases toward the Frontier Airlines counter. The bags were obviously heavy but she carried them con brio, her back straight, her low heels clicking briskly. The clerk checked them and put them on a baggage trolley. He and Sadie conferred; she passed him the ticket she had bought through a travel agency two months ago, and the clerk scribbled something on it. She took it back and turned for the gate. I lowered my head to make sure she wouldn't see me. When I looked up again, she was gone.

7

Forty long, long minutes later, a man, a woman, and two small children—a boy and a girl—passed the restaurant. The boy was holding his father's hand and chattering away. The father was looking down at him, nodding and smiling. The father was Robert Oswald.

The loudspeaker blared, "Delta's flight 194 is now arriving from Newark and Atlanta Municipal Airport. Passengers can be met at Gate 4. Delta Flight 194, now arriving."

Robert's wife—Vada, according to Al's notes—swept the little girl into her arms and hurried along faster. There was no sign of Marguerite.

I picked at my salad, chewing without tasting. My heart was beating hard.

I could hear the approaching roar of engines and saw the white nose of a DC-8 as it pulled up to the gate. Greeters piled up around the door. A waitress tapped me on the shoulder and I almost screamed.

"Sorry, sir," she said in a Texas accent that was thick enough to cut. "Jes wanted to ask if I could get y'all anything else."

"No," I said. "I'm fine."

"Well, that's good."

The first passengers began cutting across the terminal. They were all men wearing suits and prosperous haircuts. Of course. The first passengers to deplane were always from first class.

"Sure I can't get you a piece of peach pah? It's fresh today."

"No thanks."

"You sure, hon?"

Now the coach class passengers came in a flood, all of them festooned with carry-on bags. I heard a woman squeal. Was that Vada, greeting her brother-in-law?

"I'm sure," I said, and picked up my magazine.

She took the hint. I sat stirring the remains of my salad into an orange soup of French dressing and watched. Here came a man and woman with a baby, but the kid was almost a toddler, too old to be June. The passengers passed the restaurant, chattering with the friends and relatives who had come to pick them up. I saw a young man in an Army uniform pat his girlfriend's bottom. She laughed, slapped his hand, then stood on tiptoe to kiss him.

For five minutes or so the terminal was almost full. Then the crowd began to thin out. There was no sign of the Oswalds. A wild certainty came to me: they weren't on the plane. I hadn't just traveled back in time, I had bounced into some sort of parallel universe. Maybe the Yellow Card Man had been meant to stop something like that from happening, but the Yellow Card Man was dead, and I was off the hook. No Oswald? Fine, no mission. Kennedy was going to die in some other version of America, but not in this one. I could catch up with Sadie and live happily ever after.

The thought had no more than crossed my mind when I saw my target for the first time. Robert and Lee were side by side, talking animatedly. Lee was swinging what was either an oversized attaché case or a small satchel. Robert had a pink suitcase with rounded corners that looked like something out of Barbie's closet. Vada and Marina came along behind. Vada had taken one of two patchwork cloth bags; Marina had the other slung over her shoulder. She was also carrying June, now four months old, in her arms and laboring to keep up. Robert and Vada's two kids flanked her, looking at her with open curiosity.

Vada called to the men and they stopped almost in front of the restaurant. Robert grinned and took Marina's carry-bag. Lee's expression was . . . amused? Knowing? Maybe both. The tiniest suggestion of a smile dimpled the corners of his mouth. His nondescript hair was neatly combed. He was, in fact, the perfect A. J. Squared Away in his pressed white shirt, khakis, and shined shoes. He didn't look like a man who had just completed a journey halfway around the world; there wasn't a wrinkle on him and not a trace of beard-shadow on his cheeks. He was just twenty-two years old, and looked younger—like one of the teenagers in my last American Lit class.

So did Marina, who wouldn't be old enough to buy a legal drink for another month. She was exhausted, bewildered, and staring at everything. She was also beautiful, with clouds of dark hair and upturned, somehow rueful blue eyes.

June's arms and legs were swaddled in cloth diapers. Even her neck was wrapped in something, and although she wasn't crying, her face was red and sweaty. Lee took the baby. Marina smiled her gratitude, and when her lips parted, I saw that one of her teeth was missing. The others were discolored, one of them almost black. The contrast with her creamy skin and gorgeous eyes was jarring.

Oswald leaned close to her and said something that wiped the smile off her face. She looked up at him warily. He said something else, poking her shoulder with one finger as he did so. I remembered Al's story, and wondered if Oswald was saying the same thing to his wife now: *pokhoda, cyka*—walk, bitch.

But no. It was the swaddling that had upset him. He tore it away—first from the arms, then the legs—and flung the diapers at Marina, who caught them clumsily. Then she looked around to see if they were being watched.

Vada came back and touched Lee's arm. He paid no attention to her, just unwrapped the makeshift cotton scarf from around baby June's neck and flung *that* at Marina. It fell to the terminal floor. She bent and picked it up without speaking.

Robert joined them and gave his brother a friendly punch on the shoulder. The terminal had almost entirely cleared out now—the last of the deplaning passengers had passed the Oswald family— and I heard what he said clearly. "Give her a break, she just got here. She doesn't even know where here is yet."

"Look at this kid," Lee said, and raised June for inspection. At that, she finally began to cry. "She's got her wrapped up like a damn Egyptian mummy. Because that's the way they do it back home. I don't know whether to laugh or cry. *Staryj baba!* Old woman." He turned back to Marina with the bawling baby in his arms. She looked at him fearfully. *"Staryj baba!"*

She tried to smile, the way people do when they know the joke is on them, but not why. I thought fleetingly of Lennie, in *Of Mice and Men.* Then a grin, cocky and a little sideways, lit Oswald's face. It made him almost handsome. He kissed his wife gently, first on one cheek, then the other.

"USA!" he said, and kissed her again. "USA, Rina! Land of the free and home of the turds!"

Her smile became radiant. He began to speak to her in Russian, handing back the baby as he did so. He put his arm around her waist as she soothed June. She was still smiling as they left my field of vision, and shifted the baby to her shoulder so she could take his hand.

8

I went home—if I could call Mercedes Street home—and tried to take a nap. I couldn't get under, so I lay there with my hands behind my head, listening to the uneasy street noises and speaking with Al Templeton. This was a thing I found myself doing quite often, now that I was on my own. For a dead man, he always had a lot to say.

"I was stupid to come to Fort Worth," I told him. "If I try to hook up that bug to the tape recorder, someone's apt to see me. Oswald himself might see me, and that would change everything. He's already paranoid, you said so in your notes. He knew the KGB and MVD were watching him in Minsk, and he's going to be afraid that the FBI and the CIA are watching him here. And the FBI actually *will* be, at least some of the time."

"Yes, you'll have to be careful," Al agreed. "It won't be easy, but I trust you, buddy. It's why I called you in the first place."

"I don't even want to get near him. Just seeing him in the airport gave me a class-A case of the willies."

"I know you don't, but you'll have to. As someone who spent damn near his whole life cooking meals, I can tell you that no omelet was ever made without breaking eggs. And it would be a mistake to overestimate this guy. He's no super-criminal. Also, he's going to be distracted, mostly by his batshit mother. How good is he going to be at anything for awhile except shouting at his wife and knocking her around when he gets too pissed off for shouting to be enough?"

"I think he cares for her, Al. At least a little, and maybe a lot. In spite of the shouting."

"Yeah, and it's guys like him who are most likely to fuck up their women. Look at Frank Dunning. You just take care of your business, buddy."

"And what am I going to get if I do manage to hook up that bug? Tape recordings of arguments? Arguments in *Russian*? *That'll* be a big help."

"You don't need to decode the man's family life. It's George de Mohrenschildt you need to find out about. You have to make sure de Mohrenschildt isn't involved in the attempt on General Walker. Once you accomplish that, the window of uncertainty closes. And look on the bright side. If Oswald catches you spying on him, his future actions might change in a *good* way. He might not try for Kennedy after all."

"Do you really believe that?"

"No. Actually I don't."

"Neither do I. The past is obdurate. It doesn't want to be changed."

He said, "Buddy, now you're cooking . . ."

"With gas," I heard myself muttering. "Now I'm cooking with gas."

I opened my eyes. I had fallen asleep after all. Late light was coming in through the drawn curtains. Somewhere not far away, on Davenport Street in Fort Worth, the Oswald brothers and their wives would be sitting down to dinner—Lee's first meal back on his old stomping grounds.

Outside my own little bit of Fort Worth, I could hear a skip-rope chant. It sounded very familiar. I got up, went through my dim living room (furnished with two thrift-shop easy chairs but nothing else), and twitched back one of the drapes an inch or so. Those drapes had been my very first installation. I wanted to see; I didn't want to be seen.

2703 was still deserted, with the FOR RENT sign double-tacked to the railing of the rickety porch, but the lawn wasn't deserted. There, two girls were twirling a jump rope while a third stutter-stepped in and out. Of course they weren't the girls I'd seen on Kossuth Street in Derry—these three, dressed in patched and faded jeans instead of crisp new shorts, looked runty and underfed—but the chant was the same, only now with Texas accents.

"Charlie Chaplin went to *France*! Just to watch the ladies *dance*! Salute to the *Cap'un*! Salute to the *Queen*! My old man drives a sub-ma-rine!"

The skip-rope girl caught her foot and went tumbling into the crabgrass that served as 2703's front lawn. The other girls piled on top of her and all three of them rolled in the dirt. Then they got to their feet and went pelting away.

I watched them go, thinking *I saw them but they didn't see me. That's something. That's a start. But Al, where's my finish?*

De Mohrenschildt was the key to the whole deal, the only thing keeping me from killing Oswald as soon as he moved in across the street. George de Mohrenschildt, a petroleum geologist who speculated in oil leases. A man who lived the playboy lifestyle, mostly thanks to his wife's money. Like Marina, he was a Russian exile, but unlike her, from a noble family—he was, in fact, *Baron* de Mohrenschildt. The man who was going to become Lee Oswald's only friend during the few months of life Oswald had left. The man who was going to suggest to Oswald that the world would be much better off without a certain racist right-wing ex-General. If de Mohrenschildt turned out to be part of Oswald's attempt to kill Edwin Walker, my situation would be vastly complicated; all the nutty conspiracy theories would then be in play. Al, however, believed all the Russian geologist had done (or *would* do; as I've said, living in the past is confusing) was egg on a man who was already obsessed with fame and mentally unstable.

Al had written in his notes: *If Oswald was on his own on the night of April 10th, 1963, chances that there was another gunman involved in the Kennedy assassination seven months later drop to almost zero.*

Below this, in capital letters, he had added his final verdict: *GOOD ENOUGH TO TAKE THE SON OF A BITCH OUT.*

9

Seeing the little girls who hadn't seen me made me think of that old Jimmy Stewart suspenser, *Rear Window*. A person could see a lot without ever leaving his own living room. Especially if he had the right tools.

The next day, I went to a sporting goods store and bought a pair of Bausch & Lomb binoculars, reminding myself to be wary of sunflashes on the lenses. Since 2703 was on the east side of Mercedes Street, I thought I'd be safe enough in that regard anytime after noon. I poked the glasses through the gap in my drapes, and when I adjusted the focus knob, the crappy living room–kitchen across the way became so bright and detailed that I might've been standing in it.

The Leaning Lamp of Pisa was still on the old bureau where the kitchen utensils were stored, waiting for someone to turn it on and activate the bug. But it would do me no good unless it was hooked up to the cunning little Japanese reel-to-reel, which could record up to twelve hours on its slowest speed. I had tried it out, actually speaking into the spare bugged lamp (which made me feel like a character in a Woody Allen comedy), and while the playback was draggy, the words were understandable. All of which meant I was good to go.

If I dared to.

10

July Fourth on Mercedes Street was busy. Men with the day off watered lawns that were beyond saving—other than a few afternoon and evening thunderstorms, the weather had been hot and dry—then plopped down in lawn chairs, listening to baseball games on the radio and drinking beer. Subteen posses threw firecrackers at stray dogs and the few roving chickens. One of the latter was struck by a cherry bomb and exploded in a mass of blood and feathers. The child who tossed it was dragged screaming into one of the houses farther down the street by a mother wearing nothing but a slip and a Farmall baseball cap. I guessed by her unsteady gait that she had downed a few brewskis herself. The closest thing to fireworks came just after ten o'clock, when someone, possibly the same kid who slashed my convertible's tires, torched an old Studebaker that had been sitting abandoned in the parking lot of the Montgomery Ward warehouse for the last week or so. Fort Worth FD came to put it out, and everyone turned out to watch.

Hail Columbia.

The next morning I walked down to inspect the burned-out hulk, which sat sadly on the puddled remains of its tires. I spotted a telephone booth near one of the warehouse loading bays, and on impulse called Ellie Dockerty, getting the operator to find the number and connect me. I did it partly because I was lonely and homesick, mostly because I wanted news of Sadie.

Ellie answered on the second ring, and she seemed delighted to hear my voice. Standing there in an already roasting phone booth, with Mercedes Street sleeping off the Glorious Fourth behind me and the smell of charred car in my nostrils, that made me smile.

"Sadie's fine. I've had two postcards and a letter. She's working at Harrah's as a waitress." She lowered her voice. "I believe as a *cocktail* waitress, but the schoolboard will never hear that from me."

I visualized Sadie's long legs in a short cocktail waitress's skirt. I visualized businessmen trying to see the tops of her stockings or into the valley of her décolletage as she bent to put drinks on a table.

"She asked after you," Ellie said, and that made me smile again. "I didn't want to tell her that you'd sailed off the edge of the earth as far as anyone in Jodie knew, so I said you were busy with your book and doing fine."

I hadn't added a word to *The Murder Place* in a month or more, and on the two occasions when I'd picked up the manuscript and tried to read it, it all seemed to be written in third-century Punic. "I'm glad that she's doing well."

"Her residency requirement will be fulfilled by the end of the month, but she's decided to stay out there until the end of summer vacation. She says the tips are very good."

"Did you ask her for a picture of her soon-to-be ex-husband?"

"Just before she left. She said she has none. She believes her parents have several, but she refused to write them about it. Said they'd never given up on the marriage, and it would give them false hope. She also said she believed you were overreacting. *Wildly* overreacting was the phrase she used."

That sounded like my Sadie. Only she wasn't mine anymore. Now she was just *hey waitress, bring us another round . . . and bend a little lower this time.* Every man has a jealous-bone, and mine was twanging hard on the morning of July fifth.

"George? I have no doubt she still cares for you, and it might not be too late to clear this mess up."

I thought of Lee Oswald, who wouldn't make his attempt on General Edwin Walker's life for another nine months. "It's too early," I said.

"I beg pardon?"

"Nothing. It's good to talk to you, Miz Ellie, but pretty soon the operator's going to come on the line asking for more money, and I'm all out of quarters."

"I don't suppose you could get down this way for a burger and a shake, could you? At the diner? If so, I'll invite Deke Simmons to join us. He asks about you almost every day."

The thought of going back to Jodie and seeing my friends from the high school was probably the only thing that could have cheered me up that morning. "Absolutely. Would this evening be too soon? Say five o'clock?"

"It's perfect. We country mice eat early."

"Fine. I'll be there. My treat."

"I'll match you for it."

11

Al Stevens had hired a girl I knew from Business English, and I was touched by the way she lit up when she saw who was sitting with Ellie and Deke. "Mr. Amberson! Wow, it's great to see you! How're you doing?"

"Fine, Dorrie," I said.

"Well, order *big.* You've lost weight."

"It's true," Ellie said. "You need a good taking-care-of."

Deke's Mexican tan was gone, which told me he was spending most of his retirement indoors, and whatever weight I'd lost, he'd found. He shook my hand with a hard grip and told me how good it was to see me. There was no artifice in the man. Or in Ellie Dockerty, for that matter. Leaving this place for Mercedes Street, where they celebrated the Fourth by blowing up chickens, began to seem increasingly mad to me, no matter what I knew about the future. I certainly hoped Kennedy was worth it.

We ate hamburgers, french fries sizzling with grease, and apple pie à la mode. We talked about who was doing what, and had a laugh over Danny Laverty, who was finally writing his long-bruited book. Ellie said that according to Danny's wife, the first chapter was titled "I Enter the Fray."

Toward the end of the meal, as Deke stuffed his pipe with Prince Albert, Ellie lifted a tote she had stored under the table and produced a large book, which she passed above the greasy remains of our meal. "Page eighty-nine. And push back from that unsightly puddle of ketchup, if you please. This is strictly on loan, and I want to send it back in the same condition I received it."

It was a yearbook called *Tiger Tails,* and had come from a school a lot more fancy-schmancy than DCHS. *Tiger Tails* was bound in leather instead of cloth, the pages were thick and glossy, and the ad section at the back was easily a hundred pages thick. The institution it memorialized—*exalted* might be a better word—was Longacre Day School in Savannah. I thumbed through the uniformly vanilla senior section and thought there might be a black face or two there by the year 1990. Maybe.

"Holy joe," I said. "Sadie must have taken a pretty good whack in the wallet when she came to Jodie from here."

"I believe she was very anxious to get away," Deke said quietly. "And I'm sure she had her reasons."

I turned to page eighty-nine. It was headed LONGACRE SCIENCE DEPARTMENT. There was a corny group shot of four teachers in white lab coats holding bubbling beakers—paging Dr. Jekyll—and below it were four studio shots. John Clayton didn't look a bit like Lee Oswald, but he had the same sort of pleasantly forgettable face, and his lips were dimpled at the corners by the same suggestion of a smile. Was that the ghost of amusement or barely hidden contempt? Hell, maybe it was just the best the obsessive-compulsive bastard could do when the photographer told him to say cheese. The only distinguishing features were hollows at the temples, which almost matched the dimples at the corners of his mouth. The photo wasn't color, but his eyes were light enough to make me pretty sure they were either blue or gray.

I turned the book toward my friends. "See these indents on the sides of his head? Is that just a natural formation, like a hooked nose or a chin-dimple?"

They said "No" at exactly the same time. It was sort of comical.

"They're forceps marks," Deke said. "Made when some doc finally got tired of waiting and dragged him out of his mama. They usually go away, but not always. If his hair wasn't thinning on the sides, you wouldn't see them at all, would you?"

"And he hasn't been around, asking about Sadie?" I asked.

"No." They said it in unison again. Ellen added, "No one's been asking after her. Except for you, George. You damned fool." She smiled as people do when it's a joke, but not really.

I looked at my watch and said, "I've kept you folks long enough. I'll be heading on back."

"Want to take a stroll down to the football field before you go?" Deke asked. "Coach Borman said to bring you by, if I got a chance. He's got them practicing already, of course."

"In the cool of the evening, at least," Ellie said, getting up. "Thank God for small favors. Remember when the Hastings boy got a heatstroke three years ago, Deke? And how they thought it was a heart attack at first?"

"I can't imagine why he'd want to see me," I said. "I turned one of his prize defensemen to the dark side of the universe." I lowered my voice and whispered hoarsely, *"Theater arts!"*

Deke smiled. "Yeah, but you saved another one from maybe getting red-shirted at 'Bama. Or at least that's what Borman thinks. Because, my son, that's what Jim LaDue told him."

At first I didn't have any idea what he was talking about. Then I remembered the Sadie Hawkins, and grinned. "All I did was catch three of them passing a bottle of rotgut. I threw it over the fence."

Deke had stopped smiling. "One of those boys was Vince Knowles. Did you know he was drunk when he rolled that truck of his?"

"No." But it didn't surprise me. Cars and booze have always been a popular and sometimes lethal high school cocktail.

"Yessir. That, combined with whatever you said to those boys at the dance, got LaDue to swear off drinking."

"What *did* you say?" Ellie asked. She was fumbling her wallet out of her purse, but I was too lost in the memory of that night to argue with her about the check. *Do not fuck up your futures:* that was what I'd said. And Jim LaDue, he of the lazy I've-got-the-world-on-a-string smile, had actually taken it to heart. We never know which lives we influence, or when, or why. Not until the future eats the present, anyway. We know when it's too late.

"I don't remember," I said.

Ellie trotted off to pay the check.

I said, "Tell Miz Dockerty to keep an eye out for the man in that picture, Deke. You too. He may not come around, I'm starting to think I could've been wrong about that, but he might. And he's not wrapped too tightly."

Deke promised he would.

12

I almost didn't walk over to the football field. Jodie was particularly beautiful in the slanting light of that early July evening and I think part of me wanted to get my ass back to Fort Worth before I lost the will to go there. I wonder how much would have changed if I had skipped that little side trip? Maybe nothing. Maybe a lot.

Coach was running a final two or three plays with the special teams kids while the rest of the players sat on the bench with their helmets off and sweat trickling down their faces. *"Red two, red two!"* Coach shouted. He saw Deke and me and lifted a spread hand: *five minutes.* Then he turned back to the small and weary squad still on the field. *"One more time! Let's see you make that daring leap from no-ass to poor-ass, what do you say?"*

I looked across the field and saw a guy in a sport coat loud enough to scream. He was trotting up and down the sidelines with earphones on his head and what looked like a salad bowl in his hands. His glasses reminded me of someone. At first I couldn't make the connection, then I did: he looked a little like Silent Mike McEachern. My own personal Mr. Wizard.

"Who's that?" I asked Deke.

Deke squinted. "Damn if I know."

Coach clapped his hands and told his kids to shower up. He walked over to the bleachers and clapped me on the back. "Howza goin, Shakespeare?"

"Pretty good," I said, smiling gamely.

"Shakespeare, kick in the rear, that's what we used to say when we were kids." He laughed heartily.

"We used to say Coach, Coach, step on a roach."

Coach Borman looked puzzled. "Really?"

"Nah, just goofin witcha." And sort of wishing I'd acted on my first impulse and scooted out of town after supper. "How does the team look?"

"Aw, they good boys, they goan try hard, but it won't be the same without Jimmy. Did you see the new billboard out there where 109 splits off from Highway 77?" Only he said it *seb'ny-seb'n.*

"Too used to it to notice, I guess."

"Well, have a look on the way out, podna. Boosters done it up right. Jimmy's mama 'bout cried when she saw it. I understand I owe you a vote a thanks for gettin that young man to swear off the drinkin." He removed his cap with the big **C** on it, armed sweat from his forehead, put it back on, and sighed heavily. "Probably owe that fuckin nummie Vince Knowles a vote a thanks, too, but puttin him on my prayer list is the best I can do."

I recalled that Coach was a Baptist of the hard-shell variety. In addition to prayer lists, he probably believed all that shit about Noah's sons.

"No thanks necessary," I said. "Just doing my job."

He looked at me keenly. "You ought to still be doing it, not jerking off over some book. Sorry if that's too blunt, but it's how I feel."

"That's all right." It was. I liked him better for saying it. In another world, he might even have been right. I pointed across the field, where the Silent Mike look-alike was packing his salad bowl into a steel case. His earphones were still hanging around his neck. "Who's that, Coach?"

Coach snorted. "Think his name is Hale Duff. Or maybe it's Cale. New sports guy at the Big Damn." He was talking about KDAM, Denholm County's one radio station, a teensy sundowner that ran farm reports in the morning, country music in the afternoons, and rock after school let out. The kids enjoyed the station breaks as much as the music; there would be an explosion followed by an old cowboy type saying, "K-DAM! *That* was a big 'un!" In the Land of Ago, this is considered the height of risqué wit.

"What's that contraption of his, Coach?" Deke asked. "Do you know?"

"I know, all right," Coach said, "and if he thinks I'm gonna let him use it during a game broadcast, he's out of his sneaker. Think I want ever'one who's got a radio hearin me call my boys a bunch of goddam pussies when they can't deny the rush on third and short?"

I turned to him, very slowly. "What are you talking about?"

"I didn't believe him, so I tried it myself," the Coach said. Then, with mounting indignation: "I heard Boof Redford tellin one of the freshmen that my balls were bigger than my brains!"

"Really," I said. My heartbeat had picked up appreciably.

"Duffer there said he built it in his goddam garage," Coach grumbled. "Said when it's turned up to full gain, you can hear a cat fart on the next block. *That's* bullshit, accourse, but Redford was on the other side of the field when I heard him make his smart remark."

The sports guy, who looked all of twenty-four, picked up his steel equipment case and waved with his free hand. Coach waved back, then muttered under his breath, "The gameday I let him on my field with *that* thing will be the day I put a Kennedy sticker on my fucking Dodge."

13

It was almost dark when I got to the intersection of 77 and 109, but a bloated orange moon was rising in the east, and it was good enough to see the billboard. It was Jim LaDue, smiling with his football helmet in one hand, a pigskin in the other, and a lock of black hair tumbled heroically over his forehead. Above the picture, in star-spangled letters, was CONGRATULATIONS TO JIM LADUE, ALL-STATE QUARTERBACK 1960 AND 1961! GOOD LUCK AT ALABAMA! WE WILL NEVER FORGET YOU!

And below, in red letters that seemed to scream:

"JIMLA!"

14

Two days later, I walked into Satellite Electronics and waited while my host sold an iPod-sized transistor to a gum-chewing kid. When he was out the door (already pressing the little radio's earpiece into place), Silent Mike turned to me. "Why, it's my old pal Doe. How can I help you today?" Then, dropping his voice to a conspiratorial whisper: "More bugged lamps?"

"Not today," I said. "Tell me, have you ever heard of something called an omnidirectional microphone?"

His lips parted over his teeth in a smile. "My friend," he said, "you have once more come to the right place."

CHAPTER 18

1

I got a phone put in, and the first person I called was Ellen Dockerty, who was happy to give me Sadie's Reno address. "I have the telephone number of the rooming house where she's staying, too," Ellen said. "If you want it."

Of course I did, but if I had it, I would eventually give in to temptation and call. Something told me that would be a mistake.

"Just the address will be fine."

I wrote her a letter as soon as I hung up, hating the stilted, artificially chatty tone but not knowing how to get past it. The goddam broom was still between us. And what if she met some high-rolling sugar daddy out there and forgot all about me? Wasn't it possible? She'd certainly know how to give him a good time in bed; she had been a fast learner and was as agile there as she was on the dance floor. That was the jealous-bone again, and I finished the letter in a rush, knowing I probably sounded plaintive and not caring. Anything to tear through the artificiality and say something honest.

I miss you, and I'm sorry as hell for the way we left things. I just don't know how to make it better now. I have a job to do, and it won't be done until next spring. Maybe not even then, but I think it will be. I hope it will be. Please don't forget me. I love you, Sadie.

I signed it George, which seemed to cancel out any poor honesty I'd managed. Beneath it I added *Just in case you want to call,* and my new telephone number. Then I walked down to the Benbrook Library and posted the letter into the big blue mailbox out front. For the time being it was the best I could do.

2

There were three pictures clipped into Al's notebook, printed off various computer sites. One was of George de Mohrenschildt, wearing a banker-gray suit with a white hankie in the breast pocket. His hair was combed away from his brow and neatly parted in the accepted executive style of the time. The smile that creased his thickish lips reminded me of Baby Bear's bed: not too hard, not too soft, just right. There was no trace of the authentic crazy I would soon observe ripping his shirt open on the porch of 2703 Mercedes Street. Or maybe there *was* a trace. Something in the dark eyes. An arrogance. A touch of the old fuck-you.

The second picture was of the infamous shooter's nest, constructed of book cartons, on the sixth floor of the Texas School Book Depository.

The third was of Oswald, dressed in black, holding his mail-order rifle in one hand and a couple of leftist magazines in the other. The revolver he would use to kill Dallas police officer J. D. Tippit during his fucked-up getaway—unless I stopped him—was tucked in Ozzie's belt. This picture would be taken by Marina less than two weeks before the attempt on General Walker's life. The location was the enclosed side yard of a two-apartment building at 214 West Neely Street in Dallas.

While I marked time waiting for the Oswalds to move into the shack across the street from mine in Fort Worth, I visited 214 West Neely often. Dallas most assuredly sucked the big one, as my 2011 students were wont to say, but West Neely was in a slightly better neighborhood than Mercedes Street. It stank, of course—in 1962, most of central Texas smells like a malfunctioning refinery—but the odors of shit and sewage were absent. The street was crumbling but paved. And there were no chickens.

A young couple with three children currently lived upstairs at 214. After they moved out, the Oswalds would move in. It was the downstairs apartment that concerned me, because when Lee, Marina, and June moved in above, I wanted to be below.

In July of '62, the ground-floor apartment was occupied by two women and a man. The women were fat, slow-moving, and partial to wrinkled sleeveless dresses. One was in her sixties and walked with a pronounced limp. The other was in her late thirties or early forties. The facial resemblance pegged them as mother and daughter. The man was skeletal and wheelchair-bound. His hair was a thin white spray. A bag of cloudy pee attached to a fat catheter tube sat in his lap. He smoked constantly, tapping into an ashtray clamped to one of the wheelchair armrests. That summer I always saw him dressed in the same clothes: red satin basketball shorts that showed his wasted thighs almost to the crotch, a strap-style tee-shirt nearly as yellow as the urine in his catheter tube, sneakers held together by duct tape, and a large black cowboy hat with what appeared to be a snakeskin band. On the front of the hat were crossed cavalry swords. Either his wife or his daughter would push him out onto the lawn, where he would sit slumped beneath a tree, still as a statue. I began to lift my hand to him as I cruised slowly by, but he never raised his own in turn, although he came to recognize my car. Maybe he was afraid to return my wave. Maybe he thought he was being evaluated by the Angel of Death, who made his rounds in Dallas behind the wheel of an aging Ford convertible instead of on a black horse. In a way, I suppose that's what I was.

This trio looked like they'd been in residence awhile. Were they still going to be in residence next year, when I needed the place? I didn't know. Al's notes said nothing about them. For the time being, all I could do was watch and wait.

I picked up my new piece of equipment, which Silent Mike had crafted himself. I waited for my telephone to ring. Three times it did, and I leaped for it each time, hoping. Twice it was Miz Ellie, calling to chat. Once it was Deke, inviting me to dinner, an invitation I accepted gratefully.

Sadie didn't call.

3

On the third of August, a '58 Bel Air sedan pulled into 2703's excuse for a driveway. It was followed by a gleaming Chrysler. The Oswald brothers got out of the Bel Air and stood side by side, not talking.

I reached through the drapes long enough to run up my front window, letting in the street noise and a lackluster puff of hot, humid air. Then I ran for the bedroom and brought my new piece of equipment out from under the bed. Silent Mike had cut a hole in the bottom of a Tupperware bowl and taped the omnidirectional mike—which he assured me was top-of-the-line—into it, so it stuck up like a finger. I attached the microphone leads to the connecting points on the back of the tape recorder. There was a plug-in for headphones, which my electronics pal had also claimed were top-of-the-line.

I peered out and saw the Oswalds talking to the guy from the Chrysler. He was wearing a Stetson, a rancher's tie, and gaudy stitched boots. Better dressed than my landlord, but of the same tribe. I didn't have to hear the conversation; the man's gestures were textbook. *I know it ain't much, but then, you ain't got much. Do you, podna?* It had to be a hard scripture for a world traveler like Lee, who believed he was destined for fame, if not necessarily fortune.

There was an electrical socket in the baseboard. I plugged in the tape recorder, hoping I wouldn't give myself a shock or blow a fuse. The tape recorder's little red light went on. I donned the earphones and slipped the Tupperware bowl into the gap between the curtains. If they looked over here they'd be squinting into the sun, and thanks to the shadow cast by the eave above the window, they would see either nothing or an unremarkable white blur that might be anything. I reminded myself to cover the bowl with black friction tape, nevertheless. Always safe, never sorry.

And in any case, I could hear nothing.

Even the street sounds had become muffled.

Oh yeah, this is great, I thought. *This is just fucking brilliant. Thanks a pantload, Silent Mi—*

Then I noticed the VOL control on the tape recorder was sitting at zero. I twisted it all the way to the + mark, and was *blasted* by voices. I tore the earphones off my head with a curse, turned the VOL knob to the halfway point, and tried again. The result was remarkable. Like binoculars for the ears.

"Sixty a month strikes me as a little bit steep, sir," Lee Oswald was saying (considering the Templetons had been paying ten dollars a month less, it struck me that way, too). His voice was respectful, tinged by just a trace of Southern accent. "If we could agree on fifty-five . . ."

"I can respect a man who wants to dicker, but don't even bother trine," Snakeskin Boots said. He rocked back and forth on his stacked heels like a man who's anxious to be gone. "I gotta git what I gotta git. If I don't git it from you, I'm goan git it from someone else."

Lee and Robert glanced at each other.

"Might as well go in and have a look around," Lee said.

"This a good place on a fam'ly street," Snakeskin Boots said. "Y'all want to watch out for that first porch step, though, it needs a smidge of carpenterin. I got s'many of these places, and people is s'hard on them. That last bunch, law."

Watch it, asshole, I thought. *That's Ivy's people you're talking about.*

They went inside. I lost the voices, then got them again—faintly—when Snakeskin Boots ran up the front room window. It was the one Ivy had said the neighbors across the way could see into, and she was a hundred percent correct on that score.

Lee asked what his prospective landlord intended to do about the holes in the walls. There was no indignation in the query, no sarcasm, but no subservience, either, in spite of the *sir* appended to every sentence. It was a respectful yet flat mode of address he had probably learned in the Marines. *Colorless* was the best word for him. He had the face and voice of a man who was good at sliding through the cracks. In public, at least. It was Marina who saw his other face and heard his other voice.

Snakeskin Boots made vague promises, and absolutely guaranteed a new mattress for the big bedroom, on account of how "that last bunch had gone and stole" the one that had been in there. He reiterated that if Lee didn't want the place someone else would (as if it hadn't been standing vacant all year), then invited the brothers to inspect the bedrooms. I wondered how they would enjoy Rosette's artistic efforts.

I lost their voices, then got them again as they toured the kitchen area. I was happy to see them pass the Leaning Lamp of Pisa without a glance.

"—basement?" Robert asked.

"No basement!" Snakeskin Boots replied, booming it, as if the lack of a basement were an advantage. Apparently he thought it was. "Neighborhood like this, all they do is ship water. And the damp, law!" Here I lost the vocal track again as he opened the rear door to show them the backyard. Which was not a yard at all but an empty field.

Five minutes later they were out front again. This time it was Robert, the elder brother, who tried to dicker. He had no more success than Lee had.

"Will you give us a minute?" Robert asked.

Snakeskin Boots looked at his clunky chromed-up watch, and allowed as how he could do that. "But I got a 'pointment over on Church Street, so you fellas need to hurry on n make up your minds."

Robert and Lee walked to the rear of Robert's Bel Air, and although they pitched their voices low to keep Snakeskin Boots from hearing, when I tilted the bowl in their direction, I got most of it. Robert was in favor of looking at some more places. Lee said he wanted this one. It would do fine for a start.

"Lee, it's a hole," Robert said. "It's throwin your . . ." *Money away,* probably.

Lee said something I couldn't make out. Robert sighed and raised his hands in surrender. They went back to Snakeskin Boots, who gave Lee's hand a brief pump and praised the wisdom of his choice. He launched into the Landlord Scripture: first month, last month, damage deposit. Robert stepped in then, saying there would be no damage deposit until the walls were fixed and the new mattress was installed.

"New mattress, sure," Snakeskin Boots said. "And I'll see that step fixed so the little woman don't turn her ankle. But if'n I fix them walls right off, I'd have to boost the rent by five a month."

I knew from Al's notes that Lee was going to take the place, and still I expected him to walk away from this outrage. Instead, he took a limp wallet out of his back pocket and removed a thin sheaf of bills. He counted most of them into his new landlord's outstretched hand while Robert walked back to his car, shaking his head in disgust. His eyes turned briefly to my house across the street, then passed on, disinterested.

Snakeskin Boots flogged Lee's·hand again, then jumped into his Chrysler and drove off fast, leaving a scrunch of dust behind.

One of the jump-rope girls came barreling up on a rusty scooter. "You movin into Rosette's house, mister?" she asked Robert.

"No, he is," Robert said, and cocked a thumb at his brother.

She pushed her scooter to Lee and asked the man who was going to blow off the right side of Jack Kennedy's head if he had any kids.

"I've got a little girl," Lee said. He put his hands on his knees so he could get down to her level.

"She purty?"

"Not as pretty as you, nor as big."

"Can she jump rope?"

"Honey, she can't even walk yet." *Can't* came out *cain't.*

"Well bullpucky on her." She scooted away in the direction of Winscott Road.

The two brothers turned toward the house. This muffled them a little, but when I cranked the volume, I could still make out most of what they were saying.

"This . . . pig in a poke," Robert told him. "When Marina sees it, she'll be on you like flies on a dog-turd."

"I'll . . . Rina," Lee said. "But brother, if I don't . . . from Ma and out of that little apartment, I'm apt to kill her."

"She can be a . . . but . . . loves you, Lee." Robert walked a few steps toward the street. Lee joined him, and their voices came through clear as a bell.

"I know it, but she can't help herself. The other night when me n Rina's goin at it, she hollers at us from the foldout. She's sleeping in the livin room, you know. 'Take it easy on that, you two,' she hollers, 'it's too soon for another one. Wait until you can pay for the one you've got.'"

"I know it. She can be hard."

"She keeps *buyin* things, brother. Says they're for Rina, but shoves em up into *my* face." Lee laughed and walked back to the Bel Air. This time it was his eyes that skated across 2706, and it took all I had to hold still behind the drapes. And to hold the bowl still, too.

Robert joined him. They leaned on the back bumper, two men in clean blue shirts and workingmen's pants. Lee wore a tie, which he now pulled down.

"Listen to this. Ma goes to Leonard Brothers and comes back with all these clothes for Rina. She drags out a pair of shorts that are as long as bloomers, only paisley. 'Look, Reenie, aren't they purty?' she says." Lee's imitation of his mother's accent was savage.

"What'd Rina say?" Robert was smiling.

"She says, 'No, Mamochka, no, I thank but I no like, I no like. I like *this* way.' Then she puts her hand on her leg." Lee put the side of his hand on his own, about halfway up the thigh.

Robert's smile widened to a grin. "Bet Ma liked *that*."

"She says, 'Marina, shorts like that are for young girls who parade themselves on the streets looking for boyfriends, not for married women.' You're not to tell her where we are, brother. You are *not*. We got that straight?"

Robert didn't say anything for a few seconds. Perhaps he was remembering a cold day in November of 1960. His mama trotting after him along West Seventh, calling out, "*Stop,* Robert, don't walk so fast, I'm not done with you!" And although Al's notes said nothing on the subject, I doubted if she was done with Lee, either. After all, Lee was the son she really cared about. The baby of the family. The one who slept in the same bed with her until he was eleven. The one who needed regular checking to see if he'd started getting hair around his balls yet. Those things *were* in Al's notes. Next to them, in the margin, were two words you'd not ordinarily expect from a short-order cook: *hysterical fixation.*

"We got it straight, Lee, but this ain't a big town. She'll find you."

"I'll send her packing if she does. You can count on that."

They got into the Bel Air and drove away. The FOR RENT sign was gone from the porch railing. Lee and Marina's new landlord had taken it with him when he went.

I walked to the hardware store, bought a roll of friction tape, and covered the Tupperware bowl with it, outside and inside. On the whole, I thought it had been a good day, but I had entered the danger zone. And I knew it.

4

On August 10, around five in the afternoon, the Bel Air reappeared, this time pulling a small wooden trailer. It took Lee and Robert less than ten minutes to carry all of the Oswalds' worldly goods into the new manse (being careful to avoid the loose porch board, which had still not been fixed). During the moving-in process, Marina stood on the crabgrassy lawn with June in her arms, looking at her new home with an expression of dismay that needed no translation.

This time all three of the jump-rope girls appeared, two walking, the other pushing her scooter. They demanded to see the baby, and Marina complied with a smile.

"What's her name?" one of the girls asked.

"June," Marina said.

Then they all jumped in. "How old is she? Can she talk? Why don't she laugh? Does she have a dolly?"

Marina shook her head. She was still smiling. "Sorry, I no spik."

The three girls pelted off, yelling *"I no spik, I no spik!"* One of the surviving Mercedes Street chickens flew out of their way, squawking. Marina watched them go, her smile fading.

Lee came out on the lawn to join her. He was stripped to the waist, sweating hard. His skin was fishbelly white. His arms were thin and slack. He put an arm around her waist, then bent and kissed June. I thought Marina might point at the house and say *no like, I no like*—she had that much English down—but she only handed Lee the baby and climbed to the porch, tottering for a moment on the loose step, then catching her balance. It occurred to me that Sadie probably would have gone sprawling, then limped on a swollen ankle for the next ten days.

It also occurred to me that Marina was as anxious to get away from Marguerite as her husband was.

5

The tenth was a Friday. On Monday, about two hours after Lee had left for another day of putting together aluminum screen doors, a mud-colored station wagon pulled up to the curb in front of 2703. Marguerite Oswald was out on the passenger side almost before it stopped rolling. Today the red kerchief had been replaced by a white one with black polka dots, but the nurse's shoes were the same, and so was the look of dissatisfied pugnacity. She had found them, just as Robert had said she would.

Hound of heaven, I thought. *Hound of heaven.*

I was looking out through the crack between the drapes, but saw no point in powering up the mike. This was a story that needed no soundtrack.

The friend who had driven her—a portly gal—struggled out from behind the wheel and fanned the neck of her dress. The day was already another scorcher, but Marguerite cared nothing for that. She hustled her chauffeur around to the trunk of the station wagon. Inside was a high chair and a bag of groceries. Marguerite took the former; her friend hoisted the latter.

The jump-rope girl with the scooter came riding up, but Marguerite gave her short shrift. I heard "Scat, child!" and the jump-rope girl rode away with her lower lip pooched out.

Marguerite marched up the bald rut that served as a front walk. While she was eyeing the loose step, Marina came out. She was wearing a smock top and the kind of shorts Mrs. Oswald didn't approve of for married women. I wasn't surprised that Marina liked them. She had terrific legs. Her expression was one of startled alarm, and I didn't need my makeshift amplifier to hear her.

"No, Mamochka—Mamochka, no! Lee say no! Lee say no! Lee say—" Then a quick rattle of Russian as Marina expressed what her husband had said in the only way she could.

Marguerite Oswald was one of those Americans who believe foreigners are sure to understand you if you just speak *slowly* . . . and *very LOUDLY.*

"Yes . . . Lee . . . has . . . his . . . PRIDE!" she bugled. She climbed to the porch (deftly avoiding the bad step) and spoke directly into her daughter-in-law's startled face. "Nothing . . . wrong . . . with that . . . but he can't . . . let . . . my GRANDDAUGHTER . . . pay . . . the PRICE!"

She was beefy. Marina was willowy. "Mamochka" steamed inside without a second look. This was followed by a moment of silence, then a longshoreman's bellow.

"Where's that little CUTIE of mine?"

Deep in the house, probably in Rosette's old bedroom, June began to wail.

The woman who had driven Marguerite gave Marina a tentative smile, then went inside with the bag of groceries.

6

Lee came walking down Mercedes Street from the bus stop at five-thirty, banging a black dinnerbucket against one thigh. He mounted the steps, forgetting the bad one. It shifted; he tottered, dropped his dinnerbucket, then bent to pick it up.

That'll improve his mood, I thought.

He went in. I watched him cross the living room and put his dinnerbucket on the kitchen counter. He turned and saw the new high chair. He obviously knew his ma's modus operandi, because next he opened the rusty refrigerator. He was still peering into it when Marina came out of the baby's room. She had a diaper over her shoulder, and the binocs were good enough for me to see there was some spit-up on it.

She spoke to him, smiling, and he turned to her. He had the fair skin that's every easy blusher's bane, and his scowling face was bright red all the way to his thinning hair. He started shouting at her, pointing a finger at the refrigerator (the door still stood open, exhaling vapor). She turned to go back into the baby's room. He caught her by the shoulder, spun her around, and began to shake her. Her head snapped back and forth.

I didn't want to watch this, and there was no reason I should; it added nothing to what I needed to know. He was a beater, yes, but she was going to survive him, which was more than John F. Kennedy could say . . . or Officer Tippit, for that matter. So no, I didn't need to see. But sometimes you can't look away.

They argued it back and forth, Marina no doubt trying to explain that she didn't *know* how Marguerite had found them and that she'd been unable to keep "Mamochka" out of the house. And of course Lee finally hit her in the face, because he couldn't hit his ma. Even if she'd been there, he wouldn't have been able to raise a fist against her.

Marina cried out. He let her go. She spoke to him passionately, her hands held out. He tried to take one of them and she slapped it away. Then she raised those hands to the ceiling, dropped them, and walked out the front door. Lee started to follow her, then thought better of it. The brothers had put two ratty old lawn chairs on the porch. Marina sank into one of them. There was a scrape below her left eye, and her cheek was already starting to swell. She stared out into the street, and across it. I felt a stab of guilty fear even though my living room lights were out and I knew she couldn't see me. I was careful to remain still, though, with the binoculars frozen to my face.

Lee sat down at the kitchen table and propped his forehead on the heels of his palms. He remained that way for awhile, then heard something and went into the smaller of the bedrooms. He came out with June in his arms and began to walk her around the living room, rubbing her back, soothing her. Marina went inside. June saw her and held out her chubby arms. Marina went to them and Lee gave her the baby. Then, before she could walk away, he hugged her. She stood silently inside his arms for a moment, then shifted the baby so she could hug him back with one arm. His mouth was buried in her hair, and I was pretty sure I knew what he was saying: the Russian words for *I'm sorry.* I had no doubt that he was. He would be sorry next time, too. And the time after that.

Marina took June back into what had been Rosette's bedroom. Lee stood where he was for a moment, then went to the fridge, took something out, and began to eat it.

7

Late the following day, just as Lee and Marina were sitting down to supper (June lay on the living room floor, kicking her legs on a blan-

471

ket), Marguerite came puffing down the street from the Winscott Road bus stop. This evening she was wearing blue slacks that were unfortunate, considering the generous spread of her butt. She was toting a large cloth bag. Poking out of the top was the red plastic roof of a child's playhouse. She walked up the porch steps (once more deftly avoiding the bad one) and marched in without knocking.

I fought against the temptation to get my directional mike—this was another scene I did not need to be privy to—and lost. There's nothing so fascinating as a family argument, I think Leo Tolstoy said that. Or maybe it was Jonathan Franzen. By the time I got it plugged in and aimed through my open window at the open window across the street, the rhubarb was in full swing.

". . . wanted you to know where we were, I would have damn well *told* you!"

"Vada told me, she's a good girl," Marguerite said placidly. Lee's rage washed over her like a light summer shower. She was unloading mismatched dishes onto the counter with the speed of a black-jack dealer. Marina was looking at her with outright amazement. The playhouse sat on the floor, next to June's baby blanket. June kicked her legs and ignored it. Of course she ignored it. What's a four-month-old going to do with a playhouse?

"Ma, you have to leave us alone! You have to stop *bringing* things! I can take care of my family!"

Marina added her two cents' worth: "Mamochka, Lee say no."

Marguerite laughed merrily. " 'Lee say no, Lee say no.' Honey, Lee *always* say no, this little man been doin it all his life and it doesn't mean a thing. Ma takes care of him." She pinched his cheek, the way a mother would pinch the cheek of a six-year-old after he has done something naughty but undeniably cute. If Marina had tried that, I'm sure Lee would have knocked her block off.

At some point the jump-rope girls had drifted onto the bald excuse for a lawn. They watched the argument as attentively as Globe groundlings checking out the newest Shakespeare offering in the standing-room section. Only in the play we were watching, the shrew was going to come out on top.

"What did she make you for dinner, honey? Was it something good?"

"We had stew. *Zharkoye.* That guy Gregory sent some coupons for the ShopRite." His mouth worked. Marguerite waited. "Did you want some, Ma?"

"*Zharkoye* pretty okay, Mamochka," Marina said with a hopeful smile.

"No, I couldn't eat anything like that," Marguerite said.

"Hell, Ma, you don't even know what it is!"

It was as if he hadn't spoken. "It would upset my stomach. Besides, I don't want to be on a city bus after eight o'clock. There are too many drunk men on them after eight o'clock. Lee, honey, you need to fix that step before someone breaks a leg."

He muttered something, but Marguerite's attention had moved elsewhere. She swooped down like a hawk on a fieldmouse and grabbed June. With my binoculars, the baby's startled expression was unmistakable.

"How's my little CUTIE tonight? How's my DEAR ONE? How's my little DEVUSHKA?"

Her little devushka, scared shitless, began to scream her head off.

Lee made a move to take the baby. Marguerite's red lips peeled back from her teeth in what could have been a grin, but only if you wanted to be charitable. It looked more like a snarl to me. It must have to her son, too, because he stepped back. Marina was biting her lip, her eyes wide with dismay.

"Oooo, Junie! Junie-Moonie-SPOONIE!"

Marguerite marched back and forth across the threadbare green carpet, ignoring June's increasingly distressed wails just as she had ignored Lee's anger. Was she actually *feeding* on those wails? It looked that way to me. After awhile, Marina could bear it no longer. She got up and went to Marguerite, who steamed away from her, holding the baby to her breasts. Even from across the street I could imagine the sound of her big white nurse's shoes: *clud-clump-clud.* Marina followed her. Marguerite, perhaps feeling her point was made, at last surrendered the baby. She pointed at Lee, then spoke to Marina in her loud English instructor's voice.

"He gained weight . . . when you were staying with me . . . because I fixed him . . . all the things he LIKES . . . but he's still TOO . . . DAMN . . . SKINNY!"

Marina was looking at her over the top of the baby's head, her pretty eyes wide. Marguerite rolled her own, either in impatience or outright disgust, and put her face down to Marina's. The Leaning Lamp of Pisa was turned on, and the light skated across the lenses of Marguerite's cat's-eye glasses.

"FIX HIM . . . WHAT HE'LL EAT! NO . . . SOURED . . . CREAM! NO . . . YOGRIT! HE'S . . . TOO . . . SKINNY!"

"Skeeny," Marina said doubtfully. Safe in her mother's arms, June's weeping was winding down to watery hiccups.

"Yes!" Marguerite said. Then she whirled to Lee. "Fix that step!"

With that she left, only pausing to put a large smack on her granddaughter's head. When she walked back toward the bus stop, she was smiling. She looked younger.

8

On the morning after Marguerite brought the playhouse, I was up at six. I went to the drawn drapes and peeked out through the crack without even thinking about it—spying on the house across the street had become a habit. Marina was sitting in one of the lawn chairs, smoking a cigarette. She was wearing pink rayon pajamas that were far too big for her. She had a new black eye, and there were spots of blood on the pajama shirt. She smoked slowly, inhaling deeply and staring out at nothing.

After awhile she went back inside and made breakfast. Pretty soon Lee came out and ate it. He didn't look at her. He read a book.

That guy Gregory sent some coupons for the ShopRite, Lee had told his mother, perhaps to explain the meat in the stew, maybe just to inform her that he and Marina weren't alone and friendless in Fort Worth. That appeared to have passed unnoticed by Mamochka, but it didn't pass unnoticed by me. Peter Gregory was the first link in the chain that would lead George de Mohrenschildt to Mercedes Street.

Like de Mohrenschildt, Gregory was a Russian expat in the petroleum biz. He was originally from Siberia, and taught Russian one night a week at the Fort Worth Library. Lee discovered this and called for an appointment to ask if he, Lee, could possibly get work as a translator. Gregory gave him a test and found his Russian "passable." What Gregory was really interested in—what *all* the expats were interested in, Lee must have felt—was the former Marina Prusakova, a young girl from Minsk who had somehow managed to escape the clutches of the Russian bear only to wind up in those of an American boor.

Lee didn't get the job; Gregory hired Marina instead—to give his son Paul Russian lessons. It was money the Oswalds desperately needed. It was also something else for Lee to resent. She was tutoring a rich kid twice a week while he was stuck putting together screen doors.

The morning I observed Marina smoking on the porch, Paul Gregory, good-looking and about Marina's age, pulled up in a brand-new Buick. He knocked, and Marina—wearing heavy makeup that made me think of Bobbi Jill—opened the door. Either mindful of Lee's possessiveness or because of rules of propriety she had learned back home, she gave him his lesson on the porch. It lasted an hour and a half. June lay between them on her blanket, and when she cried, the two of them took turns holding her. It was a nice little scene, although Mr. Oswald would probably not have thought so.

Around noon, Paul's father pulled up behind the Buick. There were two men and two women with him. They brought groceries. The elder Gregory hugged his son, then kissed Marina on the cheek (the one that wasn't swollen). There was a lot of talk in Russian. The younger Gregory was lost, but Marina was found: she lit up like a neon sign. She invited them in. Soon they were sitting in the living room, drinking iced tea and talking. Marina's hands flew like excited birds. June went from hand to hand and lap to lap.

I was fascinated. The Russian émigré community had found the girl-woman who would become their darling. How could she be anything else? She was young, she was a stranger in a strange land, she was beautiful. Of course, beauty happened to be married to the beast—a surly young American who hit her (bad), and who believed passionately in a system these upper-middle-class folks had just as passionately rejected (far worse).

Yet Lee would accept their groceries with only occasional outbursts of temper, and when they came with furnishings—a new bed, a bright pink crib for the baby—he accepted these, too. He hoped the Russians would get him out of the hole he was in. But he didn't like them, and by the time he moved his family to Dallas in November of '62, he must have known his feelings were heartily reciprocated. Why *would* they like him, he must have thought. He was ideologically pure. They were cowards who had abandoned Mother Russia when she was on her knees in '43, who had licked the Germans' jackboots and then fled to the United States when the war was over, quickly embracing the American Way . . . which to Oswald meant saber-rattling, minority-oppressing, worker-exploiting crypto-fascism.

Some of this I knew from Al's notes. Most of it I saw played out on the stage across the street, or deduced from the only important conversation my lamp-bug picked up and recorded.

On the evening of August twenty-fifth, a Saturday, Marina dolled up in a pretty blue dress and popped June into a corduroy romper with appliquéd flowers on the front. Lee, looking sour, emerged from the bedroom in what had to be his only suit. It was a moderately hilarious wool box that could only have been made in Russia. It was a hot night, and I imagined he would be wringing with sweat before it was over. They walked carefully down the porch steps (the bad one still hadn't been fixed) and set off for the bus stop. I got into my car and drove up to the corner of Mercedes Street and Winscott Road. I could see them standing by the telephone pole with its white-painted stripe, arguing. Big surprise there. The bus came. The Oswalds got on. I followed, just as I had followed Frank Dunning in Derry.

History repeats itself is another way of saying the past harmonizes.

They got off the bus in a residential neighborhood on the north side of Dallas. I parked and watched them walk down to a small but handsome fieldstone-and-timber Tudor house. The carriage lamps at the end of the walk glowed softly in the dusk. There was no crabgrass on *this* lawn. Everything about the place shouted *America works!* Marina led the way to the house with the baby in her arms, Lee lagging slightly behind, looking lost in his double-breasted jacket, which swung almost to the backs of his knees.

Marina pushed Lee in front of her and pointed at the bell. He rang it. Peter Gregory and his son came out, and when June put her arms out to Paul, the young man laughed and took her. Lee's mouth twitched downward when he saw this.

Another man came out. I recognized him from the group that had arrived on the day of Paul Gregory's first language lesson, and he had been back to the Oswald place three or four times since, bringing groceries, toys for June, or both. I was pretty sure his name was George Bouhe (yes, another George, the past harmonizes in all sorts of ways), and although he was pushing sixty, I had an idea he was seriously crushing on Marina.

According to the short-order cook who'd gotten me into this, Bouhe was the one who persuaded Peter Gregory to throw the get-acquainted party. George de Mohrenschildt wasn't there, but he'd hear about it shortly thereafter. Bouhe would tell de Mohrenschildt about the Oswalds and their peculiar marriage. He would also tell de Mohrenschildt that Lee Oswald had made a scene at the party, praising socialism and the Russian collectives. *The young man strikes me as crazy,* Bouhe would say. De Mohrenschildt, a lifelong connoisseur of crazy, would decide he had to meet this odd couple for himself.

Why did Oswald blow his top at Peter Gregory's party, offending the well-meaning expats who might otherwise have helped him? I didn't know for sure, but I had a pretty good idea. There's Marina, charming them all (especially the men) in her blue dress. There's June, pretty as a Woolworth's baby picture in her charity jumper with the sewn-on flowers. And there's Lee, sweating in his ugly suit. He's keeping up with the rapid ebb and flow of Russian better than young Paul Gregory, but in the end, he's still left behind. It must have infuriated him to have to kowtow to these people, and to eat their salt. I hope it did. I hope it hurt.

I didn't linger. What I cared about was de Mohrenschildt, the next link in the chain. He would arrive onstage soon. Meanwhile, all three Oswalds were finally out of 2703, and would be until at least ten o'clock. Given that the following day was Sunday, maybe even later.

I drove back to activate the bug in their living room.

11

Mercedes Street was partying hearty that Saturday night, but the field behind *chez* Oswald was silent and deserted. I thought my key would work on the back door as well as the front, but that was a theory I never had to test, because the back door was unlocked. During my time in Fort Worth, I never once used the key I'd purchased from Ivy Templeton. Life is full of ironies.

The place was heartbreakingly neat. The high chair had been placed between the parents' seats at the little table in the kitchen where they took their meals, the tray wiped gleaming-clean. The same was true of the peeling surface of the counter and the sink with its rusty hard-water ring. I made a bet with myself that Marina would have left Rosette's jumper-clad girls and went into what was now June's room to check. I had brought a penlight and shined it around the walls. Yes, they were still there, although in the dark they were more ghostly than cheerful. June probably looked at them as she lay in her crib, sucking her bokkie. I wondered if she would remember them later, on some deep level of her mind. Crayola ghost-girls.

Jimla, I thought for no reason at all, and shivered.

I moved the bureau, attached the tapwire to the lamp's plug, and fed it through the hole I'd drilled in the wall. All fine, but then I had a bad moment. Very bad. When I moved the bureau back into place, it bumped against the wall and the Leaning Lamp of Pisa toppled.

If I'd had time to think, I would have frozen in place and the damn thing would have shattered on the floor. Then what? Remove the bug and leave the pieces? Hope they'd accept the idea that the lamp, unsteady to begin with, had fallen on its own? Most people would buy that, but most people don't have reason to be paranoid about the FBI. Lee might find the hole I'd drilled in the wall. If he did, the butterfly would spread its wings.

But I didn't have time to think. I reached out and caught the lamp on the way down. Then I just stood there, holding it and shaking. It was hot as an oven in the little house, and I could smell the stink of my own sweat. Would *they* smell it when they came back? How could they not?

I wondered if I were mad. Surely the smart thing would be to remove the bug . . . and then remove myself. I could reconnect with Oswald on April tenth of next year, watch him try to assassinate General Edwin Walker, and if he was on his own, I could then kill him just as I had Frank Dunning. KISS, as they say in Christy's AA meetings; keep it simple, stupid. Why in God's name was I fucking with a bugged thriftshop lamp when the future of the world was at stake?

It was Al Templeton who answered. *You're here because the window of uncertainty is still open. You're here because if George de Mohrenschildt is more than he appears, then maybe Oswald wasn't the one. You're here to save Kennedy, and making sure starts now. So put that fucking lamp back where it belongs.*

I put the lamp back where it belonged, although its unsteadiness worried me. What if Lee knocked it off the bureau himself, and saw the bug inside when the ceramic base shattered? For that matter, what if Lee and de Mohrenschildt conversed in this room, but with the lamp off and in tones too low for my long-distance mike to pick up? Then it all would have been for nothing.

You'll never make an omelet thinking that way, buddy.

What convinced me was the thought of Sadie. I loved her and she loved me—at least she had—and I'd thrown that away to come here to this shitty street. And by Christ, I wasn't going to leave without at least trying to hear what George de Mohrenschildt had to say for himself.

I slipped through the back door, and with the penlight clamped in my teeth, connected the tapwire to the tape recorder. I slid the recorder into a rusty Crisco can to protect it from the elements, then concealed it in the little nest of bricks and boards I had already prepared.

Then I went back to my own shitty little house on that shitty little street and began to wait.

12

They never used the lamp until it got almost too dark to see. Saving on the electricity bill, I suppose. Besides, Lee was a working-man. He went to bed early, and she went when he did. The first time I checked the tape, what I had was mostly Russian—and draggy Russian at that, given the super-slow speed of the recorder. If Marina tried out her English vocabulary, Lee would reprimand her. Nevertheless, he sometimes spoke to June in English if the baby was fussy, always in low, soothing tones. Sometimes he even sang to her. The super-slow recordings made him sound like an orc trying its hand at "Rockabye, Baby."

Twice I heard him hit Marina, and the second time, Russian wasn't good enough to express his rage. "You worthless, nagging cunt! I guess maybe my ma was right about you!" This was followed by the slam of a door, and the sound of Marina crying. It cut out abruptly as she turned off the lamp.

On the evening of September fourth, I saw a kid, thirteen or so, come to the Oswalds' door with a canvas sack over his shoulder. Lee, barefoot and dressed in a tee-shirt and jeans, opened up. They spoke. Lee invited him inside. They spoke some more. At one point Lee picked up a book and showed it to the kid, who looked at it dubiously. There was no chance of using the directional mike, because the weather had turned cool and the windows over there were shut. But the Leaning Lamp of Pisa was on, and when I retrieved the second tape late the following night, I was treated to an amusing conversation. By the third time I played it, I hardly heard the slow drag of the voices.

The kid was selling subscriptions to a newspaper—or maybe it was a magazine—called *Grit.* He informed the Oswalds that it had all sorts of interesting stuff the New York papers couldn't be bothered with (he labeled this "country news"), plus sports and gardening tips. It also had what he called "fiction stories" and comic strips. "You won't get *Dixie Dugan* in the *Times Herald,*" he informed them. "My mama loves Dixie."

"Well son, that's fine," Lee said. "You're quite the little businessman, aren't you?"

"Uh . . . yessir?"

"Tell me how much you make."

"I don't get but four cents on every dime, but that ain't the big thing, sir. Mostly what I like is the prizes. They're way better than the ones you get selling Cloverine Salve. Nuts to that! I goan get me a .22! My dad said I could have it."

"Son, do you know you're being exploited?"

"Huh?"

"They take the dimes. You get pennies and the promise of a rifle."

"Lee, he nice boy," Marina said. "Be nice. Leave alone."

Lee ignored her. "You need to know what's in this book, son. Can you read what's on the front?"

"Oh, yessir. It says *The Condition of the Working Class,* by Friedrik . . . Ing-gulls?"

"*Engels*. It's all about what happens to boys who think they're going to wind up millionaires by selling stuff door-to-door."

"I don't want to be no millionaire," the boy objected. "I just want a .22 so I can plink rats at the dump like my friend Hank."

"You make pennies selling their newspapers; they make dollars selling your sweat, and the sweat of a million boys like you. The free market isn't free. You need to educate yourself, son. I did, and I started when I was just your age."

Lee gave the *Grit* newsboy a ten-minute lecture on the evils of capitalism, complete with choice quotes from Karl Marx. The boy listened patiently, then asked: "So you goan buy a sup-scription?"

"Son, have you listened to a single word I've said?"

"Yessir!"

"Then you should know that this system has stolen from me just as it's stealing from you and your family."

"You broke? Why didn't you say so?"

"What I've been trying to do is explain to you *why* I'm broke."

"Well, gol-lee! I could've tried three more houses, but now I have to go home because it's almost my curfew!"

"Good luck," Marina said.

The front door squalled open on its old hinges, then rattled shut (it was too tired to thump). There was a long silence. Then Lee said, in a flat voice: "You see. That's what we're up against."

Not long after, the lamp went out.

13

My new phone stayed mostly silent. Deke called once—one of those quick howya doin duty-calls—but that was all. I told myself I couldn't expect more. School was back in, and the first few weeks were always harum-scarum. Deke was busy because Miz Ellie had unretired him. He told me that, after some grumbling, he had allowed her to put his name on the substitute list. Ellie wasn't calling because she had five thousand things to do and probably five hundred little brushfires to put out.

I realized only after Deke hung up that he hadn't mentioned Sadie . . . and two nights after Lee's lecture to the newsboy, I decided I had to talk to her. I had to hear her voice, even if all she had to say was *Please don't call me, George, it's over.*

As I reached for the phone, it rang. I picked it up and said—with complete certainty: "Hello, Sadie. Hello, honey."

14

There was a moment of silence long enough for me to think I had been wrong after all, that someone was going to say *I'm not Sadie, I'm just some putz who dialed a wrong number.* Then she said: "How did you know it was me?"

I almost said *harmonics,* and she might have understood that. But *might* wasn't good enough. This was an important call, and I didn't want to screw it up. *Desperately* didn't want to screw it up. Through most of what followed there were two of me on the phone, George who was speaking out loud and Jake on the inside, saying all the things George couldn't. Maybe there are always two on each end of the conversation when good love hangs in the balance.

"Because I've been thinking about you all day," I said. (*I've been thinking of you all summer.*)

"How are you?"

"I'm fine." *(I'm lonely.)* "How about you? How was your summer? Did you get it done?" *(Have you cut your legal ties to your weird husband?)*

"Yes," she said. "Done deal. Isn't that one of the things you say, George? Done deal?"

"I guess so. How's school? How's the library?"

"George? Are we going to talk like this, or are we going to talk?"

"All right." I sat down on my lumpy secondhand couch. "Let's talk. Are you okay?"

"Yes, but I'm unhappy. And I'm very confused." She hesitated, then said: "I was working at Harrah's, you probably know that. As a cocktail waitress. And I met somebody."

"Oh?" *(Oh, shit.)*

"Yes. A very nice man. Charming. A gentleman. Just shy of forty. His name is Roger Beaton. He's an aide to the Republican senator from California, Tom Kuchel. He's the minority whip in the Senate, you know. Kuchel, I mean, not Roger." She laughed, but not the way you do when something's funny.

"Should I be glad you met someone nice?"

"I don't know, George . . . *are* you glad?"

"No." *(I want to kill him.)*

"Roger is handsome," she said in a flat just-the-facts voice. "He's pleasant. He went to Yale. He knows how to show a girl a good time. And he's tall."

The second me would no longer keep silent. "I want to kill him."

That made her laugh, and the sound of it was a relief. "I'm not telling you this to hurt you, or make you feel bad."

"Really? Then why *are* you telling me?"

"We went out three or four times. He kissed me . . . we made out a little . . . just necking, like kids. .·. ."

(I not only want to kill him, I want to do it slowly.)

"But it wasn't the same. Maybe it could be, in time; maybe not. He gave me his number in Washington, and told me to call him if I . . . how did he put it? 'If you get tired of shelving books and carrying a torch for the one that got away.' I think that was the gist of it. He says he's going places, and that he needs a good woman to go with him. He thought I might be that woman. Of course, men say stuff like that. I'm not as naïve as I once was. But sometimes they mean it."

"Sadie . . ."

"Still, it wasn't quite the same." She sounded thoughtful, absent, and for the first time I wondered if something other than doubt about her personal life might be wrong with her. If she might be sick. "On the plus side, there was no broom in evidence. Of course, sometimes men hide the broom, don't they? Johnny did. You did, too, George."

"Sadie?"

"Yes?"

"Are *you* hiding a broom?"

There was a long moment of silence. Much longer than the one when I had answered the phone with her name, and much longer than I expected. At last she said, "I don't know what you mean."

"You don't sound like yourself, that's all."

"I told you, I'm very confused. And I'm sad. Because you're still not ready to tell me the truth, are you?"

"If I could, I would."

"You know something interesting? You have good friends in Jodie—not just me—and none of them know where you live."

"Sadie—"

"You say it's Dallas, but you're on the Elmhurst exchange, and Elmhurst is Fort Worth."

I'd never thought of that. What else hadn't I thought of?

"Sadie, all I can tell you is that what I'm doing is very impor—"

"Oh, I'm sure it is. And what Senator Kuchel's doing is very important, too. Roger was at pains to tell me that, and to tell me that if I . . . I joined him in Washington, I would be more or less sitting at the feet of greatnesss . . . or in the doorway to history . . . or something like that. Power excites him. It was one of the few things it was hard to like about him. What I thought—what I still think—is, who am I to sit at the feet of greatness? I'm just a divorced librarian."

"Who am I to stand in the doorway to history?" I said.

"What? What did you say, George?"

"Nothing, hon."

"Maybe you better not call me that."

"Sorry." *(I'm not.)* "What exactly are we talking about?"

"You and me and whether or not that still makes an *us*. It would help if you could tell me why you're in Texas. Because I *know* you didn't come to write a book or teach school."

"Telling you could be dangerous."

"We're *all* in danger," she said. "Johnny's right about that. Will I tell you something Roger told me?"

"All right." *(Where did he tell you, Sadie? And were the two of you vertical or horizontal when the conversation took place?)*

"He'd had a drink or two, and he got gossipy. We were in his hotel room, but don't worry—I kept my feet on the floor and all my clothes on."

"I wasn't worrying."

"If you weren't, I'm disappointed in you."

"All right, I was worried. What did he say?"

"He said there's a rumor that there's going to be some sort of major deal in the Caribbean this fall or winter. A flashpoint, he called it. I'm assuming he meant Cuba. He said, 'That idiot JFK is going to put us all in the soup just to show he's got balls.'"

I remembered all the end-of-the-world crap her former husband had poured into her ears. *Anyone who reads the paper can see it coming,* he'd told her. *We'll die with sores all over our bodies, and coughing up our lungs.* Stuff like that leaves an impression, especially when spoken in tones of dry scientific certainty. Leaves an impression? A scar, more like it.

"Sadie, that's crap."

"Oh?" She sounded nettled. "I suppose you have the inside scoop and Senator Kuchel doesn't?"

"Let's say I do."

"Let's not. I'll wait for you to come clean a little longer, but not much. Maybe just because you're a good dancer."

"Then let's go dancing!" I said a little wildly.

"Goodnight, George."

And before I could say anything else, she hung up.

15

I started to call her back, but when the operator said "Number, please?" sanity reasserted itself. I put the phone back in its cradle. She had said what she needed to say. Trying to get her to say more would only make things worse.

I tried to tell myself that her call had been nothing but a strata-gem to get me off the dime, a *speak for yourself, John Alden* kind of thing. It wouldn't work because that wasn't Sadie. It had seemed more like a cry for help.

I picked up the phone again, and this time when the operator asked for a number, I gave her one. The phone rang twice on the other end, and then Ellen Dockerty said, "Yes? Who is it, please?"

"Hi, Miz Ellie. It's me. George."

Maybe that moment-of-silence thing was catching. I waited. Then she said, "Hello, George. I've been neglecting you, haven't I? It's just that I've been awfully—"

"Busy, sure. I know what the first week or two's like, Ellie. I called because Sadie just called me."

"Oh?" She sounded very cautious.

"If you told her my number was on a Fort Worth exchange instead of Dallas, it's okay."

"I wasn't gossiping. I hope you understand that. I thought she had a right to know. I care for Sadie. Of course I care for you, too, George . . . but you're gone. She's not."

I *did* understand, although it hurt. The feeling of being in a space capsule bound for the outer depths recurred. "I'm fine with that, Ellie, and it really wasn't much of a fib. I expect to be moving to Dallas soon."

No response, and what could she say? *Perhaps you are, but we both know you're a bit of a liar?*

"I didn't like the way she sounded. Does she seem all right to you?"

"I'm not sure I want to answer that question. If I said no, you might come roaring down to see her, and she doesn't want to see you. Not as things stand."

Actually she *had* answered my question. "Was she okay when she came back?"

"She was fine. Glad to see us all."

"But now she sounds distracted and says she feels sad."

"Is that so surprising?" Miz Ellie spoke with asperity. "There are lots of memories here for Sadie, many of them connected to a man she still has feelings for. A nice man and a lovely teacher, but one who arrived flying false colors."

That one *really* hurt.

"It seemed like something else. She spoke about some sort of coming crisis that she heard about from—" From the Yalie who was sitting in the doorway of history? "From someone she met in Nevada. Her husband filled her head with a lot of nonsense—"

"Her head? Her pretty little head?" Not just asperity now; outright anger. It made me feel small and mean. "George, I have a stack of folders a mile high in front of me, and I need to get to them. You cannot psychoanalyze Sadie Dunhill at long distance, and I cannot help you with your love life. The only thing I can do is to advise you to come clean if you care for her. Sooner rather than later."

"You haven't seen her husband around, I suppose?"

"*No!* Goodnight, George!"

For the second time that night, a woman I cared about hung up on me. That was a new personal record.

I went into the bedroom and began to undress. *Fine* when she arrived. *Glad* to be back with all her Jodie friends. Not so fine now.

Because she was torn between the handsome, on-the-fast-track-to-success new guy and the tall dark stranger with the invisible past? That would probably be the case in a romance novel, but if it was the case here, why hadn't she been down at the mouth when she came back?

An unpleasant thought occurred to me: maybe she was drinking. A lot. Secretly. Wasn't it possible? My wife had been a secret heavy drinker for years—before I married her, in fact—and the past harmonizes with itself. It would be easy to dismiss that, to say that Miz Ellie would have spotted the signs, but drunks can be clever. Sometimes it's years before people start to get wise. If Sadie was showing up for work on time, Ellie might not notice that she was doing so with bloodshot eyes and mints on her breath.

The idea was probably ridiculous. All my suppositions were suspect, each one colored by how much I still cared for Sadie.

I lay back on my bed, looking up at the ceiling. In the living room, the oil stove gurgled—it was another cool night.

Let it go, buddy, Al said. *You have to. Remember, you're not here to get—*

The girl, the gold watch, and everything. Yeah, Al, got it.

Besides, she's probably fine. You're the one with the problem.

More than just one, actually, and it was a long time before I fell asleep.

16

The following Monday, when I made one of my regular drive-bys of 214 West Neely Street in Dallas, I observed a long gray funeral hack parked in the driveway. The two fat ladies were standing on the porch, watching a couple of men in dark suits lift a stretcher into the rear. On it was a sheeted form. On the tottery-looking balcony above the porch, the young couple from the upstairs apartment was also watching. Their youngest child was sleeping in his mother's arms.

The wheelchair with the ashtray clamped to the arm stood orphaned under the tree where the old man had spent most of his days last summer.

I pulled over and stood by my car until the hearse left. Then (although I realized the timing was rather, shall we say, crass) I crossed the street and walked up the path to the porch. At the foot of the stairs, I tipped my hat. "Ladies, I'm very sorry for your loss."

The older of the two—the wife who was now a widow, I assumed—said: "You've been here before."

Indeed I have, I thought of saying. *This thing is bigger than pro football.*

"He saw you." Not accusing; just stating a fact.

"I've been looking for an apartment in this neighborhood. Will you be keeping this one?"

"No," the younger one said. "He had some *in*-surance. Bout the only thing he did have. 'Cept for some medals in a box." She sniffed. I tell you, it broke my heart a little to see how grief-stricken those two ladies were.

"He said you was a ghost," the widow told me. "He said he could see right through you. Accourse he was as crazy as a shit-house mouse. Last three years, ever since he had his stroke and they put him on that peebag. Me n Ida's goin back to Oklahoma."

Try Mozelle, I thought. *That's where you're supposed to go when you give up your apartment.*

"What do you want?" the younger one asked. "We got to take him a suit on down to the funeary home."

"I'd like the number of your landlord," I said.

The widow's eyes gleamed. "What'd it be worth to you, mister?"

"I'll give it to you for free!" said the young woman on the second-floor balcony.

The bereaved daughter looked up and told her to shut her fucking mouth. That was the thing about Dallas. Derry, too.

Neighborly.

CHAPTER 19

1

George de Mohrenschildt made his grand entrance on the afternoon of September fifteenth, a dark and rainy Saturday. He was behind the wheel of a coffee-colored Cadillac right out of a Chuck Berry song. With him was a man I knew, George Bouhe, and one I didn't—a skinny whip of a guy with a fuzz of white hair and the ramrod back of a fellow who's spent a good deal of time in the military and is still happy about it. De Mohrenschildt went around to the back of the car and opened the trunk. I dashed to get the distance mike.

When I came back with my gear, Bouhe had a folded-up playpen under his arm, and the military-looking guy had an armload of toys. De Mohrenschildt was empty-handed, and mounted the steps in front of the other two with his head up and his chest thrown out. He was tall and powerfully built. His graying hair was combed slantwise back from his broad forehead in a way that said—to me, at least—*look on my works, ye mighty, and despair. For I am GEORGE.*

I plugged in the tape recorder, put on the headphones, and tilted the mike-equipped bowl across the street.

Marina was out of sight. Lee was sitting on the couch, reading a thick paperback by the light of the lamp on the bureau. When he heard footsteps on the porch, he looked up with a frown and tossed his book on the coffee table. *More goddam expats,* he might have been thinking.

But he went to answer the knock. He held out his hand to the silver-haired stranger on his porch, but de Mohrenschildt surprised him—and me—by pulling Lee into his arms and bussing him on both cheeks. Then he held him back by the shoulders. His voice was deep and accented—German rather than Russian, I thought. "Let me look at a young man who has journeyed so far and come back with his ideals intact!" Then he pulled Lee into another hug. Oswald's head just showed above the bigger man's shoulder, and I saw something even more surprising: Lee Harvey Oswald was smiling.

2

Marina came out of the baby's room with June in her arms. She exclaimed with pleasure when she saw Bouhe, and thanked him for the playpen and what she called, in her stilted English, the "child's playings." Bouhe introduced the skinny man as Lawrence Orlov—*Colonel* Lawrence Orlov, if you please—and de Mohrenschildt as "a friend of the Russian community."

Bouhe and Orlov went to work setting the playpen up in the middle of the floor. Marina stood with them, chatting in Russian. Like Bouhe, Orlov couldn't seem to take his eyes off the young Russian mother. Marina was wearing a smock top and shorts showcasing legs that went up forever. Lee's smile was gone. He was retreating into his usual gloom.

Only de Mohrenschildt wouldn't let him. He spotted Lee's paperback, sprang to the coffee table, and picked it up. "*Atlas Shrugged?*" Speaking just to Lee. Completely ignoring the others, who were admiring the new playpen. "Ayn Rand? What is a young revolutionary doing with *this*?"

"Know your enemy," Lee said, and when de Mohrenschildt burst into a hearty roar of laughter, Lee's smile resurfaced.

"And what do you make of Miss Rand's cri de coeur?" That struck a chord when I played the tape back. I listened to the comment twice before it clicked: it was almost exactly the same phrase Mimi Corcoran had used when asking me about *The Catcher in the Rye*.

"I think she's swallowed the poison bait," Oswald said. "Now she's making money by selling it to other people."

"Exactly, my friend. I've never heard it put better. There will come a day when the Rands of the world will answer for their crimes. Do you believe that?"

"I know it," Lee said. He spoke matter-of-factly.

De Mohrenschildt patted the couch. "Sit by me. I want to hear of your adventures in the homeland."

But first Bouhe and Orlov approached Lee and de Mohrenschildt. There was a lot of back and forth in Russian. Lee looked dubious, but when de Mohrenschildt said something to him, also in Russian, Lee nodded and spoke briefly to Marina. The way he flicked his hand at the door made it pretty clear: *Go on, then, go.*

De Mohrenschildt tossed his car keys to Bouhe, who fumbled them. De Mohrenschildt and Lee exchanged a look of shared amusement as Bouhe grubbed them off the dirty green carpet. Then they left, Marina carrying the baby in her arms, and drove off in de Mohrenschildt's boat of a Cadillac.

"Now we have peace, my friend," de Mohrenschildt said. "And the men will open their wallets, which is good, yes?"

"I get tired of them always opening their wallets," Lee said. "Rina's starting to forget that we didn't come back to America just to buy a damn freezer and a bunch of dresses."

De Mohrenschildt waved this away. "Sweat from the back of the capitalist hog. Man, isn't it enough that you live in this depressing place?"

Lee said, "It sure idn't much, is it?"

De Mohrenschildt clapped him on the back almost hard enough to knock the smaller man off the couch. "Cheer up! What you take now, you give back a thousandfold later. Isn't that what you believe?" And when Lee nodded: "Now tell me how things stand in Russia, Comrade—may I call you Comrade, or have you repudiated that form of address?"

"You can call me anything but late to dinner," Oswald said, and laughed. I could see him opening to de Mohrenschildt the way a flower opens to the sun after days of rain.

Lee talked about Russia. He was long-winded and pompous. I wasn't very interested in his rap about how the Communist bureaucracy had hijacked all the country's wonderful prewar socialist ideals (he passed over Stalin's Great Purge in the thirties). Nor was I interested in his judgment that Nikita Khrushchev was an idiot; you could hear the same idle bullshit about American leaders in any barbershop or shoeshine parlor right here. Oswald might be going to change the course of history in a mere fourteen months, but he was a bore.

What interested me was the way de Mohrenschildt listened. He did it as the world's more charming and magnetic people do, always asking the right question at the right time, never fidgeting or taking his eyes from the speaker's face, making the other guy feel like the most knowledgeable, brilliant, and intellectually savvy person on the planet. This might have been the first time in his life that Lee had been listened to in such a way.

"There's only one hope for socialism that I see," Lee finished, "and that's Cuba. There the revolution is still pure. I hope to go there one day. I may become a citizen."

De Mohrenschildt nodded gravely. "You could do far worse. I have been, many times, before the current administration made it difficult to travel there. It is a beautiful country . . . and now, thanks to Fidel, it's a beautiful country that belongs to the people who live there."

"I know it." Lee's face was shining.

"But!" De Mohrenschildt raised a lecturely finger. "If you believe the American capitalists will let Fidel, Raul, and Che work their magic without interference, you're living in a dream-world. Already the wheels are turning. You know this fellow Walker?"

My ears pricked up.

"*Edwin* Walker? The general who got fired?" Lee said it *fard*.

"The very one."

"I know him. Lives in Dallas. Ran for governor and got his ass kicked. Then he goes over to Miss'sippi to stand with Ross Barnett when James Meredith integrated Ole Miss. He's just another segregationist little Hitler."

"A racist, certainly, but for him the segregationist cause and the Klan bobos are just a blind. He sees the push for Negro rights as a club to beat at the socialist principles that so haunt him and his ilk. James Meredith? A communist! The N-double-A-C-P? A front! SNCC? Black on top, red inside!"

"Sure," Lee said, "it's how they work."

I couldn't tell if de Mohrenschildt was actually invested in the things he was saying or if he was just winding Lee up for the hell of it. "And what do the Walkers and the Barnetts and the capering revivalist preachers like Billy Graham and Billy James Hargis see as the beating heart of this evil nigger-loving communist monster? Russia!"

"I know it."

"And where do they see the grasping hand of communism just ninety miles from the shores of the United States? Cuba! Walker no longer wears the uniform, but his best friend does. Do you know who I'm talking about?"

Lee shook his head. His eyes never left de Mohrenschildt's face.

"Curtis LeMay. Another racist who sees communists behind every bush. What do Walker and LeMay insist that Kennedy do? Bomb Cuba! Then invade Cuba! Then make Cuba the fifty-first state! Their humiliation at the Bay of Pigs has only made them more determined!" De Mohrenschildt made his own exclamation marks by pounding his fist on his thigh. "Men like LeMay and Walker are far more dangerous than the Rand bitch, and not because they have guns. Because they have *followers*."

"I know the danger," Lee said. "I've started organizing a Hands Off Cuba group here in Fort Worth. I've got a dozen people interested already."

That was bold. To the best of my knowledge, the only thing Lee had been organizing in Fort Worth was a passel of aluminum screen doors, plus the backyard clothes-whirligig on the few occasions when Marina could persuade him to hang the baby's diapers on it.

"You'd better work fast," de Mohrenschildt said grimly. "Cuba's a billboard for revolution. When the suffering people of Nicaragua and Haiti and the Dominican Republic look at Cuba, they see a peaceful agrarian socialist society where the dictator has been overturned and the secret police have been sent packing, sometimes with their truncheons stuck up their fat asses!"

Lee squalled laughter.

"They see the great sugar plantations and the slave-labor farms of United Fruit turned over to the farmers. They see Standard Oil sent packing. They see the casinos, all run by the Lansky Mob—"

"I know it," Lee said.

"—shut down. The donkey-shows have stopped, my friend, and the women who used to sell their bodies . . . and their *daughters'* bodies—have found honest work again. A peon who would have died in the streets under the pig Batista can now go to a hospital and be treated like a man. And why? Because under Fidel, the doctor and the peon stand as equals!"

"I know it," Lee said. It was his default position.

De Mohrenschildt leaped from the couch and began to pace around the new playpen. "Do you think Kennedy and his Irish cabal will let that billboard stand? That *lighthouse,* flashing its message of hope?"

"I sort of like Kennedy," Lee said, as if embarrassed to admit it. "In spite of the Bay of Pigs. That was Eisenhower's plan, you know."

"Most of the GSA likes President Kennedy. Do you know what I mean by the GSA? I can assure you that the rabid she-weasel who wrote *Atlas Shrugged* knows. Great Stupid America, that's what I mean. The citizens of the USA will live happy and die content if they have a refrigerator that makes ice, two cars in their garage, and *77 Sunset Strip* on their boob tubes. Great Stupid America loves Kennedy's *smile.* Oh yes. Yes indeed. He has a wonderful smile, I admit it. But did not Shakespeare say a man can smile, and smile, and be a villain? Do you know that Kennedy has okayed a CIA plan to *assassinate* Castro? Yes! They've already tried—and failed, thank God—three or four times. I have this from my oil contacts in Haiti and the DR, Lee, and it's good information."

Lee expressed dismay.

"But Fidel has a strong friend in Russia," de Mohrenschildt went on, still pacing. "It isn't the Russia of Lenin's dreams—or yours, or mine—but they may have their own reasons for standing with Fidel if America tries another invasion. And mark my words: Kennedy is apt to try it, and soon. He'll listen to LeMay. He'll listen to Dulles and Angleton of the CIA. All he needs is the right pretext and then he'll go in, just to show the world he's got balls."

They went on talking about Cuba. When the Cadillac returned, the rear seat was full of groceries—enough for a month, it looked like.

"Shit," Lee said. "They're back."

"And we are glad to see them," de Mohrenschildt said pleasantly.

"Stay for dinner," Lee said. "Rina's not much of a cook, but—"

"I must go. My wife is waiting anxiously for my report, and I'll give her a good one! I'll bring her next time, shall I?"

"Yeah, sure."

They went to the door. Marina was talking with Bouhe and Orlov as the two men lifted cartons of canned goods from the trunk. But she wasn't just talking; she was flirting a little, too. Bouhe looked ready to fall on his knees.

On the porch, Lee said something about the FBI. De Mohrenschildt asked him how many times. Lee held up three fingers. "One agent called Fain. He came twice. Another named Hosty."

"Look them right in the eye and answer their questions!" de Mohrenschildt said. "You have nothing to fear, Lee, not just because you are innocent, but because you are in the right!"

The others were looking at him now . . . and not just them. The jump-rope girls had appeared, standing in the rut that served as a sidewalk on our block of Mercedes Street. De Mohrenschildt had an audience, and was declaiming to it.

"You are ideologically dedicated, young Mr. Oswald, so of course they come. The Hoover Gang! For all we know, they're watching now, perhaps from down the block, perhaps from that house right across the street!"

De Mohrenschildt stabbed his finger at my drawn drapes. Lee turned to look. I stood still in the shadows, glad I'd put down the sound-enhancing Tupperware bowl, even though it was now coated with black tape.

"I know who they are. Haven't they and their CIA first cousins been to visit me on many occasions, trying to browbeat me into informing on my Russian and South American friends? After the war, didn't they call me a closet Nazi? Haven't they claimed I hired the *tonton macoute* to beat and torture my competitors for oil leases in Haiti? Didn't they accuse me of bribing Papa Doc and paying for the Trujillo assassination? Yes, yes, all of that and more!"

The jump-rope girls were staring at him with their mouths open. So was Marina. Once he got going, George de Mohrenschildt swept everything before him.

"Be courageous, Lee! When they come, stand forward! Show them this!" He grasped his shirt and tore it open. Buttons popped off and clattered to the porch. The jump-rope girls gasped, too shocked to giggle. Unlike most American men of that time, de Mohrenschildt wore no undershirt. His skin was the color of oiled mahogany. Fatty breasts hung on old muscle. He pounded his right fist above his left nipple. "Tell them 'Here is my heart, and my heart is pure, and my heart belongs to my cause!' Tell them 'Even if Hoover rips my heart out of me, it will still beat, and a thousand other hearts will beat in time! Then ten thousand! Then a hundred thousand! Then a million!'"

Orlov put down the box of canned goods he was holding so he could offer a round of light satiric applause. Marina's cheeks were flaming with color. Lee's face was the most interesting one. Like Paul of Tarsus on the Damascus Road, he'd had a revelation.

The blindness had dropped from his eyes.

3

De Mohrenschildt's preaching and shirt-ripping antics—not so very different from the tent-show shenanigans of the right-wing evangelists he reviled—were deeply troubling to me. I had hoped that if I could listen in on a heart-to-heart between the two men, it might go a long way toward eliminating de Mohrenschildt as a real factor in the Walker attempt, and hence the Kennedy assassination. I'd gotten the heart-to-heart, but it made things worse instead of better.

One thing seemed clear: it was time to bid Mercedes Street a not-so-fond *adieu*. I had rented the ground-floor apartment at 214 West Neely. On the twenty-fourth of September, I packed up my aging Ford Sunliner with my few clothes, my books, and my typewriter, and moved them to Dallas.

The two fat ladies had left behind a sickroom-stenchy pigsty. I did the cleanup myself, thanking God that Al's rabbit-hole emerged in a time when aerosol air-freshener was available. I bought a portable TV at a yard sale and plunked it down on the kitchen counter next to the stove (which I thought of as the Repository of Antique Grease). As I swept, washed, scrubbed, and sprayed, I watched crime shows like *The Untouchables* and sitcoms like *Car 54, Where Are You?* When the thumps and shouts of the kids upstairs quit for the night, I turned in and slept like the dead. There were no dreams.

I held onto my place on Mercedes Street, but didn't see much at 2703. Sometimes Marina popped June into a stroller (another gift from her elderly admirer, Mr. Bouhe) and rolled her up to the warehouse parking lot and back again. In the afternoons, after school let out, the jump-rope girls often accompanied them. Marina even jumped herself a couple of times, chanting in Russian. The sight of her mother pogoing up and down with that great cloud of dark hair flying made the baby laugh. The jump-rope girls laughed, too. Marina didn't mind. She talked a lot with them, and never looked irritated when they giggled and corrected her. She looked pleased, in fact. Lee didn't want her to learn English, but she was learning it anyway. Good for her.

On October 2, 1962, I woke to eerie silence in my Neely Street apartment: no running feet overhead, no young mother yelling at the older two to get ready for school. They had moved out in the middle of the night.

I went upstairs and tried my key on their door. It didn't work, but the lock was of the spring variety and I popped it easily with a coathanger. I spied an empty bookcase in the living room. I drilled a small hole in the floor, plugged in the second bugged lamp, and fed the tapwire through the hole and into my downstairs apartment. Then I moved the bookcase over it.

The bug worked fine, but the reels of the cunning little Japanese tape recorder only turned when prospective tenants came to look at the apartment and happened to try the lamp. There were lookers, but no takers. Until the Oswalds moved in, I had the Neely Street address entirely to myself. After the bumptious carnival that was Mercedes Street, that was a relief, although I kind of missed the jump-rope girls. They were my Greek chorus.

4

I slept in my Dallas apartment at night and watched Marina stroll the baby in Fort Worth by day. While I was so occupied, another sixties watershed moment was approaching, but I ignored it. I was preoccupied with the Oswalds, who were undergoing another domestic spasm.

Lee came home early from work one day during the second week of October. Marina was out walking June. They spoke at the foot of the driveway across the street. Near the end of the conversation, Marina spoke in English. "Vut is *lay-doff* mean?"

He explained in Russian. Marina spread her hands in a what-can-you-do gesture, and hugged him. Lee kissed her cheek, then took the baby out of the stroller. June laughed as he held her high over his head, her hands reaching down to tug at his hair. They went inside together. Happy little family, bearing up under temporary adversity.

That lasted until five in the afternoon. I was getting ready to drive back to Neely Street when I spied Marguerite Oswald approaching from the bus stop on Winscott Road.

Here comes trouble, I thought, and how right I was.

Once again Marguerite avoided the still unrepaired ha-ha step; once more she entered without knocking; fireworks followed immediately. It was a warm evening and the windows were open over there. I didn't bother with the distance mike. Lee and his mother argued at full volume.

He hadn't been laid off from his job at Leslie Welding after all, it seemed; he had just walked away. The boss called Vada Oswald, looking for him because they were shorthanded, and when he got no help from Robert's wife, he called Marguerite.

"I *lied* for you, Lee!" Marguerite shouted. "I said you had the flu! Why do you always make me lie for you?"

"I don't make you do nothing!" he shouted back. They were standing nose-to-nose in the living room. "I don't make you do nothing, and you do it anyway!"

"Lee, how are you going to support your family? You need a job!"

"Oh, I'll get a job! Don't you worry about that, Ma!"

"Where?"

"I don't know—"

"Oh, *Lee*! How'll you pay the rent?"

"—but she's got plenty of friends." He jerked a thumb at Marina, who flinched. "They aren't good for much, but they'll be good for that. You need to get out of here, Ma. Go back home. Let me catch my breath."

Marguerite darted to the playpen. "Where'd this here come from?"

"The friends I told you about. Half of em's rich and the rest are trying. They like to talk to Rina." Lee sneered. "The older ones like to ogle her tits."

501

STEPHEN KING

"Lee!" Shocked voice, but a look on her face that was . . . pleased? Was Mamochka pleased at the fury she heard in her son's voice?

"Go on, Ma. Give us some peace."

"Does she understand that men who give things always want things in return? Does she, Lee?"

"Get the hell out!" Shaking his fists. Almost dancing in his impotent rage.

Marguerite smiled. "You're upset. Of course you are. I'll come back when you're feeling more in control of yourself. And I'll help. I always want to help."

Then, abruptly, she rushed at Marina and the baby. It was as if she meant to attack them. She covered June's face with kisses, then strode across the room. At the door, she turned and pointed at the playpen. "Tell her to scrub that down, Lee. People's cast-offs always have germs. If the baby gets sick, you'll never be able to afford the doctor."

"Ma! *Go!*"

"I am just now." Calm as cookies and milk. She twiddled her fingers in a girlish ta-ta gesture, and off she went.

Marina approached Lee, holding the baby like a shield. They talked. Then they shouted. Family solidarity was gone with the wind; Marguerite had seen to that. Lee took the baby, rocked her in the crook of one arm, then—with absolutely no warning—punched his wife in the face. Marina went down, bleeding from the mouth and nose and crying loudly. Lee looked at her. The baby was also crying. Lee stroked June's fine hair, kissed her cheek, rocked her some more. Marina came back into view, struggling to her feet. Lee kicked her in the side and down she went again. I could see nothing but the cloud of her hair.

Leave him, I thought, even though I knew she wouldn't. *Take the baby and leave him. Go to George Bouhe. Warm his bed if you have to, but get away from that skinny, mother-ridden monster posthaste.*

But it was Lee who left her, at least temporarily. I never saw him on Mercedes Street again.

5

It was their first separation. Lee went to Dallas to look for work. I don't know where he stayed. According to Al's notes it was the Y, but that turned out to be wrong. Maybe he found a place in one of the cheap rooming houses downtown. I wasn't concerned. I knew they'd show up together to rent the apartment above me, and for the time being, I'd had enough of him. It was a treat not to have to listen to his slowed-down voice saying *I know it* a dozen times in every conversation.

Thanks to George Bouhe, Marina landed on her feet. Not long after Marguerite's visit and Lee's decampment, Bouhe and another man arrived in a Chevy truck and moved her out. When the pickup left 2703 Mercedes, mother and daughter were riding in the bed. The pink suitcase Marina had brought from Russia had been lined with blankets, and June lay fast asleep in this make-shift nest. Marina put a steadying hand on the little girl's chest as the truck started rolling. The jump-rope girls were watching, and Marina waved to them. They waved back.

6

I found George de Mohrenschildt's address in the Dallas White Pages and followed him several times. I was curious about whom he might meet, although if it were a CIA man, a minion of the Lansky Mob, or some other possible conspirator, I doubt I would have known it. All I can say is that he met no one that seemed suspicious to me. He went to work; he went to the Dallas Country Club, where he played tennis or swam with his wife; they went out to a couple of strip clubs. He didn't bother the dancers, but had a penchant for fondling his wife's boobs and butt in public. She didn't seem to mind.

On two occasions he met with Lee. Once it was at de Mohrenschildt's favorite strip club. Lee seemed uncomfortable with the milieu, and they didn't stay long. The second time they had lunch in a Browder Street coffee shop. There they remained until almost two in the afternoon, talking over endless cups of coffee. Lee started to get up, reconsidered, and ordered something else. The waitress brought him a piece of pie, and he handed her something, which she put in her apron pocket after a cursory glance. Instead of following when they left, I approached the waitress and asked if I could see what the young man had given her.

"You c'n have it," she said, and gave me a sheet of yellow paper with black tabloid letters at the top: HANDS OFF CUBA! It urged "interested persons" to join the Dallas–Fort Worth branch of this fine organization. DON'T LET UNCLE SAM DUPE YOU! WRITE TO PO BOX 1919 FOR DETAILS OF FUTURE MEETINGS.

"What did they talk about?" I asked.

"Are you a cop?"

"No, I tip better than the cops," I said, and handed her a five-dollar bill.

"That stuff," she said, and pointed at the flyer, which Oswald had undoubtedly printed off at his new place of employment. "Cuba. Like I give a shit."

But on the night of October twenty-second, less than a week later, President Kennedy was also talking about Cuba. And then everybody gave a shit.

7

It's a blues truism that you never miss your water until the well runs dry, but until the fall of 1962, I didn't realize that also applied to the patter of little feet shaking your ceiling. With the family from upstairs gone, 214 West Neely took on a creepy haunted-house vibe. I missed Sadie, and began to worry about her almost obsessively. On second thought, you can strike the almost. Ellie Dockerty and Deke Simmons didn't take my concern about her husband seriously. Sadie herself didn't take it seriously; for all I knew, she thought I was trying to scare her about John Clayton in order to keep her from pushing me entirely out of her life. None of them knew that, if you removed the Sadie part, her name was only a syllable away from Doris Dunning. None of them knew about the harmonic effect, which I seemed to be creating myself, just by my presence in the Land of Ago. That being the case, who would be to blame if something happened to Sadie?

The bad dreams started to come back. The Jimla dreams.

I quit keeping tabs on George de Mohrenschildt and started taking long walks that began in the afternoon and didn't finish up back at West Neely Street until nine or even ten o'clock at night. I spent them thinking about Lee, now working as a photoprint trainee at a Dallas graphic arts company called Jaggars-Chiles-Stovall. Or about Marina, who had taken up temporary residence with a newly divorced woman named Elena Hall. The Hall woman worked for George Bouhe's dentist, and it was the dentist who had been behind the wheel of the pickup on the day Marina and June moved out of the dump on Mercedes Street.

Mostly what I thought about was Sadie. And Sadie. And Sadie.

On one of those strolls, feeling thirsty as well as depressed, I stopped into a neighborhood watering hole called the Ivy Room and ordered a beer. The jukebox was off and the patrons were unusually silent. When the waitress put my beer in front of me and immediately turned to face the TV over the bar, I realized that everyone was watching the man I had come to save. He was pale and grave. There were dark circles under his eyes.

"To halt this offensive buildup, a strict quarantine of all offensive equipment under shipment to Cuba is being initiated. All ships of any kind bound for Cuba, if found to contain cargoes of offensive weapons, will be turned back."

"Christ Jesus!" said a man in a cowboy hat. "What does he think the Russkies are goan do about *that*?"

"Shut up, Bill," the bartender said. "We need to hear this."

"It shall be the policy of this nation," Kennedy went on, "to regard any nuclear missile launched from Cuba against any nation in the Western Hemisphere as an attack by the Soviet Union on the United States, requiring a full retaliatory response upon the Soviet Union."

A woman at the end of the bar moaned and clutched her stomach. The man beside her put an arm around her, and she put her head on his shoulder.

What I saw on Kennedy's face was fright and determination in equal measure. What I also saw was *life*—a total engagement with the job at hand. He was exactly thirteen months from his date with the assassin's bullet.

"As a necessary military precaution, I have reinforced our base at Guantánamo and evacuated today the dependents of our personnel there."

"Drinks for the house on me," Bill the Cowboy suddenly proclaimed. "Because this looks like the end of the road, *amigos.*" He put two twenties beside his shot glass, but the bartender made no move to pick them up. He was watching Kennedy, who was now calling on Chairman Khrushchev to eliminate "this clandestine, reckless, and provocative threat to world peace."

The waitress who had served my beer, a rode-hard-and-put-away-wet peroxide blonde of fifty or so, suddenly burst into tears. That decided me. I got off my stool, wove my way around the tables where men and women sat looking at the television like solemn children, and slipped into one of the phone booths next to the Skee-Ball machine.

The operator told me to deposit forty cents for the first three minutes. I dropped in two quarters. The pay phone bonged mellowly. Faintly, I could still hear Kennedy talking in that nasal New England voice. Now he was accusing Soviet Foreign Minister Andrei Gromyko of being a liar. No waffling there.

"Connecting you now, sir," the operator said. Then she blurted: "Are you listening to the president? If you're not, you should turn on your TV or radio."

"I'm listening," I said. Sadie would be, too. Sadie, whose husband had spouted a lot of apocalyptic bullshit thinly coated with science. Sadie, whose Yalie politico friend had told her something big was going to pop in the Caribbean. A flashpoint, probably Cuba.

I had no idea what I was going to say to soothe her, but that wasn't a problem. The phone rang and rang. I didn't like it. Where was she at eight-thirty on a Monday night in Jodie? At the movies? I didn't believe it.

"Sir, your party does not answer."

"I know it," I said, and grimaced when I heard Lee's pet phrase coming out of my mouth.

My quarters clattered into the coin return when I hung up. I started to put them back in, then reconsidered. What good would it do to call Miz Ellie? I was in Miz Ellie's bad books now. Deke's too, probably. They'd tell me to go peddle my papers.

When I walked back to the bar, Walter Cronkite was showing U-2 photos of the Soviet missile bases that were under construction. He said that many members of Congress were urging Kennedy to initiate bombing missions or launch a full-scale invasion immediately. American missile bases and the Strategic Air Command had gone to DEFCON-4 for the first time in history.

"American B-52 bombers will soon be circling just outside the Soviet Union's borders," Cronkite was saying in that deep, portentous voice of his. "And—this is obvious to all of us who've covered the last seven years of this ever more frightening cold war—the chances for a mistake, a potentially *disastrous* mistake, grow with each new escalation of—"

"Don't wait!" a man standing by the pool table shouted. *"Bomb the living shit out of those commie cocksuckers right now!"*

There were a few cries of protest at this bloodthirsty sentiment, but they were mostly drowned in a wave of applause. I left the Ivy Room and jogged back to Neely Street. When I got there, I jumped into my Sunliner and rolled wheels for Jodie.

My car radio, now working again, broadcast nothing but a heaping dish of doom as I chased my headlights down Highway 77. Even the DJs had caught Nuclear Flu, saying things like "God bless America" and "Keep your powder dry." When the K-Life jock played Johnny Horton caterwauling "The Battle Hymn of the Republic," I snapped it off. It was too much like the day after 9/11.

I kept the pedal to the metal in spite of the Sunliner's increasingly distressed engine and the way the needle on the ENGINE TEMP dial kept creeping toward *H*. The roads were all but deserted, and I turned into Sadie's driveway at just a little past twelve-thirty on the morning of the twenty-third. Her yellow VW Beetle was parked in front of the closed garage doors, and the lights were on downstairs, but there was no answer when I rang the doorbell. I went around back and hammered on the kitchen door, also to no effect. I liked it less and less.

She kept a spare key under the back step. I fished it out and let myself in. The unmistakable aroma of whiskey hit my nose, and the stale smell of cigarettes.

"Sadie?"

Nothing. I crossed the kitchen to the living room. There was an overflowing ashtray on the low table in front of the couch, and liquid soaking into the *Life* and *Look* magazines spread out there. I put my fingers into it, then raised them to my nose. Scotch. Fuck.

"Sadie?"

Now I could smell something else that I remembered well from Christy's binges: the sharp aroma of vomit.

I ran down the short hall on the other side of the living room. There were two doors facing each other, one giving on her bedroom and the other leading to an office-study. The doors were shut, but the bathroom door at the end of the hall was open. The harsh fluorescent light showed vomit splattered on the ring of the toilet bowl. There was more on the pink tile floor and the rim of the bathtub. There was a bottle of pills standing beside the soapdish on the sink. The cap was off. I ran to the bedroom.

She was lying crosswise on the mussed coverlet, wearing a slip and one suede moccasin. The other had dropped off onto the floor. Her skin was the color of old candle wax, and she did not appear to be breathing. Then she took a huge snoring gasp and wheezed it back out. Her chest remained flat for a terrifying four seconds, then she jerked in another rattle of breath. There was another overflowing ashtray on the night table. A crumpled Winston pack, charred at one end by an imperfectly stubbed-out cigarette, lay on top of the dead soldiers. Beside the ashtray were a half-empty glass and a bottle of Glenlivet. Not much of the Scotch was gone—thank God for small favors—but it wasn't really the Scotch I was worried about. It was the pills. There was also a brown manila envelope on the table with what looked like photographs spilling out of it, but I didn't glance at them. Not then.

I got my arms around her and tried to pull her into a sitting position. The slip was silk and slithered through my hands. She thumped back onto the bed and took another of those rasping, labored breaths. Her hair flopped across one closed eye.

"Sadie, wake up!"

Nothing. I grabbed her by the shoulders, and hauled her against the head of the bed. It thumped and shivered.

"Lea me lone." Slurry and weak, but better than nothing.

"Wake up, Sadie! You have to wake up!"

I began to slap lightly at her cheeks. Her eyes remained shut, but her hands came up and tried—weakly—to fend me off.

"Wake up! Wake up, dammit!"

Her eyes opened, looked at me without recognition, then shut again. But she was breathing more normally. Now that she was sitting, that terrifying rasp was gone.

I went back to the bathroom, dumped her toothbrush out of the pink plastic glass, and turned on the cold tap. While I filled the glass, I looked at the label on the pill bottle. Nembutal. There were ten or a dozen capsules left, so it hadn't been a suicide attempt. At least not an overt one. I spilled them into the toilet, then ran back to the bedroom. She was sliding down from the sitting position I'd left her in, and with her head cocked forward and her chin down against her breastbone, her respiration had turned raspy again.

I put the glass of water on the nightstand, and froze for a second as I got a look at one of the photographs sticking out of the envelope. It could have been a woman—what remained of the hair was long—but it was hard to tell for sure. Where the face should have been, there was only raw meat with a hole near the bottom. The hole appeared to be screaming.

I hauled Sadie up, grabbed a handful of her hair, and pulled her head back. She moaned something that might have been *Don't, that hurts.* Then I threw the glass of water in her face. She jerked and her eyes flew open.

"Jor? Wha you doon here, Jor? Why-my wet?"

"Wake up. Wake up, Sadie." I began to slap her face again, but more gently now, almost patting. It wasn't good enough. Her eyes started to slip closed.

"Go . . . *way!*"

"Not unless you want me to call an ambulance. That way you can see your name in the paper. The schoolboard would love that. Upsa-daisy."

I managed to get my hands linked behind her and pulled her off the bed. Her slip rucked up, then fell back into place as she crumpled to her knees on the carpet. Her eyes flew open and she cried out in pain, but I got her on her feet. She swayed back and forth, slapping at my face with more strength.

"Get ow! Get ow, Jor!"

"No, ma'am." I put my arm around her waist and got her moving toward the door, half-leading and half-carrying her. We made the turn toward the bathroom, and then her knees came unhinged. I carried her, which was no mean feat, given her height and size. Thank God for adrenaline. I batted down the toilet ring and got her seated just before my own knees gave out. I was gasping for breath, partly from effort, mostly from fright. She started to tilt toward starboard, and I slapped her bare arm—*smack.*

"Sit up!" I shouted into her face. "Sit up, Christy, goddammit!"

Her eyes fought open. They were badly bloodshot. "Who Christy?"

"Lead singer with the Rolling Fucking Stones," I said. "How long have you been taking Nembutal? And how many did you take tonight?"

"Got a scrishun," she said. "None your bi'ness, Jor."

"How many? How much did you drink?"

"Go-way."

I spun the tub's cold tap all the way, then pulled the pin that turned on the shower. She saw what I meant to do, and once again began to slap.

"No, Jor! No!"

I ignored her. This wasn't the first time that I'd put a partially dressed woman into a cold shower, and some things are like riding a bike. I lifted her over the rim of the tub in a quick clean-and-jerk I'd feel in the small of my back the next day, then held on tight as the cold water smacked her and she began to flail. She reached out to grab the towel bar, yelling. Her eyes were open now. Beads of water stood in her hair. The slip turned transparent, and even under such circumstances it was impossible not to feel a moment of lust as those curves came into full view.

She tried to get out. I pushed her back.

"Stand there, Sadie. Stand there and take it."

"H-How long? It's *cold*!"

"Until I see some color come back into your cheeks."

"W-Why are you d-d-doing this?" Her teeth were chattering.

"Because you almost killed yourself!" I shouted.

She flinched. Her feet slipped, but she grabbed the towel bar and stayed upright. Reflexes returning. Good.

"The p-p-pills weren't working, so I had a d-drink, that's all. Let me get out, I'm so cold. Please G-George, *please* let me get out." Her hair was clinging to her cheeks now, she looked like a drowned rat, but she *was* getting some color in her face. Nothing but a thin flush, but it was a start.

I turned off the shower, got my arms around her in a hug, and held her as she tottered over the lip of the tub. Water from her soaked slip pattered onto the pink bathmat. I whispered into her ear: "I thought you were dead. When I came in and saw you lying there, I thought you were fucking dead. You'll never know how that felt."

I let her go. She stared at me with wide, wondering eyes. Then she said: "John was right. R-Roger, too. He called me tonight before Kennedy's speech. From Washington. So what does it matter? By this time next week, we'll *all* be dead. Or wish we were."

At first I had no idea what she was talking about. I saw Christy standing there, dripping and bedraggled and full of bullshit, and I was utterly furious. *You cowardly bitch,* I thought. She must have seen it in my eyes, because she drew back.

That cleared my head. Could I call her cowardly just because I happened to know what the landscape looked like over the horizon?

I took a bath towel from the rack over the toilet and handed it to her. "Strip off, then dry off," I said.

"Go out, then. Give me some privacy."

"I will if you tell me you're awake."

"I'm awake." She looked at me with churlish resentment and— maybe—the tiniest glint of humor. "You certainly know how to make an entrance, George."

I turned to the medicine cabinet.

"There aren't any more," she said. "What isn't in me is in the commode."

Having been married to Christy for four years, I looked any- way. Then I flushed the toilet. With that business taken care of, I slipped past her to the bathroom door. "I'll give you three min- utes," I said.

9

The return address on the manila envelope was John Clayton, 79 East Oglethorpe Avenue, Savannah, Georgia. You certainly couldn't accuse the bastard of flying under false colors, or going the anonymous route. The postmark was August twenty-eighth, so it had probably been waiting here for her when she got back from Reno. She'd had nearly two months to brood over the contents. Had she sounded sad and depressed when I'd talked to her on the night of September sixth? Well, no wonder, given the photographs her ex had so thoughtfully sent her.

We're all in danger, she'd said the last time I spoke to her on the phone. *Johnny's right about that.*

The pictures were of Japanese men, women, and children. Victims of the atomic bomb-blasts at Hiroshima, Nagasaki, or both. Some were blind. Many were bald. Most were suffering from radiation burns. A few, like the faceless woman, had been charbroiled. One picture showed a quartet of black statues in cringing postures. Four people had been standing in front of a wall when the bomb went off. The people had been vaporized, and most of the wall had been vaporized, too. The only parts that remained were the parts that had been shielded by those standing in front of it. The shapes were black because they were coated in charred flesh.

On the back of each picture, he had written the same message in his clear, neat hand: *Coming soon to America. Statistical analysis does not lie.*

"Nice, aren't they?"

Her voice was flat and lifeless. She was standing in the doorway, bundled into the towel. Her hair fell to her bare shoulders in damp ringlets.

"How much did you have to drink, Sadie?"

"Only a couple of shots when the pills wouldn't work. I think I tried to tell you that when you were shaking and slapping me."

"If you expect me to apologize, you'll wait a long time. Barbiturates and booze are a bad combination."

"It doesn't matter," she said. "I've been slapped before."

That made me think of Marina, and I winced. It wasn't the same, but slapping is slapping. And I had been angry as well as scared.

She went to the chair in the corner, sat down, and pulled the towel tighter around her. She looked like a sulky child. "My friend Roger Beaton called. Did I tell you that?"

"Yes."

"My *good* friend Roger." Her eyes dared me to make something of it. I didn't. Ultimately, it was her life. I just wanted to make sure she *had* a life.

"All right, your good friend Roger."

"He told me to be sure and watch the Irish asshole's speech tonight. That's what he called him. Then he asked me how far Jodie was from Dallas. When I told him he said, 'That should be far enough, depending on which way the wind's blowing.' He's getting out of Washington himself, lots of people are, but I don't think it will do them any good. You can't outrun a nuclear war." She began to cry then, harsh and wrenching sobs that shook her whole body. *"Those idiots are going to destroy a beautiful world! They're going to kill children! I hate them! I hate them all! Kennedy, Khrushchev, Castro, I hope they all rot in hell!"*

She covered her face with her hands. I knelt like some old-fashioned gentleman preparing to propose and embraced her. She put her arms around my neck and clung to me in what was almost a drowner's grip. Her body was still cold from the shower, but the cheek she laid against my arm was feverish.

In that moment I hated them all, too, John Clayton most of all for planting this seed in a young woman who was insecure and psychologically vulnerable. He had planted it, watered it, weeded it, and watched it grow.

And was Sadie the only one in terror tonight, the only one who had turned to the pills and the booze? How hard and fast were they drinking in the Ivy Room right now? I'd made the stupid assumption that people were going to approach the Cuban Missile Crisis much like any other temporary international dust-up, because by the time I went to college, it was just another intersection of names and dates to memorize for the next prelim. That's how things look from the future. To people in the valley (the dark valley) of the present, they look different.

"The pictures were here when I got back from Reno." She looked at me with her bloodshot, haunted eyes. "I wanted to throw them away, but I couldn't. I kept looking at them."

"It's what the bastard wanted. That's why he sent them."

She didn't seem to hear. "Statistical analysis is his hobby. He says that someday, when the computers are good enough, it will be the most important science, because statistical analysis is never wrong."

"Not true." In my mind's eye I saw George de Mohrenschildt, the charmer who was Lee's only friend. "There's always a window of uncertainty."

"I guess the day of Johnny's super-computers will never come," she said. "The people left—if there are any—will be living in caves. And the sky . . . no more blue. Nuclear darkness, that's what Johnny calls it."

"He's full of shit, Sadie. Your pal Roger, too."

She shook her head. Her bloodshot eyes regarded me sadly. "Johnny knew the Russians were going to launch a space satellite. We were just out of college then. He told me in the summer, and sure enough, they put Sputnik up in October. 'Next they'll send a dog or a monkey,' Johnny said. 'After that they'll send a man. Then they'll send two men and a bomb.'"

"And did they do that? Did they, Sadie?"

"They sent the dog, and they sent the man. The dog's name was Laika, remember? It died up there. Poor doggy. They won't have to send up the two men and the bomb, will they? They'll use their missiles. And we'll use ours. All over a shitpot island where they make *cigars*."

"Do you know what the magicians say?"

"The—? What are you talking about?"

"They say you can fool a scientist, but you can never fool another magician. Your ex may teach science, but he's sure no magician. The Russians, on the other hand, are."

"You're not making sense. Johnny says the Russians *have* to fight, and soon, because now they have missile superiority, but they won't for long. That's why they won't back down in Cuba. It's a pretext."

"Johnny's seen too much newsreel footage of missiles being trundled through Red Square on Mayday. What he *doesn't* know— and what Senator Kuchel doesn't know, either, probably—is that over half of those missiles don't have engines in them."

"You don't . . . you can't . . ."

"He doesn't know how many of their ICBMs blow up on their launch pads in Siberia because their rocketry guys are incompetent. He doesn't know that over half the missiles our U-2 planes have photographed are actually painted trees with cardboard fins. It's sleight of hand, Sadie. It fools scientists like Johnny and politicians like Senator Kuchel, but it would never fool another magician."

"That's . . . it's not . . ." She fell silent for a moment, biting at her lips. Then she said, "How could *you* know stuff like that?"

"I can't tell you."

"Then I can't believe you. Johnny said Kennedy was going to be the nominee of the Democratic party, even though everybody else thought it was going to be Humphrey on account of Kennedy being a Catholic. He analyzed the states with primaries, ran the numbers, and he was right. He said Johnson would be Kennedy's running mate because Johnson was the only Southerner who would be acceptable north of the Mason-Dixon line. He was right about that, too. Kennedy got in, and now he's going to kill us all. Statistical analysis doesn't lie."

I took a deep breath. "Sadie, I want you to listen to me. Very carefully. Are you awake enough to do that?"

For a moment there was nothing. Then I felt her nod against my upper arm.

"It's now early Tuesday morning. This standoff is going to go on for another three days. Or maybe it's four, I can't remember."

"What do you mean, you can't *remember*?"

I mean there's nothing about this in Al's notes, and my only college class in American History was almost twenty years ago. It's amazing I can remember as much as I do.

"We're going to blockade Cuba, but the only Russian ship we'll stop won't have anything in it but food and trade goods. The Russians are going to bluster, but by Thursday or Friday they're going to be scared to death and looking for a way out. One of the big Russian diplomats will initiate a backchannel meeting with some TV guy." And seemingly from nowhere, the way crossword puzzle answers sometimes come to me, I remembered the name. Or almost remembered it. "His name is John Scolari, or something like that—"

"Scali? Are you talking about John Scali, on the ABC News?"

"Yeah, that's him. This is going to happen Friday or Saturday, while the rest of the world—including your ex and your pal from Yale—is just waiting for the word to stick their heads between their legs and kiss their asses goodbye."

She heartened me by giggling.

"This Russian will more or less say . . ." Here I did a pretty good Russian accent. I had learned it listening to Lee's wife. Also from Boris and Natasha on *Rocky and Bullwinkle*. "'Get vurd to your president that ve vunt vay to back out of this vith honor. You agree take your nuclear missiles out of Turkey. You promise never to invade Kooba. Ve say okay and dismantle missiles in Kooba.' And that, Sadie, is exactly what's going to happen."

She wasn't giggling now. She was staring at me with huge saucer eyes. "You're making this up to make me feel better."

I said nothing.

"You're *not*," she whispered. "You really believe it."

"Wrong," I said. "I *know* it. Big difference."

"George . . . *nobody* knows the future."

"John Clayton claims to know, and you believe *him*. Roger from Yale claims to know, and you believe him, too."

"You're jealous of him, aren't you?"

"You're goddam right."

"I never slept with him. I never even wanted to." Solemnly, she added: "I could never sleep with a man who wears that much cologne."

"Good to know. I'm still jealous."

"Should I ask questions about how you—"

"No. I won't answer them." I probably shouldn't have told her as much as I had, but I couldn't stop myself. And in truth, I would do it again. "But I will tell you one other thing, and this you can check yourself in a couple of days. Adlai Stevenson and the Russian representative to the UN are going to face off in the General Assembly. Stevenson's going to exhibit huge photos of the missile bases the Russians are building in Cuba, and ask the Russian guy to explain what the Russians said wasn't there. The Russian guy is going to say something like, 'You must vait, I cannot respond viddout full translation.' And Stevenson, who knows the guy can speak perfect English, is going to say something that'll wind up in the history books along with *'don't fire until you see the whites of their eyes.'* He's going to tell the Russian guy he can wait until hell freezes over."

She looked at me doubtfully, turned to the night table, saw the charred pack of Winstons sitting on top of a hill of crushed butts, and said: "I think I'm out of cigarettes."

"You should be okay until morning," I said dryly. "It looks to me like you front-loaded about a week's supply."

"George?" Her voice was very small, very timid. "Will you stay with me tonight?"

"My car's parked in your—"

"If one of the neighborhood neb-noses says something, I'll tell them you came to see me after the president's speech and it wouldn't start."

Considering how the Sunliner was running these days, that was plausible. "Does your sudden concern for propriety mean you've stopped worrying about nuclear Armageddon?"

"I don't know. I only know I don't want to be alone. I'll even make love with you if that will get you to stay, but I don't think it would be much good for either of us. My head aches so *badly*."

"You don't have to make love to me, hon. It's not a business deal."

"I didn't mean—"

"Hush. I'll get the aspirin."

"And look on top of the medicine cabinet, would you? Sometimes I leave a pack of cigarettes there."

She had, but by the time she'd taken three puffs of the one I lit for her, she was wall-eyed and dozing. I took it from between her fingers and mashed it out on the lower slope of Mount Cancer. Then I took her in my arms and laid back on the pillows. We fell asleep that way.

10

When I woke to the first long light of dawn, the fly of my slacks was unzipped and a skillful hand was exploring inside my underwear. I turned to her. She was looking at me calmly. "The world is still here, George. And so are we. Come on. But be gentle. My head still aches."

I was gentle, and I made it last. *We* made it last. At the end, she lifted her hips and dug into my shoulder blades. It was her *oh dear, oh my God, oh sugar* grip.

"Anything." She was whispering, her breath in my ear making me shiver as I came. "You can be anything, do anything, just say you'll stay. And that you still love me."

"Sadie . . . I never stopped."

11

We had breakfast in her kitchen before I went back to Dallas. I told her it really *was* Dallas now, and although I didn't have a phone yet, I would give her the number as soon as I had one.

She nodded and picked at her eggs. "I meant what I said. I won't ask any more questions about your business."

"That's best. Don't ask, don't tell."

"Huh?"

"Never mind."

"Just tell me again that you're up to good rather than no good."

"Yes," I said. "I'm one of the good guys."

"Will you be able to tell me someday?"

"I hope so," I said. "Sadie, those pictures he sent—"

"I tore them up this morning. I don't want to talk about them."

"We don't have to. But I need you to tell me that's *all* the contact you've had with him. That he hasn't been around."

"He hasn't been. And the postmark on the envelope was Savannah."

I'd noticed that. But I'd also noticed the postmark was almost two months old.

"He's not big on personal confrontation. He's brave enough in his mind, but I think he's a physical coward."

That struck me as a good assessment; sending the pictures was textbook passive-aggressive behavior. Still, she had been sure Clayton wouldn't find out where she was now living and teaching, and she'd been wrong about that. "The behavior of mentally unstable people is hard to predict, honey. If you saw him, you'd call the police, right?"

"*Yes*, George." With a touch of her old impatience. "I need to ask you one question, then we won't talk about this anymore until you're ready. If you ever are."

"Okay." I tried to prepare an answer to the question I was sure would be coming: *Are you from the future, George?*

"It's going to sound crazy."

"It's been a crazy night. Go ahead."

"Are you . . ." She laughed, then started to gather the plates. She went to the sink with them, and with her back turned, she asked: "Are you human? Like, from planet Earth?"

I went to her, reached around to cup her breasts, and kissed the back of her neck. "Totally human."

She turned. Her eyes were grave. "Can I ask another?"

I sighed. "Shoot."

"I've got at least forty minutes before I have to dress for school. Do you happen to have another condom? I think I've discovered the cure for headaches."

CHAPTER 20

1

So in the end it only took the threat of nuclear war to bring us back together—how romantic is that?

Okay, maybe not.

Deke Simmons, the sort of man who took an extra hankie to sad movies, approved heartily. Ellie Dockerty did not. Here is a strange thing I've noticed: women are better at keeping secrets, but men are more comfortable with them. A week or so after the Cuban Missile Crisis ended, Ellie called Sadie into her office and shut the door—not a good sign. She was typically blunt, asking Sadie if she knew any more about me than she had before.

"No," Sadie said.

"But you've begun again."

"Yes."

"Do you even know where he lives?"

"No, but I have a telephone number."

Ellie rolled her eyes, and who could blame her. "Has he told you anything at all about his past? Whether he's been married before? Because I believe that he has been."

Sadie stayed silent.

"Has he happened to mention if he's left a dropped calf or two behind somewhere? Because sometimes men do that, and a man who's done it once will not hesitate to—"

"Miz Ellie, may I go back to the library now? I've left a student in charge, and while Helen's very responsible, I don't like to leave them too—"

"Go, go." Ellie flapped a hand at the door.

"I thought you *liked* George," Sadie said as she got up.

"I do," Ellie replied—in a tone, Sadie told me later, that said *I did.* "I'd like him even better—and like him for *you* better—if I knew what his real name was, and what he's up to."

"Don't ask, don't tell," Sadie said as she went to the door.

"What's *that* supposed to mean?"

"That I love him. That he saved my life. That all I have to give him in return is my trust, and I intend to give it."

Miz Ellie was one of those women accustomed to getting the last word in most situations, but she didn't get it that time.

2

We fell into a pattern that fall and winter. I would drive down to Jodie on Friday afternoons. Sometimes on the way, I would buy flowers at the florist in Round Hill. Sometimes I'd get my hair cut at the Jodie Barber Shop, which was a great place to catch up on all the local chatter. Also, I'd gotten used to having it short. I could remember wearing it so long it flopped in my eyes, but not why I'd put up with the annoyance. Getting used to Jockey shorts over boxers was harder, but after awhile my balls no longer claimed to be strangling.

We'd usually eat at Al's Diner on those evenings, then go to the football game. And when the football season ended, there was basketball. Sometimes Deke joined us, decked out in his school sweater with Brian the Fightin' Denton Lion on the front.

Miz Ellie, never.

Her disapproval did not stop us from going to the Candlewood Bungalows after the Friday games. I usually stayed there alone on Saturday nights, and on Sundays I'd join Sadie for services at Jodie's First Methodist Church. We shared a hymnal and sang many verses of "Bringing in the Sheaves." *Sowing in the morning, sowing seeds of kindness* . . . the melody and those well-meant sentiments still linger in my head.

After church we'd have the noon meal at her place, and after that I'd drive back to Dallas. Every time I made that drive, it seemed longer and I liked it less. Finally, on a chilly day in mid-December, my Ford threw a rod, as if expressing its own opinion that we were driving in the wrong direction. I wanted to get it fixed—that Sunliner convertible was the only car I ever truly loved—but the guy at Killeen Auto Repair told me it would take a whole new engine, and he just didn't know where he could lay his paws on one.

I dug into my still-sturdy (well . . . *relatively* sturdy) cash reserve and bought a 1959 Chevy, the kind with the bodacious gull-wing tailfins. It was a good car, and Sadie said she absolutely adored it, but for me it was never quite the same.

We spent Christmas night together at the Candlewood. I put a sprig of holly on the dresser and gave her a cardigan. She gave me a pair of loafers that are on my feet now. Some things are meant to keep.

We had dinner at her house on Boxing Day, and while I was setting the table, Deke's Ranch Wagon pulled into the driveway. That surprised me, because Sadie had said nothing about company. I was more surprised to see Miz Ellie on the passenger side. The way she stood with her arms folded, looking at my new car, told me I wasn't the only one who'd been kept in the dark about the guest list. But—credit where credit is due—she greeted me with a fair imitation of warmth and kissed me on the cheek. She was wearing a knitted ski cap that made her look like an elderly child, and offered me a tight smile of thanks when I whisked it off her head.

"I didn't get the memo, either," I said.

Deke pumped my hand. "Merry Christmas, George. Glad to see you. Gosh, something smells good."

He wandered off to the kitchen. A few moments later I heard Sadie laugh and say, "Get your fingers *out* of that, Deke, didn't your mama raise you right?"

Ellie was slowly undoing the keg buttons of her coat, never taking her eyes from my face. "Is it wise, George?" she asked. "What you and Sadie are doing—is it wise?"

Before I could answer, Sadie swept in with the turkey she'd been fussing over ever since we'd gotten back from the Candlewood Bungalows. We sat down and linked hands. "Dear Lord, please bless this food to our bodies," Sadie said, "and please bless our fellowship, one with the other, to our minds and our spirits."

I started to let go, but she was still gripping my hand with her left and Ellie's with her right. "And please bless George and Ellie with friendship. Help George remember her kindness, and help Ellie to remember that without George, there would be a girl from this town with a terribly scarred face. I love them both, and it's sad to see mistrust in their eyes. For Jesus's sake, amen."

"Amen!" Deke said heartily. "Good prayer!" He winked at Ellie.

I think part of Ellie wanted to get up and leave. It might have been the reference to Bobbi Jill that stopped her. Or maybe it was how much she'd come to respect her new school librarian. Maybe it even had a little to do with me. I like to think so.

Sadie was looking at Miz Ellie with all her old anxiety.

"That turkey looks absolutely wonderful," Ellie said, and handed me her plate. "Would you help me to a drumstick, George? And don't spare the stuffing."

Sadie could be vulnerable, and Sadie could be clumsy, but Sadie could also be very, very brave.

How I loved her.

3

Lee, Marina, and June went to the de Mohrenschildts' to see in the new year. I was left to my own lonely devices, but when Sadie called and asked if I'd take her to the New Year's Eve dance at Jodie's Bountiful Grange, I hesitated.

"I know what you're thinking," she said, "but this will be better than last year. We'll *make* it better, George."

So there we were at eight o'clock, once more dancing beneath sagging nets of balloons. This year's band was called the Dominoes. They featured a four-man horn section instead of the Dick Dale–style surf guitars that had dominated the previous year's dance, but they also knew how to lay it down. There were the same two bowls of pink lemonade and ginger ale, one soft and one spiked. There were the same smokers clustered beneath the fire escape in the chill air. But it *was* better than last year. There was a great sense of relief and happiness. The world had passed under a nuclear shadow in October . . . but then it had passed back out again. I heard several approving comments about how Kennedy had made the bad old Russian bear back down.

Around nine o'clock, during a slow dance, Sadie suddenly screamed and broke away from me. I was sure she'd spotted John Clayton, and my heart jumped into my throat. But that had been a scream of pure happiness, because the two newcomers she had spotted were Mike Coslaw—looking absurdly handsome in a tweed topcoat—and Bobbi Jill Allnut. Sadie ran to them . . . and tripped over someone's foot. Mike caught her and swung her around. Bobbi Jill waved to me, a little shyly.

I shook Mike's hand and kissed Bobbi Jill on the cheek. The disfiguring scar was now a faint pink line. "Doctor says it'll be all gone by next summer," she said. "He called me his fastest-healing patient. Thanks to you."

"I got a part in *Death of a Salesman,* Mr. A.," Mike said. "I'm playing Biff."

"Type-casting," I said. "Just watch out for flying pies."

I saw him talking to the band's lead singer during one of the breaks, and knew perfectly well what was coming. When they got back on the stand, the singer said: "I've got a special request. Do we have a George Amberson and Sadie Dunhill in the house? George and Sadie? Come on up here, George and Sadie, outta your seats and onto your feets."

We walked toward the bandstand through a storm of applause. Sadie was laughing and blushing. She shook her fist at Mike. He grinned. The boy was leaving his face; the man was coming in. A little shyly, but coming. The singer counted off, and the brass section swung into that downbeat I still hear in my dreams.

Bah-dah-dah . . . bah-dah-da-dee-dum . . .

I held my hands out to her. She shook her head, but began to swing her hips a little just the same.

"Go get him, Miz Sadie!" Bobbi Jill shouted. "Do the thing!"

The crowd joined in. *"Go! Go! Go!"*

She gave in and took my hands. We danced.

4

At midnight, the band played "Auld Lang Syne"—different arrangement from last year, same sweet song—and the balloons came drifting down. All around us, couples were kissing and embracing. We did the same.

"Happy New Year, G——" She pulled back from me, frowning. "What's wrong?"

I'd had a sudden image of the Texas School Book Depository, an ugly brick square with windows like eyes. This was the year it would become an American icon.

It won't. I'll never let you get that far, Lee. You'll never be in that sixth-floor window. That's my promise.

"George?"

"Goose walked over my grave, I guess," I said. "Happy New Year."

I went to kiss her, but she held me back for a moment. "It's almost here, isn't it? What you came to do."

"Yes," I said. "But it's not tonight. For tonight it's just us. So kiss me, honey. And dance with me."

528

I had two lives in late 1962 and early 1963. The good one was in Jodie, and at the Candlewood in Killeen. The other was in Dallas.

Lee and Marina got back together. Their first stop in Dallas was a dump just around the corner from West Neely. De Mohrenschildt helped them move in. George Bouhe wasn't in evidence. Neither were any of the other Russian émigrés. Lee had driven them away. *They hated him,* Al had written in his notes, and below that: *He wanted them to.*

The crumbling redbrick at 604 Elsbeth Street had been divided into four or five apartments bursting with poor folks who worked hard, drank hard, and produced hordes of snot-nosed yelling kids. The place actually made the Oswalds' Fort Worth domicile look good.

I didn't need electronic assistance to monitor the deteriorating condition of their marriage; Marina continued to wear shorts even after the weather turned cool, as if to taunt him with her bruises. And her sex appeal, of course. June usually sat between them in her stroller. She no longer cried much during their shouting matches, only watched, sucking her thumb or a pacifier.

One day in November of 1962, I came back from the library and observed Lee and Marina on the corner of West Neely and Elsbeth, shouting at each other. Several people (mostly women at that hour of the day) had come out on their porches to watch. June sat in the stroller wrapped in a fuzzy pink blanket, silent and forgotten.

They were arguing in Russian, but the latest bone of contention was clear enough from Lee's jabbing finger. She was wearing a straight black skirt—I don't know if they were called pencil skirts back then or not—and the zipper on her left hip was halfway down. Probably it just snagged in the cloth, but listening to him rave, you would've thought she was trolling for men.

She brushed back her hair, pointed at June, then waved a hand at the house they were now inhabiting—the broken gutters dripping black water, the trash and beer cans on the bald front lawn—and screamed at him in English: "You say happy lies, then bring wife and baby to this *peegsty*!"

He flushed all the way to his hairline and clutched his arms across his thin chest, as if to anchor his hands and keep them from doing damage. He might have succeeded—that time, at least—if she hadn't laughed, then twirled one finger around her ear in a gesture that must be common to all cultures. She started to turn away. He hauled her back, bumping the stroller and almost overturning it. Then he slugged her. She fell down on the cracked sidewalk and covered her face when he bent over her. "No, Lee, no! No more heet me!"

He didn't hit her. He yanked her to her feet and shook her, instead. Her head snapped and rolled.

"You!" a rusty voice said from my left. It made me jump. "*You*, boy!"

It was an elderly woman on a walker. She was standing on her porch in a pink flannel nightgown with a quilted jacket over it. Her graying hair stood straight up, making me think of Elsa Lanchester's twenty-thousand-volt home permanent in *The Bride of Frankenstein*.

"That man is beating on that woman! Go down there and put a stop to it!"

"No, ma'am," I said. My voice was unsteady. I thought of adding *I won't come between a man and his wife*, but that would have been a lie. The truth was that I wouldn't do anything that might disturb the future.

"You coward," she said.

Call the cops, I almost said, but bit it back just in time. If it wasn't in the old lady's head and I put it there, that could also change the course of the future. *Did* the cops come? Ever? Al's notebook didn't say. All I knew was that Oswald would never be jugged for spousal abuse. I suppose in that time and that place, few men were.

He was dragging her up the front walk with one hand and yank- ing the stroller with the other. The old woman gave me a final withering glance, then clumped back into her house. The other spectators were doing the same. Show over.

From my living room, I trained my binoculars on the redbrick monstrosity catercorner from me. Two hours later, just as I was about to give up the surveillance, Marina emerged with the small pink suitcase in one hand and the blanket-wrapped baby in the other. She had changed the offending skirt for slacks and what appeared to be two sweaters—the day had turned cold. She hurried down the street, several times looking back over her shoulder for Lee. When I was sure he wasn't going to follow her, I did.

She went as far as Mister Car Wash four blocks down West Davis, and used the pay telephone there. I sat across the street at the bus stop with a newspaper spread out in front of me. Twenty minutes later, trusty old George Bouhe showed up. She spoke to him earnestly. He led her around to the passenger side of the car and opened the door for her. She smiled and pecked him on the corner of the mouth. I'm sure he treasured both. Then he got in behind the wheel and they drove away.

6

That night there was another argument in front of the Elsbeth Street house, and once again most of the immediate neighborhood turned out to watch. Feeling there was safety in numbers, I joined them.

Someone—almost certainly Bouhe—had sent George and Jeanne de Mohrenschildt to get the rest of Marina's things. Bouhe probably figured they were the only ones who'd be able to get in without physical restraints being imposed on Lee.

"Be damned if I'll hand anything over!" Lee shouted, oblivious of the rapt neighbors taking in every word. Cords stood out on his neck; his face was once more a bright, steaming red. How he must have hated that tendency to blush like a little girl who's been caught passing love-notes.

De Mohrenschildt took the reasonable approach. "Think, my friend. This way there's still a chance. If she sends the police . . ." He gave a shrug and lifted his hands to the sky.

"Give me an hour, then," Lee said. He was showing teeth, but that expression was the farthest thing in the world from a smile. "It'll give me a chance to put a knife through ever one of her dresses and break ever one of the toys those fatcats sent to buy my daughter."

"What's going on?" a young man asked me. He was about twenty, and had pulled up on a Schwinn.

"Domestic argument, I guess."

"Osmont, or whatever his name is, right? Russian lady left him? About time, I'd say. That guy there's crazy. He's a commie, you know it?"

"I think I heard something about that."

Lee was marching up the porch steps with his head back and his spine straight—Napoleon retreating from Moscow—when Jeanne de Mohrenschildt called to him sharply. "Stop it, you stupidnik!"

Lee turned to her, his eyes wide, unbelieving . . . and hurt. He looked at de Mohrenschildt, his expression saying *can't you control your wife,* but de Mohrenschildt said nothing. He looked amused. Like a jaded theatergoer watching a play that's actually not too bad. Not great, not Shakespeare, but a perfectly acceptable time-passer.

Jeanne: "If you love your wife, Lee, for God's sake stop acting like a spoiled brat. Behave."

"You can't talk to me like that." Under stress, his Southern accent grew stronger. *Can't* became *cain't; like that* became *like-at.*

"I can, I will, I do," she said. "Let us get her things, or I'll call the police myself."

Lee said, "Tell her to shut up and mind her business, George."

De Mohrenschildt laughed cheerily. "Today you *are* our business, Lee." Then he grew serious. "I am losing respect for you,

Comrade. Let us in now. If you value my friendship as I value yours, let us in now."

Lee's shoulders slumped and he stood aside. Jeanne marched up the steps, not even sparing him a glance. But de Mohrenschildt stopped and enveloped Lee, who was now painfully thin, in a powerful embrace. After a moment or two, Oswald hugged him back. I realized (with a mixture of pity and revulsion) that the boy—that was all he was, really—had begun weeping.

"What are they," the young man with the bike asked, "couple of queers?"

"They're queer, all right," I said. "Just not the way you mean."

7

Later that month, I returned from one of my weekends with Sadie to discover Marina and June back in residence at the shithole on Elsbeth Street. For a little while, the family seemed at peace. Lee went to work—now creating photographic enlargements instead of aluminum screen doors—and came home, sometimes with flowers. Marina greeted him with kisses. Once she showed him the front lawn, where she had picked up all the garbage, and he applauded her. That made her laugh, and when she did, I saw that her teeth had been fixed. I don't know how much George Bouhe had to do with that, but my guess is plenty.

I watched this scene from the corner, and was once more startled by the rusty voice of the old lady with the walker. "It won't last, you know."

"You could be right," I said.

"He's probably goan kill her. I seen it before." Below her electric hair, her eyes surveyed me with cold contempt. "And you won't step in to do nothing, will you, Sonny Biscuit?"

"I will," I told her. "If things get bad enough, I will step in."

That was a promise I meant to keep, although not on Marina's behalf.

8

The day after Sadie's Boxing Day dinner, there was a note from Oswald in my mailbox, although it was signed A. Hidell. This alias was in Al's notes. The *A* stood for Alek, Marina's pet name for him during their Minsk days.

The communication didn't disturb me, since everyone on the street seemed to have gotten one just like it. The flyers had been printed on hot-pink paper (probably filched from Oswald's current place of employment), and I saw a dozen or more flapping up the gutters. The residents of Dallas's Oak Cliff neighborhood were not known for putting litter in its place.

PROTEST CHANNEL 9 FASCISM!
HOME OF SEGREGATIONIST BILLY JAMES HARGIS!
PROTEST FASCIST EX-GENERAL EDWIN WALKER!

During the Thursday night telemcast of the Billy James Hargis so-called "Cristian Crusade," Channel 9 will give are-time to GENERAL EDWIN WALKER, a right-wing fascist who has encouraged JFK to invade the peaceful peoples of Cuba and who has formented anti-black, anti-integration "HATE-SPEAK" all over the south. (If you have doubts about the accuracy of this information, check the "TV Guide.") These two men stand for everythig we fouht against in WWII, and their Fascist RAVINGS have no place on the are-waves. EDWIN WALKER was one of the WHITE SUPREMACISTS who tried to bar JAMES MERDITH from attending "OLE MISS." If you love America, protest the free are-time given to men who pretch HATE and VIOLENCE. Write a letter! Better still, come to Channel 9 on Dec. 27 and "sit in!"

A. Hidell
President of Hands Off Cuba
Dallas–Fort Worth Branch

I briefly pondered the misspellings, then folded the flyer and put it in the box where I kept my manuscripts.

If there was a protest at the station, it wasn't reported in the *Slimes Herald* the day after the Hargis-Walker "telemcast." I doubt that anyone turned up, including Lee himself. I certainly didn't, but I tuned in to Channel 9 on Thursday night, anxious to see the man Lee—probably Lee—was soon going to try to kill.

At first it was just Hargis, sitting behind an office-set desk and pretending to scribble important notes while a canned choir sang "The Battle Hymn of the Republic." He was a fattish fellow with a lot of plastered-back black hair. As the choir faded out, he put down his pen, looked into the camera, and said: "Welcome to the Christian Crusade, neighbors. I come with good news—*Jesus loves you.* Yes he does, every last one of you. Won't you join me in prayer?"

Hargis bent the Almighty's ear for at least ten minutes. He covered the usual stuff, thanking God for the chance to spread the gospel and instructing Him to bless those who'd sent in love-offerings. Then he got down to business, asking God to arm His Chosen People with the sword and buckler of righteousness so we could defeat communism, which had reared its ugly head just ninety miles off the shores of Florida. He asked God to grant President Kennedy the wisdom (which Hargis, being closer to the Big Guy, already possessed) to go in there and root out the tares of godlessness. He also demanded that God put an end to the growing communist threat on American college campuses—folk music seemed to have something to do with it, but Hargis kind of lost the thread on that part. He finished by thanking God for his guest tonight, the hero of Anzio and the Chosin Reservoir, General Edwin A. Walker.

Walker appeared not in uniform but in a khaki suit that closely resembled one. The creases in his pants looked sharp enough to shave with. His stony face reminded me of the cowboy actor Randolph Scott. He shook Hargis's hand and they talked about communism, which was rife not just on the college campuses, but in the halls of Congress and the scientific community as well. They touched on fluoridation. Then they schmoozed about Cuba, which Walker called "the cancer of the Caribbean."

I could see why Walker had failed so badly in his run for the Texas governorship the year before. At the front of a high school class he would have put the kids to sleep even in period one, when they were freshest. But Hargis moved him along smoothly, interjecting "Praise Jesus!" and "God's witness, brother!" whenever things got a little sticky. They discussed an upcoming barnstorm crusade through the South called Operation Midnight Ride, and then Hargis invited Walker to clear the air concerning "certain scurrilous charges of segregationism that have surfaced in the New York press and elsewhere."

Walker finally forgot he was on television and came to life. "You know that's nothing but a truckload of commie propaganda."

"I know it!" Hargis exclaimed. "And God wants you to tell it, brother."

"I spent my life in the U.S. Army, and I'll be a soldier in my heart until the day I die." (If Lee had his way, that would be in roughly three months.) "As a soldier, I always did my duty. When President Eisenhower ordered me to Little Rock during the civil disturbances of 1957—this had to do with the forced integration of Central High School, as you know—I did my duty. But Billy, I am also a soldier of God—"

"A *Christian* soldier! Praise Jesus!"

"—and as a Christian, I know that forced integration is just flat-out *wrong*. It's Constitution-wrong, states rights–wrong, and Bible-wrong."

"Tell it," Hargis said, and wiped a tear from his cheek. Or maybe it was sweat that had oozed through his makeup.

"Do I hate the Negro race? Those who say that—and those who worked to drive me from the military service I loved—are liars and communists. You know better, the men I served with know better, and *God* knows better." He leaned forward in the guest's chair. "Do you think the *Negro* teachers in Alabama and Arkansas and Louisiana and the great state of Texas want integration? They do not. They see it as a slap in the face to their own skills and hard work. Do you think that *Negro* students want to go to school with whites naturally better equipped for readin, writin, and rithmetic? Do you think real Americans want the sort of race mongrelization that will result from this sort of mingling?"

"Of course they don't! *Praaaiiise Jesus!*"

I thought about the sign I'd seen in North Carolina, the one pointing to a path bordered with poison ivy. *COLORED*, it had said. Walker didn't deserve killing, but he could certainly do with a brisk shaking. I'd give *anyone* a big old *praise Jesus* on that one.

My attention had wandered, but something Walker was now saying brought it back in a hurry.

"It was God, not General Edwin Walker, who ordained the Negro position in His world when He gave them a different skin color and a different set of talents. More *athletic* talents. What does the Bible tell us about this difference, and why the Negro race has been cursed to so much pain and travail? We only have to look at the ninth chapter of Genesis, Billy."

"Praise God for His Holy Word."

Walker closed his eyes and raised his right hand, as if testifying in court. "'And Noah drank of the wine, and was drunken, and lay uncovered. Ham saw the nakedness of his father, and told them who stood without.' But Shem and Japeth—one father of the Arab race, one father of the white race, I know you know this, Billy, but not everybody does, not everybody has the good old Bible-learning we got at our mothers' knees—"

"Praise God for Christian mothers, you tell it!"

"Shem and Japeth didn't look. And when Noah awoke and found out what had been going on, he said, 'Cursed be Canaan, he shall be a servant even unto servants, a hewer of wood and a drawer of wa—'"

I snapped the TV off.

9

What I saw of Lee and Marina during January and February of 1963 made me think of a tee-shirt Christy sometimes used to wear during the last year of our marriage. There was a fiercely grinning pirate on the front, with this message below him: THE BEATINGS WILL CONTINUE UNTIL MORALE IMPROVES. Plenty of beatings took place at 604 Elsbeth Street that winter. We in the neighborhood heard Lee's shouting and Marina's cries—sometimes of anger, sometimes of pain. Nobody did anything, and that included me.

Not that she was the only wife to take regular beatings in Oak Cliff; the Friday and Saturday Night Fights seemed to be a local tradition. All I remember wanting during those dismal gray months was for the squalid, endless soap opera to be over so I could be with Sadie full-time. I would verify that Lee was solo when he attempted to kill General Walker, then conclude my business. Oswald acting alone once didn't necessarily mean he'd been acting alone both times, but it was the best I could do. With the *i*'s dotted and the *t*'s crossed—most of them, anyway—I would pick my time and place and shoot Lee Oswald as coldly as I had shot Frank Dunning.

Time passed. Slowly, but it passed. And then one day, not long before the Oswalds moved into the apartment on Neely Street above my own, I saw Marina talking to the old lady with the walker and the Elsa Lanchester hair. They were both smiling. The old lady asked her something. Marina laughed, nodded, and held her hands out in front of her stomach.

I stood at my window with the curtain drawn back, my binoculars in one hand and my mouth hanging open. Al's notes had said nothing about *this* development, either because he didn't know or didn't care. But *I* cared.

The wife of the man I had waited over four years to kill was once again pregnant.

CHAPTER 21

1

The Oswalds became my upstairs neighbors on March 2, 1963. They hand-carried their possessions, mostly in liquor store cartons, from the crumbling brick box on Elsbeth Street. Soon the wheels of the little Japanese tape recorder were turning on a regular basis, but mostly I listened in with the earphones. That way the conversations upstairs were normal instead of slowed down, but of course I couldn't understand much of it, anyway.

The week after the Oswalds moved into their new digs, I visited one of the pawnshops on Greenville Avenue to buy a gun. The first revolver the pawnbroker showed me was the same Colt .38 model I'd bought in Derry.

"This is excellent pertection against muggers n home-breakers," the pawnbroker said. "Dead accurate up to twenty yards."

"Fifteen," I said. "I heard fifteen."

The pawnie raised his eyebrows. "Okay, say fifteen. Anyone stupid enough—"

—to try mugging me out of my cash is going to be a lot closer than that, that's how the pitch goes.

"—to brace you is gonna be in at close quarters, so what do you say?"

My first impulse, just to break that sense of chiming but slightly discordant harmony was to tell him I wanted something else, maybe a .45, but breaking the harmony might be a bad idea.

Who knew? What I *did* know was that the .38 I'd bought in Derry had done the job.

"How much?"

"Let you have it for twelve."

That was two dollars more than I'd paid in Derry, but of course that had been four and a half years ago. Adjusting for inflation, twelve seemed about right. I told him to add a box of bullets and he had a deal.

When the broker saw me putting the gun and the ammo in the briefcase I'd brought along for that purpose, he said, "Why don't you let me sell you a holster, son? You don't sound like you're from around here and you probably don't know, but you c'n carry legal in Texas, no permit needed if you don't have a felony record. You got a felony record?"

"No, but I don't expect to be mugged in broad daylight."

The broker offered a dark smile. "On Greenville Avenue you can never tell *what's* gonna happen. Man blew his own head off just a block and a half from here a few years ago."

"Really?"

"Yessir, outside a bar called the Desert Rose. Over a woman, accourse. Don't that figure?"

"I guess," I said. "Although sometimes it's politics."

"Nah, nah, at the bottom it's always a woman, son."

I'd found a parking space four blocks west of the pawnshop, and in order to get back to my new (new to me, anyway) car, I had to pass Faith Financial, where I'd laid my bet on the Miracle Pirates in the fall of 1960. The sharpie who'd paid off my twelve hundred was standing out front, having a smoke. He was wearing his green eyeshade. His eyes passed over me, but seemingly without interest or recognition.

2

That was on a Friday afternoon, and I drove straight from Greenville Avenue to Killeen, where Sadie met me at the Candlewood Bungalows. We spent the night, as was our habit that winter. The next day she drove back to Jodie, where I joined her on Sunday for church. After the benediction, during the part where we shook hands with the people all around us, saying "Peace be with you," my thoughts turned—not comfortably—to the gun now stowed in the trunk of my car.

Over the Sunday noon meal, Sadie asked: "How much longer? Until you do what you have to do?"

"If everything goes the way I hope, not much more than a month."

"And if it doesn't?"

I scrubbed my hands through my hair and went to the window. "Then I don't know. Anything else on your mind?"

"Yes," she said calmly. "There's cherry cobbler for afters. Would you like whipped cream on yours?"

"Very much," I said. "I love you, honey."

"You better," she said, getting up to fetch dessert. "Because I'm kind of out on a limb here."

I stayed at the window. A car came rolling slowly down the street—an oldie but a goodie, as the jocks on K-Life said—and I felt that harmonic chime again. But I was always feeling it now, and sometimes it meant nothing. One of Christy's AA slogans came to my mind: FEAR, standing for *false evidence appearing real.*

This time a click of association came, though. The car was a white-over-red Plymouth Fury, like the one I'd seen in the parking lot of the Worumbo mill, not far from the drying shed where the rabbit-hole into 1958 came out. I remembered touching the trunk to make sure it was real. This one had an Arkansas plate instead of a Maine one, but still . . . that chime. That harmonic chime.

Sometimes I felt that if I knew what that chime meant, I'd know everything. Probably stupid, but true.

The Yellow Card Man knew, I thought. *He knew and it killed him.*

My latest harmonic signaled left, turned at the stop sign, and disappeared toward Main Street.

"Come eat dessert, you," Sadie said from behind me, and I jumped.

The AAs say FEAR stands for something else, as well: *Fuck everything and run.*

3

When I got back to Neely Street that night, I put on the earphones and listened to the latest recording. I expected nothing but Russian, but this time I got English as well. And splashing sounds.

Marina: (Speaks Russian.)
Lee: "I can't, Mama, I'm in the tub with Junie!"
(More splashing, and laughter—Lee's and the baby's high chortle.)
Lee: "Mama, we got water on the floor! Junie *splash*! *Bad* girl!"
Marina: "Mop it up! I beezy! *Beezy!*" (But she is also laughing.)
Lee: "I can't, you want the baby to . . ." (Russian.)
Marina: (Speaks Russian—scolding and laughing at the same time.)
(More splashing. Marina is humming some pop song from KLIF. It sounds sweet.)
Lee: "Mama, bring us our toys!"
Marina: "*Da, da,* always you must have the toys."
(Splashing, loud. The door to the bathroom must be all the way open now.)
Marina: (Speaks Russian.)
Lee (pouty little boy's voice): "Mama, you forgot our rubber ball."
(Big splash—the baby screams with delight.)

Marina: "There, all toys for preence and preencessa."
(Laughter from all three—their joy turns me cold.)
Lee: "Mama, bring us a (Russian word). We have water on our ear."
Marina (laughing): "Oh my God, what next?"

I lay awake a long time that night, thinking of the three of them. Happy for once, and why not? 214 West Neely wasn't much, but it was still a step up. Maybe they were even sleeping in the same bed, June for once happy instead of scared to death.

And now a fourth in the bed, as well. The one growing in Marina's belly.

4

Things began to move faster, as they had in Derry, only now time's arrow was flying toward April 10 instead of Halloween. Al's notes, which I had depended on to get me this far, became less helpful. Leading up to the attempt on Walker's life, they concentrated almost solely on Lee's actions and movements, and that winter there was a lot more to their lives, Marina's in particular.

For one thing, she had finally made a friend—not a sugar daddy wannabe like George Bouhe, but a woman friend. Her name was Ruth Paine, and she was a Quaker lady. *Russian speaker,* Al had noted in a laconic style not much like his earlier notes. *Met at party, 2(??)/63. Marina separated from Lee and living with the Paine woman at the time of the Kennedy assassination.* And then, as if it were no more than an afterthought: *Lee stored M-C in Paine garage. Wrapped in blanket.*

By *M-C,* he meant the mail-order Mannlicher-Carcano rifle with which Lee planned to kill General Walker.

I don't know who threw the party where Lee and Marina met the Paines. I don't know who introduced them. De Mohrenschildt? Bouhe? Probably one or the other, because by then the rest of the émigrés were giving the Oswalds a wide berth. Hubby was a sneering know-it-all, wifey a punching bag who'd passed up God knew how many chances to leave him for good.

What I do know is Marina Oswald's potential escape-hatch arrived behind the wheel of a Chevrolet station wagon—white over red—on a rainy day in the middle of March. She parked at the curb and looked around dubiously, as if not sure she had come to the right address. Ruth Paine was tall (although not as tall as Sadie) and painfully thin. Her brownish hair was banged over a huge expanse of forehead in front and flipped in back, a style that did not flatter her. She wore rimless glasses on a nose splashed with freckles. To me, peering through a crack in the curtains, she looked like the kind of woman who steered clear of meat and marched in Ban the Bomb demonstrations . . . and that was pretty much who Ruth Paine was, I think, a woman who was New Age before New Age was cool.

Marina must have been watching for her, because she came clattering down the outside stairs with the baby in her arms, a blanket flipped up over June's head to protect her from the drifting drizzle. Ruth Paine smiled tentatively and spoke carefully, putting a space between each word. "Hello, Mrs. Oswald, I'm Ruth Paine. Do you remember me?"

"Da," Marina said. "Yes." Then she added something in Russian. Ruth replied in the same language . . . although haltingly.

Marina invited her in. I waited until I heard the creak of their footsteps above me, then donned the earphones connected to the lamp bug. What I heard was a conversation in mixed English and Russian. Marina corrected Ruth several times, sometimes with laughter. I understood enough to figure out why Ruth Paine had come. Like Paul Gregory, she wanted Russian lessons. I understood something else from their frequent laughter and increasingly easy conversation: they liked each other.

I was glad for Marina. If I killed Oswald after his attempt on General Walker, the New Agey Ruth Paine might take her in. I could hope.

5

Ruth only came twice to Neely Street for her lessons. After that, Marina and June got in the station wagon and Ruth drove them away. Probably to her home in the posh (at least by Oak Cliff standards) suburb of Irving. That address wasn't in Al's notes—he seemed to care little about Marina's relationship with Ruth, probably because he expected to finish Lee long before that rifle ended up in the Paines' garage—but I found it in the phone directory: 2515 West Fifth Street.

One overcast March afternoon, about two hours after Marina and Ruth had departed, Lee and George de Mohrenschildt showed up in de Mohrenschildt's car. Lee got out carrying a brown paper sack with a sombrero and PEPINO'S BEST MEXICAN printed on the side. De Mohrenschildt had a six-pack of Dos Equis. They went up the outside staircase, talking and laughing. I grabbed the earphones, heart pumping. At first there was nothing, but then one of them turned on the lamp. After that I might have been in the room with them, an unseen third.

Please don't conspire to kill Walker, I thought. *Please don't make my job harder than it already is.*

"Pardon the mess," Lee said. "She doesn't do anything much these days but sleep, watch TV, and talk about that woman she's giving lessons to."

De Mohrenschildt spoke for awhile about some oil leases he was trying to get hold of in Haiti, and spoke harshly of the repressive Duvalier regime. "At the end of the day, trucks drive through the marketplace and pick up the dead. Many of them are children who've starved to death."

"Castro and the Front will put an end to that," Lee said grimly.

"May providence hasten the day." There was the clink of bottles, probably to toast the idea of providence hastening the day. "How is work, Comrade? And how is it you're not there this afternoon?"

He wasn't there, Lee said, because he wanted to be here. Simple as that. He'd just punched out and walked away. "What can they do about it? I'm the best damn photoprint technician ole Bobby Stovall's got, and he knows it. The foreman, his name is *(I couldn't make it out—Graff? Grafe?)* says 'Quit trying to play labor organizer, Lee.' You know what I do? I laugh and say 'Okay, *svinoyeb,*' and walk away. He's a pig's dick, and ever'one knows it."

Still, it was clear Lee liked his job, although he complained about the paternalistic attitude, and how seniority counted for more than talent. At one point he said, "You know, in Minsk, on a level playing field, I'd be running the place in a year."

"I know you would, my son—it's completely evident."

Playing him up. *Winding* him up. I was sure of it. I didn't like it.

"Did you see the paper this morning?" Lee asked.

"I saw nothing but telegrams and memos this morning. Why do you think I'm here, if not to get away from my desk?"

"Walker did it," Lee said. "He joined up with Hargis's crusade— or maybe it's Walker's crusade and Hargis joined up. I cain't tell. That fucking Midnight Ride thing, anyway. Those two ninnies are going to tour the whole South, telling people that the N-double-A-C-P's a communist front. They'll set integration and voting rights back twenty years."

"Sure! And fomenting hate. How long before the massacres start?"

"Or until someone shoots Ralph Abernathy and Dr. King!"

"Of *course* King will be shot," de Mohrenschildt said, almost laughing. I was standing up, my hands pressing the earphones tight to the sides of my head, sweat trickling down my face. This was dangerous ground, indeed—the very edge of conspiracy. "It's only a matter of time."

One of them used the church key on another bottle of Mexican beer, and Lee said, "Someone should stop those two bastards."

"You're wrong to call our General Walker a ninny," de Mohrenschildt said in a lecturely tone. "Hargis, yes, okay. Hargis is a joke. What I hear is that he is—like so many of his ilk—a man of twisted sexual appetites, willing to diddle a little girl's cunt in the morning and a little boy's asshole in the afternoon."

"Man, that's *sick*!" Lee's voice broke like an adolescent's on the last word. Then he laughed.

"But Walker, ah, there's a very different kettle of shrimp. He's high in the John Birch Society—"

"Those Jew-hating fascists!"

"—and I can see a day, not long hence, when he may run it. Once he has the confidence and approval of the other right-wing nut groups, he may even run for office again . . . but this time not for governor of Texas. I suspect he has his sights aimed higher. The Senate? Perhaps. Even the White House?"

"That could never happen." But Lee sounded unsure.

"It's *unlikely* to happen," de Mohrenschildt corrected. "But never underestimate the American bourgeoisie's capacity to embrace fascism under the name of populism. Or the power of television. Without TV, Kennedy would never have beaten Nixon."

"Kennedy and his iron fist," Lee said. His approval of the current president seemed to have gone the way of blue suede shoes. "He won't never rest as long as Fidel's shitting in Batista's commode."

"And never underestimate the terror white America feels at the idea of a society in which racial equality has become the law of the land."

"Nigger, nigger, nigger, beaner, beaner, beaner!" Lee burst out, with a rage so great it was nearly anguish. "That's all I hear at work!"

"I'm sure. When the *Morning News* says 'the great state of Texas,' what they mean is 'the *hate* state of Texas.' And people listen! For a man like Walker—a *war hero* like Walker—a buffoon like Hargis is nothing but a stepping-stone. The way von Hindenberg was a stepping-stone for Hitler. With the right public relations people to smooth him out, Walker could go far. Do you know what I think? That the man who knocked off General Edwin Racist America Walker would be doing society a favor."

I dropped heavily into a chair beside the table where the little tape recorder sat, its reels spinning.

"If you really believe—" Lee began, and then there was a loud buzz that made me snatch the headphones off. There were no cries of alarm or outrage from upstairs, no swift movement of feet, so—unless they were very good at covering up on the spur of the moment—I thought I could assume the lamp bug hadn't been discovered. I put the headphones back on. Nothing. I tried the distance mike, standing on a chair and holding the Tupperware bowl almost against the ceiling. With it I could hear Lee talking and de Mohrenschildt's occasional replies, but I couldn't make out what they were saying.

My ear in the Oswald apartment had gone deaf.

The past is obdurate.

After another ten minutes of conversation—maybe about politics, maybe about the annoying nature of wives, maybe about newly hatching plans to kill General Edwin Walker—de Mohrenschildt bounded down the outside stairs and drove away.

Lee's footfalls crossed above my head—*clump, clud, clump.* I followed them into my bedroom and trained the distance mike on the place where they stopped. Nothing . . . nothing . . . then the faint but unmistakable sound of snoring. When Ruth Paine dropped off Marina and June two hours later, he was still sleeping the sleep of Dos Equis. Marina didn't wake him. I wouldn't have woken the bad-tempered little sonofabitch, either.

6

Oswald began to miss a lot more work after that day. If Marina knew, she didn't care. Maybe she didn't even notice. She was absorbed with her new friend Ruth. The beatings had abated a little, not because morale had improved, but because Lee was out almost as frequently as she was. He often took his camera.

Thanks to Al's notes, I knew where he was going and what he was doing.

One day after he'd left for the bus stop, I jumped into my car and drove to Oak Lawn Avenue. I wanted to beat Lee's crosstown bus, and I did. Handily. There was plenty of slant-style parking on both sides of Oak Lawn, but my red gull-wing Chevy was distinctive, and I didn't want to risk Lee seeing it. I put it around the corner on Wycliff Avenue, in the parking lot of an Alpha Beta grocery. Then I strolled down to Turtle Creek Boulevard. The houses there were neo-haciendas with arches and stucco siding. There were palm-lined drives, big lawns, even a fountain or two.

In front of 4011, a trim man (who bore a striking resemblance to the cowboy actor Randolph Scott) was at work with a push mower. Edwin Walker saw me looking at him and struck a curt half-salute from the side of his brow. I returned the gesture. Lee Oswald's target resumed mowing and I moved on.

7

The streets making up the Dallas block I was interested in were Turtle Creek Boulevard (where the general lived), Wycliff Avenue (where I'd parked), Avondale Avenue (which was where I went after returning Walker's wave), and Oak Lawn, a street of small businesses that ran directly behind the general's house. Oak Lawn was the one I was most interested in, because it was going to be Lee's line of approach and route of escape on the night of April 10.

I stood in front of Texas Shoes & Boots, the collar of my denim jacket raised and my hands stuffed in my pockets. About three minutes after I took up this position, the bus stopped at the corner of Oak Lawn and Wycliff. Two women with cloth shopping bags got off immediately when the doors flopped open. Then Lee descended to the sidewalk. He carried a brown paper bag, like a workman's lunchsack.

There was a big stone church on the corner. Lee sauntered over to the iron railing running in front of it, read the noticeboard, took a small notepad out of his hip pocket, and jotted something down. After that he headed in my direction, tucking the notebook into his pocket as he walked. I hadn't expected that. Al had believed Lee was going to stash his rifle near the railroad tracks on the other side of Oak Lawn Avenue, a good half a mile away. But maybe the notes were wrong, because Lee didn't even glance in that direction. He was seventy or eighty yards away, and closing in fast on my position.

He's going to notice me and he's going to speak to me, I thought. *He's going to say, "Aren't you the guy who lives downstairs? What are you doing here?"* If he did, the future would skew off in a new direction. Not good.

I stared at the shoes and boots in the show window with sweat dampening the nape of my neck and rolling down my back. When I finally took a chance and shifted my eyes to the left, Lee was gone. It was like a magic trick.

I sauntered up the street. I wished I'd put on a cap, maybe even some sunglasses—why hadn't I? What kind of half-assed secret agent was I, anyway?

I came to a coffee shop about halfway along the block, the sign in the window advertising BREAKFAST ALL DAY. Lee wasn't inside. Beyond the coffee shop was the mouth of an alley. I walked slowly across it, glanced to my right, and saw him. His back was to me. He had taken his camera out of the paper sack but wasn't shooting with it, at least not yet. He was examining trash cans. He pulled off the lids, looked inside, then replaced them.

Every bone in my body—by which I mean every instinct in my brain, I suppose—was urging me to move on before he turned and saw me, but a powerful fascination held me in place a little longer. I think it would have held most people. How many opportunities do we have, after all, to watch a guy as he goes about the business of planning a cold-blooded murder?

He moved a little deeper into the alley, then stopped at a circular iron plate set in a plug of concrete. He tried to lift it. No go.

The alley was unpaved, badly potholed, and about two hundred yards long. Halfway down its length, the chain link guarding weedy backyards and vacant lots gave way to high board fences draped in ivy that looked less than vibrant after a cold and dismal winter. Lee pushed a mat of it aside, and tried a board. It swung out and he peered into the hole behind it.

Axioms about how you have to break eggs to make an omelet were all very fine, but I felt I had pressed my luck enough. I walked on. At the end of the block I stopped at the church that had caught Lee's interest. It was the Oak Lawn Church of Latter-day Saints. The noticeboard said there were regular services every Sunday morning and special newcomers' services every Wednesday night at 7 PM, with a social hour to follow. Refreshments would be served.

April 10 was a Wednesday and Lee's plan (assuming it wasn't de Mohrenschildt's) now seemed clear enough: hide the gun in the alley ahead of time, then wait until the newcomers' service—and the social hour, of course—was over. He'd be able to hear the worshippers when they came out, laughing and talking as they headed for the bus stop. The buses ran on the quarter hour; there was always one coming along. Lee would take his shot, hide the gun behind the loose board again (*not* near the train tracks), then mingle with the church folk. When the next bus came, he'd be gone.

I glanced to my right just in time to see him emerging from the alley. The camera was back in the paper sack. He went to the bus stop and leaned against the post. A man came along and asked him something. Soon they were in conversation. Batting the breeze with a stranger, or was this perhaps another friend of de Mohrenschildt's? Just some guy on the street, or a co-conspirator? Maybe even the famous Unknown Shooter who—according to the conspiracy theorists—had been lurking on the grassy knoll near Dealey Plaza when Kennedy's motorcade approached? I told myself that was crazy, but it was impossible to know for sure. That was the hell of it.

There was no way of knowing *anything* for sure, and wouldn't be until I saw with my own eyes that Oswald was alone on April 10. Even that wouldn't be enough to put all my doubts to rest, but it would be enough to proceed on.

Enough to kill Junie's father.

The bus came growling up to the stop. Secret Agent X-19—also known as Lee Harvey Oswald, the renowned Marxist and wife-beater—got on. When the bus was out of sight, I went back to the alley and walked its length. At the end, it widened out into a big unfenced backyard. There was a '57 or '58 Chevy Biscayne parked beside a natural gas pumping station. There was a barbecue pot standing on a tripod. Beyond the barbie was the backside of a big dark brown house. The general's house.

I looked down and saw a fresh drag-mark in the dirt. A garbage can stood at one end of it. I hadn't seen Lee move the can, but I knew he had. On the night of the tenth, he meant to rest the rifle barrel on it.

8

On Monday, March 25, Lee came walking up Neely Street carrying a long package wrapped in brown paper. Peering through a tiny crack in the curtains, I could see the words REGISTERED and INSURED stamped on it in big red letters. For the first time I thought he seemed furtive and nervous, actually looking around at his exterior surroundings instead of at the spooky furniture deep in his head. I knew what was in the package: a 6.5mm Carcano rifle—also known as a Mannlicher-Carcano—complete with scope, purchased from Klein's Sporting Goods in Chicago. Five minutes after he climbed the outside stairs to the second floor, the gun Lee would use to change history was in a closet above my head. Marina took the famous pictures of him holding it just outside my living room window six days later, but I didn't see it. That was a Sunday, and I was in Jodie. As the tenth grew closer, those weekends with Sadie had become the most important, the *dearest,* things in my life.

9

I came awake with a jerk, hearing someone mutter "Still not too late" under his breath. I realized it was me and shut up.

Sadie murmured some thick protest and turned over in bed. The familiar squeak of the springs locked me in place and time: the Candlewood Bungalows, April 5, 1963. I fumbled my watch from the nightstand and peered at the luminous numbers. It was quarter past two in the morning, which meant it was actually the sixth of April.

Still not too late.

Not too late for what? To back off, to let well enough alone? Or bad enough, come to that? The idea of backing off was attractive, God knew. If I went ahead and things went wrong, this could be my last night with Sadie. Ever.

Even if you do have to kill him, you don't have to do it right away.

True enough. Oswald was going to relocate to New Orleans for awhile after the attempt on the general's life—another shitty apartment, one I'd already visited—but not for two weeks. That would give me plenty of time to stop his clock. But I sensed it would be a mistake to wait very long. I might find reasons to keep on waiting. The best one was beside me in this bed: long, lovely, and smoothly naked. Maybe she was just another trap laid by the obdurate past, but that didn't matter, because I loved her. And I could envision a scenario—all too clearly—where I'd have to run after killing Oswald. Run where? Back to Maine, of course. Hoping I could stay ahead of the cops just long enough to get to the rabbit-hole and escape into a future where Sadie Dunhill would be . . . well . . . about eighty years old. If she were alive at all. Given her cigarette habit, that would be like rolling six the hard way.

I got up and went to the window. Only a few of the bungalows were occupied on this early-spring weekend. There was a mud- or manure-splattered pickup truck with a trailer full of what looked like farm implements behind it. An Indian motorcycle with a side-car. A couple of station wagons. And a two-tone Plymouth Fury. The moon was sliding in and out of thin clouds and it wasn't possible to make out the color of the car's lower half by that stuttery light, but I was pretty sure I knew what it was, anyway.

I pulled on my pants, undershirt, and shoes. Then I slipped out of the cabin and walked across the courtyard. The chilly air bit at my bed-warm skin, but I barely felt it. Yes, the car was a Fury, and yes, it was white over red, but this one wasn't from Maine *or* Arkansas; the plate was Oklahoma, and the decal in the rear window read GO, SOONERS. I peeked in and saw a scatter of textbooks. Some student, maybe headed south to visit his folks on spring break. Or a couple of horny teachers taking advantage of the Candlewood's liberal guest policy.

Just another not-quite-on-key chime as the past harmonized with itself. I touched the trunk, as I had back in Lisbon Falls, then returned to the bungalow. Sadie had pushed the sheet down to her waist, and when I came in, the draft of cool air woke her up. She sat, holding the sheet over her breasts, then let it drop when she saw it was me.

"Can't sleep, honey?"

"I had a bad dream and went out for some air."

"What was it?"

I unbuttoned my jeans, kicked off my loafers. "Can't remember."

"Try. My mother always used to say if you tell your dreams, they won't come true."

I got into bed with her wearing nothing but my undershirt. "*My* mother used to say if you kiss your honey, they won't come true."

"Did she actually say that?"

"No."

"Well," she said thoughtfully, "it sounds possible. Let's try it."

We tried it.

One thing led to another.

10

Afterward, she lit a cigarette. I lay watching the smoke drift up and turn blue in the occasional moonlight coming through the half-drawn curtains. *I'd never leave the curtains that way at Neely Street,* I thought. *At Neely Street, in my other life, I'm always alone but still careful to close them all the way. Except when I'm peeking, that is. Lurking.*

Just then I didn't like myself very much.

"George?"

I sighed. "That's not my name."

"I know."

I looked at her. She inhaled deeply, enjoying her cigarette guilt-lessly, as people do in the Land of Ago. "I don't have any inside information, if that's what you're thinking. But it stands to reason. The rest of your past is made up, after all. And I'm glad. I don't like George all that much. It's kind of . . . what's that word you use sometimes? . . . kind of dorky."

"How does Jake suit you?"

"As in Jacob?"

"Yes."

"I like it." She turned to me. "In the Bible, Jacob wrestled an angel. And you're wrestling, too. Aren't you?"

"I suppose I am, but not with an angel." Although Lee Oswald didn't make much of a devil, either. I liked George de Mohren-schildt better for the devil role. In the Bible, Satan's a tempter who makes the offer and then stands aside. I hoped de Mohrenschildt was like that.

Sadie snubbed her cigarette. Her voice was calm, but her eyes were dark. "Are you going to be hurt?"

"I don't know."

"Are you going away? Because if you have to go away, I'm not sure I can stand it. I would have died before I said it when I was there, but Reno was a nightmare. Losing you for good . . ." She shook her head slowly. "No, I'm not sure I could stand that."

"I want to marry you," I said.

"My God," she said softly. "Just when I'm ready to say it'll never happen, Jake-alias-George says right now."

"Not right now, but if the next week goes the way I hope it does . . . will you?"

"Of course. But I *do* have to ask one teensy question."

"Am I single? Legally single? Is that what you want to know?" She nodded.

"I am," I said.

She let out a comic sigh and grinned like a kid. Then she sobered. "Can I help you? Let me help you."

The thought turned me cold, and she must have seen it. Her lower lip crept into her mouth. She bit down on it with her teeth. "That bad, then," she said musingly.

"Let's put it this way: I'm currently close to a big machine full of sharp teeth, and it's running full speed. I won't allow you next to me while I'm monkeying with it."

"When is it?" she asked. "Your . . . I don't know . . . your date with destiny?"

"Still to be determined." I had a feeling that I'd said too much already, but since I'd come this far, I decided to go a little farther. "Something's going to happen this Wednesday night. Something I have to witness. Then I'll decide."

"Is there no way I can help you?"

"I don't think so, honey."

"If it turns out I can—"

"Thanks," I said. "I appreciate that. And you really will marry me?"

"Now that I know your name is Jake? Of course."

11

On Monday morning, around ten o'clock, the station wagon pulled up at the curb and Marina went off to Irving with Ruth Paine. I had an errand of my own to run, and was just about to leave the apartment when I heard the thump of footsteps descending the outside stairs. It was Lee, looking pale and grim. His hair was mussy and his face was stippled with a bad breakout of post-adolescent acne. He was wearing jeans and an absurd trenchcoat that flapped around his shins. He walked with one arm across his chest, as if his ribs hurt.

Or as if he had something under his coat. *Before the attempt, Lee sighted in his new rifle somewhere out by Love Field,* Al had written. I didn't care where he sighted it in. What I cared about was how close I'd just come to meeting him face-to-face. I'd made the careless assumption that I'd missed him going off to work, and—

Why *wasn't* he at work on a Monday morning, come to that?

I dismissed the question and went out, carrying my school briefcase. Inside were the never-to-be-finished novel, Al's notes, and the work-in-progress describing my adventures in the Land of Ago.

If Lee wasn't alone on the night of April 10, I might be spotted and killed by one of his co-conspirators, maybe even de Mohrenschildt himself. I still thought the odds of that were unlikely, but the odds of having to run away after killing Oswald were better. So were the odds of being captured and arrested for murder. I didn't want anyone—the police, for instance—finding Al's notes or my memoir if either of those things happened.

The important thing to me on that eighth of April was to get my paperwork out of the apartment and far away from the confused and aggressive young man who lived upstairs. I drove to the First Corn Bank of Dallas, and was not surprised to see that the bank official who helped me bore a striking resemblance to the Hometown Trust banker who had helped me in Lisbon Falls. This guy's name was Link instead of Dusen, but he still looked like the old-time Cuban bandleader, Xavier Cugat.

I enquired about safe deposit boxes. Soon enough, the manuscripts were in Box 775. I drove back to Neely Street and had a moment of severe panic when I couldn't find the goddam key to the box.

Relax, I told myself. *It's in your pocket somewhere, and even if it isn't, your new pal Richard Link will be happy to give you a duplicate. Might cost you all of a buck.*

As if the thought had summoned it, I found the key hiding way down in the corner of my pocket, under my change. I put it on my key ring, where it would be safe. If I *did* have to run back to the rabbit-hole, and stepped into the past again after a return to the present, I'd still have it . . . although everything that had happened in the last four and a half years would reset. The manuscripts now in the safe deposit box would be lost in time. That was probably good news.

The bad news was that Sadie would be, too.

CHAPTER 22

1

The afternoon of April tenth was clear and warm, a foretaste of summer. I dressed in slacks and one of the sport coats I'd bought during my year teaching at Denholm Consolidated. The .38 Police Special, fully loaded, went into my briefcase. I don't remember being nervous; now that the time had come, I felt like a man encased in a cold envelope. I checked my watch: three-thirty.

My plan was to once more park in the Alpha Beta lot on Wycliff Avenue. I could be there by four-fifteen at the latest, even if the crosstown traffic was heavy. I'd scope out the alley. If it was empty, as I expected it would be at that hour, I'd check the hole behind the loose board. If Al's notes were right about Lee stashing the Carcano in advance (even though he'd been wrong about the place), it would be there.

I'd go back to my car for awhile, watching the bus stop just in case Lee showed up early. When the 7:00 P.M. newcomers' service started at the Mormon church, I'd stroll to the coffee shop that served breakfast all day and take a seat by the window. I would eat food I wasn't hungry for, dawdling, making it last, watching the buses arrive and hoping that when Lee finally got off one, he'd be alone. I would also be hoping *not* to see George de Mohrenschildt's boat of a car.

That, at least, was the plan.

I picked up my briefcase, glancing at my watch again as I did so. 3:33. The Chevy was gassed and ready to go. If I'd gone out and gotten into it then, as I'd planned to, my phone would have rung in an empty apartment. But I didn't, because someone knocked at the door just as I reached for the knob.

I opened it and Marina Oswald was standing there.

2

For a moment I just gaped, unable to move or speak. Mostly it was her unexpected presence, but there was something else, as well. Until she was standing right in front of me, I hadn't realized how much her wide blue eyes looked like Sadie's.

Marina either ignored my surprised expression or didn't notice it. She had problems of her own. "Please excuse, have you seen my hubka?" She bit her lips and shook her head a little. *"Hubs-bun."* She attempted to smile, and she had those nicely refurbished teeth to smile with, but it still wasn't very successful. "Sorry, sir, don't speak good Eenglish. Am Byelorussia."

I heard someone—I guess it was me—ask if she was talking about the man who lived upstairs.

"Yes, please, my hubs-bun, Lee. We leeve upstair. This our *malyshka*—our baby." She pointed at June, who sat at the bottom of the steps in her walker, contentedly sucking on a pacifier. "He go out now all times since he lose his work." She tried the smile again, and when her eyes crinkled, a tear spilled from the corner of the left one and tracked down her cheek.

So. Ole Bobby Stovall could get along without his best photo-print technician after all, it seemed.

"I haven't seen him, Mrs. . . ." *Oswald* almost jumped out, but I held it back in time. And that was good, because how would I know? They got no home delivery, it seemed. There were two mailboxes on the porch, but their name wasn't on either of them. Neither was mine. I got no home delivery, either.

"Os'wal," she said, and held out her hand. I shook it, more convinced than ever that this was a dream I was having. But her small dry palm was all too real. "Marina Os'wal, I am please to meet you, sir."

"I'm sorry, Mrs. Oswald, I haven't seen him today." Not true; I'd seen him go out just after noon, not long after Ruth Paine's station wagon swept Marina and June away to Irving.

"I'm worry for him," she said. "He . . . I don' know . . . sorry. No mean bother for you." She smiled again—the sweetest, saddest smile—and wiped the tear slowly from her face.

"If I see him—"

Now she looked alarmed. "No, no, say nutting. He don' like me talk to strangers. He come home supper, maybe for sure." She walked down the steps and spoke Russian to the baby, who laughed and held out her chubby arms to her mother. "Goodbye, mister sir. Many thanks. You say nutting?"

"Okay," I said. "Mum's the word." She didn't get that, but nodded and looked relieved when I put my finger across my lips.

I closed the door, sweating heavily. Somewhere I could hear not just one butterfly flapping its wings, but a whole cloud of them.

Maybe it's nothing.

I watched Marina push June's stroller down the sidewalk toward the bus stop, where she probably meant to wait for her hubs-bun . . . who was up to something. That much she knew. It had been all over her face.

I reached for the doorknob when she was out of sight, and that was when the phone rang. I almost didn't answer it, but there were only a few people with my number, and one of them was a woman I cared about very much.

"Hello?"

"Hello, Mr. Amberson," a man said. He had a soft Southern accent. I'm not sure if I knew who he was right away. I can't remember. I think I did. "Someone here has something to say to you."

I lived two lives in late 1962 and early 1963, one in Dallas and one in Jodie. They came together at 3:39 on the afternoon of April 10. In my ear, Sadie began screaming.

3

She lived in a single-story prefab ranch on Bee Tree Lane, part of a four- or five-block development of houses just like it on the west side of Jodie. An aerial photograph of the neighborhood in a 2011 history book might have been captioned MID-CENTURY STARTER HOMES. She arrived there around three o'clock that afternoon, following an after-school meeting with her student library aides. I doubt if she noticed the white-over-red Plymouth Fury parked at the curb a little way down the block.

Across the street, four or five houses down, Mrs. Holloway was washing her car (a Renault Dauphine that the rest of the neighbors eyed with suspicion). Sadie waved to her when she got out of her VW Bug. Mrs. Holloway waved back. The only owners of foreign (and somehow *alien*) cars on the block, they were casually collegial.

Sadie went up the walk to her front door and stood there for a moment, frowning. It was ajar. Had she left it that way? She went in and closed it behind her. It didn't catch because the lock had been forced, but she didn't notice. By then her whole attention was fixed on the wall over the sofa. There, written in her own lipstick, were two words in letters three feet high: DIRTY CUNT.

She should have run then, but her dismay and outrage were so great that she had no room for fear. She knew who had done it, but surely Johnny was gone. The man she had married had little taste for physical confrontation. Oh, there had been plenty of harsh words and that one slap, but nothing else.

Besides, her underwear was all over the floor.

It made a rough trail from the living room down the short hall to her bedroom. All of it—full slips, half-slips, bras, panties, the girdle she didn't need but sometimes wore—had been slashed. At the end of the hall, the door to the bathroom stood open. The towel rack had been ripped down. Printed on the tile where it had been, also in her lipstick, was another message: FILTHY FUCKER.

The door of her bedroom was also open. She went to it and stood in it with no sense at all that Johnny Clayton was standing behind it with a knife in one hand and a Smith & Wesson Victory .38 in the other. The revolver he carried that day was the same make and model as the one Lee Oswald would use to take the life of Dallas policeman J. D. Tippit.

Her little vanity bag lay open on her bed, the contents, mostly makeup, scattered across the coverlet. The accordion doors of her closet were folded open. Some of her clothes still drooped sadly from their hangers; most were on the floor. All of them had been slashed.

"Johnny, you bastard!" She wanted to scream those words, but the shock was too great. She could only whisper.

She started for the closet but didn't get far. An arm curled around her neck and a small circle of steel pressed hard against her temple. "Don't move, don't fight. If you do, I'll kill you."

She tried to pull away and he lashed her upside the head with the revolver's short barrel. At the same time the arm around her neck tightened. She saw the knife in the fist at the end of the arm that was choking her and stopped struggling. It was Johnny—she recognized the voice—but it really *wasn't* Johnny. He had changed.

I should have listened to him, she thought—meaning me. *Why didn't I listen?*

He marched her into the living room, arm still around her throat, then spun her and shoved her down on the couch, where she flopped, legs splayed.

"Pull down your dress. I can see your garters, you whore."

He was wearing bib overalls (that alone was enough to make her feel like she was dreaming) and had dyed his hair a weird orange-blond. She almost laughed.

He sat down on the hassock in front of her. The gun was aimed at her midsection. "We're going to call your cockboy."

"I don't know what—"

"Amberson. The one you play hide the salami with in that hot-sheets place over Killeen. I know all about it. I've been watching you a long time."

"Johnny, if you leave now I won't call the police. I promise. Even though you spoiled my clothes."

"Whore clothes," he said dismissively.

"I don't . . . I don't know his number."

Her address book, the one she usually kept in her little office next to the typewriter, was lying open next to the phone. "I do. It's on the first page. I looked under *C* for Cockboy first, but it wasn't there. I'll place the call, so you don't get any ideas about saying something to the operator. Then you talk to him."

"I won't, Johnny, not if you mean to hurt him."

He leaned forward. His weird orange-blond hair flopped into his eyes and he brushed it away with the hand holding the gun. Then he used the knife-hand to pluck the phone out of its cradle. The gun remained pointed steadily at her midsection. "Here's the thing, Sadie," he said, and now he sounded almost rational. "I'm going to kill one of you. The other can live. You decide which one it's going to be."

He meant every word. She could see it on his face. "What . . . what if he isn't home?"

He chuckled at her stupidity. "Then you die, Sadie."

She must have thought: *I can buy some time. It's at least three hours from Dallas to Jodie, more if the traffic's heavy. Time enough for Johnny to come to his senses. Maybe. Or for his attention to lapse just long enough for me to throw something at him and run out the door.*

He dialed 0 without looking at the address book (his memory for numbers had always been just short of perfect), and asked for WEstbrook 7-5430. Listened. Said, "Thank you, Operator."

Then, silence. Somewhere, over a hundred miles north, a telephone was ringing. She must have wondered how many rings Johnny would allow before hanging up and shooting her in the stomach.

Then his listening expression changed. He brightened, even smiled a little. His teeth were as white as ever, she observed, and why not? He had always brushed them at least half a dozen times a day. "Hello, Mr. Amberson. Someone here has something to say to you."

He got off the hassock and handed Sadie the phone. As she put it to her ear, he slashed out with the knife, quick as a striking snake, and sliced open the side of her face.

4

"What did you do to her?" I shouted. *"What did you do, you bastard?"*

"Hush, Mr. Amberson." He sounded amused. Sadie was no longer screaming, but I could hear her sobbing. "She's all right. She's bleeding pretty heavily, but that will stop." He paused, then spoke in a tone of judicious consideration. "Of course, she's not going to be pretty anymore. Now she looks like what she is, just a cheap four-dollar whore. My mother said she was, and my mother was right."

"Let her go, Clayton," I said. "Please."

"I *want* to let her go. Now that I've marked her, I *want* to. But here's what I already told her, Mr. Amberson. I am going to kill one of you. She cost me my job, you know; I had to quit and go into an electrical-treatment hospital or they were going to have me arrested." He paused. "I pushed a girl down the stairs. She tried to touch me. All this dirty bitch's fault, this one right here bleeding into her lap. I got her blood on my hands, too. I will need disinfectant." And he laughed.

"Clayton—"

"I'll give you three and a half hours. Until seven-thirty. Then I'll put two bullets in her. One in her stomach and one in her filthy cunt."

In the background, I heard Sadie scream: *"Don't you do it, Jacob!"*

"SHUT UP!" Clayton yelled at her. *"SHUT YOUR MOUTH!"* Then, to me, chillingly conversational: "Who's Jacob?"

"Me," I said. "It's my middle name."

"Does she call you that in bed when she sucks your cock, cock-boy?"

"Clayton," I said. "Johnny. Think what you're doing."

"I've been thinking about it for over a year. They gave me shock treatments in the electric hospital, you know. They said they'd stop the dreams, but they didn't. They made them worse."

"How bad is she cut? Let me talk to her."

"No."

"If you let me talk to her, maybe I'll do what you're asking. If you don't, I most certainly won't. Are you too fogged out from your shock treatments to understand that?"

It seemed he wasn't. There was a shuffling sound in my ear, then Sadie was on. Her voice was thin and trembling. "It's bad, but it's not going to kill me." Her voice dropped. "He just missed my eye—"

Then Clayton was back. "See? Your little tramp is fine. Now you just jump in your hotrod Chevrolet and get out here just as fast as the wheels will roll, how would that be? But listen to me carefully, Mr. George Jacob Amberson Cockboy: if you call the police, if I see a single blue or red light, I will kill this bitch and then myself. Do you believe that?"

"Yes."

"Good. I'm seeing an equation here where the values balance: the cockboy and the whoregirl. I'm in the middle. I'm the equals sign, Amberson, but you have to decide. Which value gets canceled out? It's your call."

"No!" she screamed. *"Don't! If you come out here he'll kill both of u—"*

The phone clicked in my ear.

5

I've told the truth so far, and I'm going to tell the truth here even though it casts me in the worst possible light: my first thought as my numb hand replaced the phone in its cradle was that he was wrong, the values *didn't* balance. In one pan of the scales was a pretty high school librarian. In the other was a man who knew the future and had—theoretically, at least—the power to change it. For a second, part of me actually thought about sacrificing Sadie and going across town to watch the alley running between Oak Lawn Avenue and Turtle Creek Boulevard to find out if the man who changed American history was on his own.

Then I got into my Chevy and headed for Jodie. Once I got out on Highway 77, I pegged the speedometer at seventy and kept it there. While I was driving, I thumbed the latches on my briefcase, took out my gun, and dropped it into the inner pocket of my sport coat.

I realized I'd have to involve Deke in this. He was old and no longer steady on his feet, but there was simply no one else. He would *want* to be involved, I told myself. He loved Sadie. I saw it in his face every time he looked at her.

And he's had his life, my cold mind said. *She hasn't. Anyway, he'll have the same chance the lunatic gave you. He doesn't have to come.*

But he would. Sometimes the things presented to us as choices aren't choices at all.

I never wished so much for my long-gone cell as I did on that drive from Dallas to Jodie. The best I could do was a gas station phone booth on SR 109, about half a mile beyond the football billboard. On the other end the phone rang three times . . . four . . . five . . .

Just as I was about to hang up, Deke said, "Hello? Hello?" He sounded irritated and out of breath.

"Deke? It's George."

"Hey, boy!" Now tonight's version of Bill Turcotte (from that popular and long-running play *The Homicidal Husband*) sounded delighted instead of irritated. "I was out in my little garden beside the house. I almost let it ring, but then—"

"Be quiet and listen. Something very bad's happened. Is still happening. Sadie's been hurt already. Maybe a lot."

There was a brief pause. When he spoke again, Deke sounded younger: like the tough man he had undoubtedly been forty years and two wives ago. Or maybe that was just hope. Tonight hope and a man in his late sixties was all I had. "You're talking about her husband, aren't you? This is my fault. I think I saw him, but that was weeks ago. And his hair was much longer than in the yearbook picture. Not the same color, either. It was almost *orange.*" A momentary pause, and then a word I had never heard from him before. *"Fuck!"*

I told him what Clayton wanted, and what I proposed to do. The plan was simple enough. Did the past harmonize with itself? Fine, I would let it. I knew Deke might have a heart attack— Turcotte had—but I wasn't going to let that stop me. I wasn't going to let anything stop me. It was Sadie.

I waited for him to ask if it wouldn't be better to turn this over to the police, but of course he knew better. Doug Reems, the Jodie constable, had poor eyesight, wore a brace on one leg, and was even older than Deke. Nor did Deke ask why I hadn't called the state police from Dallas. If he had, I would have told him I believed Clayton was serious about killing Sadie if he saw a single flashing light. It was true, but not the real reason. I wanted to take care of the son of a bitch myself.

I was very angry.

"What time does he expect you, George?"

"No later than seven-thirty."

"And it's now . . . quarter of, by my watch. Which gives us a smidge of time. The street behind Bee Tree is Apple-something. I disremember just what. That's where you'll be?"

"Right. The house behind hers."

"I can meet you there in five minutes."

"Sure, if you drive like a lunatic. Make it ten. And bring a prop, something he can see from the living room window if he looks out. I don't know, maybe—"

"Will a casserole dish do?"

"Fine. See you there in ten."

Before I could hang up, he said, "Do you have a gun?"

"Yes."

His reply was close to a dog's growl. "Good."

6

The street behind Doris Dunning's house had been Wyemore Lane. The street behind Sadie's was Apple Blossom Way. 202 Wyemore had been for sale. 140 Apple Blossom Way had no FOR SALE sign on the lawn, but it was dark and the lawn was shaggy, dotted with dandelions. I parked in front and looked at my watch. Six-fifty.

Two minutes later, Deke pulled his Ranch Wagon up behind my Chevy and got out. He was wearing jeans, a plaid shirt, and a string tie. In his hands he was holding a casserole dish with a flower on the side. It had a glass lid, and looked to contain three or four quarts of chop suey.

"Deke, I can't thank you en—"

"I don't deserve thanks, I deserve a swift kick in the pants. The day I saw him, he was coming out of the Western Auto just as I was going in. It had to've been Clayton. It was a windy day. A gust blew his hair back and I saw those hollows at his temples for just a second. But the hair . . . long and not the same color . . . he was dressed in cowboy clothes . . . shit-fire." He shook his head. "I'm getting old. If Sadie's hurt, I'll never forgive myself."

"Are you feeling all right? No chest pains, or anything like that?"

He looked at me as if I were crazy. "Are we going to stand here discussing my health, or are we going to try to get Sadie out of the trouble she's in?"

"We're going to do more than try. Go around the block to her house. While you're doing that, I'll cut through this backyard, then push through the hedge and into Sadie's." I was thinking about the Dunning house on Kossuth Street, of course, but even as I said it, I remembered that there *was* a hedge at the foot of Sadie's tiny backyard. I'd seen it many times. "You knock and say something cheery. Loud enough for me to hear. By then I'll be in the kitchen."

"What if the back door's locked?"

"She keeps a key under the step."

"Okay." Deke thought for a moment, frowning, then raised his head. "I'll say 'Avon calling, special casserole delivery.' And raise the dish so he can see me through the living room window if he looks. Will that do?"

"Yes. All I want you to do is distract him for a few seconds."

"Don't you shoot if there's any chance you might hit Sadie. Tackle the bastard. You'll do okay. The guy I saw was skinny as a rail."

We looked at each other bleakly. Such a plan would work on *Gunsmoke* or *Maverick,* but this was real life. And in real life the good guys—and gals—sometimes get their asses kicked. Or killed.

7

The yard behind the house on Apple Blossom Way wasn't quite the same as the one behind the Dunning place, but there were similarities. For one, there was a doghouse, although no sign reading YOUR POOCH BELONGS HERE. Instead, painted in a child's unsteady hand over the round door-shaped entrance, were the words BUTCHS HOWSE. And no trick-or-treating kiddies. Wrong season.

The hedge, however, looked exactly the same.

I pushed through it, barely noticing the scratches the stiff branches scrawled on my arms. I crossed Sadie's backyard in a running crouch, and tried the door. Locked. I felt beneath the step, sure that the key would be gone because the past harmonized but the past was obdurate.

It was there. I fished it out, put it in the lock, and applied slow increasing pressure. There was a faint thump from inside the door when the latch sprang back. I stiffened, waiting for a yell of alarm. None came. There were lights on in the living room, but I heard no voices. Maybe Sadie was dead already and Clayton was gone.

God, please no.

Once I eased the door open, however, I heard him. He was talking in a loud and monotonous drone, sounding like Billy James Hargis on tranquilizers. He was telling her what a whore she was, and how she had ruined his life. Or maybe it was the girl who had tried to touch him he was talking about. To Johnny Clayton they were all the same: sex-hungry disease carriers. You had to lay down the law. And, of course, the broom.

I slipped off my shoes and put them on the linoleum. The light was on over the sink. I checked my shadow to make sure it wasn't going to precede me into the doorway. I took my gun out of my sport coat pocket and started across the kitchen, meaning to stand beside the doorway to the living room until I heard *Avon calling!* Then I would go in a rush.

Only that isn't what happened. When Deke called out, there was nothing cheery about it. That was a cry of shocked fury. And it wasn't outside the front door; it was right in the house.

"Oh, my God! Sadie!"

After that, things happened very, very fast.

8

Clayton had forced the front door lock so it wouldn't latch. Sadie didn't notice, but Deke did. Instead of knocking, he pushed it open and stepped inside with the casserole dish in his hands. Clayton was still sitting on the hassock, and the gun was still pointed at Sadie, but he had put the knife down on the floor beside him. Deke said later he didn't even know Clayton *had* a knife. I doubt if he really even noticed the gun. His attention was fixed on Sadie. The top of her blue dress was now a muddy maroon. Her arm and the side of the sofa where it dangled were both covered with blood. But worst of all was her face, which was turned toward him. Her left cheek hung in two flaps, like a torn curtain.

"Oh, my God! Sadie!" The cry was spontaneous, nothing but pure shock.

Clayton turned, upper lip lifted in a snarl. He raised the gun. I saw this as I burst through the doorway between the kitchen and the living room. And I saw Sadie piston out one foot, kicking the hassock. Clayton fired, but the bullet went into the ceiling. As he tried to get up, Deke threw the casserole dish. The cover lifted off. Noodles, hamburger, green peppers, and tomato sauce sprayed in a fan. The dish, still more than half-full, hit Clayton's right arm. Chop suey poured out. The gun went flying.

I saw the blood. I saw Sadie's ruined face. I saw Clayton crouched on the blood-spotted rug and raised my own gun.

"No!" Sadie screamed. *"No, don't, please don't!"*

It cleared my mind like a slap. If I killed him, I would become the subject of police scrutiny no matter how justified the killing might be. My George Amberson identity would fall apart, and any chance I had of stopping the assassination in November would be gone. And really, how justified *would* it be? The man was disarmed.

Or so I thought, because I didn't see the knife, either. It was hidden by the overturned hassock. Even if it had been out in the open, I might have missed it.

I put the gun back in my pocket and hauled him to his feet.

"You can't hit me!" Spit flew from his lips. His eyes fluttered like those of a man having a seizure. His urine let go; I heard it pattering to the carpet. "I'm a mental patient, I'm not responsible, I can't be held responsible, I have a certificate, it's in the glove compartment of my car, I'll show it to y——"

The whine of his voice, the abject terror in his face now that he was disarmed, the way his dyed orange-blond hair hung around his face in clumps, even the smell of chop suey . . . all of these things enraged me. But mostly it was Sadie, cowering on the couch and drenched in blood. Her hair had come loose, and on the left side it hung in a clot beside her grievously wounded face. She would wear her scar in the same place Bobbi Jill wore the ghost of hers, of course she would, the past harmonizes, but Sadie's wound looked oh so much worse.

I slapped him across the right side of his face hard enough to knock spittle flying from the left side of his mouth. *"You crazy fuck, that's for the broom!"*

I went back the other way, this time knocking the spit from the right side of his mouth and relishing his howl in the bitter, unhappy way that is reserved only for the worst things, the ones where the evil is too great to be taken back. Or ever forgiven. *"That's for Sadie!"*

I balled my fist. In some other world, Deke was yelling into the phone. And was he rubbing his chest, the way Turcotte had rubbed his? No. At least not yet. In that same other world Sadie was moaning. *"And this is for me!"*

I drove my fist forward, and—I said I would tell the truth, every bit of it—when his nose splintered, his scream of pain was music to my ears. I let him go and he collapsed to the floor.

Then I turned to Sadie.

She tried to get off the couch, then fell back. She tried to hold her arms out to me, but she couldn't do that, either. They dropped into the sodden mess of her dress. Her eyes started to roll up and I was sure she was going to faint, but she held on. "You came," she whispered. "Oh, Jake, you came for me. You both did."

"Bee Tree Lane!" Deke shouted into the phone. "No, I don't know the number, I can't remember it, but you'll see an old man with chop suey on his shoes standing outside and waving his arms! Hurry! She's lost a lot of blood!"

"Sit still," I said. "Don't try to—"

Her eyes widened. She was looking over my shoulder. "Look out! Jake, *look out!*"

I turned, fumbling in my pocket for the gun. Deke also turned, holding the telephone receiver in both of his arthritis-knotted hands like a club. But although Clayton had picked up the knife he'd used to disfigure Sadie, his days of attacking anyone were over. Anyone but himself, that is.

It was another scene I'd played before, this one on Greenville Avenue, not long after I'd come to Texas. There was no Muddy

Waters blasting from the Desert Rose, but here was another badly hurt woman and another man bleeding from another broken nose, his shirt untucked and flapping almost to his knees. He was holding a knife instead of a gun, but otherwise it was just the same.

"No, Clayton!" I shouted. "Put it down!"

His eyes, visible through clumps of orange hair, were bulging as he stared at the dazed, half-fainting woman on the couch. "Is this what you want, Sadie?" he shouted. "If this is what you want, I'll give you what you want!"

Grinning desperately, he raised the knife to his throat . . . and cut.

PART 5

11/22/63

CHAPTER 23

1

From the Dallas *Morning News,* April 11, 1963 (page 1):

RIFLEMAN TAKES SHOT AT WALKER
By Eddie Hughes

A gunman with a high-powered rifle tried to kill former Maj. General Edwin A. Walker at his home Wednesday night, police said, and missed the controversial crusader by less than an inch.

Walker was working on his income taxes at 9:00 PM when the bullet crashed through a rear window and slammed into a wall next to him.

Police said a slight movement by Walker apparently saved his life.

"Somebody had a perfect bead on him," said Detective Ira Van Cleave. "Whoever it was certainly wanted to kill him."

Walker dug out several fragments of the shell's jacket from his right sleeve and was still shaking glass and slivers of the bullet out of his hair when reporters arrived.

Walker said he returned to his Dallas home Monday after the first stop of a lecture-tour called "Operation Midnight Ride." He also told reporters . . .

From the Dallas *Morning News,* April 12, 1963 (page 7):

MENTAL PATIENT SLASHES EX-WIFE, COMMITS SUICIDE
By Mack Dugas

(JODIE) 77-year-old Deacon "Deke" Simmons arrived too late on Wednesday night to save Sadie Dunhill from being wounded, but things could have been much worse for the 28-year-old Dunhill, a popular librarian in the Denholm Consolidated School District.

According to Douglas Reems, the Jodie town constable, "If Deke hadn't arrived when he did, Miss Dunhill almost certainly would have been killed." When approached by reporters, Simmons would only say, "I don't want to talk about it, it's over."

According to Constable Reems, Simmons overpowered the much younger John Clayton and wrestled away a small revolver. Clayton then produced the knife with which he had wounded his wife and used it to slash his own throat. Simmons and another man, George Amberson of Dallas, tried to stop the bleeding to no avail. Clayton was pronounced dead at the scene.

Mr. Amberson, a former teacher in the Denholm Consolidated School District who arrived shortly after Clayton had been disarmed, could not be reached for comment but told Constable Reems at the scene that Clayton—a former mental patient—may have been stalking his ex-wife for months. The staff at Denholm Consolidated High School had been alerted, and principal Ellen Dockerty had obtained a picture, but Clayton was said to have disguised his appearance.

Miss Dunhill was transported by ambulance to Parkland Memorial Hospital in Dallas, where her condition is listed as fair.

2

I wasn't able to see her until Saturday. I spent most of the intervening hours in the waiting room with a book I couldn't seem to read. Which was all right, because I had plenty of company—most of the DCHS teachers dropped by to check on Sadie's condition, as did almost a hundred students, those without licenses driven into Dallas by their parents. Many stayed to give blood to replace the pints Sadie had used. Soon my briefcase was stuffed with get-well cards and notes of concern. There were enough flowers to make the nurses' station look like a greenhouse.

I thought I'd gotten used to living in the past, but I was still shocked by Sadie's room at Parkland when I was finally allowed inside. It was an overheated single not much bigger than a closet. There was no bathroom; an ugly commode that only a dwarf could have used comfortably squatted in the corner, with a semi-opaque plastic curtain to pull across (for semi-privacy). Instead of buttons to raise and lower the bed, there was a crank, its white paint worn off by many hands. Of course there were no monitors showing computer-generated vital signs, and no TV for the patient, either.

A single glass bottle of something—maybe saline—hung from a metal stand. A tube went from it to the back of Sadie's left hand, where it disappeared beneath a bulky bandage.

Not as bulky as the one wrapped around the left side of her head, though. A sheaf of her hair had been cut off on that side, giving her a lopsided punished look . . . and of course, she *had* been punished. The docs had left a tiny slit for her eye. It and the one on the unbandaged, undamaged side of her face fluttered open when she heard my footsteps, and although she was doped up, those eyes registered a momentary flash of terror that squeezed my heart.

Then, wearily, she turned her face to the wall.

"Sadie—honey, it's me."

"Hi, me," she said, not turning back.

I touched her shoulder, which the gown left bare, and she twitched it away. "Please don't look at me."

"Sadie, it doesn't matter."

She turned back. Sad, morphine-loaded eyes looked at me, one peering out of a gauze peephole. An ugly yellowish-red stain was oozing through the bandages. Blood and some sort of ointment, I supposed.

"It matters," she said. "This isn't like what happened to Bobbi Jill." She tried to smile. "You know how a baseball looks, all those red stitches? That's what Sadie looks like now. They go up and down and all around."

"They'll fade."

"You don't get it. He cut all the way through my cheek to the inside of my mouth."

"But you're alive. And I love you."

"Say that when the bandages come off," she said in her dull, doped-up voice. "I make the Bride of Frankenstein look like Liz Taylor."

I took her hand. "I read something once—"

"I don't think I'm quite ready for a literary discussion, Jake."

She tried to turn away again, but I held onto her hand. "It was a Japanese proverb. 'If there is love, smallpox scars are as pretty as dimples.' I'll love your face no matter what it looks like. Because it's yours."

She began to cry, and I held her until she quieted. In fact, I thought she had gone to sleep when she said, "I know it's my fault, I married him, but—"

"It's not your fault, Sadie, you didn't know."

"I knew there was something not right about him. And still I went ahead. I think mostly because my mother and father wanted it so badly. They haven't come yet, and I'm glad. Because I blame them, too. That's awful, isn't it?"

"While you're serving up the blame, save a helping for me. I saw that goddam Plymouth he was driving at least twice dead on, and maybe a couple of other times out of the corner of my eye."

"You don't need to feel guilty on that score. The state police detective and the Texas Ranger who interviewed me said Johnny's trunk was full of license plates. He probably stole them at motor courts, they said. And he had a lot of stickers, whatdoyoucallums—"

"Decals." I was thinking of the one that had fooled me at the Candlewood that night. GO, SOONERS. I'd made the mistake of dismissing my repeated sightings of the white-over-red Plymouth as just another harmonic of the past. I should have known better. I *would* have known better, if half my mind hadn't been back in Dallas, with Lee Oswald and General Walker. And if blame mattered, there was a helping for Deke, too. After all, he had seen the man, had registered those deep dimples on the sides of his forehead.

Let it go, I thought. *It's happened. It can't be undone.*

Actually, it could.

"Jake, do the police know you aren't . . . quite who you say you are?"

I brushed back the hair on the right side of her face, where it was still long. "I'm fine on that score."

Deke and I had been interviewed by the same policemen who interviewed Sadie before the docs rolled her into the operating room. The state police detective had issued a tepid reprimand about men who had seen too many TV westerns. The Ranger seconded this, then shook our hands and said, "In your place, I would have done exactly the same thing."

"Deke's pretty much kept me out of it. He wants to make sure the schoolboard doesn't get pissy about you coming back next year. It seems incredible to me that being cut up by a lunatic could lead to dismissal on grounds of moral turpitude, but Deke seems to think it's best if—"

"I can't go back. I can't face the kids looking like I do now."

"Sadie, if you knew how many of them have come here—"

"That's sweet, it means a lot, and they're the very ones I couldn't face. Don't you understand? I think I could deal with the ones who'd laugh and make jokes. In Georgia I taught with a woman who had a harelip, and I learned a lot from the way she handled teenage cruelty. It's the other ones that would undo me. The well-meaning ones. The looks of sympathy . . . and the ones who can't stand to look at all." She took a deep, shuddering breath, then burst out: "Also, I'm *angry*. I know life is hard, I think *everyone* knows that in their hearts, but why does it have to be cruel, as well? Why does it have to *bite*?"

I took her in my arms. The unmarked side of her face was hot and throbbing. "I don't know, honey."

"Why are there no second chances?"

I held her. When her breathing became regular, I let her go and stood up quietly to leave. Without opening her eyes, she said, "You told me there was something you had to witness on Wednesday night. I don't think it was Johnny Clayton cutting his own throat, was it?"

"No."

"Did you miss it?"

I thought of lying, didn't. "Yes."

Now her eyes opened, but it was a struggle and they wouldn't stay open for long. "Will *you* get a second chance?"

"I don't know. It doesn't matter."

That wasn't the truth. Because it would matter to John Kennedy's wife and children; it would matter to his brothers; perhaps to Martin Luther King; almost certainly to the tens of thousands of young Americans who were now in high school and who would, if nothing changed the course of history, be invited to put on uniforms, fly to the other side of the world, spread their nether cheeks, and sit down on the big green dildo that was Vietnam.

She closed her eyes. I left the room.

3

There were no current DCHS students in the lobby when I got off the elevator, but there were a couple of alums. Mike Coslaw and Bobbi Jill Allnut were sitting in hard plastic chairs with unread magazines in their laps. Mike jumped up and shook my hand. From Bobbi Jill I got a good strong hug.

"How bad is it?" she asked. "I mean"—she rubbed the tips of her fingers over her own fading scar—"can it be fixed?"

"I don't know."

"Have you talked to Dr. Ellerton?" Mike asked. Ellerton, reputedly the best plastic surgeon in central Texas, was the doc who had worked his magic on Bobbi Jill.

"He's in the hospital this afternoon, doing rounds. Deke, Miz Ellie, and I have an appointment with him in"—I checked my watch—"twenty minutes. Would you two care to sit in?"

"Please," Bobbi Jill said. "I just *know* he can fix her. He's a genius."

"Come on, then. Let's see what the genius can do."

Mike must have read my face, because he squeezed my arm and said, "Maybe it's not as bad as you think, Mr. A."

4

It was worse.

Ellerton passed around the photographs—stark black-and-white glossies that reminded me of Weegee and Diane Arbus. Bobbi Jill gasped and turned away. Deke grunted softly, as if he'd been struck a blow. Miz Ellie shuffled through them stoically, but her face lost all color except for the two balls of rouge flaming on her cheeks.

In the first two, Sadie's cheek hung in ragged flaps. That I had seen on Wednesday night and was prepared for. What I wasn't prepared for was the stroke-victim droop of her mouth and the slack wad of the flesh below her left eye. It gave her a clownish look that made me want to thump my head on the table of the small conference room the doctor had appropriated for our meeting. Or maybe—this would be better—to rush down to the morgue where Johnny Clayton lay so I could beat on him some more.

"When this young woman's parents arrive this evening," Ellerton said, "I will be tactful and hopeful, because parents deserve tact and hope." He frowned. "Although one might have expected them sooner, given the gravity of Mrs. Clayton's condi—"

"Miss *Dunhill*," Ellie said with quiet savagery. "She was legally divorced from that monster."

"Yes, quite, I stand corrected. At any rate, you are her friends, and I believe you deserve less tact and more truth." He looked dispassionately at one of the photographs, and tapped Sadie's torn cheek with a short, clean fingernail. "This can be improved, but never put right. Not with the techniques now at my disposal. Perhaps a year from now, when the tissue has fully healed, I might be able to repair the worst of the dissymmetry."

Tears began to run down Bobbi Jill's cheeks. She took Mike's hand.

"The permanent damage to her looks is unfortunate," Ellerton said, "but there are other problems, as well. The facial nerve has been cut. She is going to have problems eating on the left side of her mouth. The droop in the eye you see in these photographs will be with her for the rest of her life, and her tear duct has been partially severed. Yet her sight may not be impaired. We'll hope not."

He sighed and spread his hands.

"Given the promise of wonderful stuff like microsurgery and nerve regeneration, we may be able to do more with cases like this in twenty or thirty years. For now, all I can say is I'll do my best to repair all the damage that is repairable."

Mike spoke up for the first time. His tone was bitter. "Too bad we don't live in 1990, huh?"

5

It was a silent, dispirited little group that walked out of the hospital that afternoon. At the edge of the parking lot, Miz Ellie touched my sleeve. "I should have listened to you, George. I am so, so sorry."

"I'm not sure it would have made any difference," I said, "but if you want to make it up to me, ask Freddy Quinlan to give me a call. He's the real estate guy who helped me when I first came to Jodie. I want to be close to Sadie this summer, and that means I need a place to rent."

"You can stay with me," Deke said. "I have plenty of room."

I turned to him. "Are you sure?"

"You'd be doing me a favor."

"I'll be happy to pay—"

He waved it away. "You can kick in for groceries. That'll be fine."

He and Ellie had come in Deke's Ranch Wagon. I watched them pull out, then trudged to my Chevrolet, which now seemed—probably unfairly—a bad-luck car. Never had I less wanted to go back to West Neely, where I would no doubt hear Lee taking out on Marina his frustrations over missing General Walker.

"Mr. A.?" It was Mike. Bobbi Jill stood a few paces back with her arms folded tightly beneath her breasts. She looked cold and unhappy.

"Yes, Mike."

"Who's going to pay Miss Dunhill's hospital bills? And for all those surgeries he talked about? Does she have insurance?"

"Some." But nowhere near enough, not for a thing like this. I thought of her parents, but the fact that they still hadn't shown up yet was troubling. They *couldn't* blame her for what Clayton had done . . . could they? I didn't see how, but I had come from a world where women were, for the most part, treated as equals. 1963 never seemed more like a foreign country to me than it did at that moment.

"I'll help as much as I can," I said, but how much would that be? My cash reserves were deep enough to get me through another few months, but not enough to pay for half a dozen facial reconstruction procedures. I didn't want to go back to Faith Financial on Greenville Avenue, but I supposed I would if I had to. The Kentucky Derby was coming up in less than a month, and according to the bookie section of Al's notes, the winner was going to be Chateaugay, a longshot. A thousand on the nose would net seven or eight grand, enough to take care of Sadie's hospital stay and—at 1963 rates—at least some of the follow-up surgeries.

"I have an idea," Mike said, then glanced over his shoulder. Bobbi Jill gave him an encouraging smile. "That is, me n Bobbi Jill do."

"Bobbi Jill and I, Mike. You're not a kid anymore, so don't talk like one."

"Right, right, sorry. If you can come back into the coffee shop for ten minutes or so, we'll lay it on you."

I went. We drank coffee. I listened to their idea. And agreed. Sometimes when the past harmonizes with itself, the wise man clears his throat and sings along.

6

There was a whopper of an argument in the apartment above me that evening. Baby June added her nickel's worth, wailing her head off. I didn't bother to eavesdrop; the yelling would be in Russian, for the most part, anyway. Then, around eight, an unaccustomed silence fell. I assumed they'd gone to bed two hours or so earlier than their usual time, and that was a relief.

I was thinking about going to bed myself when the de Mohrenschildts' yacht of a Cadillac pulled up at the curb. Jeanne slid out; George *popped* out with his usual jack-in-the-box élan. He opened the rear door behind the driver's seat and brought out a large stuffed rabbit with improbable purple fur. I gawked at this through the slit in the drapes for a moment before the penny dropped: tomorrow was Easter Sunday.

They headed for the outside stairs. She walked; George, in the lead, trotted. His pounding footfalls on the ramshackle steps shook the whole building.

I heard startled voices over my head, muffled but clearly questioning. Footfalls hurried across my ceiling, making the overhead light fixture in the living room rattle. Did the Oswalds think it was the Dallas police coming to make an arrest? Or maybe one of the FBI agents who had been keeping tabs on Lee while he and his family were living on Mercedes Street? I hoped the little bastard's heart was in his throat, choking him.

There was a flurry of knocks on the door at the top of the stairs, and de Mohrenschildt called jovially: "Open up, Lee! Open up, you heathen!"

The door opened. I donned my earphones but heard nothing. Then, just as I was deciding to try the mike in the Tupperware bowl, either Lee or Marina turned on the lamp with the bug in it. It was working again, at least for the time being.

"—for the baby," Jeanne was saying.

"Oh, thank!" Marina said. "Thank very much, Jeanne, so kind!"

"Don't just stand there, Comrade, get us something to drink!" de Mohrenschildt said. He sounded like he'd had a few belts already.

"I only have tea," Lee said. He sounded petulant and half-awake.

"Tea's fine. I've got something here in my pocket that'll get it up on its feet." I could almost see him wink.

Marina and Jeanne lapsed into Russian. Lee and de Mohrenschildt—their heavier footfalls unmistakable—started toward the kitchen area, where I knew I'd lose them. The women were standing close to the lamp, and their voices would cover the conversation of the men.

Then Jeanne, in English: "Oh my goodness, is that a *gun?*"

Everything stopped, including—so it felt—my heart.

Marina laughed. It was a tinkling little cocktail-party laugh, *hahaha,* artificial as hell. "He lose job, we have no money, and this crazy person buy rifle. I say, 'Put in closet, you crazy eediot, so it don't upset my pregnance.'"

"I wanted to do some target-shooting, that's all," Lee said. "I was pretty good in the Marines. Never shot Maggie's Drawers a single time."

Another silence. It seemed to go on forever. Then de Mohrenschildt's big hail-fellow laugh boomed out. "Come on, don't bullshit a bullshitter! How'd you miss him, Lee?"

"I don't know what the hell you're talking about."

"General Walker, boy! Someone almost splattered his Negro-hating brains all over his office wall at that house of his on Turtle Creek. You mean you didn't know?"

"I haven't been reading the papers just lately."

"Oh?" Jeanne said. "Don't I see the *Times Herald* over there on that stool?"

"I mean I don't read the news. Too depressing. Just the funny-pages and the want-ads. Big Brother says get a job or the baby starves."

"So you weren't the one who took that potshot, huh?" de Mohrenschildt asked.

Teasing him. *Baiting* him.

The question was why. Because de Mohrenschildt would never in his wildest dreams have believed a pipsqueak like Ozzie Rabbit was the shooter last Wednesday night . . . or because he knew that Lee was? Maybe because Jeanne had noticed the rifle? I wished with all my heart that the women weren't there. Given a chance to listen to Lee and his peculiar amigo talk man-to-man, my questions might have been answered. As it was, I still could not be sure.

"You think I'd be crazy enough to shoot at someone with J. Edgar Hoover looking over my shoulder?" Lee sounded like he was trying to get into the spirit of the thing, Josh Along with George instead of Sing Along with Mitch, but he wasn't doing a very good job.

"Nobody thinks you shot at anybody, Lee," Jeanne said in a placating voice. "Just promise that when your baby starts to walk, you find a safer place than the closet for that rifle of yours."

Marina replied to this in Russian, but I'd glimpsed the baby in the side yard from time to time and knew what she was saying—that June was walking already.

"Junie will enjoy the nice present," Lee said, "but we don't celebrate Easter. We're atheists."

Maybe *he* was, but according to Al's notes, Marina—with the help of her admirer, George Bouhe—had had June secretly baptized right around the time of the Missile Crisis.

"So are we," de Mohrenschildt said. "That's why we celebrate the Easter Bunny!" He had moved closer to the lamp, and his roar of laughter half-deafened me.

They talked for another ten minutes, mixing English and Russian. Then Jeanne said, "We'll leave you in peace now. I think we turned you out of bed."

"No, no, we were up," Lee said. "Thanks for dropping by."

George said, "We'll talk soon, Lee, eh? You can come to the country club. We'll organize the waiters into a collective!"

"Sure, sure." They were moving toward the door now.

De Mohrenschildt said something else, but it was too low for me to catch more than a few words. They might have been *get it back.* Or *got your back,* although I didn't think that was common slang in the sixties.

When did you get it back? Was that what he said? As in when did you get the rifle back?

I replayed the tape half a dozen times, but at super-slow speed, there was just no way to tell. I lay awake long after the Oswalds had gone to sleep; I was still awake at two in the morning, when June cried briefly and was soothed back to dreamland by her mother. I thought of Sadie, sleeping the unrestful sleep of morphine at Parkland Hospital. The room was ugly and the bed was narrow, but I would have been able to sleep there, I was sure of it.

I thought about de Mohrenschildt, that manic shirt-ripping stage actor. *What did you say, George? What did you say there at the end? Was it* when did you get it back? *Was it* cheer up, things aren't so black? *Was it* don't let this set you back? *Or something else entirely?*

At last I slept. And dreamed I was at a carnival with Sadie. We came to a shooting gallery where Lee stood with his rifle socked into the hollow of his shoulder. The guy behind the counter was George de Mohrenschildt. Lee fired three times and didn't hit a single target.

"Sorry, son," de Mohrenschildt said, "no prizes for guys who shoot Maggie's Drawers."

Then he turned to me and grinned.

"Step right up, son, you may have better luck. *Somebody's* going to kill the president, why not you?"

I woke with a start in the first weak light of day. Above me, the Oswalds slept on.

7

Easter Sunday afternoon found me back in Dealey Plaza, sitting on a park bench, looking at the forbidding brick cube of the School Book Depository, and wondering what to do next.

In ten days, Lee was going to leave Dallas for New Orleans, the city of his birth. He would get a job greasing machinery at a coffee company and rent the apartment on Magazine Street. After spending two weeks or so with Ruth Paine and her children in Irving, Marina and June would join him. I wouldn't follow. Not with Sadie facing a long period of recovery and an uncertain future.

Was I going to kill Lee between this Easter Sunday and the twenty-fourth? I probably could. Since losing his job at Jaggars-Chiles-Stovall, he spent most of his time either in the apartment or handing out Fair Play for Cuba leaflets in downtown Dallas. Once in awhile he went to the public library, where he seemed to have given up Ayn Rand and Karl Marx in favor of Zane Grey westerns.

Shooting him on the street or at the library on Young Street would be a recipe for instant incarceration, but if I did it in the upstairs apartment, while Marina was in Irving, helping Ruth Paine improve her Russian? I could knock on the door and put a bullet in his head when he opened it. Done deal. No risk of shooting Maggie's Drawers at point-blank range. The problem was the aftermath. I'd have to run. If I didn't, I'd be the first person the police would question. I was the downstairs neighbor, after all.

I could claim I wasn't there when it happened, and they might buy that for awhile, but how long would it be before they discovered that the George Amberson of West Neely Street was the same George Amberson who just happened to be at a scene of violence on Bee Tree Lane in Jodie not long before? That would merit checking, and checking would soon reveal that George Amberson's teaching certificate came from a degree-mill in Oklahoma and George Amberson's references were phony. At that point I'd very likely be arrested. The police would obtain a court order to open my safe deposit box if they found out I had one, and they probably would. Mr. Richard Link, my banker, would see my name and/or picture in the paper and come forward. What would the police make of my memoir? That I had a motive for shooting Oswald, no matter how crazy.

No, I'd have to run for the rabbit-hole, ditching the Chevy somewhere in Oklahoma or Arkansas, then taking a bus or train. And if I made it back to 2011, I could never use the rabbit-hole again without causing a reset. That would mean leaving Sadie behind forever, disfigured and alone. *Of course he ran out on me,* she would think. *He talked a good game about smallpox scars being as pretty as dimples, but once he heard Ellerton's prognosis—ugly now, ugly forever—he headed for the hills.*

She might not even blame me. That was the most rotten possibility of all.

But no. No. I could think of a worse one. Suppose I got back to 2011 and discovered that Kennedy had been assassinated on November 22 after all? I still wasn't positive Oswald was on his own. Who was I to say that ten thousand conspiracy theorists were wrong, especially based on the few scraps of information all my haunting and stalking had gleaned?

Maybe I'd check Wikipedia and discover the shooter had been on the grassy knoll, after all. Or on the roof of the combined jail and county courthouse on Houston Street, armed with a sharpshooter's rifle instead of a mail-order Mannlicher-Carcano. Or hiding in a sewer on Elm Street and watching for Kennedy's approach with a periscope, as some of the wilder conspiracy buffs claimed.

De Mohrenschildt was a CIA asset of some kind. Even Al Templeton, who was almost positive that Oswald had acted alone, acknowledged that much. Al was convinced he was just a *little* asset, passing on bits of South and Central American tittle-tattle to keep his various oil speculations afloat. But what if he was more? The CIA had loathed Kennedy ever since he refused to send in American troops to back the beleagured partisans at the Bay of Pigs. His graceful handling of the Missile Crisis had deepened that loathing; the spooks had wanted to use it as a pretext to end the cold war once and for all, because they were positive the bally-hooed "missile gap" was a fiction. You could read much of this in the daily papers, sometimes between the lines of the news stories, sometimes stated baldly in the op-ed essays.

Suppose certain rogue elements in the CIA had talked George de Mohrenschildt into a much more dangerous mission? Not killing the president himself, but recruiting several less-than-balanced individuals who would be willing to do the job? Would de Mohrenschildt say yes to such an offer? I thought he might. He and Jeanne lived big, but I had no real idea how they supported the Cadillac, the country club, and their sprawl of a house on Simpson Stuart Road. Serving as the cutout, a dead-short between a targeted U.S. president and an agency that theoretically existed to do his bidding . . . that would be dangerous work, but if the potential gain were big enough, a man living above his means might be tempted. And it wouldn't even have to be a cash payoff, that was the beauty of it. Just those wonderful oil leases in Venezuela, Haiti, and the DR. Also, such work might appeal to a grandiose strutter like de Mohrenschildt. He liked action, and he didn't care for Kennedy.

Thanks to John Clayton, I couldn't even eliminate de Mohrenschildt from the Walker attempt. It was Oswald's rifle, yes, but suppose Lee had found himself unable to fire it when the time came? I thought it would be just like the little weasel to choke at the critical moment. I could see de Mohrenschildt snatching the Carcano out of Lee's trembling hands and snarling, *Give it to me, I'll do it myself.*

Would de Mohrenschildt have felt capable of making the shot from behind the garbage can Lee meant to use as a sniper's bench? One line in Al's notes made me think the answer was yes: *Won skeet-shooting championship at country club in 1961.*

If I killed Oswald and Kennedy died anyway, it would all be for nothing. And then what? Rinse and repeat? Kill Frank Dunning again? Save Carolyn Poulin again? Drive to Dallas again?

Meet Sadie again?

She would be unmarked, and that was good. I would know what her crazy ex-husband looked like, dye-job and all, and this time I could stop him before he got close. Also good. But just thinking about going through all of it again exhausted me. Nor did I think I could kill Lee in cold blood, at least not based on the circumstantial evidence I had. With Frank Dunning, I'd known for sure. I had *seen*.

So—what was my next move?

It was quarter past four, and I decided my next move was visiting Sadie. I started for my car, which was parked on Main Street. On the corner of Main and Houston, just past the old courthouse, I had a sensation of being watched and turned around. No one was on the sidewalk behind me. It was the Depository that was watching, all those blank windows overlooking Elm Street, where the presidential motorcade would arrive some two hundred days from that Easter Sunday.

8

They were serving dinner on Sadie's floor when I arrived: chop suey. The smell brought back a vivid image of the way the blood had gushed over John Clayton's hand and forearm before he fell to the carpet, mercifully facedown.

"Hey there, Mr. Amberson," the head nurse said as I signed in. She was a graying woman in a starched white cap and uniform. A pocket watch was pinned to her formidable bosom. She was looking at me from behind a barricade of bouquets. "There was a fair amount of shouting in there last night. I'm only telling you because you're her fiancé, right?"

"Right," I said. Certainly it was what I wanted to be, slashed face or no slashed face.

The nurse leaned toward me between two overloaded vases. A few daisies brushed through her hair. "Look, I don't ordinarily gossip about my patients, and I ream out the younger nurses who do. But the way her parents treated her wasn't right. I guess I don't *entirely* blame them for riding down from Georgia with that lunatic's folks, but—"

"Wait. Are you telling me the Dunhills and the Claytons *carpooled?*"

"I guess they were all palsy-walsy back in happier days, so all right, fine, but to tell her that while they were visiting their daughter, their good friends the Claytons were downstairs signing their son's body out of the morgue . . ." She shook her head. "Daddy never said boo, but that *woman* . . ."

She looked around to make sure we were still alone, saw we were, and turned back to me. Her plain country face was grim with outrage.

"She never shut *up*. One question about how her daughter was feeling, then it was the poor Claytons this and the poor Claytons that. Your Miss Dunhill held her tongue until her mother said what a shame it was that they'd have to change churches again. Then the girl lost her temper and started shouting at them to get out."

"Good for her," I said.

"I heard her yell, 'Do you want to see what your good friends' son did to me?' and honey-pie, that's when I started running. She was trying to pull off the bandages. And the mother . . . she was *leaning forward,* Mr. Amberson. *Eager.* She actually wanted to look. I hustled them out and got one of the residents to give Miss Dunhill a shot and quiet her down. The father—a little mouse of a man—tried to apologize for his wife. 'She didn't know she was upsetting Sadie,' he says. 'Well,' I says back, 'what about you? Cat get your tongue?' And do you know what the woman said, just before they got on the elevator?"

I shook my head.

"She said, 'I can't blame him, how can I? He used to play in our yard, and he was just the sweetest boy.' Can you believe that?"

I could. Because I thought I had already met Mrs. Dunhill, in a manner of speaking. On West Seventh Street, chasing after her older son and yelling at the top of her lungs. *Stop, Robert, don't walk so fast, I'm not done with you.*

"You may find her . . . overly emotional," the nurse said. "I just wanted you to know there's a good reason for it."

9

She wasn't overly emotional. I would have preferred that. If there's such a thing as serene depression, that's where Sadie's head was at on that Easter evening. She was sitting in her chair, at least, with an untouched plate of chop suey in front of her. She'd lost weight; her long body seemed to float in the white hospital johnny she pulled around her when she saw me.

She smiled though—on the side of her face that still could—and turned her good cheek to be kissed. "Hello, George—I'd better call you that, don't you think?"

"Maybe so. How are you, honey?"

"They say I'm better, but my face feels like someone dipped it in kerosene and then set it on fire. It's because they're taking me off the pain medication. God forbid I get hooked on dope."

"If you need more, I can talk to somebody."

She shook her head. "It makes me fuzzy, and I need to think. Also, it makes it hard to keep control of my emotions. I had quite the shouting match with my mother and father."

There was only the one chair—unless you wanted to count the commode squatting in the corner—so I sat on the bed. "The head nurse filled me in. Based on what she overheard, you had every right to blow your top."

"Maybe, but what good does it do? Mom will never change. She can talk for hours about how having me almost killed her, but she has very little feeling for anyone else. It's lack of tact, but it's lack of something more. There's a word for it, but I can't remember it."

"Empathy?"

"That's it. And she has a very sharp tongue. Over the years, it's whittled my dad away to a stub. He rarely says anything these days."

"You don't need to see them again."

"I think I do." I liked her calm, detached voice less and less. "Mama says they'll fix up my old room, and I really don't have anyplace else to go."

"Your home's in Jodie. And your work."

"I think we talked about that. I'm going to tender my resignation."

"No, Sadie, no. That's a very bad idea."

She smiled as best she could. "You sound like Miz Ellie. Who didn't believe you when you said Johnny was a danger." She thought about this, then added: "Of course, neither did I. I never stopped being a fool about him, did I?"

"You have a house."

"That's true. And mortgage payments I can't make. I'll have to let it go."

"I'll make the payments."

That got through. She looked shocked. "You can't afford to do that!"

"I can, actually." Which was true . . . for awhile, at least. Plus there was always the Kentucky Derby and Chateaugay. "I'm moving out of Dallas and in with Deke. He's not charging me rent, which frees up plenty for house payments."

A tear crept to the edge of her right eye and trembled there. "You're kind of missing the point. I can't take care of myself, not yet. And I won't be 'taken in,' unless it's at home, where Mom will hire a nurse to help with the nasty bits. I've got a little pride left. Not much, but a little."

"I'll take care of you."

She stared at me, wide-eyed. "What?"

"You heard me. And when it comes to me, Sadie, you can stick your pride where the sun doesn't shine. I happen to love you. And if you love me, you'll stop talking mad shit about going home to your crocodile of a mother."

She managed a faint smile at that, then sat quiet, thinking, hands in the lap of her flimsy cover-up. "You came to Texas to do something, and it wasn't to nurse a school librarian who was too silly to know she was in danger."

"My business in Dallas is on hold."

"*Can* it be?"

"Yes." And as simply as that, it was decided. Lee was going to New Orleans, and I was going back to Jodie. The past kept fighting me, and it was going to win this round. "You need time, Sadie, and I have time. We might as well spend it together."

"You can't want me." She said this in a voice just above a whisper. "Not the way I am now."

"But I do."

She looked at me with eyes that were afraid to hope and hoped anyway. "Why would you?"

"Because you're the best thing that's ever happened to me."

The good side of her mouth began to tremble. The tear spilled onto her cheek and was followed by others. "If I didn't have to go back to Savannah . . . if I didn't have to live with them . . . with *her* . . . maybe then I could be, I don't know, just a little bit all right."

I took her into my arms. "You're going to be a lot better than that."

"Jake?" Her voice was muffled with tears. "Would you do something for me before you go?"

"What, honey?"

"Take away that goddamned chop suey. The smell is making me sick."

10

The nurse with the fullback shoulders and the watch pinned to her bosom was Rhonda McGinley, and on the eighteenth of April she insisted on pushing Sadie's wheelchair not only to the elevator but all the way out to the curb, where Deke waited with the passenger door of his station wagon open.

"Don't let me see you back here, sugar-pie," Nurse McGinley said after we'd helped Sadie into the car.

Sadie smiled distractedly and said nothing. She was—not to put too fine a point on it—stoned to the high blue sky. Dr. Ellerton had been in that morning to examine her face, an excruciating process that had necessitated extra pain medication.

McGinley turned to me. "She's going to need a lot of TLC in the next few months."

"I'll do my best."

We got rolling. Ten miles south of Dallas, Deke said, "Take that away from her and throw it out the window. I'm minding this damn traffic."

Sadie had fallen asleep with a cigarette smoldering between her fingers. I leaned over the seat and plucked it away. She moaned when I did it and said, "Oh don't, Johnny, please don't."

I met Deke's eyes. Only for a second, but enough for me to see we were thinking the same thing: *Long road ahead. Long road.*

11

I moved into Deke's Spanish-style home on Sam Houston Road. At least for public consumption. In truth, I moved in with Sadie at 135 Bee Tree Lane. I was afraid of what we might find when we first helped her inside, and I think that Sadie was, too, stoned or not. But Miz Ellie and Jo Peet from the Home Ec Department had recruited a few trustworthy girls who had spent an entire day before Sadie's return cleaning, polishing, and scrubbing every trace of Clayton's filth off the walls. The living room rug had been taken up and replaced. The new one was industrial gray, hardly an exciting color, but probably a wise choice; gray things hold so few memories. Her mutilated clothing had been whisked away and replaced with new stuff.

Sadie never said a word about the new rug and the different clothes. I'm not sure she even noticed them.

12

I spent my days there, cooking her meals, working in her little garden (which would sicken but not quite die in another hot central Texas summer), and reading *Bleak House* to her. We also became involved in several of the afternoon soaps: *The Secret Storm, Young Doctor Malone, From These Roots,* and our personal favorite, *The Edge of Night.*

She changed the parting in her hair from the center to the right, cultivating a Veronica Lake style that would cover the worst of the scarring when the bandages eventually came off. Not that they would for a long time; the first of her reconstructive surgeries—a team effort involving four doctors—was scheduled for August fifth. Ellerton said there would be at least four more.

I would drive back to Deke's after Sadie and I had our supper (which she rarely did more than pick at), because small towns are full of big eyes attached to gabby mouths. It was best that those big eyes should see my car in Deke's driveway after the sun went down. Once it was dark, I walked the two miles back to Sadie's, where I slept on the new hide-a-bed sofa until five in the morning. It was almost always broken rest, because nights when Sadie didn't awaken me, screaming and thrashing her way out of bad dreams, were rare. In the daytime, Johnny Clayton was dead. After dark he still stalked her with his gun and knife.

I would go to her and soothe her as best I could. Sometimes she would trudge out to the living room with me and smoke a cigarette before shuffling back to bed, always pressing her hair down protectively over the bad side of her face. She would not let me change the bandages. That she did herself, in the bathroom, with the door closed.

After one especially terrible nightmare, I came in to find her standing naked by her bed and sobbing. She had become shockingly thin. Her nightgown was puddled at her feet. She heard me and turned around, one arm across her breasts and the other hand over her crotch. Her hair swung back to her right shoulder, where it actually belonged, and I saw the swollen scars, the heavy stitching, the fallen, rumpled flesh over her cheekbone.

"Get out!" she screamed. *"Don't look at me like this, why can't you get out?"*

"Sadie, what is it? Why did you take off your nightgown? What's wrong?"

"I wet my bed, okay? I have to change it, *so please get out and let me put some clothes on!*"

I went to the foot of the bed, grabbed the quilt that was folded there, and wrapped it around her. When I turned one end up in a kind of collar that hid her cheek, she calmed.

"Go in the living room and be careful you don't trip on that thing. Have a smoke. I'll change the bed."

"No, Jake, it's dirty."

I took her by the shoulders. "That's what Clayton would say, and he's dead. A little piss is all it is."

"Are you sure?"

"Yes. But before you go . . ."

I turned down the makeshift collar. She flinched and closed her eyes, but stood still. Only bearing it, but I still thought it was progress. I kissed the hanging flesh that had been her cheek and then turned the quilt up again to hide it.

"How can you?" she asked without opening her eyes. "It's *awful.*"

"Nah. It's just another part of the you I love, Sadie. Now go in the other room while I change these sheets."

When it was done, I offered to get into bed with her until she fell asleep. She flinched as she had when I'd turned down the quilt and shook her head. "I can't, Jake. I'm sorry."

Little by slowly, I told myself as I plodded across town to Deke's in the first gray light of morning. *Little by slowly.*

13

On April twenty-fourth I told Deke I had something I needed to do in Dallas and asked him if he'd stay with Sadie until I got back around nine. He agreed willingly enough, and at five that afternoon I was sitting across from the Greyhound terminal on South Polk Street, near the intersection of Highway 77 and the still-new, fourlane I-20. I was reading (or pretending to read) the latest James Bond, *The Spy Who Loved Me.*

At half past the hour, a station wagon pulled into the parking lot next to the terminal. Ruth Paine was driving. Lee got out, went around to the rear, and opened the doorgate. Marina, with June in her arms, emerged from the backseat. Ruth Paine stayed behind the wheel.

Lee had only two items of luggage: an olive-green duffel bag and a quilted gun case, the kind with handles. He carried them to an idling Scenicruiser. The driver took the suitcase and the rifle and stowed them in the open luggage hold after a cursory glance at Lee's ticket.

Lee went to the door of the bus, then turned and embraced his wife, kissing her on both cheeks and then the mouth. He took the baby and nuzzled beneath her chin. June laughed. Lee laughed with her, but I saw tears in his eyes. He kissed June on the forehead, gave her a hug, then returned her to Marina and ran up the steps of the bus without looking back.

Marina walked to the station wagon, where Ruth Paine was now standing. June held her arms out to the older woman, who took her with a smile. They stood there for awhile, watching passengers board, then drove off.

I stayed where I was until the bus pulled out at 6:00 P.M., right on time. The sun, going down bloody in the west, flashed across the destination window, momentarily obscuring what was printed there. Then I could read it again, three words that meant Lee Harvey Oswald was out of my life, at least for awhile:

NEW ORLEANS EXPRESS

I watched it climb the entrance ramp to I-20 East, then walked the two blocks to where I'd parked my car and drove back to Jodie.

14

Hunch-think: that again.

I paid the May rent on the West Neely Street apartment even though I needed to start watching my dollars and had no concrete reason to do so. All I had was an unformed but strong feeling that I should keep a base of operations in Dallas.

Two days before the Kentucky Derby ran, I drove to Greenville Avenue, fully intending to put down five hundred dollars on Chateaugay to place. That, I reasoned, would be less memorable than betting on the nag to win. I parked four blocks down from Faith Financial and locked my car, a necessary precaution in that part of town even at eleven in the morning. I walked briskly at first, but then—once more for no concrete reason—my steps began to lag.

Half a block from the betting parlor masquerading as a streetfront loan operation, I came to a full stop. Once again I could see the bookie—sans eyeshade this forenoon—leaning in the doorway of his establishment and smoking a cigarette. Standing there in a strong flood of sunlight, bracketed by the sharp shadows of the doorway, he looked like a figure in an Edward Hopper painting. There was no chance he saw me that day, because he was staring at a car parked across the street. It was a cream-colored Lincoln with a green license plate. Above the numbers were the words

SUNSHINE STATE. Which did not mean it was a harmonic. Which *certainly* didn't mean it belonged to Eduardo Gutierrez of Tampa, the bookie who used to smile and say *Here comes my Yanqui from Yankeeland.* The one who had almost certainly had my beach-front house burned down.

All the same, I turned and walked back to my car with the five hundred I'd intended to bet still in my pocket.

Hunch-think.

CHAPTER 24

1

Given history's penchant for repeating itself, at least around me, you won't be surprised to find out that Mike Coslaw's plan for paying Sadie's bills was a return engagement of the *Jodie Jamboree.* He said he thought he could get the original participants to reprise their roles, as long as we scheduled it for midsummer, and he was as good as his word—almost all of them came on board. Ellie even agreed to encore her sturdy performances of "Camptown Races" and "Clinch Mountain Breakdown" on the banjo, although she claimed her fingers were still sore from the previous go-round. We picked the twelfth and thirteenth of July, but for awhile the issue was in some doubt.

The first obstacle to be surmounted was Sadie herself, who was horrified at the idea. She called it "taking charity."

"That sounds like something you might have learned at your mother's knee," I said.

She glared at me for a moment, then looked down and began stroking her hair against the bad side of her face. "What if it was? Does that make it wrong?"

"Jeez, let me think. You're talking about a life-lesson from the woman whose biggest concern after finding out her daughter had been mutilated and almost killed was her church affiliation."

"It's demeaning," she said in a low voice. "Throwing yourself on the mercy of the town is demeaning."

"You didn't feel that way when it was Bobbi Jill."

"You're hounding me, Jake. Please don't do that."

I sat down beside her and took her hand. She pulled it away. I took it again. This time she let me hold it.

"I know this isn't easy for you, honey. But there's a time to take as well as a time to give. I don't know if that one's in the Book of Ecclesiastes, but it's true, just the same. Your health insurance is a joke. Dr. Ellerton's giving us a break on his fee—"

"I never asked—"

"Hush, Sadie. Please. It's called pro bono work and he wants to do it. But there are other surgeons involved here. The bills for your surgeries are going to be enormous, and my resources will only stretch so far."

"I almost wish he'd killed me," she whispered.

"Don't you ever say that." She shrank from the anger in my voice, and the tears started. She could only cry from one eye now. "Hon, people want to do this for you. Let them. I know your mother lives in your head—almost everyone's mother does, I guess—but you can't let her have her way on this one."

"Those doctors can't fix it, anyway. It'll never be the way it was. Ellerton told me so."

"They can fix a lot of it." Which sounded marginally better than *they can fix some of it.*

She sighed. "You're braver than I am, Jake."

"You're plenty brave. Will you do this?"

"The Sadie Dunhill Charity Show. My mother would shit a brick if she found out."

"All the more reason, I'd say. We'll send her some stills."

That made her smile, but only for a moment. She lit a cigarette with fingers that trembled slightly, then began to smooth the hair against the side of her face again. "Would I have to be there? Let them see what their dollars are buying? Sort of like an American Berkshire pig on the auction block?"

"Of course not. Although I doubt if anyone would faint. Most folks around here have seen worse." As members of the faculty in a farming and ranching area, we had seen worse ourselves—Britta Carlson, for instance, who had been badly burned in a housefire, or Duffy Hendrickson, who had a left hand that looked like a hoof after a chainfall holding a truck motor slipped in his father's garage.

"I'm not ready for that kind of inspection. I don't think I ever will be."

I hoped with all my heart that didn't turn out to be true. The crazy people of the world—the Johnny Claytons, the Lee Harvey Oswalds—shouldn't get to win. If God won't make it better after they *do* have their shitty little victories, then ordinary people have to. They have to try, at least. But this wasn't the time to sermonize on the subject.

"Would it help if I said Dr. Ellerton himself has agreed to take part in the show?"

She momentarily forgot about her hair and stared at me. *"What?"*

"He wants to be the back end of Bertha." Bertha the Dancing Pony was a canvas creation of the kids in the Art Department. She wandered around during several of the skits, but her big number was a tail-waggling jig to Gene Autry's "Back in the Saddle Again." (The tail was controlled with a string pulled by the rear half of Team Bertha.) Country folk, not generally noted for their sophisticated senses of humor, found her hilarious.

Sadie began to laugh. I could see it hurt her, but she couldn't help it. She fell back against the couch, one palm pressed to the center of her forehead as if to keep her brains from exploding. "All right!" she said when she could finally talk again. "I'll let you do it just to see that." Then she glared at me. "But I'll see it during the dress rehearsal. You're not getting me up onstage where everybody can stare at me and whisper 'Oh look at that poor girl.' Have we got that straight?"

"We absolutely do," I said, and kissed her. That was one hurdle. The next would be convincing Dallas's premier plastic surgeon to come to Jodie in the July heat and prance around beneath the back half of a thirty-pound canvas costume. Because I hadn't actually asked him.

That turned out to be no problem; Ellerton lit up like a kid when I put the idea to him. "I even have practical experience," he said. "My wife's been telling me that I'm a perfect horse's ass for years now."

2

The last hurdle turned out to be the venue. In mid-June, right around the time Lee was getting kicked off a dock in New Orleans for trying to hand out his pro-Castro leaflets to the sailors of the USS *Wasp*, Deke came by Sadie's house. He kissed her on her good cheek (she averted the bad side of her face when anyone came to visit) and asked me if I'd like to step out for a cold beer.

"Go on," Sadie said. "I'll be fine."

Deke drove us to a dubiously air-conditioned tinroof called the Prairie Chicken, nine miles west of town. It was midafternoon, the place empty except for two solitary drinkers at the bar, the jukebox dark. Deke handed me a dollar. "I'll buy, you fetch. How's that for a deal?"

I went to the bar and collared two Buckhorns.

"If I'd known you were going to bring back Buckies, I would have gone myself," Deke said. "Man, this stuff is horse-piss."

"I happen to like it," I said. "Anyway, I thought you did your drinking at home. 'The asshole quotient in the local bars is a little too high for my taste,' I believe you said."

"I don't want a damn beer, anyway." Now that we were away from Sadie, I could see that he was steaming mad. "What I want to do is punch Fred Miller in the face and kick Jessica Caltrop's narra and no doubt lace-trimmed ass."

I knew the names and faces, although, having been just a humble wage-slave, I had never actually conversed with either of them. Miller and Caltrop were two-thirds of the Denholm County Schoolboard.

"Don't stop there," I said. "As long as you're in a bloodthirsty mood, tell me what you want to do to Dwight Rawson. Isn't he the other one?"

"It's Rawlings," Deke said moodily, "and I'll give him a pass. He voted on our side."

"I don't know what you're talking about."

"They won't let us use the school gym for the *Jamboree*. Even though it's the middle of summer we're talking about and it's just standing there vacant."

"Are you kidding?" Sadie had told me that certain elements of the town might take against her, and I hadn't believed her. Silly old Jake Epping, still clinging to his science-fiction fantasies of the twenty-first century.

"Son, I only wish I were. They cited fire-insurance concerns. I pointed out that they didn't have any insurance concerns when it was a benefit for a student who'd been in an accident, and the Caltrop woman—dried-up old kitty that she is—said, 'Oh yes, Deke, but that was during the *school year.*'

"They've got concerns, all right, mostly about how a member of the faculty got her face cut open by the crazy man she was married to. They're afraid it'll get mentioned in the paper or, God forbid, on one of the Dallas TV stations."

"How can it matter?" I asked. "He . . . Christ, Deke, he wasn't even *from* here! He was from *Georgia*!"

"That dudn't matter to them. What matters to them is that he *died* here, and they're afraid it'll reflect badly on the school. On the town. And on them."

I heard myself bleating, not a noble sound coming from a man in the prime of life, but I couldn't help it. "That makes no sense at all!"

"They'd fire her if they could, just to get rid of the embarrassment. Since they can't, they're hoping she'll quit before the kids have to look at what Clayton did to her face. Goddam smalltown bullshit hypocrisy at its best, my boy. When he was in his twenties, Fred Miller used to rip and roar in the Nuevo Laredo whorehouses twice a month. More, if he could get an advance on his allowance from his daddy. And I have it on damn good authority that when Jessica Caltrop was plain Jessie Trapp from Sweetwater Ranch, she got real fat when she was sixteen and real thin again about nine months later. I've a mind to tell them that my memory's even longer than their blue goddam noses, and I could embarrass them plenty if I wanted to. I wouldn't even have to work at it that hard."

"They can't really blame Sadie for her ex-husband's craziness . . . can they?"

"Grow up, George. Sometimes you act like you were born in a barn. Or some country where folks actually think straight. To them it's about sex. To folks like Fred and Jessica it's *always* about sex. They probably think Alfalfa and Spanky on *The Little Rascals* spend their spare time diddling Darla out behind the barn while Buckwheat cheers em on. And when something like this happens, it's the woman's fault. They wouldn't come right out and say so, but in their hearts they believe men are beasts and women who can't gentle em, well, be it on their own heads, son, be it on their own heads. I won't let em get away with this."

"You'll have to," I said. "If you don't, the ruckus might get back to Sadie. And she's fragile now. This might tip her over completely."

"Yeah," he said. He rummaged his pipe out of his breast pocket. "Yeah, I know that. I'm just blowin off steam. Ellie talked to the folks who run the Grange Hall just yesterday. They're happy to let us put on the show there, and it seats fifty more people. Because of the balcony, you know."

"Well there," I said, relieved. "Cooler heads prevail."

"Only one problem. They're asking four hundred for both nights. If I come up with two hundred, can you come up with the other two? You won't be getting it back from the receipts, you know. That's all earmarked for Sadie's medical work."

I knew very well about the cost of Sadie's medical work; I had already paid three hundred dollars to cover the part of her hospital stay that her shitepoke insurance wouldn't stand good for. In spite of Ellerton's good offices, the other expenses would mount up rapidly. As for me, I wasn't scraping financial bottom quite yet, but I could see it.

"George? What do you say?"

"Fifty-fifty," I agreed.

"Then drink up your shitty beer. I want to get back to town."

3

On our way out of that sad excuse for a drinking establishment, a poster propped in the window caught my eye. At the top:

SEE THE FIGHT OF THE CENTURY ON CLOSED CIRCUIT TV!
LIVE FROM MADISON SQUARE GARDEN!
DALLAS'S OWN TOM "THE HAMMER" CASE VS. DICK TIGER!
DALLAS AUDITORIUM
THURSDAY AUG. 29
ADVANCE TICKETS AVAILABLE HERE

Below were side-by-side photos of two bare-chested beefcakes with their gloved fists held up in the accepted fashion. One was young and unmarked. The other guy looked a lot older, and as if he'd had his nose broken a few times. The names were what stopped me, though. I knew them from somewhere.

"Don't even think about it," Deke said, shaking his head. "You'd get more sport out of watching a dogfight between a pit bull and a cocker spaniel. An *old* cocker spaniel."

"Really?"

"Tommy Case always had a ton of heart, but now it's a forty-year-old heart in a forty-year-old body. He got him a beergut and he can hardly move at all. Tiger's young and fast. He'll be a champ in a couple of years if the matchmakers don't slip up. In the meantime, they feed him walking tank-jobs like Case to keep him in trim."

It sounded to me like Rocky Balboa against Apollo Creed, but why not? Sometimes life imitates art.

Deke said, "TV you pay to watch in an auditorium. Boy-howdy, what next?"

"The wave of the future, I guess," I said.

"And it'll probably sell out—in Dallas, at least—but that doesn't change the fact that Tom Case is the wave of the past. Tiger'll slice him like coldcuts. Sure you're okay with this Grange thing, George?"

"Absolutely."

4

That was a strange June. On one hand, I was delighted to be rehearsing with the troupe that had put on the original *Jamboree*. It was déjà vu of the best kind. On the other hand, I found myself wondering, with greater and greater frequency, if I had ever intended to strike Lee Harvey Oswald from history's equation in the first place. I couldn't believe I lacked the guts to do it—I had already killed one bad man, and in cold blood—but it was an undeniable fact that I'd had Oswald in my sights and let him go. I told myself it was the uncertainty principle, and not the fact of his family, but I kept seeing Marina smiling and holding her hands out in front of her belly. I kept wondering if he might not be a patsy, after all. I reminded myself he'd be back in October. And then, of course, I asked myself how that would change things. His wife would still be pregnant and the window of uncertainty would still be open.

Meanwhile, there was Sadie's slow recovery to preside over, there were bills to pay, there were insurance forms to fill out (the bureaucracy every bit as infuriating in 1963 as in 2011), and those rehearsals. Dr. Ellerton could only show up for one of them, but he was a quick study and hoofed his half of Bertha the Dancing Pony with charming brio. After the run-through, he told me he wanted

612

to bring another surgeon on board, a facial specialist from Mass General. I told him—with a sinking heart—that another surgeon sounded like a grand idea.

"Can you afford it?" he asked. "Mark Anderson ain't cheap."

"We'll manage," I said.

I invited Sadie to rehearsals when the show dates grew close. She refused gently but firmly in spite of her earlier promise to come to at least one dress rehearsal. She rarely left the house, and when she did, it was only to go into the backyard garden. She hadn't been to the school—or in town—since the night John Clayton cut her face and then his own throat.

5

I spent the late morning and early afternoon of July twelfth at the Grange Hall, running a final tech rehearsal. Mike Coslaw, who had settled as naturally into the role of producer as he had that of slap-stick comedian, told me the Saturday-night show was a sellout and tonight's was at ninety percent. "We'll get enough walk-ups to fill the place, Mr. A. Count on it. I just hope me and Bobbi Jill don't mess up the encore."

"Bobbi Jill and I, Mike. And you won't mess up."

All of that was good. Less good was passing Ellen Dockerty's car turning out of Bee Tree Lane just as I was turning in, and then finding Sadie sitting by the living room window with tears on her unmarked cheek and a handkerchief in one fisted hand.

"What?" I demanded. "What did she say to you?"

Sadie surprised me by mustering a grin. It was lopsided, but not without a certain gamine charm. "Nothing that wasn't the truth. Please don't worry. I'll make you a sandwich and you can tell me how it went."

So that was what I did. And I did worry, of course, but I kept my worries to myself. Also my comments on the subject of meddle-some high school principals. That evening at six, Sadie inspected me, reknotted my tie, and then brushed some lint, real or imagined, from the shoulders of my sport coat. "I'd tell you to break a leg, but you might just go and do it."

She was wearing her old jeans and a smock top that camouflaged—a little, anyway—her weight-loss. I found myself remembering the pretty dress she'd worn to the original *Jodie Jamboree.* Pretty dress that night with a pretty girl inside it. That was then. Tonight the girl—still pretty on one side—would be at home when the curtain went up, watching a *Route 66* rerun.

"What's wrong?" she asked.

"Wishing you were going to be there, that's all."

I was sorry as soon as it was out, but it was almost okay. Her smile faded, then came back. The way the sun does when it passes behind a cloud that's only small. "*You'll* be there. Which means I will be." She looked at me with grave timidity from the one eye her Veronica Lake flip left visible. "If you love me, that is."

"I love you plenty."

"Yes, I guess you do." She kissed the corner of my mouth. "And I love you. So don't break any legs and give everybody my thanks."

"I will. You're not afraid to stay here alone?"

"I'll be okay." It wasn't actually an answer to my question, but it was the best she could do for the time being.

6

Mike was right about the walk-ups. We sold out the Friday night performance a full hour in advance of showtime. Donald Bellingham, our stage manager, lowered the houselights at 8:00 P.M. on the dot. I expected to feel a letdown after the nearly sublime original with its pie-throwing finale (which we intended to repeat on Saturday night only, the consensus being that we wanted to clean up the Grange Hall stage—and the first couple of rows—just a single time), but this one was nearly as good. For me the comedy highlight was that goddamned dancing horse. At one point Dr.

Ellerton's front-half cohort, a wildly overenthusiastic Coach Borman, almost boogied Bertha right off the stage.

The audience believed those twenty or thirty seconds of weaving around the footlights was part of the show and heartily applauded the derring-do. I, who knew better, found myself caught in an emotional paradox that will probably never be repeated. I stood in the wings next to a nearly paralytic Donald Bellingham, laughing wildly while my terrified heart fluttered at the very top of my throat.

The night's harmonic came during the encore. Mike and Bobbi Jill walked to center stage, hand in hand. Bobbi Jill faced the audience and said, "Miz Dunhill means an awful lot to me, because of her kindness and her Christian charity. She helped me when I needed help, and she made me want to learn how to do what we're going to do for you now. We thank you all for coming out tonight and showing *your* Christian charity. Don't we, Mike?"

"Yeah," he said. "You guys are the best."

He looked stage left. I pointed to Donald, who was bent over his record player with the tone arm raised, ready to stick the groove. This time Donald's father was going to know damned well that Donald had borrowed one of his big-band records, because the man was in the audience.

Glenn Miller, that long-gone bombardier, launched into "In the Mood," and onstage, to rhythmic clapping from the audience, Mike Coslaw and Bobbi Jill Allnut flew into a jet-propelled Lindy far more fervent than any I had ever managed with either Sadie or Christy. It was all youth and joy and enthusiasm, and that made it gorgeous. When I saw Mike squeeze Bobbi Jill's hand, telling her by touch to counterspin and shoot through his legs, I was suddenly back in Derry, watching Bevvie-from-the-levee and Richie-from-the-ditchie.

It's all of a piece, I thought. *It's an echo so close to perfect you can't tell which one is the living voice and which is the ghost-voice returning.*

For a moment everything was clear, and when that happens you see that the world is barely there at all. Don't we all secretly know this? It's a perfectly balanced mechanism of shouts and echoes pretending to be wheels and cogs, a dreamclock chiming beneath a mystery-glass we call life. Behind it? Below it and around it? Chaos, storms. Men with hammers, men with knives, men with guns. Women who twist what they cannot dominate and belittle what they cannot understand. A universe of horror and loss surrounding a single lighted stage where mortals dance in defiance of the dark.

Mike and Bobbi Jill danced in their time, and their time was 1963, that era of crewcuts, console televisions, and homemade garage rock. They danced on a day when President Kennedy promised to sign a nuclear test ban treaty and told reporters he had "no intention of allowing our military forces to be mired in the arcane politics and ancient grudges of southeast Asia." They danced as Bevvie and Richie had danced, as Sadie and I had danced, and they were beautiful, and I loved them not in spite of their fragility but because of it. I love them still.

They ended perfectly, hands upraised, breathing hard and facing the audience, which rose to its feet. Mike gave them a full forty seconds to pound their hands together (it's amazing how fast the footlights can transform a humble left tackle into fully fledged pressed ham) and then called for quiet. Eventually, he got it.

"Our director, Mr. George Amberson, wants to say a few words. He put a lot of effort and creativity into this show, so I hope you'll give him a big hand."

I walked out to fresh applause. I shook Mike's hand and gave Bobbi Jill a peck on the cheek. They scampered offstage. I raised my hands for quiet and launched into my carefully rehearsed speech, telling them Sadie couldn't be here tonight but thanking them all on her behalf. Every public speaker worth his salt knows to concentrate on specific members of the audience, and I focused on a pair in the third row who looked remarkably like Ma and Pa in *American Gothic*. This was Fred Miller and Jessica Caltrop, the schoolboard members who had denied us use of the school gym on the grounds that Sadie being assaulted by her ex was in bad taste and should be ignored, insofar as possible.

Four sentences in, I was interrupted by gasps of surprise. This was followed by applause—isolated at first but quickly growing to a storm. The audience took to its feet again. I had no idea what they were applauding for until I felt a light, tentative hand grip my arm above the elbow. I turned to see Sadie standing beside me in her red dress. She had put her hair up and secured it with a glittery clip. Her face—both sides of it—was completely visible. I was shocked to discover that, once fully revealed, the residual damage wasn't as awful as I had feared. There might be some sort of universal truth there, but I was too stunned to suss it out. Sure, that deep, ragged hollow and the fading hash marks of the stitches were hard to look at. So was the slack flesh and her unnaturally wide left eye, which no longer quite blinked in tandem with the right one.

But she was smiling that charming one-sided smile, and in my eyes, that made her Helen of Troy. I hugged her, and she hugged me back, laughing and crying. Beneath the dress, her whole body was thrumming like a high-tension wire. When we faced the audience again, everyone was up and cheering except for Miller and Caltrop. Who looked around, saw they were the only ones still on their fannies, and reluctantly joined the others.

"Thank you," Sadie said when they quieted. "Thank you all from the very bottom of my heart. Special thanks to Ellen Dockerty, who told me that if I didn't come here and look y'all in the eye, I'd regret it for the rest of my life. And most thanks of all to . . ."

The minutest of hesitations. I'm sure the audience didn't notice it, which made me the only one who knew how close Sadie had come to telling five hundred people my actual name.

". . . to George Amberson. I love you, George."

Which brought down the house, of course. In dark times when even the sages are uncertain, declarations of love always do.

7

Ellen took Sadie—who was exhausted—home at ten-thirty. Mike and I turned out the Grange Hall lights at midnight and stepped into the alley. "Gonna come to the after-party, Mr. A? Al said he'd keep the diner open until two, and he brought in a couple of kegs. He's not licensed for it, but I don't think anyone'll arrest him."

"Not me," I said. "I'm beat. I'll see you tomorrow night, Mike."

I drove to Deke's before going home. He was sitting on his front porch in his pajamas, smoking a final pipe.

"Pretty special night," he said.

"Yes."

"That young woman showed guts. A country mile of em."

"She did."

"Are you going to do right by her, son?"

"I'm going to try."

He nodded. "She deserves that, after the last one. And you're doing okay so far." He glanced toward my Chevy. "You could probably take your car tonight and park right out front. After tonight, I don't think anyone in town'd bat an eye."

He might have been right, but I decided better safe than sorry and hoofed it, just as I had on so many other nights. I needed the time to let my own emotions settle. I kept seeing her in the glow of the footlights. The red dress. The graceful curve of her neck. The smooth cheek . . . and the ragged one.

When I got to Bee Tree Lane and let myself in, the hide-a-bed was in its hiding state. I stood looking at this, puzzled, not sure what to make of it. Then Sadie called my name—my real one—from the bedroom. Very softly.

The lamp was on, casting a soft light across her bare shoulders and one side of her face. Her eyes were luminous and grave. "I think this is where you belong," she said. "I want you to be here. Do you?"

I took off my clothes and got in beside her. Her hand moved beneath the sheets, found me, and caressed me. "Are you hungry? Because I have poundcake if you are."

"Oh, Sadie, I'm starving."

"Then turn out the light."

8

That night in Sadie's bed was the best of my life—not because it closed the door on John Clayton, but because it opened the door on us again.

When we finished making love, I fell into the first deep sleep I'd had in months. I awoke at eight in the morning. The sun was fully up, the Angels were singing "My Boyfriend's Back" on the radio in the kitchen, and I could smell frying bacon. Soon she would call me to the table, but not yet. Not just yet.

I put my hands behind my head and looked at the ceiling, mildly stunned at how stupid—how almost willfully blind— I'd been since the day I'd allowed Lee to get on the bus to New Orleans without doing anything to stop him. Did I need to know if George de Mohrenschildt had had more to do with the attempt on Edwin Walker than just goading an unstable little man into trying it? Well, there was actually quite a simple way to determine that, wasn't there?

De Mohrenschildt knew, so I would ask him.

9

Sadie ate better than she had since the night Clayton had invaded her home, and I did pretty well myself. Together we polished off half a dozen eggs, plus toast and bacon. When the dishes were in the sink and she was smoking a cigarette with her second cup of coffee, I said I wanted to ask her something.

"If it's about coming to the show tonight, I don't think I could manage that twice."

"It's something else. But since you mention it, what exactly did Ellie say to you?"

"That it was time to stop feeling sorry for myself and rejoin the parade."

"Pretty harsh."

Sadie stroked her hair against the wounded side of her face—that automatic gesture. "Miz Ellie's not known for delicacy and tact. Did she shock me, busting in here and telling me it was time to quit lollygagging? Yes she did. Was she right? Yes she was." She stopped stroking her hair and abruptly pushed it back with the heel of her hand. "This is what I'm going to look like from now on—with some improvements—so I guess I better get used to it. Sadie's going to find out if that old saw about beauty only being skin deep is actually true."

"That's what I wanted to talk to you about."

"All right." She jetted smoke from her nostrils.

"Suppose I could take you to a place where the doctors could fix the damage to your face—not perfectly, but far better than Dr. Ellerton and his team ever could. Would you go? Even if you knew we could never come back here?"

She frowned. "Are we speaking hypothetically?"

"Actually we're not."

She crushed her cigarette out slowly and deliberately, thinking it over. "Is this like Miz Mimi going to Mexico for experimental cancer treatments? Because I don't think—"

"I'm talking about America, hon."

"Well, if it's America, I don't understand why we couldn't—"

"Here's the rest of it: *I* might have to go. With or without you."

"And never come back?" She looked alarmed.

"Never. Neither one of us could, for reasons that are difficult to explain. I suppose you think I'm crazy."

"I know you're not." Her eyes were troubled, but she spoke without hesitation.

"I may have to do something that would look very bad to law-enforcement types. It's *not* bad, but nobody would ever believe that."

"Is this . . . Jake, does this have anything to do with that thing you told me about Adlai Stevenson? What he said about hell freezing over?"

"In a way. But here's the rub. Even if I'm able to do what I have to without being caught—and I think I can—that doesn't change *your* situation. Your face is still going to be scarred to some greater or lesser degree. In this place where I could take you, there are medical resources Ellerton can only dream of."

"But we could never come back." She wasn't speaking to me; she was trying to get it straight in her mind.

"No." All else aside, if we came back to September ninth of 1958, the original version of Sadie Dunhill would already exist. That was a mind-bender I didn't even want to consider.

She got up and went to the window. She stood there with her back to me for a long time. I waited.

"Jake?"

"Yes, honey."

"Can you predict the future? You can, can't you?"

I said nothing.

In a small voice she said, "Did you come here *from* the future?"

I said nothing.

She turned from the window. Her face was very pale. "Jake, did you?"

"Yes." It was as if a seventy-pound rock had rolled off my chest. At the same time I was terrified. For both of us, but mostly for her.

"How . . . how far?"

"Honey, are you sure you—"

"Yes. *How far?*"

"Almost forty-eight years."

"Am I . . . dead?"

"I don't know. I don't want to know. This is now. And this is us."

She thought about that. The skin around the red marks of her injuries had turned very white and I wanted to go to her, but I was afraid to move. What if she screamed and ran from me?

"Why did you come?"

"To stop a man from doing something. I'll kill him if I have to. If I can make absolutely sure he deserves killing, that is. So far I haven't been able to do that."

"What's the something?"

"In four months, I'm pretty sure he's going to kill the president. He's going to kill John Ken—"

I saw her knees start to buckle, but she managed to stay on her feet just long enough to allow me to catch her before she fell.

10

I carried her to the bedroom and went into the bathroom to wet a cloth in cold water. When I returned, her eyes were already open. She looked at me with an expression I could not decipher.

"I shouldn't have told you."

"Maybe not," she said, but she didn't flinch when I sat down next to her on the bed, and made a little sighing noise of pleasure when I began to stroke her face with the cold cloth, detouring around the bad place, where all sensation except for a deep, dull pain was now gone. When I was done, she looked at me solemnly. "Tell me one thing that's going to happen. I think if I'm going to believe you, you have to do that. Something like Adlai Stevenson and hell freezing over."

"I can't. I majored in English, not American History. I studied Maine history in high school—it was a requirement—but I know next to nothing about Texas. I don't—" But I realized I did know one thing. I knew the last thing in the betting section of Al Templeton's notebook, because I'd double-checked. *In case you need a final cash transfusion,* he'd written.

"Jake?"

"I know who's going to win a prizefight at Madison Square Garden next month. His name is Tom Case, and he's going to knock out Dick Tiger in the fifth round. If that doesn't happen, I guess you're free to call for the men in the white coats. But can you keep it just between us until then? A lot depends on it."

"Yes. I can do that."

11

I half-expected Deke or Miz Ellie to buttonhole me after the second night's performance, looking grave and telling me they'd had a phone call from Sadie, saying that I'd lost my everloving mind. But that didn't happen, and when I got back to Sadie's, there was a note on the table reading *Wake me if you want a midnight snack.*

It wasn't midnight—not quite—and she wasn't asleep. The next forty minutes or so were very pleasant. Afterward, in the dark, she said: "I don't have to decide anything right now, do I?"

"No."

"And we don't have to talk about this right now."

"No."

"Maybe after the fight. The one you told me about."

"Maybe."

"I believe you, Jake. I don't know if that makes me crazy or not, but I do. And I love you."

"I love you, too."

Her eyes gleamed in the dark—the one that was almond-shaped and beautiful, the one that drooped but still saw. "I don't want anything to happen to you, and I don't want you to hurt anybody unless you absolutely have to. And never by mistake. Never *ever*. Do you promise?"

"Yes." That was easy. It was the reason Lee Oswald was still drawing breath.

"Will you be careful?"

"Yes. I'll be very—"

She stopped my mouth with a kiss. "Because no matter where

you came from, there's no future for me without you. Now let's go to sleep."

12

I thought the conversation would resume in the morning. I had no idea what—meaning how much—I would tell her when it did, but in the end I had to tell her nothing, because she didn't ask. Instead she asked me how much The Sadie Dunhill Charity Show had brought in. When I told her just over three thousand dollars, with the contents of the lobby donation box added to the gate, she threw back her head and let loose a beautiful full-throated laugh. Three grand wouldn't cover all of her bills, but it was worth a million just to hear her laugh . . . and to *not* hear her say something like *Why bother at all, when I can just get it taken care of in the future?* Because I wasn't entirely sure she really wanted to go even if she *did* believe, and because I wasn't sure I wanted to take her.

I wanted to *be* with her, yes. For as close to forever as people get. But it might be better in '63 . . . and all the years God or providence gave us after '63. *We* might be better. I could see her lost in 2011, eyeing every low-riding pair of pants and computer screen with awe and unease. I would never beat her or shout at her—no, not Sadie—but she might still become my Marina Prusakova, living in a strange place and exiled from her homeland forever.

13

There was one person in Jodie who might know how I could put Al's final betting entry to use. That was Freddy Quinlan, the real estate agent. He ran a weekly nickel-in, quarter-to-stay poker game at his house, and I'd attended a few times. During several of these games he bragged about his betting prowess in two fields: pro football and the Texas State Basketball Tournament. He saw me in his office only because, he said, it was too damn hot to play golf.

"What are we talking about here, George? Medium-sized bet or the house and lot?"

"I'm thinking five hundred dollars."

He whistled, then leaned back in his chair and laced his hands over a tidy little belly. It was only nine in the morning, but the air-conditioner was running full blast. Stacks of real estate brochures fluttered in its chilly exhaust. "That's serious cabbage. Care to let me in on a good thing?"

Since he was doing me the favor—at least I hoped so—I told him. His eyebrows shot up so high they were in danger of meeting his receding hairline.

"Holy cow! Why don't you just chuck your money down a sewer?"

"I've got a feeling, that's all."

"George, listen to your daddy. The Case-Tiger fight isn't a sporting event, it's a trial balloon for this new closed-circuit TV thing. There might be a few good fights on the undercard, but the main bout's a joke. Tiger'll have instructions to carry the poor old fella for seven or eight, then put him to sleep. Unless . . ."

He leaned forward. His chair made an unlovely *scronk* sound from somewhere underneath. "Unless you know something." He leaned back again and pursed his lips. "But how could you? You live in *Jodie,* for Chrissake. But if you did, you'd let a pal in on it, wouldn't you?"

"I don't know anything," I said, lying straight to his face (and happy to do so). "It's just a feeling, but the last time I had one this strong, I bet on the Pirates to beat the Yankees in the World Series, and I made a bundle."

"Very nice, but you know the old saying—even a stopped clock gets it right twice a day."

"Can you help me or not, Freddy?"

He gave me a comforting smile that said the fool and his money would all too soon be parted. "There's a guy in Dallas who'd be happy to take that kind of action. Name's Akiva Roth. Operates out of Faith Financial on Greenville Ave. Took over the biz from his father five or six years ago." He lowered his voice. "Word is, he's mobbed up." He lowered his voice still further. "Carlos Marcello."

That was exactly what I was afraid of, because that had also been the word on Eduardo Gutierrez. I thought again of the Lincoln with the Florida plates parked across from Faith Financial.

"I'm not sure I'd want to be seen going into a place like that. I might want to teach again, and at least two members of the schoolboard are already cheesed off at me."

"You could try Frank Frati, over in Fort Worth. He runs a pawn-shop." *Scronk* went the chair as he leaned forward to get a better look at my face. "What'd I say? Or did you inhale a bug?"

"Uh-uh. It's just that I knew a Frati once. Who also ran a pawn-shop and took bets."

"Probably they both came from the same savings-and-loan clan in Romania. Anyway, he might fade five Cs—especially a sucker bet like you're talking about. But you won't get the odds you deserve. Of course you wouldn't get em from Roth, either, but you'd get better than you would from Frank Frati."

"But with Frank I wouldn't get the Mob connection. Right?"

"I guess not, but who really knows? Bookies, even the part-time ones, ain't known for their high-class business associations."

"Probably I should take your advice and hold onto my money."

Quinlan looked horrified. "No, no, *no,* don't do that. Bet it on the Bears to win the NFL. That way you make a bundle. I practically guarantee it."

14

On July twenty-second, I told Sadie I had to run some errands in Dallas and said I'd ask Deke to check in on her. She said there was no need, that she'd be fine. She was regaining her old self. Little by slowly, yes, but she was regaining it.

She asked no questions about the nature of my errands.

My initial stop was at First Corn, where I opened my safe deposit box and triple-checked Al's notes to make sure I really remembered what I thought I had. And yes, Tom Case was going to be the upset winner, knocking out Dick Tiger in the fifth. Al must have found the fight on the internet, because he had been gone from Dallas—and the sensational sixties—long before then.

"Can I help you with anything else today, Mr. Amberson?" my banker asked as he escorted me to the door.

Well, you could say a little prayer that my old buddy Al Templeton didn't swallow a bunch of internet bullshit.

"Maybe so. Do you know where I could find a costume shop? I'm supposed to be the magician at my nephew's birthday party."

Mr. Link's secretary, after a quick glance through the Yellow Pages, directed me to an address on Young Street. There I was able to buy what I needed. I stored it at the apartment on West Neely—as long as I was paying rent on the place, it ought to be good for something. I left my revolver, too, putting it on a high shelf in the closet. The bug, which I had removed from the upstairs lamp, went into the glove compartment of my car, along with the cunning little Japanese tape recorder. I would dispose of them somewhere in the scrubland on my return to Jodie. They were of no more use to me. The apartment upstairs hadn't been re-rented, and the house was spookily silent.

Before I left Neely Street, I walked around the fenced-in side yard, where, just three months before, Marina had taken photographs of Lee holding his rifle. There was nothing to see but beaten earth and a few hardy weeds. Then, as I turned to go, I *did* see something: a flash of red under the outside stairs. It was a baby's rattle. I took it and put it in the glove compartment of my Chevy along with the bug, but unlike the bug, I held onto it. I don't know why.

15

My next stop was the sprawling ranch on Simpson Stuart Road where George de Mohrenschildt lived with his wife, Jeanne. As soon as I saw it I rejected it for the meeting I had planned. For one thing, I couldn't be sure when Jeanne would be in the house and when she'd be away, and this particular conversation had to be strictly Two Guys. For another, it wasn't quite isolated enough. Paul Quinn College, an all-black school, was close by, and summer classes must have been in. There weren't droves of kids, but I saw plenty, some walking and some on bikes. Not good for my purposes. It was possible that our discussion might be noisy. It was possible it might not be a discussion—at least in the Merriam-Webster sense—at all.

Something caught my eye. It was on the de Mohrenschildts' wide front lawn, where sprinklers flung graceful sprays in the air and created rainbows that looked small enough to put in your pocket. 1963 wasn't an election year, but in early April—right around the time somebody had taken a shot at General Edwin Walker—the representative from the Fifth District had dropped dead of a heart attack. There was going to be a run-off election for his seat on August sixth.

The sign read **ELECT JENKINS TO THE 5TH DISTRICT! ROBERT "ROBBIE" JENKINS, DALLAS'S WHITE KNIGHT!**

According to the papers, Jenkins was that for sure, a right-winger who saw eye-to-eye with Walker and Walker's spiritual advisor, Billy James Hargis. Robbie Jenkins stood for states' rights, separate-but-equal schools, and reinstituting the Missile Crisis blockade around Cuba. The same Cuba de Mohrenschildt had called "that beautiful island." The sign supported a strong feeling that I'd already developed about de Mohrenschildt. He was a dilettante who, at bottom, held no political beliefs at all. He would support whoever amused him or put money in his pocket. Lee Oswald couldn't do the latter—he was so poor he made churchmice look loaded—but his humorless dedication to socialism combined with his grandiose personal ambitions had provided de Mohrenschildt with plenty of the former.

One deduction seemed obvious: Lee had never trod the lawn or soiled the carpets of this house with his poorboy feet. This was de Mohrenschildt's other life . . . or one of them. I had a feeling he might have several, keeping them all in various watertight compartments. But that didn't answer the central question: was he so bored he would have accompanied Lee on his mission to assassinate the fascist monster Edwin Walker? I didn't know him well enough to make even an educated guess.

But I would. My heart was set on it.

16

The sign in the window of Frank Frati's pawnshop read WELCOME TO GUITAR CENTRAL, and there were plenty of them on display: acoustics, electrics, twelve-strings, and one with a double fretboard that reminded me of something I'd seen in a Mötley Crüe video. Of course there was all the other detritus of busted lives—rings, brooches, necklaces, radios, small appliances. The woman who confronted me was skinny instead of fat, she wore slacks and a Ship N Shore blouse instead of a purple dress and mocs, but the stone face was the same as that of a woman I'd met in Derry, and I heard the same words coming out of my mouth. Close enough for government work, anyway.

"I'd like to discuss a rather large sports-oriented business proposition with Mr. Frati."

"Yeah? Is that a bet when it's at home with its feet up?"

"Are you a cop?"

"Yeah, I'm Chief Curry of the Dallas Police. Can't you tell from the glasses and the jowls?"

"I don't see any glasses or jowls, ma'am."

"That's because I'm in disguise. What you want to bet on in the middle of the summer, chum? There's nothing to bet on."

"Case-Tiger."

"Which pug?"

"Case."

She rolled her eyes, then shouted back over her shoulder. "Better get out here, Dad, you got a live one."

Frank Frati was at least twice Chaz Frati's age, but the resemblance was still there. They were related, of course they were. If I mentioned I had once laid a bet with a Mr. Frati of Derry, Maine, I had no doubt we could have a pleasant little discussion about what a small world it was.

Instead of doing that, I proceeded directly to negotiations. Could I put five hundred dollars on Tom Case to win his bout against Dick Tiger in Madison Square Garden?

"Yes indeedy," Frati said. "You could also stick a red-hot branding iron up your rootie-patootie, but why would you want to?"

His daughter yapped brief, bright laughter.

"What kind of odds would I get?"

He looked at the daughter. She put up her hands. Two fingers raised on the left, one finger on the right.

"Two-to-one? That's ridiculous."

"It's a ridiculous life, my friend. Go see an Ionesco play if you don't believe me. I recommend *Victims of Duty.*"

Well, at least he didn't call me cuz, as his Derry cuz had done.

"Work with me a little on this, Mr. Frati."

He picked up an Epiphone Hummingbird acoustic and began to tune it. He was eerily quick. "Give me something to work with, then, or blow on over to Dallas. There's a place called—"

"I know the place in Dallas. I prefer Fort Worth. I used to live here."

"The fact that you moved shows more sense than wanting to bet on Tom Case."

"What about Case by a knockout somewhere in the first seven rounds? What would that get me?"

He looked at the daughter. This time she raised three fingers on her left hand.

"And Case by a knockout in the first five?"

She deliberated, then raised a fourth finger. I decided not to push it any farther. I wrote my name in his book and showed him my driver's license, holding my thumb over the Jodie address just as I had when I'd bet on the Pirates at Faith Financial almost three years ago. Then I passed over my cash, which was about a quarter of all my remaining liquidity, and tucked the receipt into my wallet. Two thousand would be enough to pay down some more of Sadie's expenses and carry me for my remaining time in Texas. Plus, I wanted to gouge this Frati no more than I'd wanted to gouge Chaz Frati, even though he *had* set Bill Turcotte on me.

"I'll be back the day after the dance," I said. "Have my money ready."

The daughter laughed and lit a cigarette. "Ain't that what the chorus girl said to the archbishop?"

"Is your name Marjorie, by any chance?" I asked.

She froze with the cigarette in front of her and smoke trickling from between her lips. "How'dja know?" She saw my expression and laughed. "Actually, it's Wanda, sport. I hope you bet better than you guess names."

Heading back to my car, I hoped the same thing.

CHAPTER 25

1

I stayed with Sadie on the morning of August fifth until they put her on a gurney and rolled her down to the operating room. There Dr. Ellerton was waiting for her, along with enough other docs to field a basketball team. Her eyes were shiny with preop dope.

"Wish me luck."

I bent and kissed her. "All the luck in the world."

It was three hours before she was wheeled back to her room—same room, same picture on the wall, same horrible squatting commode—fast asleep and snoring, the left side of her face covered in a fresh bandage. Rhonda McGinley, the nurse with the fullback shoulders, let me stay with her until she came around a little, which was a big infraction of the rules. Visiting hours are more stringent in the Land of Ago. Unless the head nurse has taken a shine to you, that is.

"How are you?" I asked, taking Sadie's hand.

"Sore. And sleepy."

"Go back to sleep then, honey."

"Maybe next time . . ." Her words trailed off in a furry *hzzzzz* sound. Her eyes closed, but she forced them open with an effort. ". . . will be better. In your place."

Then she was gone, and I had something to think about.

When I went back to the nurses' station, Rhonda told me that Dr. Ellerton was waiting for me downstairs in the cafeteria.

"We'll keep her tonight and probably tomorrow, too," he said. "The last thing we want is for any sort of infection to develop." (I thought of this later, of course—one of those things that's funny, but not very.)

"How did it go?"

"As well as can be expected, but the damage Clayton inflicted was very serious. Pending her recovery, I'm going to schedule her second go-round for November or December." He lit a cigarette, chuffed out smoke, and said: "This is a helluva surgical team, and we're going to do everything we can . . . but there are limits."

"Yes. I know." I was pretty sure I knew something else, as well: there were going to be no more surgeries. Here, at least. The next time Sadie went under the knife, it wouldn't be a knife at all. It would be a laser.

In *my* place.

2

Small economies always come back and bite you in the ass. I'd had the phone taken out of my Neely Street apartment in order to save eight or ten dollars a month, and now I wanted it. But there was a U-Tote-M four blocks away with a phone booth next to the Coke cooler. I had de Mohrenschildt's number on a scrap of paper. I dropped a dime and dialed.

"De Mohrenschildt residence, how may I help you?" Not Jeanne's voice. A maid, probably—where *did* the de Mohrenschildt bucks come from?

"I'd like to speak to George, please."

"I'm afraid he's at the office, sir."

I grabbed a pen from my breast pocket. "Can you give me that number?"

"Yes, sir. CHapel 5-6323."

"Thanks." I wrote it on the back of my hand.

"May I say who called, if you don't reach him, sir?"

I hung up. That chill was enveloping me again. I welcomed it. If I'd ever needed cold clarity, it was now.

I dropped another dime and this time got a secretary who told me I'd reached the Centrex Corporation. I told her I wanted to speak to Mr. de Mohrenschildt. She, of course, wanted to know why.

"Tell him it's about Jean-Claude Duvalier and Lee Oswald. Tell him it's to his advantage."

"Your name, sir?"

Puddentane wouldn't do here. "John Lennon."

"Please hold, Mr. Lennon, I'll see if he's available."

There was no canned music, which on the whole seemed an improvement. I leaned against the wall of the hot booth and stared at the sign reading IF YOU SMOKE, PLEASE TURN ON FAN. I didn't smoke, but turned the fan on, anyway. It didn't help much.

There was a click in my ear loud enough to make me wince, and the secretary said, "You're connected, Mr. D."

"Hello?" That jovial booming actor's voice. "Hello? Mr. Lennon?"

"Hello. Is this line secure?"

"What do you . . . ? Of course it is. Just a minute. Let me shut the door."

There was a pause, then he was back. "What's this about?"

"Haiti, my friend. And oil leases."

"What's this about *Monsieur* Duvalier and that guy Oswald?" There was no worry in his voice, just cheerful curiosity.

"Oh, you know them both much better than that," I said. "Go ahead and call them Baby Doc and Lee, why don't you?"

"I'm awfully busy today, Mr. Lennon. If you don't tell me what this is about, I'm afraid I'll have to—"

"Baby Doc can approve the oil leases in Haiti you've been wanting for the last five years. You know this; he's his father's righthand man, he runs the *tonton macoute,* and he's next in line for the big chair. He likes you, and *we* like you—"

De Mohrenschildt began to sound less like an actor and more like a real guy. "When you say *we,* do you mean—"

"We *all* like you, de Mohrenschildt, but we're worried about your association with Oswald."

"Jesus, I hardly know the guy! I haven't seen him in six or eight months!"

"You saw him on Easter Sunday. You brought his little girl a stuffed rabbit."

A very long pause. Then: "All right, I guess I did. I forgot about that."

"Did you forget about someone taking a shot at Edwin Walker?"

"What has that got to do with *me*? Or my business?" His puzzled outrage was almost impossible to disbelieve. Key word: *almost*.

"Come on, now," I said. "You accused Oswald of doing it."

"I was joking, goddammit!"

I gave him two beats, then said, "Do you know what company I work for, de Mohrenschildt? I'll give you a hint—it's *not* Standard Oil."

There was silence on the line while de Mohrenschildt ran through the bullshit I'd spouted so far. Except it *wasn't* bullshit, not entirely. I'd known about the stuffed rabbit, and I'd known about the how-did-you-miss crack he'd made after his wife spotted the rifle. The conclusion was pretty clear. My company was The Company, and the only question in de Mohrenschildt's mind right now—I hoped—was how much more of his no doubt interesting life we'd bugged.

"This is a misunderstanding, Mr. Lennon."

"I hope for your sake that it is, because it looks to us like you might have primed him to take the shot. Going on and on about what a racist Walker is, and how he's going to be the next American Hitler."

"That's totally untrue!"

I ignored this. "But it's not our chief worry. Our chief worry is that you may have accompanied Mr. Oswald on his errand last April tenth."

"Ach, mein Gott! That's insane!"

"If you can prove that—and if you promise to stay away from the unstable Mr. Oswald in the future—"

"He's in New Orleans, for God's sake!"

"Shut up," I said. "We know where he is and what he's doing. Handing out Fair Play for Cuba leaflets. If he doesn't stop soon, he'll wind up in jail." Indeed he would, and in less than a week. His uncle Dutz—the one associated with Carlos Marcello—would go his bail. "He'll be back in Dallas soon enough, but you won't see him. Your little game is over."

"I tell you I never—"

"Those leases can still be yours, but not unless you can prove you weren't with Oswald on April tenth. Can you do that?"

"I . . . let me think." There was a long pause. "Yes. Yes, I think I can."

"Then let's meet."

"When?"

"Tonight. Nine o'clock. I have people to answer to, and they'd be very unhappy with me if I gave you time to build an alibi."

"Come to the house. I'll send Jeanne out to a movie with her girlfriends."

"I have another place in mind. And you won't need directions to find it." I told him what I had in mind.

"Why there?" He sounded honestly puzzled.

"Just come. And if you don't want the Duvaliers *père* and *fils* very angry at you, my friend, come alone."

I hung up.

3

I was back at the hospital at six on the dot, and visited with Sadie for half an hour. Her head was clear again, and she claimed her pain wasn't too bad. At six-thirty I kissed her good cheek and told her I had to go.

"Your business?" she asked. "Your real business?"

"Yes."

"No one gets hurt unless it's absolutely necessary. Right?"

I nodded. "And never by mistake."

"Be careful."

"Like walking on eggs."

She tried to smile. It turned into a wince as the freshly flayed left side of her face pulled against itself. Her eyes looked over my shoulder. I turned to see Deke and Ellie in the doorway. They had dressed in their best, Deke in a summer-weight suit, string tie, and town cowboy hat, Ellie in a pink silk dress.

"We can wait, if you want us to," Ellie said.

"No, come on in. I was just leaving. But don't stay long, she's tired."

I kissed Sadie twice—dry lips and moist forehead. Then I drove back to West Neely Street, where I spread out the items I'd bought at the costume and novelty shop. I worked slowly and carefully in front of the bathroom mirror, referring often to the directions and wishing Sadie were here to help me.

I wasn't worried that de Mohrenschildt would take a look at me and say *haven't I seen you before;* what I wanted to make sure of was that he wouldn't recognize "John Lennon" later on. Depending on how believable he was, I might have to come back on him. If so, I'd want to take him by surprise.

I glued on the mustache first. It was a bushy one, making me look like an outlaw in a John Ford western. Next came the makeup, which I used on my face and hands to give myself a rancher's tan. There were horn-rimmed specs with plain glass lenses. I had briefly considered dying my hair, but that would have created a parallel with John Clayton that I couldn't have faced. Instead I yanked on a San Antonio Bullets baseball cap. When I was finished, I hardly recognized myself in the mirror.

"Nobody gets hurt unless it absolutely has to happen," I told the stranger in the mirror. "And never by mistake. Have we got that straight?"

The stranger nodded, but the eyes behind the fake glasses were cool.

The last thing I did before leaving was to take my revolver from the closet shelf and shove it in my pocket.

4

I got to the deserted parking lot at the end of Mercedes Street twenty minutes early, but de Mohrenschildt was already there, his gaudy Cadillac butted up against the brick backside of the Montgomery Ward warehouse. That meant he was anxious. Excellent.

I looked around, almost expecting to see the jump-rope girls, but of course they were in for the night—possibly sleeping and dreaming of Charlie Chaplin touring France, just to watch the ladies dance.

I parked near de Mohrenschildt's yacht, rolled down my window, stuck out my left hand, and curled the index finger in a beckoning gesture. For a moment de Mohrenschildt sat where he was, as if unsure. Then he got out. The bigtime strut wasn't in evidence. He looked frightened and furtive. That was also excellent. In one hand he held a file folder. From the flat look of it, there wasn't much inside. I hoped it wasn't just a prop. If it was, we were going to dance, and it wouldn't be the Lindy Hop.

He opened the door, leaned in, and said, "Look, you're not going to shoot me or anything, are you?"

"Nope," I said, hoping I sounded bored. "If I was from the FBI you might have to worry about that, but I'm not and you know I'm not. You've done business with us before." I hoped to God Al's notes were right about that.

"Is this car bugged? Are *you*?"

"If you're careful about what you say, you won't have anything to worry about, will you? Now get in."

He got in and shut the door. "About those leases—"

"You can discuss those another time, with other people. Oil

isn't my specialty. My specialty is dealing with people who behave indiscreetly, and your relationship with Oswald has been *very* indiscreet."

"I was curious, that's all. Here's a man who manages to defect to Russia, then *re*-defect to the United States. He's a semi-educated hillbilly, but he's surprisingly crafty. Also . . ." He cleared his throat. "I have a friend who wants to fuck his wife."

"We know about that," I said, thinking of Bouhe—just another George in a seemingly endless parade of them. How happy I would be to escape the echo chamber of the past. "My sole interest is making sure you had nothing to do with that botched Walker hit."

"Look at this. I took it from my wife's scrapbook."

He opened the folder, removed the single page of newsprint it contained, and passed it over. I turned on the Chevy's domelight, hoping my tan wouldn't look like the makeup it was. On the other hand, who cared? It would strike de Mohrenschildt as just one more bit of cloak-and-dagger spookery.

The sheet was from the April 12 *Morning News*. I knew the feature; AROUND TOWN was probably read a lot more closely by most Dallas-ites than the world and national news. There were lots of names in boldface type and lots of pix showing men and women in evening dress. De Mohrenschildt had used red ink to circle a squib halfway down. In the accompanying photo, George and Jeanne were unmistakable. He was in a tux and flashing a grin that seemed to show as many teeth as there are keys on a piano. Jeanne was displaying an amazing amount of cleavage, which the third person at the table appeared to be inspecting closely. All three held up champagne glasses.

"This is *Friday*'s paper," I said. "The Walker shooting was on Wednesday."

"These Around Town items are always two days old. Because they're about nightlife, dig? Besides . . . don't just look at the picture, *read* it, man. It's right there in black and white!"

I checked, but I knew he was telling the truth as soon as I saw the other man's name in the newspaper's hotcha-hotcha boldface type. The harmonic echo was as loud as a guitar amp set on reverb.

Local oil rajah **George de Mohrenschildt** and wife **Jeanne** lifted a glass (or maybe it was a dozen!) at the **Carousel Club** on Wednesday night, celebrating the scrump-tiddly-uptious lady's birthday. How old? The lovebirds weren't telling, but to us she doesn't look a day over twenty-three (skidoo!). They were hosted by the **Carousel's** jovial panjandrum **Jack Ruby**, who sent over a bottle o' bubbly and then joined them for a toast. Happy birthday, **Jeanne**, and long may you wave!

"The champagne was rotgut and I had a hangover until three the next afternoon, but it was worth it if you're satisfied."

I was. I was also fascinated. "How well do you know this guy Ruby?"

De Mohrenschildt sniffed—all his baronial snobbery expressed in a single quick inhale through flared nostrils. "Not well, and don't want to. He's a crazy little Jew who buys the police free drinks so they'll look the other way when he uses his fists. Which he likes to do. One day his temper will get him in trouble. Jeanne likes the strippers. They get her hot." He shrugged, as if to say who could understand women. "Now are you—" He looked down, saw the gun in my fist, and stopped talking. His eyes widened. His tongue came out and licked his lips. It made a peculiar wet slupping sound as he drew it back into his mouth.

"Am I satisfied? Was that what you were going to ask?" I prodded him with the gun barrel and took considerable pleasure in his gasp. Killing changes a man, I tell you, it coarsens him, but in my defense, if there was ever a man who deserved a salutary scare, it was this one. Marguerite was partially responsible for what her youngest son had become, and there was plenty of responsibility for Lee himself—all those half-formed dreams of glory—but de Mohrenschildt had played a part. And was it some complicated plot hatched deep in the bowels of the CIA? No. Slumming simply amused him. So did the rage and disappointment baking up from the plugged oven of Lee's disturbed personality.

"Please," de Mohrenschildt whispered.

"I'm satisfied. But listen to me, you windbag: you're never going to meet with Lee Oswald again. You're never going to talk to him on the phone. You're never going to mention a word of this conversation to his wife, to his mother, to George Bouhe, to any of the other émigrés. Do you understand that?"

"Yes. Absolutely. I was growing bored with him, anyway."

"Not half as bored as I am with you. If I find out you've talked to Lee, I'll kill you. *Capisce?*"

"Yes. And the leases . . . ?"

"Someone will be in touch. Now get the fuck out of my car."

He did so, posthaste. When he was behind the wheel of the Caddy, I reached out again with my left hand. Instead of beckoning, this time I used my index finger to point at Mercedes Street. He went.

I sat where I was a little while longer, looking at the clipping, which he in his haste had forgotten to take with him. The de Mohrenschildts and Jack Ruby, glasses raised. Was it a signpost pointing toward a conspiracy, after all? The tin-hat crew who believed in things like shooters popping up from sewers and Oswald doppelgängers probably would have thought so, but I knew better. It was just another harmonic. This was the Land of Ago, where everything echoed.

I felt I had closed Al Templeton's window of uncertainty to the merest draft. Oswald was going to return to Dallas on the third of October. According to Al's notes, he would get hired as a common laborer at the Texas School Book Depository in the middle of October. Except that wasn't going to happen, because sometime between the third and the sixteenth, I was going to end his miserable, dangerous life.

5

I was allowed to spring Sadie from the hospital on the morning of August seventh. She was quiet on the ride back to Jodie. I could tell she was still in considerable pain, but she rested a companionable hand on my thigh for most of the drive. When we turned off Highway 77 at the big Denholm Lions billboard, she said: "I'm going back to school in September."

"Sure?"

"Yes. If I could stand up in front of the whole town at the Grange, I guess I can manage it in front of a bunch of kids in the school library. Besides, I have a feeling we're going to need the money. Unless you have some source of income I don't know about, you've got to be almost broke. Thanks to me."

"I should have some money coming in at the end of the month."

"The fight?"

I nodded.

"Good. And I'll only have to listen to the whispers and the giggles for a little while, anyway. Because when you go, I'm going with you." She paused. "If it's still what you want."

"Sadie, it's *all* I want."

We turned onto Main Street. Jem Needham was just finishing his rounds in his milk truck. Bill Gavery was putting out fresh loaves of bread under cheesecloth in front of the bakery. From a passing car Jan and Dean were singing that in Surf City there were two girls for every boy.

"Will I like it, Jake? In your place?"

"I hope so, hon."

"Is it very different?"

I smiled. "People pay more for gasoline and have more buttons to push. Otherwise, it's about the same."

6

That hot August was as close to a honeymoon as we ever managed, and it was sweet. Any pretense that I was rooming with Deke Simmons pretty well went out the window, although I still kept my car in his driveway at night.

Sadie recovered quickly from the latest insult to her flesh, and although her eye sagged and her cheek was still scarred and deeply hollowed where Clayton had cut through to the inside of her mouth, there was visible improvement. Ellerton and his crew had done a good job with what they had.

We read books sitting side by side on her couch, with her fan blowing back our hair—*The Group* for her, *Jude the Obscure* for me. We had backyard picnics in the shade of her prized Chinese Pistache tree and drank gallons of iced coffee. Sadie began to cut back on the smokes again. We watched *Rawhide* and *Ben Casey* and *Route 66*. One night she tuned in *The New Adventures of Ellery Queen*, but I asked her to change the channel. I didn't like mysteries, I said.

Before bed, I carefully smoothed ointment on her wounded face, and once we were *in* bed . . . it was good. Leave it at that.

One day outside the grocery store, I ran into that upstanding schoolboard member Jessica Caltrop. She said she would like to speak to me for a moment on what she called "a delicate subject."

"What might that be, Miz Caltrop?" I asked. "Because I've got ice cream in here, and I'd like to get home with it before it melts."

She gave me a chilly smile that could have kept my French vanilla firm for hours. "Would home be on Bee Tree Lane, Mr. Amberson? With the unfortunate Miss Dunhill?"

"And that would be your business how?"

The smile froze a little more deeply. "As a member of the schoolboard, I have to make sure that the morality of our faculty is spotless. If you and Miss Dunhill are living together, that is a matter of grave concern to me. Teenagers are impressionable. They imitate what they see in their elders."

"You think? After fifteen years or so in the classroom, I would have said they observe adult behavior and then run the other way as fast as they can."

"I'm sure we could have an illuminating discussion on how you view teenage psychology, Mr. Amberson, but that's not why I asked to speak to you, uncomfortable as I find it." She didn't look a bit uncomfortable. "If you are living in sin with Miss Dunhill—"

"Sin," I said. "Now there's an interesting word. Jesus said that he without it was free to cast the first stone. Or she, I suppose. Are *you* without it, Miz Caltrop?"

"This discussion is not about me."

"But we could make it about you. *I* could make it about you. I could, for instance, start asking around about the woods colt you dropped once upon a time."

She recoiled as if slapped and took two steps back toward the brick wall of the market. I took two steps forward, my grocery bags curled in my arms.

"I find that repulsive and offensive. If you were still teaching, I'd—"

"I'm sure you would, but I'm not, so you need to listen to me very carefully. It's my understanding that you had a kid when you were sixteen and living on Sweetwater Ranch. I don't know if the father was one of your schoolmates, a saddle tramp, or even your own father—"

"You're disgusting!"

True. And sometimes it's *such* a pleasure.

"I don't care who it was, but I care about Sadie, who's been through more pain and heartache than you've felt in your whole life." Now I had her pinned against the brick wall. She was looking up at me, her eyes bright with terror. In another time and place I could have felt sorry for her. Not now. "If you say *one word* about Sadie—one word to anybody—I'll make it my business to find out where that kid of yours is now, and I'll spread the word from one end of this town to the other. Do you understand me?"

"Get out of my way! Let me pass!"

"Do you understand me?"

"Yes! *Yes!*"

"Good." I stepped back. "Live your life, Miz Caltrop. I suspect it's been pretty gray since you were sixteen—busy, though, inspecting other people's dirty laundry *does* keep a person busy—but you live it. And let us live ours."

She sidled to her left along the brick wall, in the direction of the parking lot behind the market. Her eyes were bulging. They never left me.

I smiled pleasantly. "Before this discussion becomes something that never happened, I want to give you a piece of advice, little lady. It comes straight from my heart. I love her, and you do not want to fuck with a man in love. If you mess in my business—or Sadie's—I will try my best to make you the sorriest bluenose bitch in Texas. That is my sincere promise to you."

She ran for the parking lot. She did it awkwardly, like someone who hasn't moved at a pace faster than a stately walk in a long time. In her brown shin-length skirt, opaque flesh-toned hose, and sensible brown shoes, she was the spirit of the age. Her hair was coming loose from its bun. Once I had no doubt she had worn it down, the way men like to see a woman's hair, but that had been a long time ago.

"And have a nice day!" I called after her.

7

Sadie came into the kitchen while I was putting things away in the icebox. "You were gone a long time. I was starting to worry."

"I got talking. You know how it is in Jodie. Always someone to pass the time of day with."

She smiled. The smile was coming a little more easily now. "You're a sweet guy."

I thanked Sadie and told her she was a sweet gal. I wondered if Caltrop would talk to Fred Miller, the other schoolboard member who saw himself as a guardian of town morality. I didn't think so. It wasn't just that I knew about her youthful indiscretion; I had set out to scare her. It had worked with de Mohrenschildt, and it had worked with her. Scaring people is a dirty job, but somebody has to do it.

Sadie crossed the kitchen and put an arm around me. "What would you say to a weekend at the Candlewood Bungalows before school starts? Just like in the old days? I suppose that's very forward of Sadie, isn't it?"

"Well now, that depends." I took her in my arms. "Are we talking about a dirty weekend?"

She blushed, except for around the scar. The flesh there remained white and shiny. "Absolutely feelthy, señor."

"The sooner the better, then."

8

It wasn't actually a dirty weekend, unless you believe—as the Jessica Caltrops of the world seem to—that lovemaking is dirty. It's true that we spent a lot of it in bed. But we also spent a fair amount outside. Sadie was a tireless walker, and there was a vast open field on the flank of a hill behind the Candlewood. It was rioting with late-summer wildflowers. We spent most of Saturday afternoon there. Sadie could name some of the blooms—Spanish dagger, prickly poppy, something called yucca birdweed—but at others she could only shake her head, then bend over to smell whatever aromas there were to be smelled. We walked hand in hand, with high grass brushing against our jeans and big clouds with fluffed-out tops sailing the high Texas sky. Long shutters of light and shadow slipped across the field. There was a cool breeze that day, and no refinery smell in the air. At the top of the hill we turned and looked back. The bungalows were small and insignificant on the tree-dotted sweep of the prairie. The road was a ribbon.

Sadie sat down, drew her knees to her chest, and clasped her arms around her shins. I sat down beside her.

"I want to ask you something," she said.

"All right."

"It's not about the . . . you know, where you come from . . . that's more than I want to think about just now. It's about the man you came to stop. The one you say is going to kill the president."

I considered this. "Delicate subject, hon. Do you remember me telling you that I'm close to a big machine full of sharp teeth?"

"Yes—"

"I said I wouldn't let you stand next to me while I was fooling with it. I've already said more than I meant to, and probably more than I should have. Because the past doesn't want to be changed. It fights back when you try. And the bigger the potential change, the harder it fights. I don't want you to be hurt."

"I already have been," she said quietly.

"Are you asking if that was my fault?"

"No, honey." She put a hand on my cheek. "No."

"Well, it may have been, at least partially. There's a thing called the butterfly effect—" There were hundreds of them fluttering on the slope before us, as if to illustrate that very fact.

"I know what that is," she said. "There's a Ray Bradbury story about it."

"Really?"

"It's called 'A Sound of Thunder.' It's very beautiful and very disturbing. But Jake—Johnny was crazy long before you came on the scene. I *left* him long before you came on the scene. And if you hadn't come along, some other man might have. I'm sure he wouldn't have been as nice as you, but I wouldn't have known that, would I? Time is a tree with many branches."

"What do you want to know about the guy, Sadie?"

"Mostly why you don't just call the police—anonymously, of course—and report him."

I pulled a stem of grass to chew while I thought about that. The first thing to cross my mind was something de Mohrenschildt had said in the Montgomery Ward parking lot: *He's a semi-educated hill-billy, but he's surprisingly crafty.*

It was a good assessment. Lee had escaped Russia when he was tired of it; he would also be crafty enough to escape the Book Depository after shooting the president in spite of the almost immediate police and Secret Service response. Of *course* it was a quick response; plenty of people were going to see exactly where the shots came from.

Lee would be questioned at gunpoint in the second-floor break room even before the speeding motorcade delivered the dying president to Parkland Hospital. The cop who did the questioning would recall later that the young man had been reasonable and persuasive. Once foreman Roy Truly vouched for him as an employee, the cop would let Ozzie Rabbit go and then hurry upstairs to seek the source of the gunshots. It was possible to believe that, if not for his encounter with Patrolman Tippit, Lee might not have been captured for days or weeks.

"Sadie, the Dallas cops are going to shock the world with their incompetence. I'd be nuts to trust them. They might not even act on an anonymous tip."

"But why? Why wouldn't they?"

"Right now because the guy's not even in Texas, and he doesn't mean to come back. He's planning to defect to Cuba."

"*Cuba?* Why in the world *Cuba?*"

I shook my head. "It doesn't matter, because it's not going to work. He's going to return to Dallas, but not with any plan to kill the president. He doesn't even know Kennedy's coming to Dallas. Kennedy himself doesn't know, because the trip hasn't been scheduled yet."

"But *you* know."

"Yes."

"Because in the time you come from, all this is in the history books."

"The broad strokes, yes. I got the specifics from the friend who sent me here. I'll tell you the whole story someday when this is over, but not now. Not while the machine with all those teeth is still running full tilt. The important thing is this: if the police question the guy at any point before mid-November, he's going to sound completely innocent, because he *is* innocent." Another of those vast cloud-shadows rolled over us, temporarily dropping the temperature by ten degrees or so. "For all I know, he may not have made up his mind entirely until the moment he pulled the trigger."

"You speak as if it's already happened," she marveled.

"In my world, it has."

"What's important about mid-November?"

"On the sixteenth, the *Morning News* is going to tell Dallas about Kennedy's motorcade down Main Street. L— the guy will read that and realize the cars will go right past the place where he's working. He's probably going to think it's a message from God. Or maybe the ghost of Karl Marx."

"Where's he going to work?"

I shook my head again. That wasn't safe for her to know. Of course, *none* of this was safe. Yet (I've said it before, but it bears repeating) what a relief to tell at least some of it to another person.

"If the police talked to him, they might at least frighten him out of doing it."

She was right, but what a horrifying risk. I'd already taken a smaller one by talking to de Mohrenschildt, but de Mohrenschildt wanted those oil leases. Also, I'd done more than frighten him— I'd scared the living bejesus out of him. I thought he'd keep mum. Lee, on the other hand . . .

I took Sadie's hand. "Right now I can predict where this man's going the same way I could predict where a train is going to go, because it can't leave the tracks. Once I step in, once I *meddle,* all bets are off."

"If you talked to him yourself?"

A truly nightmarish image came into my mind. I saw Lee telling the cops, *The idea was put into my head by a man named George Amberson. If it hadn't been for him, I never would have thought of it.*

"I don't think that would work, either."

In a small voice, she asked: "Will you have to kill him?"

I didn't answer. Which was an answer in itself, of course.

"And you really know this is going to happen."

"Yes."

"The way you know Tom Case is going to win that fight on the twenty-ninth."

"Yes."

"Even though everybody who knows boxing says Tiger's going to murder him."

I smiled. "You've been reading the sports pages."

"Yes. I have." She took the piece of grass from my mouth and put it in her own. "I've never been to a prizefight. Will you take me?"

"It's not exactly live, you know. It's on a big TV screen."

"I know. Will you take me?"

9

There were plenty of good-looking women in the Dallas Auditorium on fight night, but Sadie got her fair share of admiring glances. She had made herself up carefully for the occasion, but even the most skillful makeup could only minimize the damage to her face, not completely hide it. Her dress helped matters considerably. It clung smoothly to her body line, and had a deep scoop neck.

The brilliant stroke was a felt fedora given to her by Ellen Dockerty, when Sadie told her that I had asked her to go to the prizefight with me. The hat was an almost exact match for the one Ingrid Bergman wears in the final scene of *Casablanca.* With its insouciant slant, it set her face off perfectly . . . and of course it slanted to the left, putting a deep triangle of shadow over her bad cheek. It was better than any makeup job. When she came out of the bedroom for inspection, I told her she was absolutely gorgeous.

STEPHEN KING

The look of relief on her face and the excited sparkle in her eyes suggested that she knew I was doing more than trying to make her feel good.

There was heavy traffic coming into Dallas, and by the time we reached our seats, the third of five undercard matches was going on—a large black man and an even larger white man slowly pummeling each other while the crowd cheered. Not one but four enormous screens hung over the polished hardwood floor where the Dallas Spurs played (badly) during the basketball season. The picture was provided by multiple rear-screen projection systems, and although the colors were muddy—almost rudimentary—the images themselves were crisp. Sadie was impressed. In truth, so was I.

"Are you nervous?" she asked.

"Yes."

"Even though—"

"Even though. When I bet on the Pirates to win the World Series back in '60, I *knew*. Here I'm depending entirely on my friend, who got it off the internet."

"What in the world is that?"

"Sci-fi. Like Ray Bradbury."

"Oh . . . okay." Then she put her fingers between her lips and whistled. *"Hey beer-man!"*

The beer-man, decked out in a vest, cowboy hat, and silver-studded concho belt, sold us two bottles of Lone Star (glass, not plastic) with paper cups nestled over the necks. I gave him a buck and told him to keep the change.

Sadie took hers, bumped it against mine, and said: "Luck, Jake."

"If I need it, I'm in one hell of a jam."

She lit a cigarette, adding her smoke to the blue veil hanging around the lights. I was on her right, and from where I sat, she looked perfect.

I tapped her on the shoulder, and when she turned, I kissed her lightly on her parted lips. "Kid," I said, "we'll always have Paris."

She grinned. "The one in Texas, maybe."

652

A groan went up from the crowd. The black fighter had just knocked the white one on his ass.

10

The main bout commenced at nine-thirty. Close-ups of the fighters filled the screens, and when the camera centered on Tom Case, my heart sank. There were threads of gray in his curly black hair. His cheeks were becoming jowls. His midsection flabbed over his trunks. Worst of all, though, were his somehow bewildered eyes, which peered from puffy sacs of scar tissue. He didn't look entirely sure about where he was. The audience of fifteen hundred or so mostly cheered—Tom Case was a hometown boy, after all—but I also heard a healthy chorus of boos. Sitting there slumped on his stool, holding the ropes with his gloved hands, he looked like he'd already lost. Dick Tiger, on the other hand, was up on his feet, shadowboxing and skipping nimbly in his black hightops.

Sadie leaned close to me and whispered, "This doesn't look so good, honey."

That was the understatement of the century. It looked terrible.

Down front (where the screen must have seemed like a looming cliff with blurred moving figures projected on it), I saw Akiva Roth squire a mink-wearing dolly in Garbo shades to a seat that would have been ringside, if the fight hadn't been on a screen. In front of Sadie and me, a chubby man smoking a cigar turned around and said, "Who ya got, beautiful?"

"Case!" Sadie said bravely.

The chubby cigar-smoker laughed. "Well, you got a good heart, anyway. Care to put a tenspot on that?"

"Will you give me four-to-one? If Case knocks him out?"

"If *Case* knocks *Tiger* out? Lady, you're on." He stuck out a hand. Sadie shook it. Then she turned to me with a defiant little smile playing around the corner of her mouth that still worked.

"Pretty bold," I said.

"Not at all," she said. "Tiger's going down in five. I can see the future."

11

The ring announcer, wearing a tux and a pound of hair tonic, trotted to center ring, yanked down a mike on a silver cord, and gave the fighters' stats in a rolling carny-barker's voice. The National Anthem played. Men yanked off their hats and put their hands over their hearts. I could feel my own heart thudding rapidly, at least a hundred and twenty beats a minute and maybe more. The auditorium was air-conditioned, but sweat was rolling down the back of my neck and humidifying my armpits.

A girl in a swimsuit strutted around the ring in high heels, holding up a card with a big number *1* on it.

The bell clanged. Tom Case shuffled into the ring with a resigned expression on his face. Dick Tiger bounded happily to meet him, feinted with his right hand, then unleashed a compact left hook that decked Case exactly twelve seconds into the fight. The crowds—the one here and the one in the Garden, two thousand miles away—let out a disgusted groan. The hand Sadie had rested on my thigh seemed to spring claws as it tensed and dug in.

"Tell that ten to say goo'bye to his friends, beautiful," the chubby cigar-smoker said gleefully.

Al, what the fuck were you thinking?

Dick Tiger retreated to his corner and stood there bouncing nonchalantly on the balls of his feet while the ref commenced the count, sweeping his right arm up and down dramatically. On three, Case stirred. On five he sat up. On seven he took a knee. And on nine he rose and lifted his gloves. The ref took the fighter's face in his hands and asked a question. Case replied. The ref nodded, beckoned to Tiger, and stepped aside.

The Tiger Man, perhaps anxious to get to the steak dinner waiting for him at Sardi's, rushed in for the kill. Case didn't try to escape him—his speed had left him behind long ago, perhaps during some tank-town fight in Moline, Illinois, or New Haven, Connecticut—but he was able to cover up . . . and clinch. He did a lot of that, resting his head on Tiger's shoulder like a tired tango dancer and pounding his gloves weakly on Tiger's back. The crowd began to boo. When the bell rang and Case plodded back to his stool with his head down and his gloved fists dangling, they booed louder.

"He stinks, beautiful," the chubby man remarked.

Sadie looked at me anxiously. "What do you think?"

"I think he made it through the first, anyway." What I *really* thought was that someone should stick a fork in Tom Case's sagging butt, because to me he looked almost done.

The chick in the Jantzen did her thing again, this time holding up a *2*. The bell clanged. Once again Tiger bounded and Case plodded. My guy continued to move in close so he could clinch whenever possible, but I noticed he was now managing to deflect the left hook that had devastated him in the first round. Tiger worked on the older fighter's gut with piston-like shots of his right hand, but there must have been quite a lot of muscle left under that flab, because they didn't seem to affect Case very much. At one point, Tiger pushed Case back and gestured with both gloves in a *come on, come on* gesture. The crowd cheered. Case only stared at him, so Tiger moved in. Case immediately clinched. The crowd groaned. The bell rang.

"My granny could give Tiger a better show," the cigar-smoker grumbled.

"Maybe," Sadie said, lighting her third cigarette of the fight, "but he's still on his feet, isn't he?"

"Not for long, sugar. The next time one of those left hooks gets through, it's gonna be Case closed." He chortled.

The third round was more clinching and shuffling, but in the fourth, Case let his guard drop slightly and Tiger hit him with a barrage of lefts and rights to the head that brought the audience to its feet, roaring. Akiva Roth's girlfriend was with them. Mr. Roth himself retained his seat, but *did* trouble himself enough to cup his ladyfriend's ass with a beringed right hand.

Case fell back against the ropes, shooting rights at Tiger, and one of those blows got through. It looked pretty feeble, but I saw sweat fly from the Tiger Man's hair as he shook his head. There was a bewildered where-did-*that*-come-from expression on his face. Then he moved in again and went back to work. Blood began oozing from a cut beside Case's left eye. Before Tiger could increase the damage from a trickle to a gush, the bell rang.

"If you hand over that ten now, beautiful," the pudgy cigar-smoker said, "you and your boyfriend will be able to beat the traffic."

"Tell you what," Sadie said. "I'll give you one chance to call it off and save yourself forty dollars."

The pudgy cigar-smoker laughed. "Beautiful *and* a sensayuma. If that long tall helicopter you're with treats you bad, sugar, come home with me."

In Case's corner, the trainer was working frantically on the bad eye, squeezing something from a tube and mooshing it around with the tips of his fingers. It looked like Crazy Glue to me, except I don't think that had been invented yet. Then he slapped Case in the chops with a wet towel. The bell rang.

Dick Tiger bored in, jamming with his right and hooking with his left. Case dodged one left hook, and for the first time in the fight, Tiger launched a right uppercut at the older man's head. Case managed to pull back just enough to keep from taking it full on the jaw, but it connected with his cheek. The force of it distorted his entire face into a horror-house grimace. He staggered back. Tiger came at him. The crowd was up again, bellowing for blood. We rose with them. Sadie's hands were over her mouth.

Tiger had Case pinned in one of the neutral corners and was hammering him with rights and lefts. I could see Case sagging; I could see the lights in his eyes dimming. One more left hook—or that cannon-shot right—and they would go out.

"*PUT IM DOWN!*" the chubby cigar-smoker was screaming. "*PUT HIM DOWN, DICKY! KNOCK HIS BLOCK OFF!*"

656

Tiger hit him low, below the belt. Probably not on purpose, but the ref stepped in. While he cautioned Tiger about the low blow, I watched Case to see how he would use this temporary respite. I saw something come into his face that I recognized. I had seen Lee wearing the same expression on the day he'd been giving Marina hell about the zipper of her skirt. It had appeared when Marina had come back on him, accusing him of bringing her and the baby to a *peegsty* and then twirling her finger around her ear in a you're-crazy gesture.

All at once this had stopped being just a payday to Tom Case.

The ref stepped aside. Tiger bored in, but this time Case stepped to meet him. What happened during the next twenty seconds was the most electrifying, terrifying thing I have ever seen as part of an audience. The two of them simply stood toe-to-toe, slugging each other in the face, the chest, the shoulders, the gut. There was no bobbing, no weaving, no fancy footwork. They were bulls in a pasture. Case's nose broke and gushed blood. Tiger's lower lip smashed back against his teeth and split; blood poured down both sides of his chin, making him look like a vampire after a big meal.

Everyone in the auditorium was on their feet and screaming. Sadie was jumping up and down. Her fedora fell off, exposing the scarred cheek. She took no notice. Nobody else did, either. On the huge screens, World War III was in full swing.

Case lowered his head to take one of those bazooka rights, and I saw Tiger grimace as his fist connected with hard bone. He took a step backward and Case unloaded a monster uppercut. Tiger turned his head, avoiding the worst of it, but his mouthpiece flew free and rolled across the canvas.

Case moved in, throwing haymaker lefts and rights. There was no artistry to them, only raw, angry power. Tiger backpedaled, tripped over his own feet, and went down. Case stood over him, seemingly unsure what to do or—perhaps—even where he was. His frantically signaling trainer caught his eye and he plodded back to his corner. The ref commenced his count.

On four, Tiger took a knee. On six, he was on his feet. After the mandatory eight-count, the fight recommenced. I looked at the big clock in the corner of the screen and saw there were fifteen seconds left in the round.

Not enough, it's not enough time.

Case plodded forward. Tiger threw that devastating left hook. Case jerked his head to one side, and when the glove had flown past his face, he lashed out with his right. This time it was Dick Tiger's face that distorted, and when he went down he didn't get up.

The pudgy man looked at the tattered remains of his cigar, then threw it on the floor. "Jesus wept!"

"Yes!" Sadie chirruped, resetting her fedora at the proper insouciant slant. "On a stack of blueberry pancakes, and the disciples said they were the best they ever ate! Now pay up!"

12

By the time we got back to Jodie, August 29 had become August 30, but we were both too excited to sleep. We made love, then came out to the kitchen and ate pie in our underwear.

"Well?" I said. "What do you think?"

"That I never want to go to another prizefight. That was pure bloodlust. And I was up on my feet, cheering with the rest. For a few seconds—maybe even a full minute—I wanted Case to kill that dancing all-full-of-himself dandy. Then I couldn't wait to get back here and jump into bed with you. That wasn't about love just now, Jake. That was about *burning.*"

I said nothing. Sometimes there's nothing to say.

She reached across the table, plucked a crumb from my chin, and popped it into my mouth. "Tell me it's not hate."

"What's not?"

"The reason you feel you have to stop this man on your own." She saw me start to open my mouth and held up a hand to stop me. "I heard everything you said, all your reasons, but you have to tell me they *are* reasons, and not just what I saw in that man Case's eyes when Tiger hit him in the trunks. I can love you if you're a man, and I can love you if you're a hero—I guess, although for some reason that seems a lot harder—but I don't think I can love a vigilante."

I thought of how Lee looked at his wife when he wasn't mad at her. I thought about the conversation I'd overheard when he and his little girl were splashing in the bath. I thought about his tears outside the bus station, when he'd held Junie and nuzzled beneath her chin before rolling off to New Orleans.

"It's not hate," I said. "What I feel about him is . . ."

I trailed off. She watched me.

"Sorrow for a spoiled life. But you can feel sorry for a good dog that goes rabid, too. That doesn't stop you from putting him down."

She looked me in the eyes. "I want you again. But this time it should be for love, you know? Not because we just saw two men beat the hell out of each other and our guy won."

"Okay," I said. "Okay. That's good."

And it was.

13

"Well look here," said Frank Frati's daughter when I walked into the pawnshop around noon on that Friday. "It's the boxing swami with the New England accent." She offered me a glittery smile, then turned her head and shouted, *"Da-ad!* It's your Tom Case man!"

Frati came shuffling out. "Hello there, Mr. Amberson," he said. "Big as life and handsome as Satan on Saturday night. I bet you're feeling bright-eyed and bushy-tailed this fine day, aren't you?"

"Sure," I said. " Why wouldn't I? I had a lucky hit."

"I'm the one who took the hit." He pulled a brown envelope, a little bigger than standard business-size, from the back pocket of his baggy gabardine slacks. "Two grand. Feel free to count it."

"That's all right," I said. "I trust you."

He started to pass over the envelope, then pulled it back and tapped his chin with it. His blue eyes, faded but shrewd, sized me up. "Any interest in rolling this over? Football season is coming up, as is the Series."

"I don't know jack about football, and a Dodgers-Yankees Series doesn't interest me much. Hand it over."

He did so.

"Pleasure doing business with you," I said, and walked out. I could feel their eyes following me, and I had that by now very unpleasant sense of déjà vu. I couldn't pinpoint the cause. I got into my car, hoping I would never have to return to that part of Fort Worth again. Or to Greenville Avenue in Dallas. Or place another bet with another bookie named Frati.

Those were my three wishes, and they all came true.

14

My next stop was 214 West Neely Street. I'd phoned the land-lord and told him August was my last month. He tried to talk me out of it, telling me good tenants such as myself were hard to find. That was probably true—the police hadn't come once on my account, and they visited the neighborhood a lot, especially on weekends—but I suspected it had more to do with too many apartments and not enough renters. Dallas was experiencing one of its periodic lows.

I stopped at First Corn on the way and plumped up my check-ing account with Frati's two grand. That was fortunate. I realized later—much later—that if I'd had it on me when I got to Neely Street, I surely would have lost it.

My plan was to dummy-check the four rooms for any posses-sions I might have left behind, paying particular attention to those mystic points of junk-attraction beneath sofa cushions, under the bed, and at the backs of bureau drawers. And of course I'd take my

Police Special. I would want it to deal with Lee. I now had every intention of killing him, and as soon after he returned to Dallas as I possibly could. In the meantime, I didn't want to leave a trace of George Amberson behind.

As I closed in on Neely, that sense of being stuck in time's echo chamber was very strong. I kept thinking about the two Fratis, one with a wife named Marjorie, one with a daughter named Wanda.

Marjorie: *Is that a bet in regular talk?*
Wanda: *Is that a bet when it's at home with its feet up?*
Marjorie: *I'm J. Edgar Hoover, my son.*
Wanda: *I'm Chief Curry of the Dallas Police.*

And so what? It was the chiming, that was all. The harmony. A side effect of time-travel.

Nevertheless, an alarm bell began to ring far back in my head, and as I turned onto Neely Street, it moved up to the forebrain. History repeats itself, the past harmonizes, and that was what this feeling was about . . . but not *all* it was about. As I turned into the driveway of the house where Lee had laid his half-assed plan to assassinate Edwin Walker, I really listened to that alarm bell. Because now it was close. Now it was shrieking.

Akiva Roth at the fight, but not alone. With him had been a party-doll in Garbo sunglasses and a mink stole. August in Dallas was hardly mink weather, but the auditorium had been air-conditioned, and—as they say in my time—sometimes you just gotta signify.

Take away the dark glasses. Take away the stole. What do you have?

For a moment as I sat there in my car, listening to the cooling engine tick and tock, I still had nothing. Then I realized that if you replaced the mink stole with a Ship N Shore blouse, you had Wanda Frati.

Chaz Frati of Derry had set Bill Turcotte on me. That thought had even crossed my mind . . . but I had dismissed it. Bad idea.

Who had Frank Frati of Fort Worth set on me? Well, he had

to know Akiva Roth of Faith Financial; Roth was his daughter's boyfriend, after all.

Suddenly I wanted my gun, and I wanted it right away.

I got out of the Chevy and trotted up the porch steps, my keys in my hand. I was fumbling through them when a panel truck roared around the corner from Haines Avenue and scrunched to a stop in front of 214 with the leftside wheels up on the curb.

I looked around. Saw no one. The street was deserted. There's never a bystander you can scream to for help when you want one. Let alone a cop.

I jammed the right key into the lock and turned it, thinking I'd lock them out—whoever *they* were—and call the cops on the phone. I was inside and smelling the hot, stale air of the deserted apartment when I remembered that there *was* no phone.

Big men were running across the lawn. Three of them. One had a short length of pipe that looked to be wrapped in something.

No, actually there were enough guys to play bridge. The fourth was Akiva Roth, and he wasn't running. He was strolling up the walk with his hands in his pockets and a placid smile on his face.

I slammed the door. I twisted the thumb bolt. I had barely finished when it exploded open. I ran for the bedroom and got about halfway.

15

Two of Roth's goons dragged me into the kitchen. The third was the one with the pipe. It was wrapped in strips of dark felt. I saw this when he laid it carefully on the table where I had eaten a good many meals. He put on yellow rawhide gloves.

Roth leaned in the doorway, still smiling placidly. "Eduardo Gutierrez has syphilis," he announced. "It's gone to his brain. He'll be dead in eighteen months, but you know what? He don't care. He believes he's gonna come back as an Arab emirate, or sumshit. How 'bout that, huh?"

Responding to non sequiturs—at cocktail parties, on public transportation, in ticket lines at the movie theater—is dicey enough, but it's *really* hard to know what to say when you're being held by two men and about to receive a beating from a third. So I said nothing.

"The thing is, you got in his head. You won bets you weren't supposed to win. Sometimes you lost, but Eddie G got this crazy idea that when you lost, you were losing on purpose. You know? Then you hit big on the Derby, and he decided you were, I dunno, some kind of telepathic gizmo who could see the future. Did you know he burned down your house?"

I said nothing.

"Then," Roth said, "when those little wormies really started to bite his brain, he started to think you were some kind of ghoul, or devil. He put out the word all over the South, the West, the Midwest. 'Look for this guy Amberson, and bring him down. Kill him. The guy is unnatural. I could smell it on im but I didn't pay attention. Now look at me, sick and dying. And it's this guy's fault. He's a ghoul or a devil, or sumshit.' Crazy, you know? Toys in the attic."

I said nothing.

"Carmo, I don't think my friend Georgie's listening. I think he's dozing off. Give him a wake-up call."

The man in the yellow rawhide gloves swung a Tom Case uppercut, bringing it from hip level to the left side of my face. Pain exploded in my head, and for a few moments I saw everything on that side through a scarlet haze.

"Okay, you look a little more awake now," Roth said. "Where was I? Oh, I know. How you turned into Eddie G's private boogeyman. Because of the syph, we all knew that. If it hadn't been you, it would have been some barbershop dog. Or a girl who jerked him off too hard at the drive-in when he was sixteen. Sometimes he can't remember his own address, he has to call someone to come get him. Sad, huh? It's those worms in his head. But everybody humors him, because Eddie was always a good guy. He could tell a joke, man, you'd laugh until you cried. Nobody even thought you were real. Then Eddie G's boogeyman turns up in Dallas, at my shop. And what happens? The boogeyman bets on the Pirates to beat the Yankees, which everyone knows ain't gonna happen, and in seven games, which everyone knows the Series ain't gonna go."

"It was just luck," I said. My voice sounded furry, because the side of my mouth was swelling. "An impulse bet."

"That's just stupid, and stupidity always got to be paid for. Carmo, kneecap this stupid sonofabitch."

"No!" I said. "No, please don't do that!"

Carmo smiled as if I'd said something cute, plucked the felt-wrapped pipe from the table, and swung it at my left knee. I heard something down there make a popping sound. Like a big knuckle. The pain was exquisite. I bit back a scream and sagged against the men who were holding me. They yanked me back up.

Roth stood in the doorway, hands in pockets, smiling his happy placid smile. "Okay. Cool. That's gonna swell, by the way. You won't believe how big it's gonna get. But hey, you bought it, you paid for it, you own it. Meanwhile, the facts, ma'am, nothing but the facts." The goons holding me laughed.

"The facts are nobody dressed like you was on the day you came into my store makes a bet like that. For a man dressed like you was, an impulse bet is ten dollars, a double sawbuck at most. But the Pirates came through, that is also the facts. And I'm starting to think Eddie G might be right. Not that you're a devil or a ghoul or an ESP gizmo, nothing like that, but how about maybe you know somebody who knows something? Like the fix is in and the Pirates are *supposed* to win in seven?"

"Nobody fixes baseball, Roth. Not since the Black Sox in 1919. You run a book, you must know that."

He raised his eyebrows. "You know my name! Hey, maybe you *are* an ESP guy. But I ain't got all day."

He glanced at his watch, as if to confirm this. It was big and clunky, probably a Rolex.

"I try to see where you live when you come in to collect, but you hold your thumb over your address. That's okay. Lotta guys do that. I decide I'm gonna let it go. I should send some boys down the street to beat the shit out of you, maybe even kill you so that Eddie G's mind—what's left of it—can be at rest? Because some guy took shit odds and beat me out of twelve hundred? Fuck that, what Eddie G don't know won't hurt him. Besides, with you out of the way, he'd just start thinking about something else. Maybe that Henry Ford was the Annie Christ or sumshit. Carmo, he's not listening again and *that pisses me off.*"

Carmo swung the pipe at my midsection. It struck me below the ribs with paralyzing force. There was pain, first jagged, then swallowed in a growing explosion of heat, like a fireball.

"Hurts, don't it?" Carmo said. "Gets you right in the old kazeenie."

"I think you ruptured something," I said. I heard a hoarse steam-engine sound and realized that was me, panting.

"I hope he fucking *did,*" Roth said. "I let you *go,* you dumbbell! I fucking let you *go!* I *forgot* about you! Then you turn up at Frank's in Fort Worth to bet the goddam Case-Tiger fight. Exact same MO—big bet on the underdog and all the odds you can get. This time you predict the *exact fucking round.* So here's what's going to happen, my friend: you're going to tell me how you knew. If you do that, I take some pictures of you like you are now and Eddie G's satisfied. He knows he can't have you dead, because Carlos told him no, and Carlos is the one guy he listens to, even now. But if he sees you fucked up . . . aw, but you ain't fucked up enough quite yet. Fuck him up some more, Carmo. Do the face."

So Carmo hammered my face while the other two held me. He broke my nose, closed my left eye, knocked out a few teeth, and tore open my left cheek. I kept thinking, *I'll pass out or they'll kill me, either way the pain will stop.* But I didn't pass out, and at some point Carmo quit. He was breathing hard, and there were red splotches on his yellow rawhide gloves. Sunshine came in through the kitchen windows and made cheery oblongs on the faded linoleum.

"That's better," Roth said. "Get the Polaroid out of the truck, Carmo. Hustle, now. I want to finish up here."

Before leaving, Carmo stripped off his gloves and put them on the table next to the lead pipe. Some of the felt strips had come loose. They were soaked with blood. My face was throbbing, but my abdomen was worse. There, the heat continued to spread. Something was very wrong down there.

"One more time, Amberson. How'd you know the fix was in? Who told you? The truth."

"It was just a guess." I tried to tell myself I sounded like a man with a bad cold, but I didn't. I sounded like a man who'd just had the shit beaten out of him.

He picked up the pipe and tapped it against one pudgy hand. "Who told you, fuckface?"

"Nobody. Gutierrez was right. I'm a devil, and devils can see the future."

"You're running out of chances."

"Wanda's too tall for you, Roth. And too skinny. When you're on top of her, you must look like a toad trying to fuck a log. Or maybe—"

His placid face wrinkled into rage. It was a complete transformation, and it happened in less than a second. He swung the pipe at my head. I got my left arm up and heard it crack like a birch-branch overloaded with ice. This time when I sagged, the goons let me drop to the floor.

"Fuckin wiseass, how I hate a fuckin wiseass." This seemed to come from a great distance. Or a great height. Or both. I was finally getting ready to pass out, and ever so grateful to go. But I had enough vision left to see Carmo when he came back in with a Polaroid camera. It was big and bulky, the kind where the lens comes out on a kind of accordion.

"Turn im over," Roth said. "Let's get his good side." As the goons did so, Carmo handed Roth the camera, and Roth handed Carmo the pipe. Then Roth raised the camera to his face and said,

"Watch the birdie, you fuckin spunkbucket. Here's one for Eddie G . . ."

Flash.

". . . and one for my own personal collection, which I don't actually have but which I may now start . . ."

Flash.

". . . and here's one for you. To remember that when serious people ask you questions, you should answer."

Flash.

He yanked the third shot out of the camera and threw it in my direction. It landed in front of my left hand . . . which he then stepped on. Bones crunched. I whimpered and drew my hurt hand back to my chest. He had broken at least one finger, maybe as many as three.

"You want to remember to strip that in sixty seconds, or it'll get all overcooked. If you're awake, that is."

"You want to ask im some more now that he's tenderized?" Carmo asked.

"You kiddin? Look at im. He don't even know his own name anymore. Fuck him." He started to turn away, then turned back. "Hey, asshat. Here's one to grow on."

That was when he kicked me in the side of the head with what felt like a steel-toed shoe. Skyrockets exploded across my vision. Then the back of my head connected with the baseboard, and I was gone.

16

I don't think I was out for long, because the oblongs of sunlight on the linoleum didn't appear to have moved. My mouth tasted of wet copper. I spat half-congealed blood onto the floor, along with a fragment of tooth, and set about getting to my feet. I needed to hold onto one of the kitchen chairs with my one working hand, then onto the table (which nearly fell over on top of me), but on the whole it was easier than I thought. My left leg felt numb, and my pants were tight halfway down, where the knee was swelling as promised, but I thought it could have been a lot worse.

I looked out the window to make sure the panel truck was gone, then began a slow, limping journey into the bedroom. My heart was taking big soft walloping beats in my chest. Each one throbbed in my broken nose and vibrated the swelling left side of my face, where the cheekbone just about had to be broken. The back of my head throbbed, too. My neck was stiff.

Could have been worse, I reminded myself as I shuffled across the bedroom. *You're on your feet, aren't you? Just get the damn gun, put it in the glove compartment, then drive yourself to the emergency room. You're basically all right. Probably better than Dick Tiger is this morning.*

I was able to go on telling myself that until I stretched my hand up to the closet shelf. When I did that, something first pulled in my guts . . . and then seemed to *roll.* The sullen heat centered on my left side flared like coals when you throw gasoline on them. I got my fingertips on the butt of the gun, turned it, hooked a thumb into the trigger-guard, and pulled it off the shelf. It hit the floor and bounced into the bedroom.

Probably not even loaded. I bent over to get it. My left knee shrieked and gave way. I fell to the floor, and the pain in my guts whooshed up again. I got the gun, though, and rolled the cylinder. It was loaded after all. Every chamber. I put it in my pocket and tried to crawl back to the kitchen, but the knee was too painful. And the headache was worse, spreading out dark tentacles from its little cave above the nape of my neck.

I made it to the bed on my belly, using a swimming motion. Once I was there I managed to haul myself up again, using my right arm and right leg. The left leg held me, but I was losing flexion in the knee. I had to get out of there, and right away.

I must have looked like Chester, the limping deputy from *Gunsmoke,* as I made my way out of the bedroom, across the kitchen, and to the front door, which hung open with splinters around the lock. I even remember thinking *Mr. Dillon, Mr. Dillon, there's trouble down at the Longbranch!*

I crossed the porch, seized the railing in my right fist, and crabbed down to the walk. There were only four steps, but my headache got worse each time I jolted down another one. I seemed to be losing my peripheral vision, which couldn't be good. I tried to turn my head to see my Chevrolet, but my neck didn't want to cooperate. I managed a shuffling whole-body pivot instead, and when I had the car in my sights, I realized driving would be an impossibility. Even opening the passenger side door and stowing the gun in the glove compartment would be an impossibility: bending would cause the pain and heat in my side to explode again.

I fumbled the .38 out of my pocket and returned to the porch. I held the stair-rail and underhanded the gun beneath the steps. It would have to do. I straightened up again and made my slow way down the walk to the street. *Baby steps,* I told myself. *Little baby steps.*

Two kids came sailing up on bikes. I tried to tell them I needed help, but the only thing to come out of my swollen mouth was a dry *hhhahhhh* sound. They glanced at each other, then pedaled faster and swerved around me.

I turned to the right (my swollen knee made going left seem like the world's worst idea) and began to stagger down the sidewalk. My vision continued to close in; now I seemed to be peering out of a gunslit, or from the mouth of a tunnel. For a moment that made me think of the fallen smokestack at the Kitchener Ironworks, back in Derry.

Get to Haines Avenue, I told myself. *There'll be traffic on Haines Avenue. You have to get at least that far.*

But was I going toward Haines, or away from it? I couldn't remember. The visible world was down to a single sharp circle about six inches in diameter. My head was splitting; there was a forest fire in my guts. When I fell, it seemed to be in slow motion, and the sidewalk felt as soft as a feather-pillow.

Before I could pass out, something prodded me. A hard, metallic something. A rusty voice eight or ten miles above me said, "You! *You*, boy! What's wrong with you?"

I turned over. It took the last of my strength, but I managed. Towering above me was the elderly woman who'd called me a coward when I refused to step in between Lee and Marina on The Day of the Zipper. It might have *been* that day, because, August heat or no August heat, she was once more wearing the pink flannel nightgown and the quilted jacket. Perhaps because I still had boxing on what remained of my mind, her upstanding hair today reminded me of Don King instead of Elsa Lanchester. She had poked me with one of the front legs of her walker.

"Ohmydeargod," she said. "Who has beaten you?"

That was a long story, and I couldn't tell it. The dark was closing in, and I was glad because the pain in my head was killing me. *Al got lung cancer,* I thought. *I got Akiva Roth. Either way, game over. Ozzie wins.*

Not if I could help it.

Gathering all my strength, I spoke to the face far above me, the only bright thing left in the encroaching darkness. "Call . . . nine-one-one."

"What's *that*?"

Of course she didn't know. Nine-one-one hadn't been invented yet. I held on long enough to try one more time. "Ambulance."

I think I might have repeated it, but I'm not sure. That was when the darkness swallowed me.

17

I have wondered since if it was kids who stole my car, or Roth's goons. And when it happened. At any rate, the thieves didn't trash it or crash it; Deke Simmons picked it up in the DPD impound lot a week later. It was in far better shape than I was.

Time-travel is full of ironies.

CHAPTER 26

During the next eleven weeks I once more lived two lives. There was the one I hardly knew about—the outside life—and the one I knew all too well. That was the one inside, where I often dreamed of the Yellow Card Man.

In the outside life, the walker-lady (Alberta Hitchinson; Sadie sought her out and brought her a bouquet of flowers) stood over me on the sidewalk and hollered until a neighbor came out, saw the situation, and called the ambulance that took me to Parkland. The doctor who treated me there was Malcolm Perry, who would later treat both John F. Kennedy and Lee Harvey Oswald as they lay dying. With me he had better luck, although it was a close thing.

I had sustained broken teeth, a broken nose, a broken cheekbone, a fractured left knee, a broken left arm, dislocated fingers, and abdominal injuries. I had also suffered a brain injury, which was what concerned Perry the most.

I was told I woke up and howled when my belly was palpated, but I have no memory of it. I was catheterized and immediately began pissing what boxing announcers would have called "the claret." My vitals were at first stable, then began sliding. I was typed, cross-matched, and given four units of whole blood . . . which, Sadie told me later, the residents of Jodie made up a hundred times over at a community blood drive in late September. She had to tell me several times, because I kept forgetting. I was prepped for abdominal surgery, but first a neurology consult and a spinal tap—there's no such thing as CT scans or MRIs in the Land of Ago.

I'm also told I had a conversation with two of the nurses prepping me for the tap. I told them that my wife had a drinking problem. One of them said that was too bad and asked me what her name was. I told them she was a fish called Wanda and laughed quite heartily. Then I passed out again.

My spleen was trashed. They removed it.

While I was still conked out and my spleen was going wherever no longer useful but not absolutely vital organs go, I was turned over to Orthopedics. There my broken arm was put in a splint and my broken leg in a plaster cast. Many people signed it over the following weeks. Sometimes I knew the names; usually I didn't.

I was kept sedated with my head stabilized and my bed raised to exactly thirty degrees. The phenobarbital wasn't because I was conscious (although sometimes I muttered, Sadie said) but because they were afraid I might suddenly come around and damage myself further. Basically, Perry and the other docs (Ellerton also came in regularly to monitor my progress) were treating my battered chump like an unexploded bomb.

To this day I'm not entirely sure what hematocrit and hemoglobin are, but mine started to come back up and that pleased everybody. I had another spinal tap three days later. This one showed signs of old blood, and when it comes to spinal taps, old is better than new. It indicated that I had sustained significant brain trauma, but they could forgo drilling a burr-hole in my skull, a risky procedure given all the battles my body was fighting on other fronts.

But the past is obdurate and protects itself against change. Five days after I was admitted, the flesh around the splenectomy incision began to turn red and warm. The following day the incision reopened and I spiked a fever. My condition, which had been downgraded from critical to serious after the second spinal tap, zipped back up to critical. According to my chart, I was "sedated as per Dr. Perry and neurologically minimally responsive."

On September seventh, I woke up briefly. Or so I'm told. A woman, pretty despite her scarred face, and an old man with a cowboy hat in his lap were sitting by my bed.

"Do you know your name?" the woman asked.

"Puddentane," I said. "Ask me again and I'll tell you the same."

Mr. Jake George Puddentane Epping-Amberson spent seven weeks in Parkland before being moved to a rehab center—a little housing complex for sick people—on the north side of Dallas. During those seven weeks I was on IV antibiotics for the infection that had set up shop where my spleen used to be. The splint on my broken arm was replaced with a long cast, which also filled up with names I didn't know. Shortly before moving to Eden Fallows, the rehab center, I graduated to a short cast on my arm. Around that same time, a physical therapist began to torture my knee back to something resembling mobility. I was told I screamed a lot, but I don't remember.

Malcolm Perry and the rest of the Parkland staff saved my life, I have no doubt about that. They also gave me an unintended and unwelcome gift that lasted well into my time at Eden Fallows. This was a secondary infection caused by the antibiotics being pumped into my system to beat the primary one. I have hazy memories of vomiting and of spending what seemed like whole days with my ass on a bedpan. I remember thinking at one point *I have to go to the Derry Drug and see Mr. Keene. I need Kaopectate.* But who was Mr. Keene, and where was Derry?

They let me out of the hospital when I began to hold food down again, but I'd been at Eden Fallows almost two weeks before the diarrhea stopped. By then it was nearing the end of October. Sadie (usually I remembered her name; sometimes it slipped my mind) brought me a paper jack-o'-lantern. This memory is very clear, because I screamed when I saw it. They were the screams of someone who has forgotten something vitally important.

"What?" she asked me. "What is it, honey? What's wrong? Is it Kennedy? Something about Kennedy?"

"He's going to kill them all with a hammer!" I shouted at her. *"On Halloween night! I have to stop him!"*

"Who?" She took my waving hands, her face frightened. "Stop who?"

But I couldn't remember, and I fell asleep. I slept a lot, and not just because of the slowly healing head injury. I was exhausted, little more than a ghost of my former self. On the day of the beating, I had weighed one hundred and eighty-five pounds. By the time I was released from the hospital and installed in Eden Fallows, I weighed a hundred and thirty-eight.

That was the outside life of Jake Epping, a man who had been beaten badly, then nearly died in the hospital. My inside life was blackness, voices, and flashes of understanding that were like lightning: they blinded me with their brilliance and were gone again before I could get more than glimpses of the landscape by their light. I was mostly lost, but every now and then I found myself.

Found myself hellishly hot, and a woman was feeding me ice chips that tasted heavenly cool. This was THE WOMAN WITH THE SCAR, who was sometimes Sadie.

Found myself on the commode in the corner of the room with no idea how I'd gotten there, unloosing what felt like gallons of watery burning shit, my side itching and throbbing, my knee bellowing. I remember wishing someone would kill me.

Found myself trying to get out of bed, because I had to do something terribly important. It seemed to me that the whole world was depending on me to do this thing. THE MAN WITH THE COWBOY HAT was there. He caught me and helped me back into bed before I fell on the floor. "Not yet, son," he said. "You're nowhere near strong enough."

Found myself talking—or trying to talk—to a pair of uniformed policemen who had come to ask questions about the beating I'd taken. One of them had a name tag that said TIPPIT. I tried to tell him he was in danger. I tried to tell him to remember the fifth of November. It was the right month but the wrong day. I couldn't remember the actual date and began to thump at my stupid head in frustration. The cops looked at each other, puzzled. NOT-TIPPIT called for a nurse. The nurse came with a doctor, the doctor gave me a shot, and I floated away.

Found myself listening to Sadie as she read to me, first *Jude the Obscure,* then *Tess of the D'Urbervilles.* I knew those stories, and listening to them again was comforting. At one point during *Tess,* I remembered something.

"I made Tessica Caltrop leave us alone."

Sadie looked up. "Do you mean *Jessica?* Jessica Caltrop? You did? How? Do you remember?"

But I didn't. It was gone.

Found myself looking at Sadie as she stood at my little window, staring out at the rain and crying.

But mostly I was lost.

THE MAN WITH THE COWBOY HAT was Deke, but once I thought he was my grandfather, and that scared me very badly, because Grampy Epping was dead, and—

Epping, *that* was my name. *Hold onto it,* I told myself, but at first I couldn't.

Several times AN ELDERLY WOMAN WITH RED LIP-STICK came to see me. Sometimes I thought her name was Miz Mimi; sometimes I thought it was Miz Ellie; once I was quite sure she was Irene Ryan, who played Granny Clampett on *The Beverly Hillbillies.* I told her that I'd thrown my cell phone into a pond. "Now it sleeps with the fishes. I sure wish I had that sucker back."

A YOUNG COUPLE came. Sadie said, "Look, it's Mike and Bobbi Jill."

I said, "Mike Coleslaw."

THE YOUNG MAN said, "That's close, Mr. A." He smiled. A tear ran down his cheek when he did.

Later, when Sadie and Deke came to Eden Fallows, they would sit with me on the couch. Sadie would take my hand and ask, "What's his name, Jake? You never told me his *name.* How can we stop him if we don't know who he is or where he is going to be?"

I said, "I'm going to flop him." I tried very hard. It made the back of my head hurt, but I tried even harder. "Stop him."

"You couldn't stop a cinchbug without our help," Deke said.

But Sadie was too dear and Deke was too old. She shouldn't have told him in the first place. Maybe that was all right, though, because he didn't really believe it.

"The Yellow Card Man will stop you if you get involved," I said. "I'm the only one he can't stop."

"Who is the Yellow Card Man?" Sadie asked, leaning forward and taking my hands.

"I don't remember, but he can't stop me because I don't belong here."

Only he *was* stopping me. Or something was. Dr. Perry said my amnesia was shallow and transient, and he was right . . . but only up to a point. If I tried too hard to remember the things that mattered most, my head ached fiercely, my limping walk became a stumble, and my vision blurred. Worst of all was the tendency to suddenly fall asleep. Sadie asked Dr. Perry if it was narcolepsy. He said probably not, but I thought he looked worried.

"Does he wake when you call him or shake him?"

"Always," Sadie said.

"Is it more likely to happen when he's upset because he can't remember something?"

Sadie agreed that it was.

"Then I'm quite sure it will pass, the way his amnesia is passing."

At last—little by slowly—my inside world began to merge with the outside one. I was Jacob Epping, I was a teacher, and I had somehow traveled back in time to stop the assassination of President Kennedy. I tried to reject the idea at first, but I knew too much about the intervening years, and those things weren't visions. They were memories. The Rolling Stones, the Clinton impeachment hearings, the World Trade Center in flames. Christy, my troubled and troublesome ex-wife.

One night while Sadie and I were watching *Combat,* I remembered what I had done to Frank Dunning.

"Sadie, I killed a man before I came to Texas. It was in a grave-yard. I had to. He was going to murder his whole family."

She looked at me, eyes wide and mouth open.

"Turn off the TV," I said. "The guy who plays Sergeant Saunders—can't remember his name—is going to be decapitated by a helicopter blade. Please, Sadie, turn it off."

She did, then knelt before me.

"Who's going to kill Kennedy? Where is he going to be when he does it?"

I tried my hardest, and I didn't fall asleep, but I couldn't remember. I had gone from Maine to Florida, I remembered that. In the Ford Sunliner, a great car. I had gone from Florida to New Orleans, and when I left New Orleans, I'd come to Texas. I remembered listening to "Earth Angel" on the radio as I crossed the state line, doing seventy miles per hour on Highway 20. I remembered a sign: **TEXAS WELCOMES YOU**. And a billboard advertising SONNY'S B-B-Q, 27 MI. After that, a hole in the film. On the other side were emerging memories of teaching and living in Jodie. Brighter memories of swing-dancing with Sadie and lying in bed with her at the Candlewood Bungalows. Sadie told me I'd also lived in Fort Worth and Dallas, but she didn't know where; all she had were two phone numbers that no longer worked. I didn't know where, either, although I thought one of the places might have been on Cadillac Street. She checked roadmaps and said there was no Cadillac Street in either city.

I could remember a lot of things now, but not the assassin's name, or where he was going to be when he made his try. And why not? Because the past was keeping it from me. The obdurate past.

"The assassin has a child," I said. "I think her name is April."

"Jake, I'm going to ask you something. It might make you mad, but since a lot depends on this—the fate of the world, according to you—I need to."

"Go ahead." I couldn't think of anything she might ask that would make me angry.

"Are you lying to me?"

677

"No," I said. It was true. Then.

"I told Deke we needed to call the police. He showed me a piece in the *Morning News* that said there have already been two hundred death threats and tips about potential assassins. He says both the right-wingers from Dallas–Fort Worth and the left-wingers from San Antonio are trying to scare Kennedy out of Texas. He says the Dallas police are turning all the threats and tips over to the FBI and they're doing *nothing.* He says the only person J. Edgar Hoover hates more than JFK is his brother Bobby."

I didn't much care who J. Edgar Hoover hated. "Do you believe me?"

"Yes," she said, and sighed. "Is Vic Morrow really going to die?"

That was his name, sure. "He is."

"Making *Combat?*"

"No, a movie."

She burst into tears. "Don't *you* die, Jake—please. I only want you to get better."

I had a lot of bad dreams. The locations varied—sometimes it was an empty street that looked like Main Street in Lisbon Falls, sometimes it was the graveyard where I'd shot Frank Dunning, sometimes it was the kitchen of Andy Cullum, the cribbage ace— but usually it was Al Templeton's diner. We sat in a booth with the photos on his Town Wall of Celebrity looking down at us. Al was sick—dying—but his eyes were full of bright intensity.

"The Yellow Card Man's the personification of the obdurate past," Al said. "You know that, don't you?"

Yes, I knew that.

"He thought you'd die from the beating, but you didn't. He thought you'd die of the infections, but you didn't. Now he's walling off those memories—the vital ones—because he knows it's his last hope of stopping you."

"How can he? He's dead."

Al shook his head. "No, that's me."

"Who is he? *What* is he? And how can he come back to life? He cut his own throat and the card turned black! I *saw* it!"

"Dunno, buddy. All I know is that he can't stop you if you refuse to stop. *You have to get at those memories.*"

"Help me, then!" I shouted, and grabbed the hard claw of his hand. "Tell me the guy's name! Is it Chapman? Manson? Both of those ring a bell, but neither one seems right. *You got me into this, so help me!*"

At that point in the dream Al opens his mouth to do just that, but the Yellow Card Man intervenes. If we're on Main Street, he comes out of the greenfront or the Kennebec Fruit. If it's the cemetery, he rises from an open grave like a George Romero zombie. If in the diner, the door bursts open. The card he wears in the hatband of his fedora is so black it looks like a rectangular hole in the world. He's dead and decomposing. His ancient overcoat is splotched with mold. His eye-sockets are writhing balls of worms.

"He can't tell you nothing because it's double-money day!" the Yellow Card Man who is now the Black Card Man screams.

I turn back to Al, only Al has become a skeleton with a cigarette clamped in its teeth, and I wake up, sweating. I reach for the memories but the memories aren't there.

Deke brought me the newspaper stories about the impending Kennedy visit, hoping they would jog something loose. They didn't. Once, while I was lying on the couch (I was just coming out of one of my sudden sleeps), I heard the two of them arguing yet again about calling the police. Deke said an anonymous tip would be disregarded and one that came with a name attached would get all of us in trouble.

"I don't care!" Sadie shouted. "I know you think he's nuts, but what if he's right? How are you going to feel if Kennedy goes back to Washington from Dallas in a *box*?"

"If you bring the police in, they'll focus on Jake, sweetie. And according to you, he killed a man up in New England before he came here."

Sadie, Sadie, I wish you hadn't told him that.

She stopped arguing, but she didn't give up. Sometimes she

tried to surprise it out of me, the way you can supposedly surprise someone out of the hiccups. It didn't work.

"What am I going to do with you?" she asked sadly.

"I don't know."

"Try to come at it some other way. Try to sneak up on it."

"I have. I think the guy was in the Army or the Marines." I rubbed at the back of my head, where the ache was starting again. "But it might have been the Navy. Shit, Christy, I don't know."

"Sadie, Jake. I'm Sadie."

"Isn't that what I said?"

She shook her head and tried to smile.

On the twelfth, the Tuesday after Veterans Day, the *Morning News* ran a long editorial about the impending Kennedy visit and what it meant for the city. "Most residents seem ready to welcome the young and inexperienced president with open arms," the piece said. "Excitement is running high. Of course it doesn't hurt that his pretty and charismatic wife will be along for the ride."

"More dreams about the Yellow Card Man last night?" Sadie asked when she came in. She'd spent the holiday in Jodie, mostly to water her houseplants and to "show the flag," as she put it.

I shook my head. "Honey, you've been here a lot more than you've been in Jodie. What's the status of your job?"

"Miz Ellie put me on part-time. I'm getting by, and when I go with you . . . if we go . . . I guess I'll just have to see what happens."

Her gaze shifted away from me and she busied herself lighting a cigarette. Watching her take too long tamping it on the coffee table and then fiddling with her matches, I realized a dispiriting thing: Sadie was also having her doubts. I'd predicted a peaceful end to the Missile Crisis, I had known Dick Tiger was going down in the fifth . . . but she still had her doubts. And I didn't blame her. If our positions had been reversed, I would have been having mine.

Then she brightened. "But I've got a heck of a good stand-in, and I bet you can guess who."

I smiled. "Is it . . ." I couldn't get the name. I could *see* him—

the weathered, suntanned face, the cowboy hat, the string tie—but that Tuesday morning I couldn't even get close. My head started to ache in the back, where it had hit the baseboard—but what baseboard, in what house? It was so abysmally fucked up not to know.

Kennedy's coming in ten days and I can't even remember that old guy's fucking name.

"Try, Jake."

"I *am*," I said. "I *am*, Sadie!"

"Wait a sec. I've got an idea."

She laid her smoldering cigarette in one of the ashtray grooves, got up, went out the front door, closed it behind her. Then she opened it and spoke in a voice that was comically gruff and deep, saying what the old guy said each time he came to visit: "How you doin today, son? Takin any nourishment?"

"Deke," I said. "Deke Simmons. He was married to Miz Mimi, but she died in Mexico. We had a memorial assembly for her."

The headache was gone. Just like that.

Sadie clapped her hands and ran to me. I got a long and lovely kiss.

"See?" she said when she drew back. "You can do this. It's still not too late. What's his name, Jake? What's the crazy bugger's name?"

But I couldn't remember.

On November sixteenth, the *Times Herald* published the Kennedy motorcade route. It would start at Love Field and end at the Trade Mart, where he would speak to the Dallas Citizens Council and their invited guests. The nominal purpose of his speech was to salute the Graduate Research Center and congratulate Dallas on its economic progress over the last decade, but the *Times Herald* was happy to inform those who didn't already know that the real reason was pure politics. Texas had gone for Kennedy in 1960, but '64 was looking shaky in spite of having a good old Johnson City boy on the ticket. Cynics still called the vice president "Landslide Lyndon," a reference to his 1948 Senate bid, a decidedly hinky affair he won by eighty-seven votes. That was ancient history, but the nickname's longevity said a lot about the mixed feelings Texans had about him. Kennedy's job—and Jackie's, of course—was to help Landslide Lyndon and Texas governor John Connally fire up the faithful.

"Look at this," Sadie said, tracing a fingertip along the route. "Blocks and blocks of Main Street. Then Houston Street. There are high buildings all along that part. Is the man going to be on Main Street? He just about has to be, don't you think?"

I hardly listened, because I'd seen something else. "Look, Sadie, the motorcade's going to go along Turtle Creek Boulevard!"

Her eyes blazed. "Is that where it's going to happen?"

I shook my head doubtfully. Probably not, but I knew *something* about Turtle Creek Boulevard, and it had to do with the man I'd come to stop. As I considered this, something floated to the surface.

"He was going to hide the rifle and come back for it later."

"Hide it *where*?"

"It doesn't matter, because that part already happened. That part's the past." I put my hands over my face because the light in the room was suddenly too bright.

"Stop thinking about it now," she said, and snatched the newspaper story away. "Relax, or you'll get one of your headaches and need one of those pills. They make you all sloppy."

"Yes," I said. "I know."

"You need coffee. Strong coffee."

She went into the kitchen to make it. When she came back, I was snoring. I slept for almost three hours, and might have remained in the Land of Nod even longer, but she shook me awake. "What's the last thing you remember about coming to Dallas?"

"I *don't* remember it."

"Where did you stay? A hotel? A motor court? A rented room?"

For a moment I had a hazy memory of a courtyard and many windows. A doorman? Maybe. Then it was gone. The headache was cranking up again.

"I don't know. All I remember is crossing the state line on

Highway 20 and seeing a sign for barbecue. And that was miles from Dallas."

"I know, but we don't have to go that far, because if you were on 20, you stayed on 20." She glanced at her watch. "It's too late today, but tomorrow we're going for a Sunday drive."

"It probably won't work." But I felt a flicker of hope, just the same.

She stayed the night, and the next morning we left Dallas on what residents called the Honeybee Highway, headed east toward Louisiana. Sadie was at the wheel of my Chevy, which was fine once the jimmied ignition switch had been replaced. Deke had taken care of that. She drove as far as Terrell, then pulled off 20 and turned around in the potholed dirt parking lot of a side-o'-the-road church. Blood of the Redeemer, according to the message board on the fading lawn. Below the name, there was message in white stick-on letters. It was supposed to say HAVE YOU READ THE WORD OF ALMIGHTY GOD TODAY, but some of the letters had fallen off, leaving AVE YOU REA THE WORD OF AL IGHTY GOD TOD Y.

She looked at me with some trepidation. "Can you drive back, honey?"

I was pretty sure I could. It was a straight shot, and the Chevy was an automatic. I wouldn't need to use my stiff left leg at all. The only thing was . . .

"Sadie?" I asked her as I settled behind the wheel for the first time since August and ran the seat as far back as it would go.

"Yes?"

"If I fall asleep, grab the wheel and turn off the key."

She smiled nervously. "Oh, believe me."

I checked for traffic and pulled out. At first I didn't dare go much above forty-five, but it was a Sunday noon, and we had the road pretty much to ourselves. I began to relax.

"Clear your mind, Jake. Don't try to remember anything, just let it happen."

"I wish I had my Sunliner," I said.

"Make believe it *is* your Sunliner, then, and just let it go where it wants to go."

"Okay, but . . ."

"No buts. It's a beautiful day. You're coming into a new place, and you don't have to worry about Kennedy being assassinated, because that's a long time from now. Years."

Yes, it was a nice day. And no, I didn't fall asleep, although I was plenty tired—I hadn't been out for this long since the beating. My mind kept returning to the little side-o'-the-road church. Very likely a black church. They probably swung the hymns in a way the white folks never would, and read THE WORD OF AL IGHTY GOD with lots of hallelujah and praise Jesus.

We were coming into Dallas now. I made lefts and rights— probably more rights, because my left arm was still weak and turning that way hurt, even with the power steering. Soon I was lost in the side streets.

I'm lost, all right, I thought. *I need someone to give me directions the way that kid did in New Orleans. To the Hotel Moonstone.*

Only it hadn't been the Moonstone; it had been the Monteleone. And the hotel where I'd stayed when I came to Dallas was . . . it was . . .

For a moment I thought it was going to waft away, as even Sadie's name sometimes still did. But then I saw the doorman, and all those glittering windows looking down on Commerce Street, and it clicked home.

I had stayed at the Adolphus Hotel. Yes. Because it was close to . . .

It wouldn't come. That part was still blocked off.

"Honey? All right?"

"Yes," I said. "Why?"

"You kind of jumped."

"It's my leg. Cramping up a little."

"None of this looks familiar?"

"No," I said. "None of it."

She sighed. "Another idea bites the dust. I guess we better go back. Want me to drive?"

"Maybe you better." I limped around to the passenger seat, thinking *Adolphus Hotel. Write that down when you get back to Eden Fallows. So you won't forget.*

When we were back in the little three-room efficiency with the ramps, the hospital bed, and the grab-handles on either side of the toilet, Sadie told me I ought to lie down for a little while. "And take one of your pills."

I went into the bedroom, took off my shoes—a slow process—and lay down. I didn't take a pill, though. I wanted to keep my mind clear. I had to keep it clear from now on. Kennedy and Dallas were just five days apart.

You stayed in the Adolphus Hotel because it was close to something. What?

Well, it was close to the motorcade route that had been published in the paper, which narrowed things down to . . . gee, no more than two thousand buildings. Not to mention all the statues, monuments, and walls a putative sniper could hide behind. How many alleys along the route? Dozens. How many overpasses with clear fire lines down to passby-points on West Mockingbird Lane, Lemmon Avenue, Turtle Creek Boulevard? The motorcade was going to travel all of those. How many more on Main Street and Houston Street?

You need to remember either who he is or where he's going to shoot from.

If I got one of those things, I'd get the other. I knew this. But what my mind kept returning to was that church on Route 20 where we'd turned around. Blood of the Redeemer on the Honeybee Highway. Many people saw Kennedy as a redeemer. Certainly Al Templeton had. He—

My eyes widened and I stopped breathing.

In the other room the telephone rang and I heard Sadie answer, keeping her voice pitched low because she thought I was asleep.

THE WORD OF AL IGHTY GOD.

I remembered the day I had seen Sadie's full name with part of it blocked out, so all I could read was "Doris Dun." This was a harmonic of that magnitude. I closed my eyes and visualized the church signboard. Then I visualized putting my hand over IGHTY GOD.

What I was left with was THE WORD OF AL.

Al's notes. *I had his notebook!*

But where? Where was it?

The bedroom door opened. Sadie looked in. "Jake? Are you asleep?"

"No," I said. "Just lying quiet."

"Did you remember anything?"

"No," I said. "Sorry."

"There's still time."

"Yes. New things are coming back to me every day."

"Honey, that was Deke. There's a bug going around school and he's caught a good case of it. He asked if I could come in tomorrow and Tuesday. Maybe Wednesday, too."

"Go in," I said. "If you don't, he'll try to do it himself. And he's not a young guy anymore." In my mind, four words flashed on and off like bar neon: THE WORD OF AL, THE WORD OF AL, THE WORD OF AL.

She sat down next to me on the bed. "Are you sure?"

"I'll be fine. Plenty of company, too. DAVIN comes in tomorrow, remember." DAVIN was Dallas Area Visiting Nurses. Their main job in my case was to make sure I wasn't raving, which might indicate that my brain was bleeding after all.

"Right. Nine o'clock. It's on the calendar, in case you forget. And Dr. Ellerton—"

"Coming for lunch. I remember."

"Good, Jake. That's *good.*"

"He said he'd bring sandwiches. And milkshakes. Wants to fatten me up."

"You *need* fattening up."

"Plus therapy on Wednesday. Leg-torture in the morning, arm-torture in the afternoon."

"I don't like leaving you so close to . . . you know."

"If something occurs to me, I'll call you, Sadie."

She took my hand and bent close enough so I could smell her perfume and the faint aroma of tobacco on her breath. "Do you promise?"

"Yes. Of course."

"I'll be back on Wednesday night at the latest. If Deke can't come in on Thursday, the library will just have to stay closed."

"I'll be fine."

She kissed me lightly, started out of the room, then turned back. "I almost hope Deke's right and this whole thing is a delusion. I can't bear the idea that we know and still might not be able to stop it. That we might just be sitting in the living room and watching on television when somebody—"

"I'll remember," I said.

"Will you, Jake?"

"I have to."

She nodded, but even with the shades drawn, I could read the doubt on her face. "We can still have supper before I go. You close your eyes and let that pill do its work. Get some sleep."

I closed my eyes, sure I wouldn't sleep. And that was okay, because I needed to think about the Word of Al. After a little while I could smell something cooking. It smelled good. When I'd first come out of the hospital, still puking or shitting every ten minutes, all smells had revolted me. Now things were better.

I began to drift. I could see Al sitting across from me in one of the diner booths, his paper cap tilted over his left eyebrow. Photos of smalltown bigwigs looked down at us, but Harry Dunning was no longer on the wall. I had saved him. Perhaps the second time I'd saved him from Vietnam, as well. There was no way to be sure.

Still holding you back, isn't he, buddy? Al asked.

Yes. He still is.

But you're close now.

Not close enough. I have no idea where I put that goddam notebook of yours.

You put it someplace safe. Does that narrow it down any?

I started to say no, then thought: *The Word of Al is safe. Safe. Because—*

I opened my eyes, and for the first time in what felt like weeks, a big smile creased my face.

It was in a safe deposit box.

The door opened. "Are you hungry? I kept it warm."

"Huh?"

"Jake, you've been asleep for over two hours."

I sat up and swung my legs onto the floor. "Then let's eat."

CHAPTER 27

1

11/17/63 (Sunday)

Sadie wanted to do the dishes after the meal she called supper and I called dinner, but I told her to go on and pack her overnight case instead. It was small and blue, with rounded corners.

"Your knee—"

"My knee can stand up to a few dishes. You need to hit the road now if you want a full night's sleep."

Ten minutes later the dishes were done, my fingertips were pruney, and Sadie stood at the door. With her little bag in her hands and her hair curling around her face, she had never looked prettier to me.

"Jake? Tell me one good thing about the future."

Surprisingly few things came. Cell phones? No. Suicide bombers? Probably not. Melting ice caps? Perhaps another time.

Then I grinned. "I'll give you two for the price of one. The cold war is over and the president is a black man."

She started to smile, then saw I wasn't joking. Her mouth dropped open. "Are you telling me there's a *Negro* in the *White House?*"

"Yes indeed. Although in my day, such folks prefer to be called African-Americans."

"You're serious?"

"Yes. I am."

"Oh my God!"

"A great many people said that exact thing the day after the election."

"Is he . . . doing a good job?"

"Opinions vary. If you want mine, he's doing as well as anyone could expect, given the complexities."

"On that note, I think I'll drive back to Jodie." She laughed distractedly. "In a daze."

She walked down the ramp, put her case in the cubby that served as her Beetle's trunk, then blew me a kiss. She started to get in, but I couldn't let her go like that. I couldn't run—Dr. Perry said that was still eight months away, maybe even a year—but I limped down the ramp as fast as I could.

"Wait, Sadie, wait a minute!"

Mr. Kenopensky was sitting next door in his wheelchair, bundled up in a jacket and holding his battery-powered Motorola in his lap. On the sidewalk, Norma Whitten was making her slow way down toward the mailbox on the corner, using a pair of wooden sticks more like ski poles than crutches. She turned and waved to us, trying to lift the frozen side of her face into a smile.

Sadie looked at me questioningly in the twilight.

"I just wanted to tell you something," I said. "I wanted to tell you you're the best damned thing that ever happened to me."

She laughed and hugged me. "Ditto, kind sir."

We kissed a long time, and might have kissed longer but for the dry clapping sound on our right. Mr. Kenopensky was applauding.

Sadie pulled away, but took me by the wrists. "You'll call me, won't you? Keep me . . . what's that thing you say? In the loop?"

"That's it, and I will." I had no intention of keeping her in the loop. Deke or the police, either.

"Because you can't do this on your own, Jake. You're too weak."

"I know that," I said. Thinking: *I better not be.* "Call me so I know you got back safe."

When her Bug turned the corner and disappeared, Mr. Kenopensky said, "Better mind your p's and q's, Amberson. That one's a keeper."

"I know." I stayed at the foot of the driveway long enough to make sure Miz Whitten got back from the mailbox without falling down.

She made it.

I went back inside.

2

The first thing I did was to get my key ring off the top of the dresser and pick through the keys, surprised that Sadie had never shown them to me to see if they'd jog my memory . . . but of course she couldn't think of everything. There were an even dozen. I had no idea what most of them went to, although I was pretty sure the Schlage opened the front door of my house in . . . was it Sabattus? I thought that was right, but I wasn't sure.

There was one small key on the ring. Stamped on it was **FC** and 775. It was a safe deposit box key, all right, but what was the bank? First Commercial? That sounded bankish, but it wasn't right.

I closed my eyes and looked into darkness. I waited, almost sure what I wanted would come . . . and it did. I saw a checkbook in a *faux* alligator cover. I saw myself flipping it open. This was surprisingly easy. Printed on the top check was not only my Land of Ago name but my last official Land of Ago address.

214 W. Neely St. Apartment 1
Dallas, TX

I thought: *That's where my car got stolen from.*

And I thought: *Oswald. The assassin's name is Oswald Rabbit.*

No, of course not. He was a man, not a cartoon character. But it was close.

"I'm coming for you, Mr. Rabbit," I said. "Still coming."

3

The phone rang shortly before nine-thirty. Sadie was home safe. "Don't suppose anything came to you, did it? I'm a pest, I know."

"Nothing. And you're the farthest thing in the world from a pest." She was also going to be the farthest thing in the world from Oswald Rabbit, if I had anything to do about it. Not to mention his wife, whose name might or might not be Mary, and his little girl, who I felt sure was named April.

"You were pulling my leg about a Negro being in the White House, weren't you?"

I smiled. "Wait awhile. You can see for yourself."

4

11/18/63 (Monday)

The DAVIN nurses, one old and formidable, the other young and pretty, arrived at 9:00 A.M. sharp. They did their thing. When the older one felt that I had grimaced, twitched, and moaned enough, she handed me a paper envelope with two pills in it. "Pain."

"I don't really think—"

"Take em," she said—a woman of few words. "Freebies."

I popped them in my mouth, cheeked them, swallowed water, then excused myself to use the bathroom. There I spat them out.

When I returned to the kitchen, the older nurse said: "Good progress. Don't overdo."

"Absolutely not."

"Catch them?"

"Beg pardon?"

"The assholes who beat you up."

"Uh . . . not yet."

"Doing something you shouldn't have been doing?"

I gave her my widest smile, the one Christy used to say made me look like a game-show host on crack. "I don't remember."

5

Dr. Ellerton came for lunch, bringing huge roast beef sandwiches, crispy french fries dripping in grease, and the promised milkshakes. I ate as much as I could manage, which was really quite a lot. My appetite was returning.

"Mike talked up the idea of doing yet another variety show," he said. "This time to benefit you. In the end, wiser heads prevailed. A small town can only give so much." He lit a cigarette, dropped the match into the ashtray on the table, and inhaled with gusto. "Any chance the police will catch the mugs who tuned up on you? What do you hear?"

"Nothing, but I doubt it. They cleaned out my wallet, stole my car, and split."

"What were you doing on that side of Dallas, anyway? It's not exactly the high-society part of town."

Well, apparently I lived there.

"I don't remember. Visiting someone, maybe."

"Are you getting plenty of rest? Not straining the knee too much?"

"No." Although I suspected I'd be straining it plenty before much longer.

"Still falling asleep suddenly?"

"That's quite a bit better."

"Terrific. I guess—"

The phone rang. "That'll be Sadie," I said. "She calls on her lunch break."

"I have to be shoving off, anyway. It's great to see you putting on weight, George. Say hello to the pretty lady for me."

I did so. She asked me if any *pertinent memories* were coming back. I knew by her delicate phrasing that she was calling from the school's main office—and would have to pay Mrs. Coleridge for the long-distance when she was done. Besides keeping the DCHS exchequer, Mrs. Coleridge had long ears.

I told her no, no new memories, but I was going to take a nap and hope something would be there when I woke up. I added that I loved her (it was nice to say something that was the God's honest), asked after Deke, wished her a good afternoon, and hung up. But I didn't take a nap. I took my car keys and my briefcase and drove downtown. I hoped to God I'd have something in that briefcase when I came back.

6

I motored slowly and carefully, but my knee was still aching badly when I entered the First Corn Bank and presented my safe deposit box key.

My banker came out of his office to meet me, and his name clicked home immediately: Richard Link. His eyes widened with concern when I limped to meet him. "What happened to you, Mr. Amberson?"

"Car accident." Hoping he'd missed or forgotten the squib in the *Morning News*'s Police Beat page. I hadn't seen it myself, but there had been one: Mr. George Amberson of Jodie, beaten and mugged, found unconscious, taken to Parkland Hospital. "I'm mending nicely."

"*That's* good to hear."

The safe deposit boxes were in the basement. I negotiated the stairs in a series of hops. We used our keys, and Link carried the box into one of the cubicles for me. He set it on a tiny wedge of desk just big enough to hold it, then pointed to the button on the wall.

"Just ring for Melvin when you've finished. He'll assist you."

I thanked him, and when he was gone, I pulled the curtain

across the cubicle's doorway. We had unlocked the box, but it was still closed. I stared at it, my heart beating hard. John Kennedy's future was inside.

I opened it. On top was a bundle of cash and a litter of stuff from the Neely Street apartment, including my First Corn checkbook. Beneath this was a sheaf of manuscript bound by two rubber bands. THE MURDER PLACE was typed on the top sheet. No author's name, but it was my work. Below it was a blue notebook: the Word of Al. I held it in my hands, filled with a terrible certainty that when I opened it, all the pages would be blank. The Yellow Card Man would have erased them.

Please, no.

I flipped it open. On the first page, a photograph looked back at me. Narrow, not-quite-handsome face. Lips curved in a smile I knew well—hadn't I seen it with my own eyes? It was the kind of smile that says *I know what's going on and you don't, you poor boob.*

Lee Harvey Oswald. The wretched waif who was going to change the world.

7

Memories came rushing in as I sat there in the cubicle, gasping for breath.

Ivy and Rosette on Mercedes Street. Last name Templeton, like Al's.

The jump-rope girls: *My old man drives a sub-ma-rine.*

Silent Mike (Holy Mike) at Satellite Electronics.

George de Mohrenschildt ripping open his shirt like Superman.

Billy James Hargis and General Edwin A. Walker.

Marina Oswald, the assassin's beautiful hostage, standing on my doorstep at 214 West Neely: *Please excuse, have you seen my hubka?*

The Texas School Book Depository.

Sixth floor, southeast window. The one with the best view of

Dealey Plaza and Elm Street, where it curved toward the Triple Underpass.

I began shivering. I clutched my upper arms in my fists with my arms tightly locked over my chest. It made the left one—broken by the felt-wrapped pipe—ache, but I didn't mind. I was glad. It tied me to the world.

When the shakes finally passed, I loaded the unfinished book manuscript, the precious blue notebook, and everything else into my briefcase. I reached for the button that would summon Melvin, then dummy-checked the very back of the box. There I found two more items. One was the cheap pawnshop wedding ring I'd purchased to support my cover story at Satellite Electronics. The other was the red baby rattle that had belonged to the Oswalds' little girl (June, not April). The rattle went into the briefcase, the ring into the watch pocket of my slacks. I would throw it away on my drive home. If and when the time came, Sadie would have a much nicer one.

8

Knocking on glass. Then a voice: "—all right? Mister, are you all right?"

I opened my eyes, at first with no idea where I was. I looked to my left and saw a uniformed beat-cop knocking on the driver's side window of my Chevy. Then it came. Halfway back to Eden Fallows, tired and exalted and terrified all at the same time, that *I'm going to sleep* feeling had drifted into my head. I'd pulled into a handy parking space immediately. That had been around two o'clock. Now, from the look of the lowering light, it had to be around four.

I cranked my window down and said, "Sorry, Officer. All at once I started to feel very sleepy, and it seemed safer to pull over."

He nodded. "Yup, yup, booze'll do that. How many did you have before you jumped into your car?"

"None. I suffered a head injury a few months ago." I swiveled my neck so he could see the place where the hair hadn't grown back.

He was halfway convinced, but still asked me to exhale in his face. That got him the rest of the way.

"Lemme see your ticket," he said.

I showed him my Texas driver's license.

"Not thinking of motoring all the way back to Jodie, are you?"

"No, Officer, just to North Dallas. I'm staying at a rehabilitation center called Eden Fallows."

I was sweating. I hoped that if he saw it, he'd just put it down to a man who'd been snoozing in a closed car on a warmish November day. I also hoped—fervently—that he wouldn't ask to see what was in the briefcase on the bench seat beside me. In 2011, I could refuse such a request, saying that sleeping in my car wasn't probable cause. Hell, the parking space wasn't even metered. In 1963, however, a cop might just start rummaging. He wouldn't find drugs, but he *would* find loose cash, a manuscript with the word *murder* in its title, and a notebook full of delusional weirdness about Dallas and JFK. Would I be taken either to the nearest police station for questioning, or back to Parkland for psychiatric evaluation? Did the Waltons take way too long to say goodnight?

He stood there a moment, big and red-faced, a Norman Rockwell cop who belonged on a *Saturday Evening Post* cover. Then he handed back my license. "Okay, Mr. Amberson. Go on back to this Fallows place, and I suggest you park your car for the night when you get there. You're looking peaky, nap or no nap."

"That's exactly what I plan to do."

I could see him in my rearview as I drove away, watching. I felt certain I was going to fall asleep again before I got out of his sight. There'd be no warning this time; I'd just veer off the street and onto the sidewalk, maybe mowing down a pedestrian or three before winding up in the show window of a furniture store.

When I finally parked in front of my little cottage with the ramp leading up to the front door, my head was aching, my eyes were watering, my knee was throbbing . . . but my memories of Oswald remained firm and clear. I slung my briefcase on the kitchen table and called Sadie.

"I tried you when I got home from school, but you weren't there," she said. "I was worried."

"I was next door, playing cribbage with Mr. Kenopensky." These lies were necessary. I had to remember that. And I had to tell them smoothly, because she knew me.

"Well, that's good." Then, without a pause or a change of inflection: "What's his name? What's the man's name?"

Lee Oswald. She almost surprised it out of me, after all.

"I . . . I still don't know."

"You hesitated. I heard you."

I waited for the accusation, gripping the phone hard enough to hurt.

"This time it almost popped into your head, didn't it?"

"There was something," I agreed cautiously.

We talked for fifteen minutes while I looked at the briefcase with Al's notes inside it. She asked me to call her later that evening. I promised I would.

9

I decided to wait until after *The Huntley-Brinkley Report* to open the blue notebook again. I didn't think I'd find much of practical value at this point. Al's final notes were sketchy and hurried; he had never expected Mission Oswald to go on so long. Neither had I. Getting to the disaffected little twerp was like traveling on a road littered with fallen branches, and in the end the past might succeed in protecting itself, after all. But I *had* stopped Dunning. That gave me hope. I had the glimmerings of a plan that might allow me to stop Oswald without going to prison or the electric chair in Huntsville. I had excellent reasons to want to remain free.

The best one of all was in Jodie this evening, probably feeding Deke Simmons chicken soup.

I worked my way methodically through my little invalid-friendly apartment, collecting stuff. Other than my old typewriter, I didn't want to leave a trace of George Amberson behind when I left. I hoped that wouldn't be until Wednesday, but if Sadie said that Deke was better and she was planning to come back on Tuesday night, I'd have to speed things up. And where would I hide out until my job was done? A very good question.

A trumpet-blast announced the network news. Chet Huntley appeared. "After spending the weekend in Florida, where he watched the test-firing of a Polaris missile and visited his ailing father, President Kennedy had a busy Monday, making five speeches in nine hours."

A helicopter—*Marine One*—descended while a waiting crowd cheered. The next shot featured Kennedy approaching the crowd behind a makeshift barrier, brushing at his shaggy hair with one hand and his tie with the other. He strode well ahead of the Secret Service contingent, which jogged to keep up. I watched, fascinated, as he actually slipped through a break in the barrier and plunged into the waiting mass of people, shaking hands left and right. The agents with him looked dismayed as they hurried after.

"This was the scene in Tampa," Huntley continued, "where Kennedy pressed the flesh for almost ten minutes. He worries the men whose job it is to keep him safe, but you can see that the crowd loves it. And so does he, David—for all his alleged aloofness, he enjoys the demands of politics."

Kennedy was moving toward his limo now, still shaking hands and accepting the occasional lady-hug. The car was a top-down convertible, exactly like the one he'd ride in from Love Field to his appointment with Oswald's bullet. Maybe it *was* the same one. For a moment the blurry black-and-white film caught a familiar face in the crowd. I sat on my sofa and watched as the President of the United States shook the hand of my former Tampa bookie.

I had no way of knowing if Roth was correct about "the syph" or just repeating a rumor, but Eduardo Gutierrez had lost a lot of weight, his hair was thinning, and his eyes looked confused, as if he wasn't sure where he was or even who he was. Like Kennedy's Secret Service contingent, the men flanking him wore bulky suit coats in spite of the Florida heat. It was only a glimpse, and then the footage switched to Kennedy pulling away in the open car that left him so vulnerable, still waving and flashing his grin.

Back to Huntley, his craggy face now wearing a bemused smile. "The day *did* have its funny side, David. As the president was entering the International Inn ballroom, where the Tampa Chamber of Commerce was waiting to hear him speak . . . well, listen for yourself."

Back to the footage. As Kennedy entered, waving to the standing audience, an elderly gentleman in an Alpine hat and lederhosen struck up "Hail to the Chief" on an accordion bigger than he was. The president did a double take, then lifted both hands in an amiable *holy shit* gesture. For the first time I saw him as I had come to see Oswald—as an actual man. In the double take and the gesture that followed it, I saw something even more beautiful than a sense of humor: an appreciation for life's essential absurdity.

David Brinkley was also smiling. "If Kennedy's reelected, perhaps that gentleman will be invited to play at the Inaugural Ball. Probably 'The Beer Barrel Polka' rather than 'Hail to the Chief.' Meanwhile, in Geneva . . ."

I turned off the TV, returned to the sofa, and opened Al's book. As I flipped to the back, I kept seeing that double take. And the grin. A sense of humor; a sense of the absurd. The man in the sixth-floor window of the Book Depository had neither. Oswald had proved it time and again, and such a man had no business changing history.

10

I was dismayed to find that five of the last six pages in Al's note-book dealt with Lee's movements in New Orleans and his fruitless efforts to get to Cuba via Mexico. Only the last page focused on the lead-up to the assassination, and those final notes were per-functory. Al had no doubt had that part of the story by heart, and probably figured that if I hadn't gotten Oswald by the third week of November, it was going to be too late.

10/3/63: O back in Texas. He and Marina "sort of" separated. She at Ruth Paine's house, O shows up mostly on weekends. Ruth gets O a job at Book Dep thru a neighbor (Buell Frazier). Ruth calls O "a fine young man."
    O living in Dallas during the work-week. Rooming house.
    10/17/63: O starts work at Dep. Shifting books, unloading trucks, etc.
    10/18/63: O turns 24. Ruth and Marina give him a surprise party. O thanks them. Cries.
    10/20/63: 2nd daughter born: Audrey Rachel. Ruth takes Marina to hosp (Parkland) while O works. Rifle stored in Paine garage, wrapped in blanket.
    O repeatedly visited by FBI agent James Hosty. Stokes his para-noia.
    11/21/63: O comes to Paine house. Begs Marina to reunite. M refuses. Last straw for O.
    11/22/63: O leaves all his money on dresser for Marina. Also wed-ding ring. Goes from Irving to Book Dep with Buell Frazier. Has pack-age wrapped in brown paper. Buell asks about it. "Curtain rods for my new apartment," O tells him. Mann-Carc rifle probably disassembled. Buell parks in public lot 2 blocks from Book Dep. 3-min walk.
    11:50 AM: O constructs sniper's nest on SE corner of 6th floor, using cartons to shield him from workers on other side, who are lay-ing down plywood for new floor. Lunch. No one there but him. Every-one watching for Pres.
    11:55 AM: O assembles & loads Mann-Carc.
    12:29 PM: Motorcade arrives Dealey Plaza.
    12:30 PM: O shoots 3 times. 3rd shot kills JFK.

The piece of information I most wanted—the location of Oswald's rooming house—wasn't in Al's notes. I restrained an urge to throw the notebook across the room. Instead I got up, put on my coat, and went outside. It was nearly full dark, but a three-quarter moon was rising in the sky. By its light I saw Mr. Kenopensky slumped in his wheelchair. His Motorola was in his lap.

I made my way down the ramp and limped over. "Mr. K? All right?"

For a moment he didn't answer or even move, and I was sure he was dead. Then he looked up and smiled. "Just listenin to my music, son. They play swing at night on KMAT, and it really takes me back. I could lindy and bunny-hop like nobody's biz back in the old days, though you'd never know to look at me now. Ain't the moon purty?"

It was bigtime purty. We looked at it awhile without speaking, and I thought about the job I had to do. Maybe I didn't know where Lee was staying tonight, but I knew where his *rifle* was: Ruth Paine's garage, wrapped in a blanket. Suppose I went there and took it? I might not even have to break in. This was the Land of Ago, where folks in the hinterlands often didn't lock their houses, let alone their garages.

Only what if Al was wrong? He'd been wrong about the stash-point before the Walker attempt, after all. Even if it *was* there . . .

"What're you thinkin about, son?" Mr. Kenopensky asked. "You got a misery look. Not girl trouble, I hope."

"No." At least not yet. "Do you give advice?"

"Yessir, I do. It's the one thing old coots are good for when they can't swing a rope or ride a line no more."

"Suppose you knew a man was going to do a bad thing. That his heart was absolutely set on it. If you stopped a man like that once—talked him out of it, say—do you think he'd try it again, or does that moment pass forever?"

"Hard to say. Are you maybe thinking whoever scarred your young lady's face is going to come back and try to finish the job?"

"Something like that."

"Crazy fella." It wasn't a question.

"Yes."

"Sane men will often take a hint," Mr. Kenopensky said. "Crazy men rarely do. Saw it often back in the sagebrush days, before electric lights and phones. Warn em off, they come back. Beat em up, they hit from ambush—first you, then the one they're really after. Jug em up in county, they sit and wait to get out. Safest thing to do with crazy men is put em in the penitentiary for a long stretch. Or kill em."

"That's what I think, too."

"Don't let him back to spoil the rest of her pretty, if that's what he aims to do. If you care for her as much as you seem to, you've got a responsibility."

I certainly did, although Clayton was no longer the problem. I went back to my little modular apartment, made strong black coffee, and sat down with a legal pad. My plan was a little clearer now, and I wanted to start fleshing in the details.

I doodled instead. Then fell asleep.

When I woke up it was almost midnight and my cheek ached where it had been pressed against the checked oilcloth covering the kitchen table. I looked at what was on my pad. I didn't know if I'd drawn it before going to sleep or if I had wakened long enough to do it and just couldn't remember.

It was a gun. Not a Mannlicher-Carcano rifle, but a pistol. *My* pistol. The one I'd tossed beneath the porch steps at 214 West Neely. It was probably still there. I *hoped* it was still there.

I was going to need it.

11

11/19/63 (Tuesday)

Sadie called in the morning and said Deke was a little better, but she intended to make him stay home tomorrow, as well. "Otherwise he'll just try to come in, and have a setback. But I'll pack my bag before I leave for school tomorrow morning and head your way as soon as period six is over."

Period six ended at ten past one. That meant I'd have to be gone from Eden Fallows by four o'clock tomorrow afternoon at the latest. If only I knew where. "I look forward to seeing you."

"You sound all stiff and funny. Are you having one of your headaches?"

"A little one," I said. It was true.

"Go lie down with a damp cloth over your eyes."

"I'll do that." I had no intention of doing that.

"Have you thought of anything?"

I had, as a matter of fact. I'd thought that taking Lee's rifle wasn't enough. And shooting him at the Paine house was a bad option. Not just because I'd probably be caught, either. Counting Ruth's two, there were four kids in that house. I might still have tried it if Lee had been walking from a nearby bus stop, but he'd be riding with Buell Frazier, the neighbor who'd gotten him the job at Ruth Paine's request.

"No," I said. "Not yet."

"We'll think of something. You wait and see."

12

I drove (still slowly, but with increasing confidence) across town to West Neely, wondering what I'd do if the ground-floor apartment was occupied. Buy a new gun, I supposed . . . but the .38 Police Special was the one I wanted, if only because I'd had one just like it in Derry, and that mission had been a success.

According to newscaster Frank Blair on the *Today* show, Kennedy had moved on to Miami, where he was greeted by a large crowd of *cubanos.* Some held up signs reading VIVA JFK while others carried a banner reading KENNEDY IS A TRAITOR TO OUR CAUSE. If nothing changed, he had seventy-two hours left. Oswald, who had only slightly longer, would be in the Book

Depository, perhaps loading cartons into one of the freight elevators, maybe in the break room drinking coffee.

I might be able to get him there—just walk up to him and
plug him—but I'd be collared and wrestled to the floor. After the
killshot, if I was lucky. Before, if I wasn't. Either way, the next
time I saw Sadie Dunhill it would be through glass reinforced with
chickenwire. If I had to give myself up in order to stop Oswald—
to *sacrifice myself,* in hero-speak—I thought I could do that. But I
didn't want it to play out that way. I wanted Sadie and my poundcake, too.

There was a pot barbecue on the lawn at 214 West Neely, and
a new rocking chair on the porch, but the shades were drawn and
there was no car in the driveway. I parked in front, told myself that
bold is beautiful, and mounted the steps. I stood where Marina
had stood on April tenth when she came to visit me and knocked
as she had knocked. If someone answered the door, I'd be Frank
Anderson, canvassing the neighborhood on behalf of the *Encyclopaedia Britannica* (I was too old for *Grit*). If the lady of the house
expressed an interest, I'd promise to come back with my sample
case tomorrow.

No one answered. Maybe the lady of the house also worked.
Maybe she was down the block, visiting a neighbor. Maybe she
was in the bedroom that had been mine not long ago, sleeping off
a drunk. It was mix-nox to me, as we say in the Land of Ago. The
place was quiet, that was the important thing, and the sidewalk
was deserted. Even Mrs. Alberta Hitchinson, the walker-equipped
neighborhood sentry, wasn't in evidence.

I descended from the porch in my limping sidesaddle fashion,
started down the walk, turned as if I'd forgotten something, and
peered under the steps. The .38 was there, half-buried in leaves
with the short barrel poking out. I got down on my good knee,
snagged it, and dropped it into the side pocket of my sport coat. I
looked around and saw no one watching. I limped to my car, put
the gun in the glove compartment, and drove away.

13

Instead of going back to Eden Fallows, I drove into downtown Dallas, stopping at a sporting goods store on the way to buy a gun-cleaning kit and a box of fresh ammo. The last thing I wanted was to have the .38 misfire or blow up in my face.

My next stop was the Adolphus. There were no rooms available until next week, the doorman told me—every hotel in Dallas was full for the president's visit—but for a dollar tip, he was more than happy to park my car in the hotel lot. "Have to be gone by four, though. That's when the heavy check-ins start."

By then it was noon. It was only three or four blocks to Dealey Plaza, but I took my sweet time getting there. I was tired, and my headache was worse in spite of a Goody's Powder. Texans drive with their horns, and every blast dug into my brain. I rested often, leaning against the sides of buildings and standing on my good leg like a heron. An off-duty taxi driver asked if I was okay; I assured him that I was. It was a lie. I was distraught and miserable. A man with a bum knee really shouldn't have to carry the future of the world on his back.

I dropped my grateful butt onto the same bench where I'd sat in 1960, only days after arriving in Dallas. The elm that had shaded me then clattered bare branches today. I stretched out my aching knee, sighed with relief, then turned my attention to the ugly brick cube of the Book Depository. The windows overlooking Houston and Elm Streets glittered in the chilly afternoon sun. *We know a secret,* they said. *We're going to be famous, especially the one on the southeast corner of the sixth floor. We're going to be famous, and you can't stop us.* A sense of stupid menace surrounded the building. And was it just me who thought so? I watched several people cross Elm to pass the building on the other side and thought not. Lee was inside that cube right now, and I was sure he was thinking many of the things I was thinking. *Can I do this? Will I do this? Is it my destiny?*

Robert's not your brother anymore, I thought. *Now I'm your brother, Lee, your brother of the gun. You just don't know it.*

Behind the Depository, in the trainyard, an engine hooted. A flock of band-tailed pigeons took wing. They momentarily whirled above the Hertz sign on the roof of the Depository, then wheeled away toward Fort Worth.

If I killed him before the twenty-second, Kennedy would be saved but I'd almost certainly wind up in jail or a psychiatric hospital for twenty or thirty years. But if I killed him *on* the twenty-second? Perhaps as he assembled his rifle?

Waiting until so late in the game would be a terrible risk, and one I'd tried with all my might to avoid, but I thought it could be done and was now probably my best chance. It would be safer with a partner to help me run my game, but there was only Sadie, and I wouldn't involve her. Not even, I realized bleakly, if it meant that Kennedy had to die or I had to go to prison. She had been hurt enough.

I began making my slow way back to the hotel to get my car. I took one final glance back at the Book Depository over my shoulder. It was looking at me. I had no doubt of it. And of *course* it was going to end there, I'd been foolish to imagine anything else. I had been driven toward that brick hulk like a cow down a slaughterhouse chute.

14

11/20/63 (Wednesday)

I started awake at dawn from some unremembered dream, my heart beating hard.

She knows.

Knows what?

That you've been lying to her about all the things you claim not to remember.

"No," I said. My voice was rusty with sleep.

Yes. She was careful to say she was leaving after period six, because she doesn't want you to know she's planning to leave much sooner. She doesn't want you to know until she shows up. In fact, she might be on the road already. You'll be halfway through your morning therapy session, and in she'll breeze.

I didn't want to believe this, but it felt like a foregone conclusion.

So where was I going to go? As I sat there on the bed in that Wednesday morning's first light, that also seemed like a foregone conclusion. It was as if my subconscious mind had known all along. The past has resonance, it echoes.

But first I had one more chore to perform on my used typewriter. An unpleasant one.

15

November 20, 1963

Dear Sadie,

I have been lying to you. I think you've suspected
that for quite some time now. I think you're planning to
show up early today. That is why you won't see me again
until after JFK visits Dallas the day after tomorrow.

If things go as I hope, we'll have a long and happy life
together in a different place. It will be strange to you at
first, but I think you'll get used to it. I'll help you. I love
you, and that's why I can't let you be a part of this.

Please believe in me, please be patient, and please
don't be surprised if you read my name and see my
picture in the papers—if things go as I want them to,
that will probably happen. Above all, <u>do not try to find
me.</u>

All my love,

Jake

PS: You should burn this.

16

I packed my life as George Amberson into the trunk of my gull-wing Chevy, tacked a note for the therapist on the door, and drove away feeling heavy and homesick. Sadie left Jodie even earlier than I'd thought she might—before dawn. I departed Eden Fallows at nine. She pulled her Beetle up to the curb at quarter past, read the note canceling the therapy session, and let herself in with the key I'd given her. Propped against the typewriter's roller-bar was an envelope with her name on it. She tore it open, read the letter, sat down on the sofa in front of the blank television, and cried. She was still crying when the therapist showed up . . . but she had burned the note, as I requested.

17

Mercedes Street was mostly silent under an overcast sky. The jump-rope girls weren't in evidence—they'd be in school, perhaps listening raptly as their teacher told them all about the upcoming presidential visit—but the FOR RENT sign was once more tacked to the rickety porch railing, as I'd expected. There was a phone number. I drove down to the Montgomery Ward warehouse parking lot and called it from the booth near the loading dock. I had no doubt that the man who answered with a laconic "Yowp, this is Merritt" was the same guy who had rented 2703 to Lee and Marina. I could still see his Stetson hat and gaudy stitched boots.

I told him what I wanted, and he laughed in disbelief. "I don't rent by the week. That's a fine home there, podna."

"It's a dump," I said. "I've been inside. I know."

"Now wait just a doggone—"

"Nosir, *you* wait. I'll give you fifty bucks to squat in that hole through the weekend. That's almost a full month's rent, and you can put your sign back in the window come Monday."

"Why would you—"

"Because Kennedy's coming and every hotel in Dallas–Fort Worth is full. I drove a long way to see him, and I don't intend to camp out in Fair Park or on Dealey Plaza."

I heard the click and flare of a cigarette lighter as Merritt thought this over.

"Time's wasting," I said. "Tick-tock."

"What's your name, podna?"

"George Amberson." I sort of wished I'd moved in without calling at all. I almost had, but a visit from the Fort Worth PD was the last thing I needed. I doubted if the residents of a street where chickens were sometimes blown up to celebrate holidays gave much of a shit about squatters, but better safe than sorry. I was no longer just walking around the house of cards; I was living in it.

"I'll meet you out front in half an hour, forty-five minutes."

"I'll be inside," I said. "I have a key."

More silence. Then: "Where'd you get it?"

I had no intention of peaching on Ivy, even if she was still in Mozelle. "From Lee. Lee Oswald. He gave it to me so I could go in and water his plants."

"That little pissant had *plants*?"

I hung up and drove back to 2703. My temporary landlord, perhaps motivated by curiosity, arrived in his Chrysler only fifteen minutes later. He was wearing his Stetson and fancy boots. I was sitting in the front room, listening to the argumentative ghosts of people who were still living. They had a lot to say.

Merritt wanted to pump me about Oswald—was he really a damn commanist? I said no, he was a good old Louisiana boy who worked at a place that would overlook the president's motorcade on Friday. I said I hoped that Lee would let me share his vantage point.

"Fuckin Kennedy!" Merritt nearly shouted. "Now *he's* a commanist for sure. Somebody ought to shoot that sumbitch til he cain't wiggle."

"You have a nice day, now," I said, opening the door.

He went, but he wasn't happy about it. This was a fellow who was used to having tenants kowtow and cringe. He turned on the cracked and crumbling concrete walk. "You leave the place as nice as you found it, now, y'hear?"

I looked around at the living room with its moldering rug, cracked plaster, and one brokedown easy chair. "No problem there," I said.

I sat back down and tried to tune in to the ghosts again: Lee and Marina, Marguerite and de Mohrenschildt. I fell into one of my abrupt sleeps instead. When I woke up, I thought the chanting I heard must be from a fading dream.

"Charlie Chaplin went to FRANCE! Just to see the ladies DANCE!"

It was still there when I opened my eyes. I went to the window and looked out. The jump-rope girls were a little taller and older, but it was them, all right, the Terrible Trio. The one in the middle was spotty, although she looked at least four years too young for adolescent acne. Maybe it was rubella.

"Salute to the Cap'n!"

"Salute to the Queen," I muttered, and went into the bathroom to wash my face. The water that belched out of the tap was rusty, but cold enough to wake me the rest of the way up. I had replaced my broken watch with a cheap Timex and saw it was two-thirty. I wasn't hungry, but I needed to eat something, so I drove down to Mr. Lee's Bar-B-Q. On the way back, I stopped at a drugstore for another box of headache powders. I also bought a couple of John D. MacDonald paperbacks.

The jump-rope girls were gone. Mercedes Street, ordinarily raucous, was strangely silent. *Like a play before the curtain goes up on the last act,* I thought. I went in to eat my meal, but although the ribs were tangy and tender, I ended up throwing most of them away.

18

I tried to sleep in the main bedroom, but in there the ghosts of Lee and Marina were too lively. Shortly before midnight, I relocated to the smaller bedroom. Rosette Templeton's Crayola girls were still on the walls, and I somehow found their identical jumpers (Forest Green must have been Rosette's favorite crayon) and big black shoes comforting. I thought those girls would make Sadie smile, especially the one wearing the Miss America crown.

"I love you, honey," I said, and fell asleep.

19

11/21/63 (Thursday)

I didn't want breakfast any more than I'd wanted dinner the night before, but by 11:00 A.M. I needed coffee desperately. A gallon or so seemed about right. I grabbed one of my new paperbacks—*Slam the Big Door,* it was called—and drove to the Happy Egg on Braddock Highway. The TV behind the counter was on, and I watched a news story about Kennedy's impending arrival in San Antonio, where he was to be greeted by Lyndon and Lady Bird Johnson. Also to join the party: Governor John Connally and his wife, Nellie.

Over footage of Kennedy and his wife walking across the tarmac of Andrews Air Force base in Washington, heading for the blue-and-white presidential plane, a correspondent who sounded like she might soon pee in her underwear talked about Jackie's new "soft" hairdo, set off by a "jaunty black beret," and the smooth lines of her "belted two-piece shirt-dress, by her favorite designer, Oleg Cassini." Cassini might indeed be her favorite designer, but I knew Mrs. Kennedy had another outfit packed away on the plane. The designer of that one was Coco Chanel. It was pink wool, accessorized by a black collar. And of course there was a pink pillbox hat to top it off. The suit would go well with the roses she'd be handed at Love Field, not so well with the blood which would splatter the skirt and her stockings and shoes.

20

I went back to Mercedes Street and read my paperbacks. I waited for the obdurate past to swat me like a troublesome fly—for the roof to fall in or a sinkhole to open and drop 2703 deep into the ground. I cleaned my .38, loaded it, then unloaded it and cleaned it again. I almost hoped I would disappear into one of my sudden sleeps—it would at least pass the time—but that didn't happen. The minutes dragged by, turning reluctantly into a stack of hours, each one bringing Kennedy that much closer to the intersection of Houston and Elm.

No sudden sleeps today, I thought. *That will happen tomorrow. When the critical moment comes, I'll just drop into unconsciousness. The next time I open my eyes, the deed will have been done and the past will have protected itself.*

It could happen. I knew it could. If it did, I'd have a decision to make: find Sadie and marry her, or go back and start all over again. Thinking about it, I found there was really no decision to be made. I didn't have the strength to go back and start over. One way or another, this was it. The trapper's last shot.

That night, the Kennedys, Johnsons, and Connallys ate dinner in Houston, at an event put on by the League of Latin American Citzens. The cuisine was Argentinian: *ensalada rusa* and the stew known as *guiso.* Jackie made the after-dinner speech—in Spanish. I ate takeout burgers and fries . . . or tried to. After a few bites, that meal also went into the garbage can out back.

I had finished both of the MacDonald novels. I thought about getting my own unfinished book out of the trunk of my car, but the idea of reading it was sickening. I ended up just sitting in the half-busted armchair until it was dark outside. Then I went into the little bedroom where Rosette Templeton and June Oswald had slept. I lay down with my shoes off and my clothes on, using the cushion from the living room chair as a pillow. I'd left the door open and the light in the living room burning. By its glow I could see the Crayola girls in their green jumpers. I knew I was in for the sort of night that would make the long day I had just passed seem short; I'd lie here wide awake, my feet hanging over the end of the bed almost to the floor, until the first light of November twenty-second came filtering in through the window.

It *was* long. I was tortured by what-ifs, should-have-beens, and thoughts of Sadie. Those were the worst. The missing her and wanting her went so deep it felt like physical sickness. At some point, probably long after midnight (I'd given up looking at my watch; the slow movement of the hands was too depressing), I fell into a sleep that was dreamless and profound. God knows how long I would have slept the next morning if I hadn't been awakened. Someone was shaking me gently.

"Come on, Jake. Open your eyes."

I did as I was told, although when I saw who was sitting beside me on the bed, I was at first positive I was dreaming after all. I had to be. But then I reached out, touched the leg of her faded blue jeans, and felt the fabric under my palm. Her hair was tied up, her face almost devoid of makeup, the disfigurement of her left cheek clear and singular. It was Sadie. She had found me.

CHAPTER 28

1

11/22/63 (Friday)

I sat up and embraced her without even thinking about it. She hugged me back, as hard as she could. Then I kissed her, tasting her reality—the mingled flavors of tobacco and Avon. The lipstick was fainter; in her nervousness, she had nibbled most of it away. I smelled her shampoo, her deodorant, and the oily funk of tension-sweat beneath it. Most of all I touched her: hip and breast and the scarred furrow of her cheek. She was there.

"What time is it?" My trusty Timex had stopped.

"Quarter past eight."

"Are you kidding? It can't be!"

"It is. And I'm not surprised, even if you are. How long has it been since you got anything but the kind of sleep where you just pass out for a couple of hours?"

I was still trying to deal with the idea that Sadie was here, in the Fort Worth house where Lee and Marina had lived. How could it be? In God's name, *how?* And that wasn't the only thing. Kennedy was also in Fort Worth, at this very minute giving a breakfast speech to the local Chamber of Commerce at the Texas Hotel.

"My suitcase is in my car," she said. "Will we take the Beetle to wherever we're going, or your Chevy? The Beetle might be better. It's easier to park. We may have to pay a lot for a space, even so, if

715

we don't go right now. The scalpers are already out, waving their flags. I saw them."

"Sadie . . ." I shook my head in an effort to clear it and grabbed my shoes. I had thoughts in my head, plenty of them, but they were whirling around like paper in a cyclone, and I couldn't catch a single one.

"I'm here," she said.

Yes. That was the problem. "You can't come with me. It's too dangerous. I thought I explained that, but maybe I wasn't clear enough. When you try to change the past, it bites. It'll tear your throat out if you give it the chance."

"You were clear. But you can't do this alone. Face reality, Jake. You've put on a few pounds, but you're still a scarecrow. You limp when you walk, and it's a *bad* limp. You have to stop and rest your knee every two or three hundred steps. What would you do if you had to run?"

I said nothing. I was listening, though. I wound and set my watch as I did it.

"And that's not the worst of it. You—yikes! What are you doing?" I had grabbed her thigh.

"Making sure you're real. I still can't quite believe it." *Air Force One* was going to touch down at Love Field in a little over three hours. And someone was going to give Jackie Kennedy roses. At her other Texas stops, she'd been given yellow ones, but the Dallas bouquet was going to be red.

"I'm real and I'm here. Listen to me, Jake. The worst thing isn't how badly you're still banged up. The worst thing is the way you have of falling suddenly asleep. Haven't you thought of that?"

I'd thought of it a lot.

"If the past is as malevolent as you say it is, what do you think is going to happen if you do succeed in getting close to the man you're hunting before he can pull the trigger?"

The past wasn't exactly malevolent, that was the wrong word, but I saw what she was saying and had no argument against it.

"You really don't know what you're getting yourself into."

"I absolutely do. And you're forgetting something very important." She took my hands and looked into my eyes. "I'm not just
your best girl, Jake . . . if that's what I still am to you—"

"That's exactly why it's so goddam scary having you turn up
like this."

"You say a man's going to shoot the president, and I have reason
to believe you, based on the other things that you've predicted that
have come true. Even Deke's half-persuaded. 'He knew Kennedy
was coming before *Kennedy* knew it,' he said. 'Right down to the
day and the hour. And he knew the Missus was coming along for
the ride.' But you say it as if you were the only person who cared.
You're not. Deke cares. He would have been here if he wasn't still
running a fever of a hundred and one. And *I* care. I didn't vote for
him, but I happen to be an American, and that makes him not just
the president but *my* president. Does that sound corny to you?"

"No."

"Good." Her eyes were snapping. "I have no intention of letting some crazy person shoot him, and I have no intention of falling asleep."

"Sadie—"

"Let me finish. We don't have much time, so you need to dig
out your ears. Are they dug?"

"Yessum."

"Good. *You're not getting rid of me.* Let me repeat: *not.* I'm going.
If you won't let me into your Chevy, I'll follow you in my Beetle."

"Jesus Christ," I said, and didn't know if I was cursing or praying.

"If we ever get married, I'll do what you say, as long as you're
good to me. I was raised to believe that's a wife's job." (*Oh ye child of
the sixties,* I thought.) "I'm ready to leave everything I know behind
and follow you into the future. Because I love you and because
I believe that future you talk about is really there. I'll probably
never give you another ultimatum, but I'm giving you one now.
You do this with me or you don't do it at all."

I thought about this, and carefully. I asked myself if she meant
it. The answer was as clear as the scar on her face.

Sadie, meanwhile, was looking at the Crayola Girls. "Who do you suppose drew these? They're actually quite good."

"Rosette did them," I said. "Rosette Templeton. She went back to Mozelle with her mamma after her daddy had an accident."

"And then you moved in?"

"No, across the street. A little family named Oswald moved in here."

"Is that his name, Jake? Oswald?"

"Yes. Lee Oswald."

"Am I coming with you?"

"Do I have a choice?"

She smiled and put her hand on my face. Until I saw that relieved smile, I had no idea of how frightened she must have been when she shook me awake. "No, honey," she said. "Not that I can see. That's why they call it an ultimatum."

2

We put her suitcase in the Chevrolet. If we stopped Oswald (and weren't arrested), we could get her Beetle later and she could drive it back to Jodie, where it would look normal and at home in her driveway. If things didn't go well—if we failed, or succeeded only to find ourselves on the hook for Lee's murder—we'd simply have to run for it. We could run faster, farther, and more anonymously in a V-8 Chevy than in a Volkswagen Beetle.

She saw the gun when I put it into the inside pocket of my sport coat and said, "No. Outside pocket."

I raised my eyebrows.

"Where I can get at it if you all at once get tired and decide to take a nap."

We went down the walk, Sadie hitching her purse over her shoulder. Rain had been forecast, but it looked to me as if the prognosticators would have to take a penalty card on that one. The sky was clearing.

Before Sadie could get in on the passenger side, a voice from behind me spoke up. "That your girlfriend, mister?"

I turned. It was the jump-rope girl with the acne. Only it wasn't acne, it wasn't rubella, and I didn't have to ask why she wasn't in school. She had chicken pox. "Yes, she is."

"She's purty. Except for the"—she made a *gik* sound that was, in a grotesque way, sort of charming—"on her face."

Sadie smiled. My appreciation for her sheer guts continued to go up . . . and it never went down. "What's your name, honey?"

"Sadie," the jump-rope girl said. "Sadie Van Owen. What's yours?"

"Well, you're not going to believe this, but my name's Sadie, too."

The kid eyed her with a mistrustful cynicism that was all Mercedes Street Riot Grrrl. "No, it's not!"

"It really is. Sadie Dunhill." She turned to me. "That's quite a coincidence, wouldn't you say, George?"

I wouldn't, actually, and I didn't have time to discuss it. "Need to ask you something, Miss Sadie Van Owen. You know where the buses stop on Winscott Road, don't you?"

"Sure." She rolled her eyes as if to ask *how dumb do you think I am?* "Say, have you two had the chicken pox?"

Sadie nodded.

"Me, too," I said, "so we're okay on that score. Do you know which bus goes into downtown Dallas?"

"The Number Three."

"And how often does the Three run?"

"I think every half hour, but it might be every fifteen minutes. Why you want the bus when you got a car? When you got *two* cars?"

I could tell by Big Sadie's expression that she was wondering the same thing. "I've got my reasons. And by the way, my old man drives a submarine."

Sadie Van Owen cracked a huge smile. "You know that one?"

"Known it for years," I said. "Get in, Sadie. We need to roll."

I checked my new watch. It was twenty minutes to nine.

3

"Tell me why you're interested in the buses," Sadie said.

"First tell me how you found me."

"When I got to Eden Fallows and you were gone, I burned the note as you asked, then checked with the old guy next door."

"Mr. Kenopensky."

"Yes. He didn't know anything. By then the therapist lady was sitting on your steps. She wasn't happy to find you gone. She said she'd traded with Doreen so Doreen could see Kennedy today."

The Winscott Road bus stop was ahead. I slowed to see if there was a schedule inside the little shelter next to the post, but no. I pulled into a parking space a hundred yards ahead of the stop.

"What are you doing?"

"Taking out an insurance policy. If a bus doesn't come by nine, we'll go on. Finish your story."

"I called the hotels in downtown Dallas, but nobody even wanted to talk to me. They're all so *busy*. I called Deke next, and he called the police. Told them he had reliable information that someone was going to shoot the president."

I'd been watching for the bus in my rearview mirror, but now I looked at Sadie in shock. Yet I felt reluctant admiration for Deke. I had no idea how much of what Sadie had told him he actually believed, but he'd gone way out on a limb, just the same. "What happened? Did he give his name?"

"He never got the chance. They hung up on him. I think that's when I really started to believe you about how the past protects itself. And that's what all this is to you, isn't it? Just a living history book."

"Not anymore."

Here came a lumbering bus, green over yellow. The sign in the destination window read 3 MAIN STREET DALLAS 3. It stopped and the doors at the front and back flapped open on their accordion hinges. Two or three people got on, but there was no way they were going to find seats; when the bus rolled slowly past us, I saw that all of them were full. I glimpsed a woman with a row of Kennedy buttons pinned to her hat. She waved at me gaily, and although our eyes met for only a second, I could feel her excitement, delight, and anticipation.

I dropped the Chevy into gear and followed the bus. On the back, partially obscured by belching brown exhaust, a radiantly smiling Clairol girl proclaimed that if she only had one life, she wanted to live it as a blonde. Sadie waved her hand theatrically. "Uck! Drop back! It stinks!"

"That's quite a criticism, coming from a pack-a-day chick," I said, but she was right, the diesel stench was nasty. I fell back. There was no need to tailgate now that I knew Sadie Jump-Rope had been right about the number. She'd probably been right about the interval, too. The buses might run every half hour on ordinary days, but this was no ordinary day.

"I did some more crying, because I thought you were gone for sure. I was scared for you, but I hated you, too."

I could understand that and still feel I'd done the right thing, so it seemed best to say nothing.

"I called Deke again. He asked me if you'd ever said anything about having another bolt-hole, maybe in Dallas but probably in Fort Worth. I said I didn't remember you saying anything specific. He said it probably would have been while you were in the hospital, and all confused. He told me to think hard. As if I wasn't. I went back to Mr. Kenopensky on the chance you might have said something to him. By then it was almost suppertime, and getting dark. He said no, but right about then his son came by with a pot roast dinner and invited me to eat with them. Mr. K got talking— he has all kinds of stories about the old days—"

"I know." Up ahead, the bus turned east on Vickery Boulevard. I signaled and followed it but stayed far enough back so we didn't have to eat the diesel. "I've heard at least three dozen. Blood-on-the-saddle stuff."

"Listening to him was the best thing I could have done, because

I stopped racking my brains for awhile, and sometimes when you relax, things let go and float to the surface of your mind. While I was walking back to your little apartment, I suddenly remembered you saying you lived for awhile on Cadillac Street. Only you knew that wasn't quite right."

"Oh my God. I forgot all about that."

"It was my last chance. I called Deke again. He didn't have any detailed city maps, but he knew there were some at the school library. He drove down—probably coughing his head off, he's still pretty sick—got them, and called me from the office. He found a Ford Avenue in Dallas, and a Chrysler Park, and several Dodge Streets. But none of them had the feel of a Cadillac, if you know what I mean. Then he found Mercedes Street in Fort Worth. I wanted to go right away, but he told me I'd have a much better chance of spotting you or your car if I waited until morning."

She gripped my arm. Her hand was cold.

"Longest night of my life, you troublesome man. I hardly slept a wink."

"I made up for you, although I didn't finally go under until the wee hours. If you hadn't come, I might have slept right through the damn assassination."

How dismal would *that* be for an ending?

"Mercedes goes on for *blocks*. I drove and drove. Then I could see the end, at the parking lot of some big building that looks like the back of a department store."

"Close. It's a Montgomery Ward warehouse."

"And still no sign of you. I can't tell you how downhearted I was. *Then* . . ." She grinned. It was radiant in spite of the scar. "Then I saw that red Chevy with the silly tailfins that look like a woman's eyebrows. Bright as a neon sign. I shouted and pounded the dashboard of my little Beetle until my hand was sore. And now here I a—"

There was a low, crunching bang from the right front of the Chevy and suddenly we were veering at a lamppost. There was a series of hard thuds from beneath the car. I spun the wheel. It was sickeningly loose in my hands, but I got just enough steerage to avoid hitting the post head-on. Instead, Sadie's side scraped it, creating a ghastly metal-on-metal *screee.* Her door bowed inward and I yanked her toward me on the bench seat. We came to a stop with the hood hanging over the sidewalk and the car listing to the right. *That wasn't just a flat tire,* I thought. *That was a mortal fucking injury.*

Sadie looked at me, stunned. I laughed. As previously noted, sometimes there's just nothing else you can do.

"Welcome to the past, Sadie," I said. "This is how we live here."

4

She couldn't get out on her side; it was going to take a crowbar to pry the passenger door open. She slid the rest of the way across the seat and got out on mine. A few people were watching, not many.

"Gee, what happened?" a woman pushing a baby carriage asked.

That was obvious once I got around to the front of the car. The right front wheel had snapped off. It lay twenty feet behind us at the end of a curving trench in the asphalt. The jagged axle-stub gleamed in the sun.

"Busted wheel," I told the woman with the baby carriage.

"Oh, law," she said.

"What do we do?" Sadie asked in a low voice.

"We took out an insurance policy; now we file a claim. Nearest bus stop."

"My suitcase—"

Yes, I thought, *and Al's notebook. My manuscripts—the shitty novel that doesn't matter and the memoir that does. Plus my available cash.* I glanced at my watch. Quarter past nine. At the Texas Hotel, Jackie would be dressing in her pink suit. After another hour or so of politics, the motorcade would be on the move to Carswell Air Force Base, where the big plane was parked. Given the distance between Fort Worth and Dallas, the pilots would barely have time to put their wheels up.

I tried to think.

"Would you like to use my phone to call someone?" the woman with the baby carriage asked. "My house is right up the street." She scanned us, picking up on my limp and Sadie's scar. "Are you hurt?"

"We're fine," I said. I took Sadie's arm. "Would you call a service station and ask them to tow it? I know it's a lot to ask, but we're in a terrible hurry."

"I *told* him that front end was wobbly," Sadie said. She was pouring on the Georgia drawl. "Thank goodness we weren't on the highway." *Ha-way.*

"There's an Esso about two blocks up." She pointed north. "I guess I could stroll the baby over there . . ."

"Oh, that would be a lifesaver, ma'am," Sadie said. She opened her purse, removed her wallet, and took out a twenty. "Give them this on account. Sorry to ask you like this, but if I don't see Kennedy, I will just *dah.*" That made the baby carriage woman smile.

"Goodness, that much would pay for *two* tows. If you have some paper in your purse, I could scribble a receipt—"

"That's okay," I said. "We trust you. But maybe I'll put a note under the wiper."

Sadie was looking at me questioningly . . . but she was also holding out a pen and little pad with a cross-eyed cartoon kid on the cover. SKOOL DAZE, it said below his loopy grin. DEAR OLE GOLDEN SNOOZE DAZE.

A lot was riding on that note, but there was no time to think about the wording. I jotted rapidly and folded it under the wiper blade. A moment later we were around the corner and gone.

5

"Jake? Are you okay?"

"Fine. You?"

"I got bumped by the door and I'll probably have a bruise on my shoulder, but otherwise, yes. If we'd hit that post, I probably wouldn't have been. You, either. Who was the note for?"

"Whoever tows the Chevy." And I hoped to God Mr. Whoever would do as the note asked. "We'll worry about that part when we come back."

If we came back.

The next bus pole was halfway up the block. Three black women, two white women, and a Hispanic man were standing by the post, a racial mixture so balanced it looked like a casting call for *Law and Order SVU*. We joined them. I sat on the bench inside the shelter next to a sixth woman, an African-American lady whose heroic proportions were packed into a white rayon uniform that practically screamed Well-to-do White Folks' Housekeeper. On her bosom she wore a button that read ALL THE WAY WITH JFK IN '64.

"Bad leg, sir?" she asked me.

"Yes." I had four packets of headache powder in the pocket of my sport coat. I reached past the gun, got two of them, tore off the tops, and poured them into my mouth.

"Taking them that way will box your kidneys around," she said.

"I know. But I've got to keep this leg going long enough to see the president."

She broke into a large smile. "Don't I hear *that*."

Sadie was standing on the curb and looking anxiously back down the street for a Number Three.

"Buses runnin slow today," the housekeeper said, "but one be along directly. No way I'm missin Kennedy, nuh-*uh*!"

Nine-thirty came and still no bus, but the ache in my knee was down to a dull throb. God bless Goody's Powder.

Sadie came over. "Jake, maybe we ought to—"

"*Here* come a Three," the housekeeper said, and rose to her feet. She was an awesome lady, dark as ebony, taller than Sadie by at least an inch, hair plank-straight and gleaming. "How-eee, I'm gonna get me a place right there in Dealey Plaza. Got samidges in my bag. And will he hear me when I yell?"

"I bet he will," I said.

She laughed. "You better believe he will! Him and Jackie both!"

The bus was full, but the folks from the bus stop crammed on anyway. Sadie and I were the last, and the driver, who looked as harried as a stockbroker on Black Friday, held out his palm. "No more! I'm full! Got em crammed in like sardines! Wait for the next one!"

Sadie threw me an agonized look, but before I could say anything, the large lady stepped in on our behalf. "Nuh-uh, you let em on. The man he got a bum leg, and the lady got her own problems, as you can well see. Also, she skinny and he skinnier. You let em on or I'm gonna put you *off* and drive this bus myself. I can do it, too. I learned on my daddy's Bulldog."

The bus driver looked at her looming over him, then rolled his eyes and beckoned us aboard. When I reached for coins to stick in the fare-box, he covered it with a meaty palm. "Never mind the damn fare, just get behind the white line. If you can." He shook his head. "Why they didn't put on a dozen extra buses today I don't know." He yanked the chrome handle. The doors flopped shut fore and aft. The air brakes let go with a chuff and we were rolling, slow but sure.

My angel wasn't done. She began hectoring a couple of working guys, one black and one white, seated behind the driver with their dinnerbuckets in their laps. "Get on up and give your seats to this lady and gentleman, now! Can't you see he's got a bad pin? And he's still goin to see Kennedy!"

"Ma'am, that's all right," I said.

She took no notice. "Get up, now, was you raised in a woodshed?"

They got up, elbowing their way into the choked throng in the aisle. The black workingman gave the housekeeper a dirty look. "Nineteen sixty-three and I'm *still* givin the white man my seat."

"Oh, boo-hoo," his white friend said.

The black guy did a double take at my face. I don't know what he saw, but he pointed at the now-vacant seats. "Sit down before you fall down, Jackson."

I sat next to the window. Sadie murmured her thanks and sat beside me. The bus lumbered along like an old elephant that can still reach a gallop if given enough time. The housekeeper hovered protectively next to us, holding a strap and swaying her hips on the turns. There was a lot of her to sway. I looked at my watch again. The hands seemed to be leaping toward 10:00 A.M.; soon they would leap past it.

Sadie leaned close to me, her hair tickling my cheek and neck. "Where are we going, and what are we going to do when we get there?"

I wanted to turn toward her, but kept my eyes front instead, looking for trouble. Looking for the next punch. We were on West Division Street now, which was also Highway 180. Soon we'd be in Arlington, future home of George W. Bush's Texas Rangers. If all went well, we'd reach the Dallas city limits by ten-thirty, two hours before Oswald chambered the first round into his damned Italian rifle. Only, when you're trying to change the past, things rarely go well.

"Just follow my lead," I said. "And don't relax."

6

We passed south of Irving, where Lee's wife was now recuperating from the birth of her second child only a month ago. Traffic was slow and smelly. Half the passengers on our packed bus were smoking. Outside (where the air was presumably a little clearer), the streets were choked with inbound traffic. We saw one car with WE LOVE YOU JACKIE soaped on the back window, and another with GET OUT OF TEXAS YOU COMMIE RAT in the same location. The bus lurched and swayed. Larger and larger clusters of people stood at the stops; they shook their fists when our packed bus refused to even slow.

At quarter past ten we got on Harry Hines Boulevard and passed a sign pointing the way to Love Field. The accident occurred three minutes after that. I had been hoping it wouldn't happen, but I had been watching for it and waiting for it, and when the dump truck drove through the stoplight at the intersection of Hines and Inwood Avenue, I was at least halfway prepared. I'd seen one like it before, on my way to Longview Cemetery in Derry.

I grabbed Sadie's neck and pushed her head toward her lap. *"Down!"*

A second later we were thrown against the partition between the driver's seat and the passenger area. Glass broke. Metal screamed. The standees shot forward in a yelling clot of waving limbs, handbags, and dislodged for-best hats. The white workingman who'd said *Boo-hoo* was bent double over the fare machine that stood at the head of the aisle. The large housekeeper simply disappeared, buried under a human avalanche.

Sadie's nose was bleeding and there was a puffy bruise rising like bread dough under her right eye. The driver was sprawled sideways behind the wheel. The wide front window was shattered and the forward view of the street was gone, replaced by rust-flowered metal. I could read **ALLAS PUBLIC WOR**. The stench of the hot asphalt the truck had been carrying was thick.

I turned Sadie toward me. "Are you all right? Is your head clear?"

"I'm okay, just shaken up. If you hadn't shouted when you did, I wouldn't have been."

There were moans and cries of pain from the pile-up at the front of the bus. A man with a broken arm disengaged himself from the scrum and shook the driver, who rolled out of his seat. There was a wedge of glass protruding from the center of his forehead.

"Ah, Christ!" the man with the broken arm said. "I think he's fuckin dead!"

Sadie got to the guy who'd hit the fare post and helped him back to where we'd been sitting. He was white-faced and groaning. I guessed that he'd been leading with his balls when he hit the post; it was just the right height. His black friend helped me get the housekeeper to her feet, but if she hadn't been fully conscious and able to help us out, I don't think we could have done much. That was three hundred pounds of female on the hoof. She was bleeding freely from the temple, and that particular uniform was never going to be of further use to her. I asked if she was okay.

"I think so, but I fetched my head one hell of a wallop. Lawsy!"

Behind us, the bus was in an uproar. Pretty soon there was going to be a stampede. I stood in front of Sadie and got her to put her arms around my waist. Given the shape of my knee, I probably should have been holding onto her, but instinct is instinct.

"We need to let these people off the bus," I told the black workingman. "Run the handle."

He tried, but it wouldn't move. "Jammed!"

I thought that was bullshit; I thought the past was holding it shut. I couldn't help him yank, either. I only had one good arm. The housekeeper—one side of her uniform now soaked with blood—pushed past me, almost knocking me off my feet. I felt Sadie's arms jerk loose, but then she took hold again. The housekeeper's hat had come askew, and the gauze of the veil was beaded with blood. The effect was grotesquely decorative, like tiny holly-berries. She reset the hat at the proper angle, then laid hold of the chrome doorhandle with the black workingman. "I'm gonna count three, then we gonna pull this sucker," she told him. "You ready?"

He nodded.

"One . . . two . . . *three!*"

They yanked . . . or rather *she* did, and hard enough to split her dress open beneath one arm. The doors flopped open. From behind us came weak cheers.

"Thank y—" Sadie began, but then I was moving.

"Quick. Before we get trampled. Don't let go of me." We were the first ones off the bus. I turned Sadie toward Dallas. "Let's go."

"Jake, those people need help!"

"And I'm sure it's on the way. Don't look back. Look ahead, because that's where the next trouble will come from."

"How much trouble? How much more?"

"All the past can throw at us," I said.

7

It took us twenty minutes to make four blocks from where our Number Three bus had come to grief. I could feel my knee swelling. It pulsed with each beat of my heart. We came to a bench and Sadie told me to sit down.

"There's no time."

"Sit, mister." She gave me an unexpected push and I flopped onto the bench, which had an ad for a local funeral parlor on the back. Sadie nodded briskly, as a woman may when a troublesome chore has been accomplished, then stepped into Harry Hines Boulevard, opening her purse as she did so and rummaging in it. The throbbing in my knee was temporarily suspended as my heart climbed into my throat and stopped.

A car swerved around her, honking. It missed her by less than a foot. The driver shook his fist as he continued down the block, then popped up his middle finger for good measure. When I yelled at her to come back, she didn't even look in my direction. She took out her wallet as the cars whiffed past, blowing her hair back from her scarred face. She was as cool as a spring morning. She got what she wanted, dropped the wallet back into her purse, then held a greenback high over her head. She looked like a high school cheerleader at a pep rally.

"Fifty dollars!" she shouted. *"Fifty dollars for a ride into Dallas! Main Street! Main Street! Gotta see Kennedy! Fifty dollars!"*

That isn't going to work, I thought. *The only thing that's going to happen is she's going to get run over by the obdurate pa—*

A rusty Studebaker screamed to a stop in front of her. The engine bashed and clanged. There was an empty socket where one of the headlamps should have been. A man in baggy pants and a strap-style tee-shirt got out. On his head (and pulled all the way down to his ears) was a green felt cowboy hat with an Indian feather in the band. He was grinning. The grin showcased at least six missing teeth. I took one look and thought, *Here comes trouble.*

"Lady, you crazy," the Studebaker cowboy said.

"You want fifty dollars or not? Just take us to Dallas."

The man squinted at the bill, as oblivious of the swerving, honking cars as Sadie herself. He took off his hat, slapped it against the chinos hanging from his chickenbone hips, then put it back on his head, once more pulling it down until the brim rode the tops of his jug ears. "Lady, that ain't a fifty, that's a tenspot."

"I've got the rest in my billfold."

"Then why don't I just take it?" He grabbed at her big handbag and got one strap. I stepped off the curb, but I thought he'd have it and be gone before I could reach her. And if I *did* reach her, he'd probably beat me stupid. Skinny as he was, he still outweighed me. And he had two good arms.

Sadie held on. Pulled in opposite directions, the bag gaped open like an agonized mouth. She reached inside with her free hand and came out with a butcher knife that looked familiar. She swiped at him with it and opened his forearm. The cut began above his wrist and ended at the dirty crease on the inside of his elbow. He screamed in pain and surprise, let go of the strap, and stepped back, staring at her. "You crazy bitch, you cut me!"

He lunged for the open door of his car, which was still trying to beat itself to death. Sadie stepped forward and slashed the air in front of his face. Her hair had fallen in her eyes. Her lips were a grim line. Blood from the Studebaker cowboy's wounded arm pattered to the pavement. Cars continued to flow past. Incredibly, I heard someone yell, *"Give him the business, lady!"*

The Studebaker cowboy retreated toward the sidewalk, his eyes never leaving the knife. Without looking at me, Sadie said: "Over to you, Jake."

For a second I didn't understand, then remembered the .38. I took it out of my pocket and pointed at him. "See this, Tex? It's loaded."

"You're as crazy as she is." He was holding his arm against his chest now, branding his tee-shirt with blood. Sadie hurried around to the Studebaker's passenger side and opened the door. She looked at me over the roof and made an impatient cranking gesture with one hand. I wouldn't have believed I could love her more, but in that moment I saw I was wrong.

"You should have either taken the money or kept driving," I said. "Now let me see how you run. Do it immediately or I'll put a bullet in your leg so you can't do it at all."

"You're one fuckin bastard," he said.

"Yes, I am. And you're one fucking thief who will soon be sporting a bullet hole." I cocked the gun. The Studebaker cowboy didn't test me. He turned and hustled west on Hines with his head hunched and his arm cradled, cursing and spilling a blood-trail.

"Don't stop till you get to Love!" I shouted after him. "It's three miles the way you're going! Say hello to the president!"

"Get in, Jake. Get us out of here before the police come."

I slid in behind the wheel of the Studebaker, grimacing as my swollen knee protested. It was a standard shift, which meant using my bad leg on the clutch. I ran the seat back as far as it would go, hearing the litter of trash in back crunch and crackle, then got rolling.

"That knife," I said. "Is it—?"

"The one Johnny cut me with, yes. Sheriff Jones returned it after the inquest. He thought it was mine and he was probably right. But not from my place on Bee Tree. I'm almost positive Johnny brought it with him from our house in Savannah. I've been carrying it in my bag ever since. Because I wanted something to protect myself with, just in case . . ." Her eyes filled. "And this is an in-case, isn't it? This is an in-case if there ever was one."

"Put it back in your purse." I stabbed the clutch, which was horribly stiff, and managed to get the Studebaker into second. The car smelled like a chicken coop that hadn't been cleaned in roughly ten years.

"It'll get blood on everything inside."

"Put it back anyway. You can't walk around waving a knife, especially when the president's coming to town. Honey, that was beyond brave."

She put the knife away, then began wiping her eyes with her fisted hands, like a little girl who's scraped her knees. "What time is it?"

"Ten of eleven. Kennedy lands at Love Field in forty minutes."

"Everything's against us," she said. "Isn't it?"

I glanced at her and said, "Now you understand."

8

We made it to North Pearl Street before the Studebaker's engine blew. Steam boiled up from under the hood. Something metallic clanged to the road. Sadie cried out in frustration, struck her thigh with a balled fist, and used several bad words, but I was almost relieved. At least I wouldn't have to wrestle with the clutch anymore. I put the column shift in neutral and let the steaming car roll to the side of the street. It came to rest in front of an alley with DO NOT BLOCK painted on the cobbles, but this particular offense seemed minor to me after assault with a deadly weapon and car theft.

I got out and hobbled to the curb, where Sadie was already standing. "What time now?" she asked.

"Eleven-twenty."

"How far do we have to go?"

"The Texas School Book Depository is on the corner of Houston and Elm. Three miles. Maybe more." The words were no more than out of my mouth when we heard the roar of jet engines from behind us. We looked up and saw *Air Force One* on its descent path.

Sadie pushed her hair wearily back from her face. "What are we going to do?"

"Right now we're going to walk," I said.

"Put your arm around my shoulders. Let me take some of your weight."

"I don't need to do that, hon."

But a block later, I did.

9

We approached the intersection of North Pearl and Ross Avenue at eleven-thirty, right around the time Kennedy's 707 would be rolling to a stop near the official greeters . . . including, of course, the woman with the bouquet of red roses. The street corner ahead was dominated by the Cathedral Santuario de Guadalupe. On the steps, below a statue of the saint with her arms outstretched, sat a man with wooden crutches on one side and an enamel kitchen pot on the other. Propped against the pot was a sign reading I AM CRIPPLE UP *BAD*! PLEASE GIVE WHAT YOU CAN BE A GOOD SAMARIAN GOD LOVES YOU.

"Where are *your* crutches, Jake?"

"Back at Eden Fallows, in the bedroom closet."

"You forgot your *crutches*?"

Women are good at rhetorical questions, aren't they?

"I haven't been using them that much lately. For short distances, I'm pretty much okay." This sounded marginally better than admitting that the main thing on my mind had been getting the hell away from the little rehab cluster before Sadie arrived.

"Well, you could sure use a pair now."

She ran ahead with enviable fleetness and spoke to the beggar on the church steps. By the time I limped up, she was dickering with him. "A set of crutches like that costs nine dollars, and you want fifty for *one*?"

"I need at least one to get home," he said reasonably. "And your friend looks like he needs one to get *anywhere*."

"What about all that God loves you, be a good Samaritan stuff?"

"Well," the beggar said, thoughtfully rubbing his whiskery chin, "God *does* love you, but I'm just a poor old cripple fella. If you don't like my terms, make like the Pharisee and pass by on the other side. That's what I'd do."

"I bet you would. What if I just snatched them away, you money-grubbing thing?"

"I guess you could, but then God wouldn't love you anymore," he said, and burst out laughing. It was a remarkably cheerful sound for a man who was crippled up bad. He was doing better in the dental department than the Studebaker cowboy, but not a whole hell of a lot.

"Give him the money," I said. "I only need one."

"Oh, I'll give him the money. I just hate being screwed."

"Lady, that's a shame for the male population of planet Earth, if you don't mind me saying."

"Watch your mouth," I said. "That's my fiancée you're talking about." It was eleven-forty now.

The beggar took no notice of me. He was eyeing Sadie's wallet. "There's blood on that. Did you cut yourself shaving?"

"Don't try out for the *Sullivan* show just yet, sweetheart, Alan King you're not." Sadie produced the ten she'd flashed at oncoming traffic, plus two twenties. "There," she said as he took them. "I'm broke. Are you satisfied?"

"You helped a poor crippled man," the beggar said. "*You're* the one who ought to be satisfied."

"Well, I'm not!" Sadie shouted. "And I hope your damn old eyes fall out of your ugly head!"

The beggar gave me a sage guy-to-guy look. "Better get her home, Sunny Jim, I think she's gonna start on her monthly right t'irectly."

I put the crutch under my right arm—people who've been lucky with their bones think you'd use a single crutch on the injured side, but that's not the case—and took Sadie's elbow with my left hand. "Come on. No time."

As we walked away, Sadie slapped her jeans-clad rump, looked back over her shoulder, and cried: "Kiss it!"

The beggar called: "Bring it back and bend it in my direction, honeylove, that you get for free!"

10

We walked down North Pearl . . . or rather, Sadie walked and I crutched. It was a hundred times better with the crutch, but there was no way we could make the intersection of Houston and Elm before twelve-thirty.

Up ahead was a scaffolding. The sidewalk went beneath it. I steered Sadie across the street.

"Jake, why in the *world*—"

"Because it'd fall on us. Take my word for it."

"We need a ride. We *really* need . . . Jake? Why are you stopping?"

I stopped because life is a song and the past harmonizes. Usually those harmonies meant nothing (so I thought then), but every once in awhile the intrepid visitor to the Land of Ago can put one to use. I prayed with all my heart that this was one of those times.

Parked at the corner of North Pearl and San Jacinto was a 1954 Ford Sunliner convertible. Mine had been red and this one was midnight blue, but still . . . maybe . . .

I hurried to it and tried the passenger door. Locked. Of course. Sometimes you caught a break, but outright freebies? Never.

"Are you going to jump the ignition?"

I had no idea how to do that, and suspected it was probably harder than they made it look on *Bourbon Street Beat*. But I knew how to raise my crutch and slam the armpit cradle repeatedly against the window until it broke into a crack-glaze and sagged inward. No one looked at us, because there was no one on the sidewalk. All the action was to the southeast. From there we could hear the surf-roar of the crowd now gathering on Main Street in anticipation of President Kennedy's arrival.

The Saf-T-Glas sagged. I reversed the crutch and used the rubber-tipped end to push it inward. One of us would have to sit in the back. If this worked, that was. While in Derry, I'd had a copy made of the Sunliner's ignition key and taped it to the bottom of the glove compartment, underneath the paperwork. Maybe this guy had done the same. Maybe this particular harmony extended that far. It was a thin chance . . . but the chance of Sadie finding me on Mercedes Street had been thin enough to read a newspaper through, and that one had panned out. I thumbed the chrome button on this Sunliner's glove compartment and began to feel around inside.

Harmonize, you son of a bitch. Please harmonize. Give me a little help just this once.

"Jake? Why would you think—"

My fingers happened on something and I brought out a tin Sucrets box. When I opened it I found not one key, but four. I didn't know what the other three might open, but I had no doubt about the one I wanted. I could have found it in the dark, just by its shape.

Man, I loved that car.

"Bingo," I said, and almost fell over when she hugged me. "You drive, honey. I'll sit in back and rest my knee."

11

I knew better than to try Main Street; it would be blocked off with sawhorses and police cars. "Take Pacific as far as you can. After that, use the side streets. Just keep the crowd-noise on your left and I think you'll be okay."

"How much time do we have?"

"Half an hour." It was actually twenty-five minutes, but I thought half an hour sounded more comforting. Besides, I didn't want her to try any stunt driving and risk an accident. We still had time—theoretically, at least—but one more wreck and we were finished.

She didn't try any stunts, but she did drive fearlessly. We came to a downed tree blocking one of the streets (of course we did), and she bumped up over the curb, driving along the sidewalk to get past it. We made it as far as the intersection of North Record Street and Havermill. There we could go no farther, because the last two blocks of Havermill—right up to the point where it intersected Elm—no longer existed. It had become a parking lot. A man holding an orange flag waved us forward.

"Fi' bucks," he said. "Just a two-minute walk to Main Street, you folks got plenny a time." Although he cast a doubtful eye at my crutch when he said it.

"I really am broke," Sadie said. "I wasn't lying about that."

I pulled out my wallet and gave the man a five. "Put it behind the Chrysler," he said. "Pull up nice and tight."

Sadie tossed him the keys. "*You* pull it up nice and tight. Come on, honey."

"Hey, not that way!" the car-park guy yelled. "That way's Elm! You want to go over to Main! That's the way he's coming!"

"We know what we're doing!" Sadie called. I hoped she was right. We made our way through the packed cars, Sadie in the lead. I twisted and flailed with my crutch, trying to avoid jutting outside mirrors and keep up with her. Now I could hear locomotives and clanging freight cars in the trainyard behind the Book Depository.

"Jake, we're leaving a trail a mile wide."

"I know. I've got a plan." A gigantic overstatement, but it sounded good.

We came out on Elm, and I pointed at the building across the street two blocks down. "There. That's where he is."

She looked at the squat red cube with the peering windows, then turned a dismayed, wide-eyed face to me. I observed—with something like clinical interest—that large white goosebumps had broken out on her neck. "Jake, it's *horrible*!"

"I know."

"But . . . what's *wrong* with it?"

"Everything. Sadie, we have to hurry. We're nearly out of time."

12

We crossed Elm on a diagonal, me crutching along at a near run. The biggest portion of the crowd was on Main Street, but more people filled Dealey Plaza and lined Elm in front of the Book Depository. They crowded the curb all the way down to the Triple Underpass. Girls sat on their boyfriends' shoulders. Children who might soon be screaming in panic happily smeared their faces with ice cream. I saw a man selling Sno-Cones and a woman with a huge bouffant hairdo hawking dollar photos of Jack and Jackie in evening wear.

By the time we reached the shadow of the Depository, I was sweating, my armpit was hollering from the constant pressure of the crutch cradle, and my left knee had been cinched in a fiery belt. I could barely bend it. I looked up and saw Depository employees leaning from some of the windows. I couldn't see anyone in the one at the southeast corner of the sixth floor, but Lee would be there.

I looked at my watch. Twelve-twenty. We could track the motorcade's progress by the rising roar on Lower Main Street.

Sadie tried the door, then gave me an anguished glare. "Locked!"

Inside, I saw a black man wearing a poorboy cap tilted at a jaunty angle. He was smoking a cigarette. Al had been a great one for marginalia in his notebook, and near the end—casually jotted, almost doodled—he had written the names of several of Lee's co-workers. I'd made no effort to study these, because I didn't see what earthly use I could put them to. Next to one of those names—the one belonging to the guy in the poorboy cap, I had no doubt—Al had written: *First one they suspected (probably because black).* It had been an unusual name, but I still couldn't remember it, either because Roth and his goons had beaten it out of my head (along with all sorts of other stuff) or because I hadn't paid enough attention in the first place.

Or just because the past was obdurate. And did it matter? It just wouldn't come. The name was nowhere.

Sadie hammered on the door. The black man in the poorboy cap stood watching her impassively. He took a drag on his cigarette and then waved the back of his hand at her: *go on, lady, go on.*

"Jake, think of something! PLEASE!"

Twelve twenty-one.

An unusual name, yes, but *why* had it been unusual? I was surprised to find this was something I actually knew.

"Because it was a girl's," I said.

Sadie turned to me. Her cheeks were flushed except for the scar, which stood out in a white snarl. "What?"

Suddenly I was hammering on the glass. *"Bonnie!"* I shouted. *"Hey, Bonnie Ray! Let us in! We know Lee! Lee! LEE OSWALD!"*

He registered the name and crossed the lobby in a maddeningly slow amble.

"I didn't know that scrawny l'il sumbitch *had* any friends," Bonnie Ray Williams said as he opened the door, then stepped aside as we rushed inside. "He probably in the break room, watchin for the president with the rest of—"

"Listen to me," I said. "I'm not his friend and he's not in the break room. He's on the sixth floor. I think he means to shoot President Kennedy."

The big man laughed merrily. He dropped his cigarette to the floor and crushed it out with a workboot. "That little pissant wouldn't have the guts to drown a litter o' kittens in a sack. All he do is sit in the corner and read *books.*"

"I tell you—"

"I'm goan on up to two. If you want to come with me, you're welcome, I guess. But don't be talkin any more nonsense about Leela. That's what we call him, Leela. Shoot the president! *Lor!*" He waved his hand and ambled away.

I thought, *You belong in Derry, Bonnie Ray. They specialize in not seeing what's right in front of them.*

"Stairs," I told Sadie.

"The elevator would be—"

The end of any chance we might have left was what it would be.

"It would get stuck between floors. *Stairs.*"

I took her hand and pulled her toward them. The staircase was a narrow gullet with wooden risers swaybacked from years of traffic. There was a rusty iron railing on the left. At the foot, Sadie turned to me. "Give me the gun."

"No."

"You'll never make it in time. I will. *Give me the gun.*"

I almost gave it up. It wasn't that I felt I deserved to keep it; now that the actual watershed moment had come, it didn't matter who stopped Oswald as long as *someone* did. But we were only a step away from the roaring machine of the past, and I was damned if I'd risk Sadie taking that last step ahead of me, only to be sucked into its whirling belts and blades.

I smiled, then leaned forward and kissed her. "Race you," I said, and started up the stairs. Over my shoulder I called, "If I fall asleep, he's all yours!"

13

"You folks crazy," I heard Bonnie Ray Williams say in a mildly remonstrative tone of voice. Then there was the light thud of footsteps as Sadie followed me. I crutched on the right—no longer leaning on it but almost *vaulting* on it—and hauled at the railing on the left. The gun in my sport coat pocket swung and thudded against my hip. My knee was bellowing. I let it yell.

When I hit the second-floor landing, I snuck a look at my watch. It was twelve twenty-five. No; twenty-six. I could hear the roar of the crowd still approaching, a wave about to break. The motorcade had passed the intersections of Main and Ervay, Main and Akard, Main and Field. In two minutes—three at most—it would reach Houston Street, turn right, and roll past the old Dallas courthouse at fifteen miles an hour. From that point on, the President of the United States would be an available target. In the 4x scope attached to the Mannlicher-Carcano, the Kennedys and

Connallys would look as big as actors on the screen at the Lisbon Drive-In. But Lee would wait a little longer. He was no suicide-drone; he wanted to get away. If he fired too soon, the security detail in the car at the head of the motorcade would see the gun-flash and return fire. He would wait until that car—and the presidential limo—made the dogleg left onto Elm. Not just a sniper; a fucking backshooter.

I still had three minutes.

Or maybe just two and a half.

I attacked the stairs between the second and third floor, ignoring the pain in my knee, forcing myself upward like a marathoner near the end of a long race. Which, of course, I was.

From below us, I could hear Bonnie Ray yelling something that had *crazy man* and *say Leela goan shoot* in it.

Until I was halfway up the flight to the third floor, I could feel Sadie beating on my back like a rider urging a horse to go faster, but then she fell back a little. I heard her gasping for air and thought, *too many cigarettes, darlin.* My knee didn't hurt anymore; the pain had been temporarily buried in a surge of adrenaline. I kept my left leg as straight as I could, letting the crutch do the work.

Around the bend. Up to the fourth floor. Now I was gasping, too, and the stairs looked steeper. Like a mountain. The cradle-rest at the top of the beggar's crutch was slimy with sweat. My head pounded; my ears rang with the sound of the cheering crowd below. The eye of my imagination opened wide and I could see the approaching motorcade: the security car, then the presidential limo with the Harley-Davidson DPD motorcycles flanking it, the cops on them wearing white chin-strapped helmets and sunglasses.

Around another corner. The crutch skidding, then steadying. Up again. The crutch thudding. Now I could smell sweet sawdust from the sixth-floor renovations: workmen replacing the old plank boards with new ones. Not on Lee's side, though. Lee had the southeast side to himself.

I reached the fifth-floor landing and made the last turn, my mouth open to scoop in air, my shirt a drenched rag against my heaving chest. Stinging sweat ran into my eyes and I blinked it away.

Three book cartons stamped ROADS TO EVERYWHERE and 4th AND 5th GRADE READERS blocked the stairs to the sixth floor. I stood on my right leg and slammed the foot of the crutch into one of them, sending it spinning. Behind me I could hear Sadie, now between the fourth and fifth floors. So I had been right to keep the gun, it seemed, although who really knew? Judging from my own experience, knowing you are the one with the primary responsibility to change the future makes you run faster.

I squeezed through the gap I created. To do so I had to put my full weight on my left leg for a second. It gave a howl of pain. I groaned and grabbed at the railing to keep from spilling forward onto the stairs. Looked at my watch. It said twelve twenty-eight, but what if it was slow? The crowd was roaring.

"Jake . . . for God's sake hurry . . ." Sadie, still on the stairs to the fifth-floor landing.

I started up the last flight, and the sound of the crowd began to drain away into a great silence. By the time I reached the top, there was nothing but the rasp of my breath and the burning hammer-strokes of my overtaxed heart.

14

The sixth floor of the Texas School Book Depository was a shadowy square dotted with islands of stacked book cartons. The overhead lights were burning where the floor was being replaced. They were off on the side where Lee Harvey Oswald planned to make history in one hundred seconds or less. Seven windows overlooked Elm Street, the five in the middle large and semicircular, the ones on the ends square. The sixth floor was gloomy around the stairhead but filled with hazy light in the area overlooking Elm Street.

Thanks to the floating sawdust from the floor project, the sun-beams slanting in through the windows looked thick enough to cut. The beam falling through the window at the southeast corner, however, had been blocked off by a stacked barricade of book car-tons. The sniper's nest was all the way across the floor from me, on a diagonal that ran from northwest to southeast.

Behind the barricade, in the sunlight, a man with a gun stood at the window. He was stooped, peering out. The window was open. A light breeze was ruffling his hair and the collar of his shirt. He began to raise the rifle.

I broke into a shambling run, slaloming around the stacked car-tons, digging in my coat pocket for the .38.

"Lee!" I shouted. *"Stop, you son of a bitch!"*

He turned his head and looked at me, eyes wide, mouth hung open. For a moment he was just Lee—the guy who had laughed and played with Junie in the bath, the one who sometimes hugged his wife and kissed her upturned face—and then his thin and some-how prissy mouth wrinkled into a snarl that showed his upper teeth. When that happened, he changed into something mon-strous. I doubt you believe that, but I swear it's true. He stopped being a man and became the daemonic ghost that would haunt America from this day on, perverting its power and spoiling its every good intent.

If I let it.

The noise of the crowd rushed in again, thousands of people applauding and cheering and yelling their brains out. I heard them and Lee did, too. He knew what it meant: now or never. He whirled back to the window and socked the rifle's butt-plate against his shoulder.

I had the pistol, the same one I'd used to kill Frank Dunning. Not just *like* it; in that moment it was the same gun. I thought so then and I think so now. The hammer tried to catch in the pocket-lining but I dragged the .38 out, hearing cloth rip as I did so.

I fired. My shot went high and only exploded splinters from the top of the window frame, but it was enough to save John Kennedy's life. Oswald jerked at the sound of the report, and the 160-grain slug from the Mannlicher-Carcano went high, shattering a window in the county courthouse.

There were screams and bewildered shouts from below us. Lee turned toward me again, his face a mask of rage, hate, and disappointment. He raised his rifle again, and this time it wouldn't be the President of the United States he'd be aiming at. He worked the bolt—*clack-clack*—and I fired at him again. Although I was three-quarters of the way across the room, less than twenty-five feet away, I missed again. I saw the side of his shirt twitch, but that was all.

My crutch struck a stack of boxes. I tottered to the left, flailing with my gun-hand for balance, but there was no chance of that. For just a moment I thought of how, on the day I'd met her, Sadie had literally fallen into my arms. I knew what was going to happen. History doesn't repeat itself, but it harmonizes, and what it usually makes is the devil's music. This time *I* was the one who stumbled, and that was the crucial difference.

I could no longer hear her on the stairs . . . but I could still hear her rapid footfalls.

"Sadie, down!" I shouted, but it was lost in the bark of Oswald's rifle.

I heard the bullet pass above me. I heard her cry out.

Then there was more gunfire, this time from outside. The presidential limo had taken off, driving toward the Triple Underpass at breakneck speed, the two couples inside ducking and holding onto each other. But the security car had pulled up on the far side of Elm Street near Dealey Plaza. The cops on the motorcycles had stopped in the middle of the street, and at least four dozen people were acting as spotters, pointing up at the sixth-floor window, where a skinny man in a blue shirt was clearly visible.

I heard a patter of thumps, a sound like hailstones striking mud. Those were the bullets that missed the window and hit the bricks above or on either side. Many didn't miss. I saw Lee's shirt billow out as if a wind had started to blow inside it—a red one that tore holes in the fabric: one above the right nipple, one at the sternum, a third where his navel would be. A fourth tore his neck open. He danced like a doll in the hazy, sawdusty light, and that terrible snarl never left his face. He wasn't a man at the end, I tell you; he was something else. Whatever gets into us when we listen to our worst angels.

A bullet spanged one of the overhead lights, shattered the bulb, and set it to swaying. Then a bullet tore off the top of the would-be assassin's head, just as one of Lee's had torn off the top of Kennedy's in the world I'd come from. He collapsed onto his barricade of boxes, sending them tumbling to the floor.

Shouts from below. Someone yelling "Man down, I saw him go down!"

Running, ascending footfalls. I sent the .38 spinning toward Lee's body. I had just enough presence of mind to know that I would be badly beaten, perhaps even killed by the men coming up the stairs if they found me with a gun in my hand. I started to get up, but my knee would no longer hold me. That was probably just as well. I might not have been visible from Elm Street, but if I was, they'd open fire on *me*. So I crawled to where Sadie lay, supporting my weight on my hands and dragging my left leg behind me like an anchor.

The front of her blouse was soaked with blood, but I could see the hole. It was dead-center in her chest, just above the slope of her breasts. More blood poured from her mouth. She was choking on it. I got my arms under her and lifted her. Her eyes never left mine. They were brilliant in the hazy gloom.

"Jake," she rasped.

"No, honey, don't talk."

She took no notice, though—when had she ever? "Jake, the president!"

"Safe." I hadn't actually seen him all in one piece as the limo tore away, but I had seen Lee jerk as he fired his only shot at the street, and that was enough for me. And I would have told Sadie he was safe no matter what.

Her eyes closed, then opened again. The footfalls were very close now, turning from the fifth-floor landing and starting up the final flight. Far below, the crowd was bellowing its excitement and confusion.

"Jake."

"What, honey?"

She smiled. "How we danced!"

When Bonnie Ray and the others arrived, I was sitting on the floor and holding her. They stampeded past me. How many I don't know. Four, maybe. Or eight. Or a dozen. I didn't bother to look at them. I held her, rocking her head against my chest, letting her blood soak into my shirt. Dead. My Sadie. She had fallen into the machine, after all.

I have never been a crying man, but almost any man who's lost the woman he loves would, don't you think? Yes. But I didn't.

Because I knew what had to be done.

PART 6

THE GREEN
CARD MAN

Daily News EXTRA

SATURDAY, NOVEMBER 23, 1963   TEN CENTS

JFK ESCAPES ASSASSINATION,
FIRST LADY ALSO OK!

Panic Strikes
During Drive
Through Dallas
STORY PAGE 5

John Kennedy walking with wife, Jacqueline, on November 22, 1963.

CHAPTER 29

1

I wasn't exactly arrested, but I was taken into custody and driven to the Dallas police station in a squad car. On the last block of the ride, people—some of them reporters, most of them ordinary citizens—pounded on the windows and peered inside. In a clinical, distant way, I wondered if I would perhaps be dragged from the car and lynched for attempting to murder the president. I didn't care. What concerned me most was my bloodstained shirt. I wanted it off; I also wanted to wear it forever. It was Sadie's blood.

Neither of the cops in the front seat asked me any questions. I suppose someone had told them not to. If they *had* asked any, I wouldn't have replied. I was thinking. I could do that because the coldness was creeping over me again. I put it on like a suit of armor. I could fix this. I *would* fix this. But first I had some talking to do.

2

They put me in a room that was as white as ice. There was a table and three hard chairs. I sat in one of them. Outside, telephones rang and a Teletype chattered. People went back and forth talking in loud voices, sometimes shouting, sometimes laughing. The laughter had a hysterical sound. It was how men laugh when they know they've had a narrow escape. Dodged a bullet, so to speak. Perhaps Edwin Walker had laughed like that on the night of April tenth, as he talked to reporters and brushed broken glass from his hair.

The same two cops who brought me from the Book Depository searched me and took my things. I asked if I could have my last two packets of Goody's. The two cops conferred, then tore them open and poured them out on the table, which was engraved with initials and scarred with cigarette burns. One of them wetted a finger, tasted the powder, and nodded. "Do you want water?"

"No." I scooped up the powder and poured it into my mouth. It was bitter. That was fine with me.

One of the cops left. The other asked for my bloody shirt, which I reluctantly took off and handed over. Then I pointed at him. "I know it's evidence, but you treat it with respect. The blood on it came from the woman I loved. That might not mean much to you, but it's also from the woman who helped to stop the murder of President Kennedy, and that should."

"We only want it for blood-typing."

"Fine. But it goes on my receipt of personal belongings. I'll want it back."

"Sure."

The cop who'd left came back with a plain white undershirt. It looked like the one Oswald had been wearing—or *would* have been wearing—in the mugshot taken shortly after his arrest at the Texas Theatre.

3

I arrived in the little white interview room at twenty past one. About an hour later (I can't say with exactitude because there was no clock and my new Timex had been taken with the rest of my personal effects), the same two uniforms brought me some company. An old acquaintance, in fact: Dr. Malcolm Perry, toting a large black country doctor's medical bag. I regarded him with mild astonishment. He was here at the police station visiting me because he didn't have to be at Parkland Hospital, picking bits of bullet and shards of bone out of John Kennedy's brain. The river of history was already moving into its new course.

"Hello, Dr. Perry."

He nodded. "Mr. Amberson." The last time he'd seen me, he'd called me George. If I'd had any doubts about being under suspicion, that would have confirmed them. But I didn't. I'd been there, and I'd known what was about to happen. Bonnie Ray Williams would already have told them as much.

"I understand you've reinjured that knee."

"Unfortunately, yes."

"Let's have a look."

He tried to pull up my left pants leg and couldn't. The joint was too swollen. When he produced a pair of scissors, both cops stepped forward and drew their guns, keeping them pointed at the floor with their fingers outside the trigger guards. Dr. Perry looked at them with mild astonishment, then cut the leg of my pants up the seam. He looked, he touched, he produced a hypodermic needle and drew off fluid. I gritted my teeth and waited for it to be over. Then he rummaged in his bag, came out with an elastic bandage, and wrapped the knee tightly. That provided some relief.

"I can give you something for the pain, if these officers don't object."

They didn't, but I did. The most crucial hour of my life—and Sadie's—was dead ahead. I didn't want dope clouding my brain when it rolled around.

"Do you have any Goody's Headache Powder?"

Perry wrinkled his nose as if he had smelled something bad. "I have Bayer Aspirin and Emprin. The Emprin's a bit stronger."

"Give me that, then. And Dr. Perry?"

He looked up from his bag.

"Sadie and I didn't do anything wrong. She gave her life for her country . . . and I would have given mine for her. I just didn't get the chance."

"If so, let me be the first to thank you. On behalf of the whole country."

"The president. Where is he now? Do you know?"

Dr. Perry looked at the cops, eyebrows raised in a question. They looked at each other, then one of them said, "He's gone on to Austin, to give a dinner speech, just like he was scheduled to do. I don't know if that makes him crazy-brave or just stupid."

Maybe, I thought, Air Force One *was going to crash, killing Kennedy and everyone else on board. Maybe he was going to have a heart attack or a fatal stroke. Maybe some other chickenshit bravo was going to blow his handsome head off.* Did the obdurate past work against the things changed as well as against the change-agent? I didn't know. Nor much care. I had done my part. What happened to Kennedy from this point on was out of my hands.

"I heard on the radio that Jackie isn't with him," Perry said quietly. "He sent her on ahead to the vice president's ranch in Johnson City. He'll join her there for the weekend as planned. If what you say is true, George—"

"I think that's enough, doc," one of the cops said. It certainly was for me; to Mal Perry I was George again.

Dr. Perry—who had his share of doctor's arrogance—ignored him. "If what you say is true, then I see a trip to Washington in your future. And very likely a medal ceremony in the Rose Garden."

After he departed, I was left alone again. Only not really; Sadie was there, too. *How we danced,* she'd said just before she passed from this world. I could close my eyes and see her in line with the other girls, shaking her shoulders and doing the Madison. In this memory she was laughing, her hair was flying, and her face was perfect. 2011 surgical techniques could do a lot to fix what John Clayton had done to that face, but I thought I had an even better technique. If I got a chance to use it, that was.

4

I was allowed to baste in my own painful juices for two hours before the door of the interview room opened again. Two men came in. The one with the basset-hound face beneath a white Stetson hat introduced himself as Captain Will Fritz of the Dallas Police. He had a briefcase—but not *my* briefcase, so that was all right.

The other guy had heavy jowls, a drinker's complexion, and short dark hair that gleamed with hair tonic. His eyes were sharp, inquisitive, and a little worried. From the inside pocket of his suit coat he produced an ID folder and flipped it open. "James Hosty, Mr. Amberson. Federal Bureau of Investigation."

You have good reason to look worried, I thought. *You were the man in charge of monitoring Lee, weren't you, Agent Hosty?*

Will Fritz said, "Like to ask you a few questions, Mr. Amberson."

"Yes," I said. "And I'd like to get out of here. People who save the President of the United States generally don't get treated like criminals."

"Now, now," Agent Hosty said. "We sent you a doc, didn't we? And not just any doc; *your* doc."

"Ask your questions," I said.

And got ready to dance.

5

Fritz opened his briefcase and brought out a plastic bag with an evidence tag taped to it. Inside it was my .38. "We found this lying against the barricade of boxes Oswald set up, Mr. Amberson. Was it his, do you think?"

"No, that's a Police Special. It's mine. Lee had a .38, but it was a Victory model. If it wasn't on his body, you'll probably find it wherever he was staying."

Fritz and Hosty looked at each other in surprise, then back at me.

"So you admit you knew Oswald," Fritz said.

"Yes, although not well. I didn't know where he was living, or I would have gone there."

"As it happens," Hosty said, "he had a room on Beckley Street. He was registered under the name O. H. Lee. He seems to have had another alias, too. Alek Hidell. He used it to get mail."

"Wife and kiddo not with him?" I asked.

Hosty smiled. It spread his jowls approximately half a mile in either direction. "Who's asking the questions here, Mr. Amberson?"

"Both of us," I said. "I risked my life to save the president, and my fiancée *gave* hers, so I think I have a right to ask questions."

Then I waited to see how tough they'd get. If real tough, they actually believed I'd been in on it. Real easy, they didn't but wanted to be sure. It turned out to be somewhere in the middle.

Fritz used a blunt finger to spin the bag with the gun in it. "I'll tell you what might have happened, Mr. Amberson. I won't say it *did*, but you'd have to convince us otherwise."

"Uh-huh. Have you called Sadie's folks? They live in Savannah. You should also call Deacon Simmons and Ellen Dockerty, in Jodie. They were like surrogate parents to her." I considered this. "To both of us, really. I was going to ask Deke to be my best man at our wedding."

Fritz took no notice of this. "What might have happened was you and your girl were in on it with Oswald. And maybe at the end you got cold feet."

The ever-popular conspiracy theory. No home should be without one.

"Maybe you realized at the last minute that you were getting ready to shoot the most powerful man in the whole world," Hosty said. "You had a moment of clarity. So you stopped him. If it went like that, you'd get a lot of leniency."

Yes. Leniency to consist of forty, maybe even fifty years in Leavenworth eating mac and cheese instead of death in the Texas electric chair.

"Then why weren't we there with him, Agent Hosty? Instead of hammering on the door to be let in?"

Hosty shrugged. *You tell me.*

"And if we were plotting an assassination, you must have seen me with him. Because I know you had him under at least partial surveillance." I leaned forward. "Why didn't *you* stop him, Hosty? That was *your* job."

He drew back as if I'd raised a fist to him. His jowls reddened.

For a few moments at least, my grief hardened into a kind of malicious pleasure. "The FBI kept an eye on him because he defected to Russia, redefected to the United States, then tried to defect to Cuba. He was handing out pro-Fidel leaflets on street corners for months before this horror show today."

"How do you know all that?" Hosty barked.

"Because he told me. Then what happens? The president who's tried everything he can think of to knock Castro off his perch comes to Dallas. Working at the Book Depository, Lee had a ringside seat for the motorcade. You knew it and did nothing."

Fritz was staring at Hosty with something like horror. I'm sure Hosty was regretting the fact that the Dallas cop was even in the room, but what could he do? It was Fritz's station.

"We did not consider him a threat," Hosty said stiffly.

"Well, *that* was certainly a mistake. What was in the note he gave you, Hosty? I know Lee went to your office and left you one when he was told you weren't there, but he wouldn't tell me what was in it. He just gave that thin little fuck-you smile of his. We're talking about the man who killed the woman I loved, so I think I deserve to know. Did he say he was going to do something that would make the world sit up and take notice? I bet he did."

"It was nothing like that!"

"Show me the note, then. Double-dog dare you."

"Any communication from Mr. Oswald is Bureau business."

"I don't think you *can* show it. I'll bet it's ashes in your office toilet, as per Mr. Hoover's orders."

If it wasn't, it would be. It was in Al's notes.

"If you're such an innocent," Fritz said, "you'll tell us how you knew Oswald and why you were carrying a handgun."

"And why the lady had a butcher's knife with blood on it," Hosty added.

I saw red at that. *"The lady had blood everywhere!"* I shouted. *"On her clothes, on her shoes, in her purse! The son of a bitch shot her in the chest, or didn't you notice?"*

Fritz: "Calm down, Mr. Amberson. No one's accusing you of anything." The subtext: *Yet.*

I took a deep breath. "Have you talked to Dr. Perry? You sent him to examine me and take care of my knee, so you must have. Which means you know I was beaten within an inch of my life last August. The man who ordered the beating—and participated in it—is a bookie named Akiva Roth. I don't think he meant to hurt me as badly as he did, but probably I smarted off to him and made him mad. I can't remember. There's a lot I can't remember since that day."

"Why didn't you report this after it happened?"

"Because I was in a coma, Detective Fritz. When I came out of it, I didn't remember. When I *did* remember—some of it, at least—I recalled Roth saying he was hooked up with a Tampa bookie I'd done business with, and a New Orleans mobster named Carlos Marcello. That made going to the cops seem risky."

"Are you saying DPD is dirty?" I didn't know if Fritz's anger was real or faked, and didn't much care.

"I'm saying I watch *The Untouchables* and I know the Mob doesn't like rats. I bought a gun for personal protection—as is my right under the Second Amendment—and I carried it." I pointed at the evidence bag. "That gun."

Hosty: "Where'd you buy it?"

"I don't remember."

Fritz: "Your amnesia is pretty convenient, isn't it? Like something on *The Secret Storm* or *As the World Turns*."

"Talk to Perry," I repeated. "And take another look at my knee. I reinjured it racing up six flights of stairs to save the president's life. Which I will tell the press. I'll also tell them my reward for doing my duty as an American citizen was an interrogation in a hot little room without even a glass of water."

"Do you want water?" Fritz asked, and I understood that this could be all right, if I didn't misstep. The president had escaped assassination by the skin of his teeth. These two men—not to mention Dallas Police Chief Jesse Curry—would be under enormous pressure to provide a hero. Since Sadie was dead, I was what they had.

"No," I said, "but a Co'-Cola would be very nice."

6

As I waited for my Coke, I thought of Sadie saying *We're leaving a trail a mile wide.* It was true. But maybe I could make that work for me. If, that was, a certain tow truck driver from a certain Fort Worth Esso station had done as the note under the Chevrolet's windshield wiper had asked.

Fritz lit a cigarette and shoved the pack across to me. I shook my head and he took it back. "Tell us how you knew him," he said.

I said I'd met Lee on Mercedes Street, and we'd struck up an acquaintance. I listened to his rantings about the evils of fascist-imperialist America and the wonderful socialist state that would emerge in Cuba. Cuba was the ideal, he said. Russia had been taken over by worthless bureaucrats, which was why he'd left. In Cuba there was Uncle Fidel. Lee didn't come right out and say that Uncle Fidel walked on the water, but he implied it.

"I thought he was nuts, but I liked his family." That much was true. I *did* like his family, and I *did* think he was nuts.

STEPHEN KING

"How did a professional educator such as yourself come to be living on the shitass side of Fort Worth in the first place?" Fritz asked.

"I was trying to write a novel. I found out I couldn't do it while I was teaching school. Mercedes Street was a dump, but it was cheap. I thought the book would take at least a year, and that meant I had to stretch my savings. When I got depressed about the neighborhood, I tried to pretend I was living in a garret on the Left Bank."

Fritz: "Did your savings include money you won from bookies?"

Me: "I'm going to take the Fifth on that one."

At this, Will Fritz actually laughed.

Hosty: "So you met Oswald and became friendly with him."

"*Relatively* friendly. You don't become close buddies with crazy people. At least I don't."

"Go on."

Lee and his family moved out; I stayed. Then one day, out of the blue, I got a call from him saying he and Marina were living on Elsbeth Street in Dallas. He said it was a better neighborhood and the rents were cheap and plentiful. I told Fritz and Hosty that I was tired of Mercedes Street by then, so I came on over to Dallas, had lunch with Lee at the Woolworth's counter, then took a walk around the neighborhood. I rented the ground-floor apartment at 214 West Neely Street, and when the upstairs apartment went vacant, I told Lee. Kind of returning the favor.

"His wife didn't like the place on Elsbeth," I said. "The West Neely Street building was just around the corner, and much nicer. So they moved in."

I had no idea how closely they would check this story, how well the chronology would hold up, or what Marina might tell them, but those things weren't important to me. I only needed time. A story that was even halfway plausible might give it to me, especially since Agent Hosty had good reason to treat me with kid gloves. If I told what I knew about his relationship with Oswald, he might spend the rest of his career freezing his ass off in Fargo.

"Then something happened that put my ears up. Last April, this was. Right around Easter. I was sitting at the kitchen table, working on my book, when this fancy car—a Cadillac, I think— pulled up, and two people got out. A man and a woman. Well-dressed. They had a stuffed toy for Junie. She's—"

Fritz: "We know who June Oswald is."

"They went up the stairs, and I heard the guy—he had kind of a German accent and a big booming voice—I heard him say, 'Lee, how did you miss?'"

Hosty leaned forward, eyes as wide as they could get in that fleshy face. *"What?"*

"You heard me. So I checked the paper, and guess what? Someone took a shot at some retired general four or five days before. Big right-winger. Just the kind of guy Lee hated."

"What did you do?"

"Nothing. I knew he had a pistol—he showed it to me one day—but the paper said the guy who shot at Walker used a rifle. Besides, most of my attention was taken up by my girlfriend by then. You asked why she had a knife in her purse. The answer is simple—she was scared. She was also attacked, only not by Mr. Roth. It was her ex-husband. He disfigured her pretty badly."

"We saw the scar," Hosty said, "and we're sorry for your loss, Amberson."

"Thank you." *You don't look sorry enough,* I thought. "The knife she was carrying was the same one her ex—John Clayton was his name—used on her. She carried it everywhere." I thought of her saying, *Just in case.* I thought of her saying, *This is an in-case if there ever was one.*

I put my hands over my face for a minute. They waited. I dropped them into my lap and went on in a toneless Joe Friday voice. Just the facts, ma'am.

"I kept the place on West Neely, but I spent most of the summer in Jodie, taking care of Sadie. I'd pretty much given up on the book idea, was thinking about reapplying at Denholm Consolidated. Then I ran into Akiva Roth and his goons. Wound up in the hospital myself. When they let me out, I went to a rehab center called Eden Fallows."

"I know it," Fritz said. "Kind of an assisted living thing."

"Yes, and Sadie was my chief assistant. I took care of her after her husband cut her; she took care of me after Roth and his associates beat me up. Things go around that way. They make . . . I don't know . . . a kind of harmony."

"Things happen for a reason," Hosty said solemnly, and for a moment I felt like launching myself over the table and pummeling his flushed and fleshy face. Not because he was wrong, though. In my humble opinion, things *do* happen for a reason, but do we *like* the reason? Rarely.

"Near the end of October, Dr. Perry okayed me to drive short distances." This was a blatant lie, but they might not check it with Perry for awhile . . . and if they made an investment in me as an authentic American Hero, they might not check at all. "I went into Dallas on Tuesday of this week to visit the apartment house on West Neely. Mostly on a whim. I wanted to see if looking at it would bring back some more of my memories."

I had indeed gone to West Neely, but to get the gun under the porch.

"Afterward, I decided to get my lunch at Woolworth's, just like in the old days. And who should I see at the counter but Lee, having a tuna on rye. I sat down and asked him how it was going, and that was when he told me the FBI was harassing him and his wife. He said, 'I'm going to teach those bastards not to fuck with me, George. If you're watching TV on Friday afternoon, maybe you'll see something.'"

"Holy cow," Fritz said. "Did you connect that with the president's visit?"

"Not at first. I never followed Kennedy's movements all that closely; I'm a Republican." Two lies for the price of one. "Besides, Lee went right on to his favorite subject."

Hosty: "Cuba."

"Right. Cuba and viva Fidel. He didn't even ask why I was

limping. He was totally wrapped up in his own stuff, you know? But that was Lee. I bought him a custard pudding—boy, that's good at Woolworth's, and only a quarter—and asked him where he was working. He told me the Book Depository on Elm Street. Said it with a big smile, as if unloading trucks and shifting boxes around was the world's biggest deal."

I let most of his blather roll off my back, I went on, because my leg was hurting and I was getting one of my headaches. I drove home to Eden Fallows and took a nap. But when I woke up, the German guy's how-did-you-miss crack came back to me. I put on the TV, and they were talking about the president's visit. That, I said, was when I started to worry. I hunted through the pile of newspapers in the living room, found the motorcade route, and saw it went right by the Book Depository.

"I stewed about it all day Wednesday." They were leaning forward over the table now, hanging on every word. Hosty was making notes without looking down at his pad. I wondered if he'd be able to read them later. "I'd say to myself, *Maybe he really means it.* Then I'd say, *Nah, Lee's all hat and no cattle.* Back and forth like that. Yesterday morning I called Sadie, told her the whole story, and asked her what she thought. She phoned Deke—Deke Simmons, the man I called her surrogate father—then called me back. She said I should tell the police."

Fritz said, "I don't mean to add to your pain, son, but if you'd done that, your ladyfriend would still be alive."

"Wait. You haven't heard the whole story." Neither had I, of course; I was making up sizable chunks of it as I went. "I told her and Deke no cops, because if Lee was innocent, he'd really be screwed. You have to understand that the guy was barely holding on by the skin of his teeth. Mercedes Street was a dump and West Neely was only a little better, but that was okay for me—I'm a single man, and I had my book to work on. Plus a little money in the bank. Lee, though . . . he had a beautiful wife and two daughters, the second one just newborn, and he could hardly keep a roof over their heads. He wasn't a bad guy—"

At this I felt an urge to check my nose and make sure it wasn't growing.

"—but he was a world-class fuckup, pardon my French. His crazy ideas made it hard for him to hold a job. He said when he got one, the FBI would go in and queer things for him. He said it happened with his printing job."

"That's bullshit," Hosty said. "The boy blamed everyone else for problems he made himself. We agree on some things, though, Amberson. He was a world-class fuckup, and I felt sorry for his wife and kids. Sorry as hell."

"Yeah? Good for you. Anyway, he had a job and I didn't want to lose it for him if he was just running his mouth . . . which was a thing he specialized in. I told Sadie I was going over to the Book Depository tomorrow—today, now—just to check up on him. She said she'd come with me. I said no, if Lee really was off his rocker and meant to do something, she could be in danger."

"Did he *seem* off his rocker when you had lunch with him?" Fritz asked.

"No, cool as a cucumber, but he always was." I leaned toward him. "I want you to listen to this part very closely, Detective Fritz. I knew she meant to go with me no matter what I told her. I could hear it in her voice. So I got the hell out. I did that to protect her. Just in case."

And this is an in-case if there ever was one, the Sadie in my head whispered. She would live there until I saw her again in the flesh. I swore I would, no matter what.

"I thought I'd spend the night in a hotel, but the hotels were full. Then I thought of Mercedes Street. I'd turned in the key to 2706, where I lived, but I still had a key to 2703 across the street, where Lee lived. He gave it to me so I could go in and water his plants."

Hosty: "He had *plants*?"

My attention was still fixed on Will Fritz. "Sadie got alarmed when she found me gone from Eden Fallows. Deke did, too. So he did call the police. Not just once but several times. Each time, the cop who took his call told him to stop bullshitting and hung up. I don't know if anyone bothered to make a record of those calls, but Deke will tell you, and he has no reason to lie."

Now Fritz was the one turning red. "If you knew how many death threats we had . . ."

"I'm sure. And only so many men. Just don't tell me that if we'd called the police, Sadie would still be alive. Don't tell me that, okay?"

He said nothing.

"How did she find you?" Hosty asked.

That was something I didn't have to lie about, and I didn't. Next, though, they'd ask about the trip from Mercedes Street in Fort Worth to the Book Depository in Dallas. That was the part of my story most fraught with peril. I wasn't worried about the Studebaker cowboy; Sadie had cut him, but only after he tried to steal her purse. The car had been on its last legs, and I had a feeling the cowboy might not even come forward to report it stolen. Of course we had stolen another one, but given the urgency of our errand, the police would surely not file charges in the matter. The press would crucify them if they tried. What I was worried about was the red Chevrolet, the one with tailfins like a woman's eyebrows. A trunk with a couple of suitcases in it could be explained away; we'd had dirty weekends at the Candlewood Bungalows before. But if they got a look at Al Templeton's notebook . . . I didn't even want to think about that.

There was a perfunctory knock on the door of the interview room, and one of the cops who had brought me to the police station poked his head in. Behind the wheel of the cruiser, and while he and his buddy had been going through my personal belongings, he had looked stone-faced and dangerous, a bluesuit right out of a crime movie. Now, unsure of himself and bug-eyed with excitement, I saw he was no more than twenty-three, and still coping with the last of his adolescent acne. Behind him I could see a lot of people—some in uniform, some not—craning for a look at me. Fritz and Hosty turned to the uninvited newcomer with impatience.

"Sirs, I'm sorry to interrupt, but Mr. Amberson has a phone call."

The flush returned to Hosty's jowls full force. "Son, we're doing an interrogation here. I don't care if it's the President of the United States calling."

The cop swallowed. His Adam's apple went up and down like a monkey on a stick. "Uh, sirs . . . it *is* the President of the United States."

It seemed they cared, after all.

7

They took me down the hall to Chief Curry's office. Fritz had me under one arm and Hosty had the other. With them supporting sixty or seventy pounds of my weight between them, I hardly limped at all. There were reporters, TV cameras, and huge lights that must have raised the temperature to a hundred degrees. These people—one step above paparazzi—had no place in a police station in the wake of an assassination attempt, but I wasn't surprised. Along another timeline, they had crowded in after Oswald's arrest and no one had kicked them out. As far as I knew, no one had even suggested it.

Hosty and Fritz bulled their way through the scrum, stone-faced. Questions were hurled at them and at me. Hosty shouted: "Mr. Amberson will have a statement after he has been fully debriefed by the authorities!"

"When?" someone shouted.

"Tomorrow, the day after, maybe next week!"

There were groans. They made Hosty smile.

"Maybe next *month.* Right now he's got President Kennedy waiting on the line, so *y'all fall back*!"

They fell back, chattering like magpies.

The only cooling device in Chief Curry's office was a fan on a bookshelf, but the moving air felt blessed after the interrogation room and the media microwave in the hall. A big black telephone handset lay on the blotter. Beside it was a file with LEE H. OSWALD printed on the tab. It was thin.

I picked up the phone. "Hello?"

The nasal New England voice that responded sent a chill up my back. This was a man who would have now been lying on a morgue slab, if not for Sadie and me. "Mister Amberson? Jack Kennedy here. I . . . ah . . . understand that my wife and I owe you . . . ah . . . our lives. I also understand that you lost someone very dear to you." *Dear* came out *deah,* the way I'd grown up hearing it.

"Her name was Sadie Dunhill, Mr. President. Oswald shot her."

"I'm so sorry for your . . . ah . . . loss, Mr. Amberson. May I call you . . . ah . . . George?"

"If you like." Thinking: *I'm not having this conversation. It's a dream.*

"Her country will give her a great outpouring of thanks . . . and you a great outpouring of condolence, I'm sure. Let me . . . ah . . . be the first to offer both."

"Thank you, Mr. President." My throat was closing and I could hardly speak above a whisper. I saw her eyes, so bright as she lay dying in my arms. *Jake, how we danced.* Do presidents care about things like that? Do they even know about them? Maybe the best ones do. Maybe it's why they serve.

"There's . . . ah . . . someone else who wants to thank you, George. My wife's not here right now, but she . . . ah . . . plans to call you tonight."

"Mr. President, I'm not sure where I'll be tonight."

"She'll find you. She's very . . . ah . . . determined when she wants to thank someone. Now tell me, George, how are *you*?"

I told him I was all right, which I was not. He promised to see me at the White House very shortly, and I thanked him, but I didn't think any White House visit was going to happen. All during that dreamlike conversation while the fan blew on my sweaty face and the pebbled glass upper panel of Chief Curry's door glowed with the supernatural light of the TV lights outside, two words beat in my brain.

I'm safe. I'm safe. I'm safe.

The President of the United States had called from Austin to thank me for saving his life, and I was safe. I could do what I needed to do.

8

Five minutes after concluding my surreal conversation with John Fitzgerald Kennedy, Hosty and Fritz were hustling me down the back stairs and into the garage where Oswald would have been shot by Jack Ruby. Then it had been crowded in anticipation of the assassin's transfer to the county jail. Now it was so empty our footsteps echoed. My minders drove me to the Adolphus Hotel, and I felt no surprise when I found myself in the same room I'd occupied when I first came to Dallas. Everything that goes around comes around, they say, and although I've never been able to figure out who the mysteriously wise sages known as "they" might be, they're certainly right when it comes to time-travel.

Fritz told me the cops posted in the corridor and below, in the lobby, were strictly for my own protection, and to keep the press away. (Uh-huh.) Then he shook my hand. Agent Hosty also shook my hand, and when he did, I felt a folded square of paper pass from his palm to mine. "Get some rest," he said. "You've earned it."

When they were gone, I unfolded the tiny square. It was a page from his notebook. He had written three sentences, probably while I was on the phone with Jack Kennedy.

Your phone is tapped. I will see you at 9 P.M. Burn this & flush the ashes.

I burned the note as Sadie had burned mine, then picked up the phone and unscrewed the mouthpiece. Inside, clinging to the wires, was a small blue cylinder no bigger than a double-A battery. I was amused to see that the writing on it was Japanese—it made me think of my old pal Silent Mike.

I jiggered it loose, put it in my pocket, screwed the mouthpiece back on, and dialed 0. There was a very long pause at the operator's end after I said my name. I was about to hang up and try again when she started crying and babbling her thanks for saving the president. If she could do anything, she said, if anyone in the *hotel* could do anything, all I had to do was call, her name was Marie, she would do *anything* to thank me.

"You could start by putting through a call to Jodie," I said, and gave her Deke's number.

"Of course, Mr. Amberson. God bless you, sir. I'm connecting your call."

The phone burred twice, then Deke answered. His voice was heavy and laryngeal, as if his bad cold had gotten worse. "If this is another goddam reporter—"

"It's not, Deke. It's me. George." I paused. "Jake."

"Oh, Jake," he said mournfully, and then *he* started to cry. I waited, holding the phone so tightly it hurt my hand. My temples throbbed. The day was dying, but the light coming in through the windows was still too bright. In the distance, I heard a rumble of thunder. Finally he said, "Are you all right?"

"Yes. But Sadie—"

"I know. It's on the news. I heard while I was on my way to Fort Worth."

So the woman with the baby carriage and the tow truck driver from the Esso station had done as I'd hoped they would. Thank God for that. Not that it seemed very important as I sat listening to this heartbroken old man try to control his tears.

"Deke . . . do you blame me? I'd understand if you do."

"No," he said at last. "Ellie doesn't, either. When Sadie made up her mind to a thing, she carried through. And if you were on Mercedes Street in Fort Worth, I was the one who told her how to find you."

"I was there."

"Did the son of a bitch shoot her? They say on the newscasts that he did."

"Yes. He meant to shoot me, but my bad leg . . . I tripped over a box or something and fell down. She was right behind me."

"Christ." His voice strengthened a bit. "But she died doing the right thing. That's what I'm going to hold onto. It's what you have to hold onto, as well."

"Without her, I never would have gotten there. If you could have seen her . . . how determined she was . . . how brave . . ."

"Christ," he repeated. It came out in a sigh. He sounded very, very old. "It was all true. Everything you said. And everything *she* said about you. You really are from the future, aren't you?"

How glad I was that the bug was in my pocket. I doubted if they'd had time to plant listening devices in the room itself, but I still cupped my hand to the mouthpiece and lowered my voice. "Not a word about any of that to the police or the reporters."

"Good God, no!" He sounded indignant at the very idea. "You'd never breathe free air again!"

"Did you go ahead and get our luggage out of the Chevy's trunk? Even after—"

"You bet. I knew it was important, because as soon as I heard, I knew you'd be under suspicion."

"I think I'll be all right," I said, "but you need to open my brief-case and . . . do you have an incinerator?"

"Yes, behind the garage."

"There's a blue notebook in the briefcase. Put it in the incinerator and burn it. Will you do that for me?" *And for Sadie. We're both depending on you.*

"Yes. I will. Jake, I'm so sorry for your loss."

"And I'm sorry for yours. Yours and Miz Ellie's."

"It's not a fair trade!" he burst out. "I don't care if he *is* the president, it's not a fair trade!"

"No," I said. "It's not. But Deke . . . it wasn't just about the president. It's about all the bad stuff that would have happened if he had died."

"I guess I have to take your word for that. But it's hard."

"I know."

Would they have a memorial assembly for Sadie at the high school, as they had for Miz Mimi? Of course they would. The networks would send camera crews, and there wouldn't be a dry eye in America. But when the show was over, Sadie would still be dead.

Unless I changed it. It would mean going through everything again, but for Sadie I'd do that. Even if she took one look at me at the party where I'd met her and decided I was too old for her (although I would do my best to change her mind about that). There was even an upside: now that I knew Lee really had been the lone gunman, I wouldn't have to wait so long to dispatch his sorry ass.

"Jake? Are you still there?"

"Yes. And remember to call me George when you talk about me, okay?"

"No fear there. I may be old, but my brains still work pretty well. Am I going to see you again?"

Not if Agent Hosty tells me what I want to hear, I thought.

"If you don't, it's because things are working out for the best."

"All right. Jake . . . George . . . did she . . . did she say anything at the end?"

I wasn't going to tell him what her final words had been, that was private, but I could give him something. He would pass it on to Ellie, and Ellie would pass it on to all Sadie's friends in Jodie. She'd had many.

"She asked if the president was safe. When I told her he was, she closed her eyes and slipped away."

Deke began to cry again. My face was throbbing. Tears would have been a relief, but my eyes were as dry as stones.

"Goodbye," I said. "Goodbye, old friend."

I hung up gently and sat still for quite some time, watching the light of a Dallas sunset fall red through the window. *Red sky at night, sailor's delight,* the old saying has it . . . but I heard another rumble of thunder. Five minutes later, when I had myself under control, I picked up my debugged phone and once again dialed 0. I told Marie I was going to lie down, and asked for an eight-o'clock wake-up call. I also asked her to put a do-not-disturb on the phone until then.

"Oh, that's already taken care of," she said excitedly. "No incoming calls to your room, orders from the police chief." Her voice dropped a register. "Was he crazy, Mr. Amberson? I mean, he *must* have been, but did he look it?"

I remembered the cheated eyes and daemonic snarl. "Oh, yes," I said. "He certainly did. Eight o'clock, Marie. Nothing until then."

I hung up before she could say anything else. Then I took off my shoes (getting free of the left one was a slow and painful process), lay down on the bed, and put my arm over my eyes. I saw Sadie dancing the Madison. I saw Sadie telling me to come in, kind sir, did I like poundcake? I saw her in my arms, her bright dying eyes turned up to my face.

I thought about the rabbit-hole, and how every time you used it there was a complete reset.

At last I slept.

9

Hosty's knock came promptly at nine. I opened up and he ambled in. He carried a briefcase in one hand (but not *my* briefcase, so that was still all right). In the other was a bottle of champagne, the good stuff, Moët et Chandon, with a red, white, and blue bow tied around the neck. He looked very tired.

"Amberson," he said.

"Hosty," I responded.

He closed the door, then pointed to the phone. I took the bug from my pocket and displayed it. He nodded.

"There are no others?" I asked.

"No. That bug is DPD's, and this is now our case. Orders straight from Hoover. If anyone asks about the phone bug, you found it yourself."

"Okay."

He held up the champagne. "Compliments of the management. They insisted I bring it up. Would you care to toast the President of the United States?"

Considering that my beautiful Sadie now lay on a slab in the county morgue, I had no interest in toasting anything. I had succeeded, and success tasted like ashes in my mouth.

"No."

"Me, either, but I'm glad as hell he's alive. Want to know a secret?"

"Sure."

"I voted for him. I may be the only agent in the whole Bureau who did."

I said nothing.

Hosty seated himself in one of the room's two armchairs and gave a long sigh of relief. He set his briefcase between his feet, then turned the bottle so he could read the label. "Nineteen fifty-eight. Wine fanciers would probably know if that was a good year, but I'm more of a beer man, myself."

"So am I."

"Then you might enjoy the Lone Star they're holding for you downstairs. There's a case of the stuff, and a framed letter promising you a case a month for the rest of your life. More champagne, too. I saw at least a dozen bottles. Everyone from the Dallas Chamber of Commerce to the City Board of Tourism sent them. You have a Zenith color television still in the carton, a solid gold signet ring with a picture of the president in it from Calloway's Fine Jewelry, a certificate for three new suits from Dallas Menswear, and all kinds of other stuff, including a key to the city. The management has set aside a room on the first floor for your swag, and I'm guessing that by dawn tomorrow they'll have to set aside another. And the food! People are bringing cakes, pies, casseroles, roasts of beef, barbecue chicken, and enough Mexican to give you the runs for five years. We're turning them away, and they hate to go, let me tell you. There are women out there in front of the hotel that . . . well, let's just say Jack Kennedy himself would be envious, and he's a legendary cocksman. If you knew what the director has in his files on that man's sex life, you wouldn't believe it."

"My capacity for belief might surprise you."

"Dallas loves you, Amberson. Hell, the whole country loves you." He laughed. The laugh turned into a cough. When it passed, he lit a cigarette. Then he looked at his watch. "As of nine-oh-seven Central Standard Time on the evening of November twenty-second, 1963, you are America's fair-haired boy."

"What about you, Hosty? Do you love me? Does Director Hoover?"

He set his cigarette aside in the ashtray after a single drag, then leaned forward and pinned me with his eyes. They were deep-set in folds of flesh, and they were tired, but they were nonetheless very bright and aware.

"Look at me, Amberson. Dead in the eyes. Then tell me if you were or weren't in on it with Oswald. And make it the truth, because I'll know a lie."

Given his egregious mishandling of Oswald, I didn't believe that, but I believed that *he* believed it. So I locked onto his gaze and said: "I was not."

For a moment he said nothing. Then he sighed, settled back, and picked up his cigarette. "No. You weren't." He jetted smoke from his nostrils. "Who do you work for, then? The CIA? The Russians, maybe? I don't see it myself, but the director believes the Russians would gladly burn a deep-cover asset in order to stop an assassination that would spark an international incident. Maybe even World War III. Especially when folks find out about Oswald's time in Russia." He said it *Roosha,* the way the televangelist Hargis did on his broadcasts. Maybe it was Hosty's idea of a jest.

I said, "I work for no one. I'm just a guy, Hosty."

He pointed his cigarette at me. "Hold that thought." He unstrapped his briefcase and took out a file even thinner than the one on Oswald I'd spied in Curry's office. This file would be mine, and it would thicken . . . but not as quickly as it would have done in the computer-driven twenty-first century.

"Before Dallas, you were in Florida. The town of Sunset Point."

"Yes."

"You substitute-taught in the Sarasota school system."

"Correct."

"Before that, we believe you spent some time in . . . was it Derren? Derren, Maine?"

"Derry."

"Where you did exactly what?"

"Where I started my book."

"Uh-huh, and before that?"

"Here and there, all around the square."

"How much do you know about my dealings with Oswald, Amberson?"

I kept silent.

"Don't play it so cozy. It's just us girls."

"Enough to cause trouble for you and your director."

"Unless?"

"Let me put it this way. The amount of trouble I cause you will be directly proportional to the amount of trouble you cause me."

"Would it be fair to say that when it came to making trouble, you'd make up what you didn't absolutely know . . . and to our detriment?"

I said nothing.

He said, as if speaking to himself, "It doesn't surprise me that you were writing a book. You should have carried on with it, Amberson. It probably would have been a bestseller. Because you're bloody good at making things up, I'll give you that. You were pretty plausible this afternoon. And you know things you have no business knowing, which is what makes us believe you're far from a private citizen. Come on, who wound you up? Was it Angleton at the Firm? It was, wasn't it? Sly rose-growing bastard that he is."

"I'm just me," I said, "and I probably don't know as much as you think. But yes, I know enough to make the Bureau look bad. How Lee told me he came right out and told *you* that he was going to shoot Kennedy, for instance."

Hosty stubbed out his cigarette hard enough to send up a fountain of sparks. Some landed on the back of his hand, but he didn't seem to feel them. "That's a fucking lie!"

"I know," I said. "And I'll tell it with a straight face. If you force me to. Has the idea of getting rid of me come up yet, Hosty?"

"Spare me the comic-book stuff. We don't kill people."

"Tell it to the Diem brothers over in Vietnam."

He was looking at me the way a man might look at a seemingly inoffensive mouse that had suddenly bitten. And with big teeth. "How do you know America had *anything* to do with the Diem brothers? According to what I read in the papers, our hands are clean."

"Let's not get off the subject. The thing is, right now I'm too popular to kill. Or am I wrong?"

"No one wants to kill you, Amberson. And no one wants to poke holes in your story." He barked an unamused laugh. "If we started doing that, the whole thing would unravel. That's how thin it is."

"'Romance at short notice was her specialty,'" I said.

"Huh?"

"H. H. Munro. Also known as Saki. The story is called 'The Open Window.' Look it up. When it comes to the art of creating bullshit on the spur of the moment, it's very instructive."

He scanned me, his shrewd little eyes worried. "I don't understand you at all. That concerns me." In the west, out toward Midland where the oil wells thump without surcease and the gas flares dim the stars, more thunder rumbled.

"What do you want from me?" I asked.

"I think that when we trace you back a little farther from Derren or Derry or whatever it is, we're going to find . . . nothing. As if you stepped right out of thin air."

This was so close to the truth it nearly took my breath away.

"What we want is for you to go back to the nowhere you came from. The scandal-press will gin up the usual nasty speculations and conspiracy theories, but we can guarantee you that you'll come out of this looking pretty good. If you even care about such things, that is. Marina Oswald will support your story right down the line."

"You've already spoken to her, I take it."

"You take it right. She knows she'll be deported if she doesn't play ball. The gentlemen of the press haven't had a very good look at you; the photos that show up in tomorrow's papers are going to be little more than blurs."

I knew he was right. I had been exposed to the cameras only on that one quick walk down the hall to Chief Curry's office, and Fritz and Hosty, both big men, had had me under the arms, blocking the best photo sightlines. Also, I'd had my head down because the lights were so bright. There were plenty of pictures of me in Jodie—even a portrait shot in the yearbook from the year I'd taught there full-time—but in this era before JPEGs or even faxes, it would be Tuesday or Wednesday of next week before they could be found and published.

"Here's a story for you," Hosty said. "You like stories, don't you? Things like this 'Open Window'?"

"I'm an English teacher. I love stories."

"This fellow, George Amberson, is so stunned with grief over the loss of his girlfriend—"

"Fiancée."

"Fiancée, right, even better. He's so grief-stricken that he ditches the whole works and simply disappears. Wants nothing to do with publicity, free champagne, medals from the president, or ticker-tape parades. He just wants to get away and mourn his loss in privacy. That's the kind of story Americans like. They see it on TV all the time. Instead of 'The Open Window,' it's called 'The Modest Hero.' And there's this FBI agent who's willing to back up every word, and even read a statement that you left behind. How does that sound?"

It sounded like manna from heaven, but I held onto my poker face. "You must be awfully sure I can disappear."

"We are."

"And you really mean it when you tell me I won't be disappearing to the bottom of the Trinity River, as per the director's orders?"

"Nothing like that." He smiled. It was meant to be reassuring, but it made me think of an old line from my teenage years: *Don't worry, you won't get pregnant, I had the mumps when I was fourteen.*

"Because I might have left a little insurance, Agent Hosty."

One eyelid twitched. It was the only sign the idea distressed him. "We think you can disappear because we believe . . . let's just say you could call on assistance, once you were clear of Dallas."

"No press conference?"

"That's the last thing we want."

He opened his briefcase again. From it he took a yellow legal pad. He passed it over to me, along with a pen from his breast pocket. "Write me a letter, Amberson. It'll be Fritz and me who'll find it tomorrow morning when we come to pick you up, but you can head it 'To Whom It May Concern.' Make it good. Make it *genius*. You can do that, can't you?"

"Sure," I said. "Romance at short notice is my specialty."

He grinned without humor and picked up the champagne bottle. "Maybe I'll try a little of this while you're romancing. None for you, after all. You're going to have a busy night. Miles to go before you sleep, and all that."

10

I wrote carefully, but it didn't take long. In a case like this (not that there had ever in the whole history of the world been a case exactly like this), I thought shorter was better. I kept Hosty's Modest Hero idea foremost in my mind. I was very glad that I'd had a chance to sleep for a few hours. Such rest as I'd managed had been shot through with baleful dreams, but my head was relatively clear.

By the time I finished, Hosty was on his third glass of bubbly.

He had taken a number of items from his briefcase and placed them on the coffee table. I handed him the pad and he began reading over what I'd written. Outside the thunder rumbled again, and lightning briefly lit the night sky, but I thought the storm was still distant.

While he read, I examined the stuff on the coffee table. There was my Timex, the one item that for some reason hadn't been returned with the rest of my personal effects when we left the cop-shop. There was a pair of horn-rimmed spectacles. I picked them up and tried them on. The lenses were plain glass. There was a key with a hollow barrel instead of notches. An envelope containing what looked like about a thousand bucks in used twenties and fifties. A hairnet. And a white uniform in two pieces—pants and tunic. The cotton cloth looked as thin as Hosty had claimed my story to be.

"This letter's good," Hosty said, putting the pad down. "You come across kind of sad, like Richard Kimble on *The Fugitive.* You watch that one?"

I'd seen the movie version with Tommy Lee Jones, but this hardly seemed the time to bring it up. "No."

"You'll be a fugitive, all right, but only from the press and an American public that's going to want to know all about you, from what kind of juice you drink in the morning to the waist size of your skivvies. You're a human interest story, Amberson, but you're not police business. You didn't shoot your girlfriend; you didn't even shoot Oswald."

"I tried. If I hadn't missed, she'd still be alive."

"I wouldn't blame yourself too much on that score. That's a big room up there, and a .38 doesn't have much accuracy from a distance."

True. You had to get within fifteen yards. So I had been told, and more than once. But I didn't say so. I thought my brief acquaintanship with Special Agent James Hosty was almost over. Basically I couldn't wait.

"You're clean. All you need to do is to get to someplace where your people can pick you up and fly you away to spook neverland. Can you manage that?"

Neverland in my case was a rabbit-hole that would transport me forty-eight years into the future. Assuming the rabbit-hole was still there.

"I believe I'll be okay."

"You better be, because if you try to hurt us, it'll come back on you double. Mr. Hoover . . . let's just say that the director is not a forgiving man."

"Tell me how I'm getting out of the hotel."

"You'll put on those kitchen whites, the glasses, and the hairnet. The key runs the service elevator. It'll take you to B-1. You walk straight through the kitchen and out the back door. With me so far?"

"Yes."

"There'll be a Bureau car waiting for you. Get in the backseat. You don't talk to the driver. This ain't no limousine service. Off you go to the bus station. Your driver can offer you one of three tickets: Tampa at eleven-forty, Little Rock at eleven-fifty, or Albuquerque at twenty past midnight. I don't want to know which one. All *you* need to know is that's where our association ends. Your responsibility to stay out of sight becomes all your own. And whoever it is you work for, of course."

"Of course."

The telephone rang. "If it's some smartass reporter who found a way to ring through, get rid of him," Hosty said. "And if you say a word about me being here, I'll cut your throat."

I thought he was joking about that, but wasn't entirely sure. I picked up the phone. "I don't know who this is, but I'm pretty tired right now, so—"

The breathy voice on the other end said she wouldn't keep me long. To Hosty I mouthed *Jackie Kennedy.* He nodded and poured a little more of my champagne. I turned away, as if by presenting Hosty with my back I could keep him from overhearing the conversation.

"Mrs. Kennedy, you really didn't have to call," I said, "but I'm honored to hear from you, just the same."

"I wanted to thank you for what you did," she said. "I know that my husband has already thanked you on our behalf, but . . . Mr. Amberson . . ." The first lady began to cry. "I wanted to thank you on behalf of our children, who were able to say goodnight to their mother and dad on the phone tonight."

Caroline and John-John. They'd never crossed my mind until that moment.

"Mrs. Kennedy, you're more than welcome."

"I understand the young woman who died was to become your wife."

"That's right."

"You must be heartbroken. Please accept my condolences—they aren't enough, I know that, but they are all I have to offer."

"Thank you."

"If I could change it . . . if in any way I could turn back the clock . . ."

No, I thought. *That's my job, Miz Jackie.*

"I understand. Thank you."

We talked a little longer. This call was much more difficult than the one with Kennedy at the police station. Partly because that one had felt like a dream and this one didn't, but mostly I think it was the residual fear I heard in Jacqueline Kennedy's voice. She truly seemed to understand what a narrow escape they'd had. I'd gotten no sense of that from the man himself. He seemed to believe he was providentially lucky, blessed, maybe even immortal. Toward the end of the conversation I remember asking her to make sure her husband quit riding in open cars for the duration of his presidency.

She said I could count on that, then thanked me one more time. I told her she was welcome one more time, then hung up the phone. When I turned around, I saw I had the room to myself. At some point while I'd been talking to Jacqueline Kennedy, Hosty had left. All that remained of him were two butts in the ashtray, a half-finished glass of champagne, and another scribbled note, lying beside the yellow legal pad with my to-whom-it-may-concern letter on it.

Get rid of the bug before you go into the bus station, it read. And below that: *Good luck, Amberson. Very sorry for your loss. H.*

Maybe he was, but sorry is cheap, isn't it? Sorry is so cheap.

11

I put on my kitchen potboy disguise and rode down to B-1 in an elevator that smelled like chicken soup, barbecue sauce, and Jack Daniel's. When the doors opened, I walked briskly through the steamy, fragrant kitchen. I don't think anyone so much as looked at me.

I came out in an alley where a couple of winos were picking through a trash bin. They didn't look at me, either, although they glanced up when sheet lightning momentarily brightened the sky. A nondescript Ford sedan was idling at the mouth of the alley. I got into the backseat and off we went. The man behind the wheel said only one thing before pulling up to the Greyhound station: "Looks like rain."

He offered me the three tickets like a poor man's poker hand. I took the one for Little Rock. I had about an hour. I went into the gift shop and bought a cheap suitcase. If all went well, I'd eventually have something to put in it. I wouldn't need much; I had all sorts of clothes at my house in Sabattus, and although that particular domicile was almost fifty years in the future, I hoped to be there in less than a week. A paradox Einstein could love, and it never crossed my tired, grieving mind that—given the butterfly effect—it almost certainly would no longer be mine. If it was there at all.

I also bought a newspaper, an extra edition of the *Slimes Herald*. There was a single photo, maybe snapped by a professional, more likely by some lucky bystander. It showed Kennedy bent over the woman I'd been talking to not long ago, the woman who'd had no bloodstains on her pink suit when she'd finally taken it off this evening.

John F. Kennedy shields his wife with his body as the presidential limo speeds away from what was nearly a national catastrophe, the caption read. Above this was a headline in thirty-six-point type. There was room, because it was only one word:

SAVED!

I turned to page 2 and was confronted with another picture. This one was of Sadie, looking impossibly young and impossibly beautiful. She was smiling. *I have my whole life ahead of me,* the smile said.

Sitting in one of the slatted wooden chairs while late-night travelers surged around me and babies cried and servicemen with duffels laughed and businessmen got shines and the overhead speakers announced arrivals and departures, I carefully folded the newsprint around the borders of that picture so I could remove it from the page without tearing her face. When that much was accomplished, I looked at it for a long time, then folded it into my wallet. The rest of the paper I threw away. There was nothing in it I wanted to read.

Boarding for the bus to Little Rock was called at eleven-twenty, and I joined the crowd clustering around the proper door. Other than wearing the fake glasses, I made no attempt to hide my face, but no one looked at me with any particular interest; I was just one more cell in the bloodstream of Transit America, no more important than any other.

I changed your lives today, I thought as I watched those present at the turning of the day, but there was no triumph or wonder in the idea; it seemed to have no emotional charge at all, either positive or negative.

I got on the bus and sat near the back. There were a lot of guys in uniform ahead of me, probably bound for Little Rock Air Force

Base. If not for what we'd done today, some of them would have died in Vietnam. Others would have come home maimed. And now? Who knew?

The bus pulled out. When we left Dallas, the thunder was louder and the lightning brighter, but there was still no rain. By the time we reached Sulphur Springs, the threatening storm was behind us and the stars were out in their tens of thousands, brilliant as ice chips and twice as cold. I looked at them for awhile, then leaned back, shut my eyes, and listened to the Big Dog's tires eating up Interstate 30.

Sadie, the tires sang. *Sadie, Sadie, Sadie.*

At last, sometime after two in the morning, I slept.

12

In Little Rock I bought a ticket on the noon bus to Pittsburgh, with a single stop in Indianapolis. I had breakfast in the depot diner, near an old fellow who ate with a portable radio in front of him on the table. It was large and covered with shiny dials. The major story was still the attempted assassination, of course . . . and Sadie. Sadie was big, big news. She was to be given a state funeral, followed by interment at Arlington National Cemetery. There was speculation that JFK himself would deliver the eulogy. In related developments, Miss Dunhill's fiancé, George Amberson, also of Jodie, Texas, had been scheduled to appear before the press at 10:00 A.M., but that had been pushed back to late afternoon— no reason given. Hosty was providing me all the room to run that he possibly could. Good for me. Him, too, of course. And his precious director.

"The president and his heroic saviors aren't the only news coming out of Texas this morning," the old duffer's radio said, and I paused with a cup of black coffee suspended halfway between the saucer and my lips. There was a sour tingle in my mouth that I'd come to recognize. A psychologist might have termed it *presque vu*—the sense people sometimes get that something amazing is about to happen—but my name for it was much more humble: a harmony.

"At the height of a thunderstorm shortly after one A.M., a freak tornado touched down in Fort Worth, destroying a Montgomery Ward warehouse and a dozen homes. Two people are known dead, and four are missing."

That two of the houses were 2703 and 2706 Mercedes Street, I had no doubt; an angry wind had erased them like a bad equation.

CHAPTER 30

1

I stepped off my final Greyhound at the Minot Avenue station in Auburn, Maine, at a little past noon on the twenty-sixth of November. After more than eighty hours of almost nonstop riding, relieved only by short intervals of sleep, I felt like a figment of my own imagination. It was cold. God was clearing His throat and spitting casual snow from a dirty gray sky. I had bought some jeans and a couple of blue chambray workshirts to replace the kitchen-whites, but such clothes weren't nearly enough. I had forgotten the Maine weather during my time in Texas, but my body remembered in a hurry and started to shiver. I made Louie's for Men my first stop, where I found a sheepskin-lined coat in my size and took it to the clerk.

He put down his copy of the Lewiston *Sun* to wait on me, and I saw my picture—yes, the one from the DCHS yearbook—on the front page. WHERE IS GEORGE AMBERSON? the headline demanded. The clerk rang up the sale and scribbled me a receipt. I tapped my picture. "What in the world do you suppose is up with that guy?"

The clerk looked at me and shrugged. "He doesn't want the publicity and I don't blame him. I love my wife a whole darn bunch, and if she died sudden, I wouldn't want people taking my picture for the papers or putting my weepy mug on TV. Would you?"

"No," I said, "I guess not."

"If I were that guy, I wouldn't come up for air until 1970. Let the ruckus die down. How about a nice cap to go with that coat? I got some flannel ones that just came in yesterday. The earflaps are good and thick."

So I bought a cap to go with my new coat. Then I limped the two blocks back to the bus station, swinging my suitcase at the end of my good arm. Part of me wanted to go to Lisbon Falls right that minute and make sure the rabbit-hole was still there. But if it was, I'd use it, I wouldn't be able to resist, and after five years in the Land of Ago, the rational part of me knew I wasn't ready for the full-on assault of what had become, in my mind, the Land of Ahead. I needed some rest first. Real rest, not dozing in a bus seat while little kids wailed and tipsy men laughed.

There were four or five taxis parked at the curb, in snow that was now swirling instead of just spitting. I got into the first one, relishing the warm breath from the heater. The cabbie turned around, a fat guy with a badge reading LICENSED LIVERY on his battered cap. He was a complete stranger to me, but I knew that when he turned on the radio, it would be tuned to WJAB out of Portland, and when he dragged his ciggies out of his breast pocket, they would be Lucky Strikes. What goes around comes around.

"Where to, chief?"

I told him to take me to the Tamarack Motor Court, out on 196.

"You got it."

He turned on the radio and got the Miracles, singing "Mickey's Monkey."

"These modern dances!" he grunted, grabbing his smokes. "They don't do nothing but teach the kids how to bump n wiggle."

"Dancing is life," I said.

2

It was a different desk clerk, but she gave me the same room. Of course she did. The rate was a little higher and the old TV had been replaced by a newer one, but the same sign was propped against the rabbit ears on top: *DO NOT USE "TINFOIL!"* The reception was still shitty. There was no news, only soap operas.

I turned it off. I put the DO NOT DISTURB sign on the door. I drew the curtains. Then I stripped and crawled into bed, where—aside from a dreamlike stumble to the bathroom to relieve my bladder—I slept for twelve hours. When I woke up, it was the middle of the night, the power was off, and a strong northwest wind was blowing outside. A brilliant crescent moon rode high in the sky. I got the extra blanket from the closet and slept for another five hours.

When I woke up, dawn lit the Tamarack Motor Court with the clear hues and shadows of a *National Geographic* photograph. There was frost on the cars pulled up in front of a scattering of units, and I could see my breath. I tried the phone, expecting nothing, but a young man in the office answered promptly, although he sounded as if he were still half-asleep. Sure, he said, the phones were fine and he'd be happy to call me a taxi—where did I want to go?

Lisbon Falls, I told him. Corner of Main Street and the Old Lewiston Road.

"The Fruit?" he asked.

I'd been away so long that for a moment it seemed like a total non sequitur. Then it clicked. "That's right. The Kennebec Fruit."

Going home, I told myself. *God help me, I'm going home.*

Only that was wrong—2011 wasn't home, and I would only be staying there a short time—assuming, that was, I could get there at all. Perhaps only minutes. Jodie was home now. Or would be, once Sadie arrived there. Sadie the virgin. Sadie with her long legs and long hair and her propensity to trip over anything that might be in the way . . . only at the critical moment, I was the one who had taken the fall.

Sadie, with her unmarked face.

She was home.

3

That morning's taxi driver was a solidly built woman in her fifties, bundled into an old black parka and wearing a Red Sox hat instead of one with a badge reading LICENSED LIVERY. As we turned left onto 196, in the direction of The Falls, she said: "D'ja hear the news? I bet you didn't—the power's off up this way, ennit?"

"What news is that?" I asked, although a dreadful certainty had already stolen into my bones: Kennedy was dead. I didn't know if it had been an accident, a heart attack, or an assassination after all, but he was dead. The past was obdurate and Kennedy was dead.

"Earthquake in Los Angeles." She pronounced it *Las Angle-ees.* "People been sayin for years that California was just gonna drop off into the ocean, and it seems like maybe they're gonna turn out to be right." She shook her head. "I ain't gonna say it's because of the loose way they live—those movie stars and all—but I'm a pretty good Baptist, and I ain't gonna say it's not."

We were passing the Lisbon Drive-In now. CLOSED FOR THE SEASON, the marquee read. SEE YOU WITH LOTS MORE IN '64!

"How bad was it?"

"They're saying seven thousand dead, but when you hear a number like that, you know it'll go higher. Most of the damn bridges fell down, the freeways are in pieces, and there's fires everywhere. Seems like the part of town where the Negroes live has pretty much burnt flat. Warts! Ain't that a hell of a name for a part of a town? I mean, even one where black folks live? Warts! Huh!"

I didn't reply. I was thinking of Rags, the puppy we'd had when

I was nine, and still living in Wisconsin. I was allowed to play with him in the backyard on school mornings until the bus came. I was teaching him to sit, fetch, roll over, stuff like that, and he was learning—smart puppy! I loved him a lot.

When the bus came, I was supposed to close the backyard gate before I ran to get on board. Rags always lay down on the kitchen stoop. My mother would call him in and feed him breakfast after she got back from taking my dad to the local train station. I always remembered to close the gate—or at least, I don't remember ever *forgetting* to do it—but one day when I came home from school, my mother told me Rags was dead. He'd been in the street and a delivery truck had run him down. She never reproached me with her mouth, not once, but she reproached me with her eyes. Because *she* had loved Rags, too.

"I closed him in like always," I said through my tears, and—as I say—I believe that I did. Maybe because I always *had.* That evening my dad and I buried him in the backyard. *Probably not legal,* Dad said, *but I won't tell if you won't.*

I lay awake for a long, long time that night, haunted by what I couldn't remember and terrified of what I might have done. Not to mention guilty. That guilt lingered a long time, a year or more. If I could have remembered for sure, one way or the other, I'm positive it would have left me more quickly. But I couldn't. Had I shut the gate, or hadn't I? Again and again I cast my mind to my puppy's final morning and could remember nothing clearly except heaving his rawhide strip and yelling, "Fetch, Rags, fetch!"

It was like that on my taxi ride to The Falls. First I tried to tell myself that there always *had* been an earthquake in late November of 1963. It was just one of those factoids—like the attempted assassination of Edwin Walker—that I had missed. As I'd told Al Templeton I majored in English, not history.

It wouldn't wash. If an earthquake like that had happened in the America I'd lived in before going down the rabbit-hole, I would have known. There were far bigger disasters—the Indian Ocean tsunami of 2004 killed over two hundred thousand—but seven thousand was a big number for America, more than twice as many fatalities as had occurred on 9/11.

Next I asked myself how what I'd done in Dallas could possibly have caused what this sturdy woman claimed had happened in LA. The only answer I could come up with was the butterfly effect, but how could it kick into gear so *soon*? No way. Absolutely not. There was no conceivable chain of cause and effect between the two events.

And still a deep part of my mind whispered, *You did this. You caused Rags's death by either leaving the backyard gate open or not closing it firmly enough to latch . . . and you caused this. You and Al spouted a lot of noble talk about saving thousands of lives in Vietnam, but this is your first real contribution to the New History: seven thousand dead in LA.*

It simply couldn't be. Even if it was. . . .

There's no downside, Al had said. *If things turn to shit, you just take it all back. Easy as erasing a dirty word off a chalkb—*

"Mister?" my driver said. "We're here." She turned to look at me curiously. "We've been here for almost three minutes. Little early for shopping, though. Are you sure this is where you want to be?"

I only knew this was where I *had* to be. I paid what was on the meter, added a generous tip (it was the FBI's money, after all), wished her a nice day, and got out.

4

Lisbon Falls was as stinky as ever, but at least the power was on; the blinker at the intersection was flashing as it swung in the northwest wind. The Kennebec Fruit was dark, the front window still empty of the apples, oranges, and bananas that would be displayed there later on. The sign hanging in the door of the greenfront read WILL OPEN AT 10 A.M. A few cars moved on Main Street and a few pedestrians scuttled along with their collars turned up. Across the street, however, the Worumbo mill was fully operational. I could hear the *shat-HOOSH, shat-HOOSH* of the weaving flats even from where I was standing. Then I heard something else: someone was calling me, although not by either of my names.

"Jimla! Hey, Jimla!"

I turned toward the mill, thinking: *He's back. The Yellow Card Man is back from the dead, just like President Kennedy.*

Only it wasn't the Yellow Card Man any more than the taxi driver who'd picked me up at the bus station was the same one who'd taken me from Lisbon Falls to the Tamarack Motor Court in 1958. Except the two drivers were *almost* the same, because the past harmonizes, and the man across the street was similar to the one who'd asked me for a buck because it was double-money day at the greenfront. He was a lot younger than the Yellow Card Man, and his black overcoat was newer and cleaner . . . but it was *almost* the same coat.

"Jimla! Over here!" He beckoned. The wind flapped the hem of the overcoat; it made the sign to his left swing on its chain the way the blinker was swinging on its wire. I could still read it, though:

NO ADMITTANCE BEYOND THIS POINT UNTIL SEWER PIPE IS REPAIRED.

Five years, I thought, *and that pesky sewer pipe's still busted.*

"Jimla! Don't make me come over there and get you!"

He probably could; his suicidal predecessor had been able to make it all the way to the greenfront. But I felt sure that if I went limping down the Old Lewiston Road fast enough, this new version would be out of luck. He might be able to follow me to the Red & White Supermarket, where Al had bought his meat, but if I made it as far as Titus Chevron, or the Jolly White Elephant, I could turn around and thumb my nose at him. He was stuck near the rabbit-hole. If he hadn't been, I would have seen him in Dallas. I knew it as surely as I knew that gravity keeps folks from floating into outer space.

As if to confirm this, he called, "Jimla, *please!*" The desperation I saw in his face was like the wind: thin but somehow relentless.

I looked both ways for traffic, saw none, and crossed the street to where he stood. As I approached, I saw two other differences. Like his predecessor, he was wearing a fedora, but it was clean instead of filthy. And as with his predecessor, a colored card was poking up from the hatband like an old-fashioned reporter's press pass. Only this one wasn't yellow, or orange, or black.

It was green.

5

"Thank God," he said. He took one of my hands in both of his and squeezed it. The flesh of his palms was almost as cold as the air. I pulled back from him, but gently. I sensed no danger about him, only that thin and insistent desperation. Although that in itself might be dangerous; it might be as keen as the blade of the knife John Clayton had used on Sadie's face.

"Who are you?" I asked. "And why do you call me Jimla? Jim LaDue is a long way from here, mister."

"I don't know who Jim LaDue is," the Green Card Man said. "I've stayed away from your string as much as—"

He stopped. His face contorted. The sides of his hands rose to his temples and pressed there, as if to hold his brains in. But it was the card stuck in the band of his hat that captured most of my attention. The color wasn't entirely fixed. For a moment it swirled and swam, reminding me of the screensaver that takes over my computer after it's been idle for fifteen minutes or so. The green swirled into a pale canary yellow. Then, as he slowly lowered his hands, it returned to green. But maybe not as bright a green as when I'd first noticed it.

"I've stayed away from your string as much as possible," the man in the black overcoat said, "but it hasn't been *entirely* possible. Besides, there are so *many* strings now. Thanks to you and your friend the cook, there's so much *crap.*"

"I don't understand any of this," I said, but that wasn't quite true. I could at least figure out the card this man (and his wet-brain forerunner) carried. They were like the badges worn by people who worked in nuclear power plants. Only instead of measuring radiation, the cards monitored . . . what? Sanity? Green, your bag of marbles was full. Yellow, you'd started to lose them. Orange, call for the men in the white coats. And when your card turned black . . .

The Green Card Man was watching me carefully. From across the street he'd looked no older than thirty. Over here, he looked closer to forty-five. Only, when you got close enough to look into his eyes, he looked older than the ages and not right in the head.

"Are you some kind of guardian? Do you guard the rabbit-hole?"

He smiled . . . or tried to. "That's what your friend called it." From his pocket he took a pack of cigarettes. There was no label on them. That was something I'd never seen before, either here in the Land of Ago or in the Land of Ahead.

"Is this the only one?"

He produced a lighter, cupped it to keep the wind from blowing the flame out, then set fire to the end of his cigarette. The smell was sweet, more like marijuana than tobacco. But it wasn't marijuana. Although he never said, I believe it was something medicinal. Perhaps not so different from my Goody's Headache Powder.

"There are a few. Think of a glass of ginger ale that's been left out and forgotten."

"Okay . . ."

"After two or three days, almost all the carbonation is gone, but there are still a few bubbles left. What you call the rabbit-hole isn't a hole at all. It's a bubble. As far as guarding . . . no. Not really. It would be nice, but there's very little we could do that wouldn't make things worse. That's the trouble with traveling in time, Jimla."

"My name is Jake."

"Fine. What we do, Jake, is watch. Sometimes we warn. As Kyle tried to warn your friend the cook."

So the crazy guy had a name. A perfectly normal one. Kyle, for God's sake. It made things worse because it made them more real.

"He *never* tried to warn Al! All he ever did was ask for a buck to buy cheap wine with!"

The Green Card Man dragged on his cigarette and looked down at the cracked concrete, frowning as if something were written there. *Shat-HOOSH, shat-HOOSH* said the weaving flats. "He did at first," he said. "In his way. Your friend was too excited by the new world he'd found to pay attention. And by then Kyle was already tottering. It's a . . . how would you put it? An occupational hazard. What we do puts us under enormous mental strain. Do you know why?"

I shook my head.

"Think a minute. How many little explorations and shopping trips did your cook friend make even *before* he got the idea of going to Dallas to stop Oswald? Fifty? A hundred? Two hundred?"

I tried to remember how long Al's Diner had stood in the mill courtyard and couldn't. "Probably even more than that."

"And what did he tell you? Each trip was the first time?"

"Yes. A complete reset."

He laughed wearily. "Sure he did. People believe what they see. And still, he should have known better. *You* should have known better. Each trip creates its own string, and when you have enough strings, they always get snarled. Did it ever cross your friend's mind to wonder how he could buy the same meat over and over? Or why things he brought from 1958 never disappeared when he made the next trip?"

"I asked him about that. He didn't know, so he dismissed it."

He started to smile, but it turned into a wince. The green once more started to fade out of the card stuck in his hat. He dragged deep on his sweet-smelling cigarette. The color returned and steadied. "Yeah, ignoring the obvious. It's what we all do. Even after his sanity began to totter, Kyle undoubtedly knew that his trips to yonder liquor store were making his condition worse, but he went on, regardless. I don't blame him; I'm sure the wine eased

his pain. Especially toward the end. Things might have been better if he hadn't been able to get to the liquor store—if it was outside the circle—but it wasn't. And really, who can say? There is no
blaming here, Jake. No condemnation."

That was good to hear, but only because it meant we could converse about this lunatic subject like halfway rational men. Not
that his feelings mattered much to me, either way; I still had to do
what I had to do. "What's your name?"

"Zack Lang. From Seattle, originally."

"Seattle *when?*"

"It's a question with no relevance to the current discussion."

"It hurts you to be here, doesn't it?"

"Yes. My own sanity won't last much longer, if I don't get back.
And the residual effects will be with me forever. High suicide
rate among our kind, Jake. Very high. Men—and we *are* men, not
aliens or supernatural beings, if that's what you were thinking—
aren't made to hold multiple reality-strings in their heads. It's not
like using your imagination. It's not like that at all. We have training, of course, but you can still feel it eating into you. Like acid."

"So every trip *isn't* a complete reset."

"Yes and no. It leaves *residue.* Every time your cook friend—"

"His name was Al."

"Yes, I suppose I knew that, but my memory has started to break
down. It's like Alzheimer's, only it's *not* Alzheimer's. It's because
the brain can't help trying to reconcile all those thin overlays of
reality. The strings create multiple images of the future. Some are
clear, most are hazy. That's probably why Kyle thought your name
was Jimla. He must have heard it along one of the strings."

He didn't hear it, I thought. *He saw it on some kind of String-O-
Vision. On a billboard in Texas. Maybe even through my eyes.*

"You don't know how lucky you are, Jake. For you, time-travel
is simple."

Not all that *simple,* I thought.

"There *were* paradoxes," I said. "All kinds of them. Weren't
there?"

"No, that's the wrong word. It's *residue*. Didn't I just tell you that?" He honestly didn't seem sure. "It gums up the machine. Eventually a point will come where the machine simply . . . stops."

I thought of how the engine had blown in the Studebaker Sadie and I had stolen.

"Buying meat over and over again in 1958 wasn't so bad," Zack Lang said. "Oh, it was causing trouble down the line, but it was bearable. Then the *big* changes started. Saving Kennedy was the biggest of all."

I tried to speak and couldn't.

"Are you beginning to understand?"

Not entirely, but I could see the general outline, and it scared the living hell out of me. The future was on strings. Like a puppet. Good God.

"The earthquake . . . I *did* cause it. When I saved Kennedy, I . . . what? Ripped the time-space continuum?" That should have come out sounding stupid, but it didn't. It sounded very grave. My head began to throb.

"You need to go back now, Jake." He spoke gently. "You need to go back and see exactly what you've done. What all your hard and no doubt well-meaning work has accomplished."

I said nothing. I had been worried about going back, but now I was afraid, as well. Is there any phrase more ominous than *you need to see exactly what you've done*? I couldn't think of one offhand.

"Go. Have a look. Spend a little time. But only a little. If this isn't put right soon, there's going to be a catastrophe."

"How big?"

He spoke calmly. "It could destroy everything."

"The world? The solar system?" I had to put my hand on the side of the drying shed to hold myself up. "The galaxy? The universe?"

"Bigger than that." He paused, wanting to make sure I understood. The card in his hatband swirled, turned yellow, swirled back toward green. "Reality itself."

6

I walked to the chain. The sign reading **NO ADMITTANCE BEYOND THIS POINT UNTIL SEWER PIPE IS REPAIRED** squeaked in the wind. I looked back at Zack Lang, that traveler from who knew when. He looked at me without expression, the hem of his black overcoat flapping around his shins.

"Lang! The harmonies . . . I caused them all. Didn't I?"

He might have nodded. I'm not sure.

The past fought change because it was destructive to the future. Change created—

I thought of an old ad for Memorex audiotape. It showed a crystal glass being shattered by sound vibrations. By pure harmonics.

"And with every change I succeeded in making, those harmonies increased. *That's* the real danger, isn't it? Those fucking harmonies."

No answer. Perhaps he had known and forgotten; perhaps he had never known at all.

Easy, I told myself . . . as I had five years before, when the first strands of gray had yet to show up in my hair. *Just take it easy.*

I ducked under the chain, my left knee yipping, then stood for a second with the high green side of the drying shed on my left. This time there was no chunk of concrete to mark the spot where the invisible stairs began. How far away from the chain had they been? I couldn't remember.

I walked slowly, slowly, my shoes gritting on the cracked concrete. *Shat-HOOSH, shat-HOOSH,* said the weaving flats . . . and then, as I took my sixth step, and the seventh, the sound changed to *too-FAR, too-FAR.* I took another step. Then another. Soon I'd reach the end of the drying shed and be in the courtyard beyond. It was gone. The bubble had burst.

I took one more step, and although there was no stair riser, for just a moment I saw my shoe as a double exposure. It was on the concrete, but it was also on dirty green linoleum. I took another step, and *I* was a double exposure. Most of my body was standing beside the Worumbo mill drying shed in late November of 1963, but part of me was somewhere else, and it wasn't the pantry of Al's Diner.

What if I came out not in Maine, not even on earth, but in some strange other dimension? Some place with a crazy red sky and air that would poison my lungs and stop my heart?

I looked back again. Lang stood there with his coat whipping in the wind. There was still no expression on his face. *You're on your own,* that empty face seemed to say. *I can't make you do anything.*

It was true, but unless I went through the rabbit-hole into the Land of Ahead, I wouldn't be able to come back to the Land of Ago. And Sadie would stay dead forever.

I closed my eyes and managed one more step. Suddenly I could smell faint ammonia and some other, more unpleasant, odor. After you'd crossed the country at the rear of a lot of Greyhound buses, that second smell was unmistakable. It was the unlovely aroma of a toilet cubicle that needed a lot more than a Glade air-freshener on the wall to sweeten it up.

Eyes closed, I took one more step, and heard that weird popping sound inside my head. I opened my eyes. I was in a small, filthy bathroom. There was no toilet; it had been removed, leaving nothing but the dirty shadow of its footing. An ancient urine-cake, faded from its bright blue operating color to a listless gray, lay in the corner. Ants marched back and forth over it. The corner I'd come out in was blocked off by cartons filled with empty bottles and cans. It reminded me of Lee's shooter's nest.

I pushed a couple of the boxes aside and eased my way into the little room. I started for the door, then restacked the cartons. No sense making it easy for anyone to stumble down the rabbit-hole by mistake. Then I stepped outside and back into 2011.

7

It had been dark the last time I'd gone down the rabbit-hole, so of course it was dark now, because it was only two minutes later. A lot had changed in those two minutes, though. I could see that even in the gloom. At some point in the last forty-eight years, the mill had burned down. All that remained were a few blackened walls, a fallen stack (that reminded me, inevitably, of the one I'd seen at the site of the Kitchener Ironworks in Derry), and several piles of rubble. There was no sign of Your Maine Snuggery, L.L. Bean Express, or any other upscale shops. Here was a wrecked mill standing on the banks of the Androscoggin. Nothing else.

On the June night when I'd left on my five-year mission to save Kennedy, the temperature had been pleasantly mild. Now it was beastly hot. I took off the sheepskin-lined coat I'd bought in Auburn and tossed it into the ill-smelling bathroom. When I closed the door again, I saw the sign on it: **BATHROOM OUT OF ORDER! NO TOILET!!! SEWER PIPE IS BROKEN!!!**

Beautiful young presidents died and beautiful young presidents lived, beautiful young women lived and then they died, but the broken sewer pipe beneath the courtyard of the old Worumbo mill was apparently eternal.

The chain was still there, too. I walked to it along the flank of the dirty old cinderblock building that had replaced the drying shed. When I ducked under the chain and went around to the front of the building, I saw it was an abandoned convenience store called Quik-Flash. The windows were shattered and all the shelves had been taken away. The place was nothing but a shell where one emergency light, its battery almost dead, buzzed like a dying fly against a winter windowpane. There was graffiti spray-painted on the remains of the floor, and just enough light to read it: GET OUT OF TOWN YOU PAKI BASTARD.

I walked across the broken concrete of the courtyard. The lot where the millworkers had once parked was gone. Nothing had been built there; it was just a vacant rectangle filled with smashed bottles, jigsaw chunks of old asphalt, and listless clumps of trash grass. Used condoms hung from some of these like ancient party-streamers. I looked up for stars and saw none. The sky was covered with low-hanging clouds just thin enough to allow a little vague moonlight to seep through. The blinker at the intersection of Main Street and Route 196 (once known as the Old Lewiston Road) had been replaced at some point by a traffic light, but it was dark. That was all right; there was no traffic in either direction.

The Fruit was gone. There was a cellar-hole where it had stood. Across from it, where the greenfront had been in 1958 and where a bank should have been standing in 2011, was something called Province of Maine Food Cooperative. Except these windows were also broken, and any goods that might have been inside were long gone. The place was as gutted as the Quik-Flash.

Halfway across the deserted intersection, I was frozen in place by a great watery ripping sound. The only thing I could imagine making a noise like that was some kind of exotic ice-plane, melting even as it broke the sound barrier. The ground beneath my feet briefly trembled. A car alarm blurped, then quit. Dogs barked, then fell silent, one by one.

Earthquake in Los Angle-ees, I thought. *Seven thousand dead.*

Headlights splashed down Route 196, and I made it to the far sidewalk in a hurry. The vehicle turned out to be a little square bus with ROUNDABOUT in its lighted destination window. That rang a faint bell, but I don't know why. Some harmony or other, I suppose. On the roof of the bus were several revolving gadgets that looked like heat-ventilators. Wind turbines, maybe? Was that possible? There was no combustion engine sound, only a faint electrical hum. I watched until the wide crescent of its single taillight was out of sight.

Okay, so gas engines were being phased out in this version of the future—this *string,* to use Zack Lang's term. That was a good thing, wasn't it?

Possibly, but the air had a heavy, somehow dead feel as I pulled it into my lungs, and there was a kind of olfactory afterscent that reminded me of how my Lionel train transformer smelled when, as a kid, I pushed it too hard. *Time to turn it off and let it rest awhile,* my father would say.

There were a few businesses on Main Street that looked like half-going concerns, but mostly it was a shambles. The sidewalk was cracked and littered with rubbish. I saw half a dozen parked cars, and every one was either a gas-electric hybrid or equipped with the roof-spinner devices. One of them was a Honda Zephyr; one was a Takuro Spirit; another a Ford Breeze. They looked old, and a couple had been vandalized. All had pink stickers on the windshields, the black letters big enough to read even in the gloom: **PROVINCE OF MAINE "A" STICKER ALWAYS PRODUCE RATION BOOK**.

A gang of kids was idling up the other side of the street, laughing and talking. "Hey!" I called across to them. "Is the library still open?"

They looked over. I saw the firefly wink of cigarettes . . . except the smell that drifted across to me was almost surely pot. "Fuck off, man!" one of them shouted back.

Another turned, dropped his pants, and mooned me. "You find any books up there, they're all yours!"

There was general laughter and they walked on, talking in lower voices and looking back.

I didn't mind being mooned—it wasn't the first time—but I didn't like those looks, and I liked the low voices even less. There might be something conspiratorial there. Jake Epping didn't exactly believe that, but George Amberson did; George had been through a lot, and it was George who bent down, grabbed two fist-sized chunks of concrete, and stuffed them into his front pockets, just for good luck. Jake thought he was being silly but didn't object.

A block farther up, the business district (such as it was) came to an abrupt end. I saw an elderly woman hurrying along and glancing nervously at the boys, who were now a little farther up on the other side of Main. She was wearing a kerchief and what looked like a respirator—the kind of thing people with COPD or advanced emphysema use.

"Ma'am, do you know if the library—"

"Leave me alone!" Her eyes were large and scared. The moon shone briefly through a rift in the clouds, and I saw that her face was covered with sores. The one below her right eye appeared to have eaten right down to the bone. "I have a paper that says I can be out, it's got a Council stamp, so leave me alone! I'm going to see my sister! Those boys are bad enough, and soon they'll start their wilding. If you touch me, I'll buzz my beezer and a constable will come!"

I somehow doubted that.

"Ma'am, I just want to know if the library is still—"

"It's been closed for years and all the books are gone! They have Hate Meetings there now. Leave me alone, I say, or I'll buzz for a constable!"

She scuttled away, looking back over her shoulder every few seconds to make sure I wasn't coming after her. I let her put enough distance between us to make her feel comfy, then continued up Main Street. My knee was recovering a bit from my stair-climbing exertions in the Book Depository, but I was still limping, and would be for some time to come. Lights burned behind drawn curtains in a few houses, but I was pretty sure it wasn't produced by Central Maine Power. Those were Coleman lanterns and in some cases kerosene lamps. Most of the houses were dark. Some were charred wrecks. There was a Nazi swastika on one of the wrecks and the words JEW RAT spray-painted on another.

Those boys are bad enough and soon they'll start their wilding.

And . . . had she really said Hate Meetings?

In front of one of the few houses that looked in good shape—it was a mansion compared to most of them—I saw a long hitching rail, like in a western movie. And actual horses had been tied up there. When the sky lightened in another of those diffuse spasms, I could see horsepucky pats, some of them fresh. The driveway was gated. The moon had gone in again, so I couldn't read the sign on the iron slats, but I didn't need to read it to know it said KEEP OUT.

Now, from up ahead, I heard someone enunciate a single word: "Cunt!"

It didn't sound young, like one of the wild boys, and it was coming from my side of the street rather than theirs. The guy sounded pissed off. He also sounded like he might be talking to himself. I walked toward his voice.

"Mother-*fucker*!" the voice cried, exasperated. "*Shit*-ass!"

He was maybe a block up. Before I got there, I heard a loud metallic bonk and the male voice cried: "Get on with you! Goddam little wetnosed sonsabitches! Get on with you before I pull my pistol!"

Mocking laughter greeted this. It was the pot-smoking wild boys, and the voice that replied certainly belonged to the one who had mooned me. "Only pistol you got is the one in your pants, and I bet it's got a mighty limp barrel!"

More laughter. It was followed by a high metallic *spannng* sound.

"You fucks, you broke one of my spokes!" When the man yelled at them again, his voice was tinged with reluctant fear. "Nah, nah, stay on your own goddam side!"

The clouds rifted. The moon peeked through. By its chancy light I saw an old man in a wheelchair. He was halfway across one of the streets intersecting Main—Goddard, if the name hadn't changed. One of his wheels had gotten stuck in a pothole, causing the chair to cant drunkenly to the left. The boys were crossing toward him. The kid who had told me to fuck off was holding a slingshot with a good-sized rock in it. That explained the bonk and the spang.

"Got any oldbucks, grampy? For that matter, you got any newbucks or canned goods?"

"No! If you don't have the goddam decency to push me out of the hole I'm in, at least go away and leave me alone!"

But they were wilding, and they weren't going to do that. They were going to rob him of whatever small shit he might happen to have, maybe beat him up, tip him over for sure.

Jake and George came together, and both of them saw red.

The attention of the wild boys was fixed on the wheelchair-geezer and they didn't see me cutting toward them on a diagonal—just as I'd cut across the sixth floor of the School Book Depository. My left arm still wasn't much good, but my right was fine, toned up by three months of physical therapy, first in Parkland and then at Eden Fallows. And I still had some of the accuracy that had made me a varsity third baseman in high school. I pegged the first chunk of concrete from thirty feet away and caught Moon Man in the center of the chest. He screamed with pain and surprise. All the boys—there were five of them—turned toward me. When they did, I saw that their faces were as disfigured as the frightened woman's had been. The one with the slingshot, young Master Fuck Off, was the worst. There was nothing but a hole where his nose should have been.

I transferred my second chunk of concrete from my left hand to my right, and threw it at the tallest of the boys, who was wearing a huge pair of loose pants with the waistband drawn up nearly to his sternum. He raised a blocking arm. The concrete struck it, knocking the joint he was holding into the street. He took one look at my face, then wheeled and ran. Moon Man followed him. That left three.

"Walk it to em, son!" the old man in the wheelchair shrilled. *"They got it coming, by Christ!"*

I was sure they did, but they had me outnumbered and my ammo was gone. When you're dealing with teenagers, the only possible way to win in such a situation is to show no fear, only genuine adult outrage. You just keep coming, and that was what I did. I seized young Master Fuck Off by the front of his ragged tee-shirt with my right hand and snatched the slingshot away from him with the left. He stared at me, wide-eyed, and put up no resistance.

"You chickenshit," I said, getting my face right up into his . . .

and never mind the nose that wasn't. He smelled sweaty and pot-smoky and deeply dirty. "How chickenshit do you have to be to go after an old man in a wheelchair?"

"Who are y—"

"Charlie Fucking Chaplin. I went to France just to see the ladies dance. Now get out of here."

"Give me back my—"

I knew what he wanted and bonked the center of his forehead with it. It started one of his sores trickling and must have hurt like hell, because his eyes filled with tears. This disgusted me and filled me with pity, but I tried to show neither. "You get nothing, chickenshit, except a chance to get out of here before I rip your worthless balls off your no doubt diseased scrote and stuff them into the hole where your nose used to be. One chance. Take it." I drew in breath, then screamed it out at his face in a spray of noise and spit: *"Run!"*

I watched them go, feeling shame and exultation in roughly equal parts. The old Jake had been great at quelling rowdy study halls on Friday afternoons before vacations, but that was about as far as his skills went. The new Jake, however, was part George. And George had been through a lot.

From behind me came a heavy bout of coughing. It made me think of Al Templeton. When it stopped, the old man said, "Fella, I would have pissed five years' worth of kidney rocks just to see those vile dinks take to their heels like that. I don't know who you are, but I've got a little Glenfiddich left in my pantry—the real stuff—and if you push me out of this goddam hole in the road and roll me home, I'll share it with you."

The moon had gone in again, but as it came back out through the ragged clouds, I saw his face. He was wearing a long white beard and had a cannula stuffed up his nose, but even after five years, I had no trouble at all recognizing the man who had gotten me into this mess.

"Hello, Harry," I said.

CHAPTER 31

1

He still lived on Goddard Street. I rolled him up the ramp to the porch, where he produced a fearsome bundle of keys. He needed them. The front door had no less than four locks.

"Do you rent or own?"

"Oh, it's all mine," he said. "Such as it is."

"Good for you." Before, he had rented.

"You still haven't told me how you know my name."

"First, let's have that drink. I can use one."

The door opened on a parlor that took up the front half of the house. He told me to whoa, as if I were a horse, and lit a Coleman lantern. By its light I saw furniture of the type that is called "old but serviceable." There was a beautiful braided rug on the floor. No GED diploma on any of the walls—and of course no framed theme titled "The Day That Changed My Life"—but there were a great many Catholic icons and lots of pictures. It was with no surprise that I recognized some of the people in them. I had met them, after all.

"Lock that behind you, would you?"

I closed us off from the dark and disturbing Lisbon Falls, and ran both bolts.

"Deadbolt, too, if you don't mind."

I twisted it and heard a heavy clunk. Harry, meanwhile, was rolling around his parlor and lighting the same sort of longchimneyed kerosene lamps I vaguely remembered seeing in my gramma Sarie's house. It was a better light for the room than the Coleman lamp, and when I killed its hot white glow, Harry Dunning nodded approvingly.

"What's your name, sir? You already know mine."

"Jake Epping. Don't suppose that rings any bells with you, does it?"

He considered, then shook his head. "Should it?"

"Probably not."

He stuck out his hand. It shook slightly with some incipient palsy. "I'll shake with you, just the same. That could have been nasty."

I shook his hand gladly. Hello, new friend. Hello, old friend.

"Okay, now that we got that took care of, we can drink with clear consciences. I'll get us that single malt." He started for the kitchen, rolling his wheels with arms that were a little shaky but still strong. The chair had a small motor, but either it didn't work or he was saving the battery. He looked back over his shoulder at me. "Not dangerous, are you? I mean, to me?"

"Not to you, Harry." I smiled. "I'm your good angel."

"This is fucking peculiar," he said. "But these days, what isn't?"

He went into the kitchen. Soon more light glowed. Homey orange-yellow light. In here, everything seemed homey. But out there . . . in the world . . .

Just what in the hell had I done?

2

"What'll we drink to?" I asked when we had our glasses in hand.

"Better times than these. Will that work for you, Mr. Epping?"

"It works fine. And make it Jake."

We clinked. Drank. I couldn't remember the last time I'd had anything stronger than Lone Star beer. The whisky was like hot honey.

"No electricity?" I asked, looking around at the lamps. He had turned them all low, presumably to save on oil.

He made a sour face. "Not from around here, are you?"

A question I'd heard before, from Frank Anicetti, at the Fruit. On my very first trip into the past. Then I'd told a lie. I didn't want to do that now.

"I don't quite know how to answer that, Harry."

He shrugged it off. "We're supposed to get juice three days a week, and this is supposed to be one of the days, but it cut off around six P.M. I believe in Province Electric like I believe in Santa Claus."

As I considered this, I remembered the stickers on the cars. "How long has Maine been a part of Canada?"

He gave me a how-crazy-are-you look, but I could see he was enjoying this. The strangeness of it and also the *there*-ness of it. I wondered when he'd last had a real conversation with someone. "Since 2005. Did someone bump you on the head, or something?"

"As a matter of fact, yes." I went to his wheelchair, dropped on the knee that still bent willingly and without pain, and showed him the place on the back of my head where the hair had never grown back. "I took a bad beating a few months ago—"

"Yuh, I seen you limping when you ran at those kids."

"—and now there's lots of things I don't remember."

The floor suddenly shook beneath us. The flames in the kerosene lamps trembled. The pictures on the walls rattled, and a two-feet-high plaster Jesus with his arms outstretched took a jittery stroll toward the edge of the mantelpiece. He looked like a guy contemplating suicide, and given the current state of things as I had observed them, I couldn't blame him.

"Popper," Harry said matter-of-factly when the shaking stopped. "You remember those, right?"

"No." I got up, went to the mantelpiece, and pushed Jesus back beside his Holy Mother.

"Thanks. I've already lost half the damn disciples off the shelf in my bedroom, and I mourn every one. They were my mom's. Poppers are earth tremors. We get a lot of em, but most of the big-daddy quakes are in the Midwest or out California way. Europe and China too, of course."

"People tying up their boats in Idaho, are they?" I was still at the mantelpiece, now looking at the framed pictures.

"Hasn't got that bad yet, but . . . you know four of the Japanese islands are gone, right?"

I looked at him with dismay. "No."

"Three were small ones, but Hokkaido's gone, too. Dropped into the goddam ocean four years ago like it was on an elevator. The scientists say it's got something to do with the earth's crust." Matter-of-factly he added: "They say if it don't stop, it'll tear the planet apart by 2080 or so. Then the solar system'll have *two* aster-oid belts."

I drank the rest of my whisky in a single gulp, and the croc-odile tears of booze momentarily doubled my vision. When the room solidified again, I pointed to a picture of Harry at about fifty. He was still in his wheelchair, but he looked hale and healthy, at least from the waist up; the legs of his suit pants billowed over his diminished legs. Next to him was a woman in a pink dress that reminded me of Jackie Kennedy's suit on 11/22/63. I remember my mother telling me never to call a woman who wasn't beautiful "plain-faced"; they were, she said, "good-faced." This woman was good-faced.

"Your wife?"

"Ayuh. That was taken on our twenty-fifth wedding anniver-sary. She died two years later. There's a lot of that going around. The politicians will tell you the A-bombs did it—been twenty-eight or -nine swapped since Hanoi Hell in '69. They'll swear it until they're blue in the face, but everyone knows the sores and the cancer didn't start getting really bad up this way until Ver-mont Yankee went China Syndrome. That happened after years of protests about the place. 'Oh,' they said, 'there won't be any big earthquakes in Vermont, not way up here in God's Kingdom, just the usual little shakers and poppers.' Yeah. Look what happened."

"You're saying a reactor blew up in Vermont."

"Spewed radiation all over New England and southern Quebec."

"When?"

"Jake, are you pulling my leg?"

"Absolutely not."

"June nineteenth, 1999."

"I'm sorry about your wife."

"Thank you, son. She was a good woman. Lovely woman. She didn't deserve what she got." He wiped his arm slowly across his eyes. "Been a long time since I talked about her, but then, it's been a long time since I've had anyone to talk *with*. Can I pour you a little more of this joy-juice?"

I held my fingers a smidge apart. I didn't expect to be here long; I had to take in all this bogus history, this *darkness,* in a hurry. I had a lot to do, not least of all bringing my own lovely woman back to life. That would mean another chat with the Green Card Man. I didn't want to be loaded when I had it, but one more little one wouldn't hurt. I needed it. My emotions felt frozen, which was probably good, because my mind was reeling.

"Were you paralyzed during the Tet Offensive?" Thinking, *Of course you were, but it could have been worse; on the last go-round you died.*

He looked blank for a moment, then his face cleared. "I guess it *was* Tet, come to think of it. We just called it the Great Saigon Fuck-All of 1967. The helicopter I was in crashed. I was lucky. Most of the people on that bird died. Some of em were diplomats, and some of them were just kids."

"Tet of '67," I said. "Not '68."

"That's right. You wouldn't have been born, but surely you read about it in the history books."

"No." I let him pour a little more scotch into my glass—just enough to cover the bottom—and said, "I know that President Kennedy was almost assassinated in November of 1963. After that I know nothing."

He shook his head. "That's the funniest case of amnesia I ever heard of."

"Was Kennedy reelected?"

"Against Goldwater? You bet your ass he was."

"Did he keep Johnson as his running mate?"

"Sure. Kennedy needed Texas. Got it, too. Governor Connally worked like a slave for him in that election, much as he despised Kennedy's New Frontier. They called it the Embarrassment Endorsement. Because of what almost happened that day in Dallas. You sure you don't know this? Never learned any of it in school?"

"You lived it, Harry. So tell me."

"I don't mind," he said. "Drag up a rock, son. Quit lookin at those pictures. If you don't know Kennedy got reelected in '64, you're sure not apt to know any of my family."

Ah, Harry, I thought.

3

When I was just a little kid—four, maybe even three—a drunk uncle told me the story of "Little Red Riding Hood." Not the one in the standard fairy-tale books, but the R-rated version, full of screams, blood, and the dull thump of the woodsman's axe. My memory of hearing it is vivid to this day, but only a few of the details remain: the wolf's teeth bared in a shining grin, for instance, and the gore-soaked granny being reborn from the wolf's yawning belly. This is my way of saying that if you're expecting *The Concise Alternate History of the World as told by Harry Dunning to Jake Epping,* forget about it. It wasn't just the horror of discovering how badly things had gone wrong. It was my need to get back and put things right.

Yet a few things stand out. The worldwide search for George Amberson, for instance. No joy there—George was as gone as Judge Crater—but in the forty-eight years since the assassination attempt in Dallas, Amberson had become a near-mythical figure. Savior, or part of the plot? People held actual conventions to discuss it, and listening to Harry tell that part, it was impossible for me not to think of all the conspiracy theories that had sprung up around the version of Lee who had succeeded. As we know, class, the past harmonizes.

Kennedy expected to sweep Barry Goldwater away in a landslide in '64; instead he won by less than forty electoral votes, a margin only Democratic Party stalwarts thought respectable. Early in his second term, he infuriated both the right-wing voters and the military establishment by declaring North Vietnam "less a danger to our democracy than the racial inequality in our schools and cities." He didn't withdraw American troops entirely, but they were restricted to Saigon and a ring around it that was called—surprise, surprise—the Green Zone. Instead of injecting large numbers of troops, the second Kennedy administration injected large amounts of money. It's the American Way.

The great civil rights reforms of the sixties never happened. Kennedy was no LBJ, and as vice president, Johnson was uniquely powerless to help him. The Republicans and Dixiecrats filibustered for a hundred and ten days; one actually died on the floor and became a right-wing hero. When Kennedy finally gave up, he made an off-the-cuff remark that would haunt him until he died in 1983: "White America has filled its house with kindling; now it will burn."

The race riots came next. While Kennedy was preoccupied with them, the North Vietnamese armies overran Saigon—and the man who'd gotten me into this was paralyzed in a helicopter crash on the deck of a U.S. aircraft carrier. Public opinion began to swing heavily against JFK.

A month after the fall of Saigon, Martin Luther King was assassinated in Chicago. The assassin turned out to be a rogue FBI agent named Dwight Holly. Before being killed himself, he claimed to have carried out the hit on Hoover's orders. Chicago went up in flames. So did a dozen other American cities.

George Wallace was elected president. By then the earthquakes had begun in earnest. Wallace couldn't do anything about those, so he settled for firebombing Chicago into submission. That, Harry said, was in June of 1969. A year later, President Wallace offered Ho Chi Minh an ultimatum: make Saigon a free city like Berlin or see Hanoi become a dead one, like Hiroshima. Uncle Ho refused. If he thought Wallace was bluffing, he was wrong. Hanoi became a radioactive cloud on August ninth, 1969, twenty-four years to the day after Harry Truman dropped Fat Man on Nagasaki. Vice President Curtis LeMay took personal charge of the mission. In a speech to the nation, Wallace called it God's will. Most Americans concurred. Wallace's approval ratings were high, but there was at least one fellow who did not approve. His name was Arthur Bremer, and on May fifteenth, 1972, he shot Wallace dead as Wallace campaigned for reelection at a shopping mall in Laurel, Maryland.

"With what kind of gun?"

"I believe it was a .38 revolver."

Sure it was. Maybe a Police Special, but probably a Victory model, the same kind of gun that had taken Officer Tippit's life along another time-string.

This was where I began to lose the thread. Where the thought *I have to put this right, put this right, put this right* began to hammer in my head like a gong.

Hubert Humphrey became president in '72. The earthquakes worsened. The world suicide rate skyrocketed. Fundamentalism of all kinds blossomed. The terrorism fomented by religious extremists blossomed with it. India and Pakistan went to war; more mushroom clouds bloomed. Bombay never became Mumbai. What it became was radioactive ash in a cancer-wind.

Likewise, Karachi. Only when Russia, China, and the United States promised to bomb both countries back to the Stone Age did the hostilities cease.

In 1976, Humphrey lost to Ronald Reagan in a coast-to-coast landslide; The Hump couldn't hold even his native state of Minnesota.

Two thousand committed mass suicide in Jonestown, Guyana.

In November of 1979, Iranian students overran the American

embassy in Tehran and took not sixty-six hostages but over two hundred. Heads rolled on Iranian TV. Reagan had learned enough from Hanoi Hell to keep the nukes in their bomb bays and missile silos, but he sent in *beaucoup* troops. The remaining hostages were, of course, slaughtered, and an emerging terrorist group calling themselves The Base—or, in Arabic, Al-Qaeda—began planting roadside bombs here, there, and everywhere.

"The man could speechify like a motherfucker, but he had no understanding of militant Islam," Harry said.

The Beatles reunited and played a Peace Concert. A suicide bomber in the crowd detonated his vest and killed three hundred spectators. Paul McCartney was blinded.

The Mideast went up in flames shortly thereafter.

Russia collapsed.

Some group—probably exiled Russian hard-line fanatics—began selling nuclear weapons to terrorist groups, including The Base.

"By 1994," Harry said in his dry voice, "the oil fields over there were so much black glass. The kind that glows in the dark. Since then, though, the terrorism has kind of burned itself out. Someone blew up a suitcase nuke in Miami two years ago, but it didn't work very well. I mean, it'll be sixty or eighty years before anybody can party on South Beach—and of course the Gulf of Mexico is basically dead soup—but only ten thousand people have died of radiation poisoning. By then it wasn't our problem. Maine voted to become a part of Canada, and President Clinton was happy to say good riddance."

"Bill Clinton's president?"

"Gosh, no. He was a shoo-in for the '04 nomination, but he died of a heart attack at the convention. His wife stepped in. *She's* president."

"Doing a good job?"

Harry waggled his hand. "Not bad . . . but you can't legislate earthquakes. And that's what's going to do for us, in the end."

Overhead, that watery ripping sound came again. I looked up. Harry didn't.

"What is that?" I asked.

"Son," he said, "nobody seems to know. The scientists argue, but in this case I think the preachers might have the straight of it. They say it's God getting ready to tear down all the works of His hands, same way that Samson tore down the Temple of the Philistines." He drank the rest of his whisky. Thin color had bloomed in his cheeks . . . which were, as far as I could see, free of radiation sores. "And on that one, I think they might be right."

"Christ almighty," I said.

He looked at me levelly. "Heard enough history, son?"

Enough to last me a lifetime.

4

"I have to go," I said. "Will you be all right?"

"Until I'm not. Same as everyone else." He looked at me closely. "Jake, where did you drop from? And why the hell should I feel like I know you?"

"Maybe because we always know our good angels?"

"Bullshit."

I wanted to be gone. All in all, I thought my life after the next reset was going to be much simpler. But first, because this was a good man who had suffered greatly in all three of his incarnations, I approached the mantelpiece again, and took down one of the framed pictures.

"Be careful with that," Harry said tetchily. "It's my family."

"I know." I put it in his gnarled and age-spotted hands, a black-and-white photo that had, by the faintly fuzzy look of the image, been blown up from a Kodak snap. "Did your dad take this? I ask, because he's the only one not in it."

He looked at me curiously, then back down at the picture. "No," he said. "This was taken by a neighbor-lady in the summer of 1958. My dad and mom were separated by then."

I wondered if the neighbor-lady had been the one I'd seen smok-

ing a cigarette as she alternated washing the family car and spraying the family dog. Somehow I was sure it had been. From far
down in my mind, like a sound heard coming up from a deep well,
came the chanting voices of the jump-rope girls: *my old man drives
a sub-ma-rine.*

"He had a drinking problem. That wasn't such a big deal back
then, lots of men drank too much and stayed under the same roofs
with their wives, but he got mean when he drank."

"I bet he did," I said.

He looked at me again, more sharply, then smiled. Most of his
teeth were gone, but the smile was still pleasant enough. "I doubt
if you know what you're talking about. How old are you, Jake?"

"Forty." Although I was sure I looked older that night.

"Which means you were born in 1971."

Actually it had been '76, but there was no way I could tell him
that without discussing the five missing years that had fallen down
the rabbit-hole, like Alice into Wonderland. "Close enough," I
said. "That photo was taken at the house on Kossuth Street." Spoken the Derry way: *Cossut.*

I tapped Ellen, who was standing to the left of her mother,
thinking of the grown-up version I'd spoken to on the phone—
call that one Ellen 2.0. Also thinking—it was inevitable—of Ellen
Dockerty, the harmonic version I'd known in Jodie.

"Can't tell from this, but she was a little carrot-top, wasn't she?
A pint-sized Lucille Ball."

Harry said nothing, only gaped.

"Did she go into comedy? Or something else? Radio or TV?"

"She does a DJ show on Province of Maine CBC," he said faintly.
"But how . . ."

"Here's Troy . . . and Arthur, also known as Tugga . . . and here's
you, with your mother's arm around you." I smiled. "Just the way
God planned it." *If only it could stay that way. If only.*

"I . . . you . . ."

"Your father was murdered, wasn't he?"

"Yes." The cannula had come askew in his nose and he pushed

it straight, his hand moving slowly, like the hand of a man who is dreaming with his eyes open. "He was shot to death in Longview Cemetery while he was putting flowers on his parents' graves. Only a few months after this picture was taken. The police arrested a man named Bill Turcotte for it—"

Ow. I hadn't seen that one coming.

"—but he had a solid alibi and eventually they had to let him go. The killer was never caught." He took one of my hands. "Mister . . . son . . . Jake . . . this is crazy, but . . . were you the one who killed my father?"

"Don't be silly." I took the picture and hung it back on the wall. "I wasn't born until 1971, remember?"

5

I walked slowly down Main Street, back to the ruined mill and the abandoned Quik-Flash convenience store that stood in front of it. I walked with my head down, not looking for No Nose and Moon Man and the rest of that happy band. I thought if they were still anywhere in the vicinity, they'd give me a wide berth. They thought I was crazy. Probably I was.

We're all mad here was what the Cheshire Cat told Alice. Then he disappeared. Except for the grin, that is. As I recall, the grin stayed awhile.

I understood more now. Not everything, I doubt if even the Card Men understand everything (and after they've spent awhile on duty, they understand almost nothing), but that still didn't help me with the decision I had to make.

As I ducked under the chain, something exploded far in the distance. It didn't make me jump. I imagined there were a lot of explosions now. When people begin to lose hope, there's bound to be explosions.

I entered the bathroom at the back of the convenience store and almost tripped over my sheepskin jacket. I kicked it aside—

I wouldn't be needing it where I was going—and walked slowly over to the piled boxes that looked so much like Lee's sniper's nest.

Goddam harmonies.

I moved enough of them so I could get into the corner, then carefully restacked them behind me. I moved forward step by small step, once again thinking of how a man or woman feels for the top of a staircase in utter darkness. But there was no step this time, only that queer doubling. I moved forward, watched my lower body shimmer, then closed my eyes.

Another step. And another. Now I felt warmth on my legs. Two more steps and sunlight turned the black behind my eyelids to red. I took one more step and heard the pop inside my head. When that cleared, I heard the *shat-HOOSH, shat-HOOSH* of the weaving flats.

I opened my eyes. The stink of the dirty abandoned restroom had been replaced by the stink of a textile mill operating full bore in a year when the Environmental Protection Agency did not exist. There was cracked cement under my feet instead of peeling linoleum. To my left were the big metal bins filled with fabric remnants and covered with burlap. To my right was the drying shed. It was eleven fifty-eight on the morning of September ninth, 1958. Harry Dunning was once more a little boy. Carolyn Poulin was in period five at LHS, perhaps listening to the teacher, perhaps daydreaming about some boy or how she would go hunting with her father in a couple of months. Sadie Dunhill, not yet married to Mr. Have Broom Will Travel, was living in Georgia. Lee Harvey Oswald was in the South China Sea with his Marine unit. And John F. Kennedy was the junior senator from Massachusetts, dreaming presidential dreams.

I was back.

6

I walked to the chain and ducked under it. On the other side I stood perfectly still for a moment, rehearsing what I was going to do. Then I walked to the end of the drying shed. Around the corner, leaning against it, was the Green Card Man. Only Zack Lang's card was no longer green. It had turned a muddy ocher shade, halfway between green and yellow. His out-of-season overcoat was dusty, and his formerly snappy fedora had a battered, somehow defeated look. His cheeks, previously clean-shaven, were now stubbled . . . and some of that stubble was white. His eyes were bloodshot. He wasn't on the booze yet—at least I couldn't smell any—but I thought he might be soon. The greenfront was, after all, within his small circle of operation, and holding all those time-strings in your head has to hurt. Multiple pasts were bad enough, but when you added multiple futures? Anyone would turn to drink, if drink were available.

I had spent an hour in 2011. Maybe a little more. How long had it been for *him*? I didn't know. I didn't *want* to know.

"Thank God," he said . . . just as he had before. But when he once more reached to take my hand in both of his, I drew back. His nails were now long and black with dirt. The fingers shook. They were the hands—and the coat, and the hat, and the card in the brim of the hat—of a wino-in-waiting.

"You know what you have to do," he said.

"I know what you *want* me to do."

"Want has nothing to do with it. You have to go back one last time. If all is well, you'll come out in the diner. Soon it will be taken away, and when that happens, the bubble that has caused all this madness will burst. It's a miracle that it's stayed as long as it has. *You have to close the circle.*"

He reached for me again. This time I did more than draw back; I turned and ran for the parking lot. He sprinted after me. Because of my bad knee, it was closer than it would have been otherwise. I could hear him right behind me as I passed the Plymouth Fury that was the double of the car I'd seen and dismissed one night in the courtyard of the Candlewood Bungalows. Then I was at the intersection of Main and the Old Lewiston Road. On the other side, the eternal rockabilly rebel stood with one boot cocked against the siding of the Fruit.

I ran across the train tracks, afraid that my bad leg would betray me on the cinders, but Lang was the one who stumbled and fell. I heard him cry out—a desperate, lonely caw—and felt an instant of pity for him. Hard duty, the man had. But I didn't let pity slow me down. The imperatives of love are cruel.

The Lewiston Express bus was coming. I lurched across the intersection and the bus driver blared his horn at me. I thought of another bus, crowded with people who were going to see the president. And the president's lady, of course, the one in the pink suit. Roses laid between them on the seat. Not yellow but red.

"Jimla, come back!"

That was right. I was the Jimla after all, the monster in Rosette Templeton's bad dream. I limped past the Kennebec Fruit, well ahead of the Ocher Card Man now. This was a race I was going to win. I was Jake Epping, high school teacher; I was George Amberson, aspiring novelist; I was the Jimla, who was endangering the whole world with every step he took.

Yet I ran on.

I thought of Sadie, tall and cool and beautiful, and I ran on. Sadie who was accident-prone and was going to stumble over a bad man named John Clayton. On him she would bruise more than her shins. *The world well lost for love*—was that Dryden or Pope?

I stopped by Titus Chevron, panting. Across the street, the beatnik proprietor of the Jolly White Elephant was smoking his pipe and watching me. The Ocher Card Man stood at the mouth of the alley behind the Kennebec Fruit. It was apparently as far as he could go in that direction.

He held out his hands to me, which was bad. Then he fell on his knees and clasped his hands in front of him, which was ever so much worse. *"Please don't do this! You must know the cost!"*

I knew it and still hurried on. A telephone booth stood at the intersection just beyond St. Joseph's Church. I shut myself inside it, consulted the phone book, and dropped a dime.

When the cab came, the driver was smoking Luckies and his radio was tuned to WJAB.

History repeats itself.

FINAL NOTES

9/30/58

I holed up in Unit 7 at the Tamarack Motor Court.

I paid with money from an ostrich wallet that was given to me by an old buddy. Money, like meat bought at the Red & White Supermarket and shirts bought at Mason's Menswear, stays. If every trip really *is* a complete reset, those things shouldn't, but it's not and they do. The money wasn't from Al, but at least Agent Hosty let me run, which might turn out to be a good thing for the world.

Or not. I don't know.

Tomorrow will be the first of October. In Derry, the Dunning kids are looking forward to Halloween and already planning their costumes. Ellen, that little red-haired kut-up kutie, plans to go as Princess Summerfall Winterspring. She'll never get the chance. If I went to Derry today, I could kill Frank Dunning and save her Halloween, but I won't. And I won't go to Durham to save Carolyn Poulin from Andy Cullum's errant shot. The question is, will I go to Jodie? I can't save Kennedy, that is out of the question, but can the future history of the world be so fragile that it will not allow two high school teachers to meet and fall in love? To marry, to dance to Beatles tunes like "I Want to Hold Your Hand," and live unremarkable lives?

I don't know, I don't know.

She might not want to have anything to do with me. We're no longer going to be thirty-five and twenty-eight; this time I'd be forty-two or -three. I look even older. But I believe in love, you know; love is a uniquely portable magic. I don't think it's in the stars, but I *do* believe that blood calls to blood and mind calls to mind and heart to heart.

Sadie dancing the Madison, color high in her cheeks, laughing.

Sadie telling me to lick her mouth again.

Sadie asking if I'd like to come in and have poundcake.

One man and one woman. Is that too much to ask?

I don't know, I don't know.

What have I done here, you ask, now that I have laid my good-angel wings aside? I have written. I have a fountain pen—one given to me by Mike and Bobbi Jill, you remember them—and I walked up the road to a market, where I bought ten refills. The ink is black, which suits my mood. I also bought two dozen thick legal pads, and I have filled all but the last one. Near the market is a Western Auto store, where I bought a spade and a steel foot-locker, the kind with a combination. The total cost of my purchases was seventeen dollars and nineteen cents. Are these items enough to turn the world dark and filthy? What will happen to the clerk, whose ordained course has been changed—just by our brief transaction—from what it would have been otherwise?

I don't know, but I *do* know this: I once gave a high school football player the chance to shine as an actor, and his girlfriend was disfigured. You could say I wasn't responsible, but we know better, don't we? The butterfly spreads its wings.

For three weeks I wrote all day, every day. Twelve hours on some days. Fourteen on others. The pen racing and racing. My hand got sore. I soaked it, then wrote some more. Some nights I went to the Lisbon Drive-In, where there's a special price for walk-ins: thirty cents. I sat in one of the folding chairs in front of the snackbar and next to the kiddie playground. I watched *The Long, Hot Summer* again. I watched *The Bridge on the River Kwai* and *South Pacific*. I watched a HORRORIFFIC DOUBLE FEATURE consisting of *The Fly* and *The Blob*. And I wondered what I was changing. If I so much as slapped a bug, I wondered what I was changing ten years up the line. Or twenty. Or forty.

I don't know, I don't know.

Here's another thing I *do* know. The past is obdurate for the same reason a turtle's shell is obdurate: because the living flesh inside is tender and defenseless.

And something else. The multiple choices and possibilities of daily life are the music we dance to. They are like strings on a guitar. Strum them and you create a pleasing sound. A harmonic. But then start adding strings. Ten strings, a hundred strings, a thousand, a million. Because they multiply! Harry didn't know what that watery ripping sound was, but I'm pretty sure I do; that's the sound of too much harmony created by too many strings.

Sing high C in a voice that's loud enough and true enough and you can shatter fine crystal. Play the right harmonic notes through your stereo loud enough and you can shatter window glass. It follows (to me, at least) that if you put enough strings on time's instrument, you can shatter reality.

But the reset is *almost* complete each time. Sure, it leaves a residue. The Ocher Card Man said so, and I believe him. But if I don't make any *big* changes . . . if I do nothing but go to Jodie and meet Sadie again for the first time . . . if we should happen to fall in love . . .

I want that to happen, and think it probably would. Blood calls to blood, heart calls to heart. She'll want children. So, for that matter, will I. I tell myself one child more or less won't make any difference, either. Or not *much* difference. Or two. Even three. (It is, after all The Era of Big Families.) We'll live quietly. We won't make waves.

Only each child is a wave.

Every breath we take is a wave.

You have to go back one last time, the Ocher Card Man said. *You have to close the circle. Want has nothing to do with it.*

Can I really be thinking of risking the world—perhaps reality itself—for the woman I love? That makes Lee's insanity look piddling.

The man with the card tucked into the brim of his hat is waiting for me beside the drying shed. I can feel him there. Maybe he's not sending out thought-waves, but it sure feels like it. *Come back. You don't have to be the Jimla. It's not too late to be Jake again. To be the good guy, the good angel. Never mind saving the president; save the world. Do it while there's still time.*

Yes.

I will.

Probably I will.

Tomorrow.

Tomorrow will be soon enough, won't it?

10/1/58

Still here at the Tamarack. Still writing.

My uncertainty about Clayton is the worst. Clayton is what I thought about as I screwed the last of my refills into my trusty fountain pen, and he's what I'm thinking about now. If I knew she was going to be safe from him, I think I could let go. Will John Clayton still turn up at Sadie's house on Bee Tree Lane if I subtract myself from the equation? Maybe seeing us together was what finally drove him over the edge. But he followed her to Texas even *before* he knew about us, and if he does it again, this time he might cut her throat instead of her cheek. Deke and I wouldn't be there to stop him, certainly.

Only maybe he *did* know about us. Sadie might have written a friend back in Savannah, and the friend might have told a friend, and the news that Sadie was spending time with a guy—one who didn't know the imperatives of the broom—might finally have gotten back to her ex. If none of that happened because I wasn't there, Sadie would be all right.

The lady or the tiger?

I don't know, I don't know.

The weather is turning toward autumn.

10/6/58

I went to the drive-in last night. It's the last weekend for them. On Monday they'll put up a sign that says CLOSED FOR THE

SEASON and add something like TWICE AS FINE IN '59! The last program consisted of two short subjects, a Bugs Bunny cartoon, and another pair of horror movies, *Macabre* and *The Tingler.* I took my usual folding chair and watched *Macabre* without really seeing it. I was cold. I have money to buy a coat, but now I'm afraid to buy much of anything. I keep thinking about the changes it could cause.

When the first feature ended, I did go into the snackbar, however. I wanted some hot coffee. (Thinking *This can't change much,* also thinking *How do you know.*) When I came out, there was only one child in the kiddie playground that would have been full at intermission only a month ago. It was a girl wearing a jean jacket and bright red pants. She was jumping rope. She looked like Rosette Templeton.

"I went down the road, the road was a-muddy," she chanted. "I stubbed my toe, my toe was a-bloody. You all here? Count *two* an *three* an *four* and *fi'*! My true love's a *butterfly*!"

I couldn't stay. I was shivering too hard.

Maybe poets can kill the world for love, but not ordinary little guys like me. Tomorrow, supposing the rabbit-hole is still there, I'm going back. But before I do . . .

Coffee wasn't the only thing I bought in the snackbar.

10/7/58

The lockbox from the Western Auto is on the bed, standing open. The spade is in the closet (what the maid thought about that I have no idea). The ink in my last refill is running low, but that's okay; another two or three pages will bring me to the end. I'll put the manuscript in the lockbox, then bury it near the pond where I once disposed of my cell phone. I'll bury it deep in that soft dark soil. Perhaps someday, someone will find it. Maybe it will be you. If there *is* a future and there *is* a you, that is. This is something I will soon find out.

I tell myself (hopefully, fearfully) that my three weeks in the Tamarack can't have changed much; Al spent four years in the past and came back to an intact present . . . although I admit I have wondered about his possible relationship to the World Trade Center holocaust or the big Japanese earthquake. I tell myself there is no connection . . . but still I wonder.

I should also tell you that I no longer think of 2011 as the present. Philip Nolan was the Man Without a Country; I am the Man Without a Time Frame. I suspect I always will be. Even if 2011 is still there, I will be a visiting stranger.

Beside me on the desk is a postcard featuring a photo of cars pulled up in front of a big screen. That's the only kind of card they sell in the Lisbon Drive-In snackbar. I have written the message, and I have written the address: Mr. Deacon Simmons, Jodie High School, Jodie, Texas. I started to write Denholm Consolidated High School, but JHS won't become DCHS until next year or the year after.

The message reads: *Dear Deke: When your new librarian comes, watch out for her. She's going to need a good angel, particularly in April of 1963. Please believe me.*

No, Jake, I hear the Ocher Card Man whisper. *If John Clayton is supposed to kill her and doesn't, changes will occur . . . and, as you've seen for yourself, the changes are never for the better. No matter how good your intentions are.*

But it's Sadie! I tell him, and although I've never been what you'd call a crying man, now the tears begin to come. They ache, they burn. *It's Sadie and I love her! How can I just stand by when he may kill her?*

The reply is as obdurate as the past itself: *Close the circle.*

So I tear the postcard into pieces, I put them in the room's ashtray, I set them on fire. There's no smoke alarm to blare to the world what I have done. There's only the rasping sound of my sobs. It's as though I have killed her with my own hands. Soon I'll bury my lockbox with the manuscript inside, and then I'll go back to Lisbon Falls, where the Ocher Card Man will no doubt be very glad to see me. I won't call a cab; I intend to walk the whole way, under the stars. I guess I want to say goodbye. Hearts don't really break. If only they could.

Right now I'm going nowhere except over to the bed, where I will lay my wet face on the pillow and pray to a God I can't quite believe in to send my Sadie some good angel so she can live. And love. And dance.

Goodbye, Sadie.

You never knew me, but I love you, honey.

CITIZEN OF THE CENTURY (2012)

1

I imagine the Home of the Famous Fatburger is gone now, replaced by an L.L. Bean Express, but I don't know for sure; that's something I've never bothered to check on the internet. All I know is that it was still there when I got back from all my adventures. And the world around it, too.

So far, at least.

I don't know about the Bean Express because that was my last day in Lisbon Falls. I went back to my house in Sabattus, caught up on my sleep, then packed two suitcases and my cat and drove south. I stopped for gas in a small Massachusetts town called Westborough, and decided it looked good enough for a man with no particular prospects and no expectations from life.

I stayed that first night in the Westborough Hampton Inn. There was Wi-Fi. I got on the net—my heart beating so hard it sent dots flashing across my field of vision—and called up the Dallas *Morning News* website. After punching in my credit card number (a process that took several retries because of my shaking fingers), I was able to access the archives. The story about an unknown assailant taking a shot at Edwin Walker was there on April 11 of 1963, but nothing about Sadie on April 12. Nothing the following week, or the week after that. I kept hunting.

I found the story I was looking for in the issue for April 30.

2

MENTAL PATIENT SLASHES EX-WIFE, COMMITS SUICIDE
By Ernie Calvert

(JODIE) 77-year-old Deacon "Deke" Simmons and Denholm Consolidated School District Principal Ellen Dockerty arrived too late on Sunday night to save Sadie Dunhill from being seriously hurt, but things could have been much worse for the popular 28-year-old school librarian.

According to Douglas Reems, the Jodie town constable, "If Deke and Ellie hadn't arrived when they did, Miss Dunhill almost certainly would have been killed."

The two educators had come with a tuna casserole and a bread pudding. Neither wanted to talk about their heroic intervention. Simmons would only say, "I wish we'd gotten there sooner."

According to Constable Reems, Simmons overpowered the much younger John Clayton, of Savannah, Georgia, after Miss Dockerty threw the casserole at him, distracting him. Simmons wrestled away a small revolver. Clayton then produced the knife with which he had cut his ex-wife's face and used it to slash his own throat. Simmons and Miss Dockerty tried to stop the bleeding to no avail. Clayton was pronounced dead at the scene.

Miss Dockerty told Constable Reems that Clayton may have been stalking his ex-wife for months. The staff at Denholm Consolidated had been alerted that Miss Dunhill's ex-husband might be dangerous, and Miss Dunhill herself had provided a photograph of Clayton, but Principal Dockerty said he had disguised his appearance.

Miss Dunhill was transported by ambulance to Parkland Memorial Hospital in Dallas, where her condition is listed as fair.

3

Never a crying man, that's me, but I made up for it that night. That night I cried myself to sleep, and for the first time in a very long time, my sleep was deep and restful.

Alive.

She was alive.

Scarred for life—oh yes, undoubtedly—but alive.

Alive, alive, alive.

4

The world was still there, and it still harmonized . . . or perhaps I *made* it harmonize. When we make that harmony ourselves, I guess we call it habit. I caught on as a sub in the Westborough school system, then caught on full-time. It did not surprise me that the principal at the local high school was a gung-ho football freak named Borman . . . as in a certain jolly coach I'd once known in another place. I stayed in touch with my old friends from Lisbon Falls for awhile, and then I didn't. *C'est la vie.*

I checked the Dallas *Morning News* archives again, and discovered a short item in the May 29 issue from 1963: JODIE LIBRARIAN LEAVES HOSPITAL. It was short and largely uninformative. Nothing about her condition and nothing about her future plans. And no photo. Squibs buried on page 20, between ads for discount furniture and door-to-door sales opportunities, never come with photos. It's one of life's great truisms, like the way the phone always rings while you're on the john or in the shower.

In the year after I came back to the Land of Now, there were some sites and some search topics I steered clear of. Was I tempted? Of course. But the net is a double-edged sword. For every thing you find that's of comfort—like discovering that the woman you loved survived her crazy ex-husband—there are two with the power to hurt. A person searching for news of a certain someone might discover that that someone had been killed in an accident. Or died of lung cancer as a result of smoking. Or committed suicide, in the case of this particular someone most likely accomplished with a combination of booze and sleeping pills.

Sadie alone, with no one to slap her awake and stick her in a cold shower. If that had happened, I didn't want to know.

I used the internet to prep for my classes, I used it to check the movie listings, and once or twice a week I checked out the latest viral videos. What I didn't do was check for news of Sadie. I suppose that if Jodie had had a newspaper I might have been even more tempted, but it hadn't had one then and surely didn't now, when that very same internet was slowly strangling the print media. Besides, there's an old saying: *peek not through a knothole, lest ye be vexed.* Was there ever a bigger knothole in human history than the internet?

She survived Clayton. It would be best, I told myself, to let my knowledge of Sadie end there.

5

It might have, had I not gotten a transfer student in my AP English class. In April of 2012, this was; it might even have been on April 10, the forty-ninth anniversary of the attempted Edwin Walker assassination. Her name was Erin Tolliver, and her family had moved to Westborough from Killeen, Texas.

That was a name I knew well. Killeen, where I had bought rubbers from a druggist with a nastily knowing smile. *Don't do anything against the law, son,* he'd advised me. Killeen, where Sadie and I had shared a great many sweet nights at the Candlewood Bungalows.

Killeen, which had had a newspaper called *The Weekly Gazette.*

During her second week of classes—by then my new AP student had made several new girlfriends, had fascinated several boys, and was settling in nicely—I asked Erin if *The Weekly Gazette* still published. Her face lit up. "You've been to Killeen, Mr. Epping?"

"I was there a long time ago," I said—a statement that wouldn't have caused a lie detector needle to budge even slightly.

"It's still there. Mama used to say she only got it to wrap the fish in."

"Does it still run the 'Jodie Doin's' column?"

"It runs a 'Doin's' column for every little town south of Dallas," Erin said, giggling. "I bet you could find it on the net if you really wanted to, Mr. Epping. *Everything's* on the net."

She was absolutely right about that, and I held out for exactly one week. Sometimes the knothole is just too tempting.

6

My intention was simple: I would go to the archive (assuming *The Weekly Gazette* had one) and search for Sadie's name. It was against my better judgment, but Erin Tolliver had inadvertently stirred up feelings that had begun to settle, and I knew I wouldn't rest easy again until I checked. As it turned out, the archive was unnecessary. I found what I was looking for not in the 'Jodie Doin's' column but on the first page of the current issue.

JODIE PICKS "CITIZEN OF THE CENTURY" FOR JULY CENTENNIAL CELEBRATION, the headline read. And the picture below the headline . . . she was eighty now, but some faces you don't forget. The photographer might have suggested that she turn her head so the left side was hidden, but Sadie faced the camera head-on. And why not? It was an old scar now, the wound inflicted by a man many years in his grave. I thought it lent character to her face, but of course, I was prejudiced. To the loving eye, even smallpox scars are beautiful.

In late June, after school was out, I packed a suitcase and once again headed for Texas.

7

Dusk of a summer night in the town of Jodie, Texas. It's a little bigger than it was in 1963, but not much. There's a box factory in the part of town where Sadie Dunhill once lived on Bee Tree Lane. The barber shop is gone, and the Cities Service station where I once bought gas for my Sunliner is now a 7-Eleven. There's a Subway where Al Stevens once sold Prongburgers and Mesquite Fries.

The speeches commemorating Jodie's centennial are over. The one given by the woman chosen by the Historical Society and Town Council as the Citizen of the Century was charmingly brief, that of the mayor longwinded but informative. I learned that Sadie had served one term as mayor herself and four terms in the Texas State Legislature, but that was the least of it. There was her charitable work, her ceaseless efforts to improve the quality of education at DCHS, and her year's sabbatical to do volunteer work in post-Katrina New Orleans. There was the Texas State Library program for blind students, an initiative to improve hospital services for veterans, and her ceaseless (and continuing, even at eighty) efforts to provide better state services to the indigent mentally ill. In 1996 she had been offered a chance to run for the U.S. Congress but declined, saying she had plenty to do at the grassroots.

She never remarried. She never left Jodie. She's still tall, her body unbent by osteoporosis. And she's still beautiful, her long white hair flowing down her back almost to her waist.

Now the speeches are over, and Main Street has been closed off. A banner at each end of the two-block business section proclaims

STREET DANCE, 7PM–MIDNITE!
Y'ALL COME!

Sadie is surrounded by well-wishers—some of whom I think I still recognize—so I take a walk down to the DJ's platform in front of what used to be the Western Auto and is now a Walgreens. The guy fussing with the records and CDs is a sixty-something with thinning gray hair and a considerable paunch, but I'd know those square-bear pink-rimmed specs anywhere.

"Hello, Donald," I say. "See you've still got the round mound of sound."

Donald Bellingham looks up and smiles. "Never leave for the gig without it. Do I know you?"

"No," I say, "my mom. She was at a dance you DJ'd way back in the early sixties. She said you snuck in your father's big band records."

He grins. "Yeah, I caught hell for that. Who was your mother?"

"Andrea Robertson," I say, picking the name at random. Andrea was my best pupil in period two American Lit.

"Sure, I remember her." His vague smile says he doesn't.

"I don't suppose you still have any of those old records, do you?"

"God, no. Long gone. But I've got all kinds of big band stuff on CD. Do I feel a request coming on?"

"Actually, you do. But it's kind of special."

He laughs. "Ain't they all."

I tell him what I want, and Donald—as eager to please as ever—agrees. As I start back toward the end of the block, where the woman I came to see is now being helped to punch by the mayor, Donald calls after me. "I never caught your name."

"Amberson," I tell him over my shoulder. "George Amberson."

"And you want it at eight-fifteen?"

"On the dot. Time is of the essence, Donald. Let's hope it cooperates."

Five minutes later, Donald Bellingham nukes Jodie with "At the Hop" and dancers fill the street under the Texas sunset.

8

At ten past eight, Donald plays a slow Alan Jackson tune, one even grown-ups can dance to. Sadie is left alone for the first time since the speechifying ended, and I approach her. My heart beating so hard it seems to shake my whole body.

"Miz Dunhill?"

She turns, smiling and looking up a little. She's tall, but I'm taller. Always was. "Yes?"

"My name is George Amberson. I wanted to tell you how much I admire you and all the good work you've done."

Her smile grows a little puzzled. "Thank you, sir. I don't recognize you, but the name seems familiar. Are you from Jodie?"

I can no longer travel in time, and I certainly can't read minds, but I know what she's thinking, just the same. *I hear that name in my dreams.*

"I am, and I'm not." And before she can pursue it: "May I ask what sparked your interest in public service?"

Her smile is now just a lingering ghost around the corners of her mouth. "And you want to know because—?"

"Was it the assassination? The Kennedy assassination?"

"Why . . . I guess it was, in a way. I like to think I would have gotten involved in the wider world anyway, but I suppose it started there. It left this part of Texas with . . ." Her left hand rises involuntarily toward her cheek, then drops again. ". . . such a scar. Mr. Amberson, where do I know you from? Because I *do* know you, I'm sure of it."

"Can I ask another question?"

She looks at me with mounting perplexity. I glance at my watch. Eight-fourteen. Almost time. Unless Donald forgets, of course . . . and I don't think he will. To quote some old fifties song or other, some things are just meant to be.

"The Sadie Hawkins dance, back in 1961. Who did you get to chaperone with you when Coach Borman's mother broke her hip? Do you recall?"

Her mouth drops open, then slowly closes. The mayor and his wife approach, see us in deep conversation, and veer off. We are in our own little capsule here; just Jake and Sadie. The way it was once upon a time.

"Don Haggarty," she says. "It was like shapping a dance with the village idiot. Mr. Amberson—"

But before she can finish, Donald Bellingham comes in through eight tall loudspeakers, right on cue: "Okay, Jodie, here's a blast from the past, a platter that *really* matters, only the best and by request!"

Then it comes, that smooth brass intro from a long-gone band: *Bah-dah-dah . . . bah-dah-da-dee-dum . . .*

"Oh my God, 'In the Mood,'" Sadie says. "I used to lindy to this one."

I hold out my hand. "Come on. Let's do the thing."

She laughs, shaking her head. "My swing-dancing days are far behind me, I'm afraid, Mr. Amberson."

"But you're not too old to waltz. As Donald used to say in the old days, 'Out of your seats and on your feets.' And call me George. Please."

In the street, couples are jitterbugging. A few of them are even trying to lindy-hop, but none of them can swing it the way Sadie and I could swing it, back in the day. Not even close.

She takes my hand like a woman in a dream. She *is* in a dream, and so am I. Like all sweet dreams, it will be brief . . . but brevity *makes* sweetness, doesn't it? Yes, I think so. Because when the time is gone, you can never get it back.

Party lights hang over the street, yellow and red and green. Sadie stumbles over someone's chair, but I'm ready for this and catch her easily by the arm.

"Sorry, clumsy," she says.

"You always were, Sadie. One of your more endearing traits."

Before she can ask about that, I slip my arm around her waist. She slips hers around mine, still looking up at me. The lights skate across her cheeks and shine in her eyes. We clasp hands, fingers folding together naturally, and for me the years fall away like a coat that's too heavy and too tight. In that moment I hope one thing above all others: that she was not too busy to find at least one good man, one who disposed of John Clayton's fucking broom once and for all.

She speaks in a voice almost too low to be heard over the music, but I hear her—I always did. "Who *are* you, George?"

"Someone you knew in another life, honey."

Then the music takes us, the music rolls away the years, and we dance.

January 2, 2009–December 18, 2010
Sarasota, Florida
Lovell, Maine

AFTERWORD

Almost half a century has passed since John Kennedy was murdered in Dallas, but two questions linger: Was Lee Oswald really the trigger-man, and if so, did he act alone? Nothing I've written in *11/22/63* will provide answers to those questions, because time-travel is just an interesting make-believe. But if you, like me, are curious about why those questions still remain, I think I can give you a satisfactory two-word response: Karen Carlin. Not just a footnote to history, but a footnote to a footnote. And yet . . .

Jack Ruby owned a Dallas strip joint called the Carousel Club. Carlin, whose *nom du burlesque* was Little Lynn, danced there. On the night following the assassination, Ruby received a call from Miss Carlin, who was twenty-five dollars short on the December rent and desperately needed a loan to keep from being turned out into the street. Would he help?

Jack Ruby, who had other things on his mind, gave her the rough side of his tongue (in truth, it was the only side Dallas's Sparky Jack seemed to have). He was appalled that the president he revered had been killed in his home city, and he spoke repeatedly to friends and relatives about how terrible this was for Mrs. Kennedy and her children. Ruby was heartsick at the thought of Jackie having to return to Dallas for Oswald's trial. The widow would become a national spectacle, he said. Her grief would be used to sell tabloids.

Unless, of course, Lee Oswald came down with a bad case of the deads.

Everybody at the Dallas Police Department had at least a nodding acquaintance with Jack. He and his "wife"—that was what he called his little dachsund, Sheba—were frequent visitors at DPD. He handed out free passes to his clubs, and when cops showed up there, he bought them free drinks. So no one took any particular notice of him when he turned up at the station on Saturday, November twenty-third. When Oswald was paraded before the press, proclaiming his innocence and displaying a black eye, Ruby was there. He had a gun (yes, another .38, this one a Colt Cobra), and he fully intended to shoot Oswald with it. But the room was crowded; Ruby was shunted to the back; then Oswald was gone.

So Jack Ruby gave up.

Late Sunday morning, he went to the Western Union office a block or so from the DPD and sent "Little Lynn" a money order for twenty-five dollars. Then he wandered down to the cop-shop. He assumed that Oswald had already been transferred to the Dallas County Jail, and was surprised to see a crowd gathered in front of the police station. There were reporters, news vans, and your ordinary gawkers. The transfer hadn't occurred on schedule.

Ruby had his gun, and Ruby wormed his way into the police garage. No problem there. Some of the cops even said hi, and Ruby hi'd them right back. Oswald was still upstairs. At the last moment he had asked his jailers if he could put on a sweater, because his shirt had a hole in it. The detour to get the sweater took less than three minutes, but that was just enough—life turns on a dime. Ruby shot Oswald in the abdomen. As a pig-pile of cops landed on top of Sparky Jack, he managed to yell: "Hey, guys, I'm Jack Ruby! You all know me!"

The assassin died at Parkland Hospital shortly thereafter, without making a statement. Thanks to a stripper who needed twenty-five bucks and a half-assed showboat who wanted to put on a sweater, Oswald was never tried for his crime, and never had a real chance to confess. His final statement on his part in the events of 11/22/63 was "I'm a patsy." The resulting arguments over whether or not he was telling the truth have never stopped.

Early in the novel, Jake Epping's friend Al puts the probability that Oswald was the lone gunman at ninety-five percent. After reading a stack of books and articles on the subject almost as tall as I am, I'd put the probability at ninety-eight percent, maybe even ninety-nine. Because all of the accounts, including those written by conspiracy theorists, tell the same simple American story: here was a dangerous little fame-junkie who found himself in just the right place to get lucky. Were the odds of it happening just the way it did long? Yes. So are the odds on winning the lottery, but someone wins one every day.

Probably the most useful source-materials I read in preparation for writing this novel were *Case Closed,* by Gerald Posner; *Legend,* by Edward Jay Epstein (nutty Robert Ludlum stuff, but fun); *Oswald's Tale,* by Norman Mailer; and *Mrs. Paine's Garage,* by Thomas Mallon. The latter offers a brilliant analysis of the conspiracy theorists and their need to find order in what was almost a random event. The Mailer is also remarkable. He says that he went into the project (which includes extensive interviews with Russians who knew Lee and Marina in Minsk) believing that Oswald was the victim of a conspiracy, but in the end came to believe—reluctantly—that the stodgy ole Warren Commission was right: Oswald acted alone.

It is very, very difficult for a reasonable person to believe otherwise. Occam's Razor—the simplest explanation is usually the right one.

I was also deeply impressed—and moved, and shaken—by my rereading of William Manchester's *Death of a President*. He's dead wrong about some things, he's given to flights of purple prose (calling Marina Oswald "lynx-eyed," for instance), his analysis of Oswald's motives is both superficial and hostile, but this massive work, published only four years after that terrible lunch hour in Dallas, is closest in time to the assassination, written when most of the participants were still alive and their recollections were still vivid. Armed with Jacqueline Kennedy's conditional approval of the project, everyone talked to Manchester, and although his account of the aftermath is turgid, his narrative of 11/22's events is chilling and vivid, a Zapruder film in words.

Well . . . *almost* everyone talked to him. Marina Oswald did not, and Manchester's consequent harsh treatment of her may have something to do with that. Marina (still alive at this writing) had her eye on the main chance in the aftermath of her husband's cowardly act, and who could blame her? Those who want to read her full recollections can find them in *Marina and Lee,* by Priscilla Johnson McMillan. I trust very little of what she says (unless corroborated by other sources), but I salute—with some reluctance, it's true—her survival skills.

I originally tried to write this book way back in 1972. I dropped the project because the research it would involve seemed far too daunting for a man who was teaching full-time. There was another reason: even nine years after the deed, the wound was still too fresh. I'm glad I waited. When I finally decided to go ahead, it was natural for me to turn to my old friend Russ Dorr for help with the research. He provided a splendid support system for another long book, *Under the Dome,* and once more rose to the occasion. I am writing this afterword surrounded by heaps of research materials, the most valuable of which are the videos Russ shot during our exhaustive (and exhausting) travels in Dallas, and the foot-high stack of emails that came in response to my questions about everything from the 1958 World Series to mid-century bugging devices. It was Russ who located the home of Edwin Walker, which just happened to be on the 11/22 motorcade route (the past harmonizes), and it was Russ who—after much searching of various Dallas records—found the probable 1963 address of that most peculiar man, George de Mohrenschildt. And by the way, just where *was* Mr. de Mohrenschildt on the night of April 10, 1963? Probably not at the Carousel Club, but if he had an alibi for the attempted assassination of the general, I wasn't able to find it.

I hate to bore you with my Academy Awards speech—I get very annoyed with writers who do that—but I need to tip my cap to some other people, all the same. Big Number One is Gary Mack, curator of The Sixth Floor Museum in Dallas. He answered billions of questions, sometimes twice or three times before I got the info crammed into my dumb head. The tour of the Texas School Book Depository was a grim necessity that he lightened with his considerable wit and encyclopedic knowledge.

Thanks are also due to Nicola Longford, the Executive Director of The Sixth Floor Museum, and Megan Bryant, Director of Collections and Intellectual Property. Brian Collins and Rachel Howell work in the History Department of the Dallas Public Library and gave me access to old films (some of them pretty hilarious) that show how the city looked in the years 1960–63. Susan Richards, a researcher at the Dallas Historical Society, also pitched in, as did Amy Brumfield, David Reynolds, and the staff of the Adolphus Hotel. Longtime Dallas resident Martin Nobles drove Russ and me around Dallas. He took us to the now-closed but still standing Texas Theatre, where Oswald was captured, to the former residence of Edwin Walker, to Greenville Avenue (not as gruesome as Fort Worth's bar-and-whore district once was), and to Mercedes Street, where 2703 no longer exists. It did indeed blow away in a tornado . . . although not in 1963. And a tip of the cap to Mike "Silent Mike" McEachern, who donated his name for charitable purposes.

I want to thank Doris Kearns Goodwin and her husband, former Kennedy aide-de-camp Dick Goodwin, for indulging my questions about worst-case scenarios, had Kennedy lived. George Wallace as the thirty-seventh president was their idea . . . but the more I thought about it, the more plausible it seemed. My son, the novelist Joe Hill, pointed out several consequences of time-travel I hadn't considered. He also thought up a new and better ending. Joe, you rock.

And I want to thank my wife, my first reader of choice and hardest, fairest critic. An ardent Kennedy supporter, she saw him in person not long before his death, and has never forgotten it. A contrarian her whole life, Tabitha is (it does not surprise me and should not surprise you) on the side of the conspiracy theorists.

Have I gotten things wrong here? You bet. Have I changed things to suit the course of my story? Sure. As one example, it's true that Lee and Marina went to a welcome party thrown by George Bouhe and attended by most of the area's Russian émigrés, and it's true that Lee hated and resented those middle-class burghers who had turned their back on Mother Russia, but the party happened three weeks later than it does in my book. And while it's true that Lee, Marina, and baby June lived upstairs at 214 West Neely Street, I have no idea who—if anybody—lived in the downstairs apartment. But that was the one I toured (paying twenty bucks for the privilege), and it seemed a shame not to use the layout of the place. And what a desperate little place it was.

Mostly, however, I stuck to the truth.

Some people will protest that I have been excessively hard on the city of Dallas. I beg to differ. If anything, Jake Epping's first-person narrative allowed me to be too easy on it, at least as it was in 1963. On the day Kennedy landed at Love Field, Dallas was a hateful place. Confederate flags flew rightside up; American flags flew upside down. Some airport spectators held up signs reading HELP JFK STAMP OUT DEMOCRACY. Not long before that day in November, both Adlai Stevenson and Lady Bird Johnson were subjected to spit-showers by Dallas voters. Those spitting on Mrs. Johnson were middle-class housewives.

It's better today, but one still sees signs on Main Street saying HANDGUNS NOT ALLOWED IN THE BAR. This is an afterword, not an editorial, but I hold strong opinions on this subject, particularly given the current political climate of my country. If you want to know what political extremism can lead to, look at the Zapruder film. Take particular note of frame 313, where Kennedy's head explodes.

Before I finish, I want to thank one other person: the late Jack Finney, who was one of America's great fantasists and storytellers.

Besides *The Body Snatchers,* he wrote *Time and Again,* which is, in this writer's humble opinion, *the* great time-travel story. Originally I meant to dedicate this book to him, but in June of last year, a lovely little granddaughter arrived in our family, so Zelda gets the nod.

Jack, I'm sure you'd understand.

Stephen King
Bangor, Maine

Book Clubs: Travel Back to
11/22/63
with
STEPHEN KING

This book club kit contains everything you will need for an evening dedicated to *11/22/63*: suggested questions for discussion, a conversation with Stephen King about the book, a playlist, and a selection of recipes. There'll be a whole lotta shakin' goin' on!

Questions for Discussion

1. Where were you when JFK was assassinated?

2. *11/22/63* is filled with historical research—it twins real events with events and characters from King's imagination. Did you learn anything surprising about the actual events leading up to the Kennedy assassination while reading this novel?

3. Our hero Jake Epping goes on an epic journey to try to prevent Kennedy's assassination. Why choose this watershed moment in American history rather than any other moment? Would you choose a different moment, and if so, when?

4. Many great books, TV shows, and movies have investigated the idea of time travel. Do you have any particular favorite books or films that explore this?

5. When Jake lives in 1960s small town Texas, he meets some of the most important people in his life, including the lanky, lovely librarian Sadie. Why is Jake drawn to her? And why is she drawn to him? How does their relationship change over the course of the novel?

6. What is the role of romance in this book? Some reviewers of *11/22/63* cited King's optimism about love—after reading *11/22/63*, do you agree?

7. Jake (or rather George) has to spend a lot of time in Dallas, which he experiences as a malevolent place. Jodie, on the other hand, is everything idyllic small town America should be. Do you believe that certain places are evil at certain times?

8. *11/22/63* gives readers an opportunity to immerse themselves in the past, in all its casual cigarette smoking glory—the music, food, language, cars, and dancing. What are your favorite things about the '50s and '60s King creates in *11/22/63*? And least favorite?

9. Do you believe in the butterfly effect/chaos theory?

10. If you could pick any other period in history that you could go back to, which would it be?

11. Conspiracy theories abound, and numerous books have been written on the subject of the Kennedy assassination. In his afterword, King concludes (as Jake does in the book) that Lee Harvey Oswald was the lone gunman, a disturbed and grandiose man who altered world history forever all on his own. Do you agree?

Photo: Shane Leonard

A conversation with
Stephen King about 11/22/63

Where were you when JFK was assassinated?

When I got the news I was in a hearse. I was a tuition kid in a little town and there was no bus service to the high school where we went. So our parents clubbed together and paid a guy who had a converted hearse, which he turned into a kind of school bus, and we went back and forth in that.

We didn't get the news that Kennedy had been assassinated in school. But when we got into the hearse to go home, the driver, Mike, had the radio on for the first time in living memory. We heard that Kennedy had been killed. Mike, who was kind of silent, spoke up. "They'll catch the son of a bitch who did that and somebody will kill him." And that's exactly what happened.

When and why did you decide to write a novel about the Kennedy assassination?

I tried to write this novel in 1973 when I was teaching high school. At that time it was called *Split Track* and I wrote fourteen single-spaced pages. Then I stopped. The research was daunting for someone who was working full-time at another job. Also, I understood I wasn't ready—the scope was too big for me at that time. I put the book aside and thought someday maybe I'd go back to it.

I'm glad that I didn't go forward with it then. In 1973 the wound was still too fresh. Now it's going on half a century since Kennedy was assassinated. I think that's about long enough.

I recently saw Robert Redford's film *The Conspirator* about the Lincoln assassination. That was a hundred fifty years ago, but it's still kind of a shock to see the president of the United States assassinated by a lone gunman.

How does having a modern character going back in time affect the way you depict the 1950s, as opposed to simply setting a novel then?

Jake Epping, my main character, makes several different trips into the past—every trip takes him back to two minutes before noon on September 19, 1958, and every trip is a complete reset. Little by little he gets used to it, but the contrast between his twenty-first-century sensibility and the world of that late fifties and early sixties is jarring in a way that *Mad Men* isn't. And sometimes it's pretty funny, as when Jake gets caught singing a risqué Rolling Stones tune and tries to convince his girlfriend that he heard a song containing the lyrics "she tried to take me upstairs for a ride" on the radio!

We're pretty well anchored in the present, the world that we live in as it is now—a world where there's four-dollar-a-gallon gasoline, where men and women have a certain equality, where there's an African American president, where we have computers. When you first go back to 1958, the trip is jarring. Yet the longer Jake stays, the more he feels at home in that particular world. Eventually, he doesn't want to leave it. He's gotten fond of his life at a time when you didn't have to take your shoes off at the airport.

The act of writing is almost an act of hypnosis. You can remember things that are not immediately accessible to the conscious mind. I felt extremely challenged as I began this book. Could I really capture the sense of what it was like to live between 1958 and 1963? But writing, like anything imaginative, is an act of faith. You have to believe that those details will be there when you need them.

The more I wrote about those years, the more I remembered. I used research when I fell short but it was amazing how much came back to me—the sound coins made when you dropped them into the machine when you got on the bus; the smell of movie theaters when everybody was smoking; the dances, the teenage slang, books that were current, and the importance of the library in research. There's a funny sequence where Jake needs to find somebody and is very frustrated; if he had his computer he could simply run a search engine and get what he needed in two or three minutes. There weren't Jetways then; you walked out of a terminal and mounted the steps to get on a TWA plane. Now, TWA doesn't exist anymore, but that's the airline carrier that brought Lee Harvey Oswald back to Texas.

When researching the music of the day, do you listen to those songs as you write?

I've always been a pop music fan. I have a good grasp of music between 1955 and now—it's just one of the places where my head feels at home. It's also one of the indicators of how American life changes and what's going on at any particular time.

One of the epigrams for *11/22/63* is "dancing is life," and dancing is something that has always interested me. It's symbolic in so many ways of the courting ritual. The changes in dancing mirror the changes in the way we court and love and live over the years. I went to YouTube to watch videos of dances from the fifties and the sixties and that was an interesting thing, to watch people do the Stroll and the Madison, the Lindy Hop, Hell's a Poppin'—fantastic stuff. I'm crazy about music and I'm crazy about dancing and some of that's in the book.

I listen to music all the time. Not when I'm composing fresh copy, but when I'm rewriting or editing, I've always got it on and it's always turned up really loud. I also have certain touchstone songs that I go back to—they drive my wife, my kids, my grandchildren crazy. I'm the sort of guy who will play Whitney Houston's "I Will Always Love You" twenty-five times until I discover the song was written by Dolly Parton and then I listen to the Dolly Parton version forty times.

The music that made the biggest impression on me was rock 'n' roll from the early fifties. I tried to get into the book the excitement that the kids felt to hear someone like Jerry Louis, Chuck Berry, or Little Richard. The first time you heard Little Richard your life changed. The first time I heard Freddie Cannon do "Palisades Park" I thought to myself, "This makes me feel so happy to be alive."

Your *11/22/63* Playlist

Stephen King listened to these songs while writing *11/22/63*. Play them in the background during your book club gathering, and read his comments below. Enjoy!

1. "Swing the Mood," Jive Bunny and the Mastermixers:
"Most music critics of the purist stripe absolutely hated this collaboration between elderly British DJ John Pickles and his son, Andrew (aided by producer Mark 'The Hitman' Smith). For one thing, all the vocals have been speeded up, so everyone is singing an octave higher than normal. I'm no purist, and I just love this. There's a video on YouTube that's full of joyful dancing (not to mention Elvis deplaning in Germany with a dufflebag over his shoulder). The accompanying track is a variation."

2. "Screw You, We're From Texas," Ray Wylie Hubbard:
"Kind of says it all, don't it?"

3. "The Walk," the Inmates:
"I think the original was by The Diamonds, but this version is way cooler."

4. "Honky Tonk Women," the Rolling Stones

5. "That's Right (You're Not from Texas)," Lyle Lovett:
"Lots of people in Dallas will probably point this out to me. Like I don't know."

6. "She's About a Mover," Sir Douglas Quintet:
"Guest appearance at Miz Mimi's wedding party."

7. "You're Gonna Miss Me," the 13th Floor Elevators:
"Many would say the Elevators were the quintessential Texas rock band. They were from Austin, they swallowed LSD by the bushel, and frontman Roky Erikson ended up in a mental asylum. Without the Elevators, ZZ Top probably never exists. Then there was this young girl, Janis Joplin, who sometimes sang with them."

8. "Heaven's Just a Sin Away," John Fogerty:
"The ultimate cheating song. This version probably isn't as good as the honky-tonk original, by The Kendalls, but it's good. Always makes me think of Jake and Sadie at the Candlewood."

9. "Texas Time Travelin'," Cory Morrow

10. "C'mon Everybody," Eddie Cochran:
"The avatar of late '50s rock. Cochran, who died in a car crash, was the rock version of James Dean."

11. "At the Hop," Danny and the Juniors:
"The best jitterbug tune ever."

12. "The Twist," Chubby Checker

13. "The Wah Watusi," the Orlons:
"A dance that was banned in most high schools, because it involved boys and girls thrusting their pelvises at each other. Oooh, no!"

14. "Bristol Stomp," the Dovells:
"The Dovells were by far the best of the Philly doo-wop groups. They almost caused a riot when they appeared on *American Bandstand*. Those boys were handsome dogs, and they could shake it. Their signature dance-move was called The Baseball. It beggars description; all you can do is fall down and worship."

15. "Sea Cruise," Frankie Ford

16. "Whole Lotta Shakin' Goin' On," Jerry Lee Lewis:
"This record's fifty-five years old, and still nasty. But not Lewis's finest record, in my opinion—that would be 'Lewis Boogie.'"

17. "Rock and Roll Is Here to Stay," Danny and the Juniors:
"Killer song with not one but two modulations. And rock is supposed to be simple!"

18. "Do You Wanna Dance," Bobby Freeman:
"Sure we do. Dancing is life."

19. "Thriftstore Cowgirl," Red Meat:
"This is how time travel is supposed to be."

20. "In the Mood," Glenn Miller:
"Isn't this where we came in?"

Your *11/22/63* Menu

The food of the 1950s and 1960s tastes especially delicious to Jake Epping. Cook and serve one of the hearty meals he enjoys in *11/22/63*.

Recipes courtesy of *The Joy of Cooking* 75th Anniversary Edition; available from Scribner.

> There was a U-Needa-Lunch on Witcham Street, just around the corner. I ordered a hamburger, a fountain Coke, and a piece of chocolate pie. The pie was excellent—real chocolate, real cream. It filled my mouth the way Frank Anicetti's root beer had.

HAMBURGERS
4 burgers

It is a mistake to make burgers with lean beef, for they need some fat for flavor and moistness. The ideal burger is made from ground chuck.

Divide the meat into 4 equal portions and form each into a patty about 1 inch thick:

¼ pounds ground beef chuck

Sprinkle with:

Salt and black pepper

Cook, flipping once, by grilling over a hot fire, broiling under a preheated broiler, or cooking in a preheated skillet over medium-high heat. For all three methods, it will take about 3 minutes on each side for rare, 4 minutes for medium, or 5 minutes on each side for well-done. Place the burgers in or between:

4 hamburger buns or other rolls, split,
**   or 8 slices bread**

Add your choice of:

mayonnaise, mustard, sliced tomato, lettuce,
**   sliced onion, dill pickles, tomato catsup, or**
**   barbecue sauce.**

Serve at once.

I saw a little restaurant with a sign in the window reading BEST SHAKES, FRIES, AND BURGERS IN ALL OF TEXAS! It was called Al's Diner. Of course it was. I parked in one of the slant spaces out front, went in, and ordered the Pronghorn Special, which turned out to be a double cheeseburger with barbecue sauce. It came with Mesquite Fries and a Rodeo Thickshake— your choice of vanilla, chocolate, or strawberry. A Pronghorn wasn't quite as good as a Fatburger, but it wasn't bad, and the fries were just the way I like them: crispy, salty, and a little overdone.

BARBECUE SAUCE
4 cups
Combine in a medium saucepan and bring to a simmer over medium heat, stirring often:

> **1 ½ cups catsup**
> **1 cup cider vinegar or red wine vinegar**
> **¼ cup Worcestershire sauce**
> **¼ cup soy sauce**
> **1 cup packed light or dark brown sugar**
> **2 tablespoons dry mustard**
> **¼ cup chili powder, or to taste**
> **1 tablespoon grated peeled fresh ginger or**
> ** 1 teaspoon ground ginger**
> **2 garlic cloves, minced**
> **2 tablespoons vegetable oil**
> **3 lemon slices**

Simmer, stirring often, for 5 minutes. Remove the lemon slices, if desired. The sauce will keep, covered and refrigerated, for up to 2 weeks.

OVEN "FRENCH-FRIED" POTATOES
4 servings
Preheat the oven to 450°F.
Peel and cut lengthwise into ½-inch-thick strips:

> **4 medium baking potatoes (about 1 pound)**

Soak in cold water for 10 minutes, then drain and dry well between towels. Toss the potatoes with:

> **2 tablespoons vegetable or olive oil, bacon**
> ** drippings, or melted butter**

Spread on a baking sheet and bake, turning several times, until golden, 30 to 40 minutes. Turn the potatoes onto paper towels to drain briefly, then sprinkle with:

½ teaspoon salt
(paprika or black pepper to taste)

BLACK BOTTOM PIE
One 10-inch pie

Prepare a gingersnap crumb crust.
Put in a bowl, reserving a tablespoon or two
for topping, if desired:

1 ½ cups fine gingersnap crumbs

Add and stir until well blended:

¼ to ½ cup sugar, depending on sweetness
of the cookies
6 tablespoons (¾ stick) unsalted butter,
melted and cooled
(1 teaspoon ground cinnamon)

Place the crumb mixture in a pie pan, distributing the crumbs fairly evenly, then press another pie pan of the same diameter firmly into the dough. When the top pan is removed, presto!— a crust of even thickness underneath. Trim any excess that is forced over the top edge, or just pat back into the pan.

Crumb crusts do not need to be baked before filling, but if used unbaked, the crust must first be frozen for 20 minutes, or the filling will soften it. If baked before filing, they are more crunchy and flavorful; a 350°F oven for 10 to 12 minutes will do the trick. Cool the baked shell before filling.

Prepare the filling.
Pour into a small cup:

¼ cup cold water

Sprinkle over the top and let stand for 5 minutes:

½ teaspoons unflavored gelatin

Place in a small bowl:

6 ounces bittersweet or semisweet chocolate, finely
chopped, or 1 cup semisweet chocolate chips

Whisk together thoroughly in a medium heavy
saucepan:

⅓ cup sugar
4 teaspoons cornstarch

Gradually whisk in:

2 cups half-and-half or 1 cup milk plus 1 cup
heavy cream

Vigorously whisk in until no yellow streaks remain:

4 large egg yolks

Stirring constantly, bring to a simmer over medium heat and cook for 30 seconds. Immediately stir 1 cup of the mixture into the chocolate. Add the softened gelatin to the mixture remaining in the pan and stir for 30 seconds to dissolve the gelatin. Vigorously stir the chocolate mixture until smooth (if the chocolate fails to melt completely, set the bottom of the bowl in very hot water). Spread the chocolate mixture evenly over the bottom of the piecrust and refrigerate. Stir into the custard in the pan:

2 tablespoons dark rum
2 teaspoons vanilla

Beat in a large bowl until foamy:

3 large egg whites

Add:

¼ teaspoon cream of tartar

Continue to beat until soft peaks form, then gradually beat in:

⅓ cup plus 1 tablespoon sugar

Increase the speed to high and beat until the peaks are stiff and glossy. Gently fold the egg whites into the custard mixture. Spoon the filling over the chocolate mixture in the piecrust. Refrigerate for at least 3 hours, or up to 1 day. Top with **whipped cream.** If you wish, sprinkle with:

1 ounce bittersweet or semisweet chocolate,
    grated or shaved.

The pie can be refrigerated for up to 1 day.

MILK SHAKE
2 servings

Process in a blender until smooth and frothy:

2 cups any flavor ice cream
2 cups milk
(¼ cup of cocoa syrup)

Dear George—

If you still want to take me to dinner tonight, it will have to be five-ish, because I'll have early mornings all this week and next, getting ready for the Fall Book Sale. Perhaps we could come back to my place for dessert.

I have poundcake, if you'd like a slice.
Sadie

SOUR CREAM POUND CAKE
One 10-inch fluted tube or 9-inch tube cake
Stays moist for close to a week.
Have all ingredients at room temperature, about 70°F. Preheat the oven to 325°F. Grease and flour a 10-inch fluted tube pan or 9-inch plain tube pan.
Whisk together until thoroughly blended:
  3 cups sifted cake flour
  ¼ teaspoon baking soda
  ¼ teaspoon salt
Combine in a small bowl:
  1 cup sour cream
  2 teaspoons vanilla
Beat in a large bowl until creamy, about 30 seconds:
  1 cup (2 sticks) unsalted butter
Gradually add and beat on high speed until light and fluffy, 3 to 5 minutes:
  2 cups sugar
Beat in one at a time:
  6 large egg yolks
On low speed, add the flour mixture in 3 parts, alternating with the sour cream mixture in 2 parts, beating until smooth and scraping the sides of the bowl with a rubber spatula as necessary. Using clean beaters, beat in a large bowl on medium speed until soft peaks form:
  6 large egg whites
  ¼ teaspoon cream of tartar
Gradually add, beating on high speed:
  ½ cup sugar
Beat until the peaks are stiff but not dry. Use a rubber spatula to fold one-quarter of the egg whites into the sour cream mixture, then fold in the remaining whites. Scrape the batter into the pan and spread evenly. Bake until a toothpick inserted into the center comes out clean, 1 hour 10 minutes to 1 hour 20 minutes. Let cool

in the pan on a rack for 10 minutes. Slide a thin knife around the cake to detach it from the pan, invert the cake, and let cool right side up on the rack.

Once, as we ate ham-steaks and okra in her kitchen afterward, she said our courtship reminded her of that movie with Audrey Hepburn and Gary Cooper—*Love in the Afternoon*.

BROILED HAM STEAK

Traditional accompaniments are Fresh Corn Fritters and Broiled Tomatoes. Allow ⅓ pound ham per person.
Preheat the broiler. Slash in several places the fat edge of:
1 ham steak, about 1 inch thick
Place it on the broiler rack 3 inches below the heating element and broil 8 to 12 minutes on each side. If desired brush it toward the end of cooking with
a mixture of:
1 teaspoon dry mustard
1 tablespoon fresh lemon juice
¼ cup grape jelly, melted

FRIED OKRA
10 to 12 servings
In a medium bowl, combine:
½ cup cornmeal
½ teaspoon salt
½ teaspoon garlic powder or onion powder
¼ teaspoon cayenne
⅛ teaspoon ground black pepper
Dredge:
½ pound whole okra
in:
¼ cup all-purpose flour
Dip in:
1 egg beaten with 1 teaspoon water
Then dip into cornmeal mixture. Heat to 365°F in
a large skillet:
2 inches vegetable oil
Add okra to oil in batches, frying until golden, about 2 minutes. Remove okra with a slotted spoon and drain on paper towels.

Marnie gave us lunch at noon—big tuna sandwiches and bowls of homemade tomato soup.

TUNA SALAD
4 servings
Flake with a fork:
   1 cup canned or pouch tuna
Add:
   ½ to 1 cup diced celery or cucumber
In a small bowl, whisk together:
   2 tablespoons olive oil
   2 tablespoons lemon juice
or use:
   ¼ cup mayonnaise
Add:
   (1 tablespoon chopped chives)
   (1 tablespoon chopped parsley)
Combine the mixture and oil or mayonnaise with a fork.

TOMATO SOUP
About 6 cups
Fresh tomatoes can be grilled or roasted to add
a smoky flavor.
Heat in a soup pot, over medium-low heat:
   2 tablespoons olive oil
Add and cook, stirring, until tender but not browned,
5 to 10 minutes:
   1 medium onion, coarsely chopped
Stir in:
   3 pounds tomatoes, peeled, seeded, and chopped, with
       their juices, or two 28-ounce cans
       tomatoes, chopped, with their juice
Simmer until the tomatoes are covered in their own liquid, about
25 minutes. Puree the soup until smooth. Return to the pot and
stir in:
   ¾ teaspoon salt
   ¼ teaspoon black pepper
Heat through.